P9-CLP-139

THE
FOUND
AND THE
LOST

ALSO BY
URSULA K. LE GUIN

THE
FOUND
AND THE
LOST

— THE —

COLLECTED NOVELLAS

— OF —

URSULA K.
LE GUIN

SAGA PRESS

LONDON SYDNEY **NEW YORK** TORONTO NEW DELHI

SAGA PRESS

AN IMPRINT OF SIMON & SCHUSTER, INC.

1230 AVENUE OF THE AMERICAS, NEW YORK, NEW YORK 10020

This book is a work of fiction. Any references to historical events, real people, or real places are used fictitiously. Other names, characters, places, and events are products of the author's imagination, and any resemblance to actual events or places or persons, living or dead, is entirely coincidental. | Text compilation copyright © 2016 by Ursula K. Le Guin | "Vaster Than Empires and More Slow" copyright © 1975 by Ursula K. Le Guin; originally appeared in *New Dimensions 1*, 1970 | "Buffalo Gals, Won't You Come Out Tonight" copyright © 1987 by Ursula K. Le Guin; first appeared in *The Magazine of Fantasy and Science Fiction*, Nov. 1987 | "Hernes" copyright © 1991 by Ursula K. Le Guin | "The Matter of Seggri" copyright © 1994 by Ursula K. Le Guin; first appeared in *Crank!*, Spring 1994, issue no. 3 | "Another Story or a Fisherman of the Inland Sea" copyright © 1994 by Ursula K. Le Guin | "Forgiveness Day," "A Man of the People," and "A Woman's Liberation" copyright © 1994 by Ursula K. Le Guin; first appeared in *Asimov's* | "Old Music and the Slave Women" copyright © 1999 by Ursula K. Le Guin; first appeared in *Far Horizons*, edited by Robert Silverberg (Avon Eos) | "The Finder" and "On the High Marsh" copyright © 2001 by Ursula K. Le Guin | "Dragonfly" copyright © 1997 by Ursula K. Le Guin; first appeared in *Legends* | "Paradises Lost" copyright © 2002 by Ursula K. Le Guin | Jacket photograph of Thor's Well copyright © 2016 by Jun Yu/500px | All rights reserved, including the right to reproduce this book or portions thereof in any form whatsoever. For information address Saga Press Subsidiary Rights Department, 1230 Avenue of the Americas, New York, NY 10020 | SAGA PRESS and colophon are trademarks of Simon & Schuster, Inc. | For information about special discounts for bulk purchases, please contact Simon & Schuster Special Sales at 1-866-506-1949 or business@simonandschuster.com. | The Simon & Schuster Speakers Bureau can bring authors to your live event. For more information or to book an event contact the Simon & Schuster Speakers Bureau at 1-866-248-3049 or visit our website at www.simonspeakers.com. | The text for this book was set in Adobe Garamond Pro. | Manufactured in the United States of America | First Saga Press edition October 2016 | 10 9 8 7 6 5 4 3 2 1 | CIP data for this book is available from the Library of Congress. | ISBN 978-1-4814-5139-0 | ISBN 978-1-4814-5141-3 (eBook)

R0447151870

THE
FOUND
AND THE
LOST

CONTENTS

VASTER THAN
EMPIRES
AND
MORE SLOW

TREES AGAIN.

As I recall, Robert Silverberg, who first published this story in New Dimensions I, *asked very gently if I would change the title. I could see where a reader about halfway through might find the title all too descriptive of the story itself; but it was too beautiful, and too beautifully apt, to part with, and Mr. Silverberg let me keep it. It's from Marvell, "To his Coy Mistress"—*

> *Our vegetable love should grow*
> *Vaster than empires, and more slow. . . .*

Like "Nine Lives," this is not a psychomyth but a regular science fiction story, developed not for action/adventure, but psychologically. Unless physical action reflects psychic action, unless the deeds express the person, I get very bored with adventure stories; often it seems that the more action there is, the less happens. Obviously my interest is in what goes on inside. Inner space and all that. We all have forests in our minds. Forests unexplored, unending. Each of us gets lost in the forest, every night, alone.

Hidden in the foliage here is a tiny act of homage. The protagonist of "He Who Shapes" by Roger Zelazny, one of the finest science fiction stories I know, is called Charles Render. I christened a syndrome after him.

IT WAS ONLY DURING THE EARLIEST DECADES OF THE LEAGUE that the Earth sent ships out on the enormously long voyages, beyond the pale, over the stars and far away. They were seeking for worlds which had not been seeded or settled by the Founders on Hain, truly alien worlds. All the Known Worlds went back to the Hainish Origin, and the Terrans, having been not only founded but salvaged by the Hainish, resented this. They wanted to get away from the family. They wanted to find somebody new. The Hainish, like tiresomely understanding parents, supported their explorations, and contributed ships and volunteers, as did several other worlds of the League.

All these volunteers to the Extreme Survey crews shared one peculiarity: they were of unsound mind.

What sane person, after all, would go out to collect information that would not be received for five or ten centuries? Cosmic mass interference had not yet been eliminated from the operation of the ansible, and so instantaneous communication was reliable only within a range of 120 lightyears. The explorers would be quite isolated. And of course they had no idea what they might come back to, if they came back. No normal human being who had experienced time-slippage of even a few decades between League worlds would volunteer for a round trip of centuries. The Surveyors were escapists, misfits. They were nuts.

Ten of them climbed aboard the ferry at Smeming Port, and made varyingly inept attempts to get to know one another during the three days the ferry took getting to their ship, *Gum*. Gum is a Cetian nickname, on the order of Baby or Pet. There were two Cetians on the team, two Hainishmen, one Beldene, and five Terrans; the Cetian-built ship was chartered by the Government of Earth. Her motley crew came aboard wriggling through the coupling tube one by one like apprehensive spermatozoa trying to fertilize the universe. The ferry left, and the navigator put *Gum* underway. She flittered for some hours on the edge of space a few hundred million miles from Smeming Port, and then abruptly vanished.

When, after 10 hours 29 minutes, or 256 years, *Gum* reappeared in normal space, she was supposed to be in the vicinity of Star KG-E-96651. Sure enough, there was the gold pinhead of the star. Somewhere within a four-hundred-million-kilometer sphere there was also a greenish planet, World 4470, as charted by a Cetian mapmaker. The ship now had to find the planet. This was not quite so easy as it might sound, given a four-hundred-million-kilometer haystack. And *Gum* couldn't bat about in planetary space at near lightspeed; if she did, she and Star KG-E-96651 and World 4470 might all end up going bang. She had to creep, using rocket propulsion, at a few hundred thousand miles an hour. The Mathematician/Navigator, Asnanifoil, knew pretty well where the planet ought to be, and thought they might raise it within ten E-days. Meanwhile the members of the Survey team got to know one another still better.

"I can't stand him," said Porlock, the Hard Scientist (chemistry, plus physics, astronomy, geology, etc.), and little blobs of spittle appeared on his mustache. "The man is insane. I can't imagine why he was passed as fit to join a Survey team, unless this is a deliberate experiment in non-compatibility, planned by the Authority, with us as guinea pigs."

"We generally use hamsters and Hainish gholes," said Mannon, the Soft Scientist (psychology, plus psychiatry, anthropology, ecology, etc.), politely; he was one of the Hainishmen. "Instead of guinea pigs. Well, you know, Mr. Osden is really a very rare case. In fact, he's the first fully cured case of Render's Syndrome—a variety of infantile autism which was thought to be incurable. The great Terran analyst Hammergeld reasoned that the cause of the autistic condition in this case is a supernormal empathic capacity, and developed an appropriate treatment. Mr. Osden is the first patient to undergo that treatment, in fact he lived with Dr. Hammergeld until he was eighteen. The therapy was completely successful.

"Successful?"

"Why, yes. He certainly is not autistic."

"No, he's intolerable!"

"Well, you see," said Mannon, gazing mildly at the saliva-flecks on Porlock's mustache, "the normal defensive-aggressive reaction between strangers meeting—let's say you and Mr. Osden just for example—is something you're scarcely aware of; habit, manners, inattention get you past it; you've learned to ignore it, to the point where you might even deny it exists. However, Mr. Osden, being an empath, feels it. Feels his feelings, and yours, and is hard put to say which is which. Let's say that there's a normal element of hostility towards any stranger in your emotional reaction to him when you meet him, plus a spontaneous dislike of his looks, or clothes, or handshake—it doesn't matter what. He feels that dislike. As his autistic defense has been unlearned, he resorts to an aggressive-defense mechanism, a response in kind to the aggression which you have unwittingly projected onto him." Mannon went on for quite a long time.

"Nothing gives a man the right to be such a bastard," Porlock said.

"He can't tune us out?" asked Harfex, the Biologist, another Hainishman.

"It's like hearing," said Olleroo, Assistant Hard Scientist, stooping over to paint her toenails with fluorescent lacquer. "No eyelids on your ears. No Off switch on empathy. He hears our feelings whether he wants to or not."

"Does he know what we're *thinking*?" asked Eskwana, the Engineer, looking round at the others in real dread.

"No," Porlock snapped. "Empathy's not telepathy! Nobody's got telepathy."

"Yet," said Mannon, with his little smile. "Just before I left Hain there was a most interesting report in from one of the recently rediscovered worlds, a hilfer named Rocannon reporting what appears to be a teachable telepathic technique existent among a mutated hominid race; I only saw a synopsis in the HILF Bulletin, but—" He went on. The others had learned that they could talk while Mannon went on talking; he did not seem to mind, nor even to miss much of what they said.

"Then why does he hate us?" Eskwana said.

"Nobody hates you, Ander honey," said Olleroo, daubing Eskwana's left thumbnail with fluorescent pink. The engineer flushed and smiled vaguely.

"He acts as if he hated us," said Haito, the Coordinator. She was a delicate-looking woman of pure Asian descent, with a surprising voice, husky, deep, and soft, like a young bullfrog. "Why, if he suffers from our hostility, does he increase it by constant attacks and insults? I can't say I think much of Dr. Hammergeld's cure, really, Mannon; autism might be preferable. . . ."

She stopped. Osden had come into the main cabin.

He looked flayed. His skin was unnaturally white and thin, showing the channels of his blood like a faded road map in red and blue. His Adam's apple, the muscles that circled his mouth, the bones and ligaments of his wrists and hands, all stood out distinctly as if displayed for an anatomy lesson. His hair was pale rust, like long-dried blood. He had eyebrows and lashes, but they were visible only in certain lights; what one saw was the bones of the eye sockets, the veining of the lids, and the colorless eyes. They were not red eyes, for he was not really an albino, but they were not blue or grey; colors had cancelled out in Osden's eyes, leaving a cold water-like clarity, infinitely penetrable. He never looked directly at one. His face lacked expression, like an anatomical drawing, or a skinned face.

"I agree," he said in a high, harsh tenor, "that even autistic withdrawal might be preferable to the smog of cheap secondhand emotions with which you people surround me. What are you sweating hate for now, Porlock? Can't stand the sight of me? Go practice some auto-eroticism the way you were doing last night, it improves your vibes. Who the devil moved my tapes, here? Don't touch my things, any of you. I won't have it."

"Osden," said Asnanifoil in his large slow voice, "why *are* you such a bastard?"

Ander Eskwana cowered and put his hands in front of his face. Contention frightened him. Olleroo looked up with a vacant yet eager expression, the eternal spectator.

"Why shouldn't I be?" said Osden. He was not looking at Asnanifoil, and was keeping physically as far away from all of them as he could in the crowded cabin. "None of you constitute, in yourselves, any reason for my changing my behavior."

Harfex, a reserved and patient man, said, "The reason is that we shall be spending several years together. Life will be better for all of us if—"

"Can't you understand that I don't give a damn for all of you?" Osden said, took up his microtapes, and went out. Eskwana had suddenly gone to sleep. Asnanifoil was drawing slipstreams in the air with his finger and muttering the Ritual Primes. "You cannot explain his presence on the team except as a plot on the part of the Terran Authority. I saw this almost at once. This mission is meant to fail," Harfex whispered to the Coordinator, glancing over his shoulder. Porlock was fumbling with his fly-button; there were tears in his eyes. I did tell you they were all crazy, but you thought I was exaggerating.

All the same, they were not unjustified. Extreme Surveyors expected to find their fellow team members intelligent, well-trained, unstable, and personally sympathetic. They had to work together in close quarters and nasty places, and could expect one another's paranoias, depressions, manias, phobias, and compulsions to be mild enough to admit of good personal relationships, at least most of the time. Osden might be intelligent, but his training was sketchy and his personality was disastrous. He had been sent only on account of his singular gift, the power of empathy: properly speaking, of wide-range bioempathic receptivity. His talent wasn't species-specific; he could pick up emotion or sentience from anything that felt. He could share lust with a white rat, pain with a squashed cockroach, and phototropy with a moth. On an alien world, the Authority had decided, it would be useful to know if anything nearby is sentient, and if so, what its feelings towards you are. Osden's title was a new one: he was the team's Sensor.

"What is emotion, Osden?" Haito Tomiko asked him one day in the main cabin, trying to make some rapport with him for once. "What is it, exactly, that you pick up with your empathic sensitivity?"

"Muck," the man answered in his high, exasperated voice. "The psychic excreta of the animal kingdom. I wade through your faeces."

"I was trying," she said, "to learn some facts." She thought her tone was admirably calm.

"You weren't after facts. You were trying to get at me. With some fear, some curiosity, and a great deal of distaste. The way you might poke a dead dog, to see the maggots crawl. Will you understand once and for all that I don't want to be got at, that I want to be left alone?" His skin was mottled with red and violet, his voice had risen. "Go roll in your own dung, you yellow bitch!" he shouted at her silence.

"Calm down," she said, still quietly, but she left him at once and went to her cabin. Of course he had been right about her motives; her question had been largely a pretext, a mere effort to interest him. But what harm in that? Did not that effort imply respect for the other? At the moment of asking the question she had felt at most a slight distrust of him; she had mostly felt sorry for him, the poor arrogant venomous bastard, Mr. No-Skin as Olleroo called him. What did he expect, the way he acted? Love?

"I guess he can't stand anybody feeling sorry for him," said Olleroo, lying on the lower bunk, gilding her nipples.

"Then he can't form any human relationship. All his Dr. Hammergeld did was turn an autism inside out. . . ."

"Poor frot," said Olleroo. "Tomiko, you don't mind if Harfex comes in for a while tonight, do you?"

"Can't you go to his cabin? I'm sick of always having to sit in Main with that damned peeled turnip."

"You do hate him, don't you? I guess he feels that. But I slept with Harfex last night too, and Asnanifoil might get jealous, since they share the cabin. It would be nicer here."

"Service them both," Tomiko said with the coarseness of offended modesty. Her Terran subculture, the East Asian, was a puritanical one; she had been brought up chaste.

"I only like one a night," Olleroo replied with innocent serenity. Beldene, the Garden Planet, had never discovered chastity, or the wheel.

"Try Osden, then," Tomiko said. Her personal instability was seldom so plain as now: a profound self-distrust manifesting itself as destructivism. She had volunteered for this job because there was, in all probability, no use in doing it.

The little Beldene looked up, paintbrush in hand, eyes wide. "Tomiko, that was a dirty thing to say."

"Why?"

"It would be vile! I'm not attracted to Osden!"

"I didn't know it mattered to you," Tomiko said indifferently, though she did know. She got some papers together and left the cabin, remarking, "I hope you and Harfex or whoever it is finish by last bell; I'm tired."

Olleroo was crying, tears dripping on her little gilded nipples. She wept easily. Tomiko had not wept since she was ten years old.

It was not a happy ship; but it took a turn for the better when Asnanifoil and his computers raised World 4470. There it lay, a dark-green jewel, like truth at the bottom of a gravity well. As they watched the jade disc grow, a sense of mutuality grew among them. Osden's selfishness, his accurate cruelty, served now to draw the others together. "Perhaps," Mannon said, "he was sent as a beating-gron. What Terrans call a scapegoat. Perhaps his influence will be good after all." And no one, so careful were they to be kind to one another, disagreed.

They came into orbit. There were no lights on nightside, on the continents none of the lines and clots made by animals who build.

"No men," Harfex murmured.

"Of course not," snapped Osden, who had a viewscreen to himself, and his head inside a polythene bag. He claimed that the plastic cut down on the empathic noise he received from the others. "We're two lightcenturies past the limit of the Hainish Expansion, and outside that there are no men. Anywhere. You don't think Creation would have made the same hideous mistake twice?"

No one was paying him much heed; they were looking with affection at that jade immensity below them, where there was life, but not human life. They were misfits among men, and what they saw there was not desolation, but peace. Even Osden did not look quite so expressionless as usual; he was frowning.

Descent in fire on the sea; air reconnaissance; landing. A plain of something like grass, thick, green, bowing stalks, surrounded the ship, brushed against extended viewcameras, smeared the lenses with a fine pollen.

"It looks like a pure phytosphere," Harfex said. "Osden, do you pick up anything sentient?"

They all turned to the Sensor. He had left the screen and was pouring himself a cup of tea. He did not answer. He seldom answered spoken questions.

The chitinous rigidity of military discipline was quite inapplicable to these teams of mad scientists; their chain of command lay somewhere between parliamentary procedure and peck-order, and would have driven a regular service officer out of his mind. By the inscrutable decision of the Authority, however, Dr. Haito Tomiko had been given the title of Coordinator, and she now exercised her prerogative for the first time. "Mr. Sensor Osden," she said, "please answer Mr. Harfex."

"How could I 'pick up' anything from outside," Osden said without turning, "with the emotions of nine neurotic hominids pullulating around me like worms in a can? When I have anything to tell you, I'll tell you. I'm aware of my responsibility as Sensor. If you presume to give me an order again, however, Coordinator Haito, I'll consider my responsibility void."

"Very well, Mr. Sensor. I trust no orders will be needed henceforth." Tomiko's bullfrog voice was calm, but Osden seemed to flinch slightly as he stood with his back to her, as if the surge of her suppressed rancor had struck him with physical force.

The biologist's hunch proved correct. When they began field analyses they found no animals even among the microbiota. Nobody here ate anybody else. All life-forms were photosynthesizing or saprophagous, living off light or death, not off life. Plants: infinite plants, not one species known to the visitors from the house of Man. Infinite shades and intensities of green, violet, purple, brown, red. Infinite silences. Only the wind moved, swaying leaves and fronds, a warm soughing wind laden with spores and pollens, blowing the sweet pale-green dust over prairies of great grasses, heaths that bore no heather, flowerless forests where no foot had ever walked, no eye had ever looked. A warm, sad world, sad and serene. The Surveyors, wandering like picnickers over sunny plains of violet filicaliformes, spoke softly to each other. They knew their voices broke a silence of a thousand million years, the silence of wind and leaves, leaves and wind, blowing and ceasing and blowing again. They talked softly; but being human, they talked.

"Poor old Osden," said Jenny Chong, Bio and Tech, as she piloted a helijet on the North Polar Quadrating run. "All that fancy hi-fi stuff in his brain and nothing to receive. What a bust."

"He told me he hates plants," Olleroo said with a giggle.

"You'd think he'd like them, since they don't bother him like we do."

"Can't say I much like these plants myself," said Porlock, looking down at the purple undulations of the North Circumpolar Forest. "All the same. No mind. No change. A man alone in it would go right off his head."

"But it's all alive," Jenny Chong said. "And if it lives, Osden hates it."

"He's not really so bad," Olleroo said, magnanimous. Porlock looked at her sidelong and asked, "You ever slept with him, Olleroo?"

Olleroo burst into tears and cried, "You Terrans are obscene!"

"No she hasn't," Jenny Chong said, prompt to defend. "Have you, Porlock?"

The chemist laughed uneasily: ha, ha, ha. Flecks of spittle appeared on his mustache.

"Osden can't bear to be touched," Olleroo said shakily. "I just brushed against him once by accident and he knocked me off like I was some sort of dirty . . . thing. We're all just things, to him."

"He's evil," Porlock said in a strained voice, startling the two women. "He'll end up shattering this team, sabotaging it, one way or another. Mark my words. He's not fit to live with other people!"

They landed on the North Pole. A midnight sun smouldered over low hills. Short, dry, greenish-pink bryoform grasses stretched away in every direction, which was all one direction, south. Subdued by the incredible silence, the three Surveyors set up their instruments and set to work, three viruses twitching minutely on the hide of an unmoving giant.

Nobody asked Osden along on runs as pilot or photographer or recorder, and he never volunteered, so he seldom left base camp. He ran Harfex's botanical taxonomic data through the onship computers,

and served as assistant to Eskwana, whose job here was mainly repair
and maintenance. Eskwana had begun to sleep a great deal, twenty-
five hours or more out of the thirty-two-hour day, dropping off in
the middle of repairing a radio or checking the guidance circuits of a
helijet. The Coordinator stayed at base one day to observe. No one else
was home except Poswet To, who was subject to epileptic fits; Mannon
had plugged her into a therapy-circuit today in a state of preventive
catatonia. Tomiko spoke reports into the storage banks, and kept an
eye on Osden and Eskwana. Two hours passed.

"You might want to use the 860 microwaldoes in sealing that
connection," Eskwana said in his soft, hesitant voice.

"Obviously!"

"Sorry. I just saw you had the 840's there—"

"And will replace them when I take the 860's out. When I don't know
how to proceed, Engineer, I'll ask your advice."

After a minute Tomiko looked round. Sure enough, there was
Eskwana sound asleep, head on the table, thumb in his mouth.

"Osden."

The white face did not turn, he did not speak, but conveyed impatiently that he was listening.

"You can't be unaware of Eskwana's vulnerability."

"I am not responsible for his psychopathic reactions."

"But you are responsible for your own. Eskwana is essential to our
work here, and you're not. If you can't control your hostility, you must
avoid him altogether."

Osden put down his tools and stood up. "With pleasure!" he said in
his vindictive, scraping voice. "You could not possibly imagine what it's
like to experience Eskwana's irrational terrors. To have to share his horrible cowardice, to have to cringe with him at everything!"

"Are you trying to justify your cruelty towards him? I thought you
had more self-respect." Tomiko found herself shaking with spite. "If

your empathic power really makes you share Ander's misery, why does it never induce the least compassion in you?"

"Compassion," Osden said. "Compassion. What do you know about compassion?"

She stared at him, but he would not look at her.

"Would you like me to verbalize your present emotional affect regarding myself?" he said. "I can do so more precisely than you can. I'm trained to analyze such responses as I receive them. And I do receive them."

"But how can you expect me to feel kindly towards you when you behave as you do?"

"What does it matter how I *behave*, you stupid sow, do you think it makes any difference? Do you think the average human is a well of loving-kindness? My choice is to be hated or to be despised. Not being a woman or a coward, I prefer to be hated."

"That's rot. Self-pity. Every man has—"

"But I am not a man," Osden said. "There are all of you. And there is myself. I am *one*."

Awed by that glimpse of abysmal solipsism, she kept silent a while; finally she said with neither spite nor pity, clinically, "You could kill yourself, Osden."

"That's your way, Haito," he jeered. "I'm not depressive, and *seppuku* isn't my bit. What do you want me to do here?"

"Leave. Spare yourself and us. Take the aircar and a data-feeder and go do a species count. In the forest; Harfex hasn't even started the forests yet. Take a hundred-square-meter forested area, anywhere inside radio range. But outside empathy range. Report in at 8 and 24 o'clock daily."

Osden went, and nothing was heard from him for five days but laconic all-well signals twice daily. The mood at base camp changed like a stage-set. Eskwana stayed awake up to eighteen hours a day. Poswet

To got out her stellar lute and chanted the celestial harmonies (music had driven Osden into a frenzy). Mannon, Harfex, Jenny Chong, and Tomiko all went off tranquillizers. Porlock distilled something in his laboratory and drank it all by himself. He had a hangover. Asnanifoil and Poswet To held an all-night Numerical Epiphany, that mystical orgy of higher mathematics which is the chief pleasure of the religious Cetian soul. Olleroo slept with everybody. Work went well.

The Hard Scientist came towards base at a run, laboring through the high, fleshy stalks of the graminiformes. "Something—in the forest—" His eyes bulged, he panted, his mustache and fingers trembled. "Something big. Moving, behind me. I was putting in a benchmark, bending down. It came at me. As if it was swinging down out of the trees. Behind me." He stared at the others with the opaque eyes of terror or exhaustion.

"Sit down, Porlock. Take it easy. Now wait, go through this again. You *saw* something—"

"Not clearly. Just the movement. Purposive. A—an—I don't know what it could have been. Something self-moving. In the trees, the arboriformes, whatever you call 'em. At the edge of the woods."

Harfex looked grim. "There is nothing here that could attack you, Porlock. There are not even microzoa. There *could not* be a large animal."

"Could you possibly have seen an epiphyte drop suddenly, a vine come loose behind you?"

"No," Porlock said. "It was coming down at me, through the branches, fast. When I turned it took off again, away and upwards. It made a noise, a sort of crashing. If it wasn't an animal, God knows what it could have been! It was big—as big as a man, at least. Maybe a reddish color. I couldn't see, I'm not sure."

"It was Osden," said Jenny Chong, "doing a Tarzan act." She giggled nervously, and Tomiko repressed a wild feckless laugh. But Harfex was not smiling.

"One gets uneasy under the arboriformes," he said in his polite, repressed voice. "I've noticed that. Indeed that may be why I've put off working in the forests. There's a hypnotic quality in the colors and spacing of the stems and branches, especially the helically arranged ones; and the spore-throwers grow so regularly spaced that it seems unnatural. I find it quite disagreeable, subjectively speaking. I wonder if a stronger effect of that sort mightn't have produced a hallucination. . . ?"

Porlock shook his head. He wet his lips. "It was there," he said. "Something. Moving with purpose. Trying to attack me from behind."

When Osden called in, punctual as always, at 24 o'clock that night, Harfex told him Porlock's report. "Have you come on anything at all, Mr. Osden, that could substantiate Mr. Porlock's impression of a motile, sentient life-form, in the forest?"

Ssss, the radio said sardonically. "No. Bullshit," said Osden's unpleasant voice.

"You've been actually inside the forest longer than any of us," Harfex said with unmitigable politeness. "Do you agree with my impression that the forest ambiance has a rather troubling and possibly hallucinogenic effect on the perceptions?"

Ssss. "I'll agree that Porlock's perceptions are easily troubled. Keep him in his lab, he'll do less harm. Anything else?"

"Not at present," Harfex said, and Osden cut off.

Nobody could credit Porlock's story, and nobody could discredit it. He was positive that something, something big, had tried to attack him by surprise. It was hard to deny this, for they were on an alien world, and everyone who had entered the forest had felt a certain chill and foreboding under the "trees." ("Call them trees, certainly," Harfex had said. "They really are the same thing, only, of course, altogether different.") They agreed that they had felt uneasy, or had had the sense that something was watching them from behind.

"We've got to clear this up," Porlock said, and he asked to be sent as a temporary Biologist's Aide, like Osden, into the forest to explore and observe. Olleroo and Jenny Chong volunteered if they could go as a pair. Harfex sent them all off into the forest near which they were encamped, a vast tract covering four-fifths of Continent D. He forbade side-arms. They were not to go outside a fifty-mile half-circle, which included Osden's current site. They all reported in twice daily, for three days. Porlock reported a glimpse of what seemed to be a large semi-erect shape moving through the trees across the river; Olleroo was sure she had heard something moving near the tent, the second night.

"There are no animals on this planet," Harfex said, dogged.

Then Osden missed his morning call.

Tomiko waited less than an hour, then flew with Harfex to the area where Osden had reported himself the night before. But as the helijet hovered over the sea of purplish leaves, illimitable, impenetrable, she felt a panic despair. "How can we find him in this?"

"He reported landing on the riverbank. Find the aircar; he'll be camped near it, and he can't have gone far from his camp. Species-counting is slow work. There's the river."

"There's his car," Tomiko said, catching the bright foreign glint among the vegetable colors and shadows. "Here goes, then."

She put the ship in hover and pitched out the ladder. She and Harfex descended. The sea of life closed over their heads.

As her feet touched the forest floor, she unsnapped the flap of her holster; then glancing at Harfex, who was unarmed, she left the gun untouched. But her hand kept coming back up to it. There was no sound at all, as soon as they were a few meters away from the slow, brown river, and the light was dim. Great boles stood well apart, almost regularly, almost alike; they were soft-skinned, some appearing smooth and others spongy, grey or greenish-brown or brown, twined with cable-like creepers and festooned with epiphytes, extending rigid, entangled armfuls of big, saucer-shaped, dark leaves that formed a roof-layer twenty to thirty meters thick. The ground underfoot was springy as a mattress, every inch of it knotted with roots and peppered with small, fleshy-leaved growths.

"Here's his tent," Tomiko said, cowed at the sound of her voice in that huge community of the voiceless. In the tent was Osden's sleeping bag, a couple of books, a box of rations. We should be calling, shouting for him, she thought, but did not even suggest it; nor did Harfex. They circled out from the tent, careful to keep each other in sight through the thick-standing presences, the crowding gloom. She stumbled over Osden's body, not thirty meters from the tent, led to it by the whitish gleam of a dropped notebook. He lay face down between two huge-rooted trees. His head and hands were covered with blood, some dried, some still oozing red.

Harfex appeared beside her, his pale Hainish complexion quite green in the dusk. "Dead?"

"No. He's been struck. Beaten. From behind." Tomiko's fingers felt over the bloody skull and temples and nape. "A weapon or a tool . . . I don't find a fracture."

As she turned Osden's body over so they could lift him, his eyes opened. She was holding him, bending close to his face. His pale lips writhed. A deathly fear came into her. She screamed aloud two or three times and tried to run away, shambling and stumbling into the terrible dusk. Harfex caught her, and at his touch and the sound of his voice, her panic decreased. "What is it? What is it?" he was saying.

"I don't know," she sobbed. Her heartbeat still shook her, and she could not see clearly. "The fear—the . . . I panicked. When I saw his eyes."

"We're both nervous. I don't understand this—"

"I'm all right now, come on, we've got to get him under care."

Both working with senseless haste, they lugged Osden to the riverside and hauled him up on a rope under his armpits; he dangled like a sack, twisting a little, over the glutinous dark sea of leaves. They pulled him into the helijet and took off. Within a minute they were over open prairie. Tomiko locked onto the homing beam. She drew a deep breath, and her eyes met Harfex's.

"I was so terrified I almost fainted. I have never done that."

"I was . . . unreasonably frightened also," said the Hainishman, and indeed he looked aged and shaken. "Not so badly as you. But as unreasonably."

"It was when I was in contact with him, holding him. He seemed to be conscious for a moment."

"Empathy? . . . I hope he can tell us what attacked him."

Osden, like a broken dummy covered with blood and mud, half lay as they had bundled him into the rear seats in their frantic urgency to get out of the forest.

More panic met their arrival at base. The ineffective brutality of the assault was sinister and bewildering. Since Harfex stubbornly denied any possibility of animal life they began speculating about sentient plants, vegetable monsters, psychic projections. Jenny Chong's latent phobia reasserted itself and she could talk about nothing except the Dark Egos which followed people around behind their backs. She and Olleroo and Porlock had been summoned back to base; and nobody was much inclined to go outside.

Osden had lost a good deal of blood during the three or four hours he had lain alone, and concussion and severe contusions had put him in shock and semi-coma. As he came out of this and began running a low fever he called several times for "Doctor," in a plaintive voice: "Doctor Hammergeld . . ." When he regained full consciousness, two of those long days later, Tomiko called Harfex into his cubicle.

"Osden: can you tell us what attacked you?"

The pale eyes flickered past Harfex's face.

"You were attacked," Tomiko said gently. The shifty gaze was hatefully familiar, but she was a physician, protective of the hurt. "You may not remember it yet. Something attacked you. You were in the forest—"

"Ah!" he cried out, his eyes growing bright and his features contorting. "The forest—in the forest—"

"What's in the forest?"

He gasped for breath. A look of clearer consciousness came into his face. After a while he said, "I don't know."

"Did you see what attacked you?" Harfex asked.

"I don't know."

"You remember it now."

"I don't know."

"All our lives may depend on this. You must tell us what you saw!"

"I don't know," Osden said, sobbing with weakness. He was too weak to hide the fact that he was hiding the answer, yet he would not say it. Porlock, nearby, was chewing his pepper-colored mustache as he tried to hear what was going on in the cubicle. Harfex leaned over Osden and said, "You *will* tell us—" Tomiko had to interfere bodily.

Harfex controlled himself with an effort that was painful to see. He went off silently to his cubicle, where no doubt he took a double or triple dose of tranquillizers. The other men and women, scattered about the big frail building, a long main hall and ten sleeping-cubicles, said nothing, but looked depressed and edgy. Osden, as always, even now, had them all at his mercy. Tomiko looked down at him with a rush of hatred that burned in her throat like bile. This monstrous egotism that fed itself on others' emotions, this absolute selfishness, was worse than any hideous deformity of the flesh. Like a congenital monster, he should not have lived. Should not be alive. Should have died. Why had his head not been split open?

As he lay flat and white, his hands helpless at his sides, his colorless eyes were wide open, and there were tears running from the corners. He tried to flinch away. "Don't," he said in a weak hoarse voice, and tried to raise his hands to protect his head. "Don't!"

She sat down on the folding-stool beside the cot, and after a while put her hand on his. He tried to pull away, but lacked the strength.

A long silence fell between them.

"Osden," she murmured, "I'm sorry. I'm very sorry. I will you well. Let me will you well, Osden. I don't want to hurt you. Listen, I do see now. It was one of us. That's right, isn't it. No, don't answer, only tell me if I'm wrong; but I'm not. . . . Of course there are animals on this planet. Ten of them. I don't care who it was. It doesn't matter, does it. It could have been me, just now. I realize that. I didn't understand how it is, Osden. You can't see how difficult it is for us to understand. . . . But listen. If it were love, instead of hate and fear . . . Is it never love?"

"No."

"Why not? Why should it never be? Are human beings all so weak? That is terrible. Never mind, never mind, don't worry. Keep still. At least right now it isn't hate, is it? Sympathy at least, concern, well-wishing. You do feel that, Osden? Is it what you feel?"

"Among . . . other things," he said, almost inaudibly.

"Noise from my subconscious, I suppose. And everybody else in the room . . . Listen, when we found you there in the forest, when I tried to turn you over, you partly wakened, and I felt a horror of you. I was insane with fear for a minute. Was that your fear of me I felt?"

"No."

Her hand was still on his, and he was quite relaxed, sinking towards sleep, like a man in pain who has been given relief from pain. "The forest," he muttered; she could barely understand him. "Afraid."

She pressed him no further, but kept her hand on his and watched him go to sleep. She knew what she felt, and what therefore he must feel. She was confident of it: there is only one emotion, or state of being, that can thus wholly reverse itself, polarize, within one moment. In Great Hainish indeed there is one word, *ontá*, for love and for hate. She was not in love with Osden, of course, that was another kettle of fish.

What she felt for him was *ontá*, polarized hate. She held his hand and the current flowed between them, the tremendous electricity of touch, which he had always dreaded. As he slept the ring of anatomy-chart muscles around his mouth relaxed, and Tomiko saw on his face what none of them had ever seen, very faint, a smile. It faded. He slept on.

He was tough; next day he was sitting up, and hungry. Harfex wished to interrogate him, but Tomiko put him off. She hung a sheet of polythene over the cubicle door, as Osden himself had often done. "Does it actually cut down your empathic reception?" she asked, and he replied, in the dry, cautious tone they were now using to each other, "No."

"Just a warning, then."

"Partly. More faith-healing. Dr. Hammergeld thought it worked. . . . Maybe it does, a little."

There had been love, once. A terrified child, suffocating in the tidal rush and battering of the huge emotions of adults, a drowning child, saved by one man. Taught to breathe, to live, by one man. Given everything, all protection and love, by one man. Father/Mother/God: no other. "Is he still alive?" Tomiko asked, thinking of Osden's incredible loneliness, and the strange cruelty of the great doctors. She was shocked when she heard his forced, tinny laugh.

"He died at least two and a half centuries ago," Osden said. "Do you forget where we are, Coordinator? We've all left our little families behind. . . ."

Outside the polythene curtain the eight other human beings on World 4470 moved vaguely. Their voices were low and strained. Eskwana slept; Poswet To was in therapy; Jenny Chong was trying to rig lights in her cubicle so that she wouldn't cast a shadow.

"They're all scared," Tomiko said, scared. "They've all got these ideas about what attacked you. A sort of ape-potato, a giant fanged spinach, I don't know. . . . Even Harfex. You may be right not to force them to see. That would be worse, to lose confidence in one another. But why are we all so shaky, unable to face the fact, going to pieces so easily? Are we really all insane?"

"We'll soon be more so."

"Why?"

"There *is* something." He closed his mouth, the muscles of his lips stood out rigid.

"Something sentient?"

"A sentience."

"In the forest?"

 He nodded.

"What is it, then—?"

"The fear." He began to look strained again, and moved restlessly. "When I fell, there, you know, I didn't lose consciousness at once. Or I kept regaining it. I don't know. It was more like being paralyzed."

"You were."

"I was on the ground. I couldn't get up. My face was in the dirt, in that soft leaf mold. It was in my nostrils and eyes. I couldn't move. Couldn't see. As if I was in the ground. Sunk into it, part of it. I knew I was between two trees even though I never saw them. I suppose I could feel the roots. Below me in the ground, down under the ground. My hands were bloody, I could feel that, and the blood made the dirt around my face sticky. I felt the fear. It kept growing. As if they'd finally *known* I was there, lying on them there, under them, among them, the thing they feared, and yet part of their fear itself. I couldn't stop sending the fear back, and it kept growing, and I couldn't move, I couldn't get away. I would pass out, I think, and then the fear would bring me to again, and I still couldn't move. Any more than they can."

Tomiko felt the cold stirring of her hair, the readying of the apparatus of terror. "They: who are they, Osden?"

"They, it—I don't know. The fear."

"What is he talking about?" Harfex demanded when Tomiko reported this conversation. She would not let Harfex question Osden yet, feeling that she must protect Osden from the onslaught of the Hainishman's powerful, over-repressed emotions. Unfortunately this fueled the slow fire of paranoid anxiety that burned in poor Harfex, and he thought she and Osden were in league, hiding some fact of great importance or peril from the rest of the team.

"It's like the blind man trying to describe the elephant. Osden hasn't seen or heard the . . . the sentience, any more than we have."

"But he's felt it, my dear Haito," Harfex said with just-suppressed rage. "Not empathically. On his skull. It came and knocked him down and beat him with a blunt instrument. Did he not catch *one* glimpse of it?"

"What would he have seen, Harfex?" Tomiko asked, but he would not hear her meaningful tone; even he had blocked out that comprehension. What one fears is alien. The murderer is an outsider, a foreigner, not one of us. The evil is not in me!

"The first blow knocked him pretty well out," Tomiko said a little wearily, "he didn't see anything. But when he came to again, alone in the forest, he felt a great fear. Not his own fear, an empathic effect. He is certain of that. And certain it was nothing picked up from any of us. So that evidently the native life-forms are not all insentient."

Harfex looked at her a moment, grim. "You're trying to frighten me, Haito. I do not understand your motives." He got up and went off to his laboratory table, walking slowly and stiffly, like a man of eighty not of forty.

She looked round at the others. She felt some desperation. Her new, fragile, and profound interdependence with Osden gave her, she was well aware, some added strength. But if even Harfex could not keep his head, who of the others would? Porlock and Eskwana were shut in their cubicles, the others were all working or busy with something. There was something queer about their positions. For a while the

Coordinator could not tell what it was, then she saw that they were all sitting facing the nearby forest. Playing chess with Asnanifoil, Olleroo had edged her chair around until it was almost beside his.

She went to Mannon, who was dissecting a tangle of spidery brown roots, and told him to look for the pattern-puzzle. He saw it at once, and said with unusual brevity, "Keeping an eye on the enemy."

"What enemy? What do *you* feel, Mannon?" She had a sudden hope in him as a psychologist, on this obscure ground of hints and empathies where biologists went astray.

"I feel a strong anxiety with a specific spatial orientation. But I am not an empath. Therefore the anxiety is explicable in terms of the particular stress-situation, that is, the attack on a team member in the forest, and also in terms of the total stress-situation, that is, my presence in a totally alien environment, for which the archetypical connotations of the word 'forest' provide an inevitable metaphor."

Hours later Tomiko woke to hear Osden screaming in nightmare; Mannon was calming him, and she sank back into her own dark-branching pathless dreams. In the morning Eskwana did not wake. He could not be roused with stimulant drugs. He clung to his sleep, slipping farther and farther back, mumbling softly now and then until, wholly regressed, he lay curled on his side, thumb at his lips, gone.

"Two days; two down. Ten little Indians, nine little Indians . . ." That was Porlock.

"And you're the next little Indian," Jenny Chong snapped. "Go analyze your urine, Porlock!"

"He is driving us all insane," Porlock said, getting up and waving his left arm. "Can't you feel it? For God's sake, are you all deaf and blind? Can't you feel what he's doing, the emanations? It all comes from him—from his room there—from his mind. He is driving us all insane with fear!"

"Who is?" said Asnanifoil, looming precipitous and hairy over the little Terran.

"Do I have to say his name? Osden, then. Osden! Osden! Why do you think I tried to kill him? In self-defense! To save all of us! Because you won't see what he's doing to us. He's sabotaged the mission by making us quarrel, and now he's going to drive us all insane by projecting fear at us so that we can't sleep or think, like a huge radio that doesn't make any sound, but it broadcasts all the time, and you can't sleep, and you can't think. Haito and Harfex are already under his control but the rest of you can be saved. I had to do it!"

"You didn't do it very well," Osden said, standing half-naked, all rib and bandage, at the door of his cubicle. "I could have hit myself harder. Hell, it isn't me that's scaring you blind, Porlock, it's out there—there, in the woods!"

Porlock made an ineffectual attempt to assault Osden; Asnanifoil held him back, and continued to hold him effortlessly while Mannon gave him a sedative shot. He was put away shouting about giant radios. In a minute the sedative took effect, and he joined a peaceful silence to Eskwana's.

"All right," said Harfex. "Now, Osden, you'll tell us what you know and all you know."

Osden said, "I don't know anything."

He looked battered and faint. Tomiko made him sit down before he talked.

"After I'd been three days in the forest, I thought I was occasionally receiving some kind of affect."

"Why didn't you report it?"

"Thought I was going spla, like the rest of you."

"That, equally, should have been reported."

"You'd have called me back to base. I couldn't take it. You realize that my inclusion in the mission was a bad mistake. I'm not able to coexist with nine other neurotic personalities at close quarters. I was wrong to volunteer for Extreme Survey, and the Authority was wrong to accept me."

No one spoke; but Tomiko saw, with certainty this time, the flinch in Osden's shoulders and the tightening of his facial muscles, as he registered their bitter agreement.

"Anyhow, I didn't want to come back to base because I was curious. Even going psycho, how could I pick up empathic affects when there was no creature to emit them? They weren't bad, then. Very vague. Queer. Like a draft in a closed room, a flicker in the corner of your eye. Nothing really."

For a moment he had been borne up on their listening: they heard, so he spoke. He was wholly at their mercy. If they disliked him he had to be hateful; if they mocked him he became grotesque; if they listened to him he was the storyteller. He was helplessly obedient to the demands of their emotions, reactions, moods. And there were seven of them, too many to cope with, so that he must be constantly knocked about from one to another's whim. He could not find coherence. Even as he spoke and held them, somebody's attention would wander: Olleroo perhaps was thinking that he wasn't unattractive, Harfex was seeking the ulterior motive of his words, Asnanifoil's mind, which could not be long held by the concrete, was roaming off towards the eternal peace of number, and Tomiko was distracted by pity, by fear. Osden's voice faltered. He lost the thread. "I . . . I thought it must be the trees," he said, and stopped.

"It's not the trees," Harfex said. "They have no more nervous system than do plants of the Hainish Descent on Earth. None."

"You're not seeing the forest for the trees, as they say on Earth," Mannon put in, smiling elfinly; Harfex stared at him. "What about those root-nodes we've been puzzling about for twenty days—eh?"

"What about them?"

"They are, indubitably, connections. Connections among the trees. Right? Now let's just suppose, most improbably, that you knew nothing of animal brain-structure. And you were given one axon, or one detached glial cell, to examine. Would you be likely to discover what it was? Would you see that the cell was capable of sentience?"

"No. Because it isn't. A single cell is capable of mechanical response to stimulus. No more. Are you hypothesizing that individual arboriformes are 'cells' in a kind of brain, Mannon?"

"Not exactly. I'm merely pointing out that they are all interconnected, both by the root-node linkage and by your green epiphytes in the branches. A linkage of incredible complexity and physical extent. Why, even the prairie grass-forms have those root-connectors, don't they? I know that sentience or intelligence isn't a thing, you can't find it in, or analyze it out from, the cells of a brain. It's a function of the connected cells. It is, in a sense, the connection: the connectedness. It doesn't exist. I'm not trying to say it exists. I'm only guessing that Osden might be able to describe it."

And Osden took him up, speaking as if in trance. "Sentience without senses. Blind, deaf, nerveless, moveless. Some irritability, response to touch. Response to sun, to light, to water, and chemicals in the earth around the roots. Nothing comprehensible to an animal mind. Presence without mind. Awareness of being, without object or subject. Nirvana."

"Then why do you receive fear?" Tomiko asked in a low voice.

"I don't know. I can't see how awareness of objects, of others, could arise: an unperceiving response . . . But there was an uneasiness, for days. And then when I lay between the two trees and my blood was on their roots—" Osden's face glittered with sweat. "It became fear," he said shrilly, "only fear."

"If such a function existed," Harfex said, "it would not be capable of conceiving of a self-moving, material entity, or responding to one. It could no more become aware of us than we can 'become aware' of Infinity."

"'The silence of those infinite expanses terrifies me,'" muttered Tomiko. "Pascal was aware of Infinity. By way of fear."

"To a forest," Mannon said, "we might appear as forest fires. Hurricanes. Dangers. What moves quickly is dangerous, to a plant. The rootless would be alien, terrible. And if it is mind, it seems only too probable that it might become aware of Osden, whose own mind is open to connection with all others so long as he's conscious, and who was lying in pain and afraid within it, actually inside it. No wonder it was afraid—"

"Not 'it,'" Harfex said. "There is no being, no huge creature, no person! There could at most be only a function—"

"There is only a fear," Osden said.

They were all still a while, and heard the stillness outside.

"Is that what I feel all the time coming up behind me?" Jenny Chong asked, subdued.

Osden nodded. "You all feel it, deaf as you are. Eskwana's the worst off, because he actually has some empathic capacity. He could send if he learned how, but he's too weak, never will be anything but a medium."

"Listen, Osden," Tomiko said, "you can send. Then send to it—the forest, the fear out there—tell it that we won't hurt it. Since it has, or is, some sort of affect that translates into what we feel as emotion, can't you translate back? Send out a message, We are harmless, we are friendly."

"You must know that nobody can emit a false empathic message, Haito. You can't send something that doesn't exist."

"But we don't intend harm, we are friendly."

"Are we? In the forest, when you picked me up, did you feel friendly?"

"No. Terrified. But that's—it, the forest, the plants, not my own fear, isn't it?"

"What's the difference? It's all you felt. Can't you see," and Osden's voice rose in exasperation, "why I dislike you and you dislike me, all of you? Can't you see that I retransmit every negative or aggressive affect you've felt towards me since we first met? I return your hostility, with thanks. I do it in self-defense. Like Porlock. It is self-defense, though;

it's the only technique I developed to replace my original defense of total withdrawal from others. Unfortunately it creates a closed circuit, self-sustaining and self-reinforcing. Your initial reaction to me was the instinctive antipathy to a cripple; by now of course it's hatred. Can you fail to see my point? The forest-mind out there transmits only terror, now, and the only message I can send it is terror, because when exposed to it I can feel nothing except terror!"

"What must we do, then?" said Tomiko, and Mannon replied promptly, "Move camp. To another continent. If there are plant-minds there, they'll be slow to notice us, as this one was; maybe they won't notice us at all."

"It would be a considerable relief," Osden observed stiffly. The others had been watching him with a new curiosity. He had revealed himself, they had seen him as he was, a helpless man in a trap. Perhaps, like Tomiko, they had seen that the trap itself, his crass and cruel egotism, was their own construction, not his. They had built the cage and locked him in it, and like a caged ape he threw filth out through the bars. If, meeting him, they had offered trust, if they had been strong enough to offer him love, how might he have appeared to them?

None of them could have done so, and it was too late now. Given time, given solitude, Tomiko might have built up with him a slow resonance of feeling, a consonance of trust, a harmony; but there was no time, their job must be done. There was not room enough for the cultivation of so great a thing, and they must make do with sympathy, with pity, the small change of love. Even that much had given her strength, but it was nowhere near enough for him. She could see in his flayed face now his savage resentment of their curiosity, even of her pity.

"Go lie down, that gash is bleeding again," she said, and he obeyed her.

Next morning they packed up, melted down the sprayform hangar and living quarters, lifted *Gum* on mechanical drive and took her halfway round World 4470, over the red and green lands, the many warm green seas. They had picked out a likely spot on Continent G: a prairie, twenty thousand square kilos of windswept graminiformes. No forest was within a hundred kilos of the site, and there were no lone trees or groves on the plain. The plant-forms occurred only in large species-colonies, never intermingled, except for certain tiny ubiquitous saprophytes and spore-bearers. The team sprayed holomeld over structure forms, and by evening of the thirty-two-hour day were settled in to the new camp. Eskwana was still asleep and Porlock still sedated, but everyone else was cheerful. "You can breathe here!" they kept saying.

Osden got on his feet and went shakily to the doorway; leaning there he looked through twilight over the dim reaches of the swaying grass that was not grass. There was a faint, sweet odor of pollen on the wind; no sound but the soft, vast sibilance of wind. His bandaged head cocked a little, the empath stood motionless for a long time. Darkness came, and the stars, lights in the windows of the distant house of Man. The wind had ceased, there was no sound. He listened.

In the long night Haito Tomiko listened. She lay still and heard the blood in her arteries, the breathing of sleepers, the wind blowing, the dark veins running, the dreams advancing, the vast static of stars increasing as the universe died slowly, the sound of death walking. She struggled out of her bed, fled the tiny solitude of her cubicle. Eskwana alone slept. Porlock lay straitjacketed, raving softly in his obscure native tongue. Olleroo and Jenny Chong were playing cards, grim-faced. Poswet To was in the therapy niche, plugged in. Asnanifoil was drawing a mandala, the Third Pattern of the Primes. Mannon and Harfex were sitting up with Osden.

She changed the bandages on Osden's head. His lank, reddish hair, where she had not had to shave it, looked strange. It was salted with white, now. Her hands shook as she worked. Nobody had yet said anything.

"How can the fear be here too?" she said, and her voice rang flat and false in the terrific silence.

"It's not just the trees; the grasses too . . ."

"But we're twelve thousand kilos from where we were this morning, we left it on the other side of the planet."

"It's all one," Osden said. "One big green thought. How long does it take a thought to get from one side of your brain to the other?"

"It doesn't think. It isn't thinking," Harfex said, lifelessly. "It's merely a network of processes. The branches, the epiphytic growths, the roots with those nodal junctures between individuals: they must all be capable of transmitting electrochemical impulses. There are no individual plants, then, properly speaking. Even the pollen is part of the linkage, no doubt, a sort of windborne sentience, connecting overseas. But it is not conceivable. That all the biosphere of a planet should be one network of communications, sensitive, irrational, immortal, isolated. . . ."

"Isolated," said Osden. "That's it! That's the fear. It isn't that we're motile, or destructive. It's just that we are. We are other. There has never been any other."

"You're right," Mannon said, almost whispering. "It has no peers. No enemies. No relationship with anything but itself. One alone forever."

"Then what's the function of its intelligence in species-survival?"

"None, maybe," Osden said. "Why are you getting teleological, Harfex? Aren't you a Hainishman? Isn't the measure of complexity the measure of the eternal joy?"

Harfex did not take the bait. He looked ill. "We should leave this world," he said.

"Now you know why I always want to get out, get away from you," Osden said with a kind of morbid geniality. "It isn't pleasant, is it—the other's fear. . . ? If only it were an animal intelligence. I can get through to animals. I get along with cobras and tigers; superior intelligence gives one the advantage. I should have been used in a zoo, not on a human team. . . . If I could get through to the damned stupid potato! If it wasn't so overwhelming . . . I still pick up more than the fear, you know. And before it panicked it had a—there was a serenity. I couldn't take it in, then, I didn't realize how big it was. To know the whole daylight, after all, and the whole night. All the winds and lulls together. The winter stars and the summer stars at the same time. To have roots, and no enemies. To be entire. Do you see? No invasion. No others. To be whole . . ."

He had never spoken before, Tomiko thought.

"You are defenseless against it, Osden," she said. "Your personality has changed already. You're vulnerable to it. We may not all go mad, but you will, if we don't leave."

He hesitated, then he looked up at Tomiko, the first time he had ever met her eyes, a long, still look, clear as water.

"What's sanity ever done for me?" he said, mocking. "But you have a point, Haito. You have something there."

"We should get away," Harfex muttered.

"If I gave in to it," Osden mused, "could I communicate?"

"By 'give in,'" Mannon said in a rapid, nervous voice, "I assume that you mean, stop sending back the empathic information which you receive from the plant-entity: stop rejecting the fear, and absorb it. That will either kill you at once, or drive you back into total psychological with-drawal, autism."

"Why?" said Osden. "Its message is *rejection*. But my salvation is rejection. It's not intelligent. But I am."

"The scale is wrong. What can a single human brain achieve against something so vast?"

"A single human brain can perceive pattern on the scale of stars and galaxies," Tomiko said, "and interpret it as Love."

Mannon looked from one to the other of them; Harfex was silent.

"It'd be easier in the forest," Osden said. "Which of you will fly me over?"

"When?"

"Now. Before you all crack up or go violent."

"I will," Tomiko said.

"None of us will," Harfex said.

"I can't," Mannon said. "I . . . I am too frightened. I'd crash the jet."

"Bring Eskwana along. If I can pull this off, he might serve as a medium."

"Are you accepting the Sensor's plan, Coordinator?" Harfex asked formally.

"Yes."

"I disapprove. I will come with you, however."

"I think we're compelled, Harfex," Tomiko said, looking at Osden's face, the ugly white mask transfigured, eager as a lover's face.

Olleroo and Jenny Chong, playing cards to keep their thoughts from their haunted beds, their mounting dread, chattered like scared children. "This thing, it's in the forest, it'll get you—"

"Scared of the dark?" Osden jeered.

"But look at Eskwana, and Porlock, and even Asnanifoil—"

"It can't hurt you. It's an impulse passing through synapses, a wind passing through branches. It is only a nightmare."

They took off in a helijet, Eskwana curled up still sound asleep in the rear compartment, Tomiko piloting, Harfex and Osden silent, watching ahead for the dark line of forest across the vague grey miles of starlit plain.

They neared the black line, crossed it; now under them was darkness.

She sought a landing place, flying low, though she had to fight her frantic wish to fly high, to get out, get away. The huge vitality of the plant-world was far stronger here in the forest, and its panic beat in immense dark waves. There was a pale patch ahead, a bare knoll-top a little higher than the tallest of the black shapes around it; the not-trees; the rooted; the parts of the whole. She set the helijet down in the glade, a bad landing. Her hands on the stick were slippery, as if she had rubbed them with cold soap.

About them now stood the forest, black in darkness.

Tomiko cowered and shut her eyes. Eskwana moaned in his sleep.

Harfex's breath came short and loud, and he sat rigid, even when Osden reached across him and slid the door open.

Osden stood up; his back and bandaged head were just visible in the dim glow of the control panel as he paused stooping in the doorway.

Tomiko was shaking. She could not raise her head. "No, no, no, no, no, no, no," she said in a whisper. "No. No. No."

Osden moved suddenly and quietly, swinging out the doorway, down into the dark. He was gone.

I am coming! said a great voice that made no sound.

Tomiko screamed. Harfex coughed; he seemed to be trying to stand up, but did not do so.

Tomiko drew in upon herself, all centered in the blind eye in her belly, in the center of her being; and outside that there was nothing but the fear.

It ceased.

She raised her head; slowly unclenched her hands. She sat up straight. The night was dark, and stars shone over the forest. There was nothing else.

"Osden," she said, but her voice would not come. She spoke again, louder, a lone bullfrog croak. There was no reply.

She began to realize that something had gone wrong with Harfex. She was trying to find his head in the darkness, for he had slipped down from the seat, when all at once, in the dead quiet, in the dark rear compartment of the craft, a voice spoke. "Good," it said.

It was Eskwana's voice. She snapped on the interior lights and saw the engineer lying curled up asleep, his hand half over his mouth.

The mouth opened and spoke. "All well," it said.

"Osden—"

"All well," said the soft voice from Eskwana's mouth.

"Where are you?"

Silence.

"Come back."

A wind was rising. "I'll stay here," the soft voice said.

"You can't stay—"

Silence.

"You'd be alone, Osden!"

"Listen." The voice was fainter, slurred, as if lost in the sound of wind. "Listen. I will you well."

She called his name after that, but there was no answer. Eskwana lay still. Harfex lay stiller.

"Osden!" she cried, leaning out the doorway into the dark, wind-shaken silence of the forest of being. "I will come back. I must get Harfex to the base. I will come back, Osden!"

Silence and wind in leaves.

THEY FINISHED THE PRESCRIBED SURVEY OF WORLD 4470, THE eight of them; it took them forty-one days more. Asnanifoil and one or another of the women went into the forest daily at first, searching for Osden in the region around the bare knoll, though Tomiko was not in her heart sure which bare knoll they had landed on that night in the very heart and vortex of terror. They left piles of supplies for Osden, food enough for fifty years, clothing, tents, tools. They did not go on searching; there was no way to find a man alone, hiding, if he wanted to hide, in those unending labyrinths and dim corridors vine-entangled, root-floored. They might have passed within arm's reach of him and never seen him.

But he was there; for there was no fear any more.

Rational, and valuing reason more highly after an intolerable experience of the immortal mindless, Tomiko tried to understand rationally what Osden had done. But the words escaped her control. He had taken the fear into himself, and, accepting, had transcended it. He had given up his self to the alien, an unreserved surrender, that left no place for evil. He had learned the love of the Other, and thereby had been given his whole self.—But this is not the vocabulary of reason.

The people of the Survey team walked under the trees, through the vast colonies of life, surrounded by a dreaming silence, a brooding calm that was half aware of them and wholly indifferent to them. There were no hours. Distance was no matter. Had we but world enough and time . . . The planet turned between the sunlight and the great dark; winds of winter and summer blew fine, pale pollen across the quiet seas.

Gum returned after many surveys, years, and lightyears, to what had several centuries ago been Smeming Port. There were still men there, to receive (incredulously) the team's reports, and to record its losses: Biologist Harfex, dead of fear, and Sensor Osden, left as a colonist.

BUFFALO GALS,
WON'T YOU
COME OUT TONIGHT

I

"You fell out of the sky," the coyote said.

Still curled up tight, lying on her side, her back pressed against the overhanging rock, the child watched the coyote with one eye. Over the other eye she kept her hand cupped, its back on the dirt.

"There was a burned place in the sky, up there alongside the rimrock, and then you fell out of it," the coyote repeated, patiently, as if the news was getting a bit stale. "Are you hurt?"

She was all right. She was in the plane with Mr. Michaels, and the motor was so loud she couldn't understand what he said even when he shouted, and the way the wind rocked the wings was making her feel sick, but it was all right. They were flying to Canyonville. In the plane.

She looked. The coyote was still sitting there. It yawned. It was a big one, in good condition, its coat silvery and thick. The dark tear-line from its long yellow eye was as clearly marked as a tabby cat's.

She sat up, slowly, still holding her right hand pressed to her right eye.

"Did you lose an eye?" the coyote asked, interested.

"I don't know," the child said. She caught her breath and shivered. "I'm cold."

"I'll help you look for it," the coyote said. "Come on! If you move around you won't have to shiver. The sun's up."

Cold lonely brightness lay across the falling land, a hundred miles of sagebrush. The coyote was trotting busily around, nosing under clumps of rabbit-brush and cheatgrass, pawing at a rock. "Aren't you going to look?" it said, suddenly sitting down on its haunches and abandoning the search. "I knew a trick once where I could throw my eyes way up into a tree and see everything from up there, and then whistle, and they'd come back into my head. But that goddam bluejay stole them, and when I whistled nothing came. I had to stick lumps of pine pitch into my head so I could see anything. You could try that. But you've got one eye that's okay, what do you need two for? Are you coming, or are you dying there?"

The child crouched, shivering.

"Well, come if you want to," said the coyote, yawned again, snapped at a flea, stood up, turned, and trotted away among the sparse clumps of rabbit-brush and sage, along the long slope that stretched on down and down into the plain streaked across by long shadows of sagebrush. The slender, grey-yellow animal was hard to keep in sight, vanishing as the child watched.

She struggled to her feet, and without a word, though she kept saying in her mind, "Wait, please wait," she hobbled after the coyote. She could not see it. She kept her hand pressed over the right eyesocket. Seeing with one eye there was no depth; it was like a huge, flat picture. The coyote suddenly sat in the middle of the picture, looking back at her, its mouth open, its eyes narrowed, grinning. Her legs began to steady and her head did not pound so hard, though the deep, black ache was always there. She had nearly caught up to the coyote when it trotted off again. This time she spoke. "Please wait!" she said.

"Okay," said the coyote, but it trotted right on. She followed, walking downhill into the flat picture that at each step was deep.

Each step was different underfoot; each sage bush was different, and all the same. Following the coyote she came out from the shadow of the rimrock cliffs, and the sun at eyelevel dazzled her left eye. Its bright warmth soaked into her muscles and bones at once. The air, that all night had been so hard to breathe, came sweet and easy.

The sage bushes were pulling in their shadows and the sun was hot on the child's back when she followed the coyote along the rim of a gully. After a while the coyote slanted down the undercut slope and the child scrambled after, through scrub willows to the thin creek in its wide sandbed. Both drank.

The coyote crossed the creek, not with a careless charge and splashing like a dog, but singlefoot and quiet like a cat; always it carried its tail low. The child hesitated, knowing that wet shoes make blistered feet, and then waded across in as few steps as possible. Her right arm ached with the effort of holding her hand up over her eye. "I need a bandage," she said to the coyote. It cocked its head and said nothing. It stretched out its forelegs and lay watching the water, resting but alert. The child sat down nearby on the hot sand and tried to move her right hand. It was glued to the skin around her eye by dried blood. At the little tearing-away pain, she whimpered; though it was a small pain it frightened her. The coyote came over close and poked its long snout into her face. Its strong, sharp smell was in her nostrils. It began to lick the awful, aching blindness, cleaning and cleaning with its curled, precise, strong, wet tongue, until the child was able to cry a little with relief, being comforted. Her head was bent close to the grey-yellow ribs, and she saw the hard nipples, the whitish belly-fur. She put her arm around the she-coyote, stroking the harsh coat over back and ribs.

"Okay," the coyote said, "let's go!" And set off without a backward glance. The child scrambled to her feet and followed. "Where are we going?" she said, and the coyote, trotting on down along the creek, answered, "On down along the creek . . ."

† † †

THERE MUST HAVE BEEN A WHILE SHE WAS ASLEEP WHILE SHE walked, because she felt like she was waking up, but she was walking along, only in a different place. She didn't know how she knew it was different. They were still following the creek, though the gully was flattened out to nothing much, and there was still sagebrush range as far as the eye could see. The eye—the good one—felt rested. The other one still ached, but not so sharply, and there was no use thinking about it. But where was the coyote?

She stopped. The pit of cold into which the plane had fallen re-opened and she fell. She stood falling, a thin whimper making itself in her throat.

"Over here!"

The child turned. She saw a coyote gnawing at the half-dried-up carcass of a crow, black feathers sticking to the black lips and narrow jaw.

She saw a tawny-skinned woman kneeling by a campfire, sprinkling something into a conical pot. She heard the water boiling in the pot, though it was propped between rocks, off the fire. The woman's hair was yellow and gray, bound back with a string. Her feet were bare. The upturned soles looked as dark and hard as shoe soles, but the arch of the foot was high, and the toes made two neat curving rows. She wore bluejeans and an old white shirt. She looked over at the girl. "Come on, eat crow!" she said. The child slowly came toward the woman and the fire, and squatted down. She had stopped falling and felt very light and empty; and her tongue was like a piece of wood stuck in her mouth.

Coyote was now blowing into the pot or basket or whatever it was. She reached into it with two fingers, and pulled her hand away shaking it and shouting, "Ow! Shit! Why don't I ever have any spoons?" She broke off a dead twig of sagebrush, dipped it into the pot, and licked it. "Oh, boy," she said. "Come on!"

The child moved a little closer, broke off a twig, dipped. Lumpy pinkish mush clung to the twig. She licked. The taste was rich and delicate.

"What is it?" she asked after a long time of dipping and licking.

"Food. Dried salmon mush," Coyote said. "It's cooling down." She stuck two fingers into the mush again, this time getting a good load, which she ate very neatly. The child, when she tried, got mush all over her chin. It was like chopsticks, it took practice. She practiced. They ate turn and turn until nothing was left in the pot but three rocks. The child did not ask why there were rocks in the mush-pot. They licked the rocks clean. Coyote licked out the inside of the pot-basket, rinsed it once in the creek, and put it onto her head. It fit nicely, making a conical hat. She pulled off her bluejeans. "Piss on the fire!" she cried, and did so, standing straddling it. "Ah, steam between the legs!" she said. The child, embarrassed, thought she was supposed to do the same thing, but did not want to, and did not. Bareassed, Coyote danced around the dampened fire, kicking her long thin legs out and singing,

> *"Buffalo gals, won't you come out tonight,*
> *Come out tonight, come out tonight,*
> *Buffalo gals, won't you come out tonight,*
> *And dance by the light of the moon?"*

She pulled her jeans back on. The child was burying the remains of the fire in creek-sand, heaping it over, seriously, wanting to do right. Coyote watched her.

"Is that you?" she said. "A Buffalo Gal? What happened to the rest of you?"

"The rest of me?" The child looked at herself, alarmed.

"All your people."

"Oh. Well, Mom took Bobbie, he's my little brother, away with Uncle Norm. He isn't really my uncle, or anything. So Mr. Michaels was going there anyway so he was going to fly me over to my real father, in Canyonville. Linda, my stepmother, you know, she said it was okay for the summer anyhow if I was there, and then we could see. But the plane."

In the silence the girl's face became dark red, then greyish white. Coyote watched, fascinated. "Oh," the girl said, "Oh—Oh—Mr. Michaels—he must be—Did the—"

"Come on!" said Coyote, and set off walking.

The child cried, "I ought to go back—"

"What for?" said Coyote. She stopped to look round at the child, then went on faster. "Come on, Gal!" She said it as a name; maybe it was the child's name, Myra, as spoken by Coyote. The child, confused and despairing, protested again, but followed her. "Where are we going? Where *are* we?"

"This is my country," Coyote answered, with dignity, making a long, slow gesture all round the vast horizon. "I made it. Every goddam sage bush."

And they went on. Coyote's gait was easy, even a little shambling, but she covered the ground; the child struggled not to drop behind. Shadows were beginning to pull themselves out again from under the rocks and shrubs. Leaving the creek, they went up a long, low, uneven slope that ended away off against the sky in rimrock. Dark trees stood one here, another way over there; what people called a juniper forest, a desert forest, one with a lot more between the trees than trees. Each juniper they passed smelled sharply, cat-pee smell the kids at school called it, but the child liked it; it seemed to go into her mind and wake her up. She picked off a juniper berry and held it in her mouth, but after a while spat it out. The aching was coming back in huge black waves, and she kept stumbling. She found that she was sitting down on the ground. When she tried to get up her legs shook and would not go under her. She felt foolish and frightened, and began to cry.

"We're home!" Coyote called from way on up the hill.

The child looked with her one weeping eye, and saw sagebrush, juniper, cheatgrass, rimrock. She heard a coyote yip far off in the dry twilight.

She saw a little town up under the rimrock, board houses, shacks, all unpainted. She heard Coyote call again, "Come on, pup! Come on, Gal, we're home!" She could not get up, so she tried to go on all fours, the long way up the slope to the houses under the rimrock. Long before she got there, several people came to meet her. They were all children, she thought at first, and then began to understand that most of them were grown people, but all were very short; they were broad-bodied, fat, with fine, delicate hands and feet. Their eyes were bright. Some of the women helped her stand up and walk, coaxing her, "It isn't much farther, you're doing fine." In the late dusk lights shone yellow-bright through doorways and through unchinked cracks between boards. Woodsmoke hung sweet in the quiet air. The short people talked and laughed all the time, softly. "Where's she going to stay?"—"Put her in with Robin, they're all asleep already!"—"Oh, she can stay with us."

The child asked hoarsely, "Where's Coyote?"

"Out hunting," the short people said.

A deeper voice spoke: "Somebody new has come into town?"

"Yes, a new person," one of the short men answered.

Among these people the deep-voiced man bulked impressive; he was broad and tall, with powerful hands, a big head, a short neck. They made way for him respectfully. He moved very quietly, respectful of them also. His eyes when he stared down at the child were amazing. When he blinked, it was like the passing of a hand before a candle-flame.

"It's only an owlet," he said. "What have you let happen to your eye, new person?"

"I was—We were flying—"

"You're too young to fly," the big man said in his deep, soft voice. "Who brought you here?"

"Coyote."

And one of the short people confirmed: "She came here with Coyote, Young Owl."

"Then maybe she should stay in Coyote's house tonight," the big man said.

"It's all bones and lonely in there," said a short woman with fat cheeks and a striped shirt. "She can come with us."

That seemed to decide it. The fat-cheeked woman patted the child's arm and took her past several shacks and shanties to a low, windowless house. The doorway was so low even the child had to duck down to enter. There were a lot of people inside, some already there and some crowding in after the fat-cheeked woman. Several babies were fast asleep in cradle-boxes in corners. There was a good fire, and a good smell, like toasted sesame seeds. The child was given food, and ate a little, but her head swam and the blackness in her right eye kept coming across her left eye so she could not see at all for a while. Nobody asked her name or told her what to call them. She heard the children call the fat-cheeked woman Chipmunk. She got up courage finally to say, "Is there somewhere I can go to sleep, Mrs. Chipmunk?"

"Sure, come on," one of the daughters said, "in here," and took the child into a back room, not completely partitioned off from the crowded front room, but dark and uncrowded. Big shelves with mattresses and blankets lined the walls. "Crawl in!" said Chipmunk's daughter, patting the child's arm in the comforting way they had. The child climbed onto a shelf, under a blanket. She laid down her head. She thought, "I didn't brush my teeth."

II

SHE WOKE; SHE SLEPT AGAIN. IN CHIPMUNK'S SLEEPING ROOM it was always stuffy, warm, and half-dark, day and night. People came in and slept and got up and left, night and day. She dozed and slept, got down to drink from the bucket and dipper in the front room, and went back to sleep and doze.

She was sitting up on the shelf, her feet dangling, not feeling bad any more, but dreamy, weak. She felt in her jeans pockets. In the left front one was a pocket comb and a bubblegum wrapper; in the right front, two dollar bills and a quarter and a dime.

Chipmunk and another woman, a very pretty dark-eyed plump one, came in. "So you woke up for your dance!" Chipmunk greeted her, laughing, and sat down by her with an arm around her.

"Jay's giving you a dance," the dark woman said. "He's going to make you all right. Let's get you all ready!"

There was a spring up under the rimrock, that flattened out into a pool with slimy, reedy shores. A flock of noisy children splashing in it ran off and left the child and the two women to bathe. The water was warm on the surface, cold down on the feet and legs. All naked, the two soft-voiced laughing women, their round bellies and breasts, broad hips and buttocks gleaming warm in the late afternoon light, sluiced the child down, washed and stroked her limbs and hands and hair, cleaned around the cheekbone and eyebrow of her right eye with infinite softness, admired her, sudsed her, rinsed her, splashed her out of the water, dried her off, dried each other off, got dressed, dressed her, braided her hair, braided each other's hair, tied feathers on the braid-ends, admired her and each other again, and brought her back down into the little straggling town and to a kind of playing field or dirt parking lot in among the houses. There were no streets, just paths and dirt, no lawns and gardens, just sagebrush and dirt. Quite a few people were gathering or wandering around the open place, looking dressed up, wearing colorful shirts, print dresses, strings of beads, earrings. "Hey there, Chipmunk, Whitefoot!" they greeted the women.

A man in new jeans, with a bright blue velveteen vest over a clean, faded blue workshirt, came forward to meet them, very handsome, tense, and important. "All right, Gal!" he said in a harsh, loud voice, which startled among all these soft-speaking people. "We're going to get that eye fixed right up tonight! You just sit down here and don't worry about a thing." He took her wrist, gently despite his bossy, brassy manner, and led her to a woven mat that lay on the dirt near the middle of the open place. There, feeling very foolish, she had to sit down, and was told to stay still. She soon got over feeling that everybody was looking at her, since nobody paid her more attention than a checking glance or, from Chipmunk or Whitefoot and their families, a reassuring wink. Every now and then Jay rushed over to her and said something like, "Going to be as good as new!" and went off again to organize people, waving his long blue arms and shouting.

Coming up the hill to the open place, a lean, loose, tawny figure—and the child started to jump up, remembered she was to sit still, and sat still, calling out softly, "Coyote! Coyote!"

Coyote came lounging by. She grinned. She stood looking down at the child. "Don't let that Bluejay fuck you up, Gal," she said, and lounged on.

The child's gaze followed her, yearning.

People were sitting down now over on one side of the open place, making an uneven half-circle that kept getting added to at the ends until there was nearly a circle of people sitting on the dirt around the child, ten or fifteen paces from her. All the people wore the kind of clothes the child was used to, jeans and jeans-jackets, shirts, vests, cotton dresses, but they were all barefoot, and she thought they were more beautiful than the people she knew, each in a different way, as if each one had invented beauty. Yet some of them were also very strange: thin black shining people with whispery voices, a long-legged woman with eyes like jewels. The big man called Young Owl was there, sleepy-looking and dignified, like Judge McCown who owned a sixty-thousand acre ranch; and beside him was a woman the child thought might be his sister, for like him she had a hook nose and big, strong hands; but she was lean and dark, and there was a crazy look in her fierce eyes. Yellow eyes, but round, not long and slanted like Coyote's. There was Coyote sitting, yawning, scratching her armpit, bored. Now somebody was entering the circle: a man, wearing only a kind of kilt and a cloak painted or beaded with diamond shapes, dancing to the rhythm of the rattle he carried and shook with a buzzing fast beat. His limbs and body were thick yet supple, his movements smooth and pouring. The child kept her gaze on him as he danced past her, around her, past again. The rattle in his hand shook almost too fast to see, in the other hand was something thin and sharp. People were singing around the circle now, a few notes repeated in time to the rattle, soft and tuneless. It was exciting and boring, strange and familiar. The Rattler wove his dancing closer and closer to her, darting at her. The first time she flinched away, frightened by the lunging movement and by his flat, cold face with narrow eyes, but after that she sat still, knowing her part. The dancing went on, the singing went on, till they carried her past boredom into a floating that could go on forever.

Jay had come strutting into the circle, and was standing beside her. He couldn't sing, but he called out, "Hey! Hey! Hey! Hey!" in his big, harsh voice, and everybody answered from all round, and the echo came down from the rimrock on the second beat. Jay was holding up a stick with a ball on it in one hand, and something like a marble in the other. The stick was a pipe: he got smoke into his mouth from it and blew it in four directions and up and down and then over the marble, a puff each time. Then the rattle stopped suddenly, and everything was silent for several breaths. Jay squatted down and looked intently into the child's face, his head cocked to one side. He reached forward, muttering something in time to the rattle and the singing that had started up again louder than before; he touched the child's right eye in the black center of the pain. She flinched and endured. His touch was not gentle. She saw the marble, a dull yellow ball like beeswax, in his hand; then she shut her seeing eye and set her teeth.

"There!" Jay shouted. "Open up. Come on! Let's see!"

Her jaw clenched like a vise, she opened both eyes. The lid of the right one stuck and dragged with such a searing white pain that she nearly threw up as she sat there in the middle of everybody watching.

"Hey, can you see? How's it work? It looks great!" Jay was shaking her arm, railing at her. "How's it feel? Is it working?"

What she saw was confused, hazy, yellowish. She began to discover, as everybody came crowding around peering at her, smiling, stroking and patting her arms and shoulders, that if she shut the hurting eye and looked with the other, everything was clear and flat; if she used them both, things were blurry and yellowish, but deep.

There, right close, was Coyote's long nose and narrow eyes and grin. "What is it, Jay?" she was asking, peering at the new eye. "One of mine you stole that time?"

"It's pine pitch," Jay shouted furiously. "You think I'd use some stupid secondhand coyote eye? I'm a doctor!"

"Ooooh, ooooh, a doctor," Coyote said. "Boy, that is one ugly eye. Why didn't you ask Rabbit for a rabbit-dropping? That eye looks like shit." She put her lean face yet closer, till the child thought she was going to kiss her; instead, the thin, firm tongue once more licked accurate across the pain, cooling, clearing. When the child opened both eyes again the world looked pretty good.

"It works fine," she said.

"Hey!" Jay yelled. "She says it works fine! It works fine, she says so! I told you! What'd I tell you?" He went off waving his arms and yelling. Coyote had disappeared. Everybody was wandering off.

The child stood up, stiff from long sitting. It was nearly dark; only the long west held a great depth of pale radiance. Eastward the plains ran down into night.

Lights were on in some of the shanties. Off at the edge of town somebody was playing a creaky fiddle, a lonesome chirping tune.

A person came beside her and spoke quietly: "Where will you stay?"

"I don't know," the child said. She was feeling extremely hungry. "Can I stay with Coyote?"

"She isn't home much," the soft-voiced woman said. "You were staying with Chipmunk, weren't you? Or there's Rabbit, or Jackrabbit, they have families . . ."

"Do you have a family?" the girl asked, looking at the delicate, soft-eyed woman.

"Two fawns," the woman answered, smiling. "But I just came into town for the dance."

"I'd really like to stay with Coyote," the child said after a little pause, timid, but obstinate.

"Okay, that's fine. Her house is over here." Doe walked along beside the child to a ramshackle cabin on the high edge of town. No light shone from inside. A lot of junk was scattered around the front. There was no step up to the half-open door. Over the door a battered pine board, nailed up crooked, said BIDE-A-WEE.

"Hey, Coyote? Visitors," Doe said. Nothing happened.

Doe pushed the door farther open and peered in. "She's out hunting, I guess. I better be getting back to the fawns. You going to be okay? Anybody else here will give you something to eat—you know . . . okay?"

"Yeah. I'm fine. Thank you," the child said.

She watched Doe walk away through the clear twilight, a severely elegant walk, small steps, like a woman in high heels, quick, precise, very light.

Inside Bide-A-Wee it was too dark to see anything and so cluttered that she fell over something at every step. She could not figure out where or how to light a fire. There was something that felt like a bed, but when she lay down on it, it felt more like a dirty-clothes pile, and smelt like one. Things bit her legs, arms, neck, and back. She was terribly hungry. By smell she found her way to what had to be a dead fish hanging from the ceiling in one corner. By feel she broke off a greasy flake and tasted it. It was smoked dried salmon. She ate one succulent piece after another until she was satisfied, and licked her fingers clean. Near the open door starlight shone on water in a pot of some kind; the child smelled it cautiously, tasted it cautiously, and drank just enough to quench her thirst, for it tasted of mud and was warm and stale. Then she went back to the bed of dirty clothes and fleas, and lay down. She could have gone to Chipmunk's house, or other friendly households; she thought of that as she lay forlorn in Coyote's dirty bed. But she did not go. She slapped at fleas until she fell asleep.

Along in the deep night somebody said, "Move over, pup," and was warm beside her.

BREAKFAST, EATEN SITTING IN THE SUN IN THE DOORWAY, WAS dried-salmon-powder mush. Coyote hunted, mornings and evenings, but what they ate was not fresh game but salmon, and dried stuff, and any berries in season. The child did not ask about this. It made sense to her. She was going to ask Coyote why she slept at night and waked in the day like humans, instead of the other way round like coyotes, but when she framed the question in her mind she saw at once that night is when you sleep and day when you're awake; that made sense too. But one question she did ask, one hot day when they were lying around slapping fleas.

"I don't understand why you all look like people," she said.

"We are people."

"I mean, people like me, humans."

"Resemblance is in the eye," Coyote said. "How is that lousy eye, by the way?"

"It's fine. But—like you wear clothes—and live in houses—with fires and stuff—"

"That's what you think . . . If that loudmouth Jay hadn't horned in, I could have done a really good job."

The child was quite used to Coyote's disinclination to stick to any one subject, and to her boasting. Coyote was like a lot of kids she knew, in some respects. Not in others.

"You mean what I'm seeing isn't true? Isn't real—like on TV, or something?"

"No," Coyote said. "Hey, that's a tick on your collar." She reached over, flicked the tick off, picked it up on one finger, bit it, and spat out the bits.

"Yecch!" the child said. "So?"

"So, to me you're basically greyish yellow and run on four legs. To that lot"—she waved disdainfully at the warren of little houses next down the hill—"you hop around twitching your nose all the time. To Hawk, you're an egg, or maybe getting pinfeathers. See? It just depends on how you look at things. There are only two kinds of people."

"Humans and animals?"

"No. The kind of people who say, 'There are two kinds of people' and the kind of people who don't." Coyote cracked up, pounding her thigh and yelling with delight at her joke. The child didn't get it, and waited.

"Okay," Coyote said. "There's the first people, and then the others. That's the two kinds."

"The first people are—?"

"Us, the animals . . . and things. All the old ones. You know. And you pups, kids, fledglings. All first people."

"And the—others?"

"Them," Coyote said. "You know. The others. The new people. The ones who came." Her fine, hard face had gone serious, rather formidable. She glanced directly, as she seldom did, at the child, a brief gold sharpness. "We were here," she said. "We were always here. We are always here. Where we are is here. But it's their country now. They're running it . . . Shit, even I did better!"

The child pondered and offered a word she had used to hear a good deal: "They're illegal immigrants."

"Illegal!" Coyote said, mocking, sneering. "Illegal is a sick bird. What the fuck's illegal mean? You want a code of justice from a coyote? Grow up, kid!"

"I don't want to."

"You don't want to grow up?"

"I'll be the other kind if I do."

"Yeah. So," Coyote said, and shrugged. "That's life." She got up and went around the house, and the child heard her pissing in the back yard.

A lot of things were hard to take about Coyote as a mother. When her boyfriends came to visit, the child learned to go stay with Chipmunk or the Rabbits for the night, because Coyote and her friend wouldn't even wait to get on the bed but would start doing that right on the floor or even out in the yard. A couple of times Coyote came back late from hunting with a friend, and the child had to lie up against the wall in the same bed and hear and feel them doing that right next to her. It was something like fighting and something like dancing, with a beat to it, and she didn't mind too much except that it made it hard to stay asleep.

Once she woke up and one of Coyote's friends was stroking her stomach in a creepy way. She didn't know what to do, but Coyote woke up and realized what he was doing, bit him hard, and kicked him out of bed. He spent the night on the floor, and apologized next morning—"Aw, hell, Ki, I forgot the kid was there, I thought it was you—"

Coyote, unappeased, yelled, "You think I don't got any standards? You think I'd let some coyote rape a kid in my bed?" She kicked him out of the house, and grumbled about him all day. But a while later he spent the night again, and he and Coyote did that three or four times.

Another thing that was embarrassing was the way Coyote peed anywhere, taking her pants down in public. But most people here didn't seem to care. The thing that worried the child most, maybe, was when Coyote did number two anywhere and then turned around and talked to it. That seemed so awful. As if Coyote was—the way she often seemed, but really wasn't—crazy.

The child gathered up all the old dry turds from around the house one day while Coyote was having a nap, and buried them in a sandy place near where she and Bobcat and some of the other people generally went and did and buried their number twos.

Coyote woke up, came lounging out of Bide-A-Wee, rubbing her hands through her thick, fair, grayish hair and yawning, looked all around once with those narrow eyes, and said, "Hey! Where are they?" Then she shouted, "Where are you? Where are you?"

And a faint, muffled chorus came from over in the sandy draw, "Mommy! Mommy! We're here!"

Coyote trotted over, squatted down, raked out every turd, and talked with them for a long time. When she came back she said nothing, but the child, redfaced and heart pounding, said, "I'm sorry I did that."

"It's just easier when they're all around close by," Coyote said, washing her hands (despite the filth of her house, she kept herself quite clean, in her own fashion).

"I kept stepping on them," the child said, trying to justify her deed.

"Poor little shits," said Coyote, practicing dance-steps.

"Coyote," the child said timidly. "Did you ever have any children? I mean real pups?"

"Did I? Did I have children? Litters! That one that tried feeling you up, you know? That was my son. Pick of the litter . . . Listen, Gal. Have daughters. When you have anything, have daughters. At least they clear out."

III

THE CHILD THOUGHT OF HERSELF AS GAL, BUT ALSO SOMETIMES AS Myra. So far as she knew, she was the only person in town who had two names. She had to think about that, and about what Coyote had said about the two kinds of people; she had to think about where she belonged. Some persons in town made it clear that as far as they were concerned she didn't and never would belong there. Hawk's furious stare burned through her; the Skunk children made audible remarks about what she smelled like. And though Whitefoot and Chipmunk and their families were kind, it was the generosity of big families, where one more or less simply doesn't count. If one of them, or Cottontail, or Jackrabbit, had come upon her in the desert lying lost and half-blind, would they have stayed with her, like Coyote? That was Coyote's craziness, what they called her craziness. She wasn't afraid. She went between the two kinds of people, she crossed over. Buck and Doe and their beautiful children weren't really afraid, because they lived so constantly in danger. The Rattler wasn't afraid, because he was so dangerous. And yet maybe he was afraid of her, for he never spoke, and never came close to her. None of them treated her the way Coyote did. Even among the children, her only constant playmate was one younger than herself, a preposterous and fearless little boy called Horned Toad Child. They dug and built together, out among the sagebrush, and played at hunting and gathering and keeping house and holding dances, all the great games. A pale, squatty child with fringed eyebrows, he was a self-contained but loyal friend; and he knew a good deal for his age.

"There isn't anybody else like me here," she said, as they sat by the pool in the morning sunlight.

"There isn't anybody much like me anywhere," said Horned Toad Child.

"Well, you know what I mean."

"Yeah . . . There used to be people like you around, I guess."

"What were they called?"

"Oh—people. Like everybody . . ."

"But where do my people live? They have towns. I used to live in one. I don't know where they are, is all. I ought to find out. I don't know where my mother is now, but my daddy's in Canyonville. I was going there when."

"Ask Horse," said Horned Toad Child, sagaciously. He had moved away from the water, which he did not like and never drank, and was plaiting rushes.

"I don't know Horse."

"He hangs around the butte down there a lot of the time. He's waiting till his uncle gets old and he can kick him out and be the big honcho. The old man and the women don't want him around till then. Horses are weird. Anyway, he's the one to ask. He gets around a lot. And his people came here with the new people, that's what they say, anyhow."

Illegal immigrants, the girl thought. She took Horned Toad's advice, and one long day when Coyote was gone on one of her unannounced and unexplained trips, she took a pouchful of dried salmon and salmonberries and went off alone to the flat-topped butte miles away in the southwest.

There was a beautiful spring at the foot of the butte, and a trail to it with a lot of footprints on it. She waited there under willows by the clear pool, and after a while Horse came running, splendid, with copper-red skin and long, strong legs, deep chest, dark eyes, his black hair whipping his back as he ran. He stopped, not at all winded, and gave a snort as he looked at her. "Who are you?"

Nobody in town asked that—ever. She saw it was true: Horse had come here with her people, people who had to ask each other who they were.

"I live with Coyote," she said, cautiously.

"Oh, sure, I heard about you," Horse said. He knelt to drink from the pool, long deep drafts, his hands plunged in the cool water. When he had drunk he wiped his mouth, sat back on his heels, and announced, "I'm going to be king."

"King of the Horses?"

"Right! Pretty soon now. I could lick the old man already, but I can wait. Let him have his day," said Horse, vainglorious, magnanimous. The child gazed at him, in love already, forever.

"I can comb your hair, if you like," she said.

"Great!" said Horse, and sat still while she stood behind him, tugging her pocket comb through his coarse, black, shining, yard-long hair. It took a long time to get it smooth. She tied it in a massive ponytail with willowbark when she was done. Horse bent over the pool to admire himself. "That's great," he said. "That's really beautiful!"

"Do you ever go . . . where the other people are?" she asked in a low voice.

He did not reply for long enough that she thought he wasn't going to; then he said, "You mean the metal places, the glass places? The holes? I go around them. There are all the walls now. There didn't used to be so many. Grandmother said there didn't used to be any walls. Do you know Grandmother?" he asked naively, looking at her with his great, dark eyes.

"Your grandmother?"

"Well, yes—Grandmother—You know. Who makes the web. Well, anyhow, I know there's some of my people, horses, there. I've seen them across the walls. They act really crazy. You know, we brought the new people here. They couldn't have got here without us, they only have two legs, and they have those metal shells. I can tell you that whole story. The King has to know the stories."

"I like stories a lot."

"It takes three nights to tell it. What do you want to know about them?"

"I was thinking that maybe I ought to go there. Where they are."

"It's dangerous. Really dangerous. You can't go through—they'd catch you."

"I'd just like to know the way."

"I know the way," Horse said, sounding for the first time entirely adult and reliable; she knew he did know the way. "It's a long run for a colt." He looked at her again. "I've got a cousin with different-color eyes," he said, looking from her right to her left eye. "One brown and one blue. But she's an Appaloosa."

"Bluejay made the yellow one," the child explained. "I lost my own one. In the . . . when . . . You don't think I could get to those places?"

"Why do you want to?"

"I sort of feel like I have to."

Horse nodded. He got up. She stood still.

"I could take you, I guess," he said.

"Would you? When?"

"Oh, now, I guess. Once I'm King I won't be able to leave, you know. Have to protect the women. And I sure wouldn't let my people get anywhere near those places!" A shudder ran right down his magnificent body, yet he said, with a toss of his head, "They couldn't catch me, of course, but the others can't run like I do . . ."

"How long would it take us?"

Horse thought a while. "Well, the nearest place like that is over by the red rocks. If we left now we'd be back here around tomorrow noon. It's just a little hole."

She did not know what he meant by "a hole," but did not ask.

"You want to go?" Horse said, flipping back his ponytail.

"Okay," the girl said, feeling the ground go out from under her.

"Can you run?"

She shook her head. "I walked here, though."

Horse laughed, a large, cheerful laugh. "Come on," he said, and knelt and held his hands backturned like stirrups for her to mount to his shoulders. "What do they call you?" he teased, rising easily, setting right off at a jogtrot. "Gnat? Fly? Flea?"

"Tick, because I stick!" the child cried, gripping the willowbark tie of the black mane, laughing with delight at being suddenly eight feet tall and traveling across the desert without even trying, like the tumbleweed, as fast as the wind.

† † †

MOON, A NIGHT PAST FULL, ROSE TO LIGHT THE PLAINS FOR them. Horse jogged easily on and on. Somewhere deep in the night they stopped at a Pygmy Owl camp, ate a little, and rested. Most of the owls were out hunting, but an old lady entertained them at her campfire, telling them tales about the ghost of a cricket, about the great invisible people, tales that the child heard interwoven with her own dreams as she dozed and half-woke and dozed again. Then Horse put her up on his shoulders and on they went at a tireless slow lope. Moon went down behind them, and before them the sky paled into rose and gold. The soft nightwind was gone; the air was sharp, cold, still. On it, in it, there was a faint, sour smell of burning. The child felt Horse's gait change, grow tighter, uneasy.

"Hey, Prince!"

A small, slightly scolding voice: the child knew it, and placed it as soon as she saw the person sitting by a juniper tree, neatly dressed, wearing an old black cap.

"Hey, Chickadee!" Horse said, coming round and stopping. The child had observed, back in Coyote's town, that everybody treated Chickadee with respect. She didn't see why. Chickadee seemed an ordinary person, busy and talkative like most of the small birds, nothing like so endearing as Quail or so impressive as Hawk or Great Owl.

"You're going on that way?" Chickadee asked Horse.

"The little one wants to see if her people are living there," Horse said, surprising the child. Was that what she wanted?

Chickadee looked disapproving, as she often did. She whistled a few notes thoughtfully, another of her habits, and then got up. "I'll come along."

"That's great," Horse said, thankfully.

"I'll scout," Chickadee said, and off she went, surprisingly fast, ahead of them, while Horse took up his steady long lope.

The sour smell was stronger in the air.

Chickadee halted, way ahead of them on a slight rise, and stood still. Horse dropped to a walk, and then stopped. "There," he said in a low voice.

The child stared. In the strange light and slight mist before sunrise she could not see clearly, and when she strained and peered she felt as if her left eye were not seeing at all. "What is it?" she whispered.

"One of the holes. Across the wall—see?"

It did seem there was a line, a straight, jerky line drawn across the sagebrush plain, and on the far side of it—nothing? Was it mist? Something moved there—"It's cattle!" she said. Horse stood silent, uneasy. Chickadee was coming back toward them.

"It's a ranch," the child said. "That's a fence. There's a lot of Herefords." The words tasted like iron, like salt in her mouth. The things she named wavered in her sight and faded, leaving nothing—a hole in the world, a burned place like a cigarette burn. "Go closer!" she urged Horse. "I want to see."

And as if he owed her obedience, he went forward, tense but unquestioning.

Chickadee came up to them. "Nobody around," she said in her small, dry voice, "but there's one of those fast turtle things coming."

Horse nodded, but kept going forward.

Gripping his broad shoulders, the child stared into the blank, and as if Chickadee's words had focused her eyes, she saw again: the scattered whitefaces, a few of them looking up with bluish, rolling eyes—the fences—over the rise a chimneyed house-roof and a high barn—and then in the distance something moving fast, too fast, burning across the ground straight at them at terrible speed. "Run!" she yelled to Horse, "run away! Run!" As if released from bonds he wheeled and ran, flat out, in great reaching strides, away from sunrise, the fiery burning chariot, the smell of acid, iron, death. And Chickadee flew before them like a cinder on the air of dawn.

IV

"Horse?" Coyote said. "That prick? Catfood!"

Coyote had been there when the child got home to Bide-A-Wee, but she clearly hadn't been worrying about where Gal was, and maybe hadn't even noticed she was gone. She was in a vile mood, and took it all wrong when the child tried to tell her where she had been.

"If you're going to do damn fool things, next time do 'em with me, at least I'm an expert," she said, morose, and slouched out the door. The child saw her squatting down, poking an old, white turd with a stick, trying to get it to answer some question she kept asking it. The turd lay obstinately silent. Later in the day the child saw two coyote men, a young one and a mangy-looking older one, loitering around near the spring, looking over at Bide-A-Wee. She decided it would be a good night to spend somewhere else.

The thought of the crowded rooms of Chipmunk's house was not attractive. It was going to be a warm night again tonight, and moon-lit. Maybe she would sleep outside. If she could feel sure some people wouldn't come around, like the Rattler . . . She was standing indecisive halfway through town when a dry voice said, "Hey, Gal."

"Hey, Chickadee."

The trim, black-capped woman was standing on her doorstep shaking out a rug. She kept her house neat, trim like herself. Having come back across the desert with her the child now knew, though she still could not have said, why Chickadee was a respected person.

"I thought maybe I'd sleep out tonight," the child said, tentative.

"Unhealthy," said Chickadee. "What are nests for?"

"Mom's kind of busy," the child said.

"Tsk!" went Chickadee, and snapped the rug with disapproving vigor. "What about your little friend? At least they're decent people."

"Horny-toad? His parents are so shy . . ."

"Well. Come in and have something to eat, anyhow," said Chickadee.

The child helped her cook dinner. She knew now why there were rocks in the mush-pot.

"Chickadee," she said, "I still don't understand, can I ask you? Mom said it depends who's seeing it, but still, I mean if I see you wearing clothes and everything like humans, then how come you cook this way, in baskets, you know, and there aren't any—any of the things like they have—there where we were with Horse this morning?"

"I don't know," Chickadee said. Her voice indoors was quite soft and pleasant. "I guess we do things the way they always were done. When your people and my people lived together, you know. And together with everything else here. The rocks, you know. The plants and everything." She looked at the basket of willowbark, fernroot and pitch, at the blackened rocks that were heating in the fire. "You see how it all goes together . . . ?"

"But you have fire—That's different—"

"Ah!" said Chickadee, impatient, "you people! Do you think you invented the sun?"

She took up the wooden tongs, plopped the heated rocks into the water-filled basket with a terrific hiss and steam and loud bubblings. The child sprinkled in the pounded seeds, and stirred.

Chickadee brought out a basket of fine blackberries. They sat on the newly shaken-out rug, and ate. The child's two-finger scoop technique with mush was now highly refined.

"Maybe I didn't cause the world," Chickadee said, "but I'm a better cook than Coyote."

The child nodded, stuffing.

"I don't know why I made Horse go there," she said, after she had stuffed. "I got just as scared as him when I saw it. But now I feel again like I have to go back there. But I want to stay here. With my, with Coyote. I don't understand."

"When we lived together it was all one place," Chickadee said in her slow, soft home-voice. "But now the others, the new people, they live apart. And their places are so heavy. They weigh down on our place, they press on it, draw it, suck it, eat it, eat holes in it, crowd it out . . . Maybe after a while longer there'll only be one place again, their place. And none of us here. I knew Bison, out over the mountains. I knew Antelope right here. I knew Grizzly and Greywolf, up west there. Gone. All gone. And the salmon you eat at Coyote's house, those are the dream salmon, those are the true food; but in the rivers, how many salmon now? The rivers that were red with them in spring? Who dances, now, when the First Salmon offers himself? Who dances by the river? Oh, you should ask Coyote about all this. She knows more than I do! But she forgets . . . She's hopeless, worse than Raven, she has to piss on every post, she's a terrible housekeeper . . ." Chickadee's voice had sharpened. She whistled a note or two, and said no more.

After a while the child asked very softly, "Who is Grandmother?"

"Grandmother," Chickadee said. She looked at the child, and ate several blackberries thoughtfully. She stroked the rug they sat on.

"If I built the fire on the rug, it would burn a hole in it," she said. "Right? So we build the fire on sand, on dirt . . . Things are woven together. So we call the weaver the Grandmother." She whistled four notes, looking up the smokehole. "After all," she added, "maybe all this place, the other places too, maybe they're all only one side of the weaving. I don't know. I can only look with one eye at a time, how can I tell how deep it goes?"

LYING THAT NIGHT ROLLED UP IN A BLANKET IN CHICKADEE'S back yard, the child heard the wind soughing and storming in the cottonwoods down in the draw, and then slept deeply, weary from the long night before. Just at sunrise she woke. The eastern mountains were a cloudy dark red as if the level light shone through them as through a hand held before the fire. In the tobacco patch—the only farming anybody in this town did was to raise a little wild tobacco—Lizard and Beetle were singing some kind of growing song or blessing song, soft and desultory, huh-huh-huh-huh, huh-huh-huh-huh, and as she lay warm-curled on the ground the song made her feel rooted in the ground, cradled on it and in it, so where her fingers ended and the dirt began she did not know, as if she were dead, but she was wholly alive, she was the earth's life. She got up dancing, left the blanket folded neatly on Chickadee's neat and already empty bed, and danced up the hill to Bide-A-Wee. At the half-open door she sang,

> *"Danced with a gal with a hole in her stocking*
> *And her knees kept a knocking and her toes kept*
> *   a rocking,*
> *Danced with a gal with a hole in her stocking,*
> *Danced by the light of the moon!"*

Coyote emerged, tousled and lurching, and eyed her narrowly. "Sheeeoot," she said. She sucked her teeth and then went to splash water all over her head from the gourd by the door. She shook her head and the water-drops flew. "Let's get out of here," she said. "I have had it. I don't know what got into me. If I'm pregnant again, at my age, oh, shit. Let's get out of town. I need a change of air."

In the foggy dark of the house, the child could see at least two coyote men sprawled snoring away on the bed and floor. Coyote walked over to the old white turd and kicked it. "Why didn't you stop me?" she shouted.

"I *told* you," the turd muttered sulkily.

"Dumb shit," Coyote said. "Come on, Gal. Let's go. Where to?" She didn't wait for an answer. "I know. Come on!"

And she set off through town at that lazy-looking rangy walk that was so hard to keep up with. But the child was full of pep, and came dancing, so that Coyote began dancing too, skipping and pirouetting and fooling around all the way down the long slope to the level plains. There she slanted their way off north-eastward. Horse Butte was at their backs, getting smaller in the distance.

Along near noon the child said, "I didn't bring anything to eat."

"Something will turn up," Coyote said, "sure to." And pretty soon she turned aside, going straight to a tiny gray shack hidden by a couple of half-dead junipers and a stand of rabbit-brush. The place smelled terrible. A sign on the door said: FOX. PRIVATE. NO TRESPASSING!—but Coyote pushed it open, and trotted right back out with half a small smoked salmon. "Nobody home but us chickens," she said, grinning sweetly.

"Isn't that stealing?" the child asked, worried.

"Yes," Coyote answered, trotting on.

They ate the fox-scented salmon by a dried-up creek, slept a while, and went on.

Before long the child smelled the sour burning smell, and stopped. It was as if a huge, heavy hand had begun pushing her chest, pushing her away, and yet at the same time as if she had stepped into a strong current that drew her forward, helpless.

"Hey, getting close!" Coyote said, and stopped to piss by a juniper stump.

"Close to what?"

"Their town. See?" She pointed to a pair of sage-spotted hills. Between them was an area of grayish blank.

"I don't want to go there."

"We won't go all the way in. No way! We'll just get a little closer and look. It's fun," Coyote said, putting her head on one side, coaxing. "They do all these weird things in the air."

The child hung back.

Coyote became business-like, responsible. "We're going to be very careful," she announced. "And look out for big dogs, okay? Little dogs I can handle. Make a good lunch. Big dogs, it goes the other way. Right? Let's go, then."

Seemingly as casual and lounging as ever, but with a tense alertness in the carriage of her head and the yellow glance of her eyes, Coyote led off again, not looking back; and the child followed.

All around them the pressures increased. It was as if the air itself was pressing on them, as if time was going too fast, too hard, not flowing but pounding, pounding, pounding, faster and harder till it buzzed like Rattler's rattle. Hurry, you have to hurry! everything said, there isn't time! everything said. Things rushed past screaming and shuddering. Things turned, flashed, roared, stank, vanished. There was a boy—he came into focus all at once, but not on the ground: he was going along a couple of inches above the ground, moving very fast, bending his legs from side to side in a kind of frenzied swaying dance, and was gone. Twenty children sat in rows in the air all singing shrilly and then the walls closed over them. A basket no a pot no a can, a garbage can, full of salmon smelling wonderful no full of stinking deerhides and rotten cabbage stalks, keep out of it, Coyote! Where was she?

"Mom!" the child called. "Mother!"—standing a moment at the end of an ordinary small-town street near the gas station, and the next moment in a terror of blanknesses, invisible walls, terrible smells and pressures and the overwhelming rush of Time straight forward rolling her helpless as a twig in the race above a waterfall. She clung, held on, trying not to fall—"Mother!"

Coyote was over by the big basket of salmon, approaching it, wary, but out in the open, in the full sunlight, in the full current. And a boy and a man borne by the same current were coming down the long, sage-spotted hill behind the gas station, each with a gun, red hats, hunters, it was killing season. "Hell, will you look at that damn coyote in broad daylight big as my wife's ass," the man said, and cocked aimed shot all as Myra screamed and ran against the enormous drowning torrent. Coyote fled past her yelling, "Get out of here!" She turned and was borne away.

Far out of sight of that place, in a little draw among low hills, they sat and breathed air in searing gasps until after a long time it came easy again.

"Mom, that was *stupid*," the child said furiously.

"Sure was," Coyote said. "But did you see all that food!"

"I'm not hungry," the child said sullenly. "Not till we get all the way away from here."

"But they're your folks," Coyote said. "All yours. Your kith and kin and cousins and kind. Bang! Pow! There's Coyote! Bang! There's my wife's ass! Pow! There's anything—BOOOOM! Blow it away, man! BOOOOOOM!"

"I want to go home," the child said.

"Not yet," said Coyote. "I got to take a shit." She did so, then turned to the fresh turd, leaning over it. "It says I have to stay," she reported, smiling.

"It didn't say anything! I was listening!"

"You know how to understand? You hear everything, Miss Big Ears? Hears all—Sees all with her crummy gummy eye—"

"You have pine-pitch eyes too! You told me so!"

"That's a story," Coyote snarled. "You don't even know a story when you hear one! Look, do what you like, it's a free country. I'm hanging around here tonight. I like the action." She sat down and began patting her hands on the dirt in a soft four-four rhythm and singing under her breath, one of the endless tuneless songs that kept time from running too fast, that wove the roots of trees and bushes and ferns and grass in the web that held the stream in the streambed and the rock in the rock's place and the earth together. And the child lay listening.

"I love you," she said.

Coyote went on singing.

Sun went down the last slope of the west and left a pale green clarity over the desert hills.

Coyote had stopped singing. She sniffed. "Hey," she said. "Dinner." She got up and moseyed along the little draw. "Yeah," she called back softly. "Come on!"

Stiffly, for the fear-crystals had not yet melted out of her joints, the child got up and went to Coyote. Off to one side along the hill was one of the lines, a fence. She didn't look at it. It was okay. They were outside it.

"Look at that!"

A smoked salmon, a whole chinook, lay on a little cedar-bark mat. "An offering! Well, I'll be darned!" Coyote was so impressed she didn't even swear. "I haven't seen one of these for years! I thought they'd forgotten!"

"Offering to who?"

"Me! Who else? Boy, *look* at that!"

The child looked dubiously at the salmon.

"It smells funny."

"How funny?"

"Like burned."

"It's smoked, stupid! Come on."

"I'm not hungry."

"Okay. It's not your salmon anyhow. It's mine. My offering, for me. Hey, you people! You people over there! Coyote thanks you! Keep it up like this and maybe I'll do some good things for you too!"

"Don't, don't yell, Mom! They're not that far away—"

"They're all my people," said Coyote with a great gesture, and then sat down cross-legged, broke off a big piece of salmon, and ate.

Evening Star burned like a deep, bright pool of water in the clear sky. Down over the twin hills was a dim suffusion of light, like a fog. The child looked away from it, back at the star.

"Oh," Coyote said. "Oh, shit."

"What's wrong?"

"That wasn't so smart, eating that," Coyote said, and then held herself and began to shiver, to scream, to choke—her eyes rolled up, her long arms and legs flew out jerking and dancing, foam spurted out between her clenched teeth. Her body arched tremendously backward, and the child, trying to hold her, was thrown violently off by the spasms of her limbs. The child scrambled back and held the body as it spasmed again, twitched, quivered, went still.

By moonrise Coyote was cold. Till then there had been so much warmth under the tawny coat that the child kept thinking maybe she was alive, maybe if she just kept holding her, keeping her warm, she would recover, she would be all right. She held her close, not looking at the black lips drawn back from the teeth, the white balls of the eyes. But when the cold came through the fur as the presence of death, the child let the slight, stiff corpse lie down on the dirt.

She went nearby and dug a hole in the stony sand of the draw, a shallow pit. Coyote's people did not bury their dead, she knew that. But her people did. She carried the small corpse to the pit, laid it down, and covered it with her blue and white bandanna. It was not large enough; the four stiff paws stuck out. The child heaped the body over with sand and rocks and a scurf of sagebrush and tumbleweed held down with more rocks. She also went to where the salmon had lain on the cedar mat, and finding the carcass of a lamb, heaped dirt and rocks over the poisoned thing. Then she stood up and walked away without looking back.

At the top of the hill she stood and looked across the draw toward the misty glow of the lights of the town lying in the pass between the twin hills.

"I hope you all die in pain," she said aloud. She turned away and walked down into the desert.

V

IT WAS CHICKADEE WHO MET HER, ON THE SECOND EVENING, north of Horse Butte.

"I didn't cry," the child said.

"None of us do," said Chickadee. "Come with me this way now. Come into Grandmother's house."

It was underground, but very large, dark and large, and the grandmother was there at the center, at her loom. She was making a rug or blanket of the hills and the black rain and the white rain, weaving in the lightning. As they spoke she wove.

"Hello, Chickadee. Hello, New Person."

"Grandmother," Chickadee greeted her.

The child said, "I'm not one of them."

Grandmother's eyes were small and dim. She smiled and wove. The shuttle thrummed through the warp.

"Old Person, then," said Grandmother. "You'd better go back there now, Granddaughter. That's where you live."

"I lived with Coyote. She's dead. They killed her."

"Oh, don't worry about Coyote!" Grandmother said, with a little huff of laughter. "She gets killed all the time."

The child stood still. She saw the endless weaving.

"Then I—Could I go back home—to her house—?"

"I don't think it would work," Grandmother said. "Do you, Chickadee?"

Chickadee shook her head once, silent.

"It would be dark there now, and empty, and fleas . . . You got outside your people's time, into our place; but I think that Coyote was taking you back, see. Her way. If you go back now, you can still live with them. Isn't your father there?"

The child nodded.

"They've been looking for you."

"They have?"

"Oh, yes, ever since you fell out of the sky. The man was dead, but you weren't there—they kept looking."

"Serves him right. Serves them all right," the child said. She put her hands up over her face and began to cry terribly, without tears.

"Go on, little one, Granddaughter," Spider said. "Don't be afraid. You can live well there. I'll be there too, you know. In your dreams, in your ideas, in dark corners in the basement. Don't kill me, or I'll make it rain . . ."

"I'll come around," Chickadee said. "Make gardens for me."

The child held her breath and clenched her hands until her sobs stopped and let her speak.

"Will I ever see Coyote?"

"I don't know," the Grandmother replied.

The child accepted this. She said, after another silence, "Can I keep my eye?"

"Yes. You can keep your eye."

"Thank you, Grandmother," the child said. She turned away then and started up the night slope toward the next day. Ahead of her in the air of the dawn for a long way a little bird flew, black-capped, light-winged.

HERNES

To Elizabeth Johnston Buck

Fanny, 1899

I SAID WE HAD THE SAME NAME. SHE SAID SHE HAD HAD ANOTHER name, before. I asked her to say it. She wouldn't say it. She said, "Now just Indun Fanny." She said this place was called Klatsand. There was a village here, on the creek above the beach. Another up near the spring on Kelly's place on Breton Head. Two down past Wreck Point, and one at Altar Rock. All her people. "All of my people," she said. They died of smallpox and consumption and the venereal disease. They all died in the villages. All her children died of smallpox. She said there were five women left from the villages. The other four became whores so as to live, but she was too old. The other four died. "I don't get no sickness." Her eyes are like a turtle's eyes. I bought a little basket from her for two bits. It's a pretty little thing. Her children were all born before the whites settled here and all died in one year. All of them died.

Virginia, 1979

I WANTED TO WALK DOWN TO WRECK POINT, LATE THIS AFTER-
noon, I wanted a walk after writing all day. I put on my yellow slicker
and went out in the winter wind. All the vacationers are gone at last,
and there was not another soul on the beach. The storms have brought
in an endless scurf of trash, a long, thick line lying from the foot of
Breton Head to the rocks at Wreck Point. Seaweeds and litter of water-
logged twigs and branches, feathers of seabirds, scraps of white and pink
and blue and orange plastic that from a distance I take for broken sea-
shells, grains and lumps of dirty Styrofoam, worn-down bits of plastic
floats and buoys, clots of black, tarry oil from one of the spills they don't
talk about or a tanker release, all thrown up together on the sand in the
yellowish foam the storm waves leave.

It began to rain, beating down out of the dark ceiling of clouds. I put
up the oilskin hood, and the hard rain on the south wind deafened my
ears, hitting the hood over them. I couldn't look up into the rain, only
down at the water floating and sheeting on the brown sand, wind gusts
sending cat's-paws wrinkling across it towards me, and the myriad rain
hitting it, becoming it. I opened my mouth and drank rain. It increased,
increased, increased, it was hard and thick, thick as hair, as wheat, no air
between the lines of driving rain. If I turned left, east, I could look up
a little, and I could see how the rain came, not only in waves as I often
see it from the windows of the house, but spaced and crowded together
to form columns, like tall white women, immense wraiths hurrying one
after another endlessly northward up the beach, as fast as the wind and
yet solemn, processional, great grave beings hurrying by.

There was a gust of wind so hard I had to stand still to stand against
it, and another even harder. And then it began to end. It quieted. A spat-
ter of raindrops, then none. No sound but the breakers. A faint jade blue
gleamed out over the sea. I looked inland and saw the clouds still dark

above the land, and the tall figures, the rain women, hurrying up the dark clefts of the northern hills. They faded into wisps, shreds of white mist in the black trees. They were gone.

As I came back towards Breton Head the light of the sky shone placid pale blue and pink on the low-tide lagoons at the mouth of the creek. The tideline of scurf and filth and litter had been scattered and blurred away by the rain. In the quiet colors on the pools and shoals of the shallow water hundreds of gulls were standing, silent, waiting to rise up on their wings and fly out to sea, to sleep on the waves when darkness came.

Fanny, 1919

THIS IS THE INFLUENZA. I KNOW WHERE I TOOK IT. IN PORTLAND, at the theater. People were coughing, coughing and coughing, and it was cold, and smelled of hair oil and dust. Jane wanted Lily to see the moving pictures. Always wants to get the child into the city. But the child kept fidgeting and coughing. She was cold. She didn't care for the moving pictures. She never hears a story. She doesn't put one thing to the next to make the story. She will not amount to anything. My people were no great shakes, any of them, and all of them dead now, I suppose. There might be cousins yet in Ohio, Minnie's family. Jane asked me about my people. What do I know, what do I care for them? I left them, I came west. With Jack Shawe. With Mr. Shawe. I came west, in '83, to the Owyhee. The sagebrush in the snow. I left them all there where I grew up. The cow, the white cow down in the pool like silver in the evening. No, that was later, on the dairy farm, on the Calapuya. It was mother's red cow that bawled and bawled, and I said, Why is the cow crying, Mother? And she said, For her calf, child. For Pearlie. We sold the calf, she said. And I cried for my pet. But I came out with Mr.

Shawe and left all that. We had our honeymoon in the sleeping car on
the train. A bedroom. The Honeymoon Suite, ma'am! that porter said,
laughing, and Mr. Shawe tipped him five dollars. Five dollars! We got
on the train in Chicago, in Union Station, how often I have thought of
it, the high marble walls, the trains east and the trains west, the smoke
of the trains, the voices of men calling. The cold wind blew in Union
Station. And cold, cold when we got off the train in the sagebrush in the
snow. Evening, and no town. No railway platform. Five houses on the
sagebrush plain. I never will be warm again, I think. Mr. Shawe came
back from the livery stable with the buckboard to me where I waited
with our trunks, and we drove out to the ranch across the blue snow
plain. How cold it was! How Jack Shawe did laugh when he beat me at
cribbage, nights! He always beat. How his eyes shine! And he coughs,
coughing and coughing. And my son, and my son is dead. Coughing.
There were five villages. Owyhee was five houses and the livery stable.
We were thirty miles from town on the buckboard through the sagebrush, through the snow. What a fool Jack was to take on that ranch.
It killed him in five years. His bright eyes. He could have been a great
man. My people never amounted to anything. Little sister Vinnie died
of the whooping cough. Coughing, and the red cow bawling. The white
cow stands in the evening pool, water like quicksilver, and I call her,
Come, Pearlie, come! The pet, the one I hand-reared when the mother
died. And Servine and I were fools to take on that dairy farm, I guess.
Though he did know something about dairying. I wonder what that
land on the Calapuya would sell for now. I wonder had Servine lived
would I have lived there all these years and never come here to the coast,
to the end of things. Would I be there now in the valley with the hills
all round? Pretty country, like Ohio. It's the promise land, Fanny, it's
the promise land! Poor Servine. Him and Jack Shawe both, both those
men worked so hard. Worked so hard to die so young. They had hope. I
never had much, just enough to get by, to go on with. Don't you hope in

Jesus, Fanny? Servine asked me that when he was dying. What could I say? Little sister Vinnie is with Jesus now, Mother said, and I said, I hate Jesus. Why did you sell her to him? You shouldn't have sold her! Mother stared at me, she stared. Not a word.

Oh, I am ill. I smell dust.

The markings on the basket are like a bird's feather. Light brown and dark brown, light brown and dark brown, I can see it clear. I'd like to see it, to hold it. It's a pretty thing. It's on the chiffonier in Lily's room. The child keeps shells in it. I'd like to hold a shell, cool and smooth. Light brown and dark brown in rows, neat and firm, the marks on shells, on the wings of birds. Orderly, like writing. That was the only pretty thing I had then. Charlotte said she'd send me Grand-mother's opal brooch when I got settled in Oregon, but she never did. She wrote that the jeweller in Oxford said it was just glass, not real opal, and she would be ashamed to send it, not being real. I wrote her to send it, but she never did. Fool woman. I'd have liked to have it. I think of it, after all these years. Fool woman. Oh, I ache, I am aching ill. She'd come by, Indian Fanny, when it was all trees down to the dunes. Before the loggers before the houses before the roads. When the dark hills came down to the dunes and the spruce trees dropped cones and needles on the sand, when the elk walked and the heron flew, when I brought the children here because baby Johnny was chok-ing on that valley dust, that farm dust, breathing dried cow dung, and I didn't want any more farms any more ranches any more cattle any more coughing, and I sold the place and the stock to Hinman and took the children here west to the dark. Under the trees. Looking out to the bright water. I saw my daughter running on the sand. Away and away down the beach, running on the sand. And she'd come by, not often, the old woman, Indian Fanny. And I went that time to her shack down behind the Point, and we talked. I bought the basket for two bits. Not for the children. I kept it for myself, kept my hairpins in

it, on the shelf in the little shack. What are you going over there for?
Ada Hinman said. Henrietta Koop said, Whatever are you going to
do over there on the coast? Why, it's the end of the world! Not a road!
Johnny's lungs, I said. Why, there isn't a church nearer than Astoria!
I said not a word. The dark trees and the bright water and the sand
nobody can plow, nobody can graze. I have lived at the end of the
world. I have the same name as you, I said.

Lily, 1918

DEAD IS A HOLE. DEAD IS A SQUARE BLACK HOLE. MOTHER GOT
up from the table and said, Oh, Bruv, oh, Bruv. Grandmother didn't say
anything. When I listened to Mother crying, lights went up and down
behind my eyes. Grandmother said I could go and play, but she didn't say
it nicely. Lots of people came over. I played with Sammy and Baby Wanita,
and Dicky and Sammy were playing cowboys and Indians and kept running through where we were making a house under the rhododendrons.
Then I could go to Dorothy's house for dinner, but I couldn't stay over. I
had to come home and go to bed. First the room was dark, but then it got
whitey and turned solid and pressed down and squashed down all over
me so that I got all narrow inside, and everything was white, so I couldn't
breathe. Mother came, and I told her it was the Gas. She said, No, no
dear, but I know it was the Gas. Dicky Hambleton says the men with the
Gas in the War make yellow froth like Mr. Kelly's horse did when it was
dying, and Dicky held his neck and coughed, groke, groke, but he doesn't
know anything about it. His uncle didn't die. It was in the *Astorian* about
it. Pvt. John Charles Ozer A.E.F. Oregon Hero Falls. A black square hole
with green grass all round it. I'm afraid of the Gas in my room now. In bed
it begins to get white and narrow every night, and I call to Mother, and
she comes. It's all right when she comes. I want Mouser to sleep with me,

and Mother would let him, but Grandmother says he can't because of my breathing. Maybe she'll die now. I have a dead uncle. I know a dead man. He Died for his Country. I hate Dicky Hambleton.

Jane, 1902

I WRITE MY NAME IN THE BURNING SAND. THE WIND WILL BLOW it away, the sea will wash it away, and I like that. I like to write my name. I like to sign my schoolwork: Jane S. Ozer, Jane Shawe Ozer. Servine Ozer wasn't my father, only Bruv's. My father was Jack Shawe, and I remember him: the stove was going red-hot, and he stood tall and thin, with snow in his hair when he bent down to me, and he smelled like cows and boots and smoke. His breath smelled like snow. I like that, and I like my name. I like to sign my name: JANE. Plain Jane, plain Jane, loved a Swede and married a Dane, plain Jane, plain Jane, swallowed a window and died of the pane. Ha! I like signing things. I signed the beach. My beach. Private Property—Trespassers Will Be Prosecuted. This is Jane's Beach. Recoil, profane mortals! Tread not here! Do I wish Mary was here with me? No, I don't. It is entirely my beach alone this day. My ocean. Jane alone, Jane alone, run on sand, run on stone. Bare feet. I never will marry. Mary can marry, Mary be merry. I'll marry a Dane. I'll marry a man from far, far, far away. I never will marry, I'll live up in the shack on the Kelly place, the property Mother bought, the Property on Breton Head. I'll live alone and be old and scream at night like gulls, like owls. My Property. My beach. My hills. My sky. My love, my love! Whatever is to come I love. I love it here, I love my name, I love to love. My footprints on the burning sand, on the cool wet sand, write a line behind me down the beach, running in love, writing my name, Jane running alone, ten toes and two bare soles from Breton Head to Wreck Point and straight out into the sea and back with dripping skirt. You can't catch me!

Fanny, 1906

I PUT IN TO CHANGE THE NAME AS SOON AS THEY SAID WE WERE
going to get a post office at the store. Will Hambleton wanted it to be
Breton Head, for the fancy sound of it, to bring the summer people
over from Portland. Old Frank and Sandy would have gone on with
Fish Creek. I said, That's no name, every creek in Oregon's a fish
creek. This place has a name of its own. Don't your own dad call it
Klatsand Creek, Sandy? And he's lived here since the year one. So
Sandy starts nodding that's right, that's right. He says old Alec has
it written down on a map he has as "Latsand." But she told me the
name. It was the name of her village. I said, Well, Fish Creek is no
name for this town, with its own P.O., and that big hotel going up. So
Will started right in again saying we need a dignified name that would
attract desirable residents. I said, I guess I just assumed the new P.O.
was to be Klatsand, since all the real old-timers call it that. So Frank
starts nodding like a china doll. They all fancy themselves mountain
men, here since Lewis and Clark. Will Hambleton's the newcomer
and they like him to remember it. I just thought that was its proper
name, I said, and Will laughed. He knows I get my way.

When I came here from Calapuya, Janey was ten, and Johnny was
two. We lived in that shack off the Searoad that first winter. I have saved.
I have worked at the store eight years and saved. When the Hinmans
finally paid off the farm, I bought that land up on the bluff, old Kelly's
place on Breton Head. That property. Fifty acres for fifty dollars. The
old man liked me. Said anyhow he wanted fifty dollars more than he
wanted a piece of rock. It's all been logged, but they left the little stuff,
it's coming back. There's two good springs, one developed. I want to
take the old shack down, it's rubbish. I own that land and I own a half
interest in the store and I don't owe anybody anything. If Servine had
lived I guess I'd have been slaving debts out till I died. I'd like to put up

a house, up there on the property. It's going to get crowded here in town, with that Exposition Hotel going up, bringing people in. Two houses going up on Lewis Street. I might could put up a house in town myself to rent or sell. Will Hambleton's taking out all those old trees down along the Searoad, and he's buying land. There'll be houses everywhere soon.

That shack, that winter, I couldn't stop the leaks. Tarpaulins on the roof blew off, pans and buckets every time it rained. And it rained, land! I never knew rain till I came here. When the sun came out baby Johnny would try to pick up the sunshine from the ground, didn't know what it was. But you walked under the trees, dark old spruce trees that kept it dark underneath them, and then one step more, and it was all the light. Even in the rain the beach is light. The light comes back from the sea. I have seen the rain fall between the cloud and the sea in lines like the pillars of a house, and the sun strike through them. I would call that the house of glory.

The elk would come out on the beach, that first year. They don't do that any more. I see the herd inland, going through the marshes by the creek, but those days they'd walk down the dunes like a line of cattle, only tall, and looking with those bright eyes.

Well, old Frank says, siding with Will because Will's the rich man, well, what does it mean, anyhow? It don't mean nothing. I said, It means this place. It's its name. There isn't any other place called Klatsand, is there? That made them all laugh. So I got my way. The petition to change the name was already in, anyhow. I had sent it on Tuesday.

Lily, 1924

WHEN I GET MARRIED I'LL HAVE FOUR ATTENDANTS IN PINK and white organdie. My dress will be white lace with silver lace insets and veil, and my bouquet will be pink rosebuds and white rosebuds and baby's breath. My shoes will be silver kid. I'll throw the bouquet so Dorothy can catch it. The car will be a white roadster, and we'll drive to Portland after the ceremony and have the honeymoon at the Multnomah Hotel, in the Honeymoon Suite.

Maybe it will be a blue and white wedding and my attendants will wear blue organdie with puffed sleeves and white sashes and white shoes. Marjorie and Edith and Joan and Wanita will be my attendants and Dorothy will be the Maid of Honor with a silver sash and silver kid shoes. The wedding dress will be white lace and silver lace with a tiny stand-up collar like Mary Anne Beckberg's new dress, and silver kid shoes with those cunning little undercut heels, and the bouquet will be white rosebuds and some blue flowers and baby's breath, with a silver bow and a long silver ribbon.

We could all go to Portland on the train from Gearhart and have the wedding there, in that stone church with the tower. It would be in the Portland papers. Miss Lily Herne of Klatsand Weds.

Dorothy's mother has that old lace veil that's been in her family for hundreds of years and they keep it in the camphor chest wrapped up in old yellowy tissue paper. She showed it to me. I will be her Maid of Honor when she gets married. We promised. I wish we had an old lace veil. Grandmother never had anything pretty. She wore those awful old boots and lived behind the grocery store. All she left Mother was this house and the one the Browns live in and that land up on the Head that's all wild forest. I wish she'd bought the Norsman house instead and then we could live in it. Mr. Hambleton said to Mother, "That is a real mansion, Jane. I'm surprised your mother didn't buy it when she bought up the half-block." If the porch was fixed and it was all painted white with shining parquet floors it would be a real mansion, and we could have the wedding there with the wedding party coming down the stairs, and a long lace train on my wedding dress, and a cunning little flower girl in pink, and the little boy ring bearer in blue short pants could be little Edward. They play "Here Comes the Bride" as I descend the shining curving stairs.

I could go to Portland to the girls' school there and make a dear friend and be married in her house in the exclusive West Hills with parquet floors and landscape pictures in the wallpaper, and as I walk down the shining curving stairs in silver and white lace a bevy of beautiful debutantes watches and the orchestra plays "Here Comes the Bride." My friend's father gives the bride away. He is tall and distinguished with iron-grey hair just at the temples. He takes my arm. My bridal attendants arrange my train of white and silver lace. Miss Lily Herne of Klatsand. Miss Lily Frances Herne of Portland Weds. The bride's bouquet was of orange blossoms shipped from Southern California. I would still throw it to Dorothy.

Jane, 1907

THIS IS WHY I WAS BORN:

I wear the black skirt, the white shirtwaist, the white apron, and I pin the white cap on my hair. I wear my hair teased out, combed over itself, pinned up, and piled high. I take their orders, smiling. I carry trays of food. The women approve of me, watching me move so quick and neat. The men admire, looking away, looking back. I have seen their hands tremble. I pass behind them, a breath on the red nape of the neck above the celluloid collar. Thank you, Miss. I pass in and out the swinging doors between the hot shouting kitchen and the cool murmuring dining room of the Exposition Hotel. I carry trays that bear plates of food, plates of crusts and bones and smears, glasses full, glasses stained and empty. I set down the hot dish, delicately arranged and colored, odorous, appetizing. I lift up the cold, streaked, and greasy dish. I set down the wineglass and I carry it away. I am neat and light and quick and sweet, and I give food to the hungry. I leave order and plenty where I come and go. I content them all. But it is not for this that I go among the tables, brushing like a breath of wind behind their chairs. This is not why I was born! I was born because he stands a little to the left of the desk, his dark head bowed, his hands in the light of the lamp holding the register; and looks up; and sees me. I was born so that he might see me, he was born so that I might see him. He for me and I for him, for this, for this we have come into the daylight and the starlight, the sea and the dry land.

Fanny, 1908

SHE WAS ALWAYS A GOOD CHILD, A BRIGHT CHILD, HER FATHER'S child. She did well at school. The spelling prizes and the composition prizes and the mental arithmetic. She was the Spring Princess in the pageant at Union School. She was the heroine of the Senior Girls' Play at the High School in the Finn Hall in Summersea. She carried flowers, a sheaf of calla lilies in her arms, and stood and sang that song:

> *I don't care what men may think!*
> *What care I? What care I?*

She swept her skirts up like a queen and bowed. Where do they learn? How do they know? Running on the beach like a sandpiper, and the next day, "What care I?" so high and strong and sweet, standing like a queen in the lights on the stage, everybody clapping their hands for her. I couldn't clap. I couldn't unclench my hands until the curtains came together. Why did I fear for her? Why do I fear for her? She never got into harm. She always did well. Oh, your Janey! they say. Janey waited on us at the Hotel. What a beauty she's grown! When Mary ran off with that worthless Bo Voder, not even married, I did feel for Alice Morse, but what did she expect, letting Mary paint her face and drive out with every lumberjack and longshoreman? Jane was always friends with Mary, but she never would go out with her with that crowd. I never once was afraid for her that way. She knows her worth. She is a fine girl. Like Jack Shawe, tall and fine, bright eyes and a ready laugh. But proud. Johnny's going to be like Servine, easy and sweet, easygoing. I'm not afraid for Johnny. No harm will come to him. What is it I fear for my girl? I fear even to say that: "my girl." Too much at stake.

I hate a low-stakes poker game, Jack Shawe used to say. Dollar a point, Fan? he'd say, setting out the cribbage board, nights on the Owyhee ranch, dry snow ticking at the walls. I owe you ten thousand dollars already, Jack Shawe! Come on, Fan, dollar a point. No use playing for low stakes.

It isn't Lafayette I fear. I believe he's a good man for all his city ways, and I know he is in love with her. They are in love. Is it just that that I fear? What is being in love? Jack Shawe. My love's Jack Shawe. From the moment I saw him standing at the harness counter in the store in Oxford. I knew then what I was born for. It all seems so plain and clear. Everything in the world, all life at once, all in one body and one mind. All the promises kept. And all the promises broken. In love you stake it all. All the wealth of the world, all your life's worth. And it isn't that you lose, that you're beggared, so much as that it melts away and melts away into this and that, day in day out wasted, work and talk, getting cross, getting tired, getting nowhere, coughing, nothing. Nothing left. No game. What became of it, of all you were and all you were to be? What became of the love? of the promises? of the promise?

That's what I fear for her, maybe. That she'll be thrown away, like Jack. That she won't amount to anything, won't come to be who she is. What woman ever did? Not many.

It's some easier for a man. But there aren't many of much account to start with. Of either sex.

Lafayette Herne, I don't know, he might amount to something, he might not. I feel afraid for him, too. Why is that? Have I come to love the boy? Yes, I am part of their love, caught in it; I have called him son.

He carries his head well. A city man, with his fine clothes and narrow shoes, his thick dark hair well-combed. I like the way he turns his head and smiles. He's full of confidence. Competent. Assistant manager of the Exposition Hotel, and he's sure he'll have the managership of that new hotel he talked about in San Francisco. He's marrying on that expectation. High stakes. But he's doing well, at thirty. There is a brilliance in him, a promise. Women see it. And he sees women. Even me, he sees me; I know that; some men see all women. But he's mad for Jane. It will be a strange life for her, wife of a hotel manager, people coming and going, all strangers all the time, the fine food and drink and clothing, the fast living in the city. Is that what I fear for her, for them? What is it I fear? Why does my heart beat heavily, why are my hands clenched, as I wait here in the hotel room in Astoria, dressed for my daughter's wedding?

Lily, 1928

WHAT OH WHAT OH NOW OH NOW THAT'S BLOOD, THERE'S blood. I am bleeding. I am blood, blood. I am dead. Oh let me be in the black dark underground, under the roots of the trees. Go away, go away, he

He took me in his car so far, his father's car in the dark so far away from the party, far away, go away. Go away now so I can hide the blood.

Maybe it was the curse. Maybe it was the curse come early. Maybe it came in the car in the dark in the road in the forest. After the dance is over how the road turns and twists in the darkness, and on every branch of every tree of the forest an angel sits wearing white shining clothing and crying out. I knew that then, but I can see them now. Then all the angels let down drops and spots of blood. Their white what oh their shining clothes have stiff brown spots on them between the legs and there is something on the skirt that smells. The color of the old tub out behind the store, by Grandmother's stairs, it was rusted through, flaking red-brown, spotted brown, touch it and your finger's dirty red. Don't suck it, Dorothy said, you'll get poison rust, the lockjaw. Maybe it was the curse. All the angels nesting netted in the trees the stars and the huge shadows and then he

I came in and Mother called, Is that you dear? and I said yes. Last night. Now it's light I see the blood.

He turned off the switch no headlamps all dark and the engine silent and I said, Dicky, we really should be going home, and oh there's oh there's the bluejay, the jay yelling, but so far away now from the sunlight. That was so dark. Please go away. Oh please oh please oh please go away leave me be. Please stop. The blood began as just a little spot but now it will run out of the pores of my fingers and legs and arms and make spots on all my clothes, on the sheets. The spots dry stiff and brown like poison rust. I smell of that smell. I don't dare wash. I should not wash. Water is clean. If I wash the water will turn red-brown and smell like me. I'll make it stink. That's not a word for nice girls to say, Miss Eltser said, but I but I oh but I am not oh I am not a

What did I do? What has happened to me? I did what has happened to me. It is what I did. Nice girls

But I said, Why, that was the turn to Klatsand, wasn't it? Dicky

Dicky Hambleton is a college man. He went to California to college, he'll go back again in the fall. I am in love with him. We have to be in love. He said, Well, little Lily, so tenderly when I came into the living room in my new dress for the party. Lily so tenderly.

Dorothy left the party. She came and said she was going, but she had Joe Seckett to take her and I was with Dicky so how could I go with her? She said Marjorie said all the boys were going out to Danny Beckberg's car and he had bootleg and they were drinking and she had seen Dicky Hambleton there with them. But I was waiting for Dicky to come back to dance. I had to wait for him. I have to be in love. That is all tiny and bright and far away at the other end of the road, the band and the dancing and the fairy lanterns and the other girls. Dicky came back, Let's go, let's go, Lily, let's go for a picnic in the woods. But it's night, I said, I laughed. I wanted to dance, I love to dance. My white skirt was so pretty, shining in the fairy lantern light when I whirled, when Dicky whirled me dancing, and my white shoes on the floorboard of the car but the angels lean out of the huge trees and bleed the darkness and it smells of iron, and the bar of iron Oh! Oh stop! Stop! Stop! Stop! Stop! Stop! Stop! Stop!

San Francisco, Summer of 1914

THE SUMMER FOG LAY ON THE SEA. TENDRILS OF FOG REACHED up the bare hills; fog massed and moved through the Golden Gate, erasing the islands of the bay, the ships on the water, the dark mountains of Marin. Lights lay in faint lines and curves like jewellery along the East Bay shore under hills distinct against the blue-green sky. A ferry coming in to the towered building at the foot of Market Street moved splendid over twilit water.

A man and a woman in evening dress came out of the Alta California Hotel and paused a moment on the steps. Streetlamps and the glowing windows of the hotel behind them broke the dusk into brilliances and shadows. Facing the street full of voices and movements, the stepping of horses, the roll of high, light wheels, the woman drew a deep breath and held her white silk shawl a little closer. The man turned his head to look at her. He smiled.

"Shall we walk?"

She nodded.

A clerk ran out of the hotel, deferent but urgent: "Mr. Herne, sir, the wire came in from Chicago—" Lafayette Herne turned to speak to him. Jane Herne stood holding the fringed shawl loosely, aware of her own elegance and of her husband's black-clad, slender, angular body, his low voice speaking; aware also of being posed, being poised, as if on the low, wide steps of the hotel she stood aloof, solitary as a seabird on a wide shore, facing darkness.

He took her arm very firmly, possessing it. She came, compliant, gathering up her skirt with her free hand to descend the steps, and gathering it up again as they crossed the street littered with horse dung and straw. Through the flare of streetlamps and carriage lamps the wind flowed cool and vast from the sea.

"Are you warm enough?"

"Yes."

She turned to look into the window of a jeweller's shop as they passed it, black velvet knobs and satin nests emptied for the night. He said, dryly, as if her distraction annoyed him, "I have thought about what you said."

"Yes," she said, looking straight before her, stepping out, although her stride was shortened by the fitted evening skirt.

"I've decided that you should go to your mother, as you wished, with Lily, of course, for the rest of July and August. You can go whenever you like. Take a bedroom on the Starlight. I'll come up in September if I can for a day or two, and we can travel back together. I've been working very hard, Jane, and I realize I've let my concerns prevent me from paying enough attention to your wishes."

"Or my concerns," she said, smiling.

He made a little, impatient, controlled motion of his head in response, and was silent for a minute as they walked. "You've been wanting to visit your mother. I see my selfishness in keeping you here."

"You asked me to stay, and I stayed. You weren't keeping me."

"Why must you quibble over the words? All our quarrels start with that. However you want me to say it, I'm saying that I was selfish to keep you here. I'm sorry. And I'm saying go, as soon as you like."

She walked on, and he glanced sidelong at her face.

"It's what you said you wanted," he said.

"Yes. Thank you."

He drew her arm closer in his, with a movement of relief. He began to speak, and she made a little noise, perhaps a laugh of incredulity, at the same moment.

"I don't see the joke."

"We're play-acting. If we could talk, instead of fencing—"

"I tell you that you can do what you said you wanted to do, and you say I'm play-acting, fencing. Well, what is it you want, then?"

They walked on a half block before she answered. He had shortened his stride so that they went pace for pace, their heels striking the pavement smartly. They had turned north on a quieter street, less brilliantly lighted than Market.

"To be an honest woman," she said, "married to an honest man."

A dray loaded with ten-gallon cans, hauled by a powerful team of Percherons, rumbled and clattered beside them the length of the block. They crossed a street, Lafayette Herne looking left and right and holding his wife's arm close.

"So," he said lightly, "you're going to keep on making me pay."

"Pay? Pay what?"

"For that whole misunderstanding."

"Was it a misunderstanding?"

"The business with Louisa? Of course it was. A mistake, a misunderstanding. How often do I have to say so? How often do we have to go back to it?"

"As often as you lie to me. Do I make you lie?"

"If you keep going back over the same thing, if you have no belief in me—what am I to say, Jane?"

"You want me to believe you when you lie," she said, as if asking his confirmation of the statement.

"How can I say anything you will believe while you keep nursing this grudge, this spite? You won't let me make a fresh start. You said"—and his voice shook, plangent—"that we were beginning over. But you never let me begin."

After a few more steps she drew her arm out of his and caught up the trailing corner of her shawl. The fog was thickening, turning the light of the streetlamps milky in the distances.

"Lafe," she said, "I have thought about it a lot, too. I have truly tried to begin from where we—from after you left off seeing her. I know it is true that men, that some men, have this need. It seems to me kind of like a drunkard needing whiskey, but I know that's not fair. It's more like being hungry. You can't do anything about it, I guess, any more than you can keep from getting hungry and needing to eat. And I guess I do understand that. But what I can't understand is that you make it my fault. I won't let you begin again, you say. But you know that isn't fair. You've begun again, only not with me. And you want *that* to be my fault. Maybe it is. Because I don't satisfy you. But you always deny that."

"Because it's false, it's stupid! You know it's untrue!" He spoke with passion, rounding on her; she saw tears shine in his eyes. "I love you!"

"I guess you do, Lafe. But that isn't what we're talking about."

"It is! Love is all we're talking about! Our love! What does anyone else matter to me, compared to you? Don't you see, can't you believe, that you're my wife, my world? That nobody matters to me but you?"

They had stopped and stood facing each other. Beside them was the high front porch of a frame house standing among bigger, newer buildings built since the earthquake. Tall shrubs leaned out over the wooden steps, seeming to offer them a place, a protection from the publicity of the street, as if this were the porch and garden of their own house. It was nearly dark, and the chill of the air was deepening.

"I know you mean that, Lafe," she said in a timid, rueful voice. "But lying makes love worthless. It makes our being married worthless."

"Worthless? To you!" he said, fiercely accusing.

"Well, what's it worth to you?"

"You are the mother of my child!"

"Well?" Then, with a half laugh, "Well, *that's* true enough." She looked at him with a frank puzzlement that was a bid for frankness. "And you're the father of mine. So?"

"Come on," he said, taking her arm again and setting off.

She looked back at the steps and shrubbery of the house as if reluctant to leave them. "Aren't we a block too far already?"

He strode on, and she kept pace with him.

"It's past eight," she said.

"I don't care about the play."

At the corner he stopped. Looking away from her, he said, "Your belief in me is the foundation of everything, for me. Everything. To violate that, to say as you did that I wanted you out of town, out of the way, so that—for my convenience—"

"If I was wrong, I'm sorry."

"If you were wrong!" he repeated, sarcastic, bitter. She said nothing. He went on more gently: "I know I hurt you, Jane. I hurt you badly. I make no excuse for myself. I was a fool, a brute, and I'm sorry for it. I'll be sorry the rest of my life. If you could only believe that! We put it behind us. We started fresh. But if you keep going back to it, if you won't believe in my love, what can I do? Whose fault is it if I can't put up with this sort of thing indefinitely?"

"Mine?" she asked with simple incredulity.

His hold on her arm tightened, enough that she said after a moment, "Lafe, let go." He did not let her go, but relaxed his grip.

She looked into his face in the pale light of the lamp across the street.

"We do love each other, Lafe. But love, being married, even having Lily—what good is it, without trust?" Her voice, growing shrill, broke on the last word, and she gave a sharp cry, as if she had cut herself. She freed her arm and raised her clenched hands to her face.

He stood alert and uncertain, facing her on the narrow sidewalk. He whispered her name and put up his hand to touch hers, tentative, as one might reach to touch a wound.

She brought her hands down to hold her white shawl at the breast. "Tell me, Lafe. What you believe, truly, is that you have a right to do what you choose to do."

After a pause he said, gently and steadily, "A man has the right to do what he chooses. Yes."

She looked at him then with admiration. "I wish I was the kind of woman who could leave it at that."

"So do I!" he said with humor, and yet eagerly. "Oh, Janey, just tell me what it is you want—"

"I think the best thing for me to do is go north. Go home."

"For the summer."

She did not answer.

"I'll come in September."

She shook her head.

"I'll come in September," he repeated.

"*I'll* come when and if *I* choose!"

They stared at each other, startled by the leap of her anger. She drew her arms close to her sides for warmth under the shawl. The silken fringes flickered in the foggy wind.

"You're my wife, and I'll come to you," he said calmly, reassuring.

"I'm not your wife, if your wife is just one of your women."

The words sounded false, rehearsed.

"Come on. Come on home, Janey. You got yourself all keyed up to this. Now you're worn out. Come on. It wasn't the night for a play, was it?" His handsome young face looked weary. "You're shivering," he said with concern, and put his arm around her shoulders, turning her to fit her body against his, sheltering her from the wind. They started back the way they had come, walking slowly, entwined.

"I'm not a horse, Lafe," she said after a couple of blocks.

He bent his head down to her in query.

"You're treating me like Roanie when she shies at cattle. Gentle her down, talk a little nonsense, turn her round home. . . ."

"Don't be hard, Janey."

She said nothing.

"I want to hold you. To protect you. To cherish you. I hold you so dear, I need you so. You're the center of my life. But everything I do or say you twist around wrong. I can't do anything right, say anything right."

He kept his arm around her shoulders and his body inclined towards hers as they walked, but his arm was rigid, weighing heavy.

"All I have is self-respect," she said. "You were part of it. The best part of it. You were the glory of it. That's gone. I had to let it go. But it's all I will let go."

"What is it you want, for God's sake, Jane? What do you want me to do?"

"Play fair."

"What do you mean?"

"You know what playing fair means."

"Driving me crazy with hints and suspicions and accusations, is that playing fair? Is that your self-respect?"

"Sallie Edgers," she said in a whisper, with intense shame.

"What," he said flatly, and stopped. He drew back from her. After a long pause he said rather breathlessly, "I can't live with this. With this hounding jealousy. With spying, sparring for advantage. I thought you were a generous woman."

She winced, and her face in the foggy pallor of the streetlamp looked drawn and shrunken. "I did too," she said.

Presently she began to walk forward, pulling the fringed shawl close about her arms and up to her throat. She glanced back after a few steps. He had not moved. She paused.

"You're right," he said, not loud, but clearly. "It's no good. I don't know what you want. Have it your way!"

He turned and walked away from her, the clap of his shoes quick and quickly fading. She stood irresolute, watching him. His tall, straight figure blurred into the blowing fog.

She turned and went on her way, hesitantly at first, looking back more than once. The fog had thickened, dimming lights to blurs of radiance, turning buildings, lampposts, figures of people, horses, carts, cars, to bulks and wraiths without clear form or place. Before either had crossed a street the husband and wife were lost to each other's sight. On Market Street the lights of carriages and cars, brighter and more frequent, made a confusion of turning shafts and spokes of shadows in the half-opaque atmosphere, and through this beautiful and uncanny movement of wraiths and appearances the voices of children were calling and crying like seabirds. War, the young voices cried, war, war!

Virginia, 1974

GOBS AND HUMMOCKS, RIMS AND FORMS OF FOAM ARE RUN IN by the November breakers and driven up the wet beach by the wind. Luminously white out on the water, the foam is dingy as it lies on the sand. When the great kelp trees of the sea-floor forests are battered by deep waves in storms, broken fronds and stems churn and disintegrate into a froth, whipped by wave and wind into lasting foam, that rides the combers and is thrown ashore by the breakers. And so it is not salt-white, but oxidizes to dun or yellowish as the living cells decay. It's death that colors it. If it were pure foam of water the bubbles would last no longer than the bursting bubbles of a freshwater creek. But this is water of the sea, brewed, imbued, souped up with life and life's dying and decaying. It is tainted, it is profoundly impure. It is the mother-fluid, the amniotic mine-strone. From the unmotherly sea of winter, the cold drowner, the wrecker, from her lips flies the mad foam. And on the lips, on the tongue, it does not taste pure and salt, but bursts like coarse champagne with an insipid, earthy flavor, leaving a tiny grain of sand or two between your teeth.

Crosswaves pile the foam into heaps like thunderclouds and then, receding, strand the heaps, one here one there along the beach. Each foam-billow, foam-pillow shivers under the wind, shakes, quivers like fat white flesh, inescapably feminine though not female at all. Feeble, fatuous, flabby, helpless mammocks of porous lard, all that men despise and paint and write about in woman shudders now in blowsy fragments on the beach, utterly at the mercy of the muscular breakers and the keen, hard wind. The foam-fragments shatter further. Some begin to scud with a funny smooth animal motion along the wet slick of the sand; then, coming to drier sand, they stick and shake there, or break free and begin to roll over and over up to the dunes, rounding and shrinking as they go, till they stick again, quivering, and shrink away to nothing.

Whole fleets of foam-blobs slide along silent and intent under a flaw of wind, then rest, trembling a little, always shrinking, diminishing, the walls of the joined bubbles breaking and the bubbles joining and the whole fragile shapeless structure constantly collapsing inward and fragmenting away, and yet each blob, peak, flake of foam is an entity: a brief being: seen so, perceived, at the intersection of its duration and

mine, the joining of bubbles—my eyes, the sea, the windy air. How we
fly along the beach, all air and a skin bitter wet and whitish in the twilight, not to be held or caught, and if touched, gone!

Jane, 1929

I AM LOOKING, LOOKING, I MUST LOOK FOR HER. I MUST FIND
her. I did not watch as I should have done, and she is lost. My watch was
lost, was stolen. I must go to little towns hidden deep in the folds of bare,
dark hills, asking for the jeweller's shop. The jeweller receives stolen goods,
and will know where my watch can be found. I drive the Ford up roads
into canyons above invisible streams. Above the rim of the canyons is that
high desert where my mother lived when I was born. I drive deeper into
the clefts of the high, bare hills, but it is never the town where the jeweller
lives. Men stand on the street talking about money. They glance at me
sidelong, grin, and turn away. They talk low to one another and laugh.
They know where it is. A child in a black crocheted shawl runs away down
the dirt street between the hills. I follow her, but she's far ahead, running.
She turns aside into a doorway in a long wall. When I come there I see
a courtyard under shuttered windows. Nothing is in the courtyard but a
dry well with a broken coping and a broken rope.

Sewing brings the dream back. I sit at the machine and the rattle of
the needle is like the rattle of the car on those roads in the canyons of
the dream.

Lily, did you drink your milk this morning?

She went to get the milk from the icebox. She is obedient. She was
always obedient, always dreaming. But I was not always kind, or patient,
or careful, as I am, as I try to be, now.

Sewing, I dream awake. I take her down to California on the train to
Stanford, where the boy is. I find him there on the green lawns with his

rich boy friends, and I say to Lily, Look at him, look at the lout, with his thick hands and his loud laugh, Will Hambleton's prize bull-calf! How can he shame you? How could his touch be more to you than a clod of dirt touching you? Then I say things to the boy that make him shake and stare, and I strike his face with my open hand, a hard blow, and he cries and crouches and blubbers, abject. Abject.

Then we're in San Francisco not Stanford and it's Lafe standing before us. This is your father, Lily, I say to her. She looks up. She sees him. He's gone grey, half bald, he's lost his supple waist, but a fine man still, a handsome man, wearing his years well. He looks at Lily the way he did when she was a baby, when he used to rock her on his knees and sing, Hey, Lillia Lillia, hey Lillialou. But his face changes. He sees her. His eyes grow intent. What happened to you? he asks.

A dry well with a broken rope.

It was Lafe who named her. I wanted to call her Frances or Francisca, for Mother and for San Francisco. Francisca Herne. It would have been a pretty name. But Lafe wanted his Lily.

They say they're going to build a bridge across the Golden Gate.

Lily silly Lily little one, don't go down in the well in the dark, come up, look up. You're not the first girl Lily nor the last to Oh! but that she let him in! The second time! She let him in, let him in the house, our house! That she knew no better! What did I not give her, not teach her? How could I raise such a fool? Alone, in the woods, in the car, what could she do, his thick hands, his big thick body. She stayed in her room all day, she said she felt sick. I thought she had her period. I didn't look at her. I didn't think. I was busy at the post office. I didn't look at her. And he came in the night, that night, scratched at her window, whined like a dog, and she let him in. She let him in. I cannot forgive her. How can I respect her? She let him into my house. She thought she had to, she thought he loved her, she thought she belonged to him. I know, I know. But she let him in, into this house, into her bed, into her body.

He ought to marry her, Mary says. Face up to those damn Hambletons, she said. Face up to them? Make her marry him, make her lie down every night for him to rape her with his thick body with the blessing of the law? No. They bundled him back to his rich boys' school. Let him stay there. He can boast there how he raped a girl and she liked it so much she let him into her room the next night. They'll like that story, they'll believe it. He's where I want him, gone. But I don't know where Lily is.

Eyes say what's the girl doing still in town. Showing already. Flaunting. Common decency would have sent her away. Christian morality. Child of divorce. Only to be expected.

She walks among the eyes as if they did not see her, like a wraith. She is not there.

She sent herself away, is that it? Is that where she is? Maybe she's only staying away for a while. Maybe she's hiding, hiding down inside, in the dark, where the eyes don't see. But not forever. Maybe when her child comes out into the light she'll come with it. Maybe she'll come out with it. Maybe she'll be born alive, and will be able to talk then. Maybe she'll stop pulling out the hairs on her fingers and arms and thighs, the tiny, silky, hardly there hairs of a girl of seventeen with blond hair and fine, fair skin, one by one, till her skin is like a sponge damp with bloody water.

There's a bridge across the Golden Gate, a bridge laid down on fog. I follow a child, a girl running, out onto that bridge. Wait for me! Wait! I follow my daughter who was taken from me into the dark, into the fog.

Lily, 1934

THIS IS MY HOUSE. MOTHER OWNS IT, BUT SHE SAYS IT'S MINE forever. This is my room, with the window looking out into the big rhododendron bushes. That's where he came in. The branches of the rhododendrons rushed and rattled around him, and he broke them, and my heart thumped so that I saw it moving under my nightgown like an animal. He tapped on the sill and tapped on the glass. Lily, Lily, let me in! I knew he truly loved me then.

In the car in the forest in the night, that was a mistake. An accident. He was drunk, he had been drinking, he didn't know. But when he came next night to the house, to the window, it was because he loved me. He had to go away because his father is hard and cold and ambitious, but he truly loved me. It was our tragedy. I love my room. I love to put fresh sheets on the bed.

I don't like to let Baby into my room. Angels come in with her. They stand at the window to deny my comfort. They stand at the door to deny his love. The angels won't let me have my tragedy. They deny it all and drive him out of the room with their bright swords. Out the window he goes, scrambling, because he thought he heard Mother coming, and the last I see of him forever is one leg, one foot, the sole of his shoe. He didn't lace up his shoes because he was in such a hurry, and the sole of his shoe gets pulled over the windowsill after the rest of him, all in a hurry because he thought he heard Mother, but it was only the cat in the hall, and the dawn had come with its bright swords across the sky. Into the rhododendrons he goes scrambling and breaking the branches. They'll never let him back into the garden.

I watch Baby Virginia with the angels in the garden. They're often with her when she's awake. I'd like to see one watching over her when she sleeps in her crib. It would be a tall guardian in the shadows watching her with a brooding face. I saw a picture like that in a magazine. When she's running about the garden in the sunshine, when she goes out like a little soft bundle in the rain, then they're there with her. She talks to them. Yesterday she said to one of the angels in the garden, looking up, her little face so puzzled, "What Dinya *do*?" I never hear them answer her. Maybe she does.

We were sitting on the porch in the warm evening and the angels gathered and clustered so thick in the lower branches of the big spruce that I whispered to her, "Do you see them, Baby?" She didn't look at them. She looked up at me. She smiled the wisest, kindest smile. The angels never smile even when they look at her. They're stern. I took her on my lap, and she fell asleep with her little head on my arm. The angels left the tree then and walked away across the lawn, towards the hills. I think they come up from the sea, and go up into the hills. The light of their swords is the light above the mountains, the light across the sea.

One leg, one foot, the sole of a dirty shoe thrown out of heaven's window. There's no heaven. I don't go to church. Only when I'm tired of the angels, then I go to church with Dorothy to get away from them. Dorothy lets me have my tragedy. She is my true friend. If there was a heaven I could go there and be forgiven, all washed and washed away, and then I could have my tragedy. But the angels won't let me, so I go to my room.

No, Baby, not in Mama's room. Let's go to the kitchen, shall we, and make the pie for dinner. Would Baby like a blueberry pie? Would Baby Dinya like to help her Mama?

"Boolybelly pie!"

The angels won't laugh. They won't cry. I hide my tears for Dicky's love from them, because they would throw my precious tears out the window like trash, like old shoes, to rattle in the rhododendrons. I save my love from them. My love, my love! A kicking foot on a windowsill.

Last night Mother came into the room when I had done singing Baby to sleep, and I remembered how she was there in the room when Baby was born, standing so tall in the dimness, silent. But I never speak of the angels to her, that tall woman standing in the shadows with a brooding face.

Jane, 1926

AFTER ALL THESE YEARS. POOR LAFE, IT SOUNDS LIKE HE'S IN over his head this time. I'd like to see this Santa Monica woman. He never had much sense picking women, except for me. And didn't have the sense to hang on to me. At least he had the luck not to get tangled up again, till now. I liked thinking of him free. It wasn't much, compared to what we had, but it was something. Now it's nothing. I can't live without her, he writes, besotted. How can a man like that be a slave to his penis?

It's queer that I think words, now Mother's dead, that I didn't often use even in my mind, before. She wouldn't have wanted that said. Not that she was prissy. It's queer how the words change and change the world. When I left Lafe she didn't approve, but she never said I should go back to him. You did what you could, she said. But she'd be ashamed of a divorce. That wasn't one of the words she wanted said.

I'm not ashamed, but I don't want it, that sour end. Now I know I hoped for more. No more daydreams now of us both old, him falling sick, coming here, coming back. I'd give him the south room, and care for him, bring him soup and the newspaper. And he'd die, and I'd cry, and I'd go on just the same, but it would have come round again, come whole. But it doesn't do that. It doesn't come round.

He didn't think even to ask about Lily. Forgot he had a daughter.

So I'm to be a divorcée. Stupid fancy Frenchy word. Why's it only for the women? Isn't he a divorcé? With his woman who owns "beachfront property in Malibu," but I'll bet she doesn't. I'll bet she wants to own it. I'll bet there's some kind of dealing going on under the table, finagling, and Lafe fell for it, the way he always did. A taste for high meat. Poor Lafe. Poor me. I'll never be a widow. I'll never know where he's buried.

After his letter came I needed to walk, down on the beach, get the sky over me. The waves were like pearl and mother-of-pearl, coming in out of a sunlit fog. I had my walk down to Wreck Point. When I came back there were some summer people on the beach, there's always people now. That family staying at Vineys' and some from the Hotel. There was a thin boy who made me think straight off of Lafe. Twelve or thirteen, still just a child. He ran out into the water where the creek goes out to sea, the low-tide pools and shallows, such a handsome boy, kicking his feet up high, his cap pulled way down over his eyes and his nose in the air, splashing, prancing, clowning for his family, light as light. I thought, Oh, what happens to them? My heart wrung itself like a dishcloth—what happens to the lovely boys?

And then another boy, a little one. A whole family was going in a line, dragging along, worn out, been on the beach all day, it's their holiday and they can't waste it. So they were trudging along up to the dunes, and the littlest one was behind them all, standing crying. He'd dropped his collection of gull's feathers. He stood with sandy feathers all around his feet, crying, Oh, I dropped all my feathers! Tears and snivel running down his face, Oh, wait! Wait! I have to pick them up! And they didn't wait. They didn't turn around. He was six, maybe seven, too big to be crying for feathers. Time to be a man. He had to run after them, crying, and his feathers lay there on the sand.

So I came home thinking about little Edward Hambleton. They all call him Runt. The three big boys, and that mincing Wanita cadging candy every afternoon, Will of course, even Dovey calls him Runt. Dovey's afterthought! Will says, sneering, as if he'd had no part in him. Edward's no afterthought, they just never thought at all. Maybe that's why the child's not like them. Little bright fellow, he's taken a shine to Lily, follows her around, calling her Willy. Bright and sweet, and they never turn around to him. Never hear a word he says. Will pays the child no attention at all except to hit him. All in play, he says, toughen the boy up, he says. And I saw Dicky terrify the child, Get your hand out of there! What d'you think you're doing here! An eighteen-year-old bullying a child of five. Well, no doubt they'll manage to make a man of Edward. According to their lights.

Sometimes I wonder about myself as if I was another person I was looking at: Why did she come back to Klatsand? Why ever did she bring that child back here to raise? And I don't know. I loved California, I loved the city. Why did I hightail it right back here to the end of nowhere as soon as the chance came? Running home to Mother, yes, but it was more than that. When I was up there on the Property yesterday, walking the fence line against that lumber company cutting the east side of the Head, I was thinking about how I could start putting up a house there, like Mother and I used to talk about. How many times have I thought of that? A thousand times. And I thought, If I sold out my half-interest in the store to Will Hambleton, like he's been hinting at for a year now, I could put that money into real estate. I could buy that land off Main south of Klatsand Creek; there'd be ten house lots there. And the easternmost end of it would be a prime location for that lumber and supply yard Mr. Drake was talking about in Summersea last month. Jensen owns the land. He'd sell to me. If I had the cash. I'll never have it postmistressing. And it would be a relief to quit being a partner to Will Hambleton. Between keeping an eye on his hands and keeping an eye on his accounts, I told Mary, it's like doing business with a bull elephant, you have to watch both ends. If he can't snake his trunk around you, he'll sit down on you.

But it's all here, my life's all here. I take Lily in to Portland as often as I can, I don't want the child benighted. If she marries away from Klatsand, I'll be glad. There's nobody here for her; maybe when she begins to go out with the high school crowd, she'll meet some nice young people. I've thought I should send her to St. Mary's in Portland for her last year or two. Mary talked about sending Dorothy. I'm not

sure about that. Only I know that I'm fixed here. My soul goes no farther than Breton Head. I don't know why it is. All I ever wanted truly
was my freedom. And I have it.

Virginia, 1935

I ALWAYS LIKED WHAT I DREW BEFORE, AND EVERYBODY LIKED
it. But today I tried to draw the elk for Gran. I could see it, just like we
saw it up on the Property, and like the elk on the cup in the window. I
wanted to make it for her birthday. I drew it, and it was this thing like a
cigar with sticks coming out of it. I went over the lines, and then I took
black and made the lines thicker. It was so bad then I scribbled it out,
and took a new piece of paper, and I drew really, really light, so if I got
a line wrong I could erase it, but it was just the same. I could see the elk
but all I could draw was a big stupid ugly nothing. I tore it up and tried
again, and it was worse, and I began crying and got mad. I kicked the
table leg and it fell over, the stupid old card table in my room, and all my
colors got broken, and I began screaming, and they came.

Mother picked up the colors, and Gran picked me up and made me sit
on her lap till I stopped yelling. Then I tried to tell her about the elk and
her birthday present. It was hard, because I couldn't breathe right from
crying, and I felt sleepy with her holding me. I could hear her voice inside
her saying I see and That's all right then, and then Mother came and sat
down on the bed too. I leaned on her to find out if I could hear her voice
inside her too. I could, when she said, Time to wash your face now, Dinnie.

But I didn't have a present for Gran's birthday, so I told her about the
cup. I told her I tried to make an elk like the one on the cup at Viney's
store. So after lunch she said, Let's go see that cup. We went to Viney's
and it was still in the window. The elk has what Gran says is a wreath
around it, and looks majestic. Why, I think that is a majestic elk, Gran

said. We went in, and she bought it for herself with a nickel, but she said it was her birthday present from me, because if I hadn't found it for her she never would have owned it. Mr. Viney said it was a shaving mug. I guess it is for shavings. I said maybe she could use it for her coffee and she said she guessed she'd rather keep it for show on the chiffonier beside the Indian basket and the ivory mirror from San Francisco.

Lily, 1937

I WAS SITTING ON THE COUCH IN THE FRONT ROOM, MENDING, an hour after sunrise of the clear winter day. The sun struck in through the east window straight across my work. It freed itself from the spruce branches and struck my face a blow. I closed my eyes, blind with the beating of the light. Warmth shone itself through me, clear through soul and bones. I sat there, clear through, and I knew the angels. I was pierced with light and made warm. I was the sun. The angels dissolved into the radiance of the sun. They are gone.

After a while I could open my eyes. The warmth was my own breast and lap, and the piercing brightness had gone into a beam of light that struck across the air. Dust motes drifted in the beam, moving silently like worlds in space and shining like the stars they say are suns, all of us drifting together and apart, the shining dust.

Virginia, 1957

A STRONG WOMAN WHOSE STRENGTH IS HER SOLITUDE, A WEAK woman pierced by visionary raptures, those are my mothers. For a father no man, only semen. Sown, not fathered. Who is the child of the rapist and the raped?

They never tell if Persephone had a child. The King of Hell, the Judge of the Dead, the Lord of Money raped her and then kept her as his wife. Did she never conceive? Maybe the King of Hell is impotent. Maybe he is sterile. Maybe she had an abortion, there in Hell. Maybe in Hell all babies are born dead. Maybe in Hell the fetus stays forever in the womb, which they say is Heaven. All that is likely enough, but I say that Persephone bore a child, nine months after she was raped in the fields of Enna. She was gathering flowers there, spring flowers, when the black chariot came up out of the ground and the dark lord seized her. So the child would be born in the dead of winter, underground.

When the time came for Persephone to have her half-year with her mother, she climbed up the paths and stairs to the light, carrying the little one well wrapped up. She came to the house. "Mother! Look!"

Demeter took them both into her arms, like a woman gathering flowers, like a woman gathering sheaves.

The baby thrived in the sunshine, grew like a weed, and when it came time for Persephone to go back down for the autumn and winter with her husband, her mother tried to convince her to leave the child with her. "You can't take the poor little thing back to that awful place. It's not healthy, Sephy. She'll never thrive!"

And Persephone was tempted to leave the child in the big, bright house where her mother was cook-housekeeper. She thought how her husband the Judge looked at the child with his white eyes like the eyes of a poached trout, his eyes that knew everybody was guilty. She thought how dark and dank it was in the basement of the world, cramped under its sky of stone, no place for a child to run, nothing to play with but jewels and silver and gold. But she had made her bargain, as they called it. Betrayed, she had eaten the fruit of betrayal. Seven pomegranate seeds, red as her own blood, she had eaten, betraying herself. She had eaten the food of the master and so she could not be free, and her child, the slave's daughter, could not be free. She could only ever be half free.

So she took the baby in her arms and went down the dark stairs, leaving the grandmother to rage in the great, bright, empty house, and the rain to beat on the roof all winter.

Sky was Persephone's father and uncle. Hell who raped her was her uncle and husband. There was another uncle yet: the Sea.

The years passed, and Persephone and her daughter came and went between the dark house and the light. Once when they were upstairs in the world, Persephone's daughter slipped away. She needed a light foot and a quick eye, for the mother and grandmother never let her out of their sight; but they were busy in the garden, in the kitchen, planting, weeding, cooking, canning, all the housekeeping of the world. And the girl slipped away and ran off by herself, down to the beach, to the shore of the sea. Running like a deer, the girl—what was her name? I don't know Greek, I don't know her name, just the girl, any girl—she ran to the beach and walked along beside the sea. The breakers curled over in the sunlight, white horses with their manes blown back. She saw a man driving the white horses, standing in his streaming chariot, his sparkling salt chariot. "Hello, Uncle Ocean!"

"Hello, Niece! Are you out alone? It's dangerous!"

"I know," she said, but did she know? How could she be free, and know? Or even half free, and know?

Ocean drove his white-maned horses straight up on the sand and reached down to seize her, as Hell had seized her mother. He reached out his large cold hand and took hold of her arm, but the skin sparkled, the bone was nothing. He held nothing. The wind blew through the girl. She was foam. She sparkled and flickered in the wind from the sea and was gone. The King of the Sea stood in his chariot staring. The waves broke on the sand, broke around the chariot, broke in foam, and the woman was there, the girl, the foam-born, the soul of the world, daughter of the dust of stars.

She reached up and touched the King of the Sea and he turned to foam, sparkling white, that's all he ever was. She looked at the world and saw it a bubble of foam on the coasts of time, that's all it ever was. And what was she herself? A being for a moment, a bubble of foam, that's all she ever was, she who was born, who is born, who bears.

"Where's the child got to, Seph?"

"I thought she was with you!"

Oh, the fear, the piercing fear in the kitchen, in the garden, the cold clutch at the heart! Betrayed again, forever!

The child comes sauntering in at the garden gate, tossing her hair. She'll be scolded, grounded, given a good talking-to. Aren't you ashamed of yourself? Shame on you! Shame! Shame! And she'll cry. She'll be ashamed, and frightened, and consoled. They'll all cry, in the kitchen of the world. Crying together, warm tears, women in the kitchen far from the cold sea coasts, the bright, salt, shining margins of the universe. But they know where they are and who they are. They know who keeps the house.

Jane, 1935

I'VE BUILT THE HOUSE, MOTHER. ON YOUR LAND, OUR LAND, the old Kelly place, the Property on Breton Head. Money goes a long way these days, and I've saved for ten years now. Burt Brown was glad to get the work, because nobody's building much. All the frame is lumber from the old hotel, the Exposition, where I waitressed, where I met Lafe. John Hannah had it taken down last year. Take what you want, he said, and he built two houses and I built one with the lumber, the fine clear fir, the paneled doors, the white oak flooring. It's a good house, Mother. I wish you could have seen it. You kept the houses and farmed the farms your husbands bought, you bought and sold properties, you gave me the Hemlock Street house, but never had a house of your own. Lived upstairs behind the grocery. But you always said, I'd like to put a house up there on Breton Head, up there on the Property.

Last night I slept in it for the first time, though the walls aren't finished upstairs, nor the water connected, nor a thousand things yet to be done. But the beautiful wide floors lie ready for the years, and there's a cedar shake roof, and the windows look out to the sea. I slept in my room above the sea and heard the waves all night.

In the morning I was up early and saw the elk come by. The light was just enough to see them cross the wet grass and go down into the woods. Nine of them going along, easy in their majesty, carrying their crowns. One of them looked up at me as it stepped on towards the dark trees.

I got creek water, and made coffee on the fire, and stood at the window of the kitchen to drink it. The sky turned salmon red, and the great blue heron flew over, coming up from the marshes of the creek. I never know the heron as it flies, at first. What is the slow, wide-winged figure in the sky? Then I see it, like a word in a foreign language, like seeing one's own name written in a strange alphabet, and recognizing it I say it: the heron.

Summers of the Fifties, Summers of the Sixties

SUMMER VISITS, VISITS HOME, COLLEGE VACATIONS, TAKING THE train clear across the continent from those eastern shores heavy with history and industry, heavy with humanity, those old cities, ancestral, self-absorbed. Home from the college they called nourishing mother, alma mater, though to Virginia it seemed an old man, rich, famous, a grandfather, a great-uncle preoccupied with great affairs, scarcely aware of her existence. In his generous, opulent mansion she learned to live quietly, a poor relation, a good girl. Getting better all the time. But summers the train went home, across the prairies, through the mountains, away from his world, west.

She and Dave were married by a justice of the peace. "You're sure you don't want to ask your mother to come?" he said earnestly. She laughed and said, "You know we don't go in for weddings much in my family." They honeymooned in New Hampshire and Maine, at summer houses of his parents, his cousins. His fellowship paid his tuition, they lived on what she earned typing and editing theses and term papers. Dave's first visit west was the summer he was finishing his dissertation.

Gran moved down into the Hemlock Street house with Mother so that the young couple could have the house on Breton Head to themselves, no old women in the way, she said. So that Dave could work without being distracted. Men can't work in holes and corners, he needs a place to spread himself, Gran said. After a day or two he moved Gran's oak worktable from the west window downstairs and put it against an inner wall. He said it distracted him to see the sea when he looked up from his writing. It disturbed him to see the sea in the wrong direction, he said. The sun doesn't set in the sea, I'll be glad to get back to reality, he said. Great scenery out there, he would say when he was back in his world. Wide-open spaces, right between the ears. My wife comes from Ora-gahn. He said it as if it were a foreign word. It was funny, endearing to her, that he could not pronounce the name of a state of the union. I thought it was Shenek-toddy till I went east, she said. He was incredulous. Anyone knew how to pronounce Schenectady. It was not funny.

Summer, summer mornings waking in the wide bed at the wide window of the west bedroom, the first thing this side of sleep was the sky above the sea. And all through sleep and waking was the sound of the sea hushing and lulling away down at the rocks under Breton Head, the unceasing and pacific sound. Dave wrote late, stayed up always until two or three, for it wasn't real work to him unless it turned night into day, rearranged the world to suit. He would come to bed in the dark, keyed up from his writing, full of a dry, electric tension, rousing her. In the dark, roused, Virginia would pull him into the beat of the sea, the tidal swing, and then the long lulling and hushing into sleep, sleep together, together. Birds would wake her with insistent choruses at dawn. She would go out into the first light. Twice that summer she saw the elk go by between the forest and the house. The sun came up late above the blue Coast Range from the deserts, the prairies, the old cities. Later, at ten or eleven, Dave would come down, sit mute with coffee cup in hand, wake slowly, get to work at the table facing the wall, writing and rewriting his dissertation on "Imagery of Civilization in Pound and Eliot." Telephone calls to his thesis director, hours long, a panic over a lost footnote. She was lazy, giving herself up to the sun and the wind, walking down on the beach, making jelly of wild plums, playing at housekeeping in her grandmother's house. When she wrote something she put it aside unfinished. It was disloyal to write. Her work would sap and drain the energy that must be his for his hard, his important work.

It was three years after that till the next summer home. Dave had taken the job at Brown, turning down the better-paying one at Indiana. I don't want to get on a side track, he said, and she agreed, though when they visited Bloomington for his interview her heart had yearned to the place, the high groves of the campus where fireflies flickered in the sweet inland darkness. It remained a dream. Reality was east. But he knew she was homesick.

"How about that hike around Tillamook Head this summer?"

"Over it. You can't go around it, you'd fall in the sea."

It was the hike they had kept saying they'd take, the summer of the dissertation.

"Come on," he said. "Ora-gahn or bust!" And they drove west from the old cities, all across the prairies and the deserts and through the mountains, west with the sun, in the secondhand Mustang, that good little car. Gran stayed up in her own house, this time, to be visited, cooking magnificent dinners for them, poached salmon with dill mayonnaise, boeuf bourguignon, trout caught in Klatsand Creek one hour and fried the next. "When my husband managed the hotel in San Francisco," she said, "I learned to cook from the French chef."— "God, she's wonderful," Dave whispered. They slept in the little house on Hemlock Street, in the little room that had been Virginia's room all her girl-life, where an Indian basket and an ivory-backed mirror and a green glass net-float lay on the marble-topped chiffonier. They walked the beaches and hiked every trail in the Coast Range. Dave studied maps, set goals. No way down that side of Saddle Mountain, they told him, so he found a way. He triumphed, he conquered, he won the West. She followed, Sacagawea.

"I haven't seen the elk once this summer," she said the week before they left.

"Hunters," Gran said. "And logging."

"Elk?" Dave said. He asked the boys at the service station where the elk were. He drove her all over the back roads they had told him about. He drove over Neahkahnie Mountain and down Nehalem Spit until the road ran out. They walked the long dunes above the marshes between the river and the sea. "There! There!" he cried, exulting, as the crowned shadows rocked away into the shadowy marshes. He had caught the elk, he had given them to her. They drove home in the good little grey Mustang over Neahkahnie Mountain, the road turning above the twilit sea. Her mother had kept supper out for them, cold ham and three-bean salad.

"Tell me about fireflies," her mother said to Dave. He treated her as if she were a child, and she spoke to him as a child might, trustingly.

"We called them glowworms," he said. "If you got a lot of them in a jar, after a while they used to start going on and off all together." He spoke of his childhood as if it had been very long ago, as if there were no more glowworms.

Lily listened with her sweet docility. "I only knew the name," she said. "Fireflies."

"They never made it across the Rockies," Virginia said, and her mother said, "Yes. That's in your poem."

"'Sparks,'" Virginia said, startled. She hadn't known if her mother had read the book, which stood crisp and new on the bookshelf in the parlor. It had been awarded the Yale Younger Poets prize. "Yale, eh," Dave had said.

THE SUMMER HOME A COUPLE OF YEARS LATER, THE SUMMER when she cried. That was all she had of that summer, tears. Tears wept alone in the little dark bedroom, her room. Tears wept alone on the beach at evening, swallowed while she walked. Tears wept alone as she washed steamer clams at the sink in Gran's house, tears swallowed, hidden, dried. Invisible tears. Dry tears, evaporated down to crystals of salt, stinging her eyes and tightening her throat to an endless ache. Mouthfuls of salt. Silence. The summer of silence. Every night Dave called from Cambridge to tell her about the apartments he had looked at, the apartment he had found, how his book was going, the book on Robert Lowell. He had insisted that she spend the summer in the West. He had given her Ora-gahn. She needed a rest, cheering up. Summer in Cambridge was terrible, hot, muggy, he said. "Are you writing?" he asked, and she said yes, because he wanted so much to give her her writing, too. Every night he called and talked and she hung up and cried.

Her mother sat in the little back garden. Between the big rhododendrons under the bedroom window and the paling fence held up by a wild old rambler rose there was a strip of weedy grass, and on it Lily had set two lawn chairs. The evening air was fragrant with the roses. The wind blew warm from the northeast, from the land. Inland it was blistering this week, they said. Even here it was hot inside the house. "Come out and sit," her mother had said, so when she finished crying in her dark little room she washed her face, washed the salt away, and came outside. Her mother looked like her name, dim white in the dusk between the rosebush and the dark rhododendrons. There were no fireflies, but her mother said, "There used to be angels. Do you remember them, Virginia?"

She shook her head.

"In the grass, in the trees. You talked with them. I never could."

The land-wind carried the sound of the sea away. Though the tide was in, just over the dunes down Hemlock Street, they could hardly hear the waves tonight.

"Once you asked them, 'What Dinya *do*?'"

She laughed. Tears started, but freshwater tears, flowing, profuse. She drank them. "Mother," she said, "I still don't know."

"Oh, well, yes," Lily said. "Why don't you stay here in Oregon? Dave could get a job at one of the colleges, I'm sure."

"He's an assistant professor at Harvard now, mama."

"Oh, yes. You haven't called me 'mama' for years, have you?"

"No. I just wanted to. Is it all right?"

"Oh, yes. I never did feel 'mother' was right."

"What did you feel was right?"

"Oh, nothing, I suppose. I never was really a mother, you know. That's why it was so wonderful that I had you, had a daughter. But I always felt a little uncomfortable when you called me mother, because it wasn't true."

"Yes, it was true, mother, mama. Listen. I lost a baby, I had a miscarriage, early in June. I didn't want to tell you. I didn't want to make you sad. But now I want you to know."

"Oh, dear," with a long, long sigh in the dusk. "Oh, dear. Oh, and they never come back. Once they're gone."

"They can't make it across the Rockies."

SUMMER IN VERMONT. THE AIR A WARM WET WOOLEN BLANKET wrapped closed about the body, folded over mouth and nose, soft, suffocatingly soft and wet as sweat. A blanket of sweat. But no tears, wet or dry, salt or sweet.

"It's the self-centeredness that troubles me," Dave said. "I thought we had a partnership, a pretty extraordinary one. Suddenly there seem to be all these things you want that you haven't had, but I don't know what they are. What is it you really want, Virginia?"

"That is what we shall never know," she quoted unkindly; she had become unkind, unfair. "I want to finish my degree, and teach," she said.

"Are you giving up the idea of writing, then?"

"Can't I write and teach? You do."

"If I could take off time just to write—! It seems that you're trying to throw away what most writers would kill for. Free time!"

She nodded.

"Of course, poetry doesn't take the kind of time professional writing does. Well, I suppose the thing for you to do would be go over to Wellesley and take some courses."

"I want to enroll in a degree program. I'd like to do it," it was impossible, of course, it was impossible to say it, she said it, "in the West."

"A degree program? Out West?"

She nodded.

"You mean go to some college out there?"

"Yes."

"Virginia," he said with a bewildered laugh, "be rational. I teach at Harvard. You don't expect me to give that up. But you want to go to a graduate school somewhere out West? What happens to us?"

"I don't know."

Unkind, unfair. The round, close hills huddled over the cabin. The damp sky lay on the hills like a wet blanket, an electric blanket. Heat lightning flickered and flared in the clouds. The thunder never spoke.

"You're willing to simply throw away my entire career?"

Unkind, unfair. "Of course not. Anyhow your career doesn't depend on me any more."

"When did it ever depend on you?"

She stared. "When you were in grad school, when I worked—" He looked blank. "You just said we were a partnership! I worked. I was in the typing pool, I edited theses—"

"That?" He paused a moment. "You feel that that hasn't been repaid you?"

"No! I never thought of it like that. But you finished your degree. And now I want to. Is that unfair?"

"Pound of flesh, eh? No, it's not unfair. I just didn't expect it, I guess. I thought you took your writing more seriously. Well, listen. If this is really so important to you, at this stage, I can look into the chances of getting you into the Radcliffe graduate program. There might be a little static, but so long as I don't get any danger signals—"

"What can I say that you can hear?"

He finished his beer and set the can down on the cabin floor, keeping silence. At last he spoke measuredly, thoughtfully, patiently. "I'm trying to understand what it is you want. What you've always said you wanted was time for writing. You have it now. You don't have to work, we're past that stage. We certainly don't need the money you'd make teaching, if you did get a degree. And you won't get much poetry written in graduate school, you know. But I think I do see why you think you ought to finish. A kind of moral point, a kind of closure. But isn't it really the suburban housewife syndrome? Women who don't have anything to do, going back to school for 'self-improvement' or, God help us, 'self-expression.' All that's rather beneath your level, you know. And to use the doctorate as a time-filler before having children—" He shrugged. "So, what I suggest is that you take a month this autumn, at the beach, in Maine. Take the whole semester, if you want. Do your writing. I can visit weekends. But don't just play with graduate work, Virginia!

Women keep doing that, and it—I'm sorry, but it degrades the work. Scholarship, the university, isn't a sandpile, a playground."

She looked down at the beer can in her hand. "More like a battle-ground," she said. "Red in tooth and claw, the professors."

He smiled. "If you see it that way, why do you want to join the fray?"

"To get my union card."

"The Ph.D.? What for?"

"So I can get a teaching job."

"You can teach creative writing without the degree, you know."

"You don't respect creative writing courses. You've said so often. Why do you say I could teach them?"

"Because they're playschool courses," he said, and got up to go to the refrigerator in the other room of the cabin. While he spoke he opened the refrigerator, took out a can of beer, opened it, and came back to sit down in the wicker chair by the screen door. They had not lighted a lamp, and the room was nearly dark. Mosquitoes whined at the screens.

"If you want to play, fine. But you're not going to make it on the grown-up side of the fence, Virginia. The rules are different. You've had it easy. The Yale prize dropping in your lap. And then, as my wife, certain doors have been opened for you. You may not want to acknowledge just why certain reviewers have taken your work so seriously, why some editors are so receptive. You don't have to. You can write your poems and fool around with reality; that's your privilege as an artist. But don't try to bring that attitude out of the kindergarten. Where I have to live, success isn't a matter of a prize or two. It's a lifetime's hard work. Nothing, nothing is just handed to you. You earn it. So please, don't start messing around with everything I've built up for us, out of some kind of restlessness or feeling 'unfulfilled.' I've heard your artist friends going on about what they call 'the Eastern Establishment.' That's babytalk, you know. If I weren't part of the real establishment of letters, do you seriously think you'd have got your last book published where you did? You're involved in a network of influences. Success depends on it, and to rebel against it, or deny it, is simply childish irresponsibility. Toward me."

"My last book," she said in a low voice, without enough breath, "was a failure. A miscarriage, propped up in a, in a perambulator. I'm not denying anything. I just want to stop going wrong. To go right."

"'R' or 'wr'?" he asked gently, quizzically, cocking his head. "You're all worked up, Virginia. You're letting dissatisfaction with your work, and this bad luck with the miscarriages, get you down. I don't like seeing you make yourself so unhappy. Try my idea. Go to Maine, go write, go rest!"

"I want to work for a degree. On the West Coast."

"So you said. I'm trying to understand, but I don't think I do. The idea is that I'm supposed to quit a tenure-track position in the English Department at Harvard to go teach freshman comp at some junior college out in the cactus, because you've got a whim to take a doctorate at Boondock State? How am I supposed to understand that? Have you been talking with your mother lately? This sounds like one of her versions of the real world! Seriously, Virginia, I think I have a right to ask you to consider what you're asking of me before you put a strain like this on our relationship."

"Yes."

"Yes, what?"

"Yes, you have that right."

"Well?"

"It goes both ways, doesn't it?"

"What does?"

"A relationship. I can't breathe, Dave. You're getting all the oxygen. I'm not a tree. I tried to breathe nitrogen in and oxygen out, like trees do, I tried to be your elm tree, but I got the Dutch elm blight. I'm going to die if I go on trying to live here. I can't live on what you breathe out. I can't make your oxygen any more. I'm sick, I'm afraid of dying, I'm sorry that puts a strain on our relationship!"

"All right," he said, like a cleaver falling.

He stood up, looking out through the screen, filling the doorway.

"All right. Without the poetic metaphors. What is it you want, Virginia?"

"I want to take my Ph.D. at a western school, and then teach."

"You haven't heard anything I've said."

She was silent.

"Just tell me what it is you *want*," he said.

SUMMERS, PIECES OF SUMMERS, BITS AND SCRAPS, WHEN SHE would come up from Berkeley for a week or two, after summer session and before fall term, and sleep. That was all she had of those weeks, sleep. Sleep on the beach in the sun, in the hammock up on the Head in the shade, in her bed in her room. Sleep, and the sound of the sea.

And after that the summer, the long, wide, large summer when she stayed with Gran in the house on Breton Head because she was writing her dissertation. "You can't spread out all your books and papers in that poky little house. You need a place to yourself to work," Gran said.—"That's what Virginia said," Virginia said. But she slept three or four nights a week down with her mother at Hemlock Street. She got up early those mornings and went down to the beach to walk down to Wreck Point and back, walking by the waves thinking about *The Waves*, walking through the morning thinking about *The Years*, singing nonsense to the sea. Then she walked or drove up the dirt road to the house on Breton Head, the wide-floored house, the wide oak table under windows that looked over the sea where the sun went down. She wrote her dissertation. She wrote poems in the margins of the notebooks, on the backs of file cards.

"It's not Dave's child, then."

"I haven't seen him for three years, Gran."

Gran looked uneasy. She sat hunched in the Morris chair, squirmed, picked at her thumbnail like a teenager.

"Lafayette and I lived separately for twelve years," she said at last, sitting up straight and speaking rather formally. "He asked for a divorce when he wanted to remarry. But I think if there had been another man, I would have asked for the divorce myself. Particularly if there was to be a child."

"Dave doesn't want a divorce. He's been sleeping with a girl, a student, and I think he thinks if he gets divorced he'd have to marry her. Anyhow, if I'm still married when I have it, the baby is 'legitimate.' Unlike its mother. I don't mean to be flip, Gran."

"It makes a difference," her grandmother said without any particular emotion.

"I met the . . . the father this spring at Fresno. He lives down there. He's married. They have one child, she was born damaged, it's called spina bifida. It's pretty bad. Taking care of her is full-time for both of them. They don't want to institutionalize her. She's emotionally responsive, he says. His name is Jake, Jacob Wasserstein. He teaches modern history. He's a nice man. Very gentle. He has a lot of guilt about his daughter, and his wife. He's a guilt specialist. He teaches World War II, the concentration camps, the atomic bomb."

"So he . . ."

"He knows I'm pregnant. I saw him in June just before I came up home. He's very guilty and very happy, just what he likes best. I don't mean it was intentional. My diaphragm leaked." She stopped speaking, feeling her face and throat throb red. False, flip, all of it. She felt her grandmother's deep resistance, not disapproval, not judgment, but resistance: a wall. She felt herself outside the wall, flimsy and wordy, cheap. Nothing in Jane Herne's life had come cheap, she thought.

"So," Jane Herne said, seeking words. "How will you . . . will your teaching in Southern California . . ."

"I've discussed it with the chairman. They're giving me the spring term off. They're being really nice about it. This is where being Mrs. is helpful. Is necessary, actually. But I can get a divorce afterwards. Talking with you, I guess I see what I ought to do is tell Dave I do want a divorce. And file for it if he won't agree. Oh, God. I hope he agrees."

"That's all right," her grandmother said stiffly. After a pause she added, with more ease, "You generally get what you want, Virginia. Make sure you want it."

She thought that over for a while. "The baby. And the job at UCLA. That's what I want. And the next book of poems. And the Pulitzer Prize. All right?"

"Well, you'll earn what you get. You always did."

"Not the baby. I guess I kind of got him free. What do you think, is it time for a boy in this family?"

Jane Herne looked out the west window to the sky above the sea. "You don't earn them," she said. "They don't belong to you."

Fanny, 1918

MY FAT EASY BABY, MY SUNNY JOHNNY, GOOD CHILD, SAFE child, never did any harm. Never a worry to me, and I never worried over you. My boy's not in trouble. A kind, steady fellow, and they all know it, they all like Johnny Ozer. Even when I saw the terrible pictures in the magazine I only thought of those poor foreign men. So far away. All the smiling faces in the Portland station, the young men in the train windows smiling, waving their hands, waving their hats, all the pretty girls waving. The stories about the doughboys, and the jokes, and the jolly songs, over there, over there, the drums rumtumming over there. It'll be good for Johnny, a year or two in the Army, see the world. Toughen his hide a bit, Will Hambleton said, you've got a mama's boy there, Fanny, let him go, make a man of him. A man in a ditch in the mud choked to death by poison gas. I never said don't go. I never said don't go. I didn't know, but why didn't I know? Why didn't I fear for him? Why didn't I fear evil?

I lost my son. So they say. She lost her son. As if he was something I owned, a watch. I lost my watch. I lost my son. I was careless, I was a fool. But you can't keep him. You can't put him in your pocket, pin him to your dress. You have to let them go. With little sister Vinnie down by the pond, in the hot morning, making mudpies, we called it, shaping the sticky clay of the pond bank into figures, horses, houses, men. Set them on the muddy bank to dry. Forgot them, and they picked up the water, they slipped back into mud. I came again in the evening and there were only lumps and smears of mud on the mud, shapeless, not men any more. Make a man, make a man of him. Fool woman, you didn't lose your son. You threw him away. You let him go, you sent him, you forgot him and he turned to mud.

The knuckly red hands, the way he ducked his shoulder. His soft voice. He was a bright, soft boy. He would have made himself a man, a good man, a real one.

Oh, Servine, I am sorry. I am sorry, Servine, he would have done you proud.

He was crazy to get into that uniform. He thought that would do it. That's what they all said. How could he know? At twenty years old? I should have known. But I didn't fear evil. I didn't say to him the uniform won't do it, you do it yourself, John Ozer. I feared for his lungs, there in the dusty valley, on the dairy farm, that's why I ever came here to Klatsand. When he was a tiny boy he'd laugh and cough and cough. I feared for his lungs, and I let him go breathe poison gas. I cannot breathe now. I want to tell him to fear evil, fear evil, my good son, too late.

Jane, 1967

I watch the light on the ceiling, the moving light that shines up from the sea. I lived my life beside the sea, that great presence. All my doings were here, my business among the others in the world, but all along it was beside me, that other world.

I did what most of us do, pretending to keep our own world out, wrapped up in our skin, keeping ourself safe, thinking there's nothing but me. But our world goes through and through us and we through it, there's no boundary. I breathe in the air as long as I live, and breathe it out again warmed. When I could run, I ran down the beach and left my footprints behind me in the sand. Everything I thought and did the world gave me and I gave back. But the sea won't be taken in. The sea won't let tracks be made on it. It only holds you up if you flail your arms and legs till you're worn out, and then it lets you slip down as if you'd never tried to swim. The sea is unkind. And restless. All these long nights I hear its restlessness. If I could get to the east windows I could look out to the Coast Range, the blue mountains always shaped the same. They let the mind follow their curves against the sky just as they let your feet walk on them. And lying here I watch the clouds, and they're not restless, they're restful. They change slowly, melting, till the mind melts among them and changes as silently. But the sea down there bashes its white head against the rocks like an old mad king, it grinds the rocks to sand between its fingers, it eats the land. It is violent. It will not be still. On the quietest nights I hear the sea. Air's silent, unless the wind blows hard, and earth's silent, except for the children's voices, and the sky says nothing. But the sea yells, roars, hisses, booms, thunders without pause and without end, and it has made that noise since the beginning of the world and it will go on making that noise forever and never pause or stop until the sun goes out. Then will be death indeed, when the sea dies, the sea that is death to us, the uncaring otherness. To imagine the sea silent is terrible. It makes me think that peace hangs like a drop of spray, a bubble of foam, in the tumult of the waves, that all the voices sing out of the unmeaning noise. It is the noise time makes. Creeks and rivers sing running to the sea, singing back into the unbroken tuneless noise that is the one constant thing. The stars burning make that noise. In the silence of my being now I hear it. The cells of my body burn with that noise. I lie here and drift like a drop of spray, a bubble of foam, down the beach of light. I run, I run, you can't catch me!

Lily, 1943

WHEN EDWARD HAMBLETON WAS A LITTLE BOY HE LOVED ME and I loved him, little Runt, running to me red-faced and smiling, yelling, Hi, Willy! at the top of his voice. He thought my name was Willy. Because of hearing his father called Will, I guess. I called him Little Buddy. And he is my brother truly.

May and the Hambletons call his baby Stoney, but his name is Winston Churchill Hambleton. When he came early, they telephoned Edward at Fort Ord, and he said, Name him Winston Churchill. A boy needs a good name in times like these, he said.

These are the dark times. When Mother and Mary and Lorena Weisler and Hulse Chock sit talking after the newscast about the Pacific Theater, the cities in Italy, I think we live in a world that has all gone dark so that there's only the radio connecting people, and we here away out on the edge of it, on the edge of the sea where the war is. With the blackout, the town is as dark at night as if there were only forest here again. As if the town had never been and there was only the forest at the edge of the sea.

These are the dark days. Mother said that once about the other war, about my uncle John who was killed in France. Those were the dark days, she said. I can't remember him, only a shadow between me and the west windows in somebody's house, tall and laughing. And I remember riding on a horse with somebody walking along beside holding me, and Mother said that would have been Uncle John, because he worked at the livery stable for a while, and would give me rides on an old pony around the yard. And he would ride like the wind down the beach, she said. He was twenty. He was in the trenches, that was how they said it then. Edward is twenty-two now. In the South Pacific Theater. Like an actor on a dark stage. He hasn't seen the baby. I wonder if he is dead. They say it can be weeks before you hear. They say letters come from men that are dead, sometimes after they have been dead for weeks or months.

There is no use loving him. It's like a letter from a dead man. There's no use my loving anybody but Mother and Dinnie and Dorothy. I know Dovey Hambleton hates me for living here. We say good morning, Lily, good morning, Dovey. All these years. She never speaks to Dinnie. Dicky's other children are in Texas, she was talking about them to Lorena in the store, but she stopped when I came in. They are Dinnie's sisters, her other granddaughters. Those words are like knives: daughter, granddaughter. I don't say them. They cut my tongue. I say Mother, but often it cuts my tongue when I say it. Only there is Dorothy, my friend. She was never not my friend. That is a word as sweet as milk.

Dorothy's hair is turning blond, so she dyes it back to red now. Since she had her babies her neck and ankles have got thick. She doesn't move the way girls move, light and free, the way Dinnie goes down the street all legs and ponytail. Dorothy was like that when we used to play down by the creek, playing house all afternoon, playing weddings with our dolls. Now she's heavy and open and slow, like a red cow, beautiful. She knows everything. She doesn't worry. It doesn't worry her that Cal and Joe are in the war. With her the war isn't like a black empty theater but more like a construction site, men in trucks, busy. Cal's in a lot less trouble now than he was with that logger's wife in Clatskanie! she says. Army's the safest place for him! And Joe's driving a laundry truck at some base in Georgia. My war is with a million dirty skivvies, he wrote Dorothy. She reads me his letters. They're funny, he is a kind man. She misses him but she doesn't really miss him, she doesn't need him. She is complete. Like a round world. I love her because she looks at me out of her round whole world and brings me in, so that I'm not out at the edge, under the open sky. I can't walk on the beach, under the open sky, by the sea, not since the war started. Not since the angels. They're gone, but I still fear their wings, out there. Oh, Lily, she says, stop mooning. Oh, Lily, if you aren't the craziest! What do you think, Lil, is that baby of mine cute or is he cute? Lily, will you keep the kids this afternoon, I have to go up to Summersea. Lily, is that daughter of yours bright or is she bright? Dorothy can say all the words. She's not afraid. She is my true love.

Jane, 1966

"Angel child," Lily says when Jaye runs to her with a question or a flower. "Come to Lily, angel!"

Her arms are thinner than the child's arms.

I'm seventy-nine years old and I have no idea what love is. I watch my daughter dying and think she never was much to me but heartbreak. But why does the heart break?

I don't understand it. I don't know right from wrong. I thought Lily was wrong to stay home and not have the treatments. I thought Virginia was wrong to come here to be with her. Leaving everything she's worked for, the university, throwing it away. She says they'll take her on full-time at the community college in Summersea next year. She says she wants that. Wants to stay here. I thought she was wrong to have that child, some man's child she didn't even want to marry. It all seemed wrong to me. What do I know? I couldn't have managed without her. I can't look after Lily. Can't lift my arms. Can't pick up the cat, have to wait for him to jump in my lap, come on, old Punkin, and he teases me, sits and washes his face first. And that nurse. The cancer nurse.

They say the word right out, now. Never had it in the family, save for that thing Mother told me of: her mother in Ohio had what looked like a little seed stuck to her toe, and flicked it off without much thinking, and it bled all night long so the sheets were ruined. But she never got it, nor Mother, nor I.

I can't abide the woman. "The medicine makes them dopey," she says, or "They don't know what's best for them," right in front of Lily, as if Lily were a baby or an idiot! But she's strong and knows her business, I guess. And Lily is patient with her. Patient with everybody, everything. Always. Lily shames me.

I breathe free when Virginia comes in with the child, and the nurse goes. Evenings, the four of us, Jaye asleep and Lily drowsing along, Virginia and I sit and talk, or she grades her papers, or we play cribbage. I win, generally. It's one thing Virginia's no good at. I told her the other night, you win the prizes for poetry, but don't ever take up cards for a living.

Lily was right to want to die in her own house; Virginia was right to let her. I didn't want her here. I didn't want my daughter here to die. Or live. But she didn't want to come here. She was born in the City, but her life has been in the house on Hemlock Street. She never was away for as much as a week, but for that one trip to the World's Fair, before the war. But her daughter will live here, in this house, my house. The daughter conceived in the bed the mother is dying in. In that little room. The rhododendron bushes outside the window. Virginia answered me straight, the way she does: Yes, she said, yes, if you leave me the house on Breton Head I will live there. She said, I love Los Angeles but I have work to do, and I do it better here. What about your teaching? I said, and she said, I will do it as well here as I would there, and she laughed. If you leave me the house, she said, I will live in it and Jaye will grow up in it.

That gives me pleasure. She gives me pleasure. She looks like Lafe, the way she carries her head. She glances sidelong, her eyes flash. I thought she was wrong to let Lily have her way, wrong to have the child, wrong to come here to live, but I guess we think when a woman's free she's wrong.

I miss my freedom. Running down the beach, clear to Wreck Point, barefoot, alone.

When Edward came yesterday, I thought while we were talking, this is the nearest I come to running down the beach these days. Talking with Virginia, talking with Edward. When we talk I'm still on the move. As if the mind were a beach, the long empty sand, the waves, the sky. Virginia and I talk about people, students and teachers at her college, writers she meets when she travels to her prizes and meetings, people in town here, people I used to know. She likes to hear about the town back when I was growing up, and the San Francisco years. But that's a fairy tale to her. Edward's not all that much older than her, but he's got an old mind. Maybe it was being in the war. But even as a boy he was thoughtful. Virginia flies, flies like a heron, often I can't follow her. Edward plods along trying to see his way, trying to think things out, trying to know what's right. She's free; he seeks his freedom. I admire that in him. And a man that a woman can talk honestly with is a rare man. Edward got all the honesty in the Hambleton family.

Now and then I do stop and say, in words, in my mind: Edward is Virginia's uncle by blood. And I wonder if he ever thinks about that. We've never talked about it.

I never spoke to Will Hambleton from that day on. The day she told me.

Twenty years. Passed him ten thousand times on Main Street. Passing a dog, nothing.

He learned soon enough to send somebody else to the post office, Wanita or Edward or one of the grocery clerks, for the mail or to buy stamps or send parcels. I wouldn't wait on him. If he came in, I went to the back till he was gone. Stood there. At first my face would burn, then it was nothing to me. I'd find something to do till he was gone. Sometimes other people would come in while he stood there, and I'd speak to them, ask them to wait or come back later. I know what people here thought of crazy Jane Herne at the P.O., holding a grudge for twenty years, pretending a man doesn't exist, and Will Hambleton who owns half the town at that. I don't say I was right. I don't say I was wrong. I was doing what I could.

Will Hambleton brought up his eldest son to do evil and rewarded him for doing it. I could have forgiven the boy, I suppose, if there was any reason to. But not the man. I do not see a reason to forgive him.

I did what I could, and it was nothing. What can you do to evil but refuse it? Not pretend it isn't there, but look at it, and know it, and refuse it. Punishment, what is punishment? Getting even, schoolboy stuff. The Bible God, vengeance is mine! And then it flips over and goes too far the other way, forgive them for they know not what they do. Who does know? I don't. But I have tried to know. I don't forgive a person who doesn't try to know, doesn't want to know if he does evil or not. I think in their heart they know what they do, and do it because it is in their power to do it. It is their power. It is their power over others, over us. Will's power over his sons. His son's power over my daughter. I can't do much against it, but I don't have to salute it, or smile at it, or serve it. I can turn my back on it. And I did.

Virginia, 1972

STILL I ELUDE MYSELF. THERE IS A SHAPE. THE SEA-FOG WILL take shape, form: an arm, the glint of an eye, footprints in a line above the tidemark. I have to pursue, for the pursuit creates the prey. Somewhere in these mists I am.

Body's not the answer. Maybe it is the question. In the fulfillment of sexual desire I have found the other not the one I seek. I believed what all the books said; though my mothers did not say it, I believed it: The other is the foundation. But I built nothing on that foundation. A firm ground it may be, but a foreign one, the country of the other. I wandered in his kingdom, a tourist, sightseeing—a stranger, bewildered and amazed—a pilgrim, hopeful, worshipful, but never finding the way to the shrine, even when I read the signposts that said Love, Marriage, and followed the highroads beaten wide by a million feet. A failed crusader, I never got to the holy place. I built no fortresses, no house even, only shelters for a night, tents of leaves and branches, like a savage. Ashamed, I left that country, his great, old country, stowed away, sailed off to the new world. And there I sought the new life.

Body's all the question. What could be more one's body than one's child shaped in one's womb, blood, flesh, being? Seeking my being in hers before she was conceived, so I conceived her, imagining the small embodiment that I could purely cherish. But when she first moved in me, I knew she was not mine. This was the other, the other life, more purely other than any other, for if it were not, if no charge were entrusted to me, how could I purely cherish it?

So she was born out of me on that last long wave of unutterable pain, and runs free now. She returns, she comes home, home at four in the afternoon, milk and a cookie, can we play by the creek, never yet gone longer than overnight or farther than a school excursion, but she runs away from me. I feel the string stretch, the fine cord of ethereal steel that she'll keep pulling out so long over the years, so fine, so thin that when she's gone I'll hardly know it's there, not think of it for weeks, maybe, until a sharp tug makes me cry out for the pain in the roots of the womb, the jerk and twist of the heartstring. I feel that already. I felt it when she took her first steps, not to me but away from me. She saw a toy she wanted, and stood up and took her first four steps to it, and fell down on it in triumph. She went where she wanted to go. But I can't run after her. I must not pursue her, making her my prey. Not even the flesh of my flesh is the one I stumble after, my soul taking its first steps and falling flat, defeated, empty-handed, bawling for comfort.

Oh, the images, how they flock and hurry to me, comforting! lifting me up in their arms to dizzy heights! murmuring like voices heard inside a breast my ear is pressed against, don't cry, my baby, it's all right, don't cry.

Are my images all body, then? Are they soul at all? What are these words to which I have entrusted my hope of being? Will they save me, any more than I can save my child? Will they guide me in my search, or do they confuse and mislead me, the beckoning arms, the glinting eyes, laughter in the fog, a line of footprints leading down to the edge of the water and into it and not back?

I have to think they are true. I have to trust and follow them. What other guide have I than my dear images, my lovely words, beckoning me on? Sing with us, sing with us! they sing, and I sing with them. This is the world! they say, and they give me a sea-borne ball of green glass reflecting the trees, the stars. This is the world, I say, but where in it am I? And the words say, Follow us, follow us! I follow them. The pursuit creates the prey. I come up the beach in the fog from the sea, into dark woods. In a clearing in the woods a dark, short, old woman stands. She gives me something, a cup, a nest, a basket, I am not sure what she gives me, though I take it. She cannot speak to me, for her language is dead. She is silent. I am silent. All the words have gone.

San Francisco, Summer of 1939
Jane

HALF MY LIFE, SINCE I SAW THE FOG COME DRIFTING THROUGH the Golden Gate. They've put the great red bridge across the Gate, and the double bridge across the bay, and made an island full of lights and flowers and towers and fountains in the water, but the fog isn't any different. It comes in shining over the City in the sun, the crest of a great, slow wave. It breaks slowly and the bridge is gone. The City across the grey water is gone. The top of the Tower of the Sun is gone. The grey water fades away. In a luminous cold grey silence we walk, eating hot, fresh French fries from a paper cone.

I took the child to the City of Paris store to buy her a "real San Francisco dress." I had told her the ivory-backed mirror came from Gumps, and so we had to go to Gumps. I bought her a good silver-mounted brush. She'd learn to live here in no time. She flicks her eyes sidelong and sees everything. After a day at the hotel she could have been a city child, cool as a cucumber, picking up her fork in the restaurant, flirting out the big napkin on her lap, "I'll just have ice water, please!" Oh, she's the cucumber, that Virginia.

But Lily, poor Lily, to think she was born here, in the hospital right up there on the hill, my San Francisco baby, my little Francisca! She stares around her like a wild cow. Her eyes roll. And her hat, oh, land, my daughter in a hat like that. Lily isn't worldly, is what it is, and I am. I love this city.

If I saw Lafe Herne coming down the street: I thought of it when we passed where the Alta California Hotel used to be. If I saw Lafe come down the street I'd turn and go with him. Even if he had a Santa Monica woman on his arm. He has two arms. I want to tell him that I never found a man but him worth the trouble. He deserves to know that. Not that it would mean much to him. He'd be sorry for me, think I pined, think I meant I made a mistake in leaving him. I made no mistake. What's love without trust? I made no mistake, but I'd like to see him turn his head and look at me, the flash of his eyes. I'd like to see him. He's sixty now. It's all gone. It seems a world away, the Alta California torn down, all Market Street rebuilt, and it's not that I want to go back. I don't. What I'd like is to see Lafe Herne at sixty, and walk with him down the beautiful way between the fountain pools and the rainbow iceplant flowers to the Tower of the Sun. My arm in his, the way we used to walk. And watch the fireworks with him, the way we watched them on the Embarcadero, the Fourth of July, a week after we were married. But it doesn't come round like that. You don't take hands but once. And I was right to let go.

But I do get tired. In the street outside the hotel when we came back from the fair this evening, the fog was thick, and I was tired, and Lily and the child were worn out. The newsboys were calling, and my heart went cold. I thought they were calling that there was to be war.

Lily

SIX DAYS NOW TILL WE GO HOME. THIS TIME THE TRAIN WILL BE going the right direction. The Coast Starlight, that's its name, a beautiful name. And the Pullman porter was so kind, making up my berth, making jokes. He called me Missy. You all right in there, now, Missy? But when I woke in the night the mountains were turning outside the window in the moonlight across gulfs of darkness. I want to be home. Six days now. I wear out walking those long, long avenues on Treasure Island, and the wind blows so cold down the Gayway. There are great maps of the world, and a man painting a picture bigger than the side of a house, and Venus rising from the foam of the sea with the winds and the flowers about her. It is all so big, and so many people, so many many people! I can't keep up with Mother and Virginia. They want to see every sight. They wanted to see the microscopic animals and the huge horse and to go down in the mine. They wanted to see Ripley's Odditorium, but when the man blew smoke out of the hole in his forehead Mother said, Oh, pshaw, and turned away, and Virginia was glad to get out, too.

But then she wanted to see the woman cut in half with mirrors. How do they bear it all? How do they step so boldly out into the street? The cars whiz, whiz by—How do they know which streetcar to take, and where to catch the bus? How do they recognize our hotel among all the other great high buildings all alike? I was walking right past it when they laughed and made me stop. How are they so brave, so at home in this strange world full of strangers?

Virginia

I WILL NEVER IN MY LIFE FORGET THE BEAUTY AND THE GLORY of the World's Fair. I know that glory is where I will live, and I will give my life to it.

The best thing of all was the Horse. We were walking to where the bus comes to take you back to San Francisco, after all day on Treasure Island. We were tired, and oh it was so cold with the wind blowing the fog in, but I saw the sign: THE BIGGEST HORSE IN THE WORLD! And I said, Can we see that? And Gran never says no, except for Sally Rand. So we went in. At first the man was going to say he wasn't open, I think, but then Gran looked in and said, My land! What a beauty! And the man liked her, and let us in, just by ourselves without any crowd. He took the money and began to tell us about the Horse.

He was a Percheron, mottled grey like the sky over the sea sometimes is. His head was as big as I am. He turned and looked at us with his huge dark eyes with long dark lashes. I felt truly awed in that presence of majesty. He stood in a stall, very patiently, on straw. Beside him the man looked like a little boy. After a while I asked if I could touch him. The man said, Sure, honey, and I touched the shining mottled leg at the shoulder, and the Horse turned his head again. I touched his vast soft nose, and he breathed his warm breath on me. The man picked up

one of the Horse's forefeet to show us. Under the coarse, flowing fet-
locks, the hoof was as big around as a platter, with the mighty horseshoe
nailed on. The man said, Would the little lady like a ride? And Mother
said, Oh, no, and Gran said, Would you, Virginia? I could not speak.
My heart was great in me. It swelled in my bosom. The man helped me
over the fence around the stall and then just swung me up with a kind
of push, and I sat astride the Biggest Horse in the World. His back was
as wide as a bed, so my legs stuck out, and he was warm. I could touch
his mane, which was knotted into many neat, tight, whitish knots down
his great grey neck. He stood there gently. We couldn't go anywhere
because he was fastened in his stall. When do you take him out? Gran
asked, and the man said, Generally early, before the fair opens up. I take
him on a lead up and down the avenues. That would be a sight to see!
Gran said, and I imagined it: the great Horse stepping out in the silent
morning like thunder, like an earthquake, arching his neck, stamping
his mighty hooves.

Coming home on the bus and streetcar I thought all the time about
the Horse. When I am home I am going to write a poem. I will imagine
in it what I did not see, the stepping of the Great Horse in the fog on silent
avenues under the Tower of the Sun, and I will put in it the glory and the
majesty that I have seen. For this I was born, to serve glory patiently.

Jane, 1918

I CLOSE MY EYES AND SEE THE FIREWORKS. FLOWERS OF FIRE
opening, falling like bright chrysanthemums over the dark beach. Aahhh!
everybody says. Fireworks may be the nearest thing to perfect satisfaction
in this world.

All the flags and bunting and speeches in front of the hotel this afternoon. Brave boys, glorious victories, Huns on the run.

I shut my eyes and saw Bruv running on the beach, three or four years old, running ahead of Mary and me. Mother trusted us to watch him all Saturday; it made like a vacation for her working in the store. You girls, keep him in sight! He'd fly along the beach like a little thistle seed. Three or four years old. We didn't worry about him. He was afraid of going in the water.

Every time I pass the livery stable I think of him on that pretty bay colt he'd ride down onto the beach, summer before last. Every time.

At the Hambletons' picnic they'd looped red white and blue crepe paper on the fence and stuck flags in every tree in the yard. Willie Weisler kept talking about how he hopes the war will go on so he can enlist. "Even if I am only sixteen I'm big enough to kill krauts, ain't I? Ain't I?"

"Big enough fool," his mother said.

She's right, too. Talking about killing krauts, with a name like that. And in front of Mother and me. But still it troubled me she'd speak that way to him in front of us. Women talk to their sons that way, like they despise the boy for being something they expect him to be. But men glory in it. Will took Dicky around back of the house right at the picnic to whip him for some insolence, making sure everybody knew Dicky's so bad he has to be whipped. Making sure Dicky knows it. Boasting.

Even Mary's always making out Cal to be a ruffian, when the poor child's nothing but a puppy. All he needs is a pat and a kind word. But that's just what Mary and Bo won't give him. Like they thought it was their duty not to. The ruffian in that family is Dorothy. I'm glad she's taken to playing with Lily. Lily's too moony, lives inside her head, drifts by like a little moth. "City child," Mother said, when we were first home. "Never gets her little dresses dirty. As if she didn't touch the ground."

"I know I got dirty enough," I said.

She said, "You weren't any city child. Where you were born was thirty miles to the next house."

"Born dirty," I said, but it didn't amuse her. Mother's dignity never did allow for some of my jokes. And now she doesn't smile. She never looked tired till this year. I know she's pleased with my taking over the post office from her. I wish she'd go ahead with building up there on Breton Head, on the Property, like she's always wanted to. I suggested we walk up there, clean out the spring, but she put it off. I wish I could hearten her. If she won't build up there I wish she'd come live with us, but she's too independent. Those rooms above the grocery seem so dark now. It's like her life is dark. I feel that darkness when I'm with her. Yet she takes pride in me, I know that. It is the ground I stand on.

Like chrysanthemums, opening and falling in the dark. I see the fireworks down on the beach in the night, and the breakers gleaming for a moment under the colored sparks. I see Bruv riding in the evening, fast, full gallop down the beach, away and away.

"Well, now, how about a toast," Will Hambleton says, standing up at the long picnic table, "to the new owner of the Exposition Hotel!"

No doubt now who's the great white chief in Klatsand. I've never understood how Mother gets on so easy with him. She won't stand for any of his nonsense, and he knows it, I guess. But the way he crowds you and crowds you, with that barrel chest and big face and speechy voice of his, I lose patience. And Dovey cooing. And the pushing, yelling boys, and little Wanita. Now, with her they do just the opposite from what they do to the boys: they praise her for being something they despise. A little dressed-up parrot. She's a pretty child, but land! those bows and ruffles! and stood up on a chair to recite poetry! "My Country's Flag." I got one look at Mother's face.

I caught that red ruffian Dorothy behind the rhododendrons imitating her to Lily, all lispy sweet, "my tuntwee's fwag," and I did long to laugh, but I had to hush her up. Will doesn't like fun made of him or his. And he comes it pretty high over Bo and Mary. I suppose he only had them at his picnic because Mary and I are friends. I trouble him. I go up to Portland on the train. I lived in San Francisco. Lafe managed a big hotel. I might know something Will Hambleton doesn't know. I might have an idea in my head. It makes him nervous.

Well, I know what Will would start, if I gave him one word or sign. He may yet, even if I don't. There's that look in his face, no mistaking it ever. It's like smelling something. When they get fixed on you that way, when their body's attention is on you, you know it like you know it's a warm day, without thinking. But I think of Will's body naked, like a big cheese. I think of meeting, at lunchtime? where? some bedroom with the blinds down? It turns my stomach to think of it. And then he'd go home to Dovey. Like Lafe would come home to me.

And that's why he'd be doing it. Not for love and not for desire. Those are the names they call it, the excuse. Great names, like flags and speeches. What he wants is the advantage. The power. He's got it over Mother only through his money, and never to his satisfaction. She's a partner, independent. She isn't afraid of him. If he got me to cheat with him, he'd have us both at his advantage. And the satisfaction of cheating on Dovey, too. Well, Will, it would be a nice pie if you could eat it, as the joke goes.

I dream sometimes, but there isn't a man in this county I'd look at twice. I don't know what I want; I don't know that I want anything. Only to know some soul better. I don't know anyone. I never have. Mary, of course, she's a good friend, we share our whole lives, yet something's left out. It's like there's a country in me where I can't go. Lafe might have gone there, but he turned away. And other people have that country in them, but I don't know how to find it.

Lorena Weisler—she makes me think that all I know of her is some person she puts on like a dress. At the picnic, Dovey was going on about some new kind of crochet that Mrs. Somebody from Portland had shown her that uses a special tee-tiny hook and so on, and Lorena said, "Satan will find mischief still for idle hands to do." She said it in such a mild quiet tone, it went right by Dovey and Mary, and nearly by me. I looked at Lorena. Placid as a goldfish. But there are countries in her. She is a mystery. You live your whole life around the corner from someone, talk to her, and never know her. You catch a glimpse, like a shooting star, a flicker in the darkness, the last spark of the fireworks, then it's dark again. But the spark was there, the soul, whatever it is, lighting that country for one moment. Shining on the breakers in the dark.

Virginia, 1968

LAST SUMMER, THE NIGHT AFTER GRAN'S FUNERAL, EDWARD Hambleton came up to the house. He always used to call before he came; not that time. I was putting the coffee grounds out on the flower bed, the way Gran did, when I saw him walking up the drive in the evening light. It was a long summer sunset, pale gold deepening to orange and mauve, darkening to red.

Jaye was asleep. She'd been quiet at the funeral, watchful, a little awed. When we got home she thought she'd lost her stuffed lion, her Leo. She began crying, insisting we'd left it at the cemetery. And when I found the little lion out on the deck where she'd left it, she had a tantrum. I had to shut her in her room awhile, though I didn't want to; I wanted to hold her and cry too. At last she got quiet and we could rock together, silent. She was asleep before I got her into her bed. With Leo on one side, and the old cat on the other, old Punkin. He wanted company, he missed Gran.

So Edward came on foot, alone, and we stood in that flame-colored light in the garden, hearing the sea.

"I loved your grandmother. And your mother," he said.

He wanted to say more, but I didn't know what it was, and was not willing to help him say it. My heart was busy with grief and solitude and the glory of the evening. If he spoke I would listen, but I would not be his interpreter, his native guide. I think that it behooves men to learn to speak the language of the country we live in, not using us to speak for them.

He hesitated awhile, and then said, "I love you."

The great fires in the west made his face ruddy and shadowy. I moved, so that he thought I was going to speak. He held up his hand. I've often seen him raise his hand that way, talking with Gran, as he sought a word, an idea.

"When you were in college, in the late forties, you'd come home at Christmas, summers. You waitressed at the old Chowder House. You'd come into the store, shopping for your mother." He smiled, so broadly, so cheerily that I smiled too. "You were my delight," he said. "Understand me: there was nothing wrong between May and me. There never has been. I came out of the Army, you know, and found that I'd got me this wife, and a baby. And that was a wonder. It was amazing. And then Tim came along. And I loved running the store, the business. I didn't want anything but what I had. But you were my delight."

He held up his hand again, though I hadn't been about to speak.

"You went east, got married, got divorced, took your degree—I lost you for years. But I'd go into Dorothy's shop and see your mother, like a wild cottontail rabbit there behind the counter, making change. Or I'd get talking with Jane, after council meetings. And there it was. Not pleasure, not contentment, but delight. All I had with May and Stoney and Tim, I could hold. In my hands, in my arms, I could hold what I had. And that was happiness. But with you Hernes, I held nothing. I could only let go, let go. And it was the truer joy."

His sons are both in Vietnam. I turned away from him in shame and sorrow.

"There is the family of my body," he said, "my parents, my brothers and sister, my wife, my sons. But you have been my soul's family."

He stood looking out into the red sky. The wind had turned. It blew from the land, smelling of the forest and the night.

"You are my brother's daughter," he said.

"I know," I said, for I wasn't sure he knew I knew.

"It means nothing," he said, "nothing to him, to any of them—nothing but silence and lies. But to me it has meant that, however much I held, I had to let go, too. Not to hold. And now it's all letting go. Nothing left to hold. Nothing but the truth. The truth of that delight. The one perfectly true thing in all my life."

He looked across the air at me, smiling again. "So I wanted to thank you," he said.

I put out my hands, but he did not take them. He did not touch me. He turned away and went round the house to the driveway. He was walking down the road to town as the last colors faded and the light greyed to twilight.

I believed what he said. I believed in that truth, that delight. But I wanted to cry for him, for the waste of love.

Edward was my first love, when I was thirteen, fourteen. I knew who he was, but what did it matter, what did it mean? He was kind, thin, handsome, he joined the Army, he married May Beckberg. I was a kid with a crush. I saved the cigarette butt he put out in the ashtray in Mother's house when he came to say good-bye. I kept it in a locket on a chain, and never took it off. I worshiped May and the baby. I held them in holiness. Pure romance: to love what you can never touch. And was the love he thanked me for, his pure delight, ever more than that—a bubble without substance, that a touch would break?

Yet I don't know if anything is more than that. He held his sons, as I held Jaye that night, and tonight, close, close against the heart, safe, till sleep comes. We think we hold them. But they wake, they run. His sons have gone now where only death can touch them, where all their business is death.

If they die, I see him follow them. Not touching them, but following. And May, that strong woman, alone. She always was alone, maybe. He thinks he held her, but what do we ever hold?

Lily, 1965

WHEN I WAS VERY, VERY YOUNG, MOTHER TOOK ME DOWN-stairs to see the candles lighted on the Christmas tree in the lobby of the hotel, the hotel we lived in before I can remember. But I remember that, now, all at once, like a picture in a book. The page has turned, and I see the picture. All around me and above me are great shadowy branches, shining with ribbons of tinsel, and in the shadows are round worlds, many, large ones and small ones, red, silver, blue, green, and candles burning. The candle flames are repeated and repeated in the colored worlds, and around the flames is a kind of mist or glory.

They must have set me down there under the tree. Maybe I wasn't walking yet. I sat amongst and under the branches, in the pine smell and the sweet candle smell, watching the colored worlds hanging in the hazy glory and the shadows of the branches. Near my face was a very large silvered glass globe. In it were reflected all the rest of the ornaments that reflected it too, and all the flames, and the shoots and tremblings of brightness down the tinsel, and the dark feathering of the needles. And there were eyes in that shining globe, two eyes, very round. Sometimes I saw them, sometimes not. I thought they were an animal, looking at me, that the silver bubble of glass was alive, looking out at me. I thought the tree was all alive. I saw it as a world full of worlds. It is as if all my life I have seen the tree, the candles burning, the bright eyes, the colors, the deep branches going round and up forever.

Do you see the angel at the top of the tree?

A man asked that. A man's voice.

I only wanted to look into the branches of shining worlds, the universe of branches, the eyes looking back at me. I cried when he lifted me up. Do you see the angel, Lily?

Fanny, 1898

WE WAITED FOR LOW TIDE TO FORD FISH CREEK. AS THE HORSES started into the water a great bird flew suddenly down the creek between the black trees, over us. I cried out, What is that! It looked bigger than a man. The driver said, That is the great blue heron. He said, I look for it whenever I cross this creek.

There is not much to the town. End of the world, Henrietta Koop said. The General Store where I will work for Mr. Alec Macdowell and his son Mr. Sandy Macdowell. One fine house belonging to an Astoria family, the Norsmans, but they are seldom here, I'm told. The smithy and livery stable owned by Mr. Kelly. A sorry farm across the creek. And fourteen houses among the stumps. The streets are laid out good and straight but are mud two feet deep.

Mr. Sandy Macdowell had me this house ready. A man's idea of ready. It is two rooms and sets by itself under the black spruce trees just behind the sand dunes. It is some south of where the platted streets stop, but a sand road runs in front of the property. Mr. Macdowell calls it the Searoad, and spoke of a stage line they hope to run along that road, when they have cut a road across Breton Head north of the town. Mail is carried up the beaches from the south, now, when the carrier can ride through. He can't when there's high tides in winter. Mr. Macdowell apologized for the house. It is just a shack, small and dark. Stove is all right, and all the wood I want to cut lying handy. The roof is bad. He said he hoped I would not feel lonesome. It was the only house empty just now till they can fit up the place upstairs behind the store. He told me ten times there was nothing to fear, until I said, Mr. Macdowell, I am not a timid woman. I guess you're not, he said.

He said there were no Indians and nobody had shot a cougar for ten years. But there is the old woman who lives down behind Wreck Point, I have seen her twice now. And this morning I was up to light the stove while the children were still sleeping. The rain had stopped. I stood in the doorway in the first light. I saw elk walk past, going south in a line along the dunes. One walked behind the other, tall as tall horses, some with antlers like young trees. I counted them: thirty-nine. Each one as it passed looked at me from its dark, bright eye.

Virginia, 1975

THERE'S ALWAYS THE STORY, THE OFFICIAL STORY, THE ONE THAT is reported, the one that's in the archives, the history. Then there's the child of the story, born of the story, born out of wedlock, escaping from between the sealed lips, escaping from between the straining thighs, wriggling and pushing her way out, running away crying, crying out loud for freedom! freedom! until she's raped by the god and locked in the archives and turns into white-haired history; but not before her child is born, newborn.

The story tells how the grieving mother sought her daughter over land and sea. While she grieved and while she sought, no grain grew, no flower bloomed. Then, when she found the maiden, spring came. The wild grass seeded, the birds sang, the small rain fell on the western wind.

But the maiden no longer maiden must return for half the year each year to her husband in the underworld, leaving her mother in the world of light. While the daughter is dead and the mother weeps, it is the fall and winter of the year.

The story is true. It is history.

But the child is always born, and the child has her story to tell, the unofficial, the unconfirmed, the news.

She had done her time inside. She had held court as Queen of Hell for half eternity. She had shelved the law books in the archives and filed all the files of the firm. She had lived with her husband for the appointed time, and the season of her return was at hand. She knew it by the way the roots that hung down through the low stone ceilings of the underworld—taproots of great trees, oaks, beeches, chestnuts, redwoods, only the longest roots could reach down so far—by the way those roots sent tiny fibrils, curling split ends, growing out, groping out from the damp, dark grout between the rocks that make the sky there. When she saw the thin root hairs reach out she knew the trees were needing her to come and bring the spring.

She went to her husband, the judge. She went to the courthouse, appearing before him as a plaintiff. The uncomplaining multitudes of the dead, the shadows of life awaiting judgment, made way for her. She came among them as a green shoot comes through the sodden leaves at winter's end, as a freshet of black living water cracks the rotten ice. She stood before the golden throne of judgment, between the pillars of silver, on the jewelled pavement, and stated her case: "My lord, by the terms of our agreement, it is time I go."

He could not deny it, though he wanted to. Justice binds the Lord of Hell, though mercy does not. His beautiful dark face was sad and stern. He gazed at her with eyes like silver coins, and did not speak, but nodded once.

She turned and left him. Lightly she walked the long ways and stairways that led up. The dog barked and the old boatman scowled to see her stand alone on the dark side of the river, but she laughed. She stepped into his boat to be ferried over to the other shore, where the multitudes waited. Lightly she stepped out and ran up the brightening paths, and came through the narrow way at last into the sunlight.

The fields were dun and sodden after long snow and rain. Her feet, that stayed so clean in Hell, were black at once with mud. Her hair, always so dry and neat in Hell, was windblown and wet at once with rain. She laughed, she leaped like a deer, she ran like a deer, running home to Mother.

She came to the house. The garden was untended, winter-beaten. "I'll tend to that," she said. The door of the house stood open. "They're expecting me," she said. The kitchen stove was cold, the dishes had been put up, no one was in the rooms. "They must be out looking for me," she said. "I must be late. Why didn't they just wait here for me?"

She lighted the fire in the stove. She laid out the loaf and the cheese and the red wine. As evening darkened she lighted the lights so that the windows of the house would shine across the dusk, and her mother and grandmother, trudging the road in the rain, would see the light: "Look there! She's home!"

But they did not come. The night passed, and the days passed. She kept the house, she planted the garden. The fields grew green, trees leaved, flowers bloomed: daffodil, primrose, bluebell, daisy, by the garden paths. But they did not come, the mother, the grandmother. Where were they? What was keeping them? She set out across the fields to find them. And she found them soon enough.

I don't want to tell the story. I don't want to tell that a child sees her grandmother burned to death and her mother raped by the enemy by the soldiers by the guerrillas by the patriots by the believers by the infidels by the faithful by the terrorists by the partisans by the contras by the pros. By the corporations by the executives by the rank and file by the leaders by the followers the orderers the ordered the governments the machinery. To be caught in the machinery, to fall into the machine, to be a body torn to pieces, harrowed, disemboweled, crushed by a tank by a truck by a tractor, treads and wheels smash the soft arms, the bones snap, the blood and lymph and urine burst out, for flesh is not grass but meat. I don't want to tell that a child sees the god, sees what the god does. I don't want to tell the story of the child, the child who is the spring of the world, who went out of her house and saw her grandmother doused in gasoline and burning, the grey hair all afire. She saw her mother's legs pulled apart by the machinery and the barrel of the gun pushed up into her mother's womb and then the gun was fired.

She ran, ran like a woman, heavy-footed, her breasts jouncing with each step, her breath in gasps, ran to the narrow way and down, down into the dark. She did not pay the boatman, but commanded him, "Row!" In silence he obeyed her. The dog cowered down. She ran the long ways, the dark stairs, heavily, to the house, the courthouse, the palace of precious stones under the stone sky.

The anterooms and waiting rooms were full as always of shadows, fuller than ever before. They parted, making way for her.

Her husband, her father's brother, sat on his throne holding court, judging all who came to him, and all came to him.

"Your mother is dead," she said. "Your sister is dead. They have killed Earth and Time. What is there left, my lord?"

"Money," her husband said.

The seat of judgment was solid gold, the pillars were silver, the pavements were diamonds, sapphires, emeralds, and the walls were papered with thousand-dollar bills.

"I divorce you, King of Dung," she said.

Again she said, "I divorce you, King of Dung."

Once more she said, "King of Dung, I divorce you."

As she spoke the palace dwindled into a pile of excrement, and the dark judge was a beetle that ran about among the turds.

She went up then, not looking back.

When she came to the river, great black waves beat against the beaches. The dog howled. The boatman ferrying souls across tried to turn back to the far shore, but his boat spun round, capsized, and sank. The souls of the dead swam off in the black water like minnows, glimmering.

She plunged into the river. She swam the water of darkness. She let the current bear her, riding the waves, borne to the mouth of the river where the dark waters broadened to the breakers across the bar.

The sun was going down towards the sea, laying a path of light across the waves.

Wrecked on the sand of the sea-beach lay the salt chariot, the sparkling wheels broken. The bones of the white horses were scattered there. Dead seaweed like white hair lay on the stones.

She lay down on the sand among bones of seabirds and bits of broken plastic and poisoned fish in the scum of black oil. She lay down and the tide came in across the bar. The waves broke on her body and her body broke in the waves. She became foam. She was the foam that is water and air, that is not there and is there, that is all.

She got up, the woman of foam, and went across the beach and up into the dark hills. She went home to the house, where her child waited for her in the kitchen. She saw the light of the windows shine across the darkening land. Who is it that lights the light? Whose child are you, who is your child? Whose story will be told?

WE HAVE THE SAME NAME, I SAID.

THE MATTER

OF

SEGGRI

The first recorded contact with Seggri was in year 242 of Hainish Cycle 93. A Wandership six generations out from Iao (4-Taurus) came down on the planet, and the captain entered this report in his ship's log.

Captain Aolao-olao's Report

WE HAVE SPENT NEAR FORTY DAYS ON THIS WORLD THEY CALL Se-ri or Ye-ha-ri, well entertained, and leave with as good an estimation of the natives as is consonant with their unregenerate state. They live in fine great buildings they call castles, with large parks all about. Outside the walls of the parks lie well-tilled fields and abundant orchards, reclaimed by diligence from the parched and arid desert of stone that makes up the greatest part of the land. Their women live in villages and towns huddled outside the walls. All the common work of farm and mill is performed by the women, of whom there is a vast superabundance. They are ordinary drudges, living in towns which belong to the lords of the castle. They live amongst the cattle and brute animals of all kinds, who are permitted into the houses, some of which are of fair size. These women go about drably clothed, always in groups and bands. They are never allowed within the walls of the park, leaving the food and necessaries with which they provide the men at the outer gate of the castle. They evinced great fear and distrust of us. A few of my men following some girls on the road, women rushed from the town like a pack of wild beasts, so that the men thought it best to return forthwith to the castle. Our hosts advised us that it were best for us to keep away from their towns, which we did.

The men go freely about their great parks, playing at one sport or another. At night they go to certain houses which they own in the town, where they may have their pick among the women and satisfy their lust upon them as they will. The women pay them, we were told, in their money, which is copper, for a night of pleasure, and pay them yet more if they get a child on them. Their nights thus are spent in carnal satisfaction as often as they desire, and their days in a diversity of sports and games, notably a kind of wrestling, in which they throw each other through the air so that we marveled that they seemed never to take hurt, but rose up and returned to the combat with wonderful dexterity of hand and foot. Also they fence with blunt swords, and combat with long light sticks. Also they play a game with balls on a great field, using the arms to catch or throw the ball and the legs to kick the ball and trip or catch or kick the men of the other team, so that many are bruised and lamed in the passion of the sport, which was very fine to see, the teams in their contrasted garments of bright colors much gauded out with gold and finery seething now this way, now that, up and down the field in a mass, from which the balls were flung up and caught by runners breaking free of the struggling crowd and fleeting towards the one or the other goal with all the rest in hot pursuit. There is a "battlefield" as they call it of this game lying without the walls of the castle park, near to the town, so that the women may come watch and cheer, which they do heartily, calling out the names of favorite players and urging them with many uncouth cries to victory.

Boys are taken from the women at the age of eleven and brought to the castle to be educated as befits a man. We saw such a child brought into the castle with much ceremony and rejoicing. It is said that the women find it difficult to bring a pregnancy of a manchild to term, and that of those born many die in infancy despite the care lavished upon them, so that there are far more women than men. In this we see the curse of GOD laid upon this race as upon all those who acknowledge HIM not, unrepentant heathens whose ears are stopped to true discourse and blind to the light.

These men know little of art, only a kind of leaping dance, and their science is little beyond that of savages. One great man of a castle to whom I talked, who was dressed out in cloth of gold and crimson and whom all called Prince and Grandsire with much respect and deference, yet was so ignorant he believed the stars to be worlds full of people and beasts, asking us from which star we descended. They have only vessels driven by steam along the surface of the land and water, and no notion of flight either in the air or in space, nor any curiosity about such things, saying with disdain, "That is all women's work," and indeed I found that if I asked these great men about matters of common knowledge such as the working of machinery, the weaving of cloth, the transmission of holovision, they would soon chide me for taking interest in womanish things as they called them, desiring me to talk as befit a man.

In the breeding of their fierce cattle within the parks they are very knowledgeable, as in the sewing up of their clothing, which they make from cloth the women weave in their factories. The men vie in the ornamentation and magnificence of their costumes to an extent which we might indeed have thought scarcely manly, were they not withal such proper men, strong and ready for any game or sport, and full of pride and a most delicate and fiery honor.

*The log including Captain Aolao-olao's entries was (after
a 12-generation journey) returned to the Sacred Archives
of the Universe on Iao, which were dispersed during the
period called The Tumult, and eventually preserved in
fragmentary form on Hain. There is no record of further
contact with Seggri until the First Observers were sent by
the Ekumen in 93/1333: an Alterran man and a Hainish
woman, Kaza Agad and G. Merriment. After a year in
orbit mapping, photographing, recording and studying
broadcasts, and analysing and learning a major regional
language, the Observers landed. Acting upon a strong
persuasion of the vulnerability of the planetary culture,
they presented themselves as survivors of the wreck of a
fishing boat, blown far off course, from a remote island.
They were, as they had anticipated, separated at once,
Kaza Agad being taken to the Castle and Merriment into
the town. Kaza kept his name, which was plausible in the
native context; Merriment called herself Yude. We have
only her report, from which three excerpts follow.*

From Mobile Gerindu'Uttahayudetwe'Menrade Merriment's Notes for a Report to the Ekumen, 93/1334

34/223. THEIR NETWORK OF TRADE AND INFORMATION, HENCE
their awareness of what goes on elsewhere in their world, is too sophis-
ticated for me to maintain my Stupid Foreign Castaway act any longer.
Ekhaw called me in today and said, "If we had a sire here who was
worth buying or if our teams were winning their games, I'd think you
were a spy. Who are you, anyhow?"

I said, "Would you let me go to the College at Hagka?"

She said, "Why?"

"There are scientists there, I think? I need to talk with them."

This made sense to her; she made their "Mh" noise of assent.

"Could my friend go there with me?"

"Shask, you mean?"

We were both puzzled for a moment. She didn't expect a woman to call a man "friend," and I hadn't thought of Shask as a friend. She's very young, and I haven't taken her very seriously.

"I mean Kaza, the man I came with."

"A man—to the college?" she said, incredulous. She looked at me and said, "Where *do* you come from?"

It was a fair question, not asked in enmity or challenge. I wish I could have answered it, but I am increasingly convinced that we can do great damage to these people; we are facing Resehavanar's Choice here, I fear.

Ekhaw paid for my journey to Hagka, and Shask came along with me. As I thought about it I saw that of course Shask was my friend. It was she who brought me into the motherhouse, persuading Ekhaw and Azman of their duty to be hospitable; it was she who had looked out for me all along. Only she was so conventional in everything she did and said that I hadn't realised how radical her compassion was. When I tried to thank her, as our little jitney-bus purred along the road to Hagka, she said things like she always says—"Oh, we're all family," and "People have to help each other," and "Nobody can live alone."

"Don't women ever live alone?" I asked her, for all the ones I've met belong to a motherhouse or a daughterhouse, whether a couple or a big family like Ekhaw's, which is three generations: five older women, three of their daughters living at home, and four children—the boy they all coddle and spoil so, and three girls.

"Oh yes," Shask said. "If they don't want wives, they can be single-women. And old women, when their wives die, sometimes they just

live alone till they die. Usually they go live at a daughterhouse. In the
colleges, the *vev* always have a place to be alone." Conventional she may
be, but Shask always tries to answer a question seriously and completely;
she thinks about her answer. She has been an invaluable informant. She
has also made life easy for me by not asking questions about where I
come from. I took this for the incuriosity of a person securely embedded in an unquestioned way of life, and for the self-centeredness of the
young. Now I see it as delicacy.

"A vev is a teacher?"

"Mh."

"And the teachers at the college are very respected?"

"That's what vev means. That's why we call Eckaw's mother Vev Kakaw.
She didn't go to college, but she's a thoughtful person, she's learned from
life, she has a lot to teach us."

So respect and teaching are the same thing, and the only term of
respect I've heard women use for women means teacher. And so in teaching me, young Shask respects herself? And/or earns my respect? This
casts a different light on what I've been seeing as a society in which
wealth is the important thing. Zadedr, the current mayor of Reha, is
certainly admired for her very ostentatious display of possessions; but
they don't call her Vev.

I said to Shask, "You have taught me so much, may I call you Vev
Shask?"

She was equally embarrassed and pleased, and squirmed and said,
"Oh no no no no." Then she said, "If you ever come back to Reha I
would like very much to have love with you, Yude."

"I thought you were in love with Sire Zadr!" I blurted out.

"Oh, I am," she said, with that eye-roll and melted look they have
when they speak of the sires, "aren't you? Just think of him fucking you,
oh! Oh, I get all wet thinking about it!" She smiled and wriggled. I felt
embarrassed in my turn and probably showed it. "Don't you like him?"

she inquired with a naivety I found hard to bear. She was acting like a silly adolescent, and I know she's not a silly adolescent. "But I'll never be able to afford him," she said, and sighed.

So you want to make do with me, I thought nastily.

"I'm going to save my money," she announced after a minute. "I think I want to have a baby next year. Of course I can't afford Sire Zadr, he's a Great Champion, but if I don't go to the Games at Kadaki this year I can save up enough for a really good sire at our fuckery, maybe Master Rosra. I wish, I know this is silly, I'm going to say it anyway, I've been wishing you could be its lovemother. I know you can't, you have to go to the college. I just wanted to tell you. I love you." She took my hands, drew them to her face, pressed my palms on her eyes for a moment, and then released me. She was smiling, but her tears were on my hands.

"Oh, Shask," I said, floored.

"It's all right!" she said. "I have to cry a minute." And she did. She wept openly, bending over, wringing her hands, and wailing softly. I patted her arm and felt unutterably ashamed of myself. Other passengers looked round and made little sympathetic grunting noises. One old woman said, "That's it, that's right, lovey!" In a few minutes Shask stopped crying, wiped her nose and face on her sleeve, drew a long, deep breath, and said, "All right." She smiled at me. "Driver," she called, "I have to piss, can we stop?"

The driver, a tense-looking woman, growled something, but stopped the bus on the wide, weedy roadside; and Shask and another woman got off and pissed in the weeds. There is an enviable simplicity to many acts in a society which has, in all its daily life, only one gender. And which, perhaps—I don't know this but it occurred to me then, while I was ashamed of myself—has no shame?

34/245. (DICTATED) STILL NOTHING FROM KAZA. I THINK I was right to give him the ansible. I hope he's in touch with somebody. I wish it was me. I need to know what goes on in the castles.

Anyhow I understand better now what I was seeing at the Games in Reha. There are sixteen adult women for every adult man. One conception in six or so is male, but a lot of nonviable male fetuses and defective male births bring it down to one in sixteen by puberty. My ancestors must have really had fun playing with these people's chromosomes. I feel guilty, even if it was a million years ago. I have to learn to do without shame but had better not forget the one good use of guilt. Anyhow. A fairly small town like Reha shares its castle with other towns. That confusing spectacle I was taken to on my tenth day down was Awaga Castle trying to keep its place in the Maingame against a castle from up north, and losing. Which means Awaga's team can't play in the big game this year in Fadrga, the city south of here, from which the winners go on to compete in the *big* big game at Zask, where people come from all over the continent—hundreds of contestants and thousands of spectators. I saw some holos of last year's Maingame at Zask. There were 1,280 players, the comment said, and forty balls in play. It looked to me like a total mess, my idea of a battle between two unarmed armies, but I gather that great skill and strategy is involved. All the members of the winning team get a special title for the year, and another one for life, and bring glory back to their various castles and the towns that support them.

I can now get some sense of how this works, see the system from outside it, because the college doesn't support a castle. People here aren't obsessed with sports and athletes and sexy sires the way the young women in Reha were, and some of the older ones. It's a kind of obligatory obsession. Cheer your team, support your brave men, adore your local hero. It makes sense. Given their situation, they need strong, healthy men at their fuckery; it's social selection reinforcing natural selection. But I'm glad to get away from the rah-rah and the swooning and the posters of fellows with swelling muscles and huge penises and bedroom eyes.

I have made Resehavanar's Choice. I chose the option: Less than the truth. Shoggrad and Skodr and the other teachers, professors we'd call them, are intelligent, enlightened people, perfectly capable of understanding the concept of space travel, etc., making decisions about technological innovation, etc. I limit my answers to their questions to technology. I let them assume, as most people naturally assume, particularly people from a monoculture, that our society is pretty much like theirs. When they find how it differs, the effect will be revolutionary, and I have no mandate, reason, or wish to cause such a revolution on Seggri.

Their gender imbalance has produced a society in which, as far as I can tell, the men have all the privilege and the women have all the power. It's obviously a stable arrangement. According to their histories, it's lasted at least two millennia, and probably in some form or another much longer than that. But it could be quickly and disastrously destabilised by contact with us, by their experiencing the human norm. I don't know if the men would cling to their privileged status or demand freedom, but surely the women would resist giving up their power, and their sexual system and affectional relationships would break down. Even if they learned to undo the genetic program that was inflicted on them, it would take several generations to restore normal gender distribution. I can't be the whisper that starts that avalanche.

34/266. (DICTATED) SKODR GOT NOWHERE WITH THE MEN OF Awaga Castle. She had to make her inquiries very cautiously, since it would endanger Kaza if she told them he was an alien or in any way unique. They'd take it as a claim of superiority, which he'd have to defend in trials of strength and skill. I gather that the hierarchies within the castles are a rigid framework, within which a man moves up or down issuing challenges and winning or losing obligatory and optional trials. The sports and games the women watch are only the showpieces of an endless series of competitions going on inside the castles. As an untrained, grown man Kaza would be at a total disadvantage in such trials. The only way he might get out of them, she said, would be by feigning illness or idiocy. She thinks he must have done so, since he is at least alive; but that's all she could find out—"The man who was cast away at Taha-Reha is alive."

Although the women feed, house, clothe, and support the lords of the castle, they evidently take their noncooperation for granted. She seemed glad to get even that scrap of information. As I am.

But we have to get Kaza out of there. The more I hear about it from Skodr the more dangerous it sounds. I keep thinking "spoiled brats!" but actually these men must be more like soldiers in the training camps that militarists have. Only the training never ends. As they win trials they gain all kinds of titles and ranks you could translate as "generals" and the other names militarists have for all their power-grades. Some of the "generals," the Lords and Masters and so on, are the sports idols, the darlings of the fuckeries, like the one poor Shask adored; but as they get older apparently they often trade glory among the women for power among the men, and become tyrants within their castle, bossing the "lesser" men around, until they're overthrown, kicked out. Old sires often live alone, it seems, in little houses away from the main castle, and are considered crazy and dangerous—rogue males.

It sounds like a miserable life. All they're allowed to do after age eleven is compete at games and sports inside the castle, and compete in the fuckeries, after they're fifteen or so, for money and number of fucks and so on. Nothing else. No options. No trades. No skills of making. No travel unless they play in the big games. They aren't allowed into the colleges to gain any kind of freedom of mind. I asked Skodr why an intelligent man couldn't at least come study in the college, and she told me that learning was very bad for men: it weakens a man's sense of honor, makes his muscles flabby, and leaves him impotent. "'What goes to the brain takes from the testicles,'" she said. "Men have to be sheltered from education for their own good."

I tried to "be water," as I was taught, but I was disgusted. Probably she felt it, because after a while she told me about "the secret college." Some women in colleges do smuggle information to men in castles. The poor things meet secretly and teach each other. In the castles, homosexual relationships are encouraged among boys under fifteen, but not officially tolerated among grown men; she says the "secret colleges" often are run by the homosexual men. They have to be secret because if they're caught reading or talking about ideas they may be punished by their Lords and Masters. There have been some interesting works from the "secret colleges," Skodr said, but she had to think to come up with examples. One was a man who had smuggled out an interesting mathematical theorem, and one was a painter whose landscapes, though primitive in technique, were admired by professionals of the art. She couldn't remember his name.

Arts, sciences, all learning, all professional techniques, are *haggyad*, skilled work. They're all taught at the colleges, and there are no divisions and few specialists. Teachers and students cross and mix fields all the time, and being a famous scholar in one field doesn't keep you from being a student in another. Skodr is a vev of physiology, writes plays, and is currently studying history with one of the history vevs. Her thinking is informed and lively and fearless. My School on Hain could learn from this college. It's a wonderful place, full of free minds. But only minds of one gender. A hedged freedom.

I hope Kaza has found a secret college or something, some way to fit in at the castle. He's strong, but these men have trained for years for the games they play. And a lot of the games are violent. The women say don't worry, we don't let the men kill each other, we protect them, they're our treasures. But I've seen men carried off with concussions, on the holos of their martial-art fights, where they throw each other around spectacularly. "Only inexperienced fighters get hurt." Very reassuring. And they wrestle bulls. And in that melee they call the Maingame they break each other's legs and ankles deliberately. "What's a hero without

a limp?" the women say. Maybe that's the safe thing to do, get your leg
broken so you don't have to prove you're a hero any more. But what else
might Kaza have to prove?

I asked Shask to let me know if she ever heard of him being at the
Reha fuckery. But Awaga Castle services (that's their word, the same
word they use for their bulls) four towns, so he might get sent to one
of the others. But probably not, because men who don't win at things
aren't allowed to go to the fuckeries. Only the champions. And boys
between fifteen and nineteen, the ones the older women call *dippida*,
baby animals—puppy, kitty, lamby. They use the dippida for pleasure.
They only pay for a champion when they go to the fuckery to get pregnant. But Kaza's thirty-six, he isn't a puppy or a kitten or a lamb. He's a
man, and this is a terrible place to be a man.

> *Kaza Agad had been killed; the Lords of Awaga Castle*
> *finally disclosed the fact, but not the circumstances. A year*
> *later, Merriment radioed her lander and left Seggri for*
> *Hain. Her recommendation was to observe and avoid.*
> *The Stabiles, however, decided to send another pair of*
> *observers; these were both women, Mobiles Alee Iyoo and*
> *Zerin Wu. They lived for eight years on Seggri, after the*
> *third year as First Mobiles; Iyoo stayed as Ambassador*
> *another fifteen years. They made Resehavanar's Choice*
> *as "all the truth slowly." A limit of two hundred visitors*
> *from offworld was set. During the next several generations*
> *the people of Seggri, becoming accustomed to the alien*
> *presence, considered their own options as members of the*
> *Ekumen. Proposals for a planetwide referendum on genetic*
> *alteration were abandoned, since the men's vote would be*
> *insignificant unless the women's vote were handicapped.*
> *As of the date of this report the Seggri have not undertaken*

major genetic alteration, though they have learned and
applied various repair techniques, which have resulted in
a higher proportion of full-term male infants; the gender
balance now stands at about 12:1.

The following is a memoir given to Ambassador Eritho
te Ves in 93/1569 by a woman in Ush on Seggri.

YOU ASKED ME, DEAR FRIEND, TO TELL YOU ANYTHING I MIGHT
like people on other worlds to know about my life and my world. That's
not easy! Do I want anybody anywhere else to know anything about
my life? I know how strange we seem to all the others, the half-and-half
races; I know they think us backward, provincial, even perverse. Maybe
in a few more decades we'll decide that we should remake ourselves. I
won't be alive then; I don't think I'd want to be. I like my people. I
like our fierce, proud, beautiful men, I don't want them to become like
women. I like our trustful, powerful, generous women, I don't want
them to become like men. And yet I see that among you each man has
his own being and nature, each woman has hers, and I can hardly say
what it is I think we would lose.

When I was a child I had a brother a year and a half younger than me.
His name was Ittu. My mother had gone to the city and paid five years'
savings for my sire, a Master Champion in the Dancing. Ittu's sire was
an old fellow at our village fuckery; they called him "Master Fallback."
He'd never been a champion at anything, hadn't sired a child for years,
and was only too glad to fuck for free. My mother always laughed about
it—she was still suckling me, she didn't even use a preventive, and she
tipped him two coppers! When she found herself pregnant she was furious. When they tested and found it was a male fetus she was even more
disgusted at having, as they say, to wait for the miscarriage. But when
Ittu was born sound and healthy, she gave the old sire two hundred coppers, all the cash she had.

He wasn't delicate like so many boy babies, but how can you keep from protecting and cherishing a boy? I don't remember when I wasn't looking after Ittu, with it all very clear in my head what Little Brother should do and shouldn't do and all the perils I must keep him from. I was proud of my responsibility, and vain, too, because I had a brother to look after. Not one other motherhouse in my village had a son still living at home.

Ittu was a lovely child, a star. He had the fleecy soft hair that's common in my part of Ush, and big eyes; his nature was sweet and cheerful, and he was very bright. The other children loved him and always wanted to play with him, but he and I were happiest playing by ourselves, long elaborate games of make-believe. We had a herd of twelve cattle an old woman of the village had carved from gourd-shell for Ittu—people always gave him presents—and they were the actors in our dearest game. Our cattle lived in a country called Shush, where they had great adventures, climbing mountains, discovering new lands, sailing on rivers, and so on. Like any herd, like our village herd, the old cows were the leaders; the bull lived apart; the other males were gelded; and the heifers were the adventurers. Our bull would make ceremonial visits to service the cows, and then he might have to go fight with men at Shush Castle. We made the castle of clay and the men of sticks, and the bull always won, knocking the stick-men to pieces. Then sometimes he knocked the castle to pieces too. But the best of our stories were told with two of the heifers. Mine was named Op and my brother's was Utti. Once our hero heifers were having a great adventure on the stream that runs past our village, and their boat got away from us. We found it caught against a log far downstream where the stream was deep and quick. My heifer was still in it. We both dived and dived, but we never found Utti. She had drowned. The Cattle of Shush had a great funeral for her, and Ittu cried very bitterly.

He mourned his brave little toy cow so long that I asked Djerdji the cattleherd if we could work for her, because I thought being with the real cattle might cheer Ittu up. She was glad to get two cowhands for free (when Mother found out we were really working, she made Djerdji pay us a quarter-copper a day). We rode two big, goodnatured old cows, on saddles so big Ittu could lie down on his. We took a herd of two-year-old calves out onto the desert every day to forage for the *edta* that grows best when it's grazed. We were supposed to keep them from wandering off and from trampling streambanks, and when they wanted to settle down and chew the cud we were supposed to gather them in a place where their droppings would nourish useful plants. Our old mounts did most of the work. Mother came out and checked on what we were doing and decided it was all right, and being out in the desert all day was certainly keeping us fit and healthy.

We loved our riding cows, but they were serious-minded and responsible, rather like the grown-ups in our motherhouse. The calves were something else; they were all riding breed, not fine animals of course, just villagebred; but living on edta they were fat and had plenty of spirit. Ittu and I rode them bareback with a rope rein. At first we always ended up on our own backs watching a calf's heels and tail flying off. By the end of a year we were good riders, and took to training our mounts to tricks, trading mounts at a full run, and hornvaulting. Ittu was a marvelous hornvaulter. He trained a big three-year-old roan ox with lyre horns, and the two of them danced like the finest vaulters of the great castles that we saw on the holos. We couldn't keep our excellence to ourselves out in the desert; we started showing off to the other children, inviting them to come out to Salt Springs to see our Great Trick Riding Show. And so of course the adults got to hear of it.

My mother was a brave woman, but that was too much for even her, and she said to me in cold fury, "I trusted you to look after Ittu. You let me down."

All the others had been going on and on about endangering the

precious life of a boy, the Vial of Hope, the Treasurehouse of Life, and
so on, but it was what my mother said that hurt.

"I do look after Ittu, and he looks after me," I said to her, in that
passion of justice that children know, the birthright we seldom honor.
"We both know what's dangerous and we don't do stupid things and we
know our cattle and we do everything together. When he has to go to
the castle he'll have to do lots more dangerous things, but at least he'll
already know how to do one of them. And there he has to do them alone,
but we did everything together. And I didn't let you down."

My mother looked at us. I was nearly twelve, Ittu was ten. She burst
into tears, she sat down on the dirt and wept aloud. Ittu and I both went
to her and hugged her and cried. Ittu said, "I won't go. I won't go to the
damned castle. They can't make me!"

And I believed him. He believed himself. My mother knew better.

Maybe some day it will be possible for a boy to choose his life. Among
your peoples a man's body does not shape his fate, does it? Maybe some
day that will be so here.

Our Castle, Hidjegga, had of course been keeping their eye on Ittu
ever since he was born; once a year Mother would send them the doctor's report on him, and when he was five Mother and her wives took
him out there for the ceremony of Confirmation. Ittu had been embarrassed, disgusted, and flattered. He told me in secret, "There were all
these old *men* that smelled funny and they made me take off my clothes
and they had these measuring things and they measured my peepee!
And they said it was very good. They said it was a good one. What happens when you descend?" It wasn't the first question he had ever asked
me that I couldn't answer, and as usual I made up the answer. "Descend
means you can have babies," I said, which, in a way, wasn't so far off
the mark.

Some castles, I am told, prepare boys of nine and ten for the Severance,
woo them with visits from older boys, tickets to games, tours of the park

and the buildings, so that they may be quite eager to go to the castle when they turn eleven. But we "outyonders," villagers of the edge of the desert, kept to the harsh old-fashioned ways. Aside from Confirmation, a boy had no contact at all with men until his eleventh birthday. On that day everybody he had ever known brought him to the Gate and gave him to the strangers with whom he would live the rest of his life. Men and women alike believed and still believe that this absolute sever-ance makes the man.

Vev Ushiggi, who had borne a son and had a grandson, and had been mayor five or six times, and was held in great esteem even though she'd never had much money, heard Ittu say that he wouldn't go to the damned Castle. She came next day to our motherhouse and asked to talk to him. He told me what she said. She didn't do any wooing or sweetening. She told him that he was born to the service of his people and had one responsibility, to sire children when he got old enough; and one duty, to be a strong, brave man, stronger and braver than other men, so that women would choose him to sire their children. She said he had to live in the Castle because men could not live among women. At this, Ittu asked her, "Why can't they?"

"You did?" I said, awed by his courage, for Vev Ushiggi was a formi-dable old woman.

"Yes. And she didn't really answer. She took a long time. She looked at me and then she looked off somewhere and then she stared at me for a long time and then finally she said, 'Because we would destroy them.'"

"But that's crazy," I said. "Men are our treasures. What did she say that for?"

Ittu, of course, didn't know. But he thought hard about what she had said, and I think nothing she could have said would have so impressed him.

After discussion, the village elders and my mother and her wives decided that Ittu could go on practicing hornvaulting, because it really would be a useful skill for him in the Castle; but he could not herd cattle any longer, nor go with me when I did, nor join in any of the work children of the village did, nor their games. "You've done everything together with Po," they told him, "but she should be doing things together with the other girls, and you should be doing things by yourself, the way men do."

They were always very kind to Ittu, but they were stern with us girls; if they saw us even talking with Ittu they'd tell us to go on about our work, leave the boy alone. When we disobeyed—when Ittu and I sneaked off and met at Salt Springs to ride together, or just hid out in our old playplace down in the draw by the stream to talk—he got treated with cold silence to shame him, but I got punished. A day locked in the cellar of the old fiber-processing mill, which was what my village used for a jail; next time it was two days; and the third time they caught us alone together, they locked me in that cellar for ten days. A young woman called Fersk brought me food once a day and made sure I had enough water and wasn't sick, but she didn't speak; that's how they always used to punish people in the villages. I could hear the other children going by up on the street in the evening. It would get dark at last and I could sleep. All day I had nothing to do, no work, nothing to think about except the scorn and contempt they held me in for betraying their trust, and the injustice of my getting punished when Ittu didn't.

When I came out, I felt different. I felt like something had closed up inside me while I was closed up in that cellar.

When we ate at the motherhouse they made sure Ittu and I didn't sit near each other. For a while we didn't even talk to each other. I went back to school and work. I didn't know what Ittu was doing all day. I didn't think about it. It was only fifty days to his birthday.

One night I got into bed and found a note under my clay pillow: *in the draw to-nt.* Ittu never could spell; what writing he knew I had taught him in secret. I was frightened and angry, but I waited an hour till everybody was asleep, and got up and crept outside into the windy, starry night, and ran to the draw. It was late in the dry season and the stream was barely running. Ittu was there, hunched up with his arms round his knees, a little lump of shadow on the pale, cracked clay at the waterside.

The first thing I said was, "You want to get me locked up again? They said next time it would be thirty days!"

"They're going to lock me up for fifty years," Ittu said, not looking at me.

"What am I supposed to do about it? It's the way it has to be! You're a man. You have to do what men do. They won't lock you up, anyway, you get to play games and come to town to do service and all that. You don't even know what being locked up is!"

"I want to go to Seradda," Ittu said, talking very fast, his eyes shining as he looked up at me. "We could take the riding cows to the bus station in Redang, I saved my money, I have twenty-three coppers, we could take the bus to Seradda. The cows would come back home if we turned them loose."

"What do you think you'd do in Seradda?" I asked, disdainful but curious. Nobody from our village had ever been to the capital.

"The Ekkamen people are there," he said.

"The Ekumen," I corrected him. "So what?"

"They could take me away," Ittu said.

I felt very strange when he said that. I was still angry and still disdainful but a sorrow was rising in me like dark water. "Why would they do that? What would they talk to some little boy for? How would you find them? Twenty-three coppers isn't enough anyway. Seradda's way far off. That's a really stupid idea. You can't do that."

"I thought you'd come with me," Ittu said. His voice was softer, but didn't shake.

"I wouldn't do a stupid thing like that," I said furiously.

"All right," he said. "But you won't tell. Will you?"

"No, I won't tell!" I said. "But you can't run away, Ittu. You can't. It would be—it would be dishonorable."

This time when he answered his voice shook. "I don't care," he said. "I don't care about honor. I want to be free!"

We were both in tears. I sat down by him and we leaned together the way we used to, and cried a while; not long; we weren't used to crying.

"You can't do it," I whispered to him. "It won't work, Ittu."

He nodded, accepting my wisdom.

"It won't be so bad at the Castle," I said.

After a minute he drew away from me very slightly.

"We'll see each other," I said.

He said only, "When?"

"At games. I can watch you. I bet you'll be the best rider and horn-vaulter there. I bet you win all the prizes and get to be a Champion."

He nodded, dutiful. He knew and I knew that I had betrayed our love and our birthright of justice. He knew he had no hope.

That was the last time we talked together alone, and almost the last time we talked together.

Ittu ran away about ten days after that, taking the riding cow and heading for Redang; they tracked him easily and had him back in the village before nightfall. I don't know if he thought I had told them where he would be going. I was so ashamed of not having gone with him that I could not look at him. I kept away from him; they didn't have to keep me away any more. He made no effort to speak to me.

I was beginning my puberty, and my first blood was the night before Ittu's birthday. Menstruating women are not allowed to come near the Gates at conservative castles like ours, so when Ittu was made a man I stood far back among a few other girls and women, and could not see much of the ceremony. I stood silent while they sang, and looked down at the dirt and my new sandals and my feet in the sandals, and felt the ache and tug of my womb and the secret movement of the blood, and grieved. I knew even then that this grief would be with me all my life.

Ittu went in and the Gates closed.

He became a Young Champion Hornvaulter, and for two years, when he was eighteen and nineteen, came a few times to service in our village, but I never saw him. One of my friends fucked with him and started to tell me about it, how nice he was, thinking I'd like to hear, but I shut her up and walked away in a blind rage which neither of us understood.

He was traded away to a castle on the east coast when he was twenty. When my daughter was born I wrote him, and several times after that, but he never answered my letters.

I don't know what I've told you about my life and my world. I don't know if it's what I want you to know. It is what I had to tell.

The following is a short story written in 93/1586 by a popular writer of the city of Adr, Sem Gridji. The classic literature of Seggri was the narrative poem and the drama. Classical poems and plays were written collaboratively, in the original version and also by re-writers of subsequent generations, usually anonymous. Small value was placed on preserving a "true" text, since the work was seen as an ongoing process. Probably under Ekumenical influence, individual writers in the late sixteenth century began writing short prose narratives, historical and fictional. The genre became popular, particularly in the cities, though it never obtained the immense audience of the great classical epics and plays. Literally everyone knew the plots and many quotations from the epics and plays, from books and holo, and almost every adult woman had seen or participated in a staged performance of several of them. They were

one of the principal unifying influences of the Seggrian
monoculture. The prose narrative, read in silence, served
rather as a device by which the culture might question
itself, and a tool for individual moral self-examination.
Conservative Seggrian women disapproved of the genre
as antagonistic to the intensely cooperative, collaborative
structure of their society. Fiction was not included in the
curriculum of the literature departments of the colleges, and
was often dismissed contemptuously—"fiction is for men."

Sem Gridji published three books of stories. Her bare,
blunt style is characteristic of the Seggrian short story.

Love Out of Place by Sem Gridji

AZAK GREW UP IN A MOTHERHOUSE IN THE DOWNRIVER QUAR-
ter, near the textile mills. She was a bright girl, and her family and
neighborhood were proud to gather the money to send her to college.
She came back to the city as a starting manager at one of the mills.
Azak worked well with other people; she prospered. She had a clear
idea of what she wanted to do in the next few years: to find two or
three partners with whom to found a daughterhouse and a business.

A beautiful woman in the prime of youth, Azak took great pleasure in sex, especially liking intercourse with men. Though she saved
money for her plan of founding a business, she also spent a good deal at
the fuckery, going there often, sometimes hiring two men at once. She
liked to see how they incited each other to prowess beyond what they
would have achieved alone, and shamed each other when they failed.
She found a flaccid penis very disgusting, and did not hesitate to send
away a man who could not penetrate her three or four times an evening.

The castle of her district bought a Young Champion at the Southeast

Castles Dance Tournament, and soon sent him to the fuckery. Having seen him dance in the finals on the holovision and been captivated by his flowing, graceful style and his beauty, Azak was eager to have him service her. His price was twice that of any other man there, but she did not hesitate to pay it. She found him handsome and amiable, eager and gentle, skillful and compliant. In their first evening they came to orgasm together five times. When she left she gave him a large tip. Within the week she was back, asking for Toddra. The pleasure he gave her was exquisite, and soon she was quite obsessed with him.

"I wish I had you all to myself," she said to him one night as they lay still conjoined, languorous and fulfilled.

"That is my heart's desire," he said. "I wish I were your servant. None of the other women that come here arouse me. I don't want them. I want only you."

She wondered if he was telling the truth. The next time she came, she inquired casually of the manager if Toddra were as popular as they had hoped. "No," the manager said. "Everybody else reports that he takes a lot of arousing, and is sullen and careless towards them."

"How strange," Azak said.

"Not at all," said the manager. "He's in love with you."

"A man in love with a woman?" Azak said, and laughed.

"It happens all too often," the manager said.

"I thought only women fell in love," said Azak.

"Women fall in love with a man, sometimes, and that's bad too," said the manager. "May I warn you, Azak? Love should be between women. It's out of place here. It can never come to any good end. I hate to lose the money, but I wish you'd fuck with some of the other men and not always ask for Toddra. You're encouraging him, you see, in something that does harm to him."

"But he and you are making lots of money from me!" said Azak, still taking it as a joke.

"He'd make more from other women if he wasn't in love with you," said the manager. To Azak that seemed a weak argument against the pleasure she had in Toddra, and she said, "Well, he can fuck them all when I've done with him, but for now, I want him."

After their intercourse that evening, she said to Toddra, "The manager here says you're in love with me."

"I told you I was," Toddra said. "I told you I wanted to belong to you, to serve you, you alone. I would die for you, Azak."

"That's foolish," she said.

"Don't you like me? Don't I please you?"

"More than any man I ever knew," she said, kissing him. "You are beautiful and utterly satisfying, my sweet Toddra."

"You don't want any of the other men here, do you?" he asked.

"No. They're all ugly fumblers, compared to my beautiful dancer."

"Listen, then," he said, sitting up and speaking very seriously. He was a slender man of twenty-two, with long, smooth-muscled limbs, wide-set eyes, and a thin-lipped, sensitive mouth. Azak lay stroking his thigh, thinking how lovely and lovable he was. "I have a plan," he said. "When I dance, you know, in the story-dances, I play a woman, of course; I've done it since I was twelve. People always say they can't believe I really am a man, I play a woman so well. If I escaped—from here, from the Castle—as a woman—I could come to your house as a servant—"

"What?" cried Azak, astounded.

"I could live there," he said urgently, bending over her. "With you. I would always be there. You could have me every night. It would cost you nothing, except my food. I would serve you, service you, sweep your house, do anything, anything, Azak, please, my beloved, my mistress, let me be yours!" He saw that she was still incredulous, and hurried on, "You could send me away when you got tired of me—"

"If you tried to go back to the Castle after an escapade like that they'd whip you to death, you idiot!"

"I'm valuable," he said. "They'd punish me, but they wouldn't damage me."

"You're wrong. You haven't been dancing, and your value here has slipped because you don't perform well with anybody but me. The manager told me so."

Tears stood in Toddra's eyes. Azak disliked giving him pain, but she was genuinely shocked at his wild plan. "And if you were discovered, my dear," she said more gently, "I would be utterly disgraced. It is a very childish plan, Toddra. Please never dream of such a thing again. But I am truly, truly fond of you, I adore you and want no other man but you. Do you believe that, Toddra?"

He nodded. Restraining his tears, he said, "For now."

"For now and for a long, long, long time! My dear, sweet, beautiful dancer, we have each other as long as we want, years and years! Only do your duty by the other women that come, so that you don't get sold away by your Castle, please! I couldn't bear to lose you, Toddra." And she clasped him passionately in her arms, and arousing him at once, opened to him, and soon both were crying out in the throes of delight.

Though she could not take his love entirely seriously, since what could come of such a misplaced emotion, except such foolish schemes as he had proposed?—still he touched her heart, and she felt a tenderness towards him that greatly enhanced the pleasure of their intercourse. So for more than a year she spent two or three nights a week with him at the fuckery, which was as much as she could afford. The manager, trying still to discourage his love, would not lower Toddra's fee, even though he was unpopular among the other clients of the fuckery; so Azak spent a great deal of money on him, although he would never, after the first night, accept a tip from her.

Then a woman who had not been able to conceive with any of the sires at the fuckery tried Toddra, and at once conceived, and being tested found the fetus to be male. Another woman conceived by him, again a male fetus. At once Toddra was in demand as a sire. Women began coming from all over the city to be serviced by him. This meant, of course, that he must be free during their period of ovulation. There were now many evenings that he could not meet Azak, for the manager was not to be bribed. Toddra disliked his popularity, but Azak soothed and reassured him, telling him how proud she was of him, and how his work would never interfere with their love. In fact, she was not altogether sorry that he was so much in demand, for she had found another person with whom she wanted to spend her evenings.

This was a young woman named Zedr, who worked in the mill as a machine-repair specialist. She was tall and handsome; Azak noticed first how freely and strongly she walked and how proudly she stood. She found a pretext to make her acquaintance. It seemed to Azak that Zedr admired her; but for a long time each behaved to the other as a friend only, making no sexual advances. They were much in each other's company, going to games and dances together, and Azak found that she enjoyed this open and sociable life better than always being in the fuckery alone with Toddra. They talked about how they might set up a machine-repair service in partnership. As time went on, Azak found that Zedr's beautiful body was always in her thoughts. At last, one evening in her singlewoman's flat, she told her friend that she loved her, but did not wish to burden their friendship with an unwelcome desire.

Zedr replied, "I have wanted you ever since I first saw you, but I didn't want to embarrass you with my desire. I thought you preferred men."

"Until now I did, but I want to make love with you," Azak said.

She found herself quite timid at first, but Zedr was expert and subtle, and could prolong Azak's orgasms till she found such consummation as she had not dreamed of. She said to Zedr, "You have made me a woman."

"Then let's make each other wives," said Zedr joyfully.

They married, moved to a house in the west of the city, and left the mill, setting up in business together.

All this time, Azak had said nothing of her new love to Toddra, whom she had seen less and less often. A little ashamed of her cowardice, she reassured herself that he was so busy performing as a sire that he would not really miss her. After all, despite his romantic talk of love, he was a man, and to a man fucking is the most important thing, instead of being merely one element of love and life as it is to a woman.

When she married Zedr, she sent Toddra a letter, saying that their lives had drifted apart, and she was now moving away and would not see him again, but would always remember him fondly.

She received an immediate answer from Toddra, a letter begging her to come and talk with him, full of avowals of unchanging love, badly spelled and almost illegible. The letter touched, embarrassed, and shamed her, and she did not answer it.

He wrote again and again, and tried to reach her on the holonet at her new business. Zedr urged her not to make any response, saying, "It would be cruel to encourage him."

Their new business went well from the start. They were home one evening busy chopping vegetables for dinner when there was a knock at the door. "Come in," Zedr called, thinking it was Chochi, a friend they were considering as a third partner. A stranger entered, a tall, beautiful woman with a scarf over her hair. The stranger went straight to Azak, saying in a strangled voice, "Azak, Azak, please, please let me stay with you." The scarf fell back from his long hair. Azak recognised Toddra.

She was astonished and a little frightened, but she had known Toddra a long time and been very fond of him, and this habit of affection made her put out her hands to him in greeting. She saw fear and despair in his face, and was sorry for him.

But Zedr, guessing who he was, was both alarmed and angry. She kept the chopping knife in her hand. She slipped from the room and called the city police.

When she returned she saw the man pleading with Azak to let him stay hidden in their household as a servant. "I will do anything," he said. "Please, Azak, my only love, please! I can't live without you. I can't service those women, those strangers who only want to be impregnated. I can't dance any more. I think only of you, you are my only hope. I will be a woman, no one will know. I'll cut my hair, no one will know!" So he went on, almost threatening in his passion, but pitiful also. Zedr listened coldly, thinking he was mad. Azak listened with pain and shame. "No, no, it is not possible," she said over and over, but he would not hear.

When the police came to the door and he realised who they were, he bolted to the back of the house seeking escape. The policewomen caught him in the bedroom; he fought them desperately, and they subdued him brutally. Azak shouted at them not to hurt him, but they paid no heed, twisting his arms and hitting him about the head till he stopped resisting. They dragged him out. The chief of the troop stayed to take evidence. Azak tried to plead for Toddra, but Zedr stated the facts and added that she thought he was insane and dangerous.

After some days, Azak inquired at the police office and was told that Toddra had been returned to his Castle with a warning not to send him to the fuckery again for a year or until the Lords of the Castle found him capable of responsible behavior. She was uneasy thinking of how he might be punished. Zedr said, "They won't hurt him, he's too valuable," just as he himself had said. Azak was glad to believe this. She was, in fact, much relieved to know that he was out of the way.

She and Zedr took Chochi first into their business and then into their household. Chochi was a woman from the dockside quarter, tough and humorous, a hard worker and an undemanding, comfortable lovemaker. They were happy with one another, and prospered.

A year went by, and another year. Azak went to her old quarter to arrange a contract for repair work with two women from the mill where she had first worked. She asked them about Toddra. He was back at the fuckery from time to time, they told her. He had been named the year's Champion Sire of his Castle, and was much in demand, bringing an even higher price, because he impregnated so many women and so many of the conceptions were male. He was not in demand for pleasure, they said, as he had a reputation for roughness and even cruelty. Women asked for him only if they wanted to conceive. Thinking of his gentleness with her, Azak found it hard to imagine him behaving brutally. Harsh punishment at the Castle, she thought, must have altered him. But she could not believe that he had truly changed.

Another year passed. The business was doing very well, and Azak and Chochi both began talking seriously about having children. Zedr was not interested in bearing, though happy to be a mother.

Chochi had a favorite man at their local fuckery to whom she went now and then for pleasure; she began going to him at ovulation, for he had a good reputation as a sire.

Azak had not been to a fuckery since she and Zedr married. She honored fidelity highly, and made love with no one but Zedr and Chochi. When she thought of being impregnated, she found that her old interest in fucking with men had quite died out or even turned to distaste. She did not like the idea of self-impregnation from the sperm bank, but the idea of letting a strange man penetrate her was even more repulsive. Thinking what to do, she thought of Toddra, whom she had truly loved and had pleasure with. He was again a Champion Sire, known throughout the city as a reliable impregnator. There was certainly no other man with whom she could take any pleasure. And he had loved her so much he had put his career and even his life in danger, trying to be with her. That irresponsibility was over and done with. He had never written to her again, and the Castle and the managers of the fuckery would never have let him service women if they thought him mad or untrustworthy. After all this time, she thought, she could go back to him and give him the pleasure he had so desired.

She notified the fuckery of the expected period of her next ovulation, requesting Toddra. He was already engaged for that period, and they offered her another sire; but she preferred to wait till the next month.

Chochi had conceived, and was elated. "Hurry up, hurry up!" she said to Azak. "We want twins!"

Azak found herself looking forward to being with Toddra. Regretting the violence of their last encounter and the pain it must have given him, she wrote the following letter to him:

> *"My dear, I hope our long separation and the distress of our last meeting will be forgotten in the joy of being together again, and that you still love me as I still love you. I shall be very proud to bear your child, and let us hope it may be a son! I am impatient to see you again, my beautiful dancer. Your Azak."*

There had not been time for him to answer this letter when her ovulation period began. She dressed in her best clothes. Zedr still distrusted Toddra and had tried to dissuade her from going to him; she bade her "Good luck!" rather sulkily. Chochi hung a mother-charm around her neck, and she went off.

There was a new manager on duty at the fuckery, a coarse-faced young woman who told her, "Call out if he gives you any trouble. He may be a Champion but he's rough, and we don't let him get away with hurting anybody."

"He won't hurt me," Azak said, smiling, and went eagerly into the familiar room where she and Toddra had enjoyed each other so often. He was standing waiting at the window just as he had used to stand. When he turned he looked just as she remembered, long-limbed, his silky hair flowing like water down his back, his wide-set eyes gazing at her.

"Toddra!" she said, coming to him with outstretched hands.

He took her hands and said her name.

"Did you get my letter? Are you happy?"

"Yes," he said, smiling.

"And all that unhappiness, all that foolishness about love, is it over? I am so sorry you were hurt, Toddra, I don't want any more of that. Can we just be ourselves and be happy together as we used to be?"

"Yes, all that is over," he said. "And I am happy to see you." He drew her gently to him. Gently he began to undress her and caress her body, just as he had used to, knowing what gave her pleasure, and she remembering what gave him pleasure. They lay down naked together. She was fondling his erect penis, aroused and yet a little reluctant to be penetrated after so long, when he moved his arm as if uncomfortable. Drawing away from him a little, she saw that he had a knife in his hand, which he must have hidden in the bed. He was holding it concealed behind his back.

Her womb went cold, but she continued to fondle his penis and testicles, not daring to say anything and not able to pull away, for he was holding her close with the other hand.

Suddenly he moved onto her and forced his penis into her vagina with a thrust so painful that for an instant she thought it was the knife. He ejaculated instantly. As his body arched she writhed out from under him, scrambled to the door, and ran from the room crying for help.

He pursued her, striking with the knife, stabbing her in the shoulderblade before the manager and other women and men seized him. The men were very angry and treated him with a violence which the manager's protests did not lessen. Naked, bloody, and half-conscious, he was bound and taken away immediately to the Castle.

Everyone now gathered around Azak, and her wound, which was slight, was cleaned and covered. Shaken and confused, she could ask only, "What will they do to him?"

"What do you think they do to a murdering rapist? Give him a prize?" the manager said. "They'll geld him."

"But it was my fault," Azak said.

The manager stared at her and said, "Are you mad? Go home."

She went back into the room and mechanically put on her clothes. She looked at the bed where they had lain. She stood at the window where Toddra had stood. She remembered how she had seen him dance long ago in the contest where he had first been made champion. She thought, "My life is wrong." But she did not know how to make it right.

> *Alteration in Seggrian social and cultural institutions did not take the disastrous course Merriment feared. It has been slow and its direction is not clear. In 93/1602 Terhada College invited men from two neighboring castles to apply as students, and three men did so. In the next decades, most colleges opened their doors to men. Once they were graduated, male students had to return to their castle, unless they left the planet, since native men were not allowed to live anywhere but as students in a college or in a castle, until the Open Gate Law was passed in 93/1662.*
>
> *Even after passage of that law, the castles remained closed to women; and the exodus of men from the castles was much slower than opponents of the measure feared. Social adjustment to the Open Gate Law has been slow. In several regions programs to train men in basic skills such as farming and construction have met with moderate success; the men work in competitive teams, separate from and managed by the women's companies. A good many Seggri have come to Hain to study in recent years—more men than women, despite the great numerical imbalance that still exists.*

The following autobiographical sketch by one of these
men is of particular interest, since he was involved in the
event which directly precipitated the Open Gate Law.

Autobiographical Sketch by Mobile Ardar Dez

I WAS BORN IN EKUMENICAL CYCLE 93, YEAR 1641, IN RAKEDR
on Seggri. Rakedr was a placid, prosperous, conservative town, and I
was brought up in the old way, the petted boychild of a big motherhouse.
Altogether there were seventeen of us, not counting the kitchen staff—a
great-grandmother, two grandmothers, four mothers, nine daughters,
and me. We were well off; all the women were or had been managers
or skilled workers in the Rakedr Pottery, the principal industry of the
town. We kept all the holidays with pomp and energy, decorating the
house from roof to foundation with banners for Hillalli, making fantastic costumes for the Harvest Festival, and celebrating somebody's
birthday every few weeks with gifts all round. I was petted, as I said,
but not, I think, spoiled. My birthday was no grander than my sisters',
and I was allowed to run and play with them just as if I were a girl. Yet
I was always aware, as were they, that our mothers' eyes rested on me
with a different look, brooding, reserved, and sometimes, as I grew
older, desolate.

After my Confirmation, my birthmother or her mother took me
to Rakedr Castle every spring on Visiting Day. The gates of the park,
which had opened to admit me alone (and terrified) for my Confirmation, remained shut, but rolling stairs were placed against the park
walls. Up these I and a few other little boys from the town climbed, to
sit on top of the park wall in great state, on cushions, under awnings,
and watch demonstration dancing, bull-dancing, wrestling, and other
sports on the great gamefield inside the wall. Our mothers waited below,

outside, in the bleachers of the public field. Men and youths from the Castle sat with us, explaining the rules of the games and pointing out the fine points of a dancer or wrestler, treating us seriously, making us feel important. I enjoyed that very much, but as soon as I came down off the wall and started home it all fell away like a costume shrugged off, a part played in a play; and I went on with my work and play in the motherhouse with my family, my real life.

When I was ten I went to Boys' Class downtown. The class had been set up forty or fifty years before as a bridge between the motherhouses and the Castle, but the Castle, under increasingly reactionary gover-nance, had recently withdrawn from the project. Lord Fassaw forbade his men to go anywhere outside the walls but directly to the fuckery, in a closed car, returning at first light; and so no men were able to teach the class. The townswomen who tried to tell me what to expect when I went to the Castle did not really know much more than I did. However well-meaning they were, they mostly frightened and confused me. But fear and confusion were an appropriate preparation.

I cannot describe the ceremony of Severance. I really cannot describe it. Men on Seggri, in those days, had this advantage: they knew what death is. They had all died once before their body's death. They had turned and looked back at their whole life, every place and face they had loved, and turned away from it as the gate closed.

At the time of my Severance, our small Castle was internally divided into "collegials" and "traditionals," a liberal faction left from the regime of Lord Ishog and a younger, highly conservative faction. The split was already disastrously wide when I came to the Castle. Lord Fassaw's rule had grown increasingly harsh and irrational. He governed by corrup-tion, brutality, and cruelty. All of us who lived there were of course infected, and would have been destroyed if there had not been a strong, constant, moral resistance, centered around Ragaz and Kohadrat, who had been protégés of Lord Ishog. The two men were open partners; their followers were all the homosexuals in the Castle, and a good number of other men and older boys.

My first days and months in the Scrubs' dormitory were a bewildering alternation: terror, hatred, shame, as the boys who had been there a few months or years longer than I were incited to humiliate and abuse the newcomer, in order to make a man of him—and comfort, gratitude, love, as boys who had come under the influence of the collegials offered me secret friendship and protection. They helped me in the games and competitions and took me into their beds at night, not for sex but to keep me from the sexual bullies. Lord Fassaw detested adult homosexuality and would have reinstituted the death penalty if the Town Council had allowed it. Though he did not dare punish Ragaz and Kohadrat, he punished consenting love between older boys with bizarre and appalling physical mutilations—ears cut into fringes, fingers branded with red-hot iron rings. Yet he encouraged the older boys to rape the eleven- and twelve-year-olds, as a manly practice. None of us escaped. We particularly dreaded four youths, seventeen or eighteen years old when I came there, who called themselves the Lordsmen. Every few nights they raided the Scrubs' dormitory for a victim, whom they raped as a group. The collegials protected us as best they could by ordering us to their beds, where we wept and protested loudly, while they pretended to abuse us, laughing and jeering. Later, in the dark and silence, they comforted us with candy, and sometimes, as we grew older, with a desired love, gentle and exquisite in its secrecy.

There was no privacy at all in the Castle. I have said that to women who asked me to describe life there, and they thought they understood me. "Well, everybody shares everything in a motherhouse," they would say, "everybody's in and out of the rooms all the time. You're never really alone unless you have a singlewoman's flat." I could not tell them how different the loose, warm commonality of the motherhouse was from the rigid, deliberate publicity of the forty-bed, brightly-lighted Castle dormitories. Nothing in Rakedr was private: only secret, only silent. We ate our tears.

I grew up; I take some pride in that, along with my profound gratitude to the boys and men who made it possible. I did not kill myself, as several boys did during those years, nor did I kill my mind and soul, as some did so their body could survive. Thanks to the maternal care of the collegials—the resistance, as we came to call ourselves—I grew up.

Why do I say maternal, not paternal? Because there were no fathers in my world. There were only sires. I knew no such word as father or paternal. I thought of Ragaz and Kohadrat as my mothers. I still do.

Fassaw grew quite mad as the years went on, and his hold over the Castle tightened to a deathgrip. The Lordsmen now ruled us all. They were lucky in that we still had a strong Maingame team, the pride of Fassaw's heart, which kept us in the First League, as well as two Champion Sires in steady demand at the town fuckeries. Any protest the resistance tried to bring to the Town Council could be dismissed as typical male whining, or laid to the demoralising influence of the aliens. From the outside Rakedr Castle seemed all right. Look at our great team! Look at our champion studs! The women looked no further.

How could they abandon us?—the cry every Seggrian boy must make in his heart. How could she leave me here? Doesn't she know what it's like? Why doesn't she know? Doesn't she want to know?

"Of course not," Ragaz said to me when I came to him in a passion of righteous indignation, the Town Council having denied our petition to be heard. "Of course they don't want to know how we live. Why do they never come into the castles? Oh, we keep them out, yes; but do you think we could keep them out if they wanted to enter? My dear, we collude with them and they with us in maintaining the great foundation of ignorance and lies on which our civilisation rests."

"Our own mothers abandon us," I said.

"Abandon us? Who feeds us, clothes us, houses us, pays us? We're utterly dependent on them. If ever we made ourselves independent, perhaps we could rebuild society on a foundation of truth."

Independence was as far as his vision could reach. Yet I think his mind groped further, towards what he could not see, the body's obscure, inalterable dream of mutuality.

Our effort to make our case heard at the Council had no effect except within the Castle. Lord Fassaw saw his power threatened. Within a few days Ragaz was seized by the Lordsmen and their bully boys, accused of repeated homosexual acts and treasonable plots, arraigned, and sentenced by the Lord of the Castle. Everyone was summoned to the Gamefield to witness the punishment. A man of fifty with a heart ailment—he had been a Maingame racer in his twenties and had overtrained—Ragaz was tied naked across a bench and beaten with "Lord Long," a heavy leather tube filled with lead weights. The Lordsman Berhed, who wielded it, struck repeatedly at the head, the kidneys, and the genitals. Ragaz died an hour or two later in the infirmary.

The Rakedr Mutiny took shape that night. Kohadrat, older than Ragaz and devastated by his loss, could not restrain or guide us. His vision had been of a true resistance, longlasting and nonviolent, through which the Lordsmen would in time destroy themselves. We had been following that vision. Now we let it go. We dropped the truth and grabbed weapons. "How you play is what you win," Kohadrat said, but we had heard all those old saws. We would not play the patience game any more. We would win, now, once for all.

And we did. We won. We had our victory. Lord Fassaw, the Lordsmen, and their bullies had been slaughtered by the time the police got to the Gate.

I remember how those tough women strode in among us, staring at the rooms of the Castle which they had never seen, staring at the mutilated bodies, eviscerated, castrated, headless—at Lordsman Berhed, who had been nailed to the floor with "Lord Long" stuffed down his throat—at us, the rebels, the victors, with our bloody hands and defiant faces—at Kohadrat, whom we thrust forward as our leader, our spokesman.

He stood silent. He ate his tears.

The women drew closer to one another, clutching their guns, staring around. They were appalled, they thought us all insane. Their utter incomprehension drove one of us at last to speak—a young man, Tarsk, who wore the iron ring that had been forced onto his finger when it was red-hot. "They killed Ragaz," he said. "They were all mad. Look." He held out his crippled hand.

The chief of the troop, after a pause, said, "No one will leave here till this is looked into," and marched her women out of the Castle, out of the park, locking the gate behind them, leaving us with our victory.

The hearings and judgments on the Rakedr Mutiny were all broadcast, of course, and the event has been studied and discussed ever since. My own part in it was the murder of the Lordsman Tatiddi. Three of us set on him and beat him to death with exercise-clubs in the gymnasium where we had cornered him.

How we played was what we won.

We were not punished. Men were sent from several castles to form a government over Rakedr Castle. They learned enough of Fassaw's behavior to see the cause of our rebellion, but the contempt of even the most liberal of them for us was absolute. They treated us not as men, but as irrational, irresponsible creatures, untamable cattle. If we spoke they did not answer.

I do not know how long we could have endured that cold regime of shame. It was only two months after the Mutiny that the World Council enacted the Open Gate Law. We told one another that that was our victory, we had made that happen. None of us believed it. We told one another we were free. For the first time in history, any man who wanted to leave his castle could walk out the gate. We were free!

What happened to the free man outside the gate? Nobody had given it much thought.

I was one who walked out the gate, on the morning of the day the law came into force. Eleven of us walked into town together.

Several of us, men not from Rakedr, went to one or another of the fuckeries, hoping to be allowed to stay there; they had nowhere else to go. Hotels and inns of course would not accept men. Those of us who had been children in the town went to our motherhouses.

What is it like to return from the dead? Not easy. Not for the one who returns, nor for his people. The place he occupied in their world has closed up, ceased to be, filled with accumulated change, habit, the doings and needs of others. He has been replaced. To return from the dead is to be a ghost: a person for whom there is no room.

Neither I nor my family understood that, at first. I came back to them at twenty-one as trustingly as if I were the eleven-year-old who had left them, and they opened their arms to their child. But he did not exist. Who was I?

For a long time, months, we refugees from the Castle hid in our motherhouses. The men from other towns all made their way home, usually by begging a ride with teams on tour. There were seven or eight of us in Rakedr, but we scarcely ever saw one another. Men had no place on the street; for hundreds of years a man seen alone on the street had been arrested immediately. If we went out, women ran from us, or reported us, or surrounded and threatened us—"Get back into your Castle where you belong! Get back to the fuckery where you belong! Get out of our city!" They called us drones, and in fact we had no work, no function at all in the community. The fuckeries would not accept us for service, because we had no guarantee of health and good behavior from a castle.

This was our freedom: we were all ghosts, useless, frightened, frightening intruders, shadows in the corners of life. We watched life going on around us—work, love, childbearing, childrearing, getting and spending, making and shaping, governing and adventuring—the women's world, the bright, full, real world—and there was no room in it for us. All we had ever learned to do was play games and destroy one another.

My mothers and sisters racked their brains, I know, to find some place and use for me in their lively, industrious household. Two old live-in cooks had run our kitchen since long before I was born, so cooking, the one practical art I had been taught in the Castle, was superfluous. They found household tasks for me, but they were all make-work, and they and I knew it. I was perfectly willing to look after the babies, but one of the grandmothers was very jealous of that privilege, and also some of my sisters' wives were uneasy about a man touching their baby. My sister Pado broached the possibility of an apprenticeship in the clay-works, and I leaped at the chance; but the managers of the Pottery, after long discussion, were unable to agree to accept men as employees. Their hormones would make male workers unreliable, and female workers would be uncomfortable, and so on.

The holonews was full of such proposals and discussions, of course, and orations about the unforeseen consequences of the Open Gate Law, the proper place of men, male capacities and limitations, gender as destiny. Feeling against the Open Gate policy ran very strong, and it seemed that every time I watched the holo there was a woman talking grimly about the inherent violence and irresponsibility of the male, his biological unfitness to participate in social and political decision-making. Often it was a man saying the same things. Opposition to the new law had the fervent support of all the conservatives in the castles, who pleaded eloquently for the gates to be closed and men to return to their proper station, pursuing the true, masculine glory of the games and the fuckeries.

Glory did not tempt me, after the years at Rakedr Castle; the word itself had come to mean degradation to me. I ranted against the games and competitions, puzzling most of my family, who loved to watch the Maingames and wrestling, and complained only that the level of excellence of most of the teams had declined since the gates were opened. And I ranted against the fuckeries, where, I said, men were used as cattle, stud bulls, not as human beings. I would never go there again.

"But my dear boy," my mother said at last, alone with me one evening, "will you live the rest of your life celibate?"

"I hope not," I said.

"Then . . . ?"

"I want to get married."

Her eyes widened. She brooded a bit, and finally ventured, "To a man."

"No. To a woman. I want a normal, ordinary marriage. I want to have a wife and be a wife."

Shocking as the idea was, she tried to absorb it. She pondered, frowning.

"All it means," I said, for I had had a long time with nothing to do but ponder, "is that we'd live together just like any married pair. We'd set up our own daughterhouse, and be faithful to each other, and if she had a child I'd be its lovemother along with her. There isn't any reason why it wouldn't work!"

"Well, I don't know—I don't know of any," said my mother, gentle and judicious, and never happy at saying no to me. "But you do have to find the woman, you know."

"I know," I said glumly.

"It's such a problem for you to meet people," she said. "Perhaps if you went to the fuckery . . . ? I don't see why your own motherhouse couldn't guarantee you just as well as a castle. We could try—?"

But I passionately refused. Not being one of Fassaw's sycophants, I had seldom been allowed to go to the fuckery; and my few experiences there had been unfortunate. Young, inexperienced, and without recommendation, I had been selected by older women who wanted a plaything.

Their practiced skill at arousing me had left me humiliated and enraged. They patted and tipped me as they left. That elaborate, mechanical excitation and their condescending coldness were vile to me, after the tenderness of my lover-protectors in the Castle. Yet women attracted me physically as men never had; the beautiful bodies of my sisters and their wives, all around me constantly now, clothed and naked, innocent and sensual, the wonderful heaviness and strength and softness of women's bodies, kept me continually aroused. Every night I masturbated, fanta-sising my sisters in my arms. It was unendurable. Again I was a ghost, a raging, yearning impotence in the midst of untouchable reality.

I began to think I would have to go back to the Castle. I sank into a deep depression, an inertia, a chill darkness of the mind.

My family, anxious, affectionate, busy, had no idea what to do for me or with me. I think most of them thought in their hearts that it would be best if I went back through the gate.

One afternoon my sister Pado, with whom I had been closest as a child, came to my room—they had cleared out a dormer attic for me, so that I had room at least in the literal sense. She found me in my now constant lethargy, lying on the bed doing nothing at all. She breezed in, and with the indifference women often show to moods and signals, plumped down on the foot of the bed and said, "Hey, what do you know about the man who's here from the Ekumen?"

I shrugged and shut my eyes. I had been having rape fantasies lately. I was afraid of her.

She talked on about the offworlder, who was apparently in Rakedr to study the Mutiny. "He wants to talk to the resistance," she said. "Men like you. The men who opened the gates. He says they won't come for-ward, as if they were ashamed of being heroes."

"Heroes!" I said. The word in my language is gendered female. It refers to the semi-divine, semi-historic protagonists of the Epics.

"It's what you are," Pado said, intensity breaking through her assumed breeziness. "You took responsibility in a great act. Maybe you did it wrong. Sassume did it wrong in the *Founding of Emmo*, didn't she, she let Faradr get killed. But she was still a hero. She took the responsibility. So did you. You ought to go talk to this Alien. Tell him what happened. Nobody really knows what happened at the Castle. You owe us the story."

That was a powerful phrase, among my people. "The untold story mothers the lie," was the saying. The doer of any notable act was held literally *accountable* for it to the community.

"So why should I tell it to an Alien?" I said, defensive of my inertia.

"Because he'll listen," my sister said drily. "We're all too damned busy."

It was profoundly true. Pado had seen a gate for me and opened it; and I went through it, having just enough strength and sanity left to do so.

Mobile Noem was a man in his forties, born some centuries earlier on Terra, trained on Hain, widely travelled; a small, yellow-brown, quick-eyed person, very easy to talk to. He did not seem at all masculine to me, at first; I kept thinking he was a woman, because he acted like one. He got right to business, with none of the maneuvering to assert his authority or jockeying for position that men of my society felt obligatory in any relationship with another man. I was used to men being wary, indirect, and competitive. Noem, like a woman, was direct and receptive. He was also as subtle and powerful as any man or woman I had known, even Ragaz. His authority was in fact immense; but he never stood on it. He sat down on it, comfortably, and invited you to sit down with him.

I was the first of the Rakedr mutineers to come forward and tell our story to him. He recorded it, with my permission, to use in making his report to the Stabiles on the condition of our society, "the matter of Seggri," as he called it. My first description of the Mutiny took less than an hour. I thought I was done. I didn't know, then, the inexhaustible desire to learn, to understand, to hear *all* the story, that characterises the Mobiles of the Ekumen. Noem asked questions, I answered; he speculated and extrapolated, I corrected; he wanted details, I furnished them—telling the story of the Mutiny, of the years before it, of the men of the Castle, of the women of the Town, of my people, of my life— little by little, bit by bit, all in fragments, a muddle. I talked to Noem daily for a month. I learned that the story has no beginning, and no story has an end. That the story is all muddle, all middle. That the story is never true, but that the lie is indeed a child of silence.

By the end of the month I had come to love and trust Noem, and of course to depend on him. Talking to him had become my reason for being. I tried to face the fact that he would not stay in Rakedr much longer. I must learn to do without him. Do what? There were things for men to do, ways for men to live, he proved it by his mere existence; but could I find them?

He was keenly aware of my situation, and would not let me withdraw, as I began to do, into the lethargy of fear again; he would not let me be silent. He asked me impossible questions. "What would you be if you could be anything?" he asked me, a question children ask each other.

I answered at once, passionately—"A wife!"

I know now what the flicker that crossed his face was. His quick, kind eyes watched me, looked away, looked back.

"I want my own family," I said. "Not to live in my mothers' house, where I'm always a child. Work. A wife, wives—children—to be a mother. I want life, not games!"

"You can't bear a child," he said gently.

"No, but I can mother one!"

"We gender the word," he said. "I like it better your way. . . . But tell me, Ardar, what are the chances of your marrying—meeting a woman willing to marry a man? It hasn't happened, here, has it?"

I had to say no, not to my knowledge.

"It will happen, certainly, I think," he said (his certainties were always uncertain). "But the personal cost, at first, is likely to be high. Relationships formed against the negative pressure of a society are under terrible strain; they tend to become defensive, over-intense, unpeaceful. They have no room to grow."

"Room!" I said. And I tried to tell him my feeling of having no room in my world, no air to breathe.

He looked at me, scratching his nose; he laughed. "There's plenty of room in the galaxy, you know," he said.

"Do you mean . . . I could . . . That the Ekumen . . ." I didn't even know what the question I wanted to ask was. Noem did. He began to answer it thoughtfully and in detail. My education so far had been so limited, even as regards the culture of my own people, that I would have to attend a college for at least two or three years, in order to be ready to apply to an offworld institution such as the Ekumenical Schools on Hain. Of course, he went on, where I went and what kind of training I chose would depend on my interests, which I would go to a college to discover, since neither my schooling as a child nor my training at the Castle had really given me any idea of what there was to be interested in. The choices offered me had been unbelievably limited, addressing neither the needs of a normally intelligent person nor the needs of my society. And so the Open Gate Law instead of giving me freedom had left me "with no air to breathe but airless Space," said Noem, quoting some poet from some planet somewhere. My head was spinning, full of stars. "Hagka College is quite near Rakedr," Noem said, "did you never think of applying? If only to escape from your terrible Castle?"

I shook my head. "Lord Fassaw always destroyed the application forms when they were sent to his office. If any of us had tried to apply . . ."

"You would have been punished. Tortured, I suppose. Yes. Well, from the little I know of your colleges, I think your life there would be better than it is here, but not altogether pleasant. You will have work to do, a place to be; but you will be made to feel marginal, inferior. Even highly educated, enlightened women have difficulty accepting men as their intellectual equals. Believe me, I have experienced it myself! And because you were trained at the Castle to compete, to want to excel, you may find it hard to be among people who either believe you incapable of excellence, or to whom the concept of competition, of winning and defeating, is valueless. But just there, there is where you will find air to breathe."

Noem recommended me to women he knew on the faculty of Hagka College, and I was enrolled on probation. My family were delighted to pay my tuition. I was the first of us to go to college, and they were genuinely proud of me.

As Noem had predicted, it was not always easy, but there were enough other men there that I found friends and was not caught in the paralysing isolation of the motherhouse. And as I took courage, I made friends among the women students, finding many of them unprejudiced and companionable. In my third year, one of them and I managed, tentatively and warily, to fall in love. It did not work very well or last very long, yet it was a great liberation for both of us, our liberation from the belief that the only communication or commonality possible between us was sexual, that an adult man and woman had nothing to join them but their genitals. Emadr loathed the professionalism of the fuckery as I did, and our lovemaking was always shy and brief. Its true significance was not as a consummation of desire, but as proof that we could trust each other. Where our real passion broke loose was when we lay together talking, telling each other what our lives had been, how we felt about men and women and each other and ourselves, what our nightmares were, what our dreams were. We talked endlessly, in a communion that I will cherish and honor all my life, two young souls finding their wings, flying together, not for long, but high. The first flight is the highest.

Emadr has been dead two hundred years; she stayed on Seggri, married into a motherhouse, bore two children, taught at Hagka, and died in her seventies. I went to Hain, to the Ekumenical Schools, and later to Werel and Yeowe as part of the Mobile's staff; my record is herewith enclosed. I have written this sketch of my life as part of my application to return to Seggri as a Mobile of the Ekumen. I want very much to live among my people, to learn who they are, now that I know with at least an uncertain certainty who I am.

ANOTHER STORY

OR A FISHERMAN

OF THE INLAND SEA

To the Stabiles of the Ekumen on Hain, and to Gvonesh,
Director of the Churten Field Laboratories at Ve Port:
from Tiokunan'n Kideo, Farmholder of the Second
Sedoretu of Udan, Derdan'nad, Oket, on O.

I SHALL MAKE MY REPORT AS IF I TOLD A STORY, THIS HAVING been the tradition for some time now. You may, however, wonder why a farmer on the planet O is reporting to you as if he were a Mobile of the Ekumen. My story will explain that. But it does not explain itself. Story is our only boat for sailing on the river of time, but in the great rapids and the winding shallows, no boat is safe.

So: once upon a time when I was twenty-one years old I left my home and came on the NAFAL ship *Terraces of Darranda* to study at the Ekumenical Schools on Hain.

The distance between Hain and my home world is just over four light-years, and there has been traffic between O and the Hainish system for twenty centuries. Even before the Nearly As Fast As Light drive, when ships spent a hundred years of planetary time instead of four to make the crossing, there were people who would give up their old life to come to a new world. Sometimes they returned; not often. There were tales of such sad returns to a world that had forgotten the voyager. I knew also from my mother a very old story called "The Fisherman of the Inland Sea," which came from her home world, Terra. The life of a ki'O child is full of stories, but of all I heard told by her and my othermother and my fathers and grandparents and uncles and aunts and teachers, that one was my favorite. Perhaps I liked it so well because my mother told it with deep feeling, though very plainly, and always in the same words (and I would not let her change the words if she ever tried to).

The story tells of a poor fisherman, Urashima, who went out daily in his boat alone on the quiet sea that lay between his home island and the mainland. He was a beautiful young man with long, black hair, and the daughter of the king of the sea saw him as he leaned over the side of the boat and she gazed up to see the floating shadow cross the wide circle of the sky.

Rising from the waves, she begged him to come to her palace under the sea with her. At first he refused, saying, "My children wait for me at home." But how could he resist the sea king's daughter? "One night," he said. She drew him down with her under the water, and they spent a night of love in her green palace, served by strange undersea beings. Urashima came to love her dearly, and maybe he stayed more than one night only. But at last he said, "My dear, I must go. My children wait for me at home."

"If you go, you go forever," she said.

"I will come back," he promised.

She shook her head. She grieved, but did not plead with him. "Take this with you," she said, giving him a little box, wonderfully carved, and sealed shut. "Do not open it, Urashima."

So he went up onto the land, and ran up the shore to his village, to his house: but the garden was a wilderness, the windows were blank, the roof had fallen in. People came and went among the familiar houses of the village, but he did not know a single face. "Where are my children?" he cried. An old woman stopped and spoke to him: "What is your trouble, young stranger?"

"I am Urashima, of this village, but I see no one here I know!"

"Urashima!" the woman said—and my mother would look far away, and her voice as she said the name made me shiver, tears starting to my eyes—"Urashima! My grandfather told me a fisherman named Urashima was lost at sea, in the time of his grandfather's grandfather. There has been no one of that family alive for a hundred years."

So Urashima went back down to the shore; and there he opened the box, the gift of the sea king's daughter. A little white smoke came out of it and drifted away on the sea wind. In that moment Urashima's black hair turned white, and he grew old, old, old; and he lay down on the sand and died.

Once, I remember, a traveling teacher asked my mother about the fable, as he called it. She smiled and said, "In the Annals of the Emperors of my nation of Terra it is recorded that a young man named Urashima, of the Yosa district, went away in the year 477, and came back to his village in the year 825, but soon departed again. And I have heard that the box was kept in a shrine for many centuries." Then they talked about something else.

My mother, Isako, would not tell the story as often as I demanded it. "That one is so sad," she would say, and tell instead about Grandmother and the rice dumpling that rolled away, or the painted cat who came alive and killed the demon rats, or the peach boy who floated down the river. My sister and my germanes, and older people, too, listened to her tales as closely as I did. They were new stories on O, and a new story is always a treasure. The painted cat story was the general favorite, especially when my mother would take out her brush and the block of strange, black, dry ink from Terra, and sketch the animals—cat, rat—that none of us had ever seen: the wonderful cat with arched back and brave round eyes, the fanged and skulking rats, "pointed at both ends" as my sister said. But I waited always, through all other stories, for her to catch my eye, look away, smile a little and sigh, and begin, "Long, long ago, on the shore of the Inland Sea there lived a fisherman . . ."

Did I know then what that story meant to her? that it was her story? that if she were to return to her village, her world, all the people she had known would have been dead for centuries?

Certainly I knew that she "came from another world," but what that meant to me as a five-, or seven-, or ten-year-old, is hard for me now to imagine, impossible to remember. I knew that she was a Terran and had lived on Hain; that was something to be proud of. I knew that she had come to O as a Mobile of the Ekumen (more pride, vague and grandiose) and that "your father and I fell in love at the Festival of Plays in Sudiran." I knew also that arranging the marriage had been a tricky business. Getting permission to resign her duties had not been difficult—the Ekumen is used to Mobiles going native. But as a foreigner, Isako did not belong to a ki'O moiety, and that was only the first problem. I heard all about it from my othermother, Tubdu, an endless source of family history, anecdote, and scandal. "You know," Tubdu told me when I was eleven or twelve, her eyes shining and her irrepressible, slightly wheezing, almost silent laugh beginning to shake her from the inside out—"you know, she didn't even know women got married? Where she came from, she said, women don't marry."

I could and did correct Tubdu: "Only in her part of it. She told me there's lots of parts of it where they do." I felt obscurely defensive of my mother, though Tubdu spoke without a shadow of malice or contempt; she adored Isako. She had fallen in love with her "the moment I saw her—that black hair! that mouth!"—and simply found it endearingly funny that such a woman could have expected to marry only a man.

"I understand," Tubdu hastened to assure me. "I know—on Terra it's

different, their fertility was damaged, they have to think about marrying for children. And they marry in twos, too. Oh, poor Isako! How
strange it must have seemed to her! I remember how she looked at me—"
And off she went again into what we children called The Great Giggle,
her joyous, silent, seismic laughter.

To those unfamiliar with our customs I should explain that on O, a
world with a low, stable human population and an ancient climax technology, certain social arrangements are almost universal. The dispersed
village, an association of farms, rather than the city or state, is the basic
social unit. The population consists of two halves or moieties. A child
is born into its mother's moiety, so that all ki'O (except the mountain
folk of Ennik) belong either to the Morning People, whose time is
from midnight to noon, or the Evening People, whose time is from
noon to midnight. The sacred origins and functions of the moieties are
recalled in the Discussions and the Plays and in the services at every
farm shrine. The original social function of the moiety was probably to
structure exogamy into marriage and so discourage inbreeding in isolated farmholds, since one can have sex with or marry only a person of
the other moiety. The rule is severely reinforced. Transgressions, which
of course occur, are met with shame, contempt, and ostracism. One's
identity as a Morning or an Evening Person is as deeply and intimately
part of oneself as one's gender, and has quite as much to do with one's
sexual life.

A ki'O marriage, called a sedoretu, consists of a Morning woman
and man and an Evening woman and man; the heterosexual pairs are
called Morning and Evening according to the woman's moiety; the
homosexual pairs are called Day—the two women—and Night—the
two men.

So rigidly structured a marriage, where each of four people must
be sexually compatible with two of the others while never having sex
with the fourth—clearly this takes some arranging. Making sedoretu is

a major occupation of my people. Experimenting is encouraged; four-somes form and dissolve, couples "try on" other couples, mixing and matching. Brokers, traditionally elderly widowers, go about among the farmholds of the dispersed villages, arranging meetings, setting up field dances, serving as universal confidants. Many marriages begin as a love match of one couple, either homosexual or heterosexual, to which another pair or two separate people become attached. Many marriages are brokered or arranged by the village elders from beginning to end. To listen to the old people under the village great tree making a sedo-retu is like watching a master game of chess or tidhe. "If that Evening boy at Erdup were to meet young Tobo during the flour-processing at Gad'd . . ." "Isn't Hodin'n of the Oto Morning a programmer? They could use a programmer at Erdup. . . ." The dowry a prospective bride or groom can offer is their skill, or their home farm. Otherwise undesired people may be chosen and honored for the knowledge or the property they bring to a marriage. The farmhold, in turn, wants its new members to be agreeable and useful. There is no end to the making of marriages on O. I should say that all in all they give as much satisfaction as any other arrangement to the participants, and a good deal more to the marriage-makers.

Of course many people never marry. Scholars, wandering Discuss-ers, itinerant artists and experts, and specialists in the Centers seldom want to fit themselves into the massive permanence of a farmhold sedo-retu. Many people attach themselves to a brother's or sister's marriage as aunt or uncle, a position with limited, clearly defined responsibilities; they can have sex with either or both spouses of the other moiety, thus sometimes increasing the sedoretu from four to seven or eight. Children of that relationship are called cousins. The children of one mother are brothers or sisters to one another; the children of the Morning and the children of the Evening are germanes. Brothers, sisters, and first cousins may not marry, but germanes may. In some less conservative parts of

O germane marriages are looked at askance, but they are common and respected in my region.

My father was a Morning man of Udan Farmhold of Derdan'nad Village in the hill region of the Northwest Watershed of the Saduun River, on Oket, the smallest of the six continents of O. The village comprises seventy-seven farmholds, in a deeply rolling, stream-cut region of fields and forests on the watershed of the Oro, a tributary of the wide Saduun. It is fertile, pleasant country, with views west to the Coast Range and south to the great floodplains of the Saduun and the gleam of the sea beyond. The Oro is a wide, lively, noisy river full of fish and children. I spent my childhood in or on or by the Oro, which runs through Udan so near the house that you can hear its voice all night, the rush and hiss of the water and the deep drumbeats of rocks rolled in its current. It is shallow and quite dangerous. We all learned to swim very young in a quiet bay dug out as a swimming pool, and later to handle rowboats and kayaks in the swift current full of rocks and rapids. Fishing was one of the children's responsibilities. I liked to spear the fat, beady-eyed, blue ochid; I would stand heroic on a slippery boulder in midstream, the long spear poised to strike. I was good at it. But my germane Isidri, while I was prancing about with my spear, would slip into the water and catch six or seven ochid with her bare hands. She could catch eels and even the darting ei. I never could do it. "You just sort of move with the water and get transparent," she said. She could stay underwater longer than any of us, so long you were sure she had drowned. "She's too bad to drown," her mother, Tubdu, proclaimed. "You can't drown really bad people. They always bob up again."

Tubdu, the Morning wife, had two children with her husband Kap: Isidri, a year older than me, and Suudi, three years younger. Children of the Morning, they were my germanes, as was Cousin Had'd, Tubdu's son with Kap's brother Uncle Tobo. On the Evening side there were two children, myself and my younger sister. She was named Koneko, an old name in Oket, which has also a meaning in my mother's Terran language: "kitten," the young of the wonderful animal "cat" with the round back and the round eyes. Koneko, four years younger than me, was indeed round and silky like a baby animal, but her eyes were like my mother's, long, with lids that went up towards the temple, like the soft sheaths of flowers before they open. She staggered around after me, calling, "Deo! Deo! Wait!"—while I ran after fleet, fearless, ever-vanishing Isidri, calling, "Sidi! Sidi! Wait!"

When we were older, Isidri and I were inseparable companions, while Suudi, Koneko, and Cousin Had'd made a trinity, usually coated with mud, splotched with scabs, and in some kind of trouble—gates left open so the yamas got into the crops, hay spoiled by being jumped on, fruit stolen, battles with the children from Drehe Farmhold. "Bad, bad," Tubdu would say. "None of 'em will ever drown!" And she would shake with her silent laughter.

My father Dohedri was a hardworking man, handsome, silent, and aloof. I think his insistence on bringing a foreigner into the tight-woven fabric of village and farm life, conservative and suspicious and full of old knots and tangles of passions and jealousies, had added anxiety to a temperament already serious. Other ki'O had married foreigners, of course, but almost always in a "foreign marriage," a pairing; and such couples usually lived in one of the Centers, where all kinds of untraditional arrangements were common, even (so the village gossips hissed under the great tree) incestuous couplings between two Morning people! two Evening people!—Or such pairs would leave O to live on Hain, or would cut all ties to all homes and become Mobiles on the NAFAL ships, only touching different worlds at different moments and then off again into an endless future with no past.

None of this would do for my father, a man rooted to the knees in the dirt of Udan Farmhold. He brought his beloved to his home, and persuaded the Evening People of Derdan'nad to take her into their moiety, in a ceremony so rare and ancient that a Caretaker had to come by ship and train from Noratan to perform it. Then he had persuaded Tubdu to join the sedoretu. As regards her Day marriage, this was no trouble at all, as soon as Tubdu met my mother; but it presented some difficulty as regards her Morning marriage. Kap and my father had been lovers for years; Kap was the obvious and willing candidate to complete the sedoretu; but Tubdu did not like him. Kap's long love for my father led him to woo Tubdu earnestly and well, and she was far too good-natured to hold out against the interlocking wishes of three people, plus her own lively desire for Isako. She always found Kap a boring husband, I think; but his younger brother, Uncle Tobo, was a bonus. And Tubdu's relation to my mother was infinitely tender, full of honor, of delicacy, of restraint. Once my mother spoke of it. "She knew how strange it all was to me," she said. "She knows how strange it all is."

"This world? our ways?" I asked.

My mother shook her head very slightly. "Not so much that," she said in her quiet voice with the faint foreign accent. "But men and women, women and women, together—love—It is always very strange. Nothing you know ever prepares you. Ever."

The saying is, "a marriage is made by Day," that is, the relationship of the two women makes or breaks it. Though my mother and father loved each other deeply, it was a love always on the edge of pain, never easy. I have no doubt that the radiant childhood we had in that household was founded on the unshakable joy and strength Isako and Tubdu found in each other.

So, then: twelve-year-old Isidri went off on the suntrain to school at Herhot, our district educational Center, and I wept aloud, standing in the morning sunlight in the dust of Derdan'nad Station. My friend, my playmate, my life was gone. I was bereft, deserted, alone forever. Seeing her mighty eleven-year-old elder brother weeping, Koneko set up a howl too, tears rolling down her cheeks in dusty balls like raindrops on a dirt

road. She threw her arms about me, roaring, "Hideo! She'll come back!
She'll come back!"

I have never forgotten that. I can hear her hoarse little voice, and feel
her arms round me and the hot morning sunlight on my neck.

By afternoon we were all swimming in the Oro, Koneko and I and
Suudi and Had'd. As their elder, I resolved on a course of duty and stern
virtue, and led the troop off to help Second-Cousin Topi at the irrigation control station, until she drove us away like a swarm of flies, saying,
"Go help somebody else and let me get some work done!" We went and
built a mud palace.

So, then: a year later, twelve-year-old Hideo and thirteen-year-old
Isidri went off on the suntrain to school, leaving Koneko on the dusty
siding, not in tears, but silent, the way our mother was silent when
she grieved.

I loved school. I know that the first days I was achingly homesick,
but I cannot recall that misery, buried under my memories of the full,
rich years at Herhot, and later at Ran'n, the Advanced Education Center, where I studied temporal physics and engineering.

Isidri finished the First Courses at Herhot, took a year of Second in
literature, hydrology, and oenology, and went home to Udan Farmhold
of Derdan'nad Village in the hill region of the Northwest Watershed of
the Saduun.

The three younger ones all came to school, took a year or two of
Second, and carried their learning home to Udan. When she was fifteen or sixteen, Koneko talked of following me to Ran'n; but she was
wanted at home because of her excellence in the discipline we call "thick
planning"—farm management is the usual translation, but the words
have no hint of the complexity of factors involved in thick planning,
ecology politics profit tradition aesthetics honor and spirit all functioning in an intensely practical and practically invisible balance of preser-
vation and renewal, like the homeostasis of a vigorous organism. Our

"kitten" had the knack for it, and the Planners of Udan and Derdan'nad took her into their councils before she was twenty. But by then, I was gone.

Every winter of my school years I came back to the farm for the long holidays. The moment I was home I dropped school like a book bag and became pure farm boy overnight—working, swimming, fishing, hiking, putting on Plays and farces in the barn, going to field dances and house dances all over the village, falling in and out of love with lovely boys and girls of the Morning from Derdan'nad and other villages.

In my last couple of years at Ran'n, my visits home changed mood. Instead of hiking off all over the country by day and going to a different dance every night, I often stayed home. Careful not to fall in love, I pulled away from my old, dear relationship with Sota of Drehe Farmhold, gradually letting it lapse, trying not to hurt him. I sat whole hours by the Oro, a fishing line in my hand, memorizing the run of the water in a certain place just outside the entrance to our old swimming bay. There, as the water rises in clear strands racing towards two mossy, almost-submerged boulders, it surges and whirls in spirals, and while some of these spin away, grow faint, and disappear, one knots itself on a deep center, becoming a little whirlpool, which spins slowly downstream until, reaching the quick, bright race between the boulders, it loosens and unties itself, released into the body of the river, as another spiral is forming and knotting itself round a deep center upstream where the water rises in clear strands above the boulders. . . . Sometimes that winter the river rose right over the rocks and poured smooth, swollen with rain; but always it would drop, and the whirlpools would appear again.

In the winter evenings I talked with my sister and Suudi, serious, long talks by the fire. I watched my mother's beautiful hands work on the embroidery of new curtains for the wide windows of the dining room, which my father had sewn on the four-hundred-year-old sewing machine of Udan. I worked with him on reprogramming the fertilizer systems for the east fields and the yama rotations, according to our thick-planning council's directives. Now and then he and I talked a little, never very much. In the evenings we had music; Cousin Had'd was a drummer, much in demand for dances, who could always gather a group. Or I would play Word-Thief with Tubdu, a game she adored and always lost at because she was so intent to steal my words that she forgot to protect her own. "Got you, got you!" she would cry, and melt into The Great Giggle, seizing my letterblocks with her fat, tapering, brown fingers; and next move I would take all my letters back along with most of hers. "How did you see that?" she would ask, amazed, studying the scattered words. Sometimes my otherfather Kap played with us, methodical, a bit mechanical, with a small smile for both triumph and defeat.

Then I would go up to my room under the eaves, my room of dark wood walls and dark red curtains, the smell of rain coming in the window, the sound of rain on the tiles of the roof. I would lie there in the mild darkness and luxuriate in sorrow, in great, aching, sweet, youthful sorrow for this ancient home that I was going to leave, to lose forever, to sail away from on the dark river of time. For I knew, from my eighteenth birthday on, that I would leave Udan, leave O, and go out to the other worlds. It was my ambition. It was my destiny.

I have not said anything about Isidri, as I described those winter holidays. She was there. She played in the Plays, worked on the farm, went to the dances, sang the choruses, joined the hiking parties, swam in the river in the warm rain with the rest of us. My first winter home from Ran'n, as I swung off the train at Derdan'nad Station, she greeted me with a cry of delight and a great embrace, then broke away with a strange, startled laugh and stood back, a tall, dark, thin girl with an intent, watchful face. She was quite awkward with me that evening. I felt that it was because she had always seen me as a little boy, a child, and now, eighteen and a student at Ran'n, I was a man. I was complacent with Isidri, putting her at her ease, patronizing her. In the days that followed, she remained awkward, laughing inappropriately, never opening her heart to me in the kind of long talks we used to have, and even, I thought, avoiding me. My whole last tenday at home that year, Isidri spent visiting her father's relatives in Sabtodiu Village. I was offended that she had not put off her visit till I was gone.

The next year she was not awkward, but not intimate. She had become interested in religion, attending the shrine daily, studying the Discussions with the elders. She was kind, friendly, busy. I do not remember that she and I ever touched that winter until she kissed me good-bye. Among my people a kiss is not with the mouth; we lay our cheeks together for a moment, or for longer. Her kiss was as light as the touch of a leaf, lingering yet barely perceptible.

My third and last winter home, I told them I was leaving: going to Hain, and that from Hain I wanted to go on farther and forever.

How cruel we are to our parents! All I needed to say was that I was going to Hain. After her half-anguished, half-exultant cry of "I knew it!" my mother said in her usual soft voice, suggesting not stating, "After that, you might come back, for a while." I could have said, "Yes." That was all she asked. Yes, I might come back, for a while. With the impenetrable self-centeredness of youth, which mistakes itself for honesty, I refused to give her what she asked. I took from her the modest hope of seeing me after ten years, and gave her the desolation of believing that when I left she would never see me again. "If I qualify, I want to be a Mobile," I said. I had steeled myself to speak without palliations. I prided myself on my truthfulness. And all the time, though I didn't know it, nor did they, it was not the truth at all. The truth is rarely so simple, though not many truths are as complicated as mine turned out to be.

She took my brutality without the least complaint. She had left her own people, after all. She said that evening, "We can talk by ansible, sometimes, as long as you're on Hain." She said it as if reassuring me, not herself. I think she was remembering how she had said good-bye to her people and boarded the ship on Terra, and when she landed a few seeming hours later on Hain, her mother had been dead for fifty years. She could have talked to Terra on the ansible; but who was there for her to talk to? I did not know that pain, but she did. She took comfort in knowing I would be spared it, for a while.

Everything now was "for a while." Oh, the bitter sweetness of those days! How I enjoyed myself—standing, again, poised on the slick boulder amidst the roaring water, spear raised, the hero! How ready, how willing I was to crush all that long, slow, deep, rich life of Udan in my hand and toss it away!

Only for one moment was I told what I was doing, and then so briefly that I could deny it.

I was down in the boathouse workshop, on the rainy, warm afternoon of a day late in the last month of winter. The constant, hissing thunder of the swollen river was the matrix of my thoughts as I set a new thwart in the little red rowboat we used to fish from, taking pleasure in the task, indulging my anticipatory nostalgia to the full by imagining myself on another planet a hundred years away remembering this hour in the boathouse, the smell of wood and water, the river's incessant roar. A knock at the workshop door. Isidri looked in. The thin, dark, watchful face, the long braid of dark hair, not as black as mine, the intent, clear eyes. "Hideo," she said, "I want to talk to you for a minute."

"Come on in!" I said, pretending ease and gladness, though half-aware that in fact I shrank from talking with Isidri, that I was afraid of her—why?

She perched on the vise bench and watched me work in silence for a little while. I began to say something commonplace, but she spoke: "Do you know why I've been staying away from you?"

Liar, self-protective liar, I said, "Staying away from me?"

At that she sighed. She had hoped I would say I understood, and spare her the rest. But I couldn't. I was lying only in pretending that I hadn't noticed that she had kept away from me. I truly had never, never until she told me, imagined why.

"I found out I was in love with you, winter before last," she said. "I wasn't going to say anything about it because—well, you know. If you'd felt anything like that for me, you'd have known I did. But it wasn't both of us. So there was no good in it. But then, when you told us you're leaving . . . At first I thought, all the more reason to say nothing. But then I thought, that wouldn't be fair. To me, partly. Love has a right to be spoken. And you have a right to know that somebody loves you. That somebody has loved you, could love you. We all need to know that. Maybe it's what we need most. So I wanted to tell you. And because I was afraid you thought I'd kept away from you because I didn't love you, or care about you, you know. It might have looked like that. But it wasn't that." She had slipped down off the table and was at the door.

"Sidi!" I said, her name breaking from me in a strange, hoarse cry, the name only, no words—I had no words. I had no feelings, no compassion, no more nostalgia, no more luxurious suffering. Shocked out of emotion, bewildered, blank, I stood there. Our eyes met. For four or five breaths we stood staring into each other's soul. Then Isidri looked away with a wincing, desolate smile, and slipped out.

I did not follow her. I had nothing to say to her: literally. I felt that it would take me a month, a year, years, to find the words I needed to say to her. I had been so rich, so comfortably complete in myself and my ambition and my destiny, five minutes ago; and now I stood empty, silent, poor, looking at the world I had thrown away.

That ability to look at the truth lasted an hour or so. All my life since I have thought of it as "the hour in the boathouse." I sat on the high bench where Isidri had sat. The rain fell and the river roared and the early night came on. When at last I moved, I turned on a light, and began to try to defend my purpose, my planned future, from the terrible plain reality. I began to build up a screen of emotions and evasions and versions; to look away from what Isidri had shown me; to look away from Isidri's eyes.

By the time I went up to the house for dinner I was in control of myself. By the time I went to bed I was master of my destiny again, sure of my decision, almost able to indulge myself in feeling sorry for Isidri—but not quite. Never did I dishonor her with that. I will say that much for myself. I had had the pity that is self-pity knocked out of me in the hour in the boathouse. When I parted from my family at the muddy little station in the village, a few days after, I wept, not luxuriously for them, but for myself, in honest, hopeless pain. It was too much for me to bear. I had had so little practice in pain! I said to my mother, "I will come back. When I finish the course—six years, maybe seven—I'll come back, I'll stay a while."

"If your way brings you," she whispered. She held me close to her, and then released me.

So, then: I have come to the time I chose to begin my story, when I was twenty-one and left my home on the ship *Terraces of Darranda* to study at the Schools on Hain.

Of the journey itself I have no memory whatever. I think I remember entering the ship, yet no details come to mind, visual or kinetic; I cannot recollect being on the ship. My memory of leaving it is only of an overwhelming physical sensation, dizziness. I staggered and felt sick, and was so unsteady on my feet I had to be supported until I had taken several steps on the soil of Hain.

Troubled by this lapse of consciousness, I asked about it at the Ekumenical School. I was told that it is one of the many different ways in which travel at near-lightspeed affects the mind. To most people it seems merely that a few hours pass in a kind of perceptual limbo; others have curious perceptions of space and time and event, which can be seriously disturbing; a few simply feel they have been asleep when they "wake up" on arrival. I did not even have that experience. I had no experience at all. I felt cheated. I wanted to have felt the voyage, to have known, in some way, the great interval of space: but as far as I was concerned, there was no interval. I was at the spaceport on O, and then I was at Ve Port, dizzy, bewildered, and at last, when I was able to believe that I was there, excited.

My studies and work during those years are of no interest now. I will mention only one event, which may or may not be on record in the ansible reception file at Fourth Beck Tower, EY 21-11-93/1645. (The last time I checked, it was on record in the ansible transmission file at Ran'n, ET date 30-11-93/1645. Urashima's coming and going was on record, too, in the Annals of the Emperors.) 1645 was my first year on Hain. Early in the term I was asked to come to the ansible center, where they explained that they had received a garbled screen transmission, apparently from O, and hoped I could help them reconstitute it. After a date nine days later than the date of reception, it read:

> *les oku n hide problem netru emit it hurt di it may not*
> *be salv devir*

The words were gapped and fragmented. Some were standard Hainish, but *oku* and *netru* mean "north" and "symmetrical" in Sio, my native language. The ansible centers on O had reported no record of the transmission, but the Receivers thought the message might be from O because of these two words and because the Hainish phrase "it may not be salvageable" occurred in a transmission received almost simultaneously from one of the Stabiles on O, concerning a wave-damaged desalinization plant. "We call this a creased message," the Receiver told me, when I confessed I could make nothing of it and asked how often ansible messages came through so garbled. "Not often, fortunately. We can't be certain where or when they originated, or will originate. They may be effects of a double field—interference phenomena, perhaps. One of my colleagues here calls them ghost messages."

Instantaneous transmission had always fascinated me, and though I was then only a beginner in ansible principle, I developed this fortuitous acquaintance with the Receivers into a friendship with several of them. And I took all the courses in ansible theory that were offered.

When I was in my final year in the school of temporal physics, and considering going on to the Cetian Worlds for further study—after my promised visit home, which seemed sometimes a remote, irrelevant day-dream and sometimes a yearning and yet fearful need—the first reports came over the ansible from Anarres of the new theory of transilience. Not only information, but matter, bodies, people might be transported from place to place without lapse of time. "Churten technology" was suddenly a reality, although a very strange reality, an implausible fact.

I was crazy to work on it. I was about to go promise my soul and body to the School if they would let me work on churten theory when they came and asked me if I'd consider postponing my training as a Mobile for a year or so to work on churten theory. Judiciously and graciously, I consented. I celebrated all over town that night. I remember showing all my friends how to dance the fen'n, and I remember setting off fireworks in the Great Plaza of the Schools, and I think I remember singing under the Director's windows, a little before dawn. I remember what I felt like next day, too; but it didn't keep me from dragging myself over to the Ti-Phy building to see where they were installing the Churten Field Laboratory.

Ansible transmission is, of course, enormously expensive, and I had only been able to talk to my family twice during my years on Hain; but my friends in the ansible center would occasionally "ride" a screen message for me on a transmission to O. I sent a message thus to Ran'n to be posted onto the First Sedoretu of Udan Farmhold of Derdan'nad Village of the hill district of the Northwest Watershed of the Saduun,

Oket, on O, telling them that "although this research will delay my visit home, it may save me four years' travel." The flippant message revealed my guilty feeling; but we did really think then that we would have the technology within a few months.

The Field Laboratories were soon moved out to Ve Port, and I went with them. The joint work of the Cetian and Hainish churten research teams in those first three years was a succession of triumphs, postponements, promises, defeats, breakthroughs, setbacks, all happening so fast that anybody who took a week off was out-of-date. "Clarity hiding mystery," Gvonesh called it. Every time it all came clear it all grew more mysterious. The theory was beautiful and maddening. The experiments were exciting and inscrutable. The technology worked best when it was most preposterous. Four years went by in that laboratory like no time at all, as they say.

I had now spent ten years on Hain and Ve, and was thirty-one. On O, four years had passed while my NAFAL ship passed a few minutes of dilated time going to Hain, and four more would pass while I returned: so when I returned I would have been gone eighteen of their years. My parents were all still alive. It was high time for my promised visit home.

But though churten research had hit a frustrating setback in the Spring Snow Paradox, a problem the Cetians thought might be insoluble, I couldn't stand the thought of being eight years out-of-date when I got back to Hain. What if they broke the paradox? It was bad enough knowing I must lose four years going to O. Tentatively, not too hopefully, I proposed to the Director that I carry some experimental materials with me to O and set up a fixed double-field auxiliary to the ansible link between Ve Port and Ran'n. Thus I could stay in touch with Ve, as Ve stayed in touch with Urras and Anarres; and the fixed ansible link might be preparatory to a churten link. I remember I said, "If you break the paradox, we might eventually send some mice."

To my surprise my idea caught on; the temporal engineers wanted

a receiving field. Even our Director, who could be as brilliantly inscrutable as churten theory itself, said it was a good idea. "Mouses, bugs,
gholes, who knows what we send you?" she said.

So, then: when I was thirty-one years old I left Ve Port on the
NAFAL transport *Lady of Sorra* and returned to O. This time I experienced the near-lightspeed flight the way most people do, as an unnerving interlude in which one cannot think consecutively, read a clockface,
or follow a story. Speech and movement become difficult or impossible.
Other people appear as unreal half presences, inexplicably there or not
there. I did not hallucinate, but everything seemed hallucination. It is
like a high fever—confusing, miserably boring, seeming endless, yet
very difficult to recall once it is over, as if it were an episode outside
one's life, encapsulated. I wonder now if its resemblance to the "churten
experience" has yet been seriously investigated.

I went straight to Ran'n, where I was given rooms in the New Quadrangle, fancier than my old student room in the Shrine Quadrangle,
and some nice lab space in Tower Hall to set up an experimental transilience field station. I got in touch with my family right away and talked
to all my parents; my mother had been ill, but was fine now, she said. I
told them I would be home as soon as I had got things going at Ran'n.
Every tenday I called again and talked to them and said I'd be along
very soon now. I was genuinely very busy, having to catch up the lost
four years and to learn Gvonesh's solution to the Spring Snow Paradox.
It was, fortunately, the only major advance in theory. Technology had
advanced a good deal. I had to retrain myself, and to train my assistants
almost from scratch. I had had an idea about an aspect of double-field
theory that I wanted to work out before I left. Five months went by
before I called them up and said at last, "I'll be there tomorrow." And
when I did so, I realized that all along I had been afraid.

I don't know if I was afraid of seeing them after eighteen years, of the
changes, the strangeness, or if it was myself I feared.

Eighteen years had made no difference at all to the hills beside the wide Saduun, the farmlands, the dusty little station in Derdan'nad, the old, old houses on the quiet streets. The village great tree was gone, but its replacement had a pretty wide spread of shade already. The aviary at Udan had been enlarged. The yama stared haughtily, timidly at me across the fence. A road gate that I had hung on my last visit home was decrepit, needing its post reset and new hinges, but the weeds that grew beside it were the same dusty, sweet-smelling summer weeds. The tiny dams of the irrigation runnels made their multiple, soft click and thump as they closed and opened. Everything was the same, itself. Timeless, Udan in its dream of work stood over the river that ran timeless in its dream of movement.

But the faces and bodies of the people waiting for me at the station in the hot sunlight were not the same. My mother, forty-seven when I left, was sixty-five, a beautiful and fragile elderly woman. Tubdu had lost weight; she looked shrunken and wistful. My father was still handsome and bore himself proudly, but his movements were slow and he scarcely spoke at all. My otherfather Kap, seventy now, was a precise, fidgety, little old man. They were still the First Sedoretu of Udan, but the vigor of the farmhold now lay in the Second and Third Sedoretu.

I knew of all the changes, of course, but being there among them was a different matter from hearing about them in letters and transmissions. The old house was much fuller than it had been when I lived there. The south wing had been reopened, and children ran in and out of its doors and across courtyards that in my childhood had been silent and ivied and mysterious.

My sister Koneko was now four years older than I instead of four years younger. She looked very like my early memory of my mother. As the train drew in to Derdan'nad Station, she had been the first of them I recognized, holding up a child of three or four and saying, "Look, look, it's your Uncle Hideo!"

The Second Sedoretu had been married for eleven years: Koneko and Isidri, sister-germanes, were the partners of the Day. Koneko's husband was my old friend Sota, a Morning man of Drehe Farmhold. Sota and I had loved each other dearly when we were adolescents, and I had been grieved to grieve him when I left. When I heard that he and Koneko were in love I had been very surprised, so self-centered am I, but at least I am not jealous: it pleased me very deeply. Isidri's husband, a man nearly twenty years older than herself, named Hedran, had been a traveling scholar of the Discussions. Udan had given him hospitality, and his visits had led to the marriage. He and Isidri had no children. Sota and Koneko had two Evening children, a boy of ten called Murmi, and Lasako, Little Isako, who was four.

The Third Sedoretu had been brought to Udan by Suudi, my brother-germane, who had married a woman from Aster Village; their Morning pair also came from farmholds of Aster. There were six children in that sedoretu. A cousin whose sedoretu at Ekke had broken had also come to live at Udan with her two children; so the coming and going and dressing and undressing and washing and slamming and running and shouting and weeping and laughing and eating was prodigious. Tubdu would sit at work in the sunny kitchen courtyard and watch a wave of children pass. "Bad!" she would cry. "They'll never drown, not a one of 'em!" And she would shake with silent laughter that became a wheezing cough.

My mother, who had after all been a Mobile of the Ekumen, and had traveled from Terra to Hain and from Hain to O, was impatient to hear about my research. "What is it, this churtening? How does it work, what does it do? Is it an ansible for matter?"

"That's the idea," I said. "Transilience: instantaneous transference of being from one s-tc point to another."

"No interval?"

"No interval."

Isako frowned. "It sounds wrong," she said. "Explain."

I had forgotten how direct my soft-spoken mother could be; I had forgotten that she was an intellectual. I did my best to explain the incomprehensible.

"So," she said at last, "you don't really understand how it works."

"No. Nor even what it does. Except that—as a rule—when the field is in operation, the mice in Building One are instantaneously in Building Two, perfectly cheerful and unharmed. Inside their cage, if we remembered to keep their cage inside the initiating churten field. We used to forget. Loose mice everywhere."

"What's *mice*?" said a little Morning boy of the Third Sedoretu, who had stopped to listen to what sounded like a story.

"Ah," I said in a laugh, surprised. I had forgotten that at Udan mice were unknown, and rats were fanged, demon enemies of the painted cat. "Tiny, pretty, furry animals," I said, "that come from Grandmother Isako's world. They are friends of scientists. They have traveled all over the Known Worlds."

"In tiny little spaceships?" the child said hopefully.

"In large ones, mostly," I said. He was satisfied, and went away.

"Hideo," said my mother, in the terrifying way women have of passing without interval from one subject to another because they have them all present in their mind at once, "you haven't found any kind of relationship?"

I shook my head, smiling.

"None at all?"

"A man from Alterra and I lived together for a couple of years," I said. "It was a good friendship; but he's a Mobile now. And . . . oh, you know . . . people here and there. Just recently, at Ran'n, I've been with a very nice woman from East Oket."

"I hoped, if you intend to be a Mobile, that you might make a couple-marriage with another Mobile. It's easier, I think," she said. Easier than what? I thought, and knew the answer before I asked.

"Mother, I doubt now that I'll travel farther than Hain. This churten business is too interesting; I want to be in on it. And if we do learn to control the technology, you know, then travel will be nothing. There'll be no need for the kind of sacrifice you made. Things will be different. Unimaginably different! You could go to Terra for an hour and come back here: and only an hour would have passed."

She thought about that. "If you do it, then," she said, speaking slowly, almost shaking with the intensity of comprehension, "you will . . . you will shrink the galaxy—the universe?—to . . ." and she held up her left hand, thumb and fingers all drawn together to a point.

I nodded. "A mile or a light-year will be the same. There will be no distance."

"It can't be right," she said after a while. "To have event without interval . . . Where is the dancing? Where is the way? I don't think you'll be able to control it, Hideo." She smiled. "But of course you must try."

And after that we talked about who was coming to the field dance at Drehe tomorrow.

I did not tell my mother that I had invited Tasi, the nice woman from East Oket, to come to Udan with me and that she had refused, had, in fact, gently informed me that she thought this was a good time for us to part. Tasi was tall, with a braid of dark hair, not coarse, bright black like mine but soft, fine, dark, like the shadows in a forest. A typical ki'O woman, I thought. She had deflated my protestations of love skillfully and without shaming me. "I think you're in love with some-body, though," she said. "Somebody on Hain, maybe. Maybe the man from Alterra you told me about?" No, I said. No, I'd never been in love. I wasn't capable of an intense relationship, that was clear by now. I'd dreamed too long of traveling the galaxy with no attachments anywhere, and then worked too long in the churten lab, married to a damned theory that couldn't find its technology. No room for love, no time.

But why had I wanted to bring Tasi home with me?

Tall but no longer thin, a woman of forty, not a girl, not typical, not comparable, not like anyone anywhere, Isidri had greeted me quietly at the door of the house. Some farm emergency had kept her from coming to the village station to meet me. She was wearing an old smock and leggings like any field worker, and her hair, dark beginning to grey, was in a rough braid. As she stood in that wide doorway of polished wood she was Udan itself, the body and soul of that thirty-century-old farmhold, its continuity, its life. All my childhood was in her hands, and she held them out to me.

"Welcome home, Hideo," she said, with a smile as radiant as the summer light on the river. As she brought me in, she said, "I cleared the kids out of your old room. I thought you'd like to be there—would you?" Again she smiled, and I felt her warmth, the solar generosity of a woman in the prime of life, married, settled, rich in her work and being. I had not needed Tasi as a defense. I had nothing to fear from Isidri. She felt no rancor, no embarrassment. She had loved me when she was young, another person. It would be altogether inappropriate for me to feel embarrassment, or shame, or anything but the old affectionate loyalty of the years when we played and worked and fished and dreamed together, children of Udan.

So, then: I settled down in my old room under the tiles. There were new curtains, rust and brown. I found a stray toy under the chair, in the closet, as if I as a child had left my playthings there and found them now. At fourteen, after my entry ceremony in the shrine, I had carved my name on the deep window jamb among the tangled patterns of names and symbols that had been cut into it for centuries. I looked for it now. There had been some additions. Beside my careful, clear *Hideo*, surrounded by my ideogram, the cloudflower, a younger child had hacked a straggling *Dohedri*, and nearby was carved a delicate three-roofs ideogram. The sense of being a bubble in Udan's river, a moment in the permanence of life in this house on this land on this quiet world, was almost crushing, denying my identity, and profoundly reassuring, confirming my identity. Those nights of my visit home I slept as I had not slept for years, lost, drowned in the waters of sleep and darkness, and woke to the summer mornings as if reborn, very hungry.

The children were still all under twelve, going to school at home. Isidri, who taught them literature and religion and was the school planner, invited me to tell them about Hain, about NAFAL travel, about temporal physics, whatever I pleased. Visitors to ki'O farmholds are always put to use. Evening-Uncle Hideo became rather a favorite among the children, always good for hitching up the yama-cart or taking them fishing in the big boat, which they couldn't yet handle, or telling a story about his magic mice who could be in two places at the same time. I asked them if Evening-Grandmother Isako had told them about the painted cat who came alive and killed the demon rats—"And his mouf was all BLUGGY in the morning!" shouted Lasako, her eyes shining. But they didn't know the tale of Urashima.

"Why haven't you told them 'The Fisherman of the Inland Sea'?" I asked my mother.

She smiled and said, "Oh, that was your story. You always wanted it."

I saw Isidri's eyes on us, clear and tranquil, yet watchful still.

I knew my mother had had repair and healing to her heart a year before, and I asked Isidri later, as we supervised some work the older children were doing, "Has Isako recovered, do you think?"

"She seems wonderfully well since you came. I don't know. It's damage from her childhood, from the poisons in the Terran biosphere; they say her immune system is easily depressed. She was very patient about being ill. Almost too patient."

"And Tubdu—does she need new lungs?"

"Probably. All four of them are getting older, and stubborner. . . . But you look at Isako for me. See if you see what I mean."

I tried to observe my mother. After a few days I reported back that

she seemed energetic and decisive, even imperative, and that I hadn't
seen much of the patient endurance that worried Isidri. She laughed.

"Isako told me once," she said, "that a mother is connected to her
child by a very fine, thin cord, like the umbilical cord, that can stretch
light-years without any difficulty. I asked her if it was painful, and she
said, 'Oh, no, it's just there, you know, it stretches and stretches and
never breaks.' It seems to me it must be painful. But I don't know. I
have no child, and I've never been more than two days' travel from my
mothers." She smiled and said in her soft, deep voice, "I think I love
Isako more than anyone, more even than my mother, more even than
Koneko. . . ."

Then she had to show one of Suudi's children how to reprogram the
timer on the irrigation control. She was the hydrologist for the village
and the oenologist for the farm. Her life was thick-planned, very rich
in necessary work and wide relationships, a serene and steady succession of days, seasons, years. She swam in life as she had swum in the
river, like a fish, at home. She had borne no child, but all the children
of the farmhold were hers. She and Koneko were as deeply attached as
their mothers had been. Her relation with her rather fragile, scholarly
husband seemed peaceful and respectful. I thought his Night marriage
with my old friend Sota might be the stronger sexual link, but Isidri
clearly admired and depended on his intellectual and spiritual guidance.
I thought his teaching a bit dry and disputatious; but what did I know
about religion? I had not given worship for years, and felt strange, out of
place, even in the home shrine. I felt strange, out of place, in my home.
I did not acknowledge it to myself.

I was conscious of the month as pleasant, uneventful, even a little
boring. My emotions were mild and dull. The wild nostalgia, the
romantic sense of standing on the brink of my destiny, all that was
gone with the Hideo of twenty-one. Though now the youngest of my
generation, I was a grown man, knowing his way, content with his

work, past emotional self-indulgence. I wrote a little poem for the
house album about the peacefulness of following a chosen course.
When I had to go, I embraced and kissed everyone, dozens of soft or
harsh cheek-touches. I told them that if I stayed on O, as it seemed I
might be asked to do for a year or so, I would come back next winter
for another visit. On the train going back through the hills to Ran'n,
I thought with a complacent gravity how I might return to the farm
next winter, finding them all just the same; and how, if I came back
after another eighteen years or even longer, some of them would be
gone and some would be new to me and yet it would be always my
home, Udan with its wide dark roofs riding time like a dark-sailed
ship. I always grow poetic when I am lying to myself.

I got back to Ran'n, checked in with my people at the lab in Tower
Hall, and had dinner with colleagues, good food and drink—I brought
them a bottle of wine from Udan, for Isidri was making splendid wines,
and had given me a case of the fifteen-year-old Kedun. We talked about
the latest breakthrough in churten technology, "continuous-field sending," reported from Anarres just yesterday on the ansible. I went to my
rooms in the New Quadrangle through the summer night, my head
full of physics, read a little, and went to bed. I turned out the light and
darkness filled me as it filled the room. Where was I? Alone in a room
among strangers. As I had been for ten years and would always be. On
one planet or another, what did it matter? Alone, part of nothing, part
of no one. Udan was not my home. I had no home, no people. I had no
future, no destiny, any more than a bubble of foam or a whirlpool in a
current has a destiny. It is and it isn't. Nothing more.

I turned the light on because I could not bear the darkness, but the
light was worse. I sat huddled up in the bed and began to cry. I could
not stop crying. I became frightened at how the sobs racked and shook
me till I was sick and weak and still could not stop sobbing. After a long
time I calmed myself gradually by clinging to an imagination, a childish

idea: in the morning I would call Isidri and talk to her, telling her that I needed instruction in religion, that I wanted to give worship at the shrines again, but it had been so long, and I had never listened to the Discussions, but now I needed to, and I would ask her, Isidri, to help me. So, holding fast to that, I could at last stop the terrible sobbing and lie spent, exhausted, until the day came.

I did not call Isidri. In daylight the thought which had saved me from the dark seemed foolish; and I thought if I called her she would ask advice of her husband, the religious scholar. But I knew I needed help. I went to the shrine in the Old School and gave worship. I asked for a copy of the First Discussions, and read it. I joined a Discussion group, and we read and talked together. My religion is godless, argumentative, and mystical. The name of our world is the first word of its first prayer. For human beings its vehicle is the human voice and mind. As I began to rediscover it, I found it quite as strange as churten theory and in some respects complementary to it. I knew, but had never understood, that Cetian physics and religion are aspects of one knowledge. I wondered if all physics and religion are aspects of one knowledge.

At night I never slept well and often could not sleep at all. After the bountiful tables of Udan, college food seemed poor stuff; I had no appetite. But our work, my work went well—wonderfully well.

"No more mouses," said Gvonesh on the voice ansible from Hain. "Peoples."

"What people?" I demanded.

"Me," said Gvonesh.

So our Director of Research churtened from one corner of Laboratory One to another, and then from Building One to Building Two— vanishing in one laboratory and appearing in the other, smiling, in the same instant, in no time.

"What did it feel like?" they asked, of course, and Gvonesh answered, of course, "Like nothing."

Many experiments followed; mice and gholes churtened halfway around Ve and back; robot crews churtened from Anarres to Urras, from Hain to Ve, and then from Anarres to Ve, twenty-two light-years. So, then, eventually the *Shoby* and her crew of ten human beings churtened into orbit around a miserable planet seventeen light-years from Ve and returned (but words that imply coming and going, that imply distance traveled, are not appropriate) thanks only to their intelligent use of entrainment, rescuing themselves from a kind of chaos of dissolution, a death by unreality, that horrified us all. Experiments with high-intelligence life-forms came to a halt.

"The rhythm is wrong," Gvonesh said on the ansible (she said it "rith-khom.") For a moment I thought of my mother saying, "It can't be right to have event without interval." What else had Isako said? Something about dancing. But I did not want to think about Udan. I did not think about Udan. When I did I felt, far down deeper inside me than my bones, the knowledge of being no one, no where, and a shaking like a frightened animal.

My religion reassured me that I was part of the Way, and my physics absorbed my despair in work. Experiments, cautiously resumed, succeeded beyond hope. The Terran Dalzul and his psychophysics took everyone at the research station on Ve by storm; I am sorry I never met him. As he predicted, using the continuity field he churtened without a hint of trouble, alone, first locally, then from Ve to Hain, then the great jump to Tadkla and back. From the second journey to Tadkla, his three companions returned without him. He died on that far world. It did not seem to us in the laboratories that his death was in any way caused by the churten field or by what had come to be known as "the churten experience," though his three companions were not so sure.

"Maybe Dalzul was right. One people at a time," said Gvonesh; and she made herself again the subject, the "ritual animal," as the Hainish say, of the next experiment. Using continuity technology she churtened right round Ve in four skips, which took thirty-two seconds because of the time needed to set up the coordinates. We had taken to calling the non-interval in time/real interval in space a "skip." It sounded light, trivial. Scientists like to trivialize.

I wanted to try the improvement to double-field stability that I had been working on ever since I came to Ran'n. It was time to give it a test; my patience was short, life was too short to fiddle with figures forever. Talking to Gvonesh on the ansible I said, "I'll skip over to Ve Port. And then back here to Ran'n. I promised a visit to my home farm this winter." Scientists like to trivialize.

"You still got that wrinkle in your field?" Gvonesh asked. "Some kind, you know, like a fold?"

"It's ironed out, ammar," I assured her.

"Good, fine," said Gvonesh, who never questioned what one said. "Come."

So, then: we set up the fields in a constant stable churten link with ansible connection; and I was standing inside a chalked circle in the Churten Field Laboratory of Ran'n Center on a late autumn afternoon and standing inside a chalked circle in the Churten Research Station Field Laboratory in Ve Port on a late summer day at a distance of 4.2 light-years and no interval of time.

"Feel nothing?" Gvonesh inquired, shaking my hand heartily. "Good fellow, good fellow, welcome, ammar, Hideo. Good to see. No wrinkle, hah?"

I laughed with the shock and queerness of it, and gave Gvonesh the bottle of Udan Kedun '49 that I had picked up a moment ago from the laboratory table on O.

I had expected, if I arrived at all, to churten promptly back again, but Gvonesh and others wanted me on Ve for a while for discussions and tests of the field. I think now that the Director's extraordinary intuition was at work; the "wrinkle," the "fold" in the Tiokunan'n Field still bothered her. "Is unaesthetical," she said.

"But it works," I said.

"It worked," said Gvonesh.

Except to retest my field, to prove its reliability, I had no desire to return to O. I was sleeping somewhat better here on Ve, although food was still unpalatable to me, and when I was not working I felt shaky and drained, a disagreeable reminder of my exhaustion after the night which I tried not to remember when for some reason or other I had cried so much. But the work went very well.

"You got no sex, Hideo?" Gvonesh asked me when we were alone in the Lab one day, I playing with a new set of calculations and she finishing her box lunch.

The question took me utterly aback. I knew it was not as impertinent as Gvonesh's peculiar usage of the language made it sound. But Gvonesh never asked questions like that. Her own sex life was as much a mystery as the rest of her existence. No one had ever heard her mention the word, let alone suggest the act.

When I sat with my mouth open, stumped, she said, "You used to, hah," as she chewed on a cold varvet.

I stammered something. I knew she was not proposing that she and I have sex, but inquiring after my well-being. But I did not know what to say.

"You got some kind of wrinkle in your life, hah," Gvonesh said. "Sorry. Not my business."

Wanting to assure her I had taken no offense I said, as we say on O, "I honor your intent."

She looked directly at me, something she rarely did. Her eyes were clear as water in her long, bony face softened by a fine, thick, colorless down. "Maybe is time you go back to O?" she asked.

"I don't know. The facilities here—"

She nodded. She always accepted what one said. "You read Harraven's report?" she asked, changing one subject for another as quickly and definitively as my mother.

All right, I thought, the challenge was issued. She was ready for me to test my field again. Why not? After all, I could churten to Ran'n and churten right back again to Ve within a minute, if I chose, and if the Lab could afford it. Like ansible transmission, churtening draws essentially on inertial mass, but setting up the field, disinfecting it, and holding it stable in size uses a good deal of local energy. But it was Gvonesh's suggestion, which meant we had the money. I said, "How about a skip over and back?"

"Fine," Gvonesh said. "Tomorrow."

So the next day, on a morning of late autumn, I stood inside a chalked circle in the Field Laboratory on Ve and stood—

A shimmer, a shivering of everything—a missed beat—skipped—

in darkness. A darkness. A dark room. The lab? A lab—I found the light panel. In the darkness I was sure it was the laboratory on Ve. In the light I saw it was not. I didn't know where it was. I didn't know where I was. It seemed familiar yet I could not place it. What was it? A biology lab? There were specimens, an old subparticle microscope, the maker's ideogram on the battered brass casing, the lyre ideogram. . . . I was on O. In some laboratory in some building of the Center at Ran'n? It smelled like the old buildings of Ran'n, it smelled like a rainy night on O. But how could I have not arrived in the receiving field, the circle carefully chalked on the wood floor of the lab in Tower Hall? The field itself must have moved. An appalling, an impossible thought. I was alarmed and felt rather dizzy, as if my body had skipped that beat, but I was not yet frightened. I was all right, all here, all the pieces in the right places, and the mind working. A slight spatial displacement? said the mind.

I went out into the corridor. Perhaps I had myself been disoriented and left the Churten Field Laboratory and come to full consciousness somewhere else. But my crew would have been there; where were they? And that would have been hours ago; it should have been just past noon on O when I arrived. A slight temporal displacement? said the mind, working away. I went down the corridor looking for my lab, and that is when it became like one of those dreams in which you cannot find the room which you must find. It was that dream. The building was perfectly familiar: it was Tower Hall, the second floor of Tower, but there was no Churten Lab. All the labs were biology and biophysics, and all were deserted. It was evidently late at night. Nobody around. At last I saw a light under a door and knocked and opened it on a student reading at a library terminal.

"I'm sorry," I said. "I'm looking for the Churten Field Lab—"

"The what lab?"

She had never heard of it, and apologized. "I'm not in Ti Phy, just Bi Phy," she said humbly.

I apologized too. Something was making me shakier, increasing my sense of dizziness and disorientation. Was this the "chaos effect" the crew of the *Shoby* and perhaps the crew of the *Galba* had experienced? Would I begin to see the stars through the walls, or turn around and see Gvonesh here on O?

I asked her what time it was. "I should have got here at noon," I said, though that of course meant nothing to her.

"It's about one," she said, glancing at the clock on the terminal. I looked at it too. It gave the time, the tenday, the month, the year.

"That's wrong," I said.

She looked worried.

"That's not right," I said. "The date. It's not right." But I knew from the steady glow of the numbers on the clock, from the girl's round, worried face, from the beat of my heart, from the smell of the rain, that it was right, that it was an hour after midnight eighteen years ago, that I was here, now, on the day after the day I called "once upon a time" when I began to tell this story.

A major temporal displacement, said the mind, working, laboring.

"I don't belong here," I said, and turned to hurry back to what seemed a refuge, Biology Lab 6, which would be the Churten Field Lab eighteen years from now, as if I could re-enter the field, which had existed or would exist for .004 second.

The girl saw that something was wrong, made me sit down, and gave me a cup of hot tea from her insulated bottle.

"Where are you from?" I asked her, the kind, serious student.

"Herdud Farmhold of Deada Village on the South Watershed of the Saduun," she said.

"I'm from downriver," I said. "Udan of Derdan'nad." I suddenly broke into tears. I managed to control myself, apologized again, drank my tea, and set the cup down. She was not overly troubled by my fit of weeping. Students are intense people, they laugh and cry, they break down and rebuild. She asked if I had a place to spend the night: a perceptive question. I said I did, thanked her, and left.

I did not go back to the biology laboratory, but went downstairs and started to cut through the gardens to my rooms in the New Quadrangle. As I walked the mind kept working; it worked out that somebody else had been/would be in those rooms then/now.

I turned back towards the Shrine Quadrangle, where I had lived my last two years as a student before I left for Hain. If this was in fact, as the clock had indicated, the night after I had left, my room might still be empty and unlocked. It proved to be so, to be as I had left it, the mattress bare, the cyclebasket unemptied.

That was the most frightening moment. I stared at that cyclebasket for a long time before I took a crumpled bit of outprint from it and carefully smoothed it on the desk. It was a set of temporal equations scribbled on my old pocketscreen in my own handwriting, notes from Sedharad's class in Interval, from my last term at Ran'n, day before yesterday, eighteen years ago.

I was now very shaky indeed. You are caught in a chaos field, said the mind, and I believed it. Fear and stress, and nothing to do about it, not till the long night was past. I lay down on the bare bunk-mattress, ready for the stars to burn through the walls and my eyelids if I shut them. I meant to try and plan what I should do in the morning, if there was a morning. I fell asleep instantly and slept like a stone till broad daylight, when I woke up on the bare bed in the familiar room, alert, hungry, and without a moment of doubt as to who or where or when I was.

I went down into the village for breakfast. I didn't want to meet any colleagues—no, fellow students—who might know me and say, "Hideo! What are you doing here? You left on the *Terraces of Darranda* yesterday!"

I had little hope they would not recognize me. I was thirty-one now, not twenty-one, much thinner and not as fit as I had been; but my half-Terran features were unmistakable. I did not want to be recognized, to have to try to explain. I wanted to get out of Ran'n. I wanted to go home.

O is a good world to time-travel in. Things don't change. Our trains run on the same schedule to the same places for centuries. We sign for payment and pay in contracted barter or cash monthly, so I did not have to produce mysterious coins from the future. I signed at the station and took the morning train to Saduun Delta.

The little suntrain glided through the plains and hills of the South Watershed and then the Northwest Watershed, following the ever-widening river, stopping at each village. I got off in the late afternoon at the station in Derdan'nad. Since it was very early spring, the station was muddy, not dusty.

I walked out the road to Udan. I opened the road gate that I had rehung a few days/eighteen years ago; it moved easily on its new hinges. That gave me a little gleam of pleasure. The she-yamas were all in the nursery pasture. Birthing would start any day; their woolly sides stuck out, and they moved like sailboats in a slow breeze, turning their elegant, scornful heads to look distrustfully at me as I passed. Rain clouds hung over the hills. I crossed the Oro on the humpbacked wooden bridge. Four or five great blue ochid hung in a backwater by the bridgefoot; I stopped to watch them; if I'd had a spear . . . The clouds drifted overhead trailing a fine, faint drizzle. I strode on. My face felt hot and stiff as the cool rain touched it. I followed the river road and saw the house come into view, the dark, wide roofs low on the tree-crowned hill. I came past the aviary and the collectors, past the irrigation center, under the avenue of tall bare trees, up the steps of the deep porch, to the door, the wide door of Udan. I went in.

Tubdu was crossing the hall—not the woman I had last seen, in her sixties, grey-haired and tired and fragile, but Tubdu of The Great Giggle, Tubdu at forty-five, fat and rosy-brown and brisk, crossing the hall with short, quick steps, stopping, looking at me at first with mere recognition, there's Hideo, then with puzzlement, is that Hideo? and then with shock—that can't be Hideo!

"Ombu," I said, the baby word for othermother, "Ombu, it's me, Hideo, don't worry, it's all right, I came back." I embraced her, pressed my cheek to hers.

"But, but—" She held me off, looked up at my face. "But what has happened to you, darling boy?" she cried, and then, turning, called out in a high voice, "Isako! Isako!"

When my mother saw me she thought, of course, that I had not left on the ship to Hain, that my courage or my intent had failed me; and in her first embrace there was an involuntary reserve, a withholding. Had I thrown away the destiny for which I had been so ready to throw away everything else? I knew what was in her mind. I laid my cheek to hers and whispered, "I did go, mother, and I came back. I'm thirty-one years old. I came back—"

She held me away a little just as Tubdu had done, and saw my face. "Oh Hideo!" she said, and held me to her with all her strength. "My dear, my dear!"

We held each other in silence, till I said at last, "I need to see Isidri."

My mother looked up at me intently but asked no questions. "She's in the shrine, I think."

"I'll be right back."

I left her and Tubdu side by side and hurried through the halls to the central room, in the oldest part of the house, rebuilt seven centuries ago on the foundations that go back three thousand years. The walls are stone and clay, the roof is thick glass, curved. It is always cool and still there. Books line the walls, the Discussions, the discussions of the Discussions, poetry, texts and versions of the Plays; there are drums and whispersticks for meditation and ceremony; the small, round pool which is the shrine itself wells up from clay pipes and brims its bluegreen basin, reflecting the rainy sky above the skylight. Isidri was there. She had brought in fresh boughs for the vase beside the shrine, and was kneeling to arrange them.

I went straight to her and said, "Isidri, I came back. Listen—"

Her face was utterly open, startled, scared, defenseless, the soft, thin face of a woman of twenty-two, the dark eyes gazing into me.

"Listen, Isidri: I went to Hain, I studied there, I worked on a new kind of temporal physics, a new theory—transilience—I spent ten years there. Then we began experiments, I was in Ran'n and crossed over to the Hainish system in no time, using that technology, in no time, you understand me, literally, like the ansible—not at lightspeed, not faster than light, but in no time. In one place and in another place instantaneously, you understand? And it went fine, it worked, but coming back there was . . . there was a fold, a crease, in my field. I was in the same place in a different time. I came back eighteen of your years, ten of mine. I came back to the day I left, but I didn't leave, I came back, I came back to you."

I was holding her hands, kneeling to face her as she knelt by the silent pool. She searched my face with her watchful eyes, silent. On her cheekbone there was a fresh scratch and a little bruise; a branch had lashed her as she gathered the evergreen boughs.

"Let me come back to you," I said in a whisper.

She touched my face with her hand. "You look so tired," she said. "Hideo . . . Are you all right?"

"Yes," I said. "Oh, yes. I'm all right."

And there my story, so far as it has any interest to the Ekumen or to research in transilience, comes to an end. I have lived now for eighteen years as a farmholder of Udan Farm of Derdan'nad Village of the hill region of the Northwest Watershed of the Saduun, on Oket, on O. I am fifty years old. I am the Morning husband of the Second Sedoretu of Udan; my wife is Isidri; my Night marriage is to Sota of Drehe, whose Evening wife is my sister Koneko. My children of the Morning with Isidri are Latubdu and Tadri; the Evening children are Murmi and Lasako. But none of this is of much interest to the Stabiles of the Ekumen.

My mother, who had had some training in temporal engineering, asked for my story, listened to it carefully, and accepted it without question; so did Isidri. Most of the people of my farmhold chose a simpler and far more plausible story, which explained everything fairly well, even my severe loss of weight and ten-year age gain overnight. At the very last moment, just before the space ship left, they said, Hideo decided not to go to the Ekumenical School on Hain after all. He came back to Udan, because he was in love with Isidri. But it had made him quite ill, because it was a very hard decision and he was very much in love.

Maybe that is indeed the true story. But Isidri and Isako chose a stranger truth.

Later, when we were forming our sedoretu, Sota asked me for that truth. "You aren't the same man, Hideo, though you are the man I always loved," he said. I told him why, as best I could. He was sure that Koneko would understand it better than he could, and indeed she listened gravely, and asked several keen questions which I could not answer.

I did attempt to send a message to the temporal physics department of the Ekumenical Schools on Hain. I had not been home long before my mother, with her strong sense of duty and her obligation to the Ekumen, became insistent that I do so.

"Mother," I said, "what can I tell them? They haven't invented churten theory yet!"

"Apologize for not coming to study, as you said you would. And explain it to the Director, the Anarresti woman. Maybe she would understand."

"Even Gvonesh doesn't know about churten yet. They'll begin telling her about it on the ansible from Urras and Anarres about three years from now. Anyhow, Gvonesh didn't know me the first couple of years I was there." The past tense was inevitable but ridiculous; it would have been more accurate to say, "she won't know me the first couple of years I won't be there."

Or *was* I there on Hain, now? That paradoxical idea of two simultaneous existences on two different worlds disturbed me exceedingly. It was one of the points Koneko had asked about. No matter how I discounted it as impossible under every law of temporality, I could not keep from imagining that it was possible, that another I was living on Hain, and would come to Udan in eighteen years and meet myself. After all, my present existence was also and equally impossible.

When such notions haunted and troubled me I learned to replace them with a different image: the little whorls of water that slid down between the two big rocks, where the current ran strong, just above the swimming bay in the Oro. I would imagine those whirlpools forming and dissolving, or I would go down to the river and sit and watch them. And they seemed to hold a solution to my question, to dissolve it as they endlessly dissolved and formed.

But my mother's sense of duty and obligation was unmoved by such trifles as a life impossibly lived twice.

"You should try to tell them," she said.

She was right. If my double transilience field had established itself permanently, it was a matter of real importance to temporal science, not only to myself. So I tried. I borrowed a staggering sum in cash from the farm reserves, went up to Ran'n, bought a five-thousand-word ansible screen transmission, and sent a message to my director of studies at the Ekumenical School, trying to explain why, after being accepted at the School, I had not arrived—if in fact I had not arrived.

I take it that this was the "creased message" or "ghost" they asked me to try to interpret, my first year there. Some of it is gibberish, and some words probably came from the other, nearly simultaneous transmission, but parts of my name are in it, and other words may be fragments or reversals from my long message—problem, churten, return, arrived, time.

It is interesting, I think, that at the ansible center the Receivers used the word "creased" for a temporally disturbed transilient, as Gvonesh would use it for the anomaly, the "wrinkle" in my churten field. In fact, the ansible field was meeting a resonance resistance, caused by the ten-year anomaly in the churten field, which did fold the message back into itself, crumple it up, inverting and erasing. At that point, within the implication of the Tiokunan'n Double Field, my existence on O as I sent the message was simultaneous with my existence on Hain when the message was received. There was an I who sent and an I who received. Yet, so long as the encapsulated field anomaly existed, the simultaneity was literally a point, an instant, a crossing without further implication in either the ansible or the churten field.

An image for the churten field in this case might be a river winding in its floodplain, winding in deep, redoubling curves, folding back upon itself so closely that at last the current breaks through the double banks of the S and runs straight, leaving a whole reach of the water aside as a curving lake, cut off from the current, unconnected. In this analogy, my ansible message would have been the one link, other than my memory, between the current and the lake.

But I think a truer image is the whirlpools of the current itself, occurring and recurring, the same? or not the same?

I worked at the mathematics of an explanation in the early years of my marriage, while my physics was still in good working order. See the "Notes toward a Theory of Resonance Interference in Doubled Ansible and Churten Fields," appended to this document. I realize that the explanation is probably irrelevant, since, on this stretch of the river, there is no Tiokunan'n Field. But independent research from an odd direction can be useful. And I am attached to it, since it is the last temporal physics I did. I have followed churten research with intense interest, but my life's work has been concerned with vineyards, drainage, the care of yamas, the care and education of children, the Discussions, and trying to learn how to catch fish with my bare hands.

Working on that paper, I satisfied myself in terms of mathematics and physics that the existence in which I went to Hain and became a temporal physicist specializing in transilience was in fact encapsulated (enfolded, erased) by the churten effect. But no amount of theory or proof could quite allay my anxiety, my fear—which increased after my marriage and with the birth of each of my children—that there was a crossing point yet to come. For all my images of rivers and whirlpools, I could not prove that the encapsulation might not reverse at the instant of transilience. It was possible that on the day I churtened from Ve to Ran'n I might undo, lose, erase my marriage, our children, all my life at Udan, crumple it up like a bit of paper tossed into a basket. I could not endure that thought.

I spoke of it at last to Isidri, from whom I have only ever kept one secret.

"No," she said, after thinking a long time, "I don't think that can be. There was a reason, wasn't there, that you came back—here."

"You," I said.

She smiled wonderfully. "Yes," she said. She added after a while, "And Sota, and Koneko, and the farmhold . . . But there'd be no reason for you to go back there, would there?"

She was holding our sleeping baby as she spoke; she laid her cheek against the small silky head.

"Except maybe your work there," she said. She looked at me with a little yearning in her eyes. Her honesty required equal honesty of me.

"I miss it sometimes," I said. "I know that. I didn't know that I was missing you. But I was dying of it. I would have died and never known why, Isidri. And anyhow, it was all wrong—my work was wrong."

"How could it have been wrong, if it brought you back?" she said, and to that I had no answer at all.

When information on churten theory began to be published I subscribed to whatever the Center Library of O received, particularly the work done at the Ekumenical Schools and on Ve. The general progress of research was just as I remembered, racing along for three years, then hitting the hard places. But there was no reference to a Tiokunan'n Hideo doing research in the field. Nobody worked on a theory of a stabilized double field. No churten field research station was set up at Ran'n.

At last it was the winter of my visit home, and then the very day; and I will admit that, all reason to the contrary, it was a bad day. I felt waves of guilt, of nausea. I grew very shaky, thinking of the Udan of that visit, when Isidri had been married to Hedran, and I a mere visitor.

Hedran, a respected traveling scholar of the Discussions, had in fact come to teach several times in the village. Isidri had suggested inviting him to stay at Udan. I had vetoed the suggestion, saying that though he was a brilliant teacher there was something I disliked about him. I got a sidelong flash from Sidi's clear dark eyes: *Is he jealous?* She suppressed a smile. When I told her and my mother about my "other life," the one thing I had left out, the one secret I kept, was my visit to Udan. I did not want to tell my mother that in that "other life" she had been very ill. I did not want to tell Isidri that in that "other life" Hedran had been her Evening husband and she had had no children of her body. Perhaps I was wrong, but it seemed to me that I had no right to tell these things, that they were not mine to tell.

So Isidri could not know that what I felt was less jealousy than guilt. I had kept knowledge from her. And I had deprived Hedran of a life with Isidri, the dear joy, the center, the life of my own life.

Or had I shared it with him? I didn't know. I don't know.

That day passed like any other, except that one of Suudi's children broke her elbow falling out of a tree. "At least we know she won't drown," said Tubdu, wheezing.

Next came the date of the night in my rooms in the New Quadrangle, when I had wept and not known why I wept. And a while after that, the day of my return, transilient, to Ve, carrying a bottle of Isidri's wine for Gvonesh. And finally, yesterday, I entered the churten field on Ve, and left it eighteen years ago on O. I spent the night, as I sometimes do, in the shrine. The hours went by quietly; I wrote, gave worship, meditated, and slept. And I woke beside the pool of silent water.

So, now: I hope the Stabiles will accept this report from a farmer they never heard of, and that the engineers of transilience may see it as at least a footnote to their experiments. Certainly it is difficult to verify, the only evidence for it being my word, and my otherwise almost inexplicable knowledge of churten theory. To Gvonesh, who does not know me, I send my respect, my gratitude, and my hope that she will honor my intent.

FORGIVENESS
DAY

SOLLY HAD BEEN A SPACE BRAT, A MOBILE'S CHILD, LIVING ON this ship and that, this world and that; she'd traveled five hundred light-years by the time she was ten. At twenty-five she had been through a revolution on Alterra, learned *aiji* on Terra and farthinking from an old hilfer on Rokanan, breezed through the Schools on Hain, and survived an assignment as Observer in murderous, dying Kheakh, skipping another half millennium at near-lightspeed in the process. She was young, but she'd been around.

She got bored with the Embassy people in Voe Deo telling her to watch out for this, remember that; she was a Mobile herself now, after all. Werel had its quirks—what world didn't? She'd done her homework, she knew when to curtsy and when not to belch, and vice versa. It was a relief to get on her own at last, in this gorgeous little city, on this gorgeous little continent, the first and only Envoy of the Ekumen to the Divine Kingdom of Gatay.

She was high for days on the altitude, the tiny, brilliant sun pouring vertical light into the noisy streets, the peaks soaring up incredibly behind every building, the dark blue sky where great near stars burned all day, the dazzling nights under six or seven lolloping bits of moon, the tall black people with their black eyes, narrow heads, long, narrow hands and feet, gorgeous people, her people! She loved them all. Even if she saw a little too much of them.

The last time she had had completely to herself was a few hours in the passenger cabin of the airskimmer sent by Gatay to bring her across the ocean from Voe Deo. On the airstrip she was met by a delegation of priests and officials from the King and the Council, magnificent in scarlet and brown and turquoise, and swept off to the Palace, where there was a lot of curtsying and no belching, of course, for hours—an introduction to his little shrunken old majesty, introductions to High Muckamucks and Lord Hooziwhats, speeches, a banquet—all completely predictable, no problems at all, not even the impenetrable giant fried flower on her plate at the banquet. But with her, from that first moment on the airstrip and at every moment thereafter, discreetly behind or beside or very near her, were two men: her Guide and her Guard.

The Guide, whose name was San Ubattat, was provided by her hosts in Gatay; of course he was reporting on her to the government, but he was a most obliging spy, endlessly smoothing the way for her, showing her with a bare hint what was expected or what would be a gaffe, and an excellent linguist, ready with a translation when she needed one. San was all right. But the Guard was something else.

He had been attached to her by the Ekumen's hosts on this world, the dominant power on Werel, the big nation of Voe Deo. She had promptly protested to the Embassy back in Voe Deo that she didn't need or want a bodyguard. Nobody in Gatay was out to get her and even if they were, she preferred to look after herself. The Embassy sighed. Sorry, they said. You're stuck with him. Voe Deo has a military presence in Gatay, which after all is a client state, economically dependent. It's in Voe Deo's interest to protect the legitimate government of Gatay against the native terrorist factions, and you get protected as one of their interests. We can't argue with that.

She knew better than to argue with the Embassy, but she could not resign herself to the Major. His military title, rega, she translated by the archaic word "Major," from a skit she'd seen on Terra. That Major had been a stuffed uniform, covered with medals and insignia. It puffed and strutted and commanded, and finally blew up into bits of stuffing. If only this Major would blow up! Not that he strutted, exactly, or even commanded, directly. He was stonily polite, woodenly silent, stiff and cold as rigor mortis. She soon gave up any effort to talk to him; whatever she said, he replied Yessum or Nomum with the prompt stupidity of a man who does not and will not actually listen, an officer officially incapable of humanity. And he was with her in every public situation, day and night, on the street, shopping, meeting with businessmen and officials, sight-seeing, at court, in the balloon ascent above the mountains—with her everywhere, everywhere but bed.

Even in bed she wasn't quite as alone as she would often have liked; for the Guide and the Guard went home at night, but in the anteroom of her bedroom slept the Maid—a gift from His Majesty, her own private asset.

She remembered her incredulity when she first learned that word, years ago, in a text about slavery. "On Werel, members of the dominant caste are called *owners*; members of the serving class are called *assets*. Only owners are referred to as men or women; assets are called bondsmen, bondswomen."

So here she was, the owner of an asset. You don't turn down a king's gift. Her asset's name was Rewe. Rewe was probably a spy too, but it was hard to believe. She was a dignified, handsome woman some years older than Solly and about the same intensity of skin color, though Solly was pinkish brown and Rewe was bluish brown. The palms of her hands were a delicate azure. Rewe's manners were exquisite and she had tact, astuteness, an infallible sense of when she was wanted and when not. Solly of course treated her as an equal, stating right out at the beginning that she believed no human being had a right to dominate, much less

own, another, that she would give Rewe no orders, and that she hoped
they might become friends. Rewe accepted this, unfortunately, as a new
set of orders. She smiled and said yes. She was infinitely yielding. Whatever Solly said or did sank into that acceptance and was lost, leaving
Rewe unchanged: an attentive, obliging, gentle physical presence, just
out of reach. She smiled, and said yes, and was untouchable.

And Solly began to think, after the first fizz of the first days in Gatay,
that she needed Rewe, really needed her as a woman to talk with. There
was no way to meet owner women, who lived hidden away in their bezas,
women's quarters, "at home," they called it. All bondswomen but Rewe
were somebody else's property, not hers to talk to. All she ever met was
men. And eunuchs.

That had been another thing hard to believe, that a man would vol-
untarily trade his virility for a little social standing; but she met such
men all the time in King Hotat's court. Born assets, they earned partial
independence by becoming eunuchs, and as such often rose to positions of considerable power and trust among their owners. The eunuch
Tayandan, majordomo of the palace, ruled the King, who didn't rule,
but figureheaded for the Council. The Council was made up of various
kinds of lord but only one kind of priest, Tualites. Only assets worshiped Kamye, and the original religion of Gatay had been suppressed
when the monarchy became Tualite a century or so ago. If there was
one thing she really disliked about Werel, aside from slavery and gender-
dominance, it was the religions. The songs about Lady Tual were beautiful, and the statues of her and the great temples in Voe Deo were
wonderful, and the *Arkamye* seemed to be a good story though long-
winded; but the deadly self-righteousness, the intolerance, the stupidity
of the priests, the hideous doctrines that justified every cruelty in the
name of the faith! As a matter of fact, Solly said to herself, was there
anything she *did* like about Werel?

And answered herself instantly: I love it, I love it. I love this weird little bright sun and all the broken bits of moons and the mountains going up like ice walls and the people—the people with their black eyes without whites like animals' eyes, eyes like dark glass, like dark water, mysterious—I want to love them, I want to know them, I want to reach them!

But she had to admit that the pissants at the Embassy had been right about one thing: being a woman was tough on Werel. She fit nowhere. She went about alone, she had a public position, and so was a contradiction in terms: proper women stayed at home, invisible. Only bondswomen went out in the streets, or met strangers, or worked at any public job. She behaved like an asset, not like an owner. Yet she was something very grand, an envoy of the Ekumen, and Gatay very much wanted to join the Ekumen and not to offend its envoys. So the officials and courtiers and businessmen she talked to on the business of the Ekumen did the best they could: they treated her as if she were a man.

The pretense was never complete and often broke right down. The poor old King groped her industriously, under the vague impression that she was one of his bedwarmers. When she contradicted Lord Gatuyo in a discussion, he stared with the blank disbelief of a man who has been talked back to by his shoe. He had been thinking of her as a woman. But in general the disgenderment worked, allowing her to work with them; and she began to fit herself into the game, enlisting Rewe's help in making clothes that resembled what male owners wore in Gatay, avoiding anything that to them would be specifically feminine. Rewe was a quick, intelligent seamstress. The bright, heavy, close-fitted trousers were practical and becoming, the embroidered jackets were splendidly warm. She liked wearing them. But she felt unsexed by these men who could not accept her for what she was. She needed to talk to a woman.

She tried to meet some of the hidden owner women through the owner men, and met a wall of politeness without a door, without a peephole. What a wonderful idea; we will certainly arrange a visit when the

weather is better! I should be overwhelmed with the honor if the Envoy
were to entertain Lady Mayoyo and my daughters, but my foolish, provincial girls are so unforgivably timid—I'm sure you understand. Oh,
surely, surely, a tour of the inner gardens—but not at present, when the
vines are not in flower! We must wait until the vines are in flower!

There was nobody to talk to, nobody, until she met Batikam the Makil.

It was an event: a touring troupe from Voe Deo. There wasn't much
going on in Gatay's little mountain capital by way of entertainment,
except for temple dancers—all men, of course—and the soppy fluff that
passed as drama on the Werelian network. Solly had doggedly entered
some of these wet pastels, hoping for a glimpse into the life "at home,"
but she couldn't stomach the swooning maidens who died of love while
the stiff-necked jackass heroes, who all looked like the Major, died nobly
in battle, and Tual the Merciful leaned out of the clouds smiling upon
their deaths with her eyes slightly crossed and the whites showing, a
sign of divinity. Solly had noticed that Werelian men never entered the
network for drama. Now she knew why. But the receptions at the palace
and the parties in her honor given by various lords and businessmen
were pretty dull stuff: all men, always, because they wouldn't have the
slave girls in while the Envoy was there; and she couldn't flirt even with
the nicest men, couldn't remind them that they were men, since that
would remind them that she was a woman not behaving like a lady. The
fizz had definitely gone flat by the time the makil troupe came.

She asked San, a reliable etiquette advisor, if it would be all right for
her to attend the performance. He hemmed and hawed and finally, with
more than usual oily delicacy, gave her to understand that it would be
all right so long as she went dressed as a man. "Women, you know, don't
go in public. But sometimes, they want so much to see the entertainers,
you know? Lady Amatay used to go with Lord Amatay, dressed in his
clothes, every year; everybody knew, nobody said anything—you know.
For you, such a great person, it would be all right. Nobody will say

anything. Quite, quite all right. Of course, I come with you, the rega comes with you. Like friends, ha? You know, three good men friends going to the entertainment, ha? Ha?"

Ha, ha, she said obediently. What fun!—But it was worth it, she thought, to see the makils.

They were never on the network. Young girls at home were not to be exposed to their performances, some of which, San gravely informed her, were unseemly. They played only in theaters. Clowns, dancers, prostitutes, actors, musicians, the makils formed a kind of subclass, the only assets not personally owned. A talented slave boy bought by the Entertainment Corporation from his owner was thenceforth the property of the Corporation, which trained and looked after him the rest of his life.

They walked to the theater, six or seven streets away. She had forgotten that the makils were all transvestites, indeed she did not remember it when she first saw them, a troop of tall slender dancers sweeping out onto the stage with the precision and power and grace of great birds wheeling, flocking, soaring. She watched unthinking, enthralled by their beauty, until suddenly the music changed and the clowns came in, black as night, black as owners, wearing fantastic trailing skirts, with fantastic jutting jeweled breasts, singing in tiny, swoony voices, "Oh do not rape me please kind Sir, no no, not now!" They're men, they're men! Solly realized then, already laughing helplessly. By the time Batikam finished his star turn, a marvelous dramatic monologue, she was a fan. "I want to meet him," she said to San at a pause between acts. "The actor—Batikam."

San got the bland expression that signified he was thinking how it could be arranged and how to make a little money out of it. But the Major was on guard, as ever. Stiff as a stick, he barely turned his head to glance at San. And San's expression began to alter.

If her proposal was out of line, San would have signaled or said so.

The Stuffed Major was simply controlling her, trying to keep her as tied down as one of "his" women. It was time to challenge him. She turned to him and stared straight at him. "Rega Teyeo," she said, "I quite comprehend that you're under orders to keep me in order. But if you give orders to San or to me, they must be spoken aloud, and they must be justified. I will not be managed by your winks or your whims."

There was a considerable pause, a truly delicious and rewarding pause. It was difficult to see if the Major's expression changed; the dim theater light showed no detail in his blue-black face. But there was something frozen about his stillness that told her she'd stopped him. At last he said, "I'm charged to protect you, Envoy."

"Am I endangered by the makils? Is there impropriety in an envoy of the Ekumen congratulating a great artist of Werel?"

Again the frozen silence. "No," he said.

"Then I request you to accompany me when I go backstage after the performance to speak to Batikam."

One stiff nod. One stiff, stuffy, defeated nod. Score one! Solly thought, and sat back cheerfully to watch the lightpainters, the erotic dances, and the curiously touching little drama with which the evening ended. It was in archaic poetry, hard to understand, but the actors were so beautiful, their voices so tender that she found tears in her eyes and hardly knew why.

"A pity the makils always draw on the *Arkamye*," said San, with smug, pious disapproval. He was not a very high-class owner, in fact he owned no assets; but he was an owner, and a bigoted Tualite, and liked to remind himself of it. "Scenes from the *Incarnations of Tual* would be more befitting such an audience."

"I'm sure you agree, Rega," she said, enjoying her own irony.

"Not at all," he said, with such toneless politeness that at first she did not realise what he had said; and then forgot the minor puzzle in the bustle of finding their way and gaining admittance to the backstage and to the performers' dressing room.

When they realised who she was, the managers tried to clear all the other performers out, leaving her alone with Batikam (and San and the Major, of course); but she said no, no, no, these wonderful artists must not be disturbed, just let me talk a moment with Batikam. She stood there in the bustle of doffed costumes, half-naked people, smeared makeup, laughter, dissolving tension after the show, any backstage on any world, talking with the clever, intense man in elaborate archaic woman's costume. They hit it off at once. "Can you come to my house?" she asked. "With pleasure," Batikam said, and his eyes did not flick to San's or the Major's face: the first bondsman she had yet met who did not glance to her Guard or her Guide for permission to say or do anything, anything at all. She glanced at them only to see if they were shocked. San looked collusive, the Major looked rigid. "I'll come in a little while," Batikam said. "I must change."

They exchanged smiles, and she left. The fizz was back in the air. The huge close stars hung clustered like grapes of fire. A moon tumbled over the icy peaks, another jigged like a lopsided lantern above the curlicue pinnacles of the palace. She strode along the dark street, enjoying the freedom of the male robe she wore and its warmth, making San trot to keep up; the Major, long-legged, kept pace with her. A high, trilling voice called, "Envoy!" and she turned with a smile, then swung round, seeing the Major grappling momentarily with someone in the shadow of a portico. He broke free, caught up to her without a word, seized her arm in an iron grip, and dragged her into a run. "Let go!" she said, struggling; she did not want to use an aiji break on him, but nothing less was going to get her free.

He pulled her nearly off-balance with a sudden dodge into an alley; she ran with him, letting him keep hold on her arm. They came unexpectedly out into her street and to her gate, through it, into the house, which he unlocked with a word—how did he do that?—"What is all this?" she demanded, breaking away easily, holding her arm where his grip had bruised it.

She saw, outraged, the last flicker of an exhilarated smile on his face. Breathing hard, he asked, "Are you hurt?"

"Hurt? Where you yanked me, yes—what do you think you were doing?"

"Keeping the fellow away."

"What fellow?"

He said nothing.

"The one who called out? Maybe he wanted to talk to me!"

After a moment the Major said, "Possibly. He was in the shadow. I thought he might be armed. I must go out and look for San Ubattat. Please keep the door locked until I come back." He was out the door as he gave the order; it never occurred to him that she would not obey, and she did obey, raging. Did he think she couldn't look after herself? That she needed him interfering in her life, kicking slaves around, "protecting" her? Maybe it was time he saw what an aiji fall looked like. He was strong and quick, but had no real training. This kind of amateur interference was intolerable, really intolerable; she must protest to the Embassy again.

As soon she let him back in with a nervous, shamefaced San in tow, she said, "You opened my door with a password. I was not informed that you had right of entrance day and night."

He was back to his military blankness. "Nomum," he said.

"You are not to do so again. You are not to seize hold of me ever again. I must tell you that if you do, I will injure you. If something alarms you, tell me what it is and I will respond as I see fit. Now will you please go."

"With pleasure, mum," he said, wheeled, and marched out.

"Oh, Lady—Oh, Envoy," San said, "that was a dangerous person, extremely dangerous people, I am so sorry, disgraceful," and he babbled on. She finally got him to say who he thought it was, a religious dissident, one of the Old Believers who held to the original religion of Gatay and wanted to cast out or kill all foreigners and unbelievers. "A bondsman?" she asked with interest, and he was shocked—"Oh, no, no, a real person, a man—but most misguided, a fanatic, a heathen fanatic! Knifemen, they call themselves. But a man, Lady—Envoy, certainly a man!"

The thought that she might think that an asset might touch her upset him as much as the attempted assault. If such it had been.

As she considered it, she began to wonder if, since she had put the Major in his place at the theater, he had found an excuse to put her in her place by "protecting" her. Well, if he tried it again, he'd find himself upside down against the opposite wall.

"Rewe!" she called, and the bondswoman appeared instantly as always. "One of the actors is coming. Would you like to make us a little tea, something like that?" Rewe smiled, said, "Yes," and vanished. There was a knock at the door. The Major opened it—he must be standing guard outside—and Batikam came in.

It had not occurred to her that the makil would still be in women's clothing, but it was how he dressed offstage too, not so magnificently, but with elegance, in the delicate, flowing materials and dark, subtle hues that the swoony ladies in the dramas wore. It gave considerable piquancy, she felt, to her own male costume. Batikam was not as handsome as the Major, who was a stunning-looking man till he opened his mouth; but the makil was magnetic, you had to look at him. He was a dark greyish brown, not the blue-black that the owners were so vain of (though there were plenty of black assets too, Solly had noticed: of course, when every bondswoman was her owner's sexual servant). Intense, vivid intelligence and sympathy shone in his face through the makil's Stardust black makeup, as he looked around with a slow, lovely laugh at her, at San, and at the Major standing at the door. He laughed like a woman, a warm ripple, not the ha, ha of a man. He held out his hands to Solly, and she came forward and took them. "Thank you for coming, Batikam!" she said, and he said, "Thank you for asking me, Alien Envoy!"

"San," she said, "I think this is your cue?"

Only indecision about what he ought to do could have slowed San down till she had to speak. He still hesitated a moment, then smiled with unction and said, "Yes, so sorry, a very good night to you, Envoy! Noon hour at the Office of Mines, tomorrow, I believe?" Backing away, he backed right into the Major, who stood like a post in the doorway. She looked at the Major, ready to order him out without ceremony, how dare he shove back in!—and saw the expression on his face. For once his blank mask had cracked, and what was revealed was contempt. Incredulous, sickened contempt. As if he was obliged to watch someone eat a turd.

"Get out," she said. She turned her back on both of them. "Come on, Batikam; the only privacy I have is in here," she said, and led the makil to her bedroom.

HE WAS BORN WHERE HIS FATHERS BEFORE HIM WERE BORN, IN the old, cold house in the foothills above Noeha. His mother did not cry out as she bore him, since she was a soldier's wife, and a soldier's mother, now. He was named for his great-uncle, killed on duty in the Sosa. He grew up in the stark discipline of a poor household of pure veot lineage. His father, when he was on leave, taught him the arts a soldier must know; when his father was on duty the old Asset-Sergeant Habbakam took over the lessons, which began at five in the morning, summer or winter, with worship, shortsword practice, and a cross-country run. His mother and grandmother taught him the other arts a man must know, beginning with good manners before he was two, and after his second birthday going on to history, poetry, and sitting still without talking.

The child's day was filled with lessons and fenced with disciplines; but a child's day is long. There was room and time for freedom, the freedom of the farmyard and the open hills. There was the companionship of pets, foxdogs, running dogs, spotted cats, hunting cats, and the farm cattle and the greathorses; not much companionship otherwise.

The family's assets, other than Habbakam and the two housewomen, were sharecroppers, working the stony foothill land that they and their owners had lived on forever. Their children were light-skinned, shy, already stooped to their lifelong work, ignorant of anything beyond their fields and hills. Sometimes they swam with Teyeo, summers, in the pools of the river. Sometimes he rounded up a couple of them to play soldiers with him. They stood awkward, uncouth, smirking when he shouted "Charge!" and rushed at the invisible enemy. "Follow me!" he cried shrilly, and they lumbered after him, firing their tree-branch guns at random, pow, pow. Mostly he went alone, riding his good mare Tasi or afoot with a hunting cat pacing by his side.

A few times a year visitors came to the estate, relatives or fellow officers of Teyeo's father, bringing their children and their housepeople. Teyeo silently and politely showed the child guests about, introduced them to the animals, took them on rides. Silently and politely, he and his cousin Gemat came to hate each other; at age fourteen they fought for an hour in a glade behind the house, punctiliously following the rules of wrestling, relentlessly hurting each other, getting bloodier and wearier and more desperate, until by unspoken consent they called it off and returned in silence to the house, where everyone was gathering for dinner. Everyone looked at them and said nothing. They washed up hurriedly, hurried to table. Gemat's nose leaked blood all through the meal; Teyeo's jaw was so sore he could not open it to eat. No one commented.

Silently and politely, when they were both fifteen, Teyeo and Rega Toebawe's daughter fell in love. On the last day of her visit they escaped by unspoken collusion and rode out side by side, rode for hours, too shy to talk. He had given her Tasi to ride. They dismounted to water and rest the horses in a wild valley of the hills. They sat near each other, not very near, by the side of the little quiet-running stream. "I love you," Teyeo said. "I love you," Emdu said, bending her shining black face down. They did not touch or look at each other. They rode back over the hills, joyous, silent.

When he was sixteen Teyeo was sent to the Officers' Academy in the capital of his province. There he continued to learn and practice the arts of war and the arts of peace. His province was the most rural in Voe Deo; its ways were conservative, and his training was in some ways anachronistic. He was of course taught the technologies of modern warfare, becoming a first-rate pod pilot and an expert in telereconnaissance; but he was not taught the modern ways of thinking that accompanied the technologies in other schools. He learned the poetry and history of Voe Deo, not the history and politics of the Ekumen. The Alien presence on Werel remained remote, theoretical to him. His reality was the old reality of the veot class, whose men held themselves apart from all men not soldiers and in brotherhood with all soldiers, whether owners, assets, or enemies. As for women, Teyeo considered his rights over them absolute, binding him absolutely to responsible chivalry to women of his own class and protective, merciful treatment of bondswomen. He believed all foreigners to be basically hostile, untrustworthy heathens. He honored the Lady Tual, but worshiped the Lord Kamye. He expected no justice, looked for no reward, and valued above all competence, courage, and self-respect. In some respects he was utterly unsuited to the world he was to enter, in others well prepared for it, since he was to spend seven years on Yeowe fighting a war in which there was no justice, no reward, and never even an illusion of ultimate victory.

Rank among veot officers was hereditary. Teyeo entered active service as a rega, the highest of the three veot ranks. No degree of ineptitude or distinction could lower or raise his status or his pay. Material ambition was no use to a veot. But honor and responsibility were to be earned, and he earned them quickly. He loved service, loved the life, knew he was good at it, intelligently obedient, effective in command; he had come out of the Academy with the highest recommendations, and being posted to the capital, drew notice as a promising officer as well as a likable young man. At twenty-four he was absolutely fit, his body would do anything he asked of it. His austere upbringing had given him little taste for indulgence but an intense appreciation of pleasure, so the luxuries and entertainments of the capital were a discovery of delight to him. He was reserved and rather shy, but companionable and cheerful. A handsome young man, in with a set of other young men very like him, for a year he knew what it is to live a completely privileged life with complete enjoyment of it. The brilliant intensity of that enjoyment stood against the dark background of the war in Yeowe, the slave revolution on the colony planet, which had gone on all his lifetime, and was now intensifying. Without that background, he could not have been so happy. A whole life of games and diversions had no interest for him; and when his orders came, posted as a pilot and division commander to Yeowe, his happiness was pretty nearly complete.

He went home for his thirty-day leave. Having received his parents' approbation, he rode over the hills to Rega Toebawe's estate and asked for his daughter's hand in marriage. The rega and his wife told their daughter that they approved his offer and asked her, for they were not strict parents, if she would like to marry Teyeo. "Yes," she said. As a grown, unmarried woman, she lived in seclusion in the women's side of the house, but she and Teyeo were allowed to meet and even to walk together, the chaperone remaining at some distance. Teyeo told her it was a three-year posting; would she marry in haste now, or wait three years and have a proper wedding? "Now," she said, bending down her narrow, shining face. Teyeo gave a laugh of delight, and she laughed at him. They were married nine days later—it couldn't be sooner, there had to be some fuss and ceremony, even if it was a soldier's wedding— and for seventeen days Teyeo and Emdu made love, walked together, made love, rode together, made love, came to know each other, came to love each other, quarreled, made up, made love, slept in each other's arms. Then he left for the war on another world, and she moved to the women's side of her husband's house.

His three-year posting was extended year by year, as his value as an officer was recognised and as the war on Yeowe changed from scattered containing actions to an increasingly desperate retreat. In his seventh year of service an order for compassionate leave was sent out to Yeowe Headquarters for Rega Teyeo, whose wife was dying of complications of berlot fever. At that point, there was no headquarters on Yeowe; the Army was retreating from three directions towards the old colonial capital; Teyeo's division was fighting a rear-guard defense in the sea marshes; communications had collapsed.

Command on Werel continued to find it inconceivable that a mass of ignorant slaves with the crudest kind of weapons could be defeating the Army of Voe Deo, a disciplined, trained body of soldiers with an infallible communications network, skimmers, pods, every armament and device permitted by the Ekumenical Convention Agreement. A strong faction in Voe Deo blamed the setbacks on this submissive adherence to Alien rules. The hell with Ekumenical Conventions. Bomb the damned dusties back to the mud they were made of. Use the biobomb, what was it for, anyway? Get our men off the foul planet and wipe it clean. Start fresh. If we don't win the war on Yeowe, the next revolution's going to be right here on Werel, in our own cities, in our own homes! The jittery government held on against this pressure. Werel was on probation, and Voe Deo wanted to lead the planet to Ekumenical status. Defeats were minimised, losses were not made up, skimmers, pods, weapons, men were not replaced. By the end of Teyeo's seventh year, the Army on Yeowe had been essentially written off by its government. Early in the eighth year, when the Ekumen was at last permitted to send its Envoys to Yeowe, Voe Deo and the other countries that had supplied auxiliary troops finally began to bring their soldiers home.

It was not until he got back to Werel that Teyeo learned his wife was dead.

He went home to Noeha. He and his father greeted each other with a silent embrace, but his mother wept as she embraced him. He knelt to her in apology for having brought her more grief than she could bear.

He lay that night in the cold room in the silent house, listening to his heart beat like a slow drum. He was not unhappy, the relief of being at peace and the sweetness of being home were too great for that; but it was a desolate calm, and somewhere in it was anger. Not used to anger, he was not sure what he felt. It was as if a faint, sullen red flare colored every image in his mind, as he lay trying to think through the seven years on Yeowe, first as a pilot, then the ground war, then the long retreat, the killing and the being killed. Why had they been left there to be hunted down and slaughtered? Why had the government not sent them reinforcements? The questions had not been worth asking then, they were not worth asking now. They had only one answer: We do what they ask us to do, and we don't complain. I fought every step of the way, he thought without pride. The new knowledge sliced keen as a knife through all other knowledge—And while I was fighting, she was dying. All a waste, there on Yeowe. All a waste, here on Werel. He sat up in the dark, the cold, silent, sweet dark of night in the hills. "Lord Kamye," he said aloud, "help me. My mind betrays me."

During the long leave home he sat often with his mother. She wanted to talk about Emdu, and at first he had to force himself to listen. It would be easy to forget the girl he had known for seventeen days seven years ago, if only his mother would let him forget. Gradually he learned to take what she wanted to give him, the knowledge of who his wife had been. His mother wanted to share all she could with him of the joy she had had in Emdu, her beloved child and friend. Even his father, retired now, a quenched, silent man, was able to say, "She was the light of the house." They were thanking him for her. They were telling him that it had not all been a waste.

But what lay ahead of them? Old age, the empty house. They did not complain, of course, and seemed content in their severe, placid round of daily work; but for them the continuity of the past with the future was broken.

"I should remarry," Teyeo said to his mother. "Is there anyone you've noticed . . . ?"

It was raining, a grey light through the wet windows, a soft thrumming on the eaves. His mother's face was indistinct as she bent to her mending.

"No," she said. "Not really." She looked up at him, and after a pause asked, "Where do you think you'll be posted?"

"I don't know."

"There's no war now," she said, in her soft, even voice.

"No," Teyeo said. "There's no war."

"Will there be . . . ever? do you think?"

He stood up, walked down the room and back, sat down again on the cushioned platform near her; they both sat straight-backed, still except for the slight motion of her hands as she sewed; his hands lay lightly one in the other, as he had been taught when he was two.

"I don't know," he said. "It's strange. It's as if there hadn't been a war. As if we'd never been on Yeowe—the Colony, the Uprising, all of it. They don't talk about it. It didn't happen. We don't fight wars. This is a new age. They say that often on the net. The age of peace, brotherhood across the stars. So, are we brothers with Yeowe, now? Are we brothers with Gatay and Bambur and the Forty States? Are we brothers with our assets? I can't make sense of it. I don't know what they mean. I don't know where I fit in." His voice too was quiet and even.

"Not here, I think," she said. "Not yet."

After a while he said, "I thought . . . children . . ."

"Of course. When the time comes." She smiled at him. "You never could sit still for half an hour. . . . Wait. Wait and see."

She was right, of course; and yet what he saw in the net and in town tried his patience and his pride. It seemed that to be a soldier now was a disgrace. Government reports, the news and the analyses, constantly referred to the Army and particularly the veot class as fossils, costly and useless, Voe Deo's principal obstacle to full admission to the Ekumen. His own uselessness was made clear to him when his request for a posting was met by an indefinite extension of his leave on half pay. At thirty-two, they appeared to be telling him, he was superannuated.

Again he suggested to his mother that he should accept the situation, settle down, and look for a wife. "Talk to your father," she said. He did so; his father said, "Of course your help is welcome, but I can run the farm well enough for a while yet. Your mother thinks you should go to the capital, to Command. They can't ignore you if you're there. After all. After seven years' combat—your record—"

Teyeo knew what that was worth, now. But he was certainly not needed here, and probably irritated his father with his ideas of changing this or that way things were done. They were right: he should go to the capital and find out for himself what part he could play in the new world of peace.

His first half-year there was grim. He knew almost no one at Command or in the barracks; his generation was dead, or invalided out, or home on half pay. The younger officers, who had not been on Yeowe, seemed to him a cold, buttoned-up lot, always talking money and politics. Little businessmen, he privately thought them. He knew they were afraid of him—of his record, of his reputation. Whether he wanted to or not he reminded them that there had been a war that Werel had fought and lost, a civil war, their own race fighting against itself, class against class. They wanted to dismiss it as a meaningless quarrel on another world, nothing to do with them.

Teyeo walked the streets of the capital, watched the thousands of bondsmen and bondswomen hurrying about their owners' business, and wondered what they were waiting for.

"The Ekumen does not interfere with the social, cultural, or economic arrangements and affairs of any people," the Embassy and the government spokesmen repeated. "Full membership for any nation or people that wishes it is contingent only on absence, or renunciation, of certain specific methods and devices of warfare," and there followed the list of terrible weapons, most of them mere names to Teyeo, but a few of them inventions of his own country: the biobomb, as they called it, and the neuronics.

He personally agreed with the Ekumen's judgment on such devices, and respected their patience in waiting for Voe Deo and the rest of Werel to prove not only compliance with the ban, but acceptance of the principle. But he very deeply resented their condescension. They sat in judgment on everything Werelian, viewing from above. The less they said about the division of classes, the clearer their disapproval was. "Slavery is of very rare occurrence in Ekumenical worlds," said their books, "and disappears completely with full participation in the Ekumenical polity." Was that what the Alien Embassy was really waiting for?

"By our Lady!" said one of the young officers—many of them were Tualites, as well as businessmen—"the Aliens are going to admit the dusties before they admit us!" He was sputtering with indignant rage, like a red-faced old rega faced with an insolent bondsoldier. "Yeowe— a damned planet of savages, tribesmen, regressed into barbarism— preferred over us!"

"They fought well," Teyeo observed, knowing he should not say it as he said it, but not liking to hear the men and women he had fought against called dusties. Assets, rebels, enemies, yes.

The young man stared at him and after a moment said, "I suppose you love 'em, eh? The dusties?"

"I killed as many as I could," Teyeo replied politely, and then changed the conversation. The young man, though nominally Teyeo's superior at Command, was an oga, the lowest rank of veot, and to snub him further would be ill-bred.

They were stuffy, he was touchy; the old days of cheerful good fellowship were a faint, incredible memory. The bureau chiefs at Command listened to his request to be put back on active service and sent him endlessly on to another department. He could not live in barracks, but had to find an apartment, like a civilian. His half pay did not permit him indulgence in the expensive pleasures of the city. While waiting for appointments to see this or that official, he spent his days in the library net of the Officers' Academy. He knew his education had been incomplete and was out of date. If his country was going to join the Ekumen, in order to be useful he must know more about the Alien ways of thinking and the new technologies. Not sure what he needed to know, he floundered about in the network, bewildered by the endless information available, increasingly aware that he was no intellectual and no scholar and would never understand Alien minds, but doggedly driving himself on out of his depth.

A man from the Embassy was offering an introductory course in Ekumenical history in the public net. Teyeo joined it, and sat through eight or ten lecture-and-discussion periods, straight-backed and still, only his hands moving slightly as he took full and methodical notes. The lecturer, a Hainishman who translated his extremely long Hainish name as Old Music, watched Teyeo, tried to draw him out in discussion, and at last asked him to stay in after session. "I should like to meet you, Rega," he said, when the others had dropped out.

They met at a café. They met again. Teyeo did not like the Alien's manners, which he found effusive; he did not trust his quick, clever mind; he felt Old Music was using him, studying him as a specimen of The Veot, The Soldier, probably The Barbarian. The Alien, secure in his superiority, was indifferent to Teyeo's coldness, ignored his distrust,

insisted on helping him with information and guidance, and shame-
lessly repeated questions Teyeo had avoided answering. One of these
was, "Why are you sitting around here on half pay?"

"It's not by my own choice, Mr. Old Music," Teyeo finally answered,
the third time it was asked. He was very angry at the man's impudence,
and so spoke with particular mildness. He kept his eyes away from Old
Music's eyes, bluish, with the whites showing like a scared horse. He
could not get used to Aliens' eyes.

"They won't put you back on active service?"

Teyeo assented politely. Could the man, however alien, really be
oblivious to the fact that his questions were grossly humiliating?

"Would you be willing to serve in the Embassy Guard?"

That question left Teyeo speechless for a moment; then he committed the extreme rudeness of answering a question with a question. "Why
do you ask?"

"I'd like very much to have a man of your capacity in that corps," said
Old Music, adding with his appalling candor, "Most of them are spies
or blockheads. It would be wonderful to have a man I knew was neither.
It's not just sentry duty, you know. I imagine you'd be asked by your
government to give information; that's to be expected. And we would
use you, once you had experience and if you were willing, as a liaison
officer. Here or in other countries. We would not, however, ask you to
give information to us. Am I clear, Teyeo? I want no misunderstanding
between us as to what I am and am not asking of you."

"You would be able . . . ?" Teyeo asked cautiously.

Old Music laughed and said, "Yes. I have a string to pull in your
Command. A favor owed. Will you think it over?"

Teyeo was silent a minute. He had been nearly a year now in the
capital and his requests for posting had met only bureaucratic evasion
and, recently, hints that they were considered insubordinate. "I'll accept
now, if I may," he said, with a cold deference.

The Hainishman looked at him, his smile changing to a thoughtful, steady gaze. "Thank you," he said. "You should hear from Command in a few days."

So Teyeo put his uniform back on, moved back to the City Barracks, and served for another seven years on alien ground. The Ekumenical Embassy was, by diplomatic agreement, a part not of Werel but of the Ekumen—a piece of the planet that no longer belonged to it. The Guardsmen furnished by Voe Deo were protective and decorative, a highly visible presence on the Embassy grounds in their white-and-gold dress uniform. They were also visibly armed, since protest against the Alien presence still broke out erratically in violence.

Rega Teyeo, at first assigned to command a troop of these guards, soon was transferred to a different duty, that of accompanying members of the Embassy staff about the city and on journeys. He served as a bodyguard, in undress uniform. The Embassy much preferred not to use their own people and weapons, but to request and trust Voe Deo to protect them. Often he was also called upon to be a guide and interpreter, and sometimes a companion. He did not like it when visitors from somewhere in space wanted to be chummy and confiding, asked him about himself, invited him to come drinking with them. With perfectly concealed distaste, with perfect civility, he refused such offers. He did his job and kept his distance. He knew that that was precisely what the Embassy valued him for. Their confidence in him gave him a cold satisfaction.

His own government had never approached him to give information, though he certainly learned things that would have interested them. Voe Dean intelligence did not recruit their agents among veots. He knew who the agents in the Embassy Guard were; some of them tried to get information from him, but he had no intention of spying for spies.

Old Music, whom he now surmised to be the head of the Embassy's intelligence system, called him in on his return from a winter leave at home.

The Hainishman had learned not to make emotional demands on Teyeo, but could not hide a note of affection in his voice greeting him. "Hullo, Rega! I hope your family's well? Good. I've got a particularly tricky job for you. Kingdom of Gatay. You were there with Kemehan two years ago, weren't you? Well, now they want us to send an Envoy. They say they want to join. Of course the old King's a puppet of your government; but there's a lot else going on there. A strong religious separatist movement. A Patriotic Cause, kick out all the foreigners, Voe Deans and Aliens alike. But the King and Council requested an Envoy, and all we've got to send them is a new arrival. She may give you some problems till she learns the ropes. I judge her a bit headstrong. Excellent material, but young, very young. And she's only been here a few weeks. I requested you, because she needs your experience. Be patient with her, Rega. I think you'll find her likable."

He did not. In seven years he had got accustomed to the Aliens' eyes and their various smells and colors and manners. Protected by his flaw-less courtesy and his stoical code, he endured or ignored their strange or shocking or troubling behavior, their ignorance and their different knowledge. Serving and protecting the foreigners entrusted to him, he kept himself aloof from them, neither touched nor touching. His charges learned to count on him and not to presume on him. Women were often quicker to see and respond to his Keep Out signs than men; he had an easy, almost friendly relationship with an old Terran Observer whom he had accompanied on several long investigatory tours. "You are as peaceful to be with as a cat, Rega," she told him once, and he valued the compliment. But the Envoy to Gatay was another matter.

She was physically splendid, with clear red-brown skin like that of a baby, glossy swinging hair, a free walk—too free: she flaunted her ripe, slender body at men who had no access to it, thrusting it at him, at everyone, insistent, shameless. She expressed her opinion on everything with coarse self-confidence. She could not hear a hint and refused to take an order. She was an aggressive, spoiled child with the sexuality of an adult, given the responsibility of a diplomat in a dangerously unstable country. Teyeo knew as soon as he met her that this was an impossible assignment. He could not trust her or himself. Her sexual immodesty aroused him as it disgusted him; she was a whore whom he must treat as a princess. Forced to endure and unable to ignore her, he hated her.

He was more familiar with anger than he had used to be, but not used to hating. It troubled him extremely. He had never in his life asked for a reposting, but on the morning after she had taken the makil into her room, he sent a stiff little appeal to the Embassy. Old Music responded to him with a sealed voice-message through the diplomatic link: "Love of god and country is like fire, a wonderful friend, a terrible enemy; only children play with fire. I don't like the situation. There's nobody here I can replace either of you with. Will you hang on a while longer?"

He did not know how to refuse. A veot did not refuse duty. He was ashamed at having even thought of doing so, and hated her again for causing him that shame.

The first sentence of the message was enigmatic, not in Old Music's usual style but flowery, indirect, like a coded warning. Teyeo of course knew none of the intelligence codes either of his country or of the Ekumen. Old Music would have to use hints and indirection with him. "Love of god and country" could well mean the Old Believers and the Patriots, the two subversive groups in Gatay, both of them fanatically opposed to foreign influence; the Envoy could be the child playing with fire. Was she being approached by one group or the other? He had seen no evidence of it, unless the man in the shadows that night had been not a knifeman but a messenger. She was under his eyes all day, her house watched all night by soldiers under his command. Surely the makil, Batikam, was not acting for either of those groups. He might well be a member of the Hame, the asset liberation underground of Voe Deo, but as such would not endanger the Envoy, since the Hame saw the Ekumen as their ticket to Yeowe and to freedom.

Teyeo puzzled over the words, replaying them over and over, knowing his own stupidity faced with this kind of subtlety, the ins and outs
of the political labyrinth. At last he erased the message and yawned, for
it was late; bathed, lay down, turned off the light, said under his breath,
"Lord Kamye, let me hold with courage to the one noble thing!" and
slept like a stone.

THE MAKIL CAME TO HER HOUSE EVERY NIGHT AFTER THE
theater, Teyeo tried to tell himself there was nothing wrong in it. He
himself had spent nights with the makils, back in the palmy days before
the war. Expert, artistic sex was part of their business. He knew by hearsay that rich city women often hired them to come supply a husband's
deficiencies. But even such women did so secretly, discreetly, not in this
vulgar, shameless way, utterly careless of decency, flouting the moral
code, as if she had some kind of right to do whatever she wanted wherever and whenever she wanted it. Of course Batikam colluded eagerly
with her, playing on her infatuation, mocking the Gatayans, mocking
Teyeo—and mocking her, though she didn't know it. What a chance for
an asset to make fools of all the owners at once!

Watching Batikam, Teyeo felt sure he was a member of the Hame.
His mockery was very subtle; he was not trying to disgrace the Envoy.
Indeed his discretion was far greater than hers. He was trying to keep
her from disgracing herself. The makil returned Teyeo's cold courtesy
in kind, but once or twice their eyes met and some brief, involuntary
understanding passed between them, fraternal, ironic.

There was to be a public festival, an observation of the Tualite Feast
of Forgiveness, to which the Envoy was pressingly invited by the King
and Council. She was put on show at many such events. Teyeo thought
nothing about it except how to provide security in an excited holiday
crowd, until San told him that the festival day was the highest holy day
of the old religion of Gatay, and that the Old Believers fiercely resented

the imposition of the foreign rites over their own. The little man seemed genuinely worried. Teyeo worried too when next day San was suddenly replaced by an elderly man who spoke little but Gatayan and was quite unable to explain what had become of San Ubattat. "Other duties, other duties call," he said in very bad Voe Dean, smiling and bobbing, "very great relishes time, aha? Relishes duties call."

During the days that preceded the festival tension rose in the city; graffiti appeared, symbols of the old religion smeared across walls; a Tualite temple was desecrated, after which the Royal Guard was much in evidence in the streets. Teyeo went to the palace and requested, on his own authority, that the Envoy not be asked to appear in public during a ceremony that was "likely to be troubled by inappropriate demonstrations." He was called in and treated by a Court official with a mixture of dismissive insolence and conniving nods and winks, which left him really uneasy. He left four men on duty at the Envoy's house that night. Returning to his quarters, a little barracks down the street which had been handed over to the Embassy Guard, he found the window of his room open and a scrap of writing, in his own language, on his table: *Fest F is set up for assasnation.*

He was at the Envoy's house promptly the next morning and asked her asset to tell her he must speak to her. She came out of her bedroom pulling a white wrap around her naked body. Batikam followed her, half-dressed, sleepy, and amused. Teyeo gave him the eye-signal *go*, which he received with a serene, patronising smile, murmuring to the woman, "I'll go have some breakfast. Rewe? have you got something to feed me?" He followed the bondswoman out of the room. Teyeo faced the Envoy and held out the scrap of paper.

"I received this last night, ma'am," he said. "I must ask you not to attend the festival tomorrow."

She considered the paper, read the writing, and yawned. "Who's it from?"

"I don't know, ma'am."

"What's it mean? *Assassination?* They can't spell, can they?"

After a moment, he said, "There are a number of other indications—enough that I must ask you—"

"Not to attend the festival of Forgiveness, yes. I heard you." She went to a window seat and sat down, her robe falling wide to reveal her legs; her bare, brown feet were short and supple, the soles pink, the toes small and orderly. Teyeo looked fixedly at the air beside her head. She twiddled the bit of paper. "If you think it's dangerous, Rega, bring a guardsman or two with you," she said, with the faintest tone of scorn. "I really have to be there. The King requested it, you know. And I'm to light the big fire, or something. One of the few things women are allowed to do in public here. . . . I can't back out of it." She held out the paper, and after a moment he came close enough to take it. She looked up at him smiling; when she defeated him she always smiled at him. "Who do you think would want to blow me away, anyhow? The Patriots?"

"Or the Old Believers, ma'am. Tomorrow is one of their holidays."

"And your Tualites have taken it away from them? Well, they can't exactly blame the Ekumen, can they?"

"I think it possible that the government might permit violence in order to excuse retaliation, ma'am."

She started to answer carelessly, realised what he had said, and frowned. "You think the Council's setting me up? What evidence have you?"

After a pause he said, "Very little, ma'am. San Ubattat—"

"San's been ill. The old fellow they sent isn't much use, but he's scarcely dangerous! Is that all?" He said nothing, and she went on, "Until you have real evidence, Rega, don't interfere with my obligations. Your militaristic paranoia isn't acceptable when it spreads to the people I'm dealing with here. Control it, please! I'll expect an extra guardsman or two tomorrow; and that's enough."

"Yes, ma'am," he said, and went out. His head sang with anger. It occurred to him now that her new guide had told him San Ubattat had been kept away by religious duties, not by illness. He did not turn back. What was the use? "Stay on for an hour or so, will you, Seyem?" he said to the guard at her gate, and strode off down the street, trying to walk away from her, from her soft brown thighs and the pink soles of her feet and her stupid, insolent, whorish voice giving him orders. He tried to let the bright icy sunlit air, the stepped streets snapping with banners for the festival, the glitter of the great mountains and the clamor of the markets fill him, dazzle and distract him; but he walked seeing his own shadow fall in front of him like a knife across the stones, knowing the futility of his life.

"THE VEOT LOOKED WORRIED," BATIKAM SAID IN HIS VELVET voice, and she laughed, spearing a preserved fruit from the dish and popping it, dripping, into his mouth.

"I'm ready for breakfast now, Rewe," she called, and sat down across from Batikam. "I'm starving! He was having one of his phallocratic fits. He hasn't saved me from anything lately. It's his only function, after all. So he has to invent occasions. I wish, I wish he was out of my hair. It's so nice not to have poor little old San crawling around like some kind of pubic infestation. If only I could get rid of the Major now!"

"He's a man of honor," the makil said; his tone did not seem ironical.

"How can an owner of slaves be an honorable man?"

Batikam watched her from his long, dark eyes. She could not read Werelian eyes, beautiful as they were, filling their lids with darkness.

"Male hierarchy members always yatter about their precious honor," she said. "And 'their' women's honor, of course."

"Honor is a great privilege," Batikam said. "I envy it. I envy him."

"Oh, the hell with all that phony dignity, it's just pissing to mark your territory. All you need envy him, Batikam, is his freedom."

He smiled. "You're the only person I've ever known who was neither owned nor owner. That is freedom. *That* is freedom. I wonder if you know it?"

"Of course I do," she said. He smiled, and went on eating his breakfast, but there had been something in his voice she had not heard before. Moved and a little troubled, she said after a while, "You're going away soon."

"Mind reader. Yes. In ten days, the troupe goes on to tour the Forty States."

"Oh, Batikam, I'll miss you! You're the only man, the only person here I can talk to—let alone the sex—"

"Did we ever?"

"Not often," she said, laughing, but her voice shook a little. He held out his hand; she came to him and sat on his lap, the robe dropping open. "Little pretty Envoy breasts," he said, lipping and stroking, "little soft Envoy belly . . ." Rewe came in with a tray and softly set it down. "Eat your breakfast, little Envoy," Batikam said, and she disengaged herself and returned to her chair, grinning.

"Because you're free you can be honest," he said, fastidiously peeling a pini fruit. "Don't be too hard on those of us who aren't and can't." He cut a slice and fed it to her across the table. "It has been a taste of freedom to know you," he said. "A hint, a shadow . . ."

"In a few years at most, Batikam, you *will* be free. This whole idiotic structure of masters and slaves will collapse completely when Werel comes into the Ekumen."

"If it does."

"Of course it will."

He shrugged. "My home is Yeowe," he said.

She stared, confused. "You come from Yeowe?"

"I've never been there," he said. "I'll probably never go there. What use have they got for makils? But it is my home. Those are my people. That is my freedom. When will you see . . ." His fist was clenched; he opened it with a soft gesture of letting something go. He smiled and returned to his breakfast. "I've got to get back to the theater," he said. "We're rehearsing an act for the Day of Forgiveness."

She wasted all day at court. She had made persistent attempts to obtain permission to visit the mines and the huge government-run farms on the far side of the mountains, from which Gatay's wealth flowed. She had been as persistently foiled—by the protocol and bureaucracy of the government, she had thought at first, their unwillingness to let a diplomat do anything but run round to meaningless events; but some businessmen had let something slip about conditions in the mines and on the farms that made her think they might be hiding a more brutal kind of slavery than any visible in the capital. Today she got nowhere, waiting for appointments that had not been made. The old fellow who was standing in for San misunderstood most of what she said in Voe Dean, and when she tried to speak Gatayan he misunderstood it all, through stupidity or intent. The Major was blessedly absent most of the morning, replaced by one of his soldiers, but turned up at court, stiff and silent and set-jawed, and attended her until she gave up and went home for an early bath.

Batikam came late that night. In the middle of one of the elaborate fantasy games and role reversals she had learned from him and found so exciting, his caresses grew slower and slower, soft, dragging across her like feathers, so that she shivered with unappeased desire and, pressing her body against his, realised that he had gone to sleep. "Wake up," she said, laughing and yet chilled, and shook him a little. The dark eyes opened, bewildered, full of fear.

"I'm sorry," she said at once, "go back to sleep, you're tired. No, no, it's all right, it's late." But he went on with what she now, whatever his skill and tenderness, had to see was his job.

In the morning at breakfast she said, "Can you see me as an equal, do you, Batikam?"

He looked tired, older than he usually did. He did not smile. After a while he said, "What do you want me to say?"

"That you do."

"I do," he said quietly.

"You don't trust me," she said, bitter.

After a while he said, "This is Forgiveness Day. The Lady Tual came to the men of Asdok, who had set their hunting cats upon her followers. She came among them riding on a great hunting cat with a fiery tongue, and they fell down in terror, but she blessed them, forgiving them." His voice and hands enacted the story as he told it. "Forgive me," he said.

"You don't need any forgiveness!"

"Oh, we all do. It's why we Kamyites borrow the Lady Tual now and then. When we need her. So, today you'll be the Lady Tual, at the rites?"

"All I have to do is light a fire, they said," she said anxiously, and he laughed. When he left she told him she would come to the theater to see him, tonight, after the festival.

The horse-race course, the only flat area of any size anywhere near the city, was thronged, vendors calling, banners waving; the Royal motorcars drove straight into the crowd, which parted like water and closed behind. Some rickety-looking bleachers had been erected for lords and owners, with a curtained section for ladies. She saw a motorcar drive up to the bleachers; a figure swathed in red cloth was bundled out of it and hurried between the curtains, vanishing. Were there peepholes for them to watch the ceremony through? There were women in the crowds, but bondswomen only, assets. She realised that she, too, would be kept hidden until her moment of the ceremony arrived: a red tent awaited her, alongside the bleachers, not far from the roped enclosure where priests were chanting. She was rushed out of the car and into the tent by obsequious and determined courtiers.

Bondswomen in the tent offered her tea, sweets, mirrors, makeup, and hair oil, and helped her put on the complex swathing of fine red-and-yellow cloth, her costume for her brief enactment of Lady Tual. Nobody had told her very clearly what she was to do, and to her questions the women said, "The priests will show you, Lady, you just go with them. You just light the fire. They have it all ready." She had the impression that they knew no more than she did; they were pretty girls, court assets, excited at being part of the show, indifferent to the religion. She knew the symbolism of the fire she was to light: into it faults and transgressions could be cast and burnt up, forgotten. It was a nice idea.

The priests were whooping it up out there; she peeked out—there were indeed peepholes in the tent fabric—and saw the crowd had thickened. Nobody except in the bleachers and right against the enclosure ropes could possibly see anything, but everybody was waving red-and-yellow banners, munching fried food, and making a day of it, while the priests kept up their deep chanting. In the far right of the little, blurred field of vision through the peephole was a familiar arm: the Major's, of course. They had not let him get into the motorcar with her. He must have been furious. He had got here, though, and stationed himself on guard. "Lady, Lady," the court girls were saying, "here come the priests now," and they buzzed around her making sure her headdress was on straight and the damnable, hobbling skirts fell in the right folds. They were still plucking and patting as she stepped out of the tent, dazzled by the daylight, smiling and trying to hold herself very straight and dignified as a Goddess ought to do. She really didn't want to fuck up their ceremony.

Two men in priestly regalia were waiting for her right outside the tent door. They stepped forward immediately, taking her by the elbows and saying, "This way, this way, Lady." Evidently she really wouldn't have to figure out what to do. No doubt they considered women incapable of it, but in the circumstances it was a relief. The priests hurried her along faster than she could comfortably walk in the tight-drawn skirt. They were behind the bleachers now; wasn't the enclosure in the other direction? A car was coming straight at them, scattering the few people who were in its way. Somebody was shouting; the priests suddenly began yanking her, trying to run; one of them yelled and let go her arm, felled by a flying darkness that had hit him with a jolt—she was in the middle of a melee, unable to break the iron hold on her arm, her legs imprisoned in the skirt, and there was a noise, an enormous noise, that hit her head and bent it down, she couldn't see or hear, blinded, struggling, shoved face first into some dark place with her face pressed into a stifling, scratchy darkness and her arms held locked behind her.

A car, moving. A long time. Men, talking low. They talked in Gatayan. It was very hard to breathe. She did not struggle; it was no use. They had taped her arms and legs, bagged her head. After a long time she was hauled out like a corpse and carried quickly, indoors, down stairs, set down on a bed or couch, not roughly though with the same desperate haste. She lay still. The men talked, still almost in whispers. It made no sense to her. Her head was still hearing that enormous noise, had it been real? had she been struck? She felt deaf, as if inside a wall of cotton. The cloth of the bag kept getting stuck on her mouth, sucked against her nostrils as she tried to breathe.

It was plucked off; a man stooping over her turned her so he could untape her arms, then her legs, murmuring as he did so, "Don't to be scared, Lady, we don't to hurt you," in Voe Dean. He backed away from her quickly. There were four or five of them; it was hard to see, there was very little light. "To wait here," another said, "everything all right. Just to keep happy." She was trying to sit up, and it made her dizzy. When her head stopped spinning, they were all gone. As if by magic. Just to keep happy.

A small very high room. Dark brick walls, earthy air. The light was from a little biolume plaque stuck on the ceiling, a weak, shadowless glow. Probably quite sufficient for Werelian eyes. Just to keep happy. I have been kidnapped. How about that. She inventoried: the thick mattress she was on; a blanket; a door; a small pitcher and a cup; a drainhole, was it, over in the corner? She swung her legs off the mattress and her feet struck something lying on the floor at the foot of it—she coiled up, peered at the dark mass, the body lying there. A man. The uniform, the skin so black she could not see the features, but she knew him. Even here, even here, the Major was with her.

She stood up unsteadily and went to investigate the drainhole, which was simply that, a cement-lined hole in the floor, smelling slightly chemical, slightly foul. Her head hurt, and she sat down on the bed again to massage her arms and ankles, easing the tension and pain and getting herself back into herself by touching and confirming herself, rhythmically, methodically. I have been kidnapped. How about that. Just to keep happy. What about him?

Suddenly knowing that he was dead, she shuddered and held still.

After a while she leaned over slowly, trying to see his face, listening. Again she had the sense of being deaf. She heard no breath. She reached out, sick and shaking, and put the back of her hand against his face. It was cool, cold. But warmth breathed across her fingers, once, again. She crouched on the mattress and studied him. He lay absolutely still, but when she put her hand on his chest she felt the slow heartbeat.

"Teyeo," she said in a whisper. Her voice would not go above a whisper.

She put her hand on his chest again. She wanted to feel that slow, steady beat, the faint warmth; it was reassuring. Just to keep happy.

What else had they said? Just to wait. Yes. That seemed to be the program. Maybe she could sleep. Maybe she could sleep and when she woke up the ransom would have come. Or whatever it was they wanted.

SHE WOKE UP WITH THE THOUGHT THAT SHE STILL HAD HER watch, and after sleepily studying the tiny silver readout for a while decided she had slept three hours; it was still the day of the Festival, too soon for ransom probably, and she wouldn't be able to go to the theater to see the makils tonight. Her eyes had grown accustomed to the low

light and when she looked she could see, now, that there was dried blood
all over one side of the man's head. Exploring, she found a hot lump like
a fist above his temple, and her fingers came away smeared. He had got
himself crowned. That must have been him, launching himself at the
priest, the fake priest, all she could remember was a flying shadow and
a hard thump and an ooof! like an aiji attack, and then there had been
the huge noise that confused everything. She clicked her tongue, tapped
the wall, to check her hearing. It seemed to be all right; the wall of cotton had disappeared. Maybe she had been crowned herself? She felt her
head, but found no lumps. The man must have a concussion, if he was
still out after three hours. How bad? When would the men come back?

She got up and nearly fell over, entangled in the damned Goddess
skirts. If only she was in her own clothes, not this fancy dress, three
pieces of flimsy stuff you had to have servants to put on you! She got out
of the skirt piece, and used the scarf piece to make a kind of tied skirt
that came to her knees. It wasn't warm in this basement or whatever it
was; it was dank and rather cold. She walked up and down, four steps
turn, four steps turn, four steps turn, and did some warm-ups. They
had dumped the man onto the floor. How cold was it? Was shock part
of concussion? People in shock needed to be kept warm. She dithered
a long time, puzzled at her own indecision, at not knowing what to do.
Should she try to heave him up onto the mattress? Was it better not to
move him? Where the hell were the men? Was he going to die?

She stooped over him and said sharply, "Rega! Teyeo!" and after a
moment he caught his breath.

"Wake up!" She remembered now, she thought she remembered, that
it was important not to let concussed people lapse into a coma. Except
he already had.

He caught his breath again, and his face changed, came out of the
rigid immobility, softened; his eyes opened and closed, blinked, unfo-
cused. "Oh Kamye," he said very softly.

She couldn't believe how glad she was to see him. Just to keep happy. He evidently had a blinding headache, and admitted that he was seeing double. She helped him haul himself up onto the mattress and covered him with the blanket. He asked no questions, and lay mute, lapsing back to sleep soon. Once he was settled she went back to her exercises, and did an hour of them. She looked at her watch. It was two hours later, the same day, the Festival day. It wasn't evening yet. When were the men going to come?

They came early in the morning, after the endless night that was the same as the afternoon and the morning. The metal door was unlocked and thrown clanging open, and one of them came in with a tray while two of them stood with raised, aimed guns in the doorway. There was nowhere to put the tray but the floor, so he shoved it at Solly, said, "Sorry, Lady!" and backed out; the door clanged shut, the bolts banged home. She stood holding the tray. "Wait!" she said.

The man had waked up and was looking groggily around. After finding him in this place with her she had somehow lost his nickname, did not think of him as the Major, yet shied away from his name. "Here's breakfast, I guess," she said, and sat down on the edge of the mattress. A cloth was thrown over the wicker tray; under it was a pile of Gatayan grainrolls stuffed with meat and greens, several pieces of fruit, and a capped water carafe of thin, fancily beaded metal alloy. "Breakfast, lunch, and dinner, maybe," she said. "Shit. Oh well. It looks good. Can you eat? Can you sit up?"

He worked himself up to sit with his back against the wall, and then shut his eyes.

"You're still seeing double?"

He made a small noise of assent.

"Are you thirsty?"

Small noise of assent.

"Here." She passed him the cup. By holding it in both hands he got it to his mouth, and drank the water slowly, a swallow at a time. She meanwhile devoured three grainrolls one after the other, then forced herself to stop, and ate a pini fruit. "Could you eat some fruit?" she asked him, feeling guilty. He did not answer. She thought of Batikam feeding her the slice of pini at breakfast, when, yesterday, a hundred years ago.

The food in her stomach made her feel sick. She took the cup from the man's relaxed hand—he was asleep again—and poured herself water, and drank it slowly, a swallow at a time.

When she felt better she went to the door and explored its hinges, lock, and surface. She felt and peered around the brick walls, the poured concrete floor, seeking she knew not what, something to escape with, something. . . . She should do exercises. She forced herself to do some, but the queasiness returned, and a lethargy with it. She went back to the mattress and sat down. After a while she found she was crying. After a while she found she had been asleep. She needed to piss. She squatted over the hole and listened to her urine fall into it. There was nothing to clean herself with. She came back to the bed and sat down on it, stretching out her legs, holding her ankles in her hands. It was utterly silent.

She turned to look at the man; he was watching her. It made her start. He looked away at once. He still lay half-propped up against the wall, uncomfortable, but relaxed.

"Are you thirsty?" she asked.

"Thank you," he said. Here where nothing was familiar and time was broken off from the past, his soft, light voice was welcome in its familiarity. She poured him a cup full and gave it to him. He managed it much more steadily, sitting up to drink. "Thank you," he whispered again, giving her back the cup.

"How's your head?"

He put up his hand to the swelling, winced, and sat back.

"One of them had a stick," she said, seeing it in a flash in the jumble of her memories—"a priest's staff. You jumped the other one."

"They took my gun," he said. "Festival." He kept his eyes closed.

"I got tangled in those damn clothes. I couldn't help you at all. Listen. Was there a noise, an explosion?"

"Yes. Diversion, maybe."

"Who do you think these boys are?"

"Revolutionaries. Or . . ."

"You said you thought the Gatayan government was in on it."

"I don't know," he murmured.

"You were right, I was wrong, I'm sorry," she said with a sense of virtue at remembering to make amends.

He moved his hand very slightly in an it-doesn't-matter gesture.

"Are you still seeing double?"

He did not answer; he was phasing out again.

She was standing, trying to remember Selish breathing exercises, when the door crashed and clanged, and the same three men were there, two with guns, all young, black-skinned, short-haired, very nervous. The lead one stooped to set a tray down on the floor, and without the least premeditation Solly stepped on his hand and brought her weight down on it. "You wait!" she said. She was staring straight into the faces and gun muzzles of the other two. "Just wait a moment, listen! He has a head injury, we need a doctor, we need more water, I can't even clean his wound, there's no toilet paper, who the hell are you people anyway?"

The one she had stomped was shouting, "Get off! Lady to get off my hand!" but the others heard her. She lifted her foot and got out of his way as he came up fast, backing into his buddies with the guns. "All right, Lady, we are sorry to have trouble," he said, tears in his eyes, cradling his hand. "We are Patriots. You send messish to this Pretender, like our messish. Nobody is to hurt. All right?" He kept backing up, and one of the gunmen swung the door to. Crash, rattle.

She drew a deep breath and turned. Teyeo was watching her. "That was dangerous," he said, smiling very slightly.

"I know it was," she said, breathing hard. "It was stupid. I can't get hold of myself. I feel like pieces of me. But they shove stuff in and run, damn it! We have to have some water!" She was in tears, the way she always was for a moment after violence or a quarrel. "Let's see, what have they brought this time." She lifted the tray up onto the mattress; like the other, in a ridiculous semblance of service in a hotel or a house with slaves, it was covered with a cloth. "All the comforts," she murmured. Under the cloth was a heap of sweet pastries, a little plastic hand mirror, a comb, a tiny pot of something that smelled like decayed flowers, and a box of what she identified after a while as Gatayan tampons.

"It's things for the lady," she said, "God damn them, the stupid Goddamn pricks! A mirror!" She flung the thing across the room. "Of course I can't last a day without looking in the mirror! God *damn* them!" She flung everything else but the pastries after the mirror, knowing as she did so that she would pick up the tampons and keep them under the mattress and, oh, God forbid, use them if she had to, if they had to stay here, how long would it be? ten days or more—"Oh, God," she said again. She got up and picked everything up, put the mirror and the little pot, the empty water jug and the fruit skins from the last meal, onto one of the trays and set it beside the door. "Garbage," she said in Voe Dean. Her outburst, she realised, had been in another language; Alterran, probably. "Have you any idea," she said, sitting down on the mattress again, "how hard you people make it to be a woman? You could turn a woman against being one!"

"I think they meant well," Teyeo said. She realised that there was not the faintest shade of mockery, even of amusement in his voice. If he was enjoying her shame, he was ashamed to show her that he was. "I think they're amateurs," he said.

After a while she said, "That could be bad."

"It might." He had sat up and was gingerly feeling the knot on his head. His coarse, heavy hair was blood-caked all around it. "Kidnapping," he said. "Ransom demands. Not assassins. They didn't have guns. Couldn't have got in with guns. I had to give up mine."

"You mean these aren't the ones you were warned about?"

"I don't know." His explorations caused him a shiver of pain, and he desisted. "Are we very short of water?"

She brought him another cupful. "Too short for washing. A stupid Goddamn mirror when what we need is water!"

He thanked her and drank and sat back, nursing the last swallows in the cup. "They didn't plan to take me," he said.

She thought about it and nodded. "Afraid you'd identify them?"

"If they had a place for me, they wouldn't put me in with a lady." He spoke without irony. "They had this ready for you. It must be somewhere in the city."

She nodded. "The car ride was half an hour or less. My head was in a bag, though."

"They've sent a message to the Palace. They got no reply, or an unsatisfactory one. They want a message from you."

"To convince the government they really have me? Why do they need convincing?"

They were both silent.

"I'm sorry," he said, "I can't think." He lay back. Feeling tired, low, edgy after her adrenaline rush, she lay down alongside him. She had rolled up the Goddess's skirt to make a pillow; he had none. The blanket lay across their legs.

"Pillow," she said. "More blankets. Soap. What else?"

"Key," he murmured.

They lay side by side in the silence and the faint unvarying light.

NEXT MORNING ABOUT EIGHT, ACCORDING TO SOLLY'S WATCH, the Patriots came into the room, four of them. Two stood on guard at the door with their guns ready; the other two stood uncomfortably in what floor space was left, looking down at their captives, both of whom sat cross-legged on the mattress. The new spokesman spoke better Voe Dean than the others. He said they were very sorry to cause the lady discomfort and would do what they could to make it comfortable for her, and she must be patient and write a message by hand to the Pretender King, explaining that she would be set free unharmed as soon as the King commanded the Council to rescind their treaty with Voe Deo.

"He won't," she said. "They won't let him."

"Please do not discuss," the man said with frantic harshness. "This is writing materials. This is the message." He set the papers and a stylo down on the mattress, nervously, as if afraid to get close to her.

She was aware of how Teyeo effaced himself, sitting without a motion, his head lowered, his eyes lowered; the men ignored him.

"If I write this for you, I want water, a lot of water, and soap and blankets and toilet paper and pillows and a doctor, and I want somebody to come when I knock on that door, and I want some decent clothes. Warm clothes. Men's clothes."

"No doctor!" the man said. "Write it! Please! Now!" He was jumpy, twitchy, she dared push him no further. She read their statement, copied it out in her large, childish scrawl—she seldom handwrote anything—and handed both to the spokesman. He glanced over it and without a word hurried the other men out. Clash went the door.

"Should I have refused?"

"I don't think so," Teyeo said. He stood up and stretched, but sat down again looking dizzy. "You bargain well," he said.

"We'll see what we get. Oh, God. What is going *on*?"

"Maybe," he said slowly, "Gatay is unwilling to yield to these demands. But when Voe Deo—and your Ekumen—get word of it, they'll put pressure on Gatay."

"I wish they'd get moving. I suppose Gatay is horribly embarrassed, saving face by trying to conceal the whole thing—is that likely? How long can they keep it up? What about your people? Won't they be hunting for you?"

"No doubt," he said, in his polite way.

It was curious how his stiff manner, his manners, which had always shunted her aside, cut her out, here had quite another effect: his restraint and formality reassured her that she was still part of the world outside this room, from which they came and to which they would return, a world where people lived long lives.

What did long life matter? she asked herself, and didn't know. It was nothing she had ever thought about before. But these young Patriots lived in a world of short lives. Demands, violence, immediacy, and death, for what? for a bigotry, a hatred, a rush of power.

"Whenever they leave," she said in a low voice, "I get really frightened."

Teyeo cleared his throat and said, "So do I."

EXERCISES.

"Take hold—no, take *hold*, I'm not made of glass!—Now—"

"Ha!" he said, with his flashing grin of excitement, as she showed him the break, and he in turn repeated it, breaking from her.

"All right, now you'd be waiting—here"—thump—"see?"

"Ai!"

"I'm sorry—I'm sorry, Teyeo—I didn't think about your head—Are you all right? I'm really sorry—"

"Oh, Kamye," he said, sitting up and holding his black, narrow head between his hands. He drew several deep breaths. She knelt penitent and anxious.

"That's," he said, and breathed some more, "that's not, not fair play."

"No of course it's not, it's aiji—all's fair in love and war, they say that on Terra—Really, I'm sorry, I'm terribly sorry, that was so stupid of me!"

He laughed, a kind of broken and desperate laugh, shook his head, shook it again. "Show me," he said. "I don't know what you did."

† † †

EXERCISES.

"What do you do with your mind?"

"Nothing."

"You just let it wander?"

"No. Am I and my mind different beings?"

"So . . . you don't focus on something? You just wander with it?"

"No."

"So you *don't* let it wander."

"Who?" he said, rather testily.

A pause.

"Do you think about—"

"No," he said. "Be still."

A very long pause, maybe a quarter hour.

"Teyeo, I can't. I itch. My mind itches. How long have you been doing this?"

A pause, a reluctant answer: "Since I was two."

He broke his utterly relaxed motionless pose, bent his head to stretch his neck and shoulder muscles. She watched him.

"I keep thinking about long life, about living long," she said. "I don't mean just being alive a long time, hell, I've been alive about eleven hundred years, what does that mean, nothing. I mean . . . Something about thinking of life as long makes a difference. Like having kids does. Even thinking about having kids. It's like it changes some balance. It's funny I keep thinking about that now, when my chances for a long life have kind of taken a steep fall. . . ."

He said nothing. He was able to say nothing in a way that allowed her to go on talking. He was one of the least talkative men she had ever known. Most men were so wordy. She was fairly wordy herself. He was quiet. She wished she knew how to be quiet.

"It's just practice, isn't it?" she asked. "Just sitting there."

He nodded.

"Years and years and years of practice. . . . Oh, God. Maybe . . ."

"No, no," he said, taking her thought immediately.

"But why don't they *do* something? What are they *waiting* for? It's been nine *days*!"

FROM THE BEGINNING, BY UNPLANNED, UNSPOKEN AGREEMENT, the room had been divided in two: the line ran down the middle of the mattress and across to the facing wall. The door was on her side, the left; the shit-hole was on his side, the right. Any invasion of the other's space was requested by some almost invisible cue and permitted the same way. When one of them used the shit-hole the other unobtrusively faced away. When they had enough water to take cat-baths, which was seldom, the same arrangement held. The line down the middle of the mattress was absolute. Their voices crossed it, and the sounds and smells of their bodies. Sometimes she felt his warmth; Werelian body temperature was somewhat higher than hers, and in the dank, still air she felt that faint radiance as he slept. But they never crossed the line, not by a finger, not in the deepest sleep.

Solly thought about this, finding it, in some moments, quite funny. At other moments it seemed stupid and perverse. Couldn't they both use some human comfort? The only time she had touched him was the first day, when she had helped him get onto the mattress, and then when they had enough water she had cleaned his scalp wound and little by little washed the clotted, stinking blood out of his hair, using the comb, which had after all been a good thing to have, and pieces of the Goddess's skirt, an invaluable source of washcloths and bandages. Then once his head healed, they practiced aiji daily; but aiji had an impersonal, ritual purity to its clasps and grips that was a long way from creature comfort. The rest of the time his bodily presence was clearly, invariably uninvasive and untouchable.

He was only maintaining, under incredibly difficult circumstances, the rigid restraint he had always shown. Not just he, but Rewe, too; all of them, all of them but Batikam; and yet was Batikam's instant yielding to her whim and desire the true contact she had thought it? She thought of the fear in his eyes, that last night. Not restraint, but constraint.

It was the mentality of a slave society: slaves and masters caught in the same trap of radical distrust and self-protection.

"Teyeo," she said, "I don't understand slavery. Let me say what I mean," though he had shown no sign of interruption or protest, merely civil attention. "I mean, I do understand how a social institution comes about and how an individual is simply part of it—I'm not saying why don't you agree with me in seeing it as wicked and unprofitable, I'm not asking you to defend it or renounce it. I'm trying to understand what it feels like to believe that two-thirds of the human beings in your world are actually, rightfully your property. Five-sixths, in fact, including women of your caste."

After a while he said, "My family owns about twenty-five assets."

"Don't quibble."

He accepted the reproof.

"It seems to me that you cut off human contact. You don't touch slaves and slaves don't touch you, in the way human beings ought to touch, in mutuality. You have to keep yourselves separate, always working to maintain that boundary. Because it isn't a natural boundary—it's totally artificial, man-made. I can't tell owners and assets apart physically. Can you?"

"Mostly."

"By cultural, behavioral clues—right?"

After thinking a while, he nodded.

"You are the same species, race, people, exactly the same in every way, with a slight selection towards color. If you brought up an asset child as an owner it would *be* an owner in every respect, and vice versa. So you spend your lives keeping up this tremendous division that doesn't exist. What I don't understand is how you can fail to see how appallingly wasteful it is. I don't mean economically!"

"In the war," he said, and then there was a very long pause; though Solly had a lot more to say, she waited, curious. "I was on Yeowe," he said, "you know, in the civil war."

That's where you got all those scars and dents, she thought; for however scrupulously she averted her eyes, it was impossible not to be familiar with his spare, onyx body by now, and she knew that in aiji he had to favor his left arm, which had a considerable chunk out of it just above the bicep.

"The slaves of the Colonies revolted, you know, some of them at first, then all of them. Nearly all. So we Army men there were all owners. We couldn't send asset soldiers, they might defect. We were all veots and volunteers. Owners fighting assets. I was fighting my equals. I learned that pretty soon. Later on I learned I was fighting my superiors. They defeated us."

"But that—" Solly said, and stopped; she did not know what to say.

"They defeated us from beginning to end," he said. "Partly because my government didn't understand that they could. That they fought better and harder and more intelligently and more bravely than we did."

"Because they were fighting for their freedom!"

"Maybe so," he said in his polite way.

"So . . ."

"I wanted to tell you that I respect the people I fought."

"I know so little about war, about fighting," she said, with a mixture of contrition and irritation. "Nothing, really. I was on Kheakh, but that wasn't war, it was racial suicide, mass slaughter of a biosphere. I guess there's a difference. . . . That was when the Ekumen finally decided on the Arms Convention, you know. Because of Orint and then Kheakh destroying themselves. The Terrans had been pushing for the Convention for ages. Having nearly committed suicide themselves a while back.

I'm half-Terran. My ancestors rushed around their planet slaughtering each other. For millennia. They were masters and slaves, too, some of them, a lot of them. . . . But I don't know if the Arms Convention was a good idea. If it's right. Who are we to tell anybody what to do and not to do? The idea of the Ekumen was to offer a way. To open it. Not to bar it to anybody."

He listened intently, but said nothing until after some while. "We learn to . . . close ranks. Always. You're right, I think, it wastes . . . energy, the spirit. You are open."

His words cost him so much, she thought, not like hers that just came dancing out of the air and went back into it. He spoke from his marrow. It made what he said a solemn compliment, which she accepted gratefully, for as the days went on she realized occasionally how much confidence she had lost and kept losing: self-confidence, confidence that they would be ransomed, rescued, that they would get out of this room, that they would get out of it alive.

"Was the war very brutal?"

"Yes," he said. "I can't . . . I've never been able to—to see it—Only something comes like a flash—" He held his hands up as if to shield his eyes. Then he glanced at her, wary. His apparently cast-iron self-respect was, she knew now, vulnerable in many places.

"Things from Kheakh that I didn't even know I saw, they come that way," she said. "At night." And after a while, "How long were you there?"

"A little over seven years."

She winced. "Were you lucky?"

It was a queer question, not coming out the way she meant, but he took it at value. "Yes," he said. "Always. The men I went there with were killed. Most of them in the first few years. We lost three hundred thousand men on Yeowe. They never talk about it. Two-thirds of the veot men in Voe Deo were killed. If it was lucky to live, I was lucky." He looked down at his clasped hands, locked into himself.

After a while she said softly, "I hope you still are."

He said nothing.

"HOW LONG HAS IT BEEN?" HE ASKED, AND SHE SAID, CLEARING her throat, after an automatic glance at her watch, "Sixty hours."

Their captors had not come yesterday at what had become a regular time, about eight in the morning. Nor had they come this morning.

With nothing left to eat and now no water left, they had grown increasingly silent and inert. It was hours since either had said anything. He had put off asking the time as long as he could prevent himself.

"This is horrible," she said, "this is so horrible. I keep thinking . . ."

"They won't abandon you," he said. "They feel a responsibility."

"Because I'm a woman?"

"Partly."

"Shit."

He remembered that in the other life her coarseness had offended him.

"They've been taken, shot. Nobody bothered to find out where they were keeping us," she said.

Having thought the same thing several hundred times, he had nothing to say.

"It's just such a horrible *place* to die," she said. "It's sordid. I stink. I've stunk for twenty days. Now I have diarrhea because I'm scared. But I can't shit anything. I'm thirsty and I can't drink."

"Solly," he said sharply. It was the first time he had spoken her name. "Be still. Hold fast."

She stared at him.

"Hold fast to what?"

He did not answer at once and she said, "You won't let me touch you!"

"Not to me—"

"Then to what? There isn't anything!" He thought she was going to cry, but she stood up, took the empty tray, and beat it against the door till it smashed into fragments of wicker and dust. "Come! God damn you! Come, you bastards!" she shouted. "Let us out of here!"

After that she sat down again on the mattress. "Well," she said.

"Listen," he said.

They had heard it before: no city sounds came down to this cellar, wherever it was, but this was something bigger, explosions, they both thought.

The door rattled.

They were both afoot when it opened: not with the usual clash and clang, but slowly. A man waited outside; two men came in. One, armed, they had never seen; the other, the tough-faced young man they called the spokesman, looked as if he had been running or fighting, dusty, worn-out, a little dazed. He closed the door. He had some papers in his hand. The four of them stared at one another in silence for a minute.

"Water," Solly said. "You bastards!"

"Lady," the spokesman said, "I'm sorry." He was not listening to her. His eyes were not on her. He was looking at Teyeo, for the first time. "There is a lot of fighting," he said.

"Who's fighting?" Teyeo asked, hearing himself drop into the even tone of authority, and the young man respond to it as automatically: "Voe Deo. They sent troops. After the funeral, they said they would send troops unless we surrendered. They came yesterday. They go through the city killing. They know all the Old Believer centers. Some of ours." He had a bewildered, accusing note in his voice.

"What funeral?" Solly said.

When he did not answer, Teyeo repeated it: "What funeral?"

"The lady's funeral, yours. Here—I brought net prints—A state funeral. They said you died in the explosion."

"What Goddamned explosion?" Solly said in her hoarse, parched voice, and this time he answered her: "At the Festival. The Old Believers.

The fire, Tual's fire, there were explosives in it. Only it went off too soon. We knew their plan. We rescued you from that, Lady," he said, suddenly turning to her with that same accusatory tone.

"Rescued me, you asshole!" she shouted, and Teyeo's dry lips split in a startled laugh, which he repressed at once.

"Give me those," he said, and the young man handed him the papers.

"Get us water!" Solly said.

"Stay here, please. We need to talk," Teyeo said, instinctively holding on to his ascendancy. He sat down on the mattress with the net prints. Within a few minutes he and Solly had scanned the reports of the shocking disruption of the Festival of Forgiveness, the lamentable death of the Envoy of the Ekumen in a terrorist act executed by the cult of Old Believers, the brief mention of the death of a Voe Dean Embassy guard in the explosion, which had killed over seventy priests and onlookers, the long descriptions of the state funeral, reports of unrest, terrorism, reprisals, then reports of the Palace gratefully accepting offers of assistance from Voe Deo in cleaning out the cancer of terrorism. . . .

"So," he said finally. "You never heard from the Palace. Why did you keep us alive?"

Solly looked as if she thought the question lacked tact, but the spokesman answered with equal bluntness, "We thought your country would ransom you."

"They will," Teyeo said. "Only you have to keep your government from knowing we're alive. If you—"

"Wait," Solly said, touching his hand. "Hold on. I want to think about this stuff. You'd better not leave the Ekumen out of the discussion. But getting in touch with them is the tricky bit."

"If there are Voe Dean troops here, all I need is to get a message to anyone in my command, or the Embassy Guards."

Her hand was still on his, with a warning pressure. She shook the other one at the spokesman, finger outstretched: "You kidnapped an Envoy of the Ekumen, you asshole! Now you have to do the thinking you didn't do ahead of time. And I do too, because I don't want to get blown away by your Goddamned little government for turning up alive and embarrassing them. Where are you hiding, anyhow? Is there any chance of us getting out of this room, at least?"

The man, with that edgy, frantic look, shook his head. "We are all down here now," he said. "Most of the time. You stay here safe."

"Yes, you'd better keep your passports safe!" Solly said. "Bring us some water, damn it! Let us talk a while. Come back in an hour."

The young man leaned towards her suddenly, his face contorted. "What the hell kind of lady you are," he said. "You foreign filthy stinking cunt."

Teyeo was on his feet, but her grip on his hand had tightened: after a moment of silence, the spokesman and the other man turned to the door, rattled the lock, and were let out.

"Ouf," she said, looking dazed.

"Don't," he said, "don't—" He did not know how to say it. "They don't understand," he said. "It's better if I talk."

"Of course. Women don't give orders. Women don't talk. Shitheads! I thought you said they felt so responsible for me!"

"They do," he said. "But they're young men. Fanatics. Very frightened." And you talk to them as if they were assets, he thought, but did not say.

"Well so am I frightened!" she said, with a little spurt of tears. She wiped her eyes and sat down again among the papers. "God," she said. "We've been dead for twenty days. Buried for fifteen. Who do you think they buried?"

Her grip was powerful; his wrist and hand hurt. He massaged the place gently, watching her.

"Thank you," he said. "I would have hit him."

"Oh, I know. Goddamn chivalry. And the one with the gun would have blown your head off. Listen, Teyeo. Are you sure all you have to do is get word to somebody in the Army or the Guard?"

"Yes, of course."

"You're sure your country isn't playing the same game as Gatay?"

He stared at her. As he understood her, slowly the anger he had stifled and denied, all these interminable days of imprisonment with her, rose in him, a fiery flood of resentment, hatred, and contempt.

He was unable to speak, afraid he would speak to her as the young Patriot had done.

He went around to his side of the room and sat on his side of the mattress, somewhat turned from her. He sat cross-legged, one hand lying lightly in the other.

She said some other things. He did not listen or reply.

After a while she said, "We're supposed to be talking, Teyeo. We've only got an hour. I think those kids might do what we tell them, if we tell them something plausible—something that'll work."

He would not answer. He bit his lip and held still.

"Teyeo, what did I say? I said something wrong. I don't know what it was. I'm sorry."

"They would—" He struggled to control his lips and voice. "They would not betray us."

"Who? The Patriots?"

He did not answer.

"Voe Deo, you mean? Wouldn't betray us?"

In the pause that followed her gentle, incredulous question, he knew that she was right; that it was all collusion among the powers of the world; that his loyalty to his country and service was wasted, as futile as the rest of his life. She went on talking, palliating, saying he might very well be right. He put his head into his hands, longing for tears, dry as stone.

She crossed the line. He felt her hand on his shoulder.

"Teyeo, I am very sorry," she said. "I didn't mean to insult you! I honor you. You've been all my hope and help."

"It doesn't matter," he said. "If I—If we had some water."

She leapt up and battered on the door with her fists and a sandal.

"Bastards, bastards," she shouted.

Teyeo got up and walked, three steps and turn, three steps and turn, and halted on his side of the room. "If you're right," he said, speaking slowly and formally, "we and our captors are in danger not only from Gatay but from my own people, who may . . . who have been further-ing these anti-Government factions, in order to make an excuse to bring troops here . . . to *pacify* Gatay. That's why they know where to find the factionalists. We are . . . we're lucky our group were . . . were genuine."

She watched him with a tenderness that he found irrelevant.

"What we don't know," he said, "is what side the Ekumen will take. That is . . . There really is only one side."

"No, there's ours, too. The underdogs. If the Embassy sees Voe Deo pulling a takeover of Gatay, they won't interfere, but they won't approve. Especially if it involves as much repression as it seems to."

"The violence is only against the anti-Ekumen factions."

"They still won't approve. And if they find out I'm alive, they're going to be quite pissed at the people who claimed I went up in a bonfire. Our problem is how to get word to them. I was the only person representing the Ekumen in Gatay. Who'd be a safe channel?"

"Any of my men. But . . ."

"They'll have been sent back; why keep Embassy Guards here when the Envoy's dead and buried? I suppose we could try. Ask the boys to try, that is." Presently she said wistfully, "I don't suppose they'd just let us go—in disguise? It would be the safest for them."

"There is an ocean," Teyeo said.

She beat her head. "Oh, why don't they bring some *water*. . . ." Her voice was like paper sliding on paper. He was ashamed of his anger, his grief, himself. He wanted to tell her that she had been a help and hope to him too, that he honored her, that she was brave beyond belief; but none of the words would come. He felt empty, worn-out. He felt old. If only they would bring water!

Water was given them at last; some food, not much and not fresh. Clearly their captors were in hiding and under duress. The spokesman— he gave them his war-name, Kergat, Gatayan for Liberty—told them that whole neighborhoods had been cleared out, set afire, that Voe Dean troops were in control of most of the city including the Palace, and that almost none of this was being reported in the net. "When this is over Voe Deo will own my country," he said with disbelieving fury.

"Not for long," Teyeo said.

"Who can defeat them?" the young man said.

"Yeowe. The idea of Yeowe."

Both Kergat and Solly stared at him.

"Revolution," he said. "How long before Werel becomes New Yeowe?"

"The assets?" Kergat said, as if Teyeo had suggested a revolt of cattle or of flies. "They'll never organise."

"Look out when they do," Teyeo said mildly.

"You don't have any assets in your group?" Solly asked Kergat, amazed. He did not bother to answer. He had classed her as an asset, Teyeo saw. He understood why; he had done so himself, in the other life, when such distinctions made sense.

"Your bondswoman, Rewe," he asked Solly—"was she a friend?"

"Yes," Solly said, then, "No. I wanted her to be."

"The makil?"

After a pause she said, "I think so."

"Is he still here?"

She shook her head. "The troupe was going on with their tour, a few days after the Festival."

"Travel has been restricted since the Festival," Kergat said. "Only government and troops."

"He's Voe Dean. If he's still here, they'll probably send him and his troupe home. Try and contact him, Kergat."

"A makil?" the young man said, with that same distaste and incredulity. "One of your Voe Dean homosexual clowns?"

Teyeo shot a glance at Solly: Patience, patience.

"Bisexual actors," Solly said, disregarding him, but fortunately Kergat was determined to disregard her.

"A clever man," Teyeo said, "with connections. He could help us. You and us. It could be worth it. If he's still here. We must make haste."

"Why would he help us? He is Voe Dean."

"An asset, not a citizen," Teyeo said. "And a member of Hame, the asset underground, which works against the government of Voe Deo. The Ekumen admits the legitimacy of Hame. He'll report to the Embassy that a Patriot group has rescued the Envoy and is holding her safe, in hiding, in extreme danger. The Ekumen, I think, will act promptly and decisively. Correct, Envoy?"

Suddenly reinstated, Solly gave a short, dignified nod. "But discreetly," she said. "They'll avoid violence, if they can use political coercion."

The young man was trying to get it all into his mind and work it through. Sympathetic to his weariness, distrust, and confusion, Teyeo sat quietly waiting. He noticed that Solly was sitting equally quietly, one hand lying in the other. She was thin and dirty and her unwashed, greasy hair was in a lank braid. She was brave, like a brave mare, all nerve. She would break her heart before she quit.

Kergat asked questions; Teyeo answered them, reasoning and reassuring. Occasionally Solly spoke, and Kergat was now listening to her again, uneasily, not wanting to, not after what he had called her. At last he left, not saying what he intended to do; but he had Batikam's name and an identifying message from Teyeo to the Embassy: "Half-pay veots learn to sing old songs quickly."

"What on earth!" Solly said when Kergat was gone.

"Did you know a man named Old Music, in the Embassy?"

"Ah! Is he a friend of yours?"

"He has been kind."

"He's been here on Werel from the start. A First Observer. Rather a powerful man—Yes, and 'quickly,' all right. . . . My mind really isn't working at all. I wish I could lie down beside a little stream, in a meadow, you know, and drink. All day. Every time I wanted to, just stretch my neck out and slup, slup, slup. . . . Running water . . . In the sunshine . . . Oh God, oh God, sunshine. Teyeo, this is very difficult. This is harder than ever. Thinking that there maybe is really a way out of here. Only not knowing. Trying not to hope and not to not hope. Oh, I am so tired of sitting here!"

"What time is it?"

"Half past twenty. Night. Dark out. Oh God, darkness! Just to be in the darkness . . . Is there any way we could cover up that damned biolume? Partly? To pretend we had night, so we could pretend we had day?"

"If you stood on my shoulders, you could reach it. But how could we fasten a cloth?"

They pondered, staring at the plaque.

"I don't know. Did you notice there's a little patch of it that looks like it's dying? Maybe we don't have to worry about making darkness. If we stay here long enough. Oh, God!"

"Well," he said after a while, curiously self-conscious, "I'm tired." He stood up, stretched, glanced for permission to enter her territory, got a drink of water, returned to his territory, took off his jacket and shoes, by which time her back was turned, took off his trousers, lay down, pulled up the blanket, and said in his mind, "Lord Kamye, let me hold fast to the one noble thing." But he did not sleep.

He heard her slight movements; she pissed, poured a little water, took off her sandals, lay down.

A long time passed.

"Teyeo."

"Yes."

"Do you think . . . that it would be a mistake . . . under the circumstances . . . to make love?"

A pause.

"Not under the circumstances," he said, almost inaudibly. "But—in the other life—"

A pause.

"Short life versus long life," she murmured.

"Yes."

A pause.

"No," he said, and turned to her. "No, that's wrong." They reached out to each other. They clasped each other, cleaved together, in blind haste, greed, need, crying out together the name of God in their different languages and then like animals in the wordless voice. They huddled together, spent, sticky, sweaty, exhausted, reviving, rejoined, reborn in the body's tenderness, in the endless exploration, the ancient discovery, the long flight to the new world.

He woke slowly, in ease and luxury. They were entangled, his face was against her arm and breast; she was stroking his hair, sometimes his neck and shoulder. He lay for a long time aware only of that lazy rhythm and the cool of her skin against his face, under his hand, against his leg.

"Now I know," she said, her half whisper deep in her chest, near his ear, "that I don't know you. Now I need to know you." She bent forward to touch his face with her lips and cheek.

"What do you want to know?"

"Everything. Tell me who Teyeo is. . . ."

"I don't know," he said. "A man who holds you dear."

"Oh, God," she said, hiding her face for a moment in the rough, smelly blanket.

"Who is God?" he asked sleepily. They spoke Voe Dean, but she usually swore in Terran or Alterran; in this case it had been Alterran, *Seyt*, so he asked, "Who is Seyt?"

"Oh—Tual—Kamye—what have you. I just say it. It's just bad language. Do you believe in one of them? I'm sorry! I feel like such an oaf with you, Teyeo. Blundering into your soul, invading you—We *are* invaders, no matter how pacifist and priggish we are—"

"Must I love the whole Ekumen?" he asked, beginning to stroke her breasts, feeling her tremor of desire and his own.

"Yes," she said, "yes, yes."

It was curious, Teyeo thought, how little sex changed anything. Everything was the same, a little easier, less embarrassment and inhibition; and there was a certain and lovely source of pleasure for them, when they had enough water and food to have enough vitality to make love. But the only thing that was truly different was something he had no word for. Sex, comfort, tenderness, love, trust, no word was the right word, the whole word. It was utterly intimate, hidden in the mutuality of their bodies, and it changed nothing in their circumstances, nothing in the world, even the tiny wretched world of their imprisonment. They were still trapped. They were getting very tired and were hungry most of the time. They were increasingly afraid of their increasingly desperate captors.

"I will be a lady," Solly said. "A good girl. Tell me how, Teyeo."

"I don't want you to give in," he said, so fiercely, with tears in his eyes, that she went to him and held him in her arms.

"Hold fast," he said.

"I will," she said. But when Kergat or the others came in she was sedate and modest, letting the men talk, keeping her eyes down. He could not bear to see her so, and knew she was right to do so.

The doorlock rattled, the door clashed, bringing him up out of a wretched, thirsty sleep. It was night or very early morning. He and Solly had been sleeping close entangled for the warmth and comfort of it; and seeing Kergat's face now he was deeply afraid. This was what he had feared, to show, to prove her sexual vulnerability. She was still only half-awake, clinging to him.

Another man had come in. Kergat said nothing. It took Teyeo some time to recognise the second man as Batikam.

When he did, his mind remained quite blank. He managed to say the makil's name. Nothing else.

"Batikam?" Solly croaked. "Oh, my God!"

"This is an interesting moment," Batikam said in his warm actor's voice. He was not transvestite, Teyeo saw, but wore Gatayan men's clothing. "I meant to rescue you, not to embarrass you, Envoy, Rega. Shall we get on with it?"

Teyeo had scrambled up and was pulling on his filthy trousers. Solly had slept in the ragged pants their captors had given her. They both had kept on their shirts for warmth.

"Did you contact the Embassy, Batikam?" she was asking, her voice shaking, as she pulled on her sandals.

"Oh, yes. I've been there and come back, indeed. Sorry it took so long. I don't think I quite realised your situation here."

"Kergat has done his best for us," Teyeo said at once, stiffly.

"I can see that. At considerable risk. I think the risk from now on is low. That is . . ." He looked straight at Teyeo. "Rega, how do you feel about putting yourself in the hands of Hame?" he said. "Any problems with that?"

"Don't, Batikam," Solly said. "Trust him!"

Teyeo tied his shoe, straightened up, and said, "We are all in the hands of the Lord Kamye."

Batikam laughed, the beautiful full laugh they remembered.

"In the Lord's hands, then," he said, and led them out of the room.

IN THE *ARKAMYE* IT IS SAID, "TO LIVE SIMPLY IS MOST COMPLICATED."

Solly requested to stay on Werel, and after a recuperative leave at the seashore was sent as Observer to South Voe Deo. Teyeo went straight home, being informed that his father was very ill. After his father's death, he asked for indefinite leave from the Embassy Guard, and stayed on the farm with his mother until her death two years later. He and Solly, a continent apart, met only occasionally during those years.

When his mother died, Teyeo freed his family's assets by act of irrevocable manumission, deeded over their farms to them, sold his now almost valueless property at auction, and went to the capital. He knew Solly was temporarily staying at the Embassy. Old Music told him where to find her. He found her in a small office of the palatial building. She looked older, very elegant. She looked at him with a stricken and yet wary face. She did not come forward to greet or touch him. She said, "Teyeo, I've been asked to be the first Ambassador of the Ekumen to Yeowe."

He stood still.

"Just now—I just came from talking on the ansible with Hain—"

She put her face in her hands. "Oh, my God!" she said.

He said, "My congratulations, truly, Solly."

She suddenly ran at him, threw her arms around him, and cried, "Oh, Teyeo, and your mother died, I never thought, I'm so sorry, I never, I never do—I thought we could—What are you going to do? Are you going to stay there?"

"I sold it," he said. He was enduring rather than returning her embrace. "I thought I might return to the service."

"You sold your *farm*? But I never saw it!"

"I never saw where you were born," he said.

There was a pause. She stood away from him, and they looked at
each other.

"You would come?" she said.

"I would," he said.

SEVERAL YEARS AFTER YEOWE ENTERED THE EKUMEN, MOBILE
Solly Agat Terwa was sent as an Ekumenical liaison to Terra; later she
went from there to Hain, where she served with great distinction as a
Stabile. In all her travels and posts she was accompanied by her husband,
a Werelian army officer, a very handsome man, as reserved as she was
outgoing. People who knew them knew their passionate pride and trust
in each other. Solly was perhaps the happier person, rewarded and fulfilled in her work; but Teyeo had no regrets. He had lost his world, but
he had held fast to the one noble thing.

A MAN
OF THE
PEOPLE

Stse

HE SAT BESIDE HIS FATHER BY THE GREAT IRRIGATION TANK.
Fire-colored wings soared and dipped through the twilight air. Trembling circles enlarged, interlocked, faded on the still surface of the water. "What makes the water go that way?" he asked, softly because it was mysterious, and his father answered softly, "It's where the araha touch it when they drink." So he understood that in the center of each circle was a desire, a thirst. Then it was time to go home, and he ran before his father, pretending he was an araha flying, back through the dusk into the steep, bright-windowed town.

His name was Mattinyehedarheddyuragamurus-kets Havzhiva. The word *havzhiva* means "ringed pebble," a small stone with a quartz inclusion running through it that shows as a stripe round it. The people of Stse are particular about stones and names. Boys of the Sky, the Other Sky, and the Static Interference lineages are traditionally given the names of stones or desirable manly qualities such as courage, patience, and grace. The Yehedarhed family were traditionalists, strong on family and lineage. "If you know who your people are, you know who you are," said Havzhiva's father, Granite. A kind, quiet man who took his paternal responsibility seriously, he spoke often in sayings.

Granite was Havzhiva's mother's brother, of course; that is what a father was. The man who had helped his mother conceive Havzhiva lived on a farm; he stopped in sometimes to say hello when he was in town. Havzhiva's mother was the Heir of the Sun. Sometimes Havzhiva envied his cousin Aloe, whose father was only six years older than she was and played with her like a big brother. Sometimes he envied children whose mothers were unimportant. His mother was always fasting or dancing or traveling, had no husband, and rarely slept at home. It was exciting to be with her, but difficult. He had to be important when he was with her. It was always a relief to be home with nobody there but his father and his undemanding grandmother and her sister the Winter Dancekeeper and her husband and whichever Other Sky relatives from farms and other pueblos were visiting at the moment.

There were only two Other Sky households in Stse, and the Yehedarheds were more hospitable than the Doyefarads, so all the relatives came and stayed with them. They would have been hard put to afford it if the visitors hadn't brought all sorts of farm stuff, and if Tovo hadn't been Heir of the Sun. She got paid richly for teaching and for performing the rituals and handling the protocol at other pueblos. She gave all she earned to her family, who spent it all on their relatives and on ceremonies, festivities, celebrations, and funerals.

"Wealth can't stop," Granite said to Havzhiva. "It has to keep going. Like the blood circulating. You keep it, it gets stopped—that's a heart attack. You die."

"Will Hezhe-old-man die?" the boy asked. Old Hezhe never spent anything on a ritual or a relative; and Havzhiva was an observant child.

"Yes," his father answered. "His araha is already dead."

Araha is enjoyment; honor; the particular quality of one's gender, manhood or womanhood; generosity; the savor of good food or wine.

It is also the name of the plumed, fire-colored, quick-flying mammal that Havzhiva used to see come to drink at the irrigation ponds, tiny flames darting above the darkening water in the evening.

Stse is an almost-island, separated from the mainland of the great south continent by marshes and tidal bogs, where millions of wading birds gather to mate and nest. Ruins of an enormous bridge are visible on the landward side, and another half-sunk fragment of ruin is the basis of the town's boat pier and breakwater. Vast works of other ages encumber all Hain, and are no more and no less venerable or interesting to the Hainish than the rest of the landscape. A child standing on the pier to watch his mother sail off to the mainland might wonder why people had bothered to build a bridge when there were boats and flyers to ride. They must have liked to walk, he thought. I'd rather sail in a boat. Or fly.

But the silver flyers flew over Stse, not landing, going from somewhere else to somewhere else, where historians lived. Plenty of boats came in and out of Stse harbor, but the people of his lineage did not sail them. They lived in the Pueblo of Stse and did the things that their people and their lineage did. They learned what people needed to learn, and lived their knowledge.

"People have to learn to be human," his father said. "Look at Shell's baby. It keeps saying 'Teach me! Teach me!'"

"Teach me," in the language of Stse, is "aowa."

"Sometimes the baby says 'ngaaaaa,'" Havzhiva observed.

Granite nodded. "She can't speak human words very well yet," he said.

Havzhiva hung around the baby that winter, teaching her to say human words. She was one of his Etsahin relatives, his second cousin once removed, visiting with her mother and her father and his wife. The family watched Havzhiva with approval as he patiently said "baba" and "gogo" to the fat, placid, staring baby. Though he had no sister and thus

could not be a father, if he went on studying education with such seriousness, he would probably have the honor of being the adopted father
of a baby whose mother had no brother.

He also studied at school and in the temple, studied dancing, and
studied the local version of soccer. He was a serious student. He was
good at soccer but not as good as his best friend, a Buried Cable girl
named Iyan Iyan (a traditional name for Buried Cable girls, a seabird
name). Until they were twelve, boys and girls were educated together
and alike. Iyan Iyan was the best soccer player on the children's team.
They always had to put her on the other side at halftime so that the
score would even out and they could go home for dinner without anybody having lost or won badly. Part of her advantage was that she had
got her height very early, but most of it was pure skill.

"Are you going to work at the temple?" she asked Havzhiva as they sat
on the porch roof of her house watching the first day of the Enactment
of the Unusual Gods, which took place every eleven years. No unusual
things were happening yet, and the amplifiers weren't working well, so
the music in the plaza sounded faint and full of static. The two children
kicked their heels and talked quietly. "No, I think I'll learn weaving
from my father," the boy said.

"Lucky you. Why do only stupid boys get to use looms?" It was a
rhetorical question, and Havzhiva paid it no attention. Women were not
weavers. Men did not make bricks. Other Sky people did not operate
boats but did repair electronic devices. Buried Cable people did not castrate animals but did maintain generators. There were things one could
do and things one could not do; one did those things for people and
people did those things for one. Coming up on puberty, Iyan Iyan and
Havzhiva were making a first choice of their first profession. Iyan Iyan
had already chosen to apprentice in house-building and repair, although
the adult soccer team would probably claim a good deal of her time.

A globular silver person with spidery legs came down the street in long bounds, emitting a shower of sparks each time it landed. Six people in red with tall white masks ran after it, shouting and throwing speckled beans at it. Havzhiva and Iyan Iyan joined in the shouting and craned from the roof to see it go bounding round the corner towards the plaza. They both knew that this Unusual God was Chert, a young man of the Sky lineage, a goalkeeper for the adult soccer team; they both also knew that it was a manifestation of deity. A god called Zarstsa or Ball-Lighting was using Chert to come into town for the ceremony, and had just bounded down the street pursued by shouts of fear and praise and showers of fertility. Amused and entertained by the spectacle, they judged with some acuteness the quality of the god's costume, the jumping, and the fireworks, and were awed by the strangeness and power of the event. They did not say anything for a long time after the god had passed, but sat dreamily in the foggy sunlight on the roof. They were children who lived among the daily gods. Now they had seen one of the unusual gods. They were content. Another one would come along, before long. Time is nothing to the gods.

AT FIFTEEN, HAVZHIVA AND IYAN IYAN BECAME GODS TOGETHER.

Stse people between twelve and fifteen were vigilantly watched; there would be a great deal of grief and deep, lasting shame if a child of the house, the family, the lineage, the people, should change being prematurely and without ceremony. Virginity was a sacred status, not to be carelessly abandoned; sexual activity was a sacred status, not to be carelessly undertaken. It was assumed that a boy would masturbate and make some homosexual experiments, but not a homosexual pairing; adolescent boys who paired off, and those who incurred suspicion of trying to get alone with a girl, were endlessly lectured and hectored and badgered by older men. A grown man who made sexual advances to a virgin of either sex would forfeit his professional status, his religious offices, and his houseright.

Changing being took a while. Boys and girls had to be taught how to recognise and control their fertility, which in Hainish physiology is a matter of personal decision. Conception does not happen: it is performed. It cannot take place unless both the woman and the man have chosen it. At thirteen, boys began to be taught the technique of deliberately releasing potent sperm. The teachings were full of warnings, threats, and scoldings, though the boys were never actually punished. After a year or two came a series of tests of achieved potency, a threshold ritual, frightening, formal, extremely secret, exclusively male. To have passed the tests was, of course, a matter of intense pride; yet Havzhiva, like most boys, came to his final change-of-being rites very apprehensive, hiding fear under a sullen stoicism.

The girls had been differently taught. The people of Stse believed that a woman's cycle of fertility made it easy for her to learn when and how to conceive, and so the teaching was easy too. Girls' threshold rituals were celebratory, involving praise rather than shame, arousing anticipation rather than fear. Women had been telling them for years, with demonstrations, what a man wants, how to make him stand up tall, how to show him what a woman wants. During this training, most girls asked if they couldn't just go on practicing with each other, and got scolded and lectured. No, they couldn't. Once they had changed status they could do as they pleased, but everybody must go through "the twofold door" once.

The change-of-being rites were held whenever the people in charge of them could get an equal number of fifteen-year-old boys and girls from the pueblo and its farms. Often a boy or girl had to be borrowed from one of the related pueblos to even out the number or to pair the lineages correctly. Magnificently masked and costumed, silent, the participants danced and were honored all day in the plaza and in the house consecrated to the ceremony; in the evening they ate a ritual meal in silence; then they were led off in pairs by masked and silent ritualists. Many of them kept their masks on, hiding their fear and modesty in that sacred anonymity.

Because Other Sky people have sex only with Original and Buried Cable people and they were the only ones of those lineages in the group, Iyan Iyan and Havzhiva had known they must be paired. They had recognised each other as soon as the dancing began. When they were left alone in the consecrated room, they took off their masks at once. Their eyes met. They looked away.

They had been kept apart most of the time for the past couple of years, and completely apart for the last months. Havzhiva had begun to get his growth, and was nearly as tall as she was now. Each saw a stranger. Decorous and serious, they approached each other, each thinking, "Let's get it over with." So they touched, and that god entered them, becoming them; the god for whom they were the doorway; the meaning for which they were the word. It was an awkward god at first, clumsy, but became an increasingly happy one.

When they left the consecrated house the next day, they both went to Iyan Iyan's house. "Havzhiva will live here," Iyan Iyan said, as a woman has a right to say. Everybody in her family made him welcome and none of them seemed surprised.

When he went to get his clothes from his grandmother's house, nobody there seemed surprised, everybody congratulated him, an old woman cousin from Etsahin made some embarrassing jokes, and his father said, "You are a man of this house now; come back for dinner."

So he slept with Iyan Iyan at her house, ate breakfast there, ate dinner at his house, kept his daily clothes at her house, kept his dance clothes at his house, and went on with his education, which now had mostly to do with rug-weaving on the power broadlooms and with the nature of the cosmos. He and Iyan Iyan both played on the adult soccer team.

He began to see more of his mother, because when he was seventeen she asked him if he wanted to learn Sun-stuff with her, the rites and protocols of trade, arranging fair exchange with farmers of Stse and bargaining with other pueblos of the lineages and with foreigners. The rituals were learned by rote, the protocols were learned by practice. Havzhiva went with his mother to the market, to outlying farms, and across the bay to the mainland pueblos. He had been getting restless with weaving, which filled his mind with patterns that left no room outside themselves. The travel was welcome, the work was interesting, and he admired Tovo's authority, wit, and tact. Listening to her and a group of old merchants and Sun people maneuvering around a deal was an education in itself. She did not push him; he played a very minor role in these negotiations. Training in complicated business such as Sun-stuff took years, and there were other, older people in training before him. But she was satisfied with him. "You have a knack for persuading," she told him one afternoon as they were sailing home across the golden water, watching the roofs of Stse solidify out of mist and sunset light. "You could inherit the Sun, if you wanted to."

Do I want to? he thought. There was no response in him but a sense of darkening or softening, which he could not interpret. He knew he liked the work. Its patterns were not closed. It took him out of Stse, among strangers, and he liked that. It gave him something to do which he didn't know how to do, and he liked that.

"The woman who used to live with your father is coming for a visit," Tovo said.

Havzhiva pondered. Granite had never married. The women who had borne the children Granite sired both lived in Stse and always had. He asked nothing, a polite silence being the adult way of signifying that one doesn't understand.

"They were young. No child came," his mother said. "She went away after that. She became a historian."

"Ah," Havzhiva said in pure, blank surprise.

He had never heard of anybody who became a historian. It had never occurred to him that a person could become one, any more than a person could become a Stse. You were born what you were. You were what you were born.

The quality of his polite silence was desperately intense, and Tovo certainly was not unaware of it. Part of her tact as a teacher was knowing when a question needed an answer. She said nothing.

As their sail slackened and the boat slid in towards the pier built on the ancient bridge foundations, he asked, "Is the historian Buried Cable or Original?"

"Buried Cable," his mother said. "Oh, how stiff I am! Boats are such stiff creatures!" The woman who had sailed them across, a ferrywoman of the Grass lineage, rolled her eyes, but said nothing in defense of her sweet, supple little boat.

"A relative of yours is coming?" Havzhiva said to Iyan Iyan that night.

"Oh, yes, she templed in." Iyan Iyan meant a message had been received in the information center of Stse and transmitted to the recorder in her household. "She used to live in your house, my mother said. Who did you see in Etsahin today?"

"Just some Sun people. Your relative is a historian?"

"Crazy people," Iyan Iyan said with indifference, and came to sit naked on naked Havzhiva and massage his back.

The historian arrived, a little short thin woman of fifty or so called Mezha. By the time Havzhiva met her she was wearing Stse clothing and eating breakfast with everybody else. She had bright eyes and was cheerful but not talkative. Nothing about her showed that she had broken the social contract, done things no woman does, ignored her lineage, become another kind of being. For all he knew she was married to the father of her children, and wove at a loom, and castrated animals. But nobody shunned her, and after breakfast the old people of the household took her off for a returning-traveler ceremony, just as if she were still one of them.

He kept wondering about her, wondering what she had done. He asked Iyan Iyan questions about her till Iyan Iyan snapped at him, "I don't know what she does, I don't know what she thinks. Historians are crazy. Ask her yourself!"

When Havzhiva realised that he was afraid to do so, for no reason, he understood that he was in the presence of a god who was requiring something of him. He went up to one of the sitting holes, rock cairns on the heights above the town. Below him the black tile roofs and white walls of Stse nestled under the bluffs, and the irrigation tanks shone silver among fields and orchards. Beyond the tilled land stretched the long sea marshes. He spent a day sitting in silence, looking out to sea and into his soul. He came back down to his own house and slept there. When he turned up for breakfast at Iyan Iyan's house she looked at him and said nothing.

"I was fasting," he said.

She shrugged a little. "So eat," she said, sitting down by him. After breakfast she left for work. He did not, though he was expected at the looms.

"Mother of All Children," he said to the historian, giving her the most respectful title a man of one lineage can give a woman of another, "there are things I do not know, which you know."

"What I know I will teach you with pleasure," she said, as ready with the formula as if she had lived here all her life. She then smiled and forestalled his next oblique question. "What was given me I give," she said, meaning there was no question of payment or obligation. "Come on, let's go to the plaza."

Everybody goes to the plaza in Stse to talk, and sits on the steps or around the fountain or on hot days under the arcades, and watches other people come and go and sit and talk. It was perhaps a little more public than Havzhiva would have liked, but he was obedient to his god and his teacher.

They sat in a niche of the fountain's broad base and conversed, greeting people every sentence or two with a nod or a word.

"Why did—" Havzhiva began, and stuck.

"Why did I leave? Where did I go?" She cocked her head, bright-eyed as an araha, checking that those were the questions he wanted answered. "Yes. Well, I was crazy in love with Granite, but we had no child, and he wanted a child. . . . You look like he did then. I like to look at you. . . . So, I was unhappy. Nothing here was any good to me. And I knew how to do everything here. Or that's what I thought."

Havzhiva nodded once.

"I worked at the temple. I'd read messages that came in or came by and wonder what they were about. I thought, all that's going on in the world! Why should I stay here my whole life? Does my mind have to stay here? So I began to talk with some of them in other places in the temple: who are you, what do you do, what is it like there. . . . Right away they put me in touch with a group of historians who were born in the pueblos, who look out for people like me, to make sure they don't waste time or offend a god."

This language was completely familiar to Havzhiva, and he nodded again, intent.

"I asked them questions. They asked me questions. Historians have to do a lot of that. I found out they have schools, and asked if I could go to one. Some of them came here and talked to me and my family and other people, finding out if there would be trouble if I left. Stse is a conservative pueblo. There hadn't been a historian from here for four hundred years."

She smiled; she had a quick, catching smile, but the young man listened with unchanging, intense seriousness. Her look rested on his face tenderly.

"People here were upset, but nobody was angry. So after they talked about it, I left with those people. We flew to Kathhad. There's a school there. I was twenty-two. I began a new education. I changed being. I learned to be a historian."

"How?" he asked, after a long silence.

She drew a long breath. "By asking hard questions," she said. "Like you're doing now. . . . And by giving up all the knowledge I had—throwing it away."

"How?" he asked again, frowning. "Why?"

"Like this. When I left, I knew I was a Buried Cable woman. When I was there, I had to unknow that knowledge. There, I'm not a Buried Cable woman. I'm a woman. I can have sex with any person I choose. I can take up any profession I choose. Lineage matters, here. It does not matter, there. It has meaning here, and a use. It has no meaning and no use, anywhere else in the universe." She was as intense as he, now. "There are two kinds of knowledge, local and universal. There are two kinds of time, local and historical."

"Are there two kinds of gods?"

"No," she said. "There are no gods there. The gods are here."

She saw his face change.

She said after a while, "There are souls, there. Many, many souls, minds, minds full of knowledge and passion. Living and dead. People who lived on this earth a hundred, a thousand, a hundred thousand years ago. Minds and souls of people from worlds a hundred light-years from this one, all of them with their own knowledge, their own history. The world is sacred, Havzhiva. The cosmos is sacred. That's not a knowledge I ever had to give up. All I learned, here and there, only increased it. There's nothing that is not sacred." She spoke slowly and quietly, the way most people talked in the pueblo. "You can choose the local sacredness or the great one. In the end they're the same. But not in the life one lives. 'To know there is a choice is to have to make the choice: change or stay: river or rock.' The Peoples are the rock. The historians are the river."

After a while he said, "Rocks are the river's bed."

She laughed. Her gaze rested on him again, appraising and affectionate. "So I came home," she said. "For a rest."

"But you're not—you're no longer a woman of your lineage?"

"Yes; here. Still. Always."

"But you've changed being. You'll leave again."

"Yes," she said decisively. "One can be more than one kind of being. I have work to do, there."

He shook his head, slower, but equally decisive. "What good is work without the gods? It makes no sense to me, Mother of All Children. I don't have the mind to understand."

She smiled at the double meaning. "I think you'll understand what you choose to understand, Man of my People," she said, addressing him formally to show that he was free to leave when he wanted.

He hesitated, then took his leave. He went to work, filling his mind and world with the great repeated patterns of the broadloom rugs.

That night he made it up to Iyan Iyan so ardently that she was left spent and a bit amazed. The god had come back to them burning, consuming.

"I want a child," Havzhiva said as they lay melded, sweated together, arms and legs and breasts and breath all mingled in the musky dark.

"Oh," Iyan Iyan sighed, not wanting to talk, decide, resist. "Maybe . . . Later . . . Soon . . ."

"Now," he said, "now."

"No," she said softly. "Hush."

He was silent. She slept.

MORE THAN A YEAR LATER, WHEN THEY WERE NINETEEN, IYAN Iyan said to him before he put out the light, "I want a baby."

"It's too soon."

"Why? My brother's nearly thirty. And his wife would like a baby around. After it's weaned I'll come sleep with you at your house. You always said you'd like that."

"It's too soon," he repeated. "I don't want it."

She turned to him, laying aside her coaxing, reasonable tone. "What do you want, Havzhiva?"

"I don't know."

"You're going away. You're going to leave the People. You're going crazy. That woman, that damned witch!"

"There are no witches," he said coldly. "That's stupid talk. Superstition."

They stared at each other, the dear friends, the lovers.

"Then what's wrong with you? If you want to move back home, say so. If you want another woman, go to her. But you could give me my child, first! when I ask you for it! Have you lost your araha?" She gazed at him with tearful eyes, fierce, unyielding.

He put his face in his hands. "Nothing is right," he said. "Nothing is right. Everything I do, I have to do because that's how it's done, but it—it doesn't make sense—there are other ways—"

"There's one way to live rightly," Iyan Iyan said, "that I know of. And this is where I live. There's one way to make a baby. If you know another, you can do it with somebody else!" She cried hard after this, convulsively, the fear and anger of months breaking out at last, and he held her to calm and comfort her.

When she could speak, she leaned her head against him and said miserably, in a small, hoarse voice, "To have when you go, Havzhiva."

At that he wept for shame and pity, and whispered, "Yes, yes." But that night they lay holding each other, trying to console each other, till they fell asleep like children.

"I AM ASHAMED," GRANITE SAID PAINFULLY.

"Did you make this happen?" his sister asked, dry.

"How do I know? Maybe I did. First Mezha, now my son. Was I too stern with him?"

"No, no."

"Too lax, then. I didn't teach him well. Why is he crazy?"

"He isn't crazy, brother. Let me tell you what I think. As a child he always asked why, why, the way children do. I would answer: That's how it is, that's how it's done. He understood. But his mind has no peace. My mind is like that, if I don't remind myself. Learning the Sun-stuff, he always asked, why thus? why this way, not another way? I answered: Because in what we do daily and in the way we do it, we enact the gods. He said: Then the gods are only what we do. I said: In what we do rightly, the gods are: that is the truth. But he wasn't satisfied by the truth. He isn't crazy, brother, but he is lame. He can't walk. He can't walk with us. So, if a man can't walk, what should he do?"

"Sit still and sing," Granite said slowly.

"If he can't sit still? He can fly."

"Fly?"

"They have wings for him, brother."

"I am ashamed," Granite said, and hid his face in his hands.

Tovo went to the temple and sent a message to Mezha at Kathhad: "Your pupil wishes to join you." There was some malice in the words. Tovo blamed the historian for upsetting her son's balance, off-centering him till, as she said, his soul was lamed. And she was jealous of the woman who in a few days had outdone the teachings of years. She knew she was jealous and did not care. What did her jealousy or her brother's humiliation matter? What they had to do was grieve.

As the boat for Daha sailed away, Havzhiva looked back and saw Stse: a quilt of a thousand shades of green, the sea marshes, the pastures, fields, hedgerows, orchards; the town clambering up the bluffs above, pale granite walls, white stucco walls, black tile roofs, wall above wall and roof above roof. As it diminished it looked like a seabird perched there, white and black, a bird on its nest. Above the town the heights of the island came in view, grey-blue moors and high, wild hills fading into the clouds, white skeins of marsh birds flying.

At the port in Daha, though he was farther from Stse than he had ever been and people had a strange accent, he could understand them and read the signs. He had never seen signs before, but their usefulness was evident. Using them, he found his way to the waiting room for the Kathhad flyer. People were sleeping on the cots provided, in their own blankets. He found an empty cot and lay on it, wrapped in the blanket Granite had woven for him years ago. After a short, strange night, people came in with fruit and hot drinks. One of them gave Havzhiva his ticket. None of the passengers knew anyone else; they were all strangers; they kept their eyes down. Announcements were made, and they all went outside and went into the machine, the flyer.

Havzhiva made himself look at the world as it fell out from under him. He whispered the Staying Chant soundlessly, steadily. The stranger in the seat next to him joined in.

When the world began to tilt and rush up towards him he shut his eyes and tried to keep breathing.

One by one they filed out of the flyer onto a flat, black place where it was raining. Mezha came to him through the rain, saying his name. "Havzhiva, Man of my People, welcome! Come on. There's a place for you at the School."

Kathhad and Ve

By the third year at Kathhad Havzhiva knew a great many things that distressed him. The old knowledge had been difficult but not distressing. It had been all paradox and myth, and it had made sense. The new knowledge was all fact and reason, and it made no sense.

For instance, he knew now that historians did not study history. No human mind could encompass the history of Hain: three million years of it. The events of the first two million years, the Fore-Eras, like layers of metamorphic rock, were so compressed, so distorted by the weight of the succeeding millennia and their infinite events that one could reconstruct only the most sweeping generalities from the tiny surviving details. And if one did chance to find some miraculously preserved document from a thousand millennia ago, what then? A king ruled in Azbahan; the Empire fell to the Infidels; a fusion rocket has landed on Ve. . . . But there had been uncountable kings, empires, inventions, billions of lives lived in millions of countries, monarchies, democracies, oligarchies, anarchies, ages of chaos and ages of order, pantheon upon pantheon of gods, infinite wars and times of peace, incessant discoveries and forgettings, innumerable horrors and triumphs, an endless repetition of unceasing novelty. What is the use trying to describe the flowing of a river at any one moment, and then at the next moment, and then at the next, and the next, and the next? You wear out. You say: There is a great river, and it flows through this land, and we have named it History.

To Havzhiva the knowledge that his life, any life was one flicker of light for one moment on the surface of that river was sometimes distressing, sometimes restful.

What the historians mostly did was explore, in an easy and unhurried fashion, the local reach and moment of the river. Hain itself had been for several thousand years in an unexciting period marked by the coexistence of small, stable, self-contained societies, currently called pueblos, with a high-technology, low-density network of cities and information centers, currently called the temple. Many of the people of the temple, the historians, spent their lives traveling to and gathering knowledge about the other inhabited planets of the nearby Orion Arm, colonised by their ancestors a couple of million years ago during the Fore-Eras. They acknowledged no motive in these contacts and explorations other than curiosity and fellow-feeling. They were getting in touch with their long-lost relatives. They called that greater network of worlds by an alien word, Ekumen, which meant "the household."

By now Havzhiva knew that everything he had learned in Stse, all the knowledge he had had, could be labeled: *typical pueblo culture of northwestern coastal South Continent.* He knew that the beliefs, practices, kinship systems, technologies, and intellectual organising patterns of the different pueblos were entirely different one from another, wildly different, totally bizarre—just as bizarre as the system of Stse—and he knew that such systems were to be met with on every Known World that contained human populations living in small, stable groups with a technology adapted to their environment, a low, constant birth rate, and a political life based on consent.

At first such knowledge had been intensely distressing. It had been painful. It had made him ashamed and angry. First he thought the historians kept their knowledge from the pueblos, then he thought the pueblos kept knowledge from their own people. He accused; his teachers mildly denied. No, they said. You were taught that certain things were true, or necessary; and those things are true and necessary. They are the local knowledge of Stse.

They are childish, irrational beliefs! he said. They looked at him, and he knew he had said something childish and irrational.

Local knowledge is not partial knowledge, they said. There are different ways of knowing. Each has its own qualities, penalties, rewards. Historical knowledge and scientific knowledge are a way of knowing. Like local knowledge, they must be learned. The way they know in the Household isn't taught in the pueblos, but it wasn't hidden from you, by your people or by us. Everybody anywhere on Hain has access to all the information in the temple.

This was true; he knew it to be true. He could have found out for himself, on the screens of the temple of Stse, what he was learning now. Some of his fellow students from other pueblos had indeed taught themselves how to learn from the screens, and had entered history before they ever met a historian.

Books, however, books that were the body of history, the durable reality of it, barely existed in Stse, and his anger sought justification there. You keep the books from us, all the books in the Library of Hain! No, they said mildly. The pueblos choose not to have many books. They prefer the live knowledge, spoken or passing on the screens, passing from the breath to the breath, from living mind to living mind. Would you give up what you learned that way? Is it less than, is it inferior to what you've learned here from books? There's more than one kind of knowledge, said the historians.

By his third year, Havzhiva had decided that there was more than one kind of people. The pueblans, able to accept that existence is fundamentally arbitrary, enriched the world intellectually and spiritually. Those who couldn't be satisfied with mystery were more likely to be of use as historians, enriching the world intellectually and materially.

Meanwhile he had got quite used to people who had no lineage, no relatives, and no religion. Sometimes he said to himself with a glow of pride, "I am a citizen of all history, of the millions of years of Hainish history, and my country is the whole galaxy!" At other times he felt miserably small, and he would leave his screens or his books and go look for company among his fellow students, especially the young women who were so friendly, so companionable.

AT THE AGE OF TWENTY-FOUR HAVZHIVA, OR ZHIV AS HE WAS now called, had been at the Ekumenical School on Ve for a year.

Ve, the next planet out from Hain, was colonised eons ago, the first step in the vast Hainish expansion of the Fore-Eras. It has gone through many phases as a satellite or partner of Hainish civilizations; at this period it is inhabited entirely by historians and Aliens.

In their current (that is, for at least the past hundred millennia) mood of not tampering, the Hainish have let Ve return to its own norms of coldness, dryness, and bleakness—a climate within human tolerance, but likely to truly delight only people from the Terran Altiplano or the uplands of Chiffewar. Zhiv was out hiking through this stern landscape with his companion, friend, and lover, Tiu.

They had met two years before, in Kathhad. At that point Zhiv had still been reveling in the availability of all women to himself and himself to all women, a freedom that had only gradually dawned on him, and about which Mezha had warned him gently. "You will think there are no rules," she said. "There are always rules." He had been conscious mainly of his own increasingly fearless and careless transgression of what had been the rules. Not all the women wanted to have sex, and not all the women wanted to have sex with men, as he had soon discovered, but that still left an infinite variety. He found that he was considered attractive. And being Hainish was a definite advantage with the Alien women.

The genetic alteration that made the Hainish able to control their fertility was not a simple bit of gene-splicing; involving a profound and radical reconstruction of human physiology, it had probably taken up to twenty-five generations to establish—so say the historians of Hain, who think they know in general terms the steps such a transformation must have followed. However the ancient Hainish did it, they did not do it for any of their colonists. They left the peoples of their colony worlds to work out their own solutions to the First Heterosexual Problem. These have been, of course, various and ingenious; but in all cases so far, to avoid conception you have to do something or have done something or take something or use something—unless you have sex with the Hainish.

Zhiv had been outraged when a girl from Beldene asked him if he was sure he wouldn't get her pregnant. "How do you *know*?" she said. "Maybe I should take a zapper just to be *safe*." Insulted in the quick of his manhood, he disentangled himself, said, "Maybe it is only safe not to be with me," and stalked out. Nobody else questioned his integrity, fortunately, and he cruised happily on, until he met Tiu.

She was not an Alien. He had sought out women from offworld; sleeping with Aliens added exoticism to transgression, or, as he put it, was an enrichment of knowledge such as every historian should seek. But Tiu was Hainish. She had been born and brought up in Darranda, as had her ancestors before her. She was a child of the Historians as he was a child of the People. He realised very soon that this bond and division was far greater than any mere foreignness: that their unlikeness was true difference and their likeness was true kinship. She was the country he had left his own country to discover. She was what he sought to be. She was what he sought.

What she had—so it seemed to him—was perfect equilibrium. When he was with her he felt that for the first time in his life he was learning to walk. To walk as she did: effortless, unself-conscious as an animal, and yet conscious, careful, keeping in mind all that might unbalance her and using it as tightrope walkers use their long poles. . . . This, he thought, this is a dweller in true freedom of mind, this is a woman free to be fully human, this perfect measure, this perfect grace.

He was utterly happy when he was with her. For a long time he asked nothing beyond that, to be with her. And for a long time she was wary of him, gentle but distant. He thought she had every right to keep her distance. A pueblo boy, a fellow who couldn't tell his uncle from his father—he knew what he was, here, in the eyes of the ill-natured and the insecure. Despite their vast knowledge of human ways of being, historians retained the vast human capacity for bigotry. Tiu had no such prejudices, but what did he have to offer her? She had and was everything. She was complete. Why should she look at him? If she would only let him look at her, be with her, it was all he wanted.

She looked at him, liked him, found him appealing and a little frightening. She saw how he wanted her, how he needed her, how he had made her into the center of his life and did not even know it. That would not do. She tried to be cold, to turn him away. He obeyed. He did not plead. He stayed away.

But after fifteen days he came to her and said, "Tiu, I cannot live without you," and knowing that he was speaking the plain truth she said, "Then live with me a while." For she had missed the passion his presence filled the air with. Everybody else seemed so tame, so balanced.

Their lovemaking was an immediate, immense, and continual delight. Tiu was amazed at herself, at her obsession with Zhiv, at her letting him pull her out of her orbit so far. She had never expected to adore anybody, let alone to be adored. She had led an orderly life, in which the controls were individual and internal, not social and external as they had been in Zhiv's life in Stse. She knew what she wanted to be and do. There was a direction in her, a true north, that she would always follow. Their first year together was a series of continual shifts and changes in their relationship, a kind of exciting love dance, unpredictable and ecstatic. Very gradually, she began to resist the tension, the intensity, the ecstasy. It was lovely but it wasn't right, she thought. She wanted to go on. That constant direction began to pull her away from him again; and then he fought for his life against it.

That was what he was doing, after a long day's hike in the Desert of Asu Asi on Ve, in their miraculously warm Gethenian-made tent. A dry, icy wind moaned among cliffs of crimson stone above them, polished by the endless winds to a shine like lacquer and carved by a lost civilization with lines of some vast geometry.

They might have been brother and sister, as they sat in the glow of the Chabe stove: their red-bronze coloring was the same, their thick, glossy, black hair, their fine, compact body type. The pueblan decorum and quietness of Zhiv's movements and voice met in her an articulate, quicker, more vivid response.

But she spoke now slowly, almost stiffly.

"Don't force me to choose, Zhiv," she said. "Ever since I started in the Schools I've wanted to go to Terra. Since before. When I was a kid. All my life. Now they offer me what I want, what I've worked for. How can you ask me to refuse?"

"I don't."

"But you want me to put it off. If I do, I may lose the chance forever. Probably not. But why risk it—for one year? You can follow me next year!"

He said nothing.

"If you want to," she added stiffly. She was always too ready to forgo her claim on him. Perhaps she had never believed fully in his love for her. She did not think of herself as lovable, as worthy of his passionate loyalty. She was frightened by it, felt inadequate, false. Her self-respect was an intellectual thing. "You make a god of me," she had told him, and did not understand when he replied with happy seriousness, "We make the god together."

"I'm sorry," he said now. "It's a different form of reason. Superstition, if you like. I can't help it, Tiu. Terra is a hundred and forty light-years away. If you go, when you get there, I'll be dead."

"You will not! You'll have lived another year here, you'll be on your way there, you'll arrive a year after I do!"

"I know that. Even in Stse we learned that," he said patiently. "But I'm superstitious. We die to each other if you go. Even in Kathhad you learned that."

"I didn't. It's not true. How can you ask me to give up this chance for what you admit is a superstition? Be fair, Zhiv!"

After a long silence, he nodded.

She sat stricken, understanding that she had won. She had won badly.

She reached across to him, trying to comfort him and herself. She was scared by the darkness in him, his grief, his mute acceptance of

betrayal. But it wasn't betrayal—she rejected the word at once. She
wouldn't betray him. They were in love. They loved each other. He
would follow her in a year, two years at the most. They were adults, they
must not cling together like children. Adult relationships are based on
mutual freedom, mutual trust. She told herself all these things as she
said them to him. He said yes, and held her, and comforted her. In the
night, in the utter silence of the desert, the blood singing in his ears, he
lay awake and thought, "It has died unborn. It was never conceived."

They stayed together in their little apartment at the School for the few
more weeks before Tiu left. They made love cautiously, gently, talked
about history and economics and ethnology, kept busy. Tiu had to prepare herself to work with the team she was going with, studying the
Terran concepts of hierarchy; Zhiv had a paper to write on social-energy
generation on Werel. They worked hard. Their friends gave Tiu a big
farewell party. The next day Zhiv went with her to Ve Port. She kissed
and held him, telling him to hurry, hurry and come to Terra. He saw
her board the flyer that would take her up to the NAFAL ship waiting
in orbit. He went back to the apartment on the South Campus of the
School. There a friend found him three days later sitting at his desk in
a curious condition, passive, speaking very slowly if at all, unable to eat
or drink. Being pueblo-born, the friend recognised this state and called
in the medicine man (the Hainish do not call them doctors). Having
ascertained that he was from one of the Southern pueblos, the medicine
man said, "Havzhiva! The god cannot die in you here!"

After a long silence the young man said softly in a voice which did
not sound like his voice, "I need to go home."

"That is not possible now," said the medicine man, "But we can
arrange a Staying Chant while I find a person able to address the god."
He promptly put out a call for students who were ex–People of the South.
Four responded. They sat all night with Havzhiva singing the Staying
Chant in two languages and four dialects, until Havzhiva joined them

in a fifth dialect, whispering the words hoarsely, till he collapsed and slept for thirty hours.

He woke in his own room. An old woman was having a conversation with nobody beside him. "You aren't here," she said. "No, you are mistaken. You can't die here. It would not be right, it would be quite wrong. You know that. This is the wrong place. This is the wrong life. You know that! What are you doing here? Are you lost? Do you want to know the way home? Here it is. Listen." She began singing in a thin, high voice, an almost tuneless, almost wordless song that was familiar to Havzhiva, as if he had heard it long ago. He fell asleep again while the old woman went on talking to nobody.

When he woke again she was gone. He never knew who she was or where she came from; he never asked. She had spoken and sung in his own language, in the dialect of Stse.

He was not going to die now, but he was very unwell. The medicine man ordered him to the Hospital at Tes, the most beautiful place on all Ve, an oasis where hot springs and sheltering hills make a mild local climate and flowers and forests can grow. There are paths endlessly winding under great trees, warm lakes where you can swim forever, little misty ponds from which birds rise crying, steam-shrouded hot springs, and a thousand waterfalls whose voices are the only sound all night. There he was sent to stay till he was recovered.

He began to speak into his noter, after he had been at Tes twenty days or so; he would sit in the sunlight on the doorstep of his cottage in a glade of grasses and ferns and talk quietly to himself by way of the little recording machine. "What you select from, in order to tell your story, is nothing less than everything," he said, watching the branches of the old trees dark against the sky. "What you build up your world from, your local, intelligible, rational, coherent world, is nothing less than everything. And so all selection is arbitrary. All knowledge is partial— infinitesimally partial. Reason is a net thrown out into an ocean. What truth it brings in is a fragment, a glimpse, a scintillation of the whole truth. All human knowledge is local. Every life, each human life, is local, is arbitrary, the infinitesimal momentary glitter of a reflection of . . ." His voice ceased; the silence of the glade among the great trees continued.

After forty-five days he returned to the School. He took a new apartment. He changed fields, leaving social science, Tiu's field, for Ekumenical service training, which was intellectually closely related but led to a different kind of work. The change would lengthen his time at the School by at least a year, after which if he did well he could hope for a post with the Ekumen. He did well, and after two years was asked, in the polite fashion of the Ekumenical councils, if he would care to go to Werel. Yes, he said, he would. His friends gave a big farewell party for him.

"I thought you were aiming for Terra," said one of his less-astute classmates. "All that stuff about war and slavery and class and caste and gender—isn't that Terran history?"

"It's current events in Werel," Havzhiva said.

He was no longer Zhiv. He had come back from the Hospital as Havzhiva.

Somebody else was stepping on the unastute classmate's foot, but she paid no attention. "I thought you were going to follow Tiu," she said. "I thought that's why you never slept with anybody. God, if I'd only known!" The others winced, but Havzhiva smiled and hugged her apologetically.

In his own mind it was quite clear. As he had betrayed and forsaken Iyan Iyan, so Tiu had betrayed and forsaken him. There was no going back and no going forward. So he must turn aside. Though he was one of them, he could no longer live with the People; though he had become one of them, he did not want to live with the historians. So he must go live among Aliens.

He had no hope of joy. He had bungled that, he thought. But he knew that the two long, intense disciplines that had filled his life, that of the gods and that of history, had given him an uncommon knowledge, which might be of use somewhere; and he knew that the right use of knowledge is fulfillment.

The medicine man came to visit him the day before he left, checked him over, and then sat for a while saying nothing. Havzhiva sat with him. He had long been used to silence, and still sometimes forgot that it was not customary among historians.

"What's wrong?" the medicine man said. It seemed to be a rhetorical question, from its meditative tone; at any rate, Havzhiva made no answer.

"Please stand up," the medicine man said, and when Havzhiva had done so, "Now walk a little." He walked a few steps; the medicine man observed him. "You're out of balance," he said. "Did you know it?"

"Yes."

"I could get a Staying Chant together this evening."

"It's all right," Havzhiva said. "I've always been off-balance."

"There's no need to be," the medicine man said. "On the other hand, maybe it's best, since you're going to Werel. So: Good-bye for this life."

They embraced formally, as historians did, especially when as now it was absolutely certain that they would never see one another again. Havzhiva had to give and get a good many formal embraces that day. The next day he boarded the *Terraces of Darranda* and went across the darkness.

Yeowe

DURING HIS JOURNEY OF EIGHTY LIGHT-YEARS AT NAFAL speed, his mother died, and his father, and Iyan Iyan, everyone he had known in Stse, everyone he knew in Kathhad and on Ve. By the time the ship landed, they had all been dead for years. The child Iyan Iyan had borne had lived and grown old and died.

This was a knowledge he had lived with ever since he saw Tiu board her ship, leaving him to die. Because of the medicine man, the four people who had sung for him, the old woman, and the waterfalls of Tes, he had lived; but he had lived with that knowledge.

Other things had changed as well. At the time he left Ve, Werel's colony planet Yeowe had been a slave world, a huge work camp. By the time he arrived on Werel, the War of Liberation was over, Yeowe had declared its independence, and the institution of slavery on Werel itself was beginning to disintegrate.

Havzhiva longed to observe this terrible and magnificent process, but the Embassy sent him promptly off to Yeowe. A Hainishman called Sohikelwenyanmurkeres Esdardon Aya counseled him before he left. "If you want danger, it's dangerous," he said, "and if you like hope, it's hopeful. Werel is unmaking itself, while Yeowe's trying to make itself. I don't know if it's going to succeed. I tell you what, Yehedarhed Havzhiva: there are great gods loose on these worlds."

Yeowe had got rid of its Bosses, its Owners, the Four Corporations who had run the vast slave plantations for three hundred years; but though the thirty years of the War of Liberation were over, the fighting had not stopped. Chiefs and warlords among the slaves who had risen to power during the Liberation now fought to keep and extend their power. Factions had battled over the question of whether to kick all foreigners off the planet forever or to admit Aliens and join the Ekumen. The isolationists had finally been voted down, and there was a new Ekumenical Embassy in the old colonial capital. Havzhiva spent a while there learning "the language and the table manners," as they said. Then the Ambassador, a clever young Terran named Solly, sent him south to the region called Yotebber, which was clamoring for recognition.

History is infamy, Havzhiva thought as he rode the train through the ruined landscapes of the world.

The Werelian capitalists who colonised the planet had exploited it and their slaves recklessly, mindlessly, in a long orgy of profit-making. It takes a while to spoil a world, but it can be done. Strip-mining and single-crop agriculture had defaced and sterilised the earth. The rivers were polluted, dead. Huge dust storms darkened the eastern horizon.

The Bosses had run their plantations by force and fear. For over a century they had shipped male slaves only, worked them till they died, imported fresh ones as needed. Work gangs in these all-male compounds developed into tribal hierarchies. At last, as the price of slaves on Werel and the cost of shipping rose, the Corporations began to buy bondswomen for Yeowe Colony. So over the next two centuries the slave population grew, and slave-cities were founded, "Assetvilles" and "Dustytowns" spreading out from the old compounds of the plantations. Havzhiva knew that the Liberation movement had arisen first among the women in the tribal compounds, a rebellion against male domination, before it became a war of all slaves against their owners.

The slow train stopped in city after city: miles of shacks and cabins, treeless, whole tracts bombed or burnt out in the war and not yet rebuilt; factories, some of them gutted ruins, some functioning but ancient-looking, rattletrap, smoke-belching. At each station hundreds of people got off the train and onto it, swarming, crowding, shouting out bribes to the porters, clambering up onto the roofs of the cars, brutally shoved off again by uniformed guards and policemen. In the north of the long continent, as on Werel, he had seen many black-skinned people, blue-black; but as the train went farther south there were fewer of these, until in Yotebber the people in the villages and on the desolate sidings were much paler than he was, a bluish, dusty color. These were the "dust people," the descendants of a hundred generations of Werelian slaves.

Yotebber had been an early center of the Liberation. The Bosses had made reprisal with bombs and poison gas; thousands of people had died. Whole towns had been burned to get rid of the unburied dead, human and animal. The mouth of the great river had been dammed with rotting bodies. But all that was past. Yeowe was free, a new member of the Ekumen of the Worlds, and Havzhiva in the capacity of Sub-Envoy was on his way to help the people of Yotebber Region to begin their new history. Or from the point of view of a Hainishman, to rejoin their ancient history.

He was met at the station in Yotebber City by a large crowd surging and cheering and yelling behind barricades manned by policemen and soldiers; in front of the barricades was a delegation of officials wearing splendid robes and sashes of office and variously ornate uniforms: big men, most of them, dignified, very much public figures. There were speeches of welcome, reporters and photographers for the holonet and the neareal news. It wasn't a circus, however. The big men were definitely in control. They wanted their guest to know he was welcome, he was popular, he was—as the Chief said in his brief, impressive speech—the Envoy from the Future.

That night in his luxurious suite in an Owner's city mansion converted to a hotel, Havzhiva thought: If they knew that their man from the future grew up in a pueblo and never saw a neareal till he came here . . .

He hoped he would not disappoint these people. From the moment he had first met them on Werel he had liked them, despite their monstrous society. They were full of vitality and pride, and here on Yeowe they were full of dreams of justice. Havzhiva thought of justice what an ancient Terran said of another god: I believe in it because it is impossible. He slept well, and woke early in the warm, bright morning, full of anticipation. He walked out to begin to get to know the city, his city.

The doorman—it was disconcerting to find that people who had fought so desperately for their freedom had servants—the doorman tried hard to get him to wait for a car, a guide, evidently distressed at the great man's going out so early, afoot, without a retinue. Havzhiva explained that he wanted to walk and was quite able to walk alone. He set off, leaving the unhappy doorman calling after him, "Oh, sir, please, avoid the City Park, sir!"

Havzhiva obeyed, thinking the park must be closed for a ceremony or replanting. He came on a plaza where a market was in full swing, and there found himself likely to become the center of a crowd; people inevitably noticed him. He wore the handsome Yeowan clothes, singlet, breeches, a light narrow robe, but he was the only person with red-brown skin in a city of four hundred thousand people. As soon as they saw his skin, his eyes, they knew him: the Alien. So he slipped away from the market and kept to quiet residential streets, enjoying the soft, warm air and the decrepit, charming colonial architecture of the houses. He stopped to admire an ornate Tualite temple. It looked rather shabby and desolate, but there was, he saw, a fresh offering of flowers at the feet of the image of the Mother at the doorway. Though her nose had been knocked off during the war, she smiled serenely, a little cross-eyed. People called out behind him. Somebody said close to him, "Foreign shit, get off our world," and his arm was seized as his legs were kicked out from under him. Contorted faces, screaming, closed in around him. An enormous, sickening cramp seized his body, doubling him into a red darkness of struggle and voices and pain, then a dizzy shrinking and dwindling away of light and sound.

AN OLD WOMAN WAS SITTING BY HIM, WHISPERING AN ALMOST tuneless song that seemed dimly familiar.

She was knitting. For a long time she did not look at him; when she did she said, "Ah." He had trouble making his eyes focus, but he made out that her face was bluish, a pale bluish tan, and there were no whites to her dark eyes.

She rearranged some kind of apparatus that was attached to him somewhere, and said, "I'm the medicine woman—the nurse. You have a concussion, a slight skull fracture, a bruised kidney, a broken shoulder,

and a knife wound in your gut; but you'll be all right; don't worry." All
this was in a foreign language, which he seemed to understand. At least
he understood "don't worry," and obeyed.

He thought he was on the *Terraces of Darranda* in NAFAL mode.
A hundred years passed in a bad dream but did not pass. People and
clocks had no faces. He tried to whisper the Staying Chant and it had
no words. The words were gone. The old woman took his hand. She
held his hand and slowly, slowly brought him back into time, into local
time, into the dim, quiet room where she sat knitting.

It was morning, hot, bright sunlight in the window. The Chief of
Yotebber Region stood by his bedside, a tower of a man in white-and-
crimson robes.

"I'm very sorry," Havzhiva said, slowly and thickly because his mouth
was damaged. "It was stupid of me to go out alone. The fault was
entirely mine."

"The villains have been caught and will be tried in a court of justice,"
said the Chief.

"They were young men," Havzhiva said. "My ignorance and folly
caused the incident—"

"They will be punished," the Chief said.

The day nurses always had the holoscreen up and watched the news
and the dramas as they sat with him. They kept the sound down, and
Havzhiva could ignore it. It was a hot afternoon; he was watching faint
clouds move slowly across the sky, when the nurse said, using the formal
address to a person of high status, "Oh, quick—if the gentleman will
look, he can see the punishment of the bad men who attacked him!"

Havzhiva obeyed. He saw a thin human body suspended by the feet,
the arms and hands twitching, the intestines hanging down over the
chest and face. He cried out aloud and hid his face in his arm. "Turn
it off," he said, "turn it off!" He retched and gasped for air. "You are
not people!" he cried in his own language, the dialect of Stse. There

was some coming and going in the room. The noise of a yelling crowd ceased abruptly. He got control of his breath and lay with his eyes shut, repeating one phrase of the Staying Chant over and over until his mind and body began to steady and find a little balance somewhere, not much.

They came with food; he asked them to take it away.

The room was dim, lit only by a night-light somewhere low on the wall and the lights of the city outside the window. The old woman, the night nurse, was there, knitting in the half dark.

"I'm sorry," Havzhiva said at random, knowing he didn't know what he had said to them.

"Oh, Mr. Envoy," the old woman said with a long sigh. "I read about your people. The Hainish people. You don't do things like we do. You don't torture and kill each other. You live in peace. I wonder, I wonder what we seem to you. Like witches, like devils, maybe."

"No," he said, but he swallowed down another wave of nausea.

"When you feel better, when you're stronger, Mr. Envoy, I have a thing I want to speak to you about." Her voice was quiet and full of an absolute, easy authority, which probably could become formal and formidable. He had known people who talked that way all his life.

"I can listen now," he said, but she said, "Not now. Later. You are tired. Would you like me to sing?"

"Yes," he said, and she sat and knitted and sang voicelessly, tunelessly, in a whisper. The names of her gods were in the song: Tual, Kamye. They are not my gods, he thought, but he closed his eyes and slept, safe in the rocking balance.

HER NAME WAS YERON, AND SHE WAS NOT OLD. SHE WAS FORTY-seven. She had been through a thirty-year war and several famines. She had artificial teeth, something Havzhiva had never heard of, and wore eyeglasses with wire frames; body mending was not unknown on Werel, but on Yeowe most people couldn't afford it, she said. She was very thin,

and her hair was thin. She had a proud bearing, but moved stiffly from
an old wound in the left hip. "Everybody, everybody in this world has
a bullet in them, or whipping scars, or a leg blown off, or a dead baby
in their heart," she said. "Now you're one of us, Mr. Envoy. You've been
through the fire."

He was recovering well. There were five or six medical specialists on
his case. The Regional Chief visited every few days and sent officials
daily. The Chief was, Havzhiva realised, grateful. The outrageous attack
on a representative of the Ekumen had given him the excuse and strong
popular support for a strike against the diehard isolationist World Party
led by his rival, another warlord hero of the Liberation. He sent glowing
reports of his victories to the Sub-Envoy's hospital room. The holonews
was all of men in uniforms running, shooting, flyers buzzing over desert
hills. As he walked the halls, gaining strength, Havzhiva saw patients
lying in bed in the wards wired in to the neareal net, "experiencing" the
fighting, from the point of view, of course, of the ones with guns, the
ones with cameras, the ones who shot.

At night the screens were dark, the nets were down, and Yeron came
and sat by him in the dim light from the window.

"You said there was something you had to tell me," he said. The city
night was restless, full of noises, music, voices down in the street below
the window she had opened wide to let in the warm, many-scented air.

"Yes, I did." She put her knitting down. "I am your nurse, Mr. Envoy,
but also a messenger. When I heard you'd been hurt, forgive me, but
I said, 'Praise the Lord Kamye and the Lady of Mercy!' Because I had
not known how to bring my message to you, and now I knew how."
Her quiet voice paused a minute. "I ran this hospital for fifteen years.
During the war. I can still pull a few strings here." Again she paused.
Like her voice, her silences were familiar to him. "I'm a messenger to
the Ekumen," she said, "from the women. Women here. Women all
over Yeowe. We want to make an alliance with you. . . . I know, the

government already did that. Yeowe is a member of the Ekumen of the Worlds. We know that. But what does it mean? To us? It means nothing. Do you know what women are, here, in this world? They are nothing. They are not part of the government. Women made the Liberation. They worked and they died for it just like the men. But they weren't generals, they aren't chiefs. They are nobody. In the villages they are less than nobody, they are work animals, breeding stock. Here it's some better. But not good. I was trained in the Medical School at Besso. I am a doctor, not a nurse. Under the Bosses, I ran this hospital. Now a man runs it. Our men are the owners now. And we're what we always were. Property. I don't think that's what we fought the long war for. Do you, Mr. Envoy? I think what we have is a new liberation to make. We have to finish the job."

After a long silence, Havzhiva asked softly, "Are you organised?"

"Oh, yes. Oh, yes! Just like the old days. We can organise in the dark!" She laughed a little. "But I don't think we can win freedom for ourselves alone by ourselves alone. There has to be a change. The men think they have to be bosses. They have to stop thinking that. Well, one thing we have learned in my lifetime, you don't change a mind with a gun. You kill the boss and you become the boss. We must change that mind. The old slave mind, boss mind. We have got to change it, Mr. Envoy. With your help. The Ekumen's help."

"I'm here to be a link between your people and the Ekumen. But I'll need time," he said. "I need to learn."

"All the time in the world. We know we can't turn the boss mind around in a day or a year. This is a matter of education." She said the word as a sacred word. "It will take a long time. You take your time. If we just know that you will *listen*."

"I will listen," he said.

She drew a long breath, took up her knitting again. Presently she said, "It won't be easy to hear us."

He was tired. The intensity of her talk was more than he could yet handle. He did not know what she meant. A polite silence is the adult way of signifying that one doesn't understand. He said nothing.

She looked at him. "How are we to come to you? You see, that's a problem. I tell you, we are nothing. We can come to you only as your nurse. Your housemaid. The woman who washes your clothes. We don't mix with the chiefs. We aren't on the councils. We wait on table. We don't eat the banquet."

"Tell me—" he hesitated. "Tell me how to start. Ask to see me if you can. Come as you can, as it . . . if it's safe?" He had always been quick to learn his lessons. "I'll listen. I'll do what I can." He would never learn much distrust.

She leaned over and kissed him very gently on the mouth. Her lips were light, dry, soft.

"There," she said, "no chief will give you that."

She took up her knitting again. He was half-asleep when she asked, "Your mother is living, Mr. Havzhiva?"

"All my people are dead."

She made a little soft sound. "Bereft," she said. "And no wife?"

"No."

"We will be your mothers, your sisters, your daughters. Your people. I kissed you for that love that will be between us. You will see."

"THE LIST OF THE PERSONS INVITED TO THE RECEPTION, MR. Yehedarhed," said Doranden, the Chief's chief liaison to the Sub-Envoy.

Havzhiva looked through the list on the hand-screen carefully, ran it past the end, and said, "Where is the rest?"

"I'm so sorry, Mr. Envoy—are there omissions? This is the entire list."

"But these are all men."

In the infinitesimal silence before Doranden replied, Havzhiva felt the balance of his life poised.

"You wish the guests to bring their wives? Of course! If this is the Ekumenical custom, we shall be delighted to invite the ladies!"

There was something lip-smacking in the way Yeowan men said "the ladies," a word which Havzhiva had thought was applied only to women of the owner class on Werel. The balance dipped. "What ladies?" he asked, frowning. "I'm talking about women. Do they have no part in this society?"

He became very nervous as he spoke, for he now knew his ignorance of what constituted danger here. If a walk on a quiet street could be nearly fatal, embarrassing the Chief's liaison might be completely so. Doranden was certainly embarrassed—floored. He opened his mouth and shut it.

"I'm sorry, Mr. Doranden," Havzhiva said, "please pardon my poor efforts at jocosity. Of course I know that women have all kinds of responsible positions in your society. I was merely saying, in a stupidly unfortunate manner, that I should be very glad to have such women and their husbands, as well as the wives of these guests, attend the reception. Unless I am truly making an enormous blunder concerning your customs? I thought you did not segregate the sexes socially, as they do on Werel. Please, if I was wrong, be so kind as to excuse the ignorant foreigner once again."

Loquacity is half of diplomacy, Havzhiva had already decided. The other half is silence.

Doranden availed himself of the latter option, and with a few earnest reassurances got himself away. Havzhiva remained nervous until the following morning, when Doranden reappeared with a revised list containing eleven new names, all female. There was a school principal and a couple of teachers; the rest were marked "retired."

"Splendid, splendid!" said Havzhiva. "May I add one more name?"—Of course, of course, anyone Your Excellency desires—"Dr. Yeron," he said.

Again the infinitesimal silence, the grain of dust dropping on the scales. Doranden knew that name. "Yes," he said.

"Dr. Yeron nursed me, you know, at your excellent hospital. We became friends. An ordinary nurse might not be an appropriate guest among such very distinguished people; but I see there are several other doctors on our list."

"Quite," said Doranden. He seemed bemused. The Chief and his people had become used to patronising the Sub-Envoy, ever so slightly and politely. An invalid, though now well recovered; a victim; a man of peace, ignorant of attack and even of self-defense; a scholar, a foreigner, unworldly in every sense: they saw him as something like that, he knew. Much as they valued him as a symbol and as a means to their ends, they thought him an insignificant man. He agreed with them as to the fact, but not as to the quality, of his insignificance. He knew that what he did might signify. He had just seen it.

"SURELY *YOU* UNDERSTAND THE REASON FOR HAVING A BODY-guard, Envoy," the General said with some impatience.

"This is a dangerous city, General Denkam, yes, I understand that. Dangerous for everyone. I see on the net that gangs of young men, such as those who attacked me, roam the streets quite beyond the control of the police. Every child, every woman needs a bodyguard. I should be distressed to know that the safety which is every citizen's right was my special privilege."

The General blinked but stuck to his guns. "We can't let you get assassinated," he said.

Havzhiva loved the bluntness of Yeowan honesty. "I don't want to be assassinated," he said. "I have a suggestion, sir. There are policewomen, female members of the city police force, are there not? Find me body-guards among them. After all, an armed woman is as dangerous as an armed man, isn't she? And I should like to honor the great part women played in winning Yeowe's freedom, as the Chief said so eloquently in his talk yesterday."

The General departed with a face of cast iron.

Havzhiva did not particularly like his bodyguards. They were hard, tough women, unfriendly, speaking a dialect he could hardly understand. Several of them had children at home, but they refused to talk about their children. They were fiercely efficient. He was well protected. He saw when he went about with these cold-eyed escorts that he began to be looked at differently by the city crowds: with amusement and a kind of fellow-feeling. He heard an old man in the market say, "That fellow has some sense."

EVERYBODY CALLED THE CHIEF THE CHIEF EXCEPT TO HIS face. "Mr. President," Havzhiva said, "the question really isn't one of Ekumenical principles or Hainish customs at all. None of that is or should be of the least weight, the least importance, here on Yeowe. This is your world."

The Chief nodded once, massively.

"Into which," said Havzhiva, by now insuperably loquacious, "immigrants are beginning to come from Werel now, and many, many more will come, as the Werelian ruling class tries to lessen revolutionary pressure by allowing increasing numbers of the underclass to emigrate. You, sir, know far better than I the opportunities and the problems that this great influx of population will cause here in Yotebber. Now of course at least half the immigrants will be female, and I think it worth considering that there is a very considerable difference between Werel and Yeowe in what is called the construction of gender—the roles, the expectations, the behavior, the relationships of men and women. Among the Werelian immigrants most of the decision-makers, the people of authority, will be female. The Council of the Hame is about nine-tenths women, I believe. Their speakers and negotiators are mostly women. These people are coming into a society governed and represented entirely by men. I think there is the possibility of misunderstandings and conflict, unless the situation is carefully considered beforehand. Perhaps the use of some women as representatives—"

"Among slaves on the Old World," the Chief said, "women were chiefs. Among our people, men are chiefs. That is how it is. The slaves of the Old World will be the free men of the New World."

"And the women, Mr. President?"

"A free man's women are free," said the Chief.

"WELL, THEN," YERON SAID, AND SIGHED HER DEEP SIGH. "I guess we have to kick up some dust."

"What dust people are good at," said Dobibe.

"Then we better kick up a whole lot," said Tualyan. "Because no matter what we do, they'll get hysterical. They'll yell and scream about castrating dykes who kill boy babies. If there's five of us singing some damn song, it'll get into the neareals as five hundred of us with machine guns and the end of civilisation on Yeowe. So I say let's go for it. Let's have five thousand women out singing. Let's stop the trains. Lie down on the tracks. Fifty thousand women lying on the tracks all over Yotebber. You think?"

The meeting (of the Yotebber City and Regional Educational Aid Association) was in a schoolroom of one of the city schools. Two of Havzhiva's bodyguards, in plain clothes, waited unobtrusively in the hall. Forty women and Havzhiva were jammed into small chairs attached to blank netscreens.

"Asking for?" Havzhiva said.

"The secret ballot!"

"No job discrimination!"

"Pay for our work!"

"The secret ballot!"

"Child care!"

"The secret ballot!"

"Respect!"

Havzhiva's noter scribbled away madly. The women went on shouting for a while and then settled down to talk again.

One of the bodyguards spoke to Havzhiva as she drove him home. "Sir," she said. "Was those all teachers?"

"Yes," he said. "In a way."

"Be damn," she said. "Different from they used to be."

"YEHEDARHED! WHAT THE HELL ARE YOU DOING DOWN THERE?"

"Ma'am?"

"You were on the news. Along with about a million women lying across railroad tracks and all over flyer pads and draped around the President's Residence. You were talking to women and smiling."

"It was hard not to."

"When the Regional Government begins shooting, will you stop smiling?"

"Yes. Will you back us?"

"How?"

"Words of encouragement to the women of Yotebber from the Ambassador of the Ekumen. Yeowe a model of true freedom for immigrants from the Slave World. Words of praise to the Government of Yotebber—Yotebber a model for all Yeowe of restraint, enlightenment, et cetera."

"Sure. I hope it helps. Is this a revolution, Havzhiva?"

"It is education, ma'am."

THE GATE STOOD OPEN IN ITS MASSIVE FRAME; THERE WERE NO walls.

"In the time of the Colony," the Elder said, "this gate was opened twice in the day: to let the people out to work in the morning, to let the people in from work in the evening. At all other times it was locked and barred." He displayed the great broken lock that hung on the outer face of the gate, the massive bolts rusted in their hasps. His gesture was solemn, measured, like his words, and again Havzhiva admired the dignity these people had kept in degradation, the stateliness they had maintained in, or against, their enslavement. He had begun to appreciate the immense influence of their sacred text, the *Arkamye*, preserved in oral tradition. "This was what we had. This was our belonging," an old man in the city had told him, touching the book which, at sixty-five or seventy, he was learning to read.

Havzhiva himself had begun to read the book in its original language. He read it slowly, trying to understand how this tale of fierce courage and abnegation had for three millennia informed and nourished the minds of people in bondage. Often he heard in its cadences the voices he had heard speak that day.

He was staying for a month in Hayawa Tribal Village, which had been the first slave compound of the Agricultural Plantation Corporation of Yeowe in Yotebber, three hundred fifty years ago. In this immense, remote region of the eastern coast, much of the society and culture of plantation slavery had been preserved. Yeron and other women of the Liberation Movement had told him that to know who the Yeowans were he must know the plantations and the tribes.

He knew that the compounds had for the first century been a domain of men without women and without children. They had developed an internal government, a strict hierarchy of force and favoritism. Power was won by tests and ordeals and kept by a nimble balancing of independence and collusion. When women slaves were brought in at last, they entered this rigid system as the slaves of slaves. By bondsmen as by Bosses, they were used as servants and sexual outlets. Sexual loyalty and partnership continued to be recognized only between men, a nexus of passion, negotiation, status, and tribal politics. During the next centuries the presence of children in the compounds had altered and enriched tribal customs, but the system of male dominance, so entirely advantageous to the slave-owners, had not essentially changed.

"We hope to have your presence at the initiation tomorrow," the Elder said in his grave way, and Havzhiva assured him that nothing could please or honor him more than attendance at a ceremony of such importance. The Elder was sedately but visibly gratified. He was a man over fifty, which meant he had been born a slave and had lived as a boy and man through the years of the Liberation. Havzhiva looked for scars, remembering what Yeron had said, and found them: the Elder was thin, meager, lame, and had no upper teeth; he was marked all through by famine and war. Also he was ritually scarred, four parallel ridges running from neck to elbow over the point of the shoulder like long epaulets, and a dark blue open eye tattooed on his forehead, the sign, in this tribe, of assigned, unalterable chiefdom. A slave chief, a chattel master of chattels, till the walls went down.

The Elder walked on a certain path from the gate to the longhouse, and Havzhiva following him observed that no one else used this path: men, women, children trotted along a wider, parallel road that diverged off to a different entrance to the longhouse. This was the chiefs' way, the narrow way.

That night, while the children to be initiated next day fasted and kept vigil over on the women's side, all the chiefs and elders gathered for a feast. There were inordinate amounts of the heavy food Yeowans were accustomed to, spiced and ornately served, the marsh rice that was the basis of everything fancied up with colorings and herbs; above all there was meat. Women slipped in and out serving ever more elaborate platters, each one with more meat on it—cattle flesh, Boss food, the sure and certain sign of freedom.

Havzhiva had not grown up eating meat, and could count on it giving him diarrhea, but he chewed his way manfully through the stews and steaks, knowing the significance of the food and the meaning of plenty to those who had never had enough.

After huge baskets of fruit finally replaced the platters, the women disappeared and the music began. The tribal chief nodded to his leos, a word meaning "sexual favorite/adopted brother/not heir/not son." The young man, a self-assured, good-natured beauty, smiled; he clapped his long hands very softly once, then began to brush the grey-blue palms in a subtle rhythm. As the table fell silent he sang, but in a whisper.

Instruments of music had been forbidden on most plantations; most Bosses had allowed no singing except the ritual hymns to Tual at the tenthday service. A slave caught wasting Corporation time in singing might have acid poured down his throat. So long as he could work there was no need for him to make noise.

On such plantations the slaves had developed this almost silent music, the touch and brush of palm against palm, a barely voiced, barely varied, long line of melody. The words sung were deliberately broken, distorted, fragmented, so that they seemed meaningless. *Shesh*, the owners had called it, rubbish, and slaves were permitted to "pat hands and sing rubbish" so long as they did it so softly it could not be heard outside the compound walls. Having sung so for three hundred years, they sang so now.

To Havzhiva it was unnerving, almost frightening, as voice after voice joined, always at a whisper, increasing the complexity of the rhythms till the cross-beats nearly, but never quite, joined into a single texture of hushing sibilant sound, threaded by the long-held, quarter-tonal melody sung on syllables that seemed always about to make a word but never did. Caught in it, soon almost lost in it, he kept thinking now—now one of them will raise his voice—now the leos will give a shout, a shout of triumph, letting his voice free!—But he did not. None did. The soft, rushing, waterlike music with its infinitely delicate shifting rhythm went on and on. Bottles of the orange Yote wine passed up and down the table. They drank. They drank freely, at least. They got drunk. Laughter and shouts began to interrupt the music. But they never once sang above a whisper.

They all reeled back to the longhouse on the chiefs' path, embracing, peeing companionably, one or two pausing to vomit here and there. A kind, dark man who had been seated next to Havzhiva now joined him in his bed in his alcove of the longhouse.

Earlier in the evening this man had told him that during the night and day of the initiation heterosexual intercourse was forbidden, as it would change the energies. The initiation would go crooked, and the boys might not become good members of the tribe. Only a witch, of course, would deliberately break the taboo, but many women were witches and would try to seduce a man out of malice. Regular, that is, homosexual, intercourse would encourage the energies, keep the initiation straight, and give the boys strength for their ordeal. Hence every man leaving the banquet would have a partner for the night. Havzhiva was glad he had been assigned to this man, not to one of the chiefs, whom he found daunting, and who might have expected a properly energetic performance. As it was, as well as he could remember in the morning, he and his companion had been too drunk to do much but fall asleep amidst well-intended caresses.

Too much Yote wine left a ringing headache, he knew that already, and his whole skull reconfirmed the knowledge when he woke.

At noon his friend brought him to a place of honor in the plaza, which was filling up with men. Behind them were the men's longhouses, in front of them the ditch that separated the women's side, the inside, from the men's or gate side—still so-called, though the compound walls were gone and the gate alone stood, a monument, towering above the huts and longhouses of the compound and the flat grain-fields that stretched away in all directions, shimmering in the windless, shadowless heat.

From the women's huts, six boys came at a run to the ditch. It was wider than a thirteen-year-old could jump, Havzhiva thought; but two of the boys made it. The other four leapt valiantly, fell short, clambered out, one of them hobbling, having hurt a leg or foot in his fall. Even the two who had made the jump successfully looked exhausted and frightened, and all six were bluish grey from fasting and staying awake. Elders surrounded them and got them standing in line in the plaza, naked and shivering, facing the crowd of all the men of the tribe.

No women at all were visible, over on the women's side.

A catechism began, chiefs and elders barking questions which must evidently be answered without delay, sometimes by one boy, sometimes by all together, depending on the questioner's pointing or sweeping gesture. They were questions of ritual, protocol, and ethics. The boys had been well drilled, delivering their answers in prompt yelps. The one who had lamed himself in the jump suddenly vomited and then fainted, slipping quietly down in a little heap. Nothing was done, and some questions were still pointed to him, followed by a moment of painful silence. After a while the boy moved, sat up, sat a while shuddering, then struggled to his feet and stood with the others. His bluish lips moved in answer to all the questions, though no voice reached the audience.

Havzhiva kept his apparent attention fixed on the ritual, though his mind wandered back a long time, a long way. We teach what we know, he thought, and all our knowledge is local.

After the inquisition came the marking: a single deep cut from the base of the neck over the point of the shoulder and down the outer arm to the elbow, made with a hard, sharp stake of wood dragged gouging through skin and flesh to leave, when it healed, the furrowed scar that proved the man. Slaves would not have been allowed any metal tools inside the gate, Havzhiva reflected, watching steadily as behooved a visitor and guest. After each arm and each boy, the officiating elders stopped to resharpen the stake, rubbing it on a big grooved stone that sat in the plaza. The boys' pale blue lips drew back, baring their white teeth; they writhed, half-fainting, and one of them screamed aloud, silencing himself by clapping his free hand over his mouth. One bit on his thumb till blood flowed from it as well as from his lacerated arms. As each boy's marking was finished the Tribal Chief washed the wounds and smeared some ointment on them. Dazed and wobbling, the boys stood again in line; and now the old men were tender with them, smiling, calling them "tribesman," "hero." Havzhiva drew a long breath of relief.

But now six more children were being brought into the plaza, led across the ditch-bridge by old women. These were girls, decked with anklets and bracelets, otherwise naked. At the sight of them a great cheer went up from the audience of men. Havzhiva was surprised. Women were to be made members of the tribe too? That at least was a good thing, he thought.

Two of the girls were barely adolescent, the others were younger, one of them surely not more than six. They were lined up, their backs to the audience, facing the boys. Behind each of them stood the veiled woman who had led her across the bridge; behind each boy stood one of the naked elders. As Havzhiva watched, unable to turn his eyes or mind from what he saw, the little girls lay down face up on the bare, greyish ground of the plaza. One of them, slow to lie down, was tugged and forced down by the woman behind her. The old men came around the boys, and each one lay down on one of the girls, to a great noise of cheering, jeering, and laughter and a chant of "ha-ah-ha-ah!" from the spectators. The veiled women crouched at the girls' heads. One of them reached out and held down a thin, flailing arm. The elders' bare buttocks pumped, whether in actual coitus or an imitation Havzhiva could not tell. "That's how you do it, watch, watch!" the spectators shouted to the boys, amid jokes and comments and roars of laughter. The elders one by one stood up, each shielding his penis with curious modesty.

When the last had stood up, the boys stepped forward. Each lay down on a girl and pumped his buttocks up and down, though not one of them, Havzhiva saw, had had an erection. The men around him grasped their own penises, shouting, "Here, try mine!" and cheering and chanting until the last boy scrambled to his feet. The girls lay flat, their legs parted, like little dead lizards. There was a slight, terrible movement towards them in the crowd of men. But the old women were hauling the girls to their feet, yanking them up, hurrying them back across the bridge, followed by a wave of howls and jeers from the audience.

"They're drugged, you know," said the kind, dark man who had shared Havzhiva's bed, looking into his face. "The girls. It doesn't hurt them."

"Yes, I see," said Havzhiva, standing still in his place of honor.

"These ones are lucky, privileged to assist initiation. It's important that girls cease to be virgin as soon as possible, you know. Always more than one man must have them, you know. So that they can't make claims—'this is your son,' 'this baby is the chief's son,' you know. That's all witchcraft. A son is chosen. Being a son has nothing to do with bondswomen's cunts. Bondswomen have to be taught that early. But the girls are given drugs now. It's not like the old days, under the Corporations."

"I understand," Havzhiva said. He looked into his friend's face, thinking that his dark skin meant he must have a good deal of owner blood, perhaps indeed was the son of an owner or a Boss. Nobody's son, begotten on a slave woman. A son is chosen. All knowledge is local, all knowledge is partial. In Stse, in the Schools of the Ekumen, in the compounds of Yeowe.

"You still call them bondswomen," he said. His tact, all his feelings were frozen, and he spoke in mere stupid intellectual curiosity.

"No," the dark man said, "no, I'm sorry, the language I learned as a boy—I apologize—"

"Not to me."

Again Havzhiva spoke only and coldly what was in his head. The man winced and was silent, his head bowed.

"Please, my friend, take me to my room now," Havzhiva said, and the dark man gratefully obeyed him.

† † †

HE TALKED SOFTLY INTO HIS NOTER IN HAINISH IN THE DARK. "You can't change anything from outside it. Standing apart, looking down, taking the overview, you see the pattern. What's wrong, what's missing. You want to fix it. But you can't patch it. You have to be in it, weaving it. You have to be part of the weaving." This last phrase was in the dialect of Stse.

FOUR WOMEN SQUATTED ON A PATCH OF GROUND ON THE WOMEN'S side, which had roused his curiosity by its untrodden smoothness: some kind of sacred space, he had thought. He walked towards them. They squatted gracelessly, hunched forward between their knees, with the indifference to their appearance, the carelessness of men's gaze, that he had noticed before on the women's side. Their heads were shaved, their skin chalky and pale. Dust people, dusties, was the old epithet, but to Havzhiva their color was more like clay or ashes. The azure tinge of palms and soles and wherever the skin was fine was almost hidden by the soil they were handling. They had been talking fast and quietly, but went silent as he came near. Two were old, withered up, with knobby, wrinkled knees and feet. Two were young women. They all glanced sidelong from time to time as he squatted down near the edge of the smooth patch of ground.

On it, he saw, they had been spreading dust, colored earth, making some kind of pattern or picture. Following the boundaries between colors he made out a long pale figure a little like a hand or a branch, and a deep curve of earthen red.

Having greeted them, he said nothing more, but simply squatted there. Presently they went back to what they were doing, talking in whispers to one another now and then.

When they stopped working, he said, "Is it sacred?"

The old women looked at him, scowled, and said nothing.

"You can't see it," said the darker of the young women, with a flashing, teasing smile that took Havzhiva by surprise.

"I shouldn't be here, you mean."

"No. You can be here. But you can't see it."

He rose and looked over the earth painting they had made with grey and tan and red and umber dust. The lines and forms were in a definite relationship, rhythmical but puzzling.

"It's not all there," he said.

"This is only a little, little bit of it," said the teasing woman, her dark eyes bright with mockery in her dark face.

"Never all of it at once?"

"No," she said, and the others said, "No," and even the old women smiled.

"Can you tell me what the picture is?"

She did not know the word "picture." She glanced at the others; she pondered, and looked up at him shrewdly.

"We make what we know, here," she said, with a soft gesture over the softly colored design. A warm evening breeze was already blurring the boundaries between the colors.

"They don't know it," said the other young woman, ashen-skinned, in a whisper.

"The men?—They never see it whole?"

"Nobody does. Only us. We have it here." The dark woman did not touch her head but her heart, covering her breasts with her long, work-hardened hands. She smiled again.

The old women stood up; they muttered together, one said something sharply to the young women, a phrase Havzhiva did not understand; and they stumped off.

"They don't approve of your talking of this work to a man," he said.

"A city man," said the dark woman, and laughed. "They think we'll run away."

"Do you want to run away?"

She shrugged. "Where to?"

She rose to her feet in one graceful movement and looked over the earth painting, a seemingly random, abstract pattern of lines and colors, curves and areas.

"Can you see it?" she asked Havzhiva, with that liquid teasing flash of the eyes.

"Maybe someday I can learn to," he said, meeting her gaze.

"You'll have to find a woman to teach you," said the woman the color of ashes.

"WE ARE A FREE PEOPLE NOW," SAID THE YOUNG CHIEF, THE Son and Heir, the Chosen.

"I haven't yet known a free people," Havzhiva said, polite, ambiguous.

"We won our freedom. We made ourselves free. By courage, by sacrifice, by holding fast to the one noble thing. We are a free people." The Chosen was a strong-faced, handsome, intelligent man of forty. Six gouged lines of scarring ran down his upper arms like a rough mantle, and an open blue eye stared between his eyes, unwinking.

"You are free men," Havzhiva said.

There was a silence.

"Men of the cities do not understand our women," the Chosen said. "Our women do not want a man's freedom. It is not for them. A woman holds fast to her baby. That is the noble thing for her. That is how the Lord Kamye made woman, and the Merciful Tual is her example. In other places it may be different. There may be another kind of woman, who does not care for her children. That may be. Here it is as I have said."

Havzhiva nodded, the deep, single nod he had learned from the Yeowans, almost a bow. "That is so," he said.

The Chosen looked gratified.

"I have seen a picture," Havzhiva went on.

The Chosen was impassive; he might or might not know the word. "Lines and colors made with earth on earth may hold knowledge in them. All knowledge is local, all truth is partial," Havzhiva said with an easy, colloquial dignity that he knew was an imitation of his mother, the Heir of the Sun, talking to foreign merchants. "No truth can make another truth untrue. All knowledge is a part of the whole knowledge. A true line, a true color. Once you have seen the larger pattern, you cannot go back to seeing the part as the whole."

The Chosen stood like a grey stone. After a while he said, "If we come to live as they live in the cities, all we know will be lost." Under his dogmatic tone was fear and grief.

"Chosen One," Havzhiva said, "you speak the truth. Much will be lost. I know it. The lesser knowledge must be given to gain the greater. And not once only."

"The men of this tribe will not deny our truth," the Chosen said. His unseeing, unwinking central eye was fixed on the sun that hung in a yellow dust-haze above the endless fields, though his own dark eyes gazed downward at the earth.

His guest looked from that alien face to the fierce, white, small sun that still blazed low above the alien land. "I am sure of that," he said.

WHEN HE WAS FIFTY-FIVE, STABILE YEHEDARHED HAVZHIVA went back to Yotebber for a visit. He had not been there for a long time. His work as Ekumenical Advisor to the Yeowan Ministry of Social Justice had kept him in the north, with frequent trips to the other hemisphere. He had lived for years in the Old Capital with his partner, but often visited the New Capital at the request of a new Ambassador who wanted to draw on his expertise. His partner—they had lived together for eighteen years, but there was no marriage on Yeowe—had a book she was trying to finish, and admitted that she would like to have the apartment to herself for a couple of weeks while she wrote. "Take that trip south you keep mooning about," she said. "I'll fly down as soon as I'm done. I won't tell any damned politicians where you are. Escape! Go, go, go!"

He went. He had never liked flying, though he had had to do a great deal of it, and so he made the long journey by train. They were good, fast trains, terribly crowded, people at every station swarming and rushing and shouting bribes to the conductors, though not trying to ride the roofs of the cars, not at 130 kmh. He had a private room in a through car to Yotebber City. He spent the long hours in silence watching the landscape whirl by, the reclamation projects, the old wastelands, the young forests, the swarming cities, miles of shacks and cabins and cottages and houses and apartment buildings, sprawling Werel-style compounds with connected houses and kitchen gardens and worksheds, factories, huge new plants; and then suddenly the country again, canals and irrigation tanks reflecting the colors of the evening sky, a bare-legged child walking with a great white ox past a field of shadowy grain. The nights were short, a dark, rocking sweetness of sleep.

On the third afternoon he got off the train in Yotebber City Station. No crowds. No chiefs. No bodyguards. He walked through the hot, familiar streets, past the market, through the City Park. A little bravado, there. Gangs, muggers were still about, and he kept his eye alert and his feet on the main pathways. On past the old Tualite temple. He had picked up a white flower that had dropped from a shrub in the park. He set it at the Mother's feet. She smiled, looking cross-eyed at her missing nose. He walked on to the big, rambling new compound where Yeron lived.

She was seventy-four and had retired recently from the hospital where she had taught, practiced, and been an administrator for the last fifteen years. She was little changed from the woman he had first seen sitting by his bedside, only she seemed smaller all over. Her hair was quite gone, and

she wore a glittering kerchief tied round her head. They embraced hard
and kissed, and she stroked him and patted him, smiling irrepressibly.
They had never made love, but there had always been a desire between
them, a yearning to the other, a great comfort in touch. "Look at that,
look at that grey!" she cried, petting his hair, "how beautiful! Come in
and have a glass of wine with me! How is your Araha? When is she coming? You walked right across the city carrying that bag? You're still crazy!"

He gave her the gift he had brought her, a treatise on *Certain Diseases
of Werel-Yeowe* by a team of Ekumenical medical researchers, and she
seized it greedily. For some while she conversed only between plunges
into the table of contents and the chapter on berlot. She poured out the
pale orange wine. They had a second glass. "You look fine, Havzhiva,"
she said, putting the book down and looking at him steadily. Her eyes
had faded to an opaque bluish darkness. "Being a saint agrees with you."

"It's not that bad, Yeron."

"A hero, then. You can't deny that you're a hero."

"No," he said with a laugh. "Knowing what a hero is, I won't deny it."

"Where would we be without you?"

"Just where we are now. . . ." He sighed. "Sometimes I think we're
losing what little we've ever won. This Tualbeda, in Detake Province,
don't underestimate him, Yeron. His speeches are pure misogyny and
anti-immigrant prejudice, and people are eating it up—"

She made a gesture that utterly dismissed the demagogue. "There is
no end to that," she said. "But I knew what you were going to be to us.
Right away. When I heard your name, even. I knew."

"You didn't give me much choice, you know."

"Bah. You chose, man."

"Yes," he said. He savored the wine. "I did." After a while he said,
"Not many people have the choices I had. How to live, whom to live
with, what work to do. Sometimes I think I was able to choose because
I grew up where all choices had been made for me."

"So you rebelled, made your own way," she said, nodding.

He smiled. "I'm no rebel."

"Bah!" she said again. "No rebel? You, in the thick of it, in the heart of our movement all the way?"

"Oh yes," he said. "But not in a rebellious spirit. That had to be your spirit. My job was acceptance. To keep an acceptant spirit. That's what I learned growing up. To accept. Not to change the world. Only to change the soul. So that it can be in the world. Be rightly in the world."

She listened but looked unconvinced. "Sounds like a woman's way of being," she said. "Men generally want to change things to suit."

"Not the men of my people," he said.

She poured them a third glass of wine. "Tell me about your people. I was always afraid to ask. The Hainish are so old! So learned! They know so much history, so many worlds! Us here with our three hundred years of misery and murder and ignorance—you don't know how small you make us feel."

"I think I do," Havzhiva said. After a while he said, "I was born in a town called Stse."

He told her about the pueblo, about the Other Sky people, his father who was his uncle, his mother the Heir of the Sun, the rites, the festivals, the daily gods, the unusual gods; he told her about changing being; he told her about the historian's visit, and how he had changed being again, going to Kathhad.

"All those rules!" Yeron said. "So complicated and unnecessary. Like our tribes. No wonder you ran away."

"All I did was go learn in Kathhad what I wouldn't learn in Stse," he said, smiling. "What the rules are. Ways of needing one another. Human ecology. What have we been doing here, all these years, but trying to find a good set of rules—a pattern that makes sense?" He stood up, stretched his shoulders, and said, "I'm drunk. Come for a walk with me."

They went out into the sunny gardens of the compound and walked slowly along the paths between vegetable plots and flower beds. Yeron nodded to people weeding and hoeing, who looked up and greeted her by name. She held Havzhiva's arm firmly, with pride. He matched his steps to hers.

"When you have to sit still, you want to fly," he said, looking down at her pale, gnarled, delicate hand on his arm. "If you have to fly, you want to sit still. I learned sitting, at home. I learned flying, with the historians. But I still couldn't keep my balance."

"Then you came here," she said.

"Then I came here."

"And learned?"

"How to walk," he said. "How to walk with my people."

A WOMAN'S
LIBERATION

ᴠ. Shomeke

Mʏ ᴅᴇᴀʀ ꜰʀɪᴇɴᴅ ʜᴀꜱ ᴀꜱᴋᴇᴅ ᴍᴇ ᴛᴏ ᴡʀɪᴛᴇ ᴛʜᴇ ꜱᴛᴏʀʏ ᴏꜰ ᴍʏ life, thinking it might be of interest to people of other worlds and times. I am an ordinary woman, but I have lived in years of mighty changes and have been advantaged to know with my very flesh the nature of servitude and the nature of freedom.

I did not learn to read or write until I was a grown woman, which is all the excuse I will make for the faults of my narrative.

I was born a slave on the planet Werel. As a child I was called Shomekes' Radosse Rakam. That is, Property of the Shomeke Family, Granddaughter of Dosse, Granddaughter of Kamye. The Shomeke family owned an estate on the eastern coast of Voe Deo. Dosse was my grandmother. Kamye is the Lord God.

The Shomekes possessed over four hundred assets, mostly used to cultivate the fields of gede, to herd the saltgrass cattle, to work in the mills, and as domestics in the House. The Shomeke family had been great in history. Our Owner was an important man politically, often away in the capital.

Assets took their name from their grandmother because it was the
grandmother that raised the child. The mother worked all day, and
there was no father. Women were always bred to more than one man.
Even if a man knew his child he could not care for it. He might be sold
or traded away at any time. Young men were seldom kept long on the
estates. If they were valuable, they were traded to other estates or sold to
the factories. If they were worthless, they were worked to death.

Women were not often sold. The young ones were kept for work and
breeding, the old ones to raise the young and keep the compound in
order. On some estates women bore a baby a year till they died, but on
ours most had only two or three children. The Shomekes valued women
as workers. They did not want the men always getting at the women. The
grandmothers agreed with them and guarded the young women closely.

I say men, women, children, but you are to understand that we were
not called men, women, children. Only our owners were called so. We
assets or slaves were called bondsmen, bondswomen, and pups or young.
I will use those words, though I have not heard or spoken them for
many years, and never before on this blessed world.

The bondsmen's part of the compound, the gateside, was ruled by
the Bosses, who were men, some relations of the Shomeke family, others hired by them. On the inside the young and the bondswomen lived.
There two cutfrees, castrated bondsmen, were the Bosses in name, but
the grandmothers ruled. Indeed nothing in the compound happened
without the grandmothers' knowledge.

If the grandmothers said an asset was too sick to work, the Bosses
would let that one stay home. Sometimes the grandmothers could save
a bondsman from being sold away, sometimes they could protect a girl
from being bred by more than one man, or could give a delicate girl a
contraceptive. Everybody in the compound obeyed the council of the
grandmothers. But if one of them went too far, the Bosses would have
her flogged or blinded or her hands cut off. When I was a young child,

there lived in our compound a woman we called Great-Grandmother, who had holes for eyes and no tongue. I thought that she was thus because she was so old. I feared that my grandmother Dosse's tongue would wither in her mouth. I told her that. She said, "No. It won't get any shorter, because I don't let it get too long."

I lived in the compound. My mother birthed me there, and was allowed to stay three months to nurse me; then I was weaned to cow's milk, and my mother returned to the House. Her name was Shomekes' Rayowa Yowa. She was light-skinned like most of the assets, but very beautiful, with slender wrists and ankles and delicate features. My grandmother, too, was light, but I was dark, darker than anybody else in the compound.

My mother came to visit, the cutfrees letting her in by their ladder-door. She found me rubbing grey dust on my body. When she scolded me, I told her that I wanted to look like the others.

"Listen, Rakam," she said to me, "they are dust people. They'll never get out of the dust. You're something better. And you will be beauti-ful. Why do you think you're so black?" I had no idea what she meant. "Someday I'll tell you who your father is," she said, as if she were promis-ing me a gift. I knew that the Shomekes' stallion, a prized and valuable animal, serviced mares from other estates. I did not know a father could be human.

That evening I boasted to my grandmother: "I'm beautiful because the black stallion is my father!" Dosse struck me across the head so that I fell down and wept. She said, "Never speak of your father."

I knew there was anger between my mother and my grandmother, but it was a long time before I understood why. Even now I am not sure I understand all that lay between them.

We little pups ran around in the compound. We knew nothing outside the walls. All our world was the bondswomen's huts and the bondsmen's longhouses, the kitchens and kitchen gardens, the bare plaza beaten hard by bare feet. To me, the stockade wall seemed a long way off.

When the field and mill hands went out the gate in the early morning I didn't know where they went. They were just gone. All day long the whole compound belonged to us pups, naked in the summer, mostly naked in the winter too, running around playing with sticks and stones and mud, keeping away from the grandmothers, until we begged them for something to eat or they put us to work weeding the gardens for a while.

In the evening or the early night the workers would come back, trooping in the gate guarded by the Bosses. Some were worn out and grim, others would be cheerful and talking and calling back and forth. The great gate was slammed behind the last of them. Smoke went up from all the cooking stoves. The burning cowdung smelled sweet. People gathered on the porches of the huts and longhouses. Bondsmen and bondswomen lingered at the ditch that divided the gateside from the inside, talking across the ditch. After the meal the freedmen led prayers to Tual's statue, and we lifted our own prayers to Kamye, and then people went to their beds, except for those who lingered to "jump the ditch." Some nights, in the summer, there would be singing, or a dance was allowed. In the winter one of the grandfathers—poor old broken men, not strong people like the grandmothers—would "sing the word." That is what we called reciting the *Arkamye*. Every night, always, some of the people were teaching and others were learning the sacred verses. On winter nights one of these old worthless bondsmen kept alive by the grandmothers' charity would begin to sing the word. Then even the pups would be still to listen to that story.

The friend of my heart was Walsu. She was bigger than I, and was my defender when there were fights and quarrels among the young or when older pups called me "Blackie" and "Bossie." I was small but had a fierce temper. Together, Walsu and I did not get bothered much. Then

Walsu was sent out the gate. Her mother had been bred and was now stuffed big, so that she needed help in the fields to make her quota. Gede must be hand-harvested. Every day as a new section of the bearing stalk comes ripe it has to be picked, and so gede pickers go through the same field over and over for twenty or thirty days, and then move on to a later planting. Walsu went with her mother to help her pick her rows. When her mother fell ill, Walsu took her place, and with help from other hands she kept up her mother's quota. She was then six years old by owner's count, which gave all assets the same birthday, new year's day at the beginning of spring. She might have truly been seven. Her mother remained ill both before birthing and after, and Walsu took her place in the gede field all that time. She never afterward came back to play, only in the evenings to eat and sleep. I saw her then and we could talk. She was proud of her work. I envied her and longed to go through the gate. I followed her to it and looked through it at the world. Now the walls of the compound seemed very close.

I told my grandmother Dosse that I wanted to go to work in the fields. "You're too young."

"I'll be seven at the new year."

"Your mother made me promise not to let you go out."

Next time my mother visited the compound, I said, "Grandmother won't let me go out. I want to go work with Walsu."

"Never," my mother said. "You were born for better than that."

"What for?"

"You'll see."

She smiled at me. I knew she meant the House, where she worked. She had told me often of the wonderful things in the House, things that shone and were colored brightly, things that were thin and delicate, clean things. It was quiet in the House, she said. My mother herself wore a beautiful red scarf, her voice was soft, and her clothing and body were always clean and fresh.

"When will I see?"

I teased her until she said, "All right! I'll ask my lady."

"Ask her what?"

All I knew of my-lady was that she too was delicate and clean, and that my mother belonged to her in some particular way, of which she was proud. I knew my-lady had given my mother the red scarf.

"I'll ask her if you can come begin training at the House."

My mother said "the House" in a way that made me see it as a great sacred place like the place in our prayer: *May I enter in the clear house, in the rooms of peace.*

I was so excited I began to dance and sing, "I'm going to the House, to the House!" My mother slapped me to make me stop and scolded me for being wild. She said, "You are too young! You can't behave! If you get sent away from the House, you can never come back."

I promised to be old enough.

"You must do everything right," Yowa told me. "You must do everything I say when I say it. Never question. Never delay. If my lady sees that you're wild, she'll send you back here. And that will be the end of you forever."

I promised to be tame. I promised to obey at once in everything, and not to speak. The more frightening she made it, the more I desired to see the wonderful, shining House.

When my mother left I did not believe she would speak to my-lady. I was not used to promises being kept. But after some days she returned, and I heard her speaking to my grandmother. Dosse was angry at first, speaking loudly. I crept under the window of the hut to listen. I heard my grandmother weep. I was frightened and amazed. My grandmother was patient with me, always looked after me, and fed me well. It had never entered my mind that there was anything more to it than that, until I heard her crying. Her crying made me cry, as if I were part of her.

"You could let me keep her one more year," she said. "She's just a baby.

I would never let her out the gate." She was pleading, as if she were powerless, not a grandmother. "She is my joy, Yowa!"

"Don't you want her to do well, then?"

"Just a year more. She's too wild for the House."

"She's run wild too long. She'll get sent out to the fields if she stays. A year of that and they won't have her at the House. She'll be dust. Anyhow, there's no use crying about it. I asked my lady, and she's expected. I can't go back without her."

"Yowa, don't let her come to harm," Dosse said very low, as if ashamed to say this to her daughter, and yet with strength in her voice.

"I'm taking her to keep her out of harm," my mother said. Then she called me, and I wiped my tears and came.

It is queer, but I do not remember my first walk through the world outside the compound or my first sight of the House. I suppose I was frightened and kept my eyes down, and everything was so strange to me that I did not understand what I saw. I know it was a number of days before my mother took me to show me to Lady Tazeu. She had to scrub me and train me and make sure I would not disgrace her. I was terrified when at last she took my hand, scolding me in a whisper all the time, and brought me out of the bondswomen's quarters, through halls and doorways of painted wood, into a bright, sunny room with no roof, full of flowers growing in pots.

I had hardly ever seen a flower, only the weeds in the kitchen gardens, and I stared and stared at them. My mother had to jerk my hand to make me look at the woman lying in a chair among the flowers, in clothes soft and brightly colored like the flowers. I could hardly tell them apart. The woman's hair was long and shining, and her skin was shining and black. My mother pushed me, and I did what she had made me practice over and over: I went and knelt down beside the chair and waited, and when the woman put out her long, narrow, soft hand, black above and azure on the palm, I touched my forehead to it.

I was supposed to say "I am your slave Rakam, ma'am," but my voice would not come out.

"What a pretty little thing," she said. "So dark." Her voice changed a little on the last words.

"The Bosses came in . . . that night," Yowa said in a timid, smiling way, looking down as if embarrassed.

"No doubt about that," the woman said. I was able to glance up at her again. She was beautiful. I did not know a person could be so beautiful. I think she saw my wonder. She put out her long, soft hand again and caressed my cheek and neck. "Very, very pretty, Yowa," she said. "You did quite right to bring her here. Has she been bathed?"

She would not have asked that if she had seen me when I first came, filthy and smelling of the cowdung we made our fires with. She knew nothing of the compound at all. She knew nothing beyond the beza, the women's side of the House. She was kept there just as I had been kept in the compound, ignorant of anything outside. She had never smelled cowdung, as I had never seen flowers.

My mother assured her I was clean, and she said, "Then she can come to bed with me tonight. I'd like that. Will you like to come sleep with me, pretty little—" She glanced at my mother, who murmured, "Rakam." Ma'am pursed her lips at the name. "I don't like that," she murmured. "So ugly. Toti. Yes. You can be my new Toti. Bring her this evening, Yowa."

She had had a foxdog called Toti, my mother told me. Her pet had died. I did not know animals ever had names, and so it did not seem odd to me to be given an animal's name, but it did seem strange at first not to be Rakam. I could not think of myself as Toti.

That night my mother bathed me again and oiled my skin with sweet oil and dressed me in a soft gown, softer even than her red scarf. Again she scolded and warned me, but she was excited, too, and pleased with me, as we went to the beza again, through other halls, meeting some other bondswomen on the way, and to the lady's bedroom. It was a wonderful room, hung with mirrors and draperies and paintings. I did not understand what the mirrors were, or the paintings, and was frightened when I saw people in them. Lady Tazeu saw that I was frightened. "Come, little one," she said, making a place for me in her great, wide, soft bed strewn with pillows, "come and cuddle up." I crawled in beside her, and she stroked my hair and skin and held me in her warm, soft arms until I was comfortable and at ease. "There, there, little Toti," she said, and so we slept.

I became the pet of Lady Tazeu Wehoma Shomeke. I slept with her almost every night. Her husband was seldom home and when he was there did not come to her, preferring bondswomen for his pleasure. Sometimes she had my mother or other, younger bondswomen come into her bed, and she sent me away at those times, until I was older, ten or eleven, when she began to keep me and have me join in with them, teaching me how to be pleasured. She was gentle, but she was the mistress in love, and I was her instrument which she played.

I was also trained in household arts and duties. She taught me to sing with her, as I had a true voice. All those years I was never punished and never made to do hard work. I who had been wild in the compound was perfectly obedient in the Great House. I had been rebellious to my grandmother and impatient of her commands, but whatever my lady ordered me to do I gladly did. She held me fast to her by the only kind of love she had to give me. I thought that she was the Merciful Tual come down upon the earth. That is not a way of speaking, that is the truth. I thought she was a higher being, superior to myself.

Perhaps you will say that I could not or should not have had pleasure in being used without my consent by my mistress, and if I did, I should not speak of it, showing even so little good in so great an evil. But I knew nothing of consent or refusal. Those are freedom words.

She had one child, a son, three years older than I. She lived quite alone among us bondswomen. The Wehomas were nobles of the Islands, old-fashioned people whose women did not travel, so she was cut off from her family. The only company she had was when Owner Shomeke brought friends with him from the capital, but those were all men, and she could be with them only at table.

I seldom saw the Owner and only at a distance. I thought he too was a superior being, but a dangerous one.

As for Erod, the Young Owner, we saw him when he came to visit his mother daily or when he went out riding with his tutors. We girls would peep at him and giggle to each other when we were eleven or twelve, because he was a handsome boy, night-black and slender like his mother. I knew that he was afraid of his father, because I had heard him weep when he was with his mother. She would comfort him with candy and caresses, saying, "He'll be gone again soon, my darling," I too felt sorry for Erod, who was like a shadow, soft and harmless. He was sent off to school for a year at fifteen, but his father brought him back before the year was up. Bondsmen told us the Owner had beaten him cruelly and had forbidden him even to ride off the estate.

Bondswomen whom the Owner used told us how brutal he was, showing us where he had bruised and hurt them. They hated him, but my mother would not speak against him. "Who do you think you are?" she said to a girl who was complaining of his use of her. "A lady to be treated like glass?" And when the girl found herself pregnant, stuffed was the word we used, my mother had her sent back to the compound. I did not understand why. I thought Yowa was hard and jealous. Now I think she was also protecting the girl from our lady's jealousy.

I do not know when I understood that I was the Owner's daughter. Because she had kept that secret from our lady, my mother believed it was a secret from all. But the bondswomen all knew it. I do not know what I heard or overheard, but when I saw Erod, I would study him and think that I looked much more like our father than he did, for by then

I knew what a father was. And I wondered that Lady Tazeu did not see it. But she chose to live in ignorance.

During these years I seldom went to the compound. After I had been a halfyear or so at the House, I was eager to go back and see Walsu and my grandmother and show them my fine clothes and clean skin and shining hair; but when I went, the pups I used to play with threw dirt and stones at me and tore my clothes. Walsu was in the fields. I had to hide in my grandmother's hut all day. I never wanted to go back. When my grandmother sent for me, I would go only with my mother and always stayed close by her. The people in the compound, even my grandmother, came to look coarse and foul to me. They were dirty and smelled strongly. They had sores, scars from punishment, lopped fingers, ears, or noses. Their hands and feet were coarse, with deformed nails. I was no longer used to people who looked so. We domestics of the Great House were entirely different from them, I thought. Serving the higher beings, we became like them.

When I was thirteen and fourteen Lady Tazeu still kept me in her bed, making love to me often. But also she had a new pet, the daughter of one of the cooks, a pretty little girl though white as clay. One night she made love to me for a long time in ways that she knew gave me great ecstasy of the body. When I lay exhausted in her arms she whispered "good-bye, good-bye," kissing me all over my face and breasts. I was too spent to wonder at this.

The next morning my lady called in my mother and myself to tell us that she intended to give me to her son for his seventeenth birthday. "I shall miss you terribly, Toti darling," she said, with tears in her eyes. "You have been my joy. But there isn't another girl on the place that I could let Erod have. You are the cleanest, dearest, sweetest of them all. I know you are a virgin," she meant a virgin to men, "and I know my boy will enjoy you. And he'll be kind to her, Yowa," she said earnestly to my mother. My mother bowed and said nothing. There was nothing she could say. And she said nothing to me. It was too late to speak of the secret she had been so proud of.

Lady Tazeu gave me medicine to prevent conception, but my mother, not trusting the medicine, went to my grandmother and brought me contraceptive herbs. I took both faithfully that week.

If a man in the House visited his wife he came to the beza, but if he wanted a bondswoman she was "sent across." So on the night of the Young Owner's birthday I was dressed all in red and led over, for the first time in my life, to the men's side of the House.

My reverence for my lady extended to her son, and I had been taught that owners were superior by nature to us. But he was a boy whom I had known since childhood, and I knew that his blood and mine were half the same. It gave me a strange feeling towards him.

I thought he was shy, afraid of his manhood. Other girls had tried to tempt him and failed. The women had told me what I was to do, how to offer myself and encourage him, and I was ready to do that. I was brought to him in his great bedroom, all of stone carved like lace, with high, thin windows of violet glass. I stood timidly near the door for a while, and he stood near a table covered with papers and screens. He came forward at last, took my hand, and led me to a chair. He made me sit down, and spoke to me standing, which was all improper, and confused my mind.

"Rakam," he said—"that's your name, isn't it?"—I nodded—"Rakam, my mother means only kindness, and you must not think me ungrateful to her, or blind to your beauty. But I will not take a woman who cannot freely offer herself. Intercourse between owner and slave is rape." And he talked on, talking beautifully, as when my lady read aloud from one of her books. I did not understand much, except that I was to come whenever he sent for me and sleep in his bed, but he would never touch me. And I was not to speak of this to anyone. "I am sorry, I am very sorry to ask you to lie," he said, so earnestly that I wondered if it hurt

him to lie. That made him seem more like a god than a human being. If
it hurt to lie, how could you stay alive?

"I will do just as you say, Lord Erod," I said.

So, most nights, his bondsmen came to bring me across. I would sleep
in his great bed, while he worked at the papers on his table. He slept on a
couch beneath the windows. Often he wanted to talk to me, sometimes
for a long time, telling me his ideas. When he was in school in the capital he had become a member of a group of owners who wished to abolish slavery, called The Community. Getting wind of this, his father had
ordered him out of school, sent him home, and forbidden him to leave
the estate. So he too was a prisoner. But he corresponded constantly with
others in The Community through the net, which he knew how to operate without his father's knowledge, or the government's.

His head was so full of ideas he had to speak them. Often Geu and
Ahas, the young bondsmen who had grown up with him, who always
came to fetch me across, stayed with us while he talked to all of us about
slavery and freedom and many other things. Often I was sleepy, but I
did listen, and heard much I did not know how to understand or even
believe. He told us there was an organization among assets, called the
Hame, that worked to steal slaves from the plantations. These slaves
would be brought to members of The Community, who would make
out false papers of ownership and treat them well, renting them to
decent work in the cities. He told us about the cities, and I loved to hear
all that. He told us about Yeowe Colony, saying that there was a revolution there among the slaves.

Of Yeowe I knew nothing. It was a great blue-green star that set after
the sun or rose before it, brighter than the smallest of the moons. It was
a name in an old song they sang in the compound:

> *O, O, Ye-o-we,*
> *Nobody never comes back.*

I had no idea what a revolution was. When Erod told me that it meant that assets on plantations in this place called Yeowe were fighting their owners, I did not understand how assets could do that. From the beginning it was ordained that there should be higher and lower beings, the Lord and the human, the man and the woman, the owner and the owned. All my world was Shomeke Estate and it stood on that one foundation. Who would want to overturn it? Everyone would be crushed in the ruins.

I did not like Erod to call assets slaves, an ugly word that took away our value. I decided in my mind that here on Werel we were assets, and in that other place, Yeowe Colony, there were slaves, worthless bondspeople, intractables. That was why they had been sent there. It made good sense.

By this you know how ignorant I was. Sometimes Lady Tazeu had let us watch shows on the holonet with her, but she watched only dramas, not the reports of events. Of the world beyond the estate I knew nothing but what I learned from Erod, and that I could not understand.

Erod liked us to argue with him. He thought it meant our minds were growing free. Geu was good at it. He would ask questions like, "But if there's no assets, who'll do the work?" Then Erod could answer at length. His eyes shone, his voice was eloquent. I loved him very much when he talked to us. He was beautiful and what he said was beautiful. It was like hearing the old men "singing the word," reciting the *Arkamye*, when I was a little pup in the compound.

I gave the contraceptives my lady gave me every month to girls who needed them. Lady Tazeu had aroused my sexuality and accustomed me to being used sexually. I missed her caresses. But I did not know how to approach any of the bondswomen, and they were afraid to approach me, since I belonged to the Young Owner. Being with Erod often, while he talked I yearned to him in my body. I lay in his bed and dreamed that he came and stooped over me and did with me as my lady used to do. But he never touched me.

Geu also was a handsome young man, clean and well mannered, rather dark-skinned, attractive to me. His eyes were always on me. But he would not approach me, until I told him that Erod did not touch me.

Thus I broke my promise to Erod not to tell anyone; but I did not think myself bound to keep promises, as I did not think myself bound to speak the truth. Honor of that kind was for owners, not for us.

After that, Geu used to tell me when to meet him in the attics of the House. He gave me little pleasure. He would not penetrate me, believing that he must save my virginity for our master. He had me take his penis in my mouth instead. He would turn away in his climax, for the slave's sperm must not defile the master's woman. That is the honor of a slave.

Now you may say in disgust that my story is all of such things, and there is far more to life, even a slave's life, than sex. That is very true. I can say only that it may be in our sexuality that we are most easily enslaved, both men and women. It may be there, even as free men and women, that we find freedom hardest to keep. The politics of the flesh are the roots of power.

I was young, full of health and desire for joy. And even now, even here, when I look back across the years from this world to that, to the compound and the House of Shomeke, I see images like those in a bright dream. I see my grandmother's big, hard hands. I see my mother smiling, the red scarf about her neck. I see my lady's black, silky body among the cushions. I smell the smoke of the cowdung fires, and the perfumes of the beza. I feel the soft, fine clothing on my young body, and my lady's hands and lips. I hear the old men singing the word, and my voice twining with my lady's voice in a love song, and Erod telling us of freedom. His face is illuminated with his vision. Behind him the windows of stone lace and violet glass keep out the night. I do not say I would go back. I would die before I would go back to Shomeke. I would die before I left this free world, my world, to go back to the place of slavery. But whatever I knew in my youth of beauty, of love, and of hope, was there.

And there it was betrayed. All that is built upon that foundation in the end betrays itself.

I was sixteen years old in the year the world changed.

The first change I heard about was of no interest to me except that my lord was excited about it, and so were Geu and Ahas and some of the other young bondsmen. Even my grandmother wanted to hear about it when I visited her. "That Yeowe, that slave world," she said, "they made freedom? They sent away their owners? They opened the gates? My lord, my sweet Lord Kamye, how can that be? Praise his name, praise his marvels!" She rocked back and forth as she squatted in the dust, her arms about her knees. She was an old, shrunken woman now. "Tell me!" she said.

I knew little else to tell her. "All the soldiers came back here," I said. "And those other people, those alemens, they're there on Yeowe. Maybe they're the new owners. That's all somewhere way out there," I said, flipping my hand at the sky.

"What's alemens?" my grandmother asked, but I did not know.

It was all mere words to me.

But when our Owner, Lord Shomeke, came home sick, that I understood. He came on a flyer to our little port. I saw him carried by on a stretcher, the whites showing in his eyes, his black skin mottled grey. He was dying of a sickness that was ravaging the cities. My mother, sitting with Lady Tazeu, saw a politician on the net who said that the alemens had brought the sickness to Werel. He talked so fearsomely that we thought everybody was going to die. When I told Geu about it he snorted. "Aliens, not alemens," he said, "and they've got nothing to do with it. My lord talked with the doctors. It's just a new kind of pusworm."

That dreadful disease was bad enough. We knew that any asset found to be infected with it was slaughtered at once like an animal and the corpse burned on the spot.

They did not slaughter the Owner. The House filled with doctors, and Lady Tazeu spent day and night by her husband's bed. It was a cruel death. It went on and on. Lord Shomeke in his suffering made terrible sounds, screams, howls. One would not believe a man could cry out hour after hour as he did. His flesh ulcerated and fell away, he went mad, but he did not die.

As Lady Tazeu became like a shadow, worn and silent, Erod filled with strength and excitement. Sometimes when we heard his father howling his eyes would shine. He would whisper, "Lady Tual have mercy on him," but he fed on those cries. I knew from Geu and Ahas, who had been brought up with him, how the father had tormented and despised him, and how Erod had vowed to be everything his father was not and to undo all he did.

But it was Lady Tazeu who ended it. One night she sent away the other attendants, as she often did, and sat alone with the dying man. When he began his moaning howl, she took her little sewing knife and cut his throat. Then she cut the veins in her arms across and across, and lay down by him, and so died. My mother was in the next room all night. She said she wondered a little at the silence, but was so weary that she fell asleep; and in the morning she went in and found them lying in their cold blood.

All I wanted to do was weep for my lady, but everything was in confusion. Everything in the sickroom must be burned, the doctors said, and the bodies must be burned without delay. The House was under quarantine, so only the priests of the House could hold the funeral. No one was to leave the estate for twenty days. But several of the doctors themselves left when Erod, who was now Lord Shomeke, told them what he intended to do. I heard some confused word of it from Ahas, but in my grief I paid little heed.

That evening, all the House assets stood outside the Lady's Chapel during the funeral service to hear the songs and prayers within. The Bosses and cutfrees had brought the people from the compound, and they stood behind us. We saw the procession come out, the white biers carried by, the pyres lighted, and the black smoke go up. Long before the smoke ceased rising, the new Lord Shomeke came to us all where we stood.

Erod stood up on the little rise of ground behind the chapel and spoke in a strong voice such as I had never heard from him. Always in the House it had been whispering in the dark. Now it was broad day and a strong voice. He stood there black and straight in his white mourning clothes. He was not yet twenty years old. He said, "Listen, you people: you have been slaves, you will be free. You have been my property, you will own your own lives now. This morning I sent to the Government the Order of Manumission for every asset on the estate, four hundred and eleven men, women, and children. If you will come to my office in the Counting House in the morning, I will give you your papers. Each of you is named in those papers as a free person. You can never be enslaved again. You are free to do as you please from tomorrow on. There will be money for each one of you to begin your new life with. Not what you deserve, not what you have earned in all your work for us, but what I have to give you. I am leaving Shomeke. I will go to the capital, where I will work for the freedom of every slave on Werel. The Freedom Day that came to Yeowe is coming to us, and soon. Any of you who wish to come with me, come! There's work for us all to do!"

I remember all he said. Those are his words as he spoke them. When one does not read and has not had one's mind filled up by the images on the nets, words spoken strike down deep in the mind.

There was such a silence when he stopped speaking as I had never heard.

One of the doctors began talking, protesting to Erod that he must not break the quarantine.

"The evil has been burned away," Erod said, with a great gesture to the black smoke rising. "This has been an evil place, but no more harm will go forth from Shomeke!"

At that a slow sound began among the compound people standing behind us, and it swelled into a great noise of jubilation mixed with wailing, crying, shouting, singing. "Lord Kamye! Lord Kamye!" the men shouted. An old woman came forward: my grandmother. She strode through us House assets as if we were a field of grain. She stopped a good way from Erod. People fell silent to listen to the grandmother. She said, "Lord Master, are you turning us out of our homes?"

"No," he said. "They are yours. The land is yours to use. The profit of the fields is yours. This is your home, and you are free!"

At that the shouts rose up again so loud I cowered down and covered my ears, but I was crying and shouting too, praising Lord Erod and Lord Kamye in one voice with the rest of them.

We danced and sang there in sight of the burning pyres until the sun went down. At last the grandmothers and the cutfrees got the people to go back to the compound, saying they did not have their papers yet. We domestics went straggling back to the House, talking about tomorrow, when we would get our freedom and our money and our land.

All that next day Erod sat in the Counting House and made out the papers for each slave and counted out the same amount of money for each: a hundred kue in cash, and a draft for five hundred kue on the district bank, which could not be drawn for forty days. This was, he explained to each one, to save them from exploitation by the unscrupulous before they knew how best to use their money. He advised them to form a cooperative, to pool their funds, to run the estate democratically.

"Money in the bank, Lord!" an old crippled man came out crying, jig-ging on his twisted legs. "Money in the bank, Lord!"

If they wanted, Erod said over and over, they could save their money and contact the Hame, who would help them buy passage to Yeowe with it.

"*O, O, Ye-o-we,*" somebody began singing, and they changed the words:

> "*Everybody's going to go.*
> *O, O, Ye-o-we,*
> *Everybody's going to go!*"

They sang it all day long. Nothing could change the sadness of it. I want to weep now, remembering that song, that day.

The next morning Erod left. He could not wait to get away from the place of his misery and begin his life in the capital working for free-dom. He did not say good-bye to me. He took Geu and Ahas with him. The doctors and their aides and assets had all left the day before. We watched his flyer go up into the air.

We went back to the House. It was like something dead. There were no owners in it, no masters, no one to tell us what to do.

My mother and I went in to pack up our clothing. We had said little to each other, but felt we could not stay there. We heard other women running through the beza, rummaging in Lady Tazeu's rooms, going through her closets, laughing and screaming with excitement, finding jewelry and valuables. We heard men's voices in the hall: Bosses' voices. Without a word my mother and I took what we had in our hands and went out by a back door, slipped through the hedges of the garden, and ran all the way to the compound.

The great gate of the compound stood wide open.

How can I tell you what that was to us, to see that, to see that gate stand open? How can I tell you?

2. Zeskra

Erod knew nothing about how the estate was run, because the Bosses ran it. He was a prisoner too. He had lived in his screens, his dreams, his visions.

The grandmothers and others in the compound had spent all that night trying to make plans, to draw our people together so they could defend themselves. That morning when my mother and I came, there were bondsmen guarding the compound with weapons made of farm tools. The grandmothers and cutfrees had made an election of a headman, a strong, well-liked field hand. In that way they hoped to keep the young men with them.

By the afternoon that hope was broken. The young men ran wild. They went up to the House to loot it. The Bosses shot them from the windows, killing many; the others fled away. The Bosses stayed holed up in the House, drinking the wine of the Shomekes. Owners of other plantations were flying reinforcements to them. We heard the flyers land, one after another. The bondswomen who had stayed in the House were at their mercy now.

As for us in the compound, the gates were closed again. We had moved the great bars from the outside to the inside, so we thought ourselves safe for the night at least. But in the midnight they came with heavy tractors and pushed down the wall, and a hundred men or more, our Bosses and owners from all the plantations of the region, came swarming in. They were armed with guns. We fought them with farm tools and pieces of wood. One or two of them were hurt or killed. They killed as many of us as they wanted to kill and then began to rape us. It went on all night.

A group of men took all the old women and men and held them and shot them between the eyes, the way they kill cattle. My grandmother was one of them. I do not know what happened to my mother. I did not see any bondsmen living when they took me away in the morning. I saw white papers lying in the blood on the ground. Freedom papers.

Several of us girls and young women still alive were herded into a truck and taken to the port field. There they made us enter a flyer, shoving and using sticks, and we were carried off in the air. I was not then in my right mind. All I know of this is what the others told me later.

We found ourselves in a compound, like our compound in every way. I thought they had brought us back home. They shoved us in by the cutfrees' ladder. It was still morning and the hands were out at work, only the grandmothers and pups and old men in the compound. The grandmothers came to us fierce and scowling. I could not understand at first why they were all strangers. I looked for my grandmother.

They were frightened of us, thinking we must be runaways. Plantation slaves had been running away, the last years, trying to get to the cities. They thought we were intractables and would bring trouble with us. But they helped us clean ourselves, and gave us a place near the cutfrees' tower. There were no huts empty, they said. They told us this was Zeskra Estate. They did not want to hear about what had happened at Shomeke. They did not want us to be there. They did not need our trouble.

We slept there on the ground without shelter. Some of the bondsmen came across the ditch in the night and raped us because there was nothing to prevent them from it, no one to whom we were of any value. We were too weak and sick to fight them. One of us, a girl named Abye, tried to fight. The men beat her insensible. In the morning she could not talk or walk. She was left there when the Bosses came and took us away. Another girl was left behind too, a big farmhand with white scars on her head like parts in her hair. As we were going I looked at her and saw that it was Walsu, who had been my friend. We had not recognised each other. She sat in the dirt, her head bowed down.

Five of us were taken from the compound to the Great House of

Zeskra, to the bondswomen's quarters. There for a while I had a little hope, since I knew how to be a good domestic asset. I did not know then how different Zeskra was from Shomeke. The House at Zeskra was full of people, full of owners and bosses. It was a big family, not a single Lord as at Shomeke but a dozen of them with their retainers and relations and visitors, so there might be thirty or forty men staying on the men's side and as many women in the beza, and a House staff of fifty or more. We were not brought as domestics, but as use-women.

After we were bathed we were left in the use-women's quarters, a big room without any private places. There were ten or more use-women already there. Those of them who liked their work were not glad to see us, thinking of us as rivals; others welcomed us, hoping we might take their places and they might be let to join the domestic staff. But none were very unkind, and some were kind, giving us clothes, for we had been naked all this time, and comforting the youngest of us, Mio, a little compound girl of ten or eleven whose white body was mottled all over with brown-and-blue bruises.

One of them was a tall woman called Sezi-Tual. She looked at me with an ironic face. Something in her made my soul awaken.

"You're not a dusty," she said. "You're as black as old Lord Devil Zeskra himself. You're a Bossbaby, aren't you?"

"No ma'am," I said. "A lord's child. And the Lord's child. My name is Rakam."

"Your Grandfather hasn't treated you too well lately," she said. "Maybe you should pray to the Merciful Lady Tual."

"I don't look for mercy," I said. From then on Sezi-Tual liked me, and I had her protection, which I needed.

We were sent across to the men's side most nights. When there were dinner parties, after the ladies left the dinner room we were brought in to sit on the owners' knees and drink wine with them. Then they would use us there on the couches or take us to their rooms. The men of Zeskra were not cruel. Some liked to rape, but most preferred to think that we desired them and wanted whatever they wanted. Such men could be satisfied, the one kind if we showed fear or submission, the other kind if we showed yielding and delight. But some of their visitors were another kind of man.

There was no law or rule against damaging or killing a use-woman. Her owner might not like it, but in his pride he could not say so: he was supposed to have so many assets that the loss of one or another did not matter at all. So some men whose pleasure lay in torture came to hospitable estates like Zeskra for their pleasure. Sezi-Tual, a favorite of the Old Lord, could and did protest to him, and such guests were not invited back. But while I was there, Mio, the little girl who had come with us from Shomeke, was murdered by a guest. He tied her down to the bed. He made the knot across her neck so tight that while he used her she strangled to death.

I will say no more of these things. I have told what I must tell. There are truths that are not useful. All knowledge is local, my friend has said. Is it true, where is it true, that that child had to die in that way? Is it true, where is it true, that she did not have to die in that way?

I was often used by Lord Yaseo, a middle-aged man, who liked my dark skin, calling me "My Lady." Also he called me "Rebel," because what had happened at Shomeke they called a rebellion of the slaves. Nights when he did not send for me I served as a common-girl.

After I had been at Zeskra two years Sezi-Tual came to me one morning early. I had come back late from Lord Yaseo's bed. Not many others were there, for there had been a drinking party the night before, and all the common-girls had been sent for. Sezi-Tual woke me. She had strange hair, curly, in a bush. I remember her face above me, that hair curling out all about it. "Rakam," she whispered, "one of the visitor's assets spoke to me last night. He gave me this. He said his name is Suhame."

"Suhame," I repeated. I was sleepy. I looked at what she was holding out to me: some dirty crumpled paper. "I can't read!" I said, yawning, impatient.

But I looked at it and knew it. I knew what it said. It was the freedom paper. It was my freedom paper. I had watched Lord Erod write my name on it. Each time he wrote a name he had spoken it aloud so that we would know what he was writing. I remembered the big flourish of the first letter of both my names: Radosse Rakam. I took the paper in my hand, and my hand was shaking. "Where did you get this?" I whispered.

"Better ask this Suhame," she said. Now I heard what that name meant: "from the Hame." It was a password name. She knew that too. She was watching me, and she bent down suddenly and leaned her forehead against mine, her breath catching in her throat. "If I can, I'll help," she whispered.

I met with "Suhame" in one of the pantries. As soon as I saw him I knew him: Ahas, who had been Lord Erod's favorite along with Geu. A slight, silent young man with dusty skin, he had never been much in my mind. He had watchful eyes, and I had thought when Geu and I spoke that he looked at us with ill will. Now he looked at me with a strange face, still watchful, yet blank.

"Why are you here with that Lord Boeba?" I said. "Aren't you free?"

"I am as free as you are," he said.

I did not understand him, then.

"Didn't Lord Erod protect even you?" I asked.

"Yes. I am a free man." His face began to come alive, losing that dead blankness it had when he first saw me. "Lady Boeba's a member of The Community. I work with the Hame. I've been trying to find people from Shomeke. We heard several of the women were here. Are there others still alive, Rakam?"

His voice was soft, and when he said my name my breath caught and my throat swelled. I said his name and went to him, holding him. "Ratual, Ramayo, Keo are still here," I said. He held me gently. "Walsu is in the compound," I said, "if she's still alive." I wept. I had not wept since Mio's death. He too was in tears.

We talked, then and later. He explained to me that we were indeed, by law, free, but that law meant nothing on the Estates. The government would not interfere between owners and those they claimed as their assets. If we claimed our rights, the Zeskras would probably kill us, since they considered us stolen goods and did not want to be shamed. We must run away or be stolen away, and get to the city, the capital, before we could have any safety at all.

We had to be sure that none of the Zeskra assets would betray us out of jealousy or to gain favor. Sezi-Tual was the only one I trusted entirely.

Ahas arranged our escape with Sezi-Tual's help. I pleaded once with her to join us, but she thought that since she had no papers she would have to live always in hiding, and that would be worse than her life at Zeskra.

"You could go to Yeowe," I said.

She laughed. "All I know about Yeowe is nobody ever came back. Why run from one hell to the next one?"

Ratual chose not to come with us; she was a favorite of one of the young lords and content to remain so. Ramayo, the oldest of us from Shomeke, and Keo, who was now about fifteen, wanted to come. Sezi-Tual went down to the compound and found that Walsu was alive, working as a field hand. Arranging her escape was far more difficult than ours. There was no escape from a compound. She could get away only in daylight, in the fields, under the overseer's and the Boss's eyes. It was difficult even to talk to her, for the grandmothers were distrustful. But Sezi-Tual managed it, and Walsu told her she would do whatever she must do "to see her paper again."

Lady Boeba's flyer waited for us at the edge of a great gede field that had just been harvested. It was late summer. Ramayo, Keo, and I walked away from the House separately at different times of the morning. Nobody watched over us closely, as there was nowhere for us to go. Zeskra lies among other great estates, where a runaway slave would find no friends for hundreds of miles. One by one, taking different ways, we came through the fields and woods, crouching and hiding all the way to the flyer where Ahas waited for us. My heart beat and beat so I could not breathe. There we waited for Walsu.

"There!" said Keo, perched up on the wing of the flyer. She pointed across the wide field of stubble.

Walsu came running from the strip of trees on the far side of the field. She ran heavily, steadily, not as if she were afraid. But all at once she halted. She turned. We did not know why for a moment. Then we saw two men break from the shadow of the trees in pursuit of her.

She did not run from them, leading them towards us. She ran back at them. She leapt at them like a hunting cat. As she made that leap, one of them fired a gun. She bore one man down with her, falling. The other fired again and again. "In," Ahas said, "now." We scrambled into the flyer and it rose into the air, seemingly all in one instant, the same instant in which Walsu made that great leap, she too rising into the air, into her death, into her freedom.

3. The City

I HAD FOLDED UP MY FREEDOM PAPER INTO A TINY PACKET. I carried it in my hand all the time we were in the flyer and while we landed and went in a public car through the city streets. When Ahas found what I was clutching, he said I need not worry about it. Our manumission was on record in the Government Office and would be honored, here in the City. We were free people, he said. We were gareots, that is, owners who have no assets. "Just like Lord Erod," he said. That meant nothing to me. There was too much to learn. I kept hold of my freedom paper until I had a place to keep it safe. I have it still.

We walked a little way in the streets and then Ahas led us into one of the huge houses that stood side by side on the pavement. He called it a compound, but we thought it must be an owners' house. There a middle-aged woman welcomed us. She was pale-skinned, but talked and behaved like an owner, so that I did not know what she was. She said she was Ress, a rentswoman and an elderwoman of the house.

Rentspeople were assets rented out by their owners to a company. If they were hired by a big company, they lived in the company compounds, but there were many, many rentspeople in the City who worked for small companies or businesses they managed themselves, and they occupied buildings run for profit, called open compounds. In such places the occupants must keep curfew, the doors being locked at night, but that was all; they were self-governed. This was such an open compound. It was supported by The Community. Some of the occupants were rentspeople, but many were like us, gareots who had been slaves. Over a hundred people lived there in forty apartments. It was supervised by several women, whom I would have called grandmothers, but here they were called elderwomen.

On the estates deep in the country, deep in the past, where the life was protected by miles of land and by the custom of centuries and by determined ignorance, any asset was absolutely at the mercy of any owner. From there we had come into this great crowd of two million people where nothing and nobody was protected from chance or change, where we had to learn as fast as we could how to stay alive, but where our life was in our own hands.

I had never seen a street. I could not read a word. I had much to learn.

Ress made that clear at once. She was a City woman, quick-thinking and quick-talking, impatient, aggressive, sensitive. I could not like or understand her for a long time. She made me feel stupid, slow, a clod. Often I was angry at her.

There was anger in me now. I had not felt anger while I lived at Zeskra. I could not. It would have eaten me. Here there was room for it, but I found no use for it. I lived with it in silence. Keo and Ramayo had a big room together, I had a small one next to theirs. I had never had a room to myself. At first I felt lonely in it and as if ashamed, but soon I came to like it. The first thing I did freely, as a free woman, was to shut my door.

Nights, I would shut my door and study. Days, we had work training in the morning, classes in the afternoon: reading and writing, arithmetic, history. My work training was in a small shop which made boxes of paper and thin wood to hold cosmetics, candies, jewelry, and such things. I was trained in all the different steps and crafts of making and ornamenting the boxes, for that is how most work was done in the City, by artisans who knew all their trade. The shop was owned by a member of The Community. The older workers were rentspeople. When my training was finished I too would be paid wages.

Till then Lord Erod supported me as well as Keo and Ramayo and some men from Shomeke compound, who lived in a different house. Erod never came to the house. I think he did not want to see any of the people he had so disastrously freed. Ahas and Geu said he had sold most of the land at Shomeke and used the money for The Community and to make his way in politics, as there was now a Radical Party which favored emancipation.

Geu came a few times to see me. He had become a City man, dapper and knowing. I felt when he looked at me he was thinking I had been a use-woman at Zeskra, and I did not like to see him.

Ahas, whom I had never thought about in the old days, I now admired, knowing him brave, resolute, and kind. It was he who had looked for us, found us, rescued us. Owners had paid the money but

Ahas had done it. He came often to see us. He was the only link that
had not broken between me and my childhood.

And he came as a friend, a companion, never driving me back into
my slave body. I was angry now at every man who looked at me as men
look at women. I was angry at women who looked at me seeing me
sexually. To Lady Tazeu all I had been was my body. At Zeskra that
was all I had been. Even to Erod who would not touch me that was all
I had been. Flesh to touch or not to touch, as they pleased. To use or
not to use, as they chose. I hated the sexual parts of myself, my genitals
and breasts and the swell of my hips and belly. Ever since I was a child,
I had been dressed in soft clothing made to display all that sexuality of
a woman's body. When I began to be paid and could buy or make my
own clothing, I dressed in hard, heavy cloth. What I liked of myself was
my hands, clever at their work, and my head, not clever at learning, but
still learning, no matter how long it took.

What I loved to learn was history. I had grown up without any history. There was nothing at Shomeke or Zeskra but the way things were.
Nobody knew anything about any time when things had been different.
Nobody knew there was any place where things might be different. We
were enslaved by the present time.

Erod had talked of change, indeed, but the owners were going to
make the change. We were to be changed, we were to be freed, just as
we had been owned. In history I saw that any freedom has been made,
not given.

The first book I read by myself was a history of Yeowe, written very
simply. It told about the days of the Colony, of the Four Corporations,
of the terrible first century when the ships carried slave men to Yeowe
and precious ores back. Slave men were so cheap then they worked them
to death in a few years in the mines, bringing in new shipments continually. *O, O, Yeowe, nobody never comes back.* Then the Corporations
began to send women slaves to work and breed, and over the years the

assets spilled out of the compounds and made cities—whole great cities like this one I was living in. But not run by the owners or Bosses. Run by the assets, the way this house was run by us. On Yeowe the assets had belonged to the Corporations. They could rent their freedom by paying the Corporation a part of what they earned, the way sharecropper assets paid their owners in parts of Voe Deo. On Yeowe they called those assets freedpeople. Not free people, but freedpeople. And then, this history I was reading said, they began to think, why aren't we free people? So they made the revolution, the Liberation. It began on a plantation called Nadami, and spread from there. Thirty years they fought for their freedom. And just three years ago they had won the war, they had driven the Corporations, the owners, the bosses, off their world. They had danced and sung in the streets, freedom, freedom! This book I was reading (slowly, but reading it) had been printed there—there on Yeowe, the Free World. The Aliens had brought it to Werel. To me it was a sacred book.

I asked Ahas what it was like now on Yeowe, and he said they were making their government, writing a perfect Constitution to make all men equal under the Law.

On the net, on the news, they said they were fighting each other on Yeowe, there was no government at all, people were starving, savage tribesmen in the countryside and youth gangs in the cities running amuck, law and order broken down. Corruption, ignorance, a doomed attempt, a dying world, they said.

Ahas said that the Government of Voe Deo, which had fought and lost the war against Yeowe, now was afraid of a Liberation on Werel. "Don't believe any news," he counseled me. "Especially don't believe the neareals. Don't ever go into them. They're just as much lies as the rest, but if you feel and see a thing, you will believe it. And they know that. They don't need guns if they own our minds." The owners had no reporters, no cameras on Yeowe, he said; they invented their "news," using actors. Only some of the Aliens of the Ekumen were allowed on Yeowe, and the Yeowans were debating whether they should send them away, keeping the world they had won for themselves alone.

"But then what about us?" I said, for I had begun dreaming of going there, going to the Free World, when the Hame could charter ships and send people.

"Some of them say assets can come. Others say they can't feed so many, and would be overwhelmed. They're debating it democratically. It will be decided in the first Yeowan elections, soon." Ahas was dreaming of going there too. We talked together of our dream the way lovers talk of their love.

But there were no ships going to Yeowe now. The Hame could not act openly and The Community was forbidden to act for them. The Ekumen had offered transportation on their own ships to anyone who wanted to go, but the government of Voe Deo refused to let them use any spaceport for that purpose. They could carry only their own people. No Werelian was to leave Werel.

It had been only forty years since Werel had at last allowed the Aliens to land and maintain diplomatic relations. As I went on reading history I began to understand a little of the nature of the dominant people of Werel. The black-skinned race that conquered all the other peoples of the Great Continent, and finally all the world, those who call themselves the owners, have lived in the belief that there is only one way to be. They have believed they are what people should be, do as people should do, and know all the truth that is known. All the other peoples of Werel, even when they resisted them, imitated them, trying to become them, and so became their property. When a people came out of the sky looking differently, doing differently, knowing differently, and would not let themselves be conquered or enslaved, the owner race wanted nothing to do with them. It took them four hundred years to admit that they had equals.

I was in the crowd at a rally of the Radical Party, at which Erod spoke, as beautifully as ever. I noticed a woman beside me in the crowd listening. Her skin was a curious orange-brown, like the rind of a pini, and the whites showed in the corners of her eyes. I thought she was sick—I thought of the pusworm, how Lord Shomeke's skin had changed and his eyes had shown their whites. I shuddered and drew away. She glanced at me, smiling a little, and returned her attention to the speaker. Her hair curled in a bush or cloud, like Sezi-Tual's. Her clothing was of a delicate cloth, a strange fashion. It came upon me very slowly what she was, that she had come here from a world unimaginably far. And the wonder of it was that for all her strange skin and eyes and hair and mind, she was human, as I am human: I had no doubt of that. I felt it. For a moment it disturbed me deeply. Then it ceased to trouble me and I felt a great curiosity, almost a yearning, a drawing to her. I wished to know her, to know what she knew.

In me the owner's soul was struggling with the free soul. So it will do all my life.

Keo and Ramayo stopped going to school after they had learned to read and write and use the calculator, but I kept on. When there were no more classes to take from the school the Hame kept, the teachers helped me find classes in the net. Though the government controlled such courses, there were fine teachers and groups from all over the world, talking about literature and history and the sciences and arts. Always I wanted more history.

Ress, who was a member of the Hame, first took me to the Library of Voe Deo. As it was open only to owners, it was not censored by the government. Freed assets, if they were light-skinned, were kept out by the librarians on one pretext or another. I was dark-skinned, and had learned here in the City to carry myself with an indifferent pride that spared one many insults and offenses. Ress told me to stride in as if I owned the place. I did so, and was given all privileges without question.

So I began to read freely, to read any book I wanted in that great library, every book in it if I could. That was my joy, that reading. That was the heart of my freedom.

Beyond my work at the boxmaker's, which was well paid, pleasant, and among pleasant companions, and my learning and reading, there was not much to my life. I did not want more. I was lonely, but felt that loneliness was no high price to pay for what I wanted.

Ress, whom I had disliked, was a friend to me. I went with her to meetings of the Hame, and also to entertainments that I would have known nothing about without her guidance. "Come on, Bumpkin," she would say. "Got to educate the plantation pup." And she would take me to the makil theater, or to asset dance halls where the music was good. She always wanted to dance. I let her teach me, but was not very happy dancing. One night as we were dancing the "slow-go" her hands began pressing me to her, and looking in her face I saw the mask of sexual desire on it, soft and blank. I broke away. "I don't want to dance," I said.

We walked home. She came up to my room with me, and at my door she tried to hold and kiss me. I was sick with anger. "I don't want that!" I said.

"I'm sorry, Rakam," she said, more gently than I had ever heard her speak. "I know how you must feel. But you've got to get over that, you've got to have your own life. I'm not a man, and I do want you."

I broke in—"A woman used me before a man ever did. Did you ask me if I wanted you? I will never be used again!"

That rage and spite came bursting out of me like poison from an infection. If she had tried to touch me again, I would have hurt her. I slammed my door in her face. I went trembling to my desk, sat down, and began to read the book that was open on it.

Next day we were both ashamed and stiff. But Ress had patience under her City quickness and roughness. She did not try to make love to me again, but she got me to trust her and talk to her as I could not talk to anybody else. She listened intently and told me what she thought. She said, "Bumpkin, you have it all wrong. No wonder. How could you have got it right? You think sex is something that gets done to you. It's not. It's something you do. With somebody else. Not to them. You never had any sex. All you ever knew was rape."

"Lord Erod told me all that a long time ago," I said. I was bitter. "I don't care what it's called. I had enough of it. For the rest of my life. And I'm glad to be without it."

Ress made a face. "At twenty-two?" she said. "Maybe for a while. If you're happy, then fine. But think about what I said. It's a big part of life to just cut out."

"If I have to have sex, I can pleasure myself," I said, not caring if I hurt her. "Love has nothing to do with it."

"That's where you're wrong," she said, but I did not listen. I would learn from teachers and books which I chose for myself, but I would not take advice I had not asked for. I refused to be told what to do or what to think. If I was free, I would be free by myself. I was like a baby when it first stands up.

Ahas had been giving me advice too. He said it was foolish to pursue education so far. "There's nothing useful you can do with so much book learning," he said. "It's self-indulgent. We need leaders and members with practical skills."

"We need teachers!"

"Yes," he said, "but you knew enough to teach a year ago. What's the good of ancient history, facts about alien worlds? We have a revolution to make!"

I did not stop my reading, but I felt guilty. I took a class at the Hame school teaching illiterate assets and freedpeople to read and write, as I myself had been taught only three years before. It was hard work. Reading is hard for a grown person to learn, tired, at night, after work all day. It is much easier to let the net take one's mind over.

I kept arguing with Ahas in my mind, and one day I said to him, "Is there a Library on Yeowe?"

"I don't know."

"You know there isn't. The Corporations didn't leave any libraries there. They didn't have any. They were ignorant people who knew nothing but profit. Knowledge is a good in itself. I keep on learning so that I can bring my knowledge to Yeowe. If I could, I'd bring them the whole Library!"

He stared. "What owners thought, what owners did—that's all their books are about. They don't need that on Yeowe."

"Yes they do," I said, certain he was wrong, though again I could not say why.

At the school they soon called on me to teach history, one of the teachers having left. These classes went well. I worked hard preparing them. Presently I was asked to speak to a study group of advanced students, and that, too, went well. People were interested in the ideas I drew from history and the comparisons I had learned to make of our world with other worlds. I had been studying the way various peoples bring up their children, who takes the responsibility for them and how that responsibility is understood, since this seemed to me a place where a people frees or enslaves itself.

To one of these talks a man from the Embassy of the Ekumen came. I was frightened when I saw the alien face in my audience. I was worse frightened when I recognised him. He had taught the first course in Ekumenical History that I had taken in the net. I had listened to it devotedly though I never participated in the discussion. What I learned had had a great influence on me. I thought he would find me presumptuous for talking of things he truly knew. I stammered on through my lecture, trying not to see his white-cornered eyes.

He came up to me afterwards, introduced himself politely, complimented my talk, and asked if I had read such-and-such a book. He engaged me so deftly and kindly in conversation that I had to like and trust him. And he soon earned my trust. I needed his guidance, for much foolishness has been written and spoken, even by wise people, about the balance of power between men and women, on which depend the lives of children and the value of their education. He knew useful books to read, from which I could go on by myself.

His name was Esdardon Aya. He worked in some high position, I was not sure what, at the Embassy. He had been born on Hain, the Old World, humanity's first home, from which all our ancestors came.

Sometimes I thought how strange it was that I knew about such things, such vast and ancient matters, I who had not known anything outside the compound walls till I was six, who had not known the name of the country I lived in till I was eighteen! When I was new to the City someone had spoken of "Voe Deo," and I had asked, "Where is that?" They had all stared at me. A woman, a hard-voiced old City rentswoman, had said, "Here, Dusty. Right here's Voe Deo. Your country and mine!"

I told Esdardon Aya that. He did not laugh. "A country, a people," he said. "Those are strange and very difficult ideas."

"My country was slavery," I said, and he nodded.

By now I seldom saw Ahas. I missed his kind friendship, but it had all turned to scolding. "You're puffed up, publishing, talking to audiences all the time," he said. "You're putting yourself before our cause."

I said, "But I talk to people in the Hame, I write about things we need to know. Everything I do is for freedom."

"The Community is not pleased with that pamphlet of yours," he said, in a serious, counseling way, as if telling me a secret I needed to know. "I've been asked to tell you to submit your writings to the committee before you publish again. That press is run by hotheads. The Hame is causing a good deal of trouble to our candidates."

"Our candidates!" I said in a rage. "No owner is my candidate! Are you still taking orders from the Young Owner?"

That stung him. He said, "If you put yourself first, if you won't cooperate, you bring danger on us all."

"I don't put myself first—politicians and capitalists do that. I put freedom first. Why can't you cooperate with me? It goes two ways, Ahas!"

He left angry, and left me angry.

I think he missed my dependence on him. Perhaps he was jealous, too, of my independence, for he did remain Lord Erod's man. His was a loyal heart. Our disagreement gave us both much bitter pain. I wish I knew what became of him in the troubled times that followed.

There was truth in his accusation. I had found that I had the gift in speaking and writing of moving people's minds and hearts. Nobody told me that such a gift is as dangerous as it is strong. Ahas said I was putting myself first, but I knew I was not doing that. I was wholly in the service of the truth and of liberty. No one told me that the end cannot purify the means, since only the Lord Kamye knows what the end may be. My grandmother could have told me that. The *Arkamye* would have reminded me of it, but I did not often read in it, and in the City there were no old men singing the word, evenings. If there had been, I would not have heard them over the sound of my beautiful voice speaking the beautiful truth.

I believe I did no harm, except as we all did, in bringing it to the attention of the rulers of Voe Deo that the Hame was growing bolder and the Radical Party was growing stronger, and that they must move against us.

The first sign was a divisive one. In the open compounds, as well as the men's side and the women's side there were several apartments for couples. This was a radical thing. Any kind of marriage between assets was illegal. They were allowed to live in pairs only by their owners' indulgence. Assets' only legitimate loyalty was to their owner. The child did not belong to the mother, but to the owner. But since gareots were living in the same place as owned assets, these apartments for couples had been tolerated or ignored. Now suddenly the law was invoked, asset couples were arrested, fined if they were wage earners, separated, and sent to company-run compound houses. Ress and the other elderwomen who ran our house were fined and warned that if "immoral arrangements" were discovered again, they would be held responsible and sent to the labor camps. Two little children of one of the couples were not on the government's list and so were left, abandoned, when their parents were taken off. Keo and Ramayo took them in. They became wards of the women's side, as orphans in the compounds always did.

There were fierce debates about this in meetings of the Hame and The Community. Some said the right of assets to live together and to bring up their children was a cause the Radical Party should support. It was not directly threatening to ownership, and might appeal to the natural instincts of many owners, especially the women, who could not vote but who were valuable allies. Others said that private affections must be overridden by loyalty to the cause of liberty, and that any personal issue must take second place to the great issue of emancipation. Lord Erod spoke thus at a meeting. I rose to answer him. I said that there was no freedom without sexual freedom, and that until women were allowed and men were willing to take responsibility for their children, no woman, whether owner or asset, would be free.

"Men must bear the responsibility for the public side of life, the greater world the child will enter; women, for the domestic side of life, the moral and physical upbringing of the child. This is a division enjoined by God and Nature," Erod answered.

"Then will emancipation for a woman mean she's free to enter the beza, be locked in on the women's side?"

"Of course not," he began, but I broke in again, fearing his golden tongue—"Then what is freedom for a woman? Is it different from freedom for a man? Or is a free person free?"

The moderator was angrily thumping his staff, but some other asset women took up my question. "When will the Radical Party speak for us?" they said, and one elderwoman cried, "Where are your women, you owners who want to abolish slavery? Why aren't they here? Don't you let them out of the beza?"

The moderator pounded and finally got order restored. I was half-triumphant and half-dismayed. I saw Erod and also some of the people from the Hame now looking at me as an open troublemaker. And indeed my words had divided us. But were we not already divided?

A group of us women went home talking through the streets, talking aloud. These were my streets now, with their traffic and lights and dangers and life. I was a City woman, a free woman. That night I was an owner. I owned the City. I owned the future.

The arguments went on. I was asked to speak at many places. As I was leaving one such meeting, the Hainishman Esdardon Aya came to me and said in a casual way, as if discussing my speech, "Rakam, you're in danger of arrest."

I did not understand. He walked along beside me away from the others and went on: "A rumor has come to my attention at the Embassy. . . . The government of Voe Deo is about to change the status of manumitted assets. You're no longer to be considered gareots. You must have an owner-sponsor."

This was bad news, but after thinking it over I said, "I think I can find an owner to sponsor me. Lord Boeba, maybe."

"The owner-sponsor will have to be approved by the government. . . . This will tend to weaken The Community both through the asset and the owner members. It's very clever, in its way," said Esdardon Aya.

"What happens to us if we don't find an approved sponsor?"

"You'll be considered runaways."

That meant death, the labor camps, or auction.

"O Lord Kamye," I said, and took Esdardon Aya's arm, because a curtain of dark had fallen across my eyes.

We had walked some way along the street. When I could see again I saw the street, the high houses of the City, the shining lights I had thought were mine.

"I have some friends," said the Hainishman, walking on with me, "who are planning a trip to the Kingdom of Bambur."

After a while I said, "What would I do there?"

"A ship to Yeowe leaves from there."

"To Yeowe," I said.

"So I hear," he said, as if we were talking about a streetcar line. "In a few years, I expect Voe Deo will begin offering rides to Yeowe. Exporting intractables, troublemakers, members of the Hame. But that will involve recognising Yeowe as a nation state, which they haven't brought themselves to do yet. They are, however, permitting some semilegitimate trade arrangements by their client states. . . . A couple of years ago, the King of Bambur bought one of the old Corporation ships, a genuine old Colony Trader. The King thought he'd like to visit the moons of Werel. But he found the moons boring. So he rented the ship to a consortium of scholars from the University of Bambur and businessmen from his capital. Some manufacturers in Bambur carry on a little trade with Yeowe in it, and some scientists at the university make scientific expeditions in it at the same time. Of course each trip is very expensive, so they carry as many scientists as they can whenever they go."

I heard all this not hearing it, yet understanding it.

"So far," he said, "they've gotten away with it."

He always sounded quiet, a little amused, yet not superior.

"Does The Community know about this ship?" I asked.

"Some members do, I believe. And people in the Hame. But it's very dangerous to know about. If Voe Deo were to find out that a client state was exporting valuable property . . . In fact, we believe they may have some suspicions. So this is a decision that can't be made lightly. It is both dangerous and irrevocable. Because of that danger, I hesitated to speak of it to you. I hesitated so long that you must make it very quickly. In fact, tonight, Rakam."

I looked from the lights of the City up to the sky they hid. "I'll go," I said. I thought of Walsu.

"Good," he said. At the next corner he changed the direction we had been walking, away from my house, towards the Embassy of the Ekumen.

I never wondered why he did this for me. He was a secret man, a man of secret power, but he always spoke truth, and I think he followed his own heart when he could.

As we entered the Embassy grounds, a great park softly illuminated in the winter night by ground-lights, I stopped. "My books," I said. He looked his question. "I wanted to take my books to Yeowe," I said. Now my voice shook with a rush of tears, as if everything I was leaving came down to that one thing. "They need books on Yeowe, I think," I said.

After a moment he said, "I'll have them sent on our next ship. I wish I could put you on that ship," he added in a lower voice. "But of course the Ekumen can't give free rides to runaway slaves. . . ."

I turned and took his hand and laid my forehead against it for a moment, the only time in my life I ever did that of my own free will.

He was startled. "Come, come," he said, and hurried me along.

The Embassy hired Werelian guards, mostly veots, men of the old warrior caste. One of them, a grave, courteous, very silent man, went with me on the flyer to Bambur, the island kingdom east of the Great Continent. He had all the papers I needed. From the flyer port he took me to the Royal Space Observatory, which the King had built for his spaceship. There without delay I was taken to the ship, which stood in its great scaffolding ready to depart.

I imagine that they had made comfortable apartments up front for the King when he went to see the moons. The body of the ship, which had belonged to the Agricultural Plantation Corporation, still consisted of great compartments for the produce of the Colony. It would be bringing back grain from Yeowe in four of the cargo bays that now held farm machinery made in Bambur. The fifth compartment held assets.

The cargo bay had no seats. They had laid felt pads on the floor, and we lay down and were strapped to stanchions, as cargo would have been. There were about fifty "scientists." I was the last to come aboard and be strapped in. The crew were hasty and nervous and spoke only the language of Bambur. I could not understand the instructions we were given. I needed very badly to relieve my bladder, but they had shouted "No time, no time!" So I lay in torment while they closed the great doors of the bay, which made me think of the doors of Shomeke compound. Around me people called out to one another in their language. A baby screamed. I knew that language. Then the great noise began, beneath us. Slowly I felt my body pressed down on the floor, as if a huge soft foot were stepping on me, till my shoulder blades felt as if they were cutting into the mat, and my tongue pressed back into my throat as if to choke me, and with a sharp stab of pain and hot relief my bladder released its urine.

Then we began to be weightless—to float in our bonds. Up was down and down was up, either was both or neither. I heard people all around me calling out again, saying one another's names, saying what must be, "Are you all right? Yes, I'm all right." The baby had never ceased its fierce, piercing yells. I began to feel at my restraints, for I saw the woman next to me sitting up and rubbing her arms and chest where the straps had held her. But a great blurry voice came bellowing over the loudspeaker, giving orders in the language of Bambur and then in Voe Dean: "Do not unfasten the straps! Do not attempt to move about! The ship is under attack! The situation is extremely dangerous!"

So I lay floating in my little mist of urine, listening to the strangers around me talk, understanding nothing. I was utterly miserable, and yet fearless as I had never been. I was carefree. It was like dying. It would be foolish to worry about anything while one died.

The ship moved strangely, shuddering, seeming to turn. Several people were sick. The air filled with the smell and tiny droplets of vomit. I freed my hands enough to draw the scarf I was wearing up over my face as a filter, tucking the ends under my head to hold it.

Inside the scarf I could no longer see the huge vault of the cargo bay stretching above or below me, making me feel I was about to fly or fall into it. It smelled of myself, which was comforting. It was the scarf I often wore when I dressed up to give a talk, fine gauze, pale red with a silver thread woven in at intervals. When I bought it at a City market, paying my own earned money for it, I had thought of my mother's red scarf, given her by Lady Tazeu. I thought she would have liked this one, though it was not as bright. Now I lay and looked into the pale red dimness it made of the vault, starred with the lights at the hatches, and thought of my mother, Yowa. She had probably been killed that morning in the compound. Perhaps she had been carried to another estate as a use-woman, but Ahas had never found any trace of her. I thought of the way she had of carrying her head a little to the side, deferent yet alert, gracious. Her eyes had been full and bright, "eyes that hold the seven moons," as the song says. I thought then: But I will never see the moons again.

At that I felt so strange that to comfort myself and distract my mind I began to sing under my breath, there alone in my tent of red gauze warm with my own breath. I sang the freedom songs we sang in the Hame, and then I sang the love songs Lady Tazeu had taught me. Finally I sang "O, O, Yeowe," softly at first, then a little louder. I heard a voice somewhere out in that soft red mist world join in with me, a man's voice, then a woman's. Assets from Voe Deo all know that song. We sang it together. A Bambur man's voice picked it up and put words in his own language to it, and others joined in singing it. Then the singing died away. The baby's crying was weak now. The air was very foul.

We learned many hours later, when at last clean air entered the vents and we were told we could release our bonds, that a ship of the Voe Dean

Space Defense Fleet had intercepted the freighter's course just above the atmosphere and ordered it to stop. The captain chose to ignore the signal. The warship had fired, and though nothing hit the freighter the blast had damaged the controls. The freighter had gone on, and had seen and heard nothing more of the warship. We were now about eleven days from Yeowe. The warship, or a group of them, might be in wait for us near Yeowe. The reason they gave for ordering the freighter to halt was "suspected contraband merchandise."

That fleet of warships had been built centuries ago to protect Werel from the attacks they expected from the Alien Empire, which is what they then called the Ekumen. They were so frightened by that imagined threat that they put all their energy into the technology of space flight; and the colonisation of Yeowe was a result. After four hundred years without any threat of attack, Voe Deo had finally let the Ekumen send envoys and ambassadors. They had used the Defense Fleet to transport troops and weapons during the War of Liberation. Now they were using them the way estate owners used hunting dogs and hunting cats, to hunt down runaway slaves.

I found the two other Voe Deans in the cargo bay, and we moved our "bedstraps" together so we could talk. Both of them had been brought to Bambur by the Hame, who had paid their fare. It had not occurred to me that there was a fare to be paid. I knew who had paid mine.

"Can't fly a spaceship on love," the woman said. She was a strange person. She really was a scientist. Highly trained in chemistry by the company that rented her, she had persuaded the Hame to send her to Yeowe because she was sure her skills would be needed and in demand. She had been making higher wages than many gareots did, but she expected to do still better on Yeowe. "I'm going to be rich," she said.

The man, only a boy, a mill hand in a northern city, had simply run away and had the luck to meet people who could save him from death or the labor camps. He was sixteen, ignorant, noisy, rebellious, sweet-natured. He became a general favorite, like a puppy. I was in demand because I knew the history of Yeowe and through a man who knew both our languages I could tell the Bamburs something about where they were going—the centuries of Corporation slavery, Nadami, the War, the Liberation. Some of them were rentspeople from the cities, others were a group of estate slaves bought at auction by the Hame with false money and under a false name and hurried onto this flight, knowing very little of where they were going. It was that trick that had drawn Voe Deo's attention to this flight.

Yoke, the mill boy, speculated endlessly about how the Yeowans would welcome us. He had a story, half a joke, half a dream, about the bands playing and the speeches and the big dinner they would have for us. The dinner grew more and more elaborate as the days went on. They were long, hungry days, floating in the featureless great space of the cargo bay, marked only by the alternation every twelve hours of brighter and dimmer lighting and the issuing of two meals during the "day," food and water in tubes you squeezed into your mouth. I did not think much about what might happen. I was between happenings. If the warships found us, we would probably die. If we got to Yeowe, it would be a new life. Now we were floating.

4. Yeowe

THE SHIP CAME DOWN SAFE AT THE PORT OF YEOWE. THEY unloaded the crates of machinery first, then the other cargo. We came out staggering and holding on to one another, not able to stand up to the great pull of this new world drawing us down to its center, blinded by the light of the sun that we were closer to than we had ever been.

"Over here! Over here!" a man shouted. I was grateful to hear my language, but the Bamburs looked apprehensive.

Over here—in here—strip—wait—All we heard when we were first on the Free World was orders. We had to be decontaminated, which was painful and exhausting. We had to be examined by doctors. Anything we had brought with us had to be decontaminated and examined and listed. That did not take long for me. I had brought the clothes I wore and had worn for two weeks now. I was glad to get decontaminated. Finally we were told to stand in line in one of the big empty cargo sheds. The sign over the doors still read APCY—Agricultural Plantation Corporation of Yeowe. One by one we were processed for entry. The man who processed me was short, white, middle-aged, with spectacles, like any clerk asset in the City, but I looked at him with reverence. He was the first Yeowan I had spoken to. He asked me questions from a form and wrote down my answers. "Can you read?"—"Yes."—"Skills?"—I stammered a moment and said, "Teaching—I can teach reading and history." He never looked up at me.

I was glad to be patient. After all, the Yeowans had not asked us to come. We were admitted only because they knew if they sent us back, we would die horribly in a public execution. We were a profitable cargo to Bambur, but to Yeowe we were a problem. But many of us had skills they must need, and I was glad they asked us about them.

When we had all been processed, we were separated into two groups: men and women. Yoke hugged me and went off to the men's side laughing and waving. I stood with the women. We watched all the men led off to the shuttle that went to the Old Capital. Now my patience failed and my hope darkened. I prayed, "Lord Kamye, not here, not here too!" Fear made me angry. When a man came giving us orders again, come on, this way, I went up to him and said, "Who are you? Where are we going? We are free women!"

He was a big fellow with a round, white face and bluish eyes. He looked down at me, huffy at first, then smiling. "Yes, Little Sister, you're free," he said. "But we've all got to work, don't we? You ladies are going south. They need people on the rice plantations. You do a little work, make a little money, look around a little, all right? If you don't like it down there, come on back. We can always use more pretty little ladies round here."

I had never heard the Yeowan country accent, a singing, blurry softening, with long, clear vowels. I had never heard asset women called ladies. No one had ever called me Little Sister. He did not mean the word "use" as I took it, surely. He meant well. I was bewildered and said no more. But the chemist, Tualtak, said, "Listen, I'm no field hand, I'm a trained scientist—"

"Oh, you're all scientists," the Yeowan said with his big smile. "Come on now, ladies!" He strode ahead, and we followed. Tualtak kept talking. He smiled and paid no heed.

We were taken to a train car waiting on a siding. The huge, bright sun was setting. All the sky was orange and pink, full of light. Long shadows ran black along the ground. The warm air was dusty and sweet-smelling. While we stood waiting to climb up into the car I stooped and picked up a little reddish stone from the ground. It was round, with a tiny stripe of white clear through it. It was a piece of Yeowe. I held Yeowe in my hand. That little stone, too, I still have.

Our car was shunted along to the main yards and hooked onto a train. When the train started we were served dinner, soup from great kettles wheeled through the car, bowls of sweet, heavy marsh rice, pini fruit—a luxury on Werel, here a commonplace. We ate and ate. I watched the last light die away from the long, rolling hills that the train was passing through. The stars came out. No moons. Never again. But I saw Werel rising in the east. It was a great blue-green star, looking as Yeowe looks from Werel. But you would never see Yeowe rising after sunset. Yeowe followed the sun.

I'm alive and I'm here, I thought. I'm following the sun. I let the rest go, and fell asleep to the swaying of the train.

We were taken off the train on the second day at a town on the great river Yot. Our group of twenty-three was separated there, and ten of us were taken by oxcart to a village, Hagayot. It had been an APCY compound, growing marsh rice to feed the Colony slaves. Now it was a cooperative village, growing marsh rice to feed the Free People. We were enrolled as members of the cooperative. We lived share and share alike with the villagers until payout, when we could pay them back what we owed the cooperative.

It was a reasonable way to handle immigrants without money who did not know the language or who had no skills. But I did not understand why they had ignored our skills. Why had they sent the men from Bambur plantations, field hands, into the city, not here? Why only women?

I did not understand why, in a village of free people, there was a men's side and a women's side, with a ditch between them.

I did not understand why, as I soon discovered, the men made all the decisions and gave all the orders. But, it being so, I did understand that they were afraid of us Werelian women, who were not used to taking orders from our equals. And I understood that I must take orders and not even look as if I thought of questioning them. The men of Hagayot Village watched us with fierce suspicion and a whip as ready as any Boss's. "Maybe you told men what to do back over there," the foreman told us the first morning in the fields. "Well, that's back over there. That's not here. Here we free people work together. You think you're Bosswomen. There aren't any Bosswomen here."

There were grandmothers on the women's side, but they were not the powers our grandmothers had been. Here, where for the first century there had been no slave women at all, the men had had to make their own life, set up their own powers. When women slaves at last were sent into those slave-kingdoms of men, there was no power for them at all. They had no voice. Not till they got away to the cities did they ever have a voice on Yeowe.

I learned silence.

But it was not as bad for me and Tualtak as for our eight Bambur companions. We were the first immigrants any of these villagers had ever seen. They knew only one language. They thought the Bambur women were witches because they did not talk "like human beings." They whipped them for talking to each other in their own language.

I will confess that in my first year on the Free World my heart was as low as it had been at Zeskra. I hated standing all day in the shallow water of the rice paddies. Our feet were always sodden and swollen and full of tiny burrowing worms we had to pick out every night. But it was needed work and not too hard for a healthy woman. It was not the work that bore me down.

Hagayot was not a tribal village, not as conservative as some of the old villages I learned about later. Girls here were not ritually raped, and a woman was safe on the women's side. She "jumped the ditch" only with a man she chose. But if a woman went anywhere alone, or even got separated from the other women working in the paddies, she was supposed to be "asking for it," and any man thought it his right to force himself on her.

I made good friends among the village women and the Bamburs. They were no more ignorant than I had been a few years before and some were wiser than I would ever be. There was no possibility of having a friend among men who thought themselves our owners. I could not see how life here would ever change. My heart was very low, nights, when I lay among the sleeping women and children in our hut and thought, Is this what Walsu died for?

In my second year there, I resolved to do what I could to keep above the misery that threatened me. One of the Bambur women, meek and slow of understanding, whipped and beaten by both women and men for speaking her language, had drowned in one of the great rice paddies. She had lain down there in the warm shallow water not much deeper than her ankles, and had drowned. I feared that yielding, that water of despair. I made up my mind to use my skill, to teach the village women and children to read.

I wrote out some little primers on rice cloth and made a game of it for the little children, first. Some of the older girls and women were curious. Some of them knew that people in the towns and cities could read. They saw it as a mystery, a witchcraft that gave the city people their great power. I did not deny this.

For the women, I first wrote down verses and passages of the *Arkamye*, all I could remember, so that they could have it and not have to wait for one of the men who called themselves "priests" to recite it. They were proud of learning to read these verses. Then I had my friend Seugi tell me a story, her own recollection of meeting a wild hunting cat in the marshes as a child. I wrote it down, entitling it "The Marsh Lion, by Aro Seugi," and read it aloud to the author and a circle of girls and women. They marveled and laughed. Seugi wept, touching the writing that held her voice.

The chief of the village and his headmen and foremen and honorary sons, all the hierarchy and government of the village, were suspicious and not pleased by my teaching, yet did not want to forbid me. The government of Yotebber Region had sent word that they were establishing country schools where village children were to be sent for half the year. The village men knew that their sons would be advantaged if they could already read and write when they went there.

The Chosen Son, a big, mild, pale man, blind in one eye from a war wound, came to me at last. He wore his coat of office, a tight, long coat such as Werelian owners had worn three hundred years ago. He told me that I should not teach girls to read, only boys.

I told him I would teach all the children who wanted to learn or none of them.

"Girls do not want to learn this," he said.

"They do. Fourteen girls have asked to be in my class. Eight boys. Do you say girls do not need religious training, Chosen Son?"

This gave him pause. "They should learn the life of the Merciful Lady," he said.

"I will write the Life of Tual for them," I said at once. He walked away, saving his dignity.

I had little pleasure in my victory, such as it was. At least I went on teaching.

Tualtak was always at me to run away, run away to the city downriver. She had grown very thin, for she could not digest the heavy food. She hated the work and the people. "It's all right for you, you were a plantation pup, a dusty, but I never was, my mother was a rentswoman, we lived in fine rooms on Haba Street, I was the brightest trainee they ever had in the laboratory," and on and on, over and over, living in the world she had lost.

Sometimes I listened to her talk about running away. I tried to remember the maps of Yeowe in my lost books. I remembered the great river, the Yot, running from far inland three thousand kilos to the South Sea. But where were we on its vast length, how far from Yotebber City on its delta? Between Hagayot and the city might be a hundred villages like this one. "Have you been raped?" I asked Tualtak.

She took offense. "I'm a rentswoman, not a use-woman," she snapped.

I said, "I was a use-woman for two years. If I was raped again, I would kill the man or kill myself. I think two Werelian women walking alone here would be raped. I can't do it, Tualtak."

"It can't all be like this place!" she cried, so desperate that I felt my own throat close up with tears.

"Maybe when they open the schools—there will be people from the cities then—" It was all I had to offer her, or myself, as hope. "Maybe if the harvest's good this year, if we can get our money, we can get on the train. . . ."

That indeed was our best hope. The problem was to get our money from the chief and his cohorts. They kept the cooperative's income in a stone hut which they called the Bank of Hagayot, and only they ever saw the money. Each individual had an account, and they kept tally faithfully, the old Banker Headman scratching your account out in the dirt if you asked for it. But women and children could not withdraw money from their account. All we could get was a kind of scrip, clay pieces marked by the Banker Headman, good to buy things from one another, things people in the village made, clothes, sandals, tools, bead necklaces, rice beer. Our real money was safe, we were told, in the bank. I thought of that old lame bondsman at Shomeke, jigging and singing, "Money in the bank, Lord! Money in the bank!"

Before we ever came, the women had resented this system. Now there were nine more women resenting it.

One night I asked my friend Seugi, whose hair was as white as her skin, "Seugi, do you know what happened at a place called Nadami?"

"Yes," she said. "The women opened the door. All the women rose up and then the men rose up against the Bosses. But they needed weapons. And a woman ran in the night and stole the key from the owner's box and opened the door of the strong place where the Bosses kept their guns and bullets, and she held it open with the strength of her body, so that the slaves could arm themselves. And they killed the Corporations and made that place, Nadami, free."

"Even on Werel they tell that story," I said. "Even there women tell about Nadami, where the women began the Liberation. Men tell it too. Do men here tell it? Do they know it?"

Seugi and the other women nodded.

"If a woman freed the men of Nadami," I said, "maybe the women of Hagayot can free their money."

Seugi laughed. She called out to a group of grandmothers, "Listen to Rakam! Listen to this!"

After plenty of talk for days and weeks, it ended in a delegation of women, thirty of us. We crossed the ditch bridge onto the men's side and ceremoniously asked to see the chief. Our principal bargaining counter was shame. Seugi and other village women did the speaking, for they knew how far they could shame the men without goading them into anger and retaliation. Listening to them, I heard dignity speak to dignity, pride speak to pride. For the first time since I came to Yeowe I felt I was one of these people, that this pride and dignity were mine.

Nothing happens fast in a village. But by the next harvest, the women of Hagayot could draw their own earned share out of the bank in cash.

"Now for the vote," I said to Seugi, for there was no secret ballot in the village. When there was a regional election, even in the worldwide Ratification of the Constitution, the chiefs polled the men and filled out the ballots. They did not even poll the women. They wrote in the votes they wanted cast.

But I did not stay to help bring about that change at Hagayot. Tualtak was really ill and half-crazy with her longing to get out of the marshes, to the city. And I too longed for that. So we took our wages, and Seugi and other women drove us in an oxcart on the causeway across the marshes to the freight station. There we raised the flag that signaled the next train to stop for passengers.

It came along in a few hours, a long train of boxcars loaded with marsh rice, heading for the mills of Yotebber City. We rode in the crew car with the train crew and a few other passengers, village men. I had a big knife in my belt, but none of the men showed us any disrespect. Away from their compounds they were timid and shy. I sat up in my bunk in that car watching the great, wild, plumy marshes whirl by, and the villages on the banks of the wide river, and wished the train would go on forever.

But Tualtak lay in the bunk below me, coughing and fretful. When we got to Yotebber City she was so weak I knew I had to get her to a doctor. A man from the train crew was kind, telling us how to get to the hospital on the public cars. As we rattled through the hot, crowded city streets in the crowded car, I was still happy. I could not help it.

At the hospital they demanded our citizen's registration papers.

I had never heard of such papers. Later I found that ours had been given to the chiefs at Hagayot, who had kept them, as they kept all "their" women's papers. At the time, all I could do was stare and say, "I don't know anything about registration papers."

I heard one of the women at the desk say to the other, "Lord, how dusty can you get?"

I knew what we looked like. I knew we looked dirty and low. I knew I seemed ignorant and stupid. But when I heard that word "dusty" my pride and dignity woke up again. I put my hand into my pack and brought out my freedom paper, that old paper with Erod's writing on it, all crumpled and folded, all dusty.

"This is my Citizen's Registration paper," I said in a loud voice, making those women jump and turn. "My mother's blood and my grandmother's blood is on it. My friend here is sick. She needs a doctor. Now bring us to a doctor!"

A thin little woman came forward from the corridor. "Come on this way," she said. One of the deskwomen started to protest. This little woman gave her a look.

We followed her to an examination room.

"I'm Dr. Yeron," she said, then corrected herself. "I'm serving as a nurse," she said. "But I am a doctor. And you—you come from the Old World? from Werel? Sit down there, now, child, take off your shirt. How long have you been here?"

Within a quarter of an hour she had diagnosed Tualtak and got her a bed in a ward for rest and observation, found out our histories, and sent me off with a note to a friend of hers who would help me find a place to live and a job.

"Teaching!" Dr. Yeron said. "A teacher! Oh, woman, you are rain to the dry land!"

Indeed the first school I talked to wanted to hire me at once, to teach anything I wanted. Because I come of a capitalist people, I went to other schools to see if I could make more money at them. But I came back to the first one. I liked the people there.

Before the War of Liberation, the cities of Yeowe, which were cities of Corporation-owned assets who rented their own freedom, had had their own schools and hospitals and many kinds of training programs. There was even a University for assets in the Old Capital. The Corporations, of course, had controlled all the information that came to such institutions, and watched and censored all teaching and writing, keeping everything aimed towards the maximization of their profits. But within that narrow frame the assets had been free to use the information they had as they pleased, and city Yeowans had valued education deeply. During the long war, thirty years, all that system of gathering and teaching knowledge had broken down. A whole generation grew up learning nothing but fighting and hiding, famine and disease. The head of my school said to me, "Our children grew up illiterate, ignorant. Is it any wonder the plantation chiefs just took over where the Corporation Bosses left off? Who was to stop them?"

These men and women believed with a fierce passion that only education would lead to freedom. They were still fighting the War of Liberation.

Yotebber City was a big, poor, sunny, sprawling city with wide streets, low buildings, and huge old shady trees. The traffic was mostly afoot, with cycles tinging and public cars clanging along among the slow crowds. There were miles of shacks and shanties down in the old floodplain of the river behind the levees, where the soil was rich for gardening. The center of the city was on a low rise, the mills and train yards spreading out from it. Downtown it looked like the City of Voe

Deo, only older and poorer and gentler. Instead of big stores for owners, people bought and sold everything from stalls in open markets. The air was soft here in the south, a warm, soft sea air full of mist and sunlight. I stayed happy. I have by the grace of the Lord a mind that can leave misfortune behind, and I was happy in Yotebber City.

Tualtak recovered her health and found a good job as a chemist in a factory. I saw her seldom, as our friendship had been a matter of necessity, not choice. Whenever I saw her she talked about Haba Street and her laboratory on Werel and complained about her work and the people here.

Dr. Yeron did not forget me. She wrote a note and told me to come visit her, which I did. Presently, when I was settled, she asked me to come with her to a meeting of an educational society. This, I found, was a group of democrats, mostly teachers, who sought to work against the autocratic power of the tribal and regional chiefs under the new Constitution, and to counteract what they called the slave mind, the rigid, misogynistic hierarchy that I had encountered in Hagayot. My experience was useful to them, for they were all city people who had met the slave mind only when they found themselves governed by it. The women of the group were the angriest. They had lost the most at Liberation and now had less to lose. In general the men were gradualists, the women ready for revolution. As a Werelian, ignorant of politics on Yeowe, I listened and did not talk. It was hard for me not to talk. I am a talker, and sometimes I had plenty to say. But I held my tongue and heard them. They were people worth hearing.

Ignorance defends itself savagely, and illiteracy, as I well knew, can be shrewd. Though the Chief, the President of Yotebber Region, elected by a manipulated ballot, might not understand our counter-manipulations of the school curriculum, he did not waste much energy trying to control the schools, merely sending his inspectors to meddle with our classes and censor our books. But what he saw as important

was the fact that, just as the Corporations had, he controlled the net.
The news, the information programs, the puppets of the neareals, all
danced to his strings. Against that, what harm could a lot of teachers
do? Parents who had no schooling had children who entered the net
to hear and see and feel what the Chief wanted them to know: that
freedom is obedience to leaders, that virtue is violence, that manhood
is domination. Against the enactment of such truths in daily life and
in the heightened sensational experience of the neareals, what good
were words?

"Literacy is irrelevant," one of our group said sorrowfully. "The chiefs
have jumped right over our heads into the postliterate information
technology."

I brooded over that, hating her fancy words, irrelevant, postliterate,
because I was afraid she was right.

To the next meeting of our group, to my surprise, an Alien came: the
Sub-Envoy of the Ekumen. He was supposed to be a great feather in
our Chief's cap, sent down from the Old Capital apparently to support
the Chief's stand against the World Party, which was still strong down
here and still clamoring that Yeowe should keep out all foreigners. I had
heard vaguely that such a person was here, but I had not expected to
meet him at a gathering of subversive schoolteachers.

He was a short man, red-brown, with white corners to his eyes, but
handsome if one could ignore that. He sat in the seat in front of me. He
sat perfectly still, as if accustomed to sitting still, and listened without
speaking, as if accustomed to listening. At the end of the meeting he
turned around and his queer eyes looked straight at me.

"Radosse Rakam?" he said.

I nodded, dumb.

"I'm Yehedarhed Havzhiva," he said. "I have some books for you from
Old Music."

I stared. I said, "Books?"

"From Old Music," he said again. "Esdardon Aya, on Werel."

"My books?" I said.

He smiled. He had a broad, quick smile.

"Oh, where?" I cried.

"They're at my house. We can get them tonight, if you like. I have a car." There was something ironic and light in how he said that, as if he was a man who did not expect to have a car, though he might enjoy it.

Dr. Yeron came over. "So you found her," she said to the Sub-Envoy. He looked at her with such a bright face that I thought, these two are lovers. Though she was much older than he, there was nothing unlikely in the thought. Dr. Yeron was a magnetic woman. It was odd to me to think it, though, for my mind was not given to speculating about people's sexual affairs. That was no interest of mine.

He put his hand on her arm as they talked, and I saw with peculiar intensity how gentle his touch was, almost hesitant, yet trustful. That is love, I thought. Yet they parted, I saw, without that look of private understanding that lovers often give each other.

He and I rode in his government electric car, his two silent body-guards, policewomen, sitting in the front seat. We spoke of Esdardon Aya, whose name, he explained to me, meant Old Music. I told him how Esdardon Aya had saved my life by sending me here. He listened in a way that made it easy to talk to him. I said, "I was sick to leave my books, and I've thought about them, missing them, as if they were my family. But I think maybe I'm a fool to feel that way."

"Why a fool?" he asked. He had a foreign accent, but he had the Yeowan lilt already, and his voice was beautiful, low and warm.

I tried to explain everything at once: "Well, they mean so much to me because I was illiterate when I came to the City, and it was the books that gave me freedom, gave me the world—the worlds—But now, here, I see how the net, the holos, the neareals mean so much more to people, giving them the present time. Maybe it's just clinging to the past to cling to books. Yeowans have to go towards the future. And we'll never change people's minds just with words."

He listened intently, as he had done at the meeting, and then answered slowly, "But words are an essential way of thinking. And books keep the words true. . . . I didn't read till I was an adult, either."

"You didn't?"

"I knew how, but I didn't. I lived in a village. It's cities that have to have books," he said, quite decisively, as if he had thought about this matter. "If they don't, we keep on starting over every generation. It's a waste. You have to save the words."

When we got to his house, up at the top end of the old part of town, there were four crates of books in the entrance hall.

"These aren't all mine!" I said.

"Old Music said they were yours," Mr. Yehedarhed said, with his quick smile and a quick glance at me. You can tell where an Alien is looking much better than you can tell with us. With us, except for the few people with bluish eyes, you have to be close enough to see the dark pupil move in the dark eye.

"I haven't got anywhere to put so many," I said, amazed, realising how that strange man, Old Music, had helped me to freedom yet again.

"At your school, maybe? The school library?"

It was a good idea, but I thought at once of the Chief's inspectors pawing through them, perhaps confiscating them. When I spoke of that, the Sub-Envoy said, "What if I present them as a gift from the Embassy? I think that might embarrass the inspectors."

"Oh," I said, and burst out, "Why are you so kind? You, and he—Are you Hainish too?"

"Yes," he said, not answering my other question. "I was. I hope to be Yeowan."

He asked me to sit down and drink a little glass of wine with him before his guard drove me home. He was easy and friendly, but a quiet man. I saw he had been hurt. There were scars on his face and a gap in his hair where he had had a head injury. He asked me what my books were, and I said, "History."

At that he smiled, slowly this time. He said nothing, but he raised his glass to me. I raised mine, imitating him, and we drank.

Next day he had the books delivered to our school. When we opened and shelved them, we realised we had a great treasure. "There's nothing like this at the University," said one of the teachers, who had studied there for a year.

There were histories and anthropologies of Werel and of the worlds of the Ekumen, works of philosophy and politics by Werelians and by people of other worlds, there were compendiums of literature, poetry and stories, encyclopedias, books of science, atlases, dictionaries. In a corner of one of the crates were my own few books, my own treasure, even that first little crude *History of Yeowe, Printed at Yeowe University in the Year One of Liberty.* Most of my books I left in the school library, but I took that one and a few others home for love, for comfort.

I had found another love and comfort not long since. A child at school had brought me a present, a spotted-cat kitten, just weaned. The boy gave it to me with such loving pride that I could not refuse it. When I tried to pass it on to another teacher they all laughed at me. "You're elected, Rakam!" they said. So unwillingly I took the little being home, afraid of its frailty and delicacy and near to feeling a disgust for it. Women in the beza at Zeskra had had pets, spotted cats and foxdogs, spoiled little animals fed better than we were. I had been called by the name of a pet animal once.

I alarmed the kitten taking it out of its basket, and it bit my thumb to the bone. It was tiny and frail but it had teeth. I began to have some respect for it.

That night I put it to sleep in its basket, but it climbed up on my bed and sat on my face until I let it under the covers. There it slept perfectly still all night. In the morning it woke me by dancing on me, chasing dust motes in a sunbeam. It made me laugh, waking, which is a pleasant thing. I felt that I had never laughed very much, and wanted to.

The kitten was all black, its spots showing only in certain lights, black on black. I called it Owner. I found it pleasant to come home evenings to be greeted by my little Owner.

Now for the next half year we were planning the great demonstration of women. There were many meetings, at some of which I met the Sub-Envoy again, so that I began to look for him. I liked to watch him listen to our arguments. There were those who argued that the demonstration must not be limited to the wrongs and rights of women, for equality must be for all. Others argued that it should not depend in any way on the support of foreigners, but should be a purely Yeowan movement. Mr. Yehedarhed listened to them, but I got angry. "I'm a foreigner," I said. "Does that make me no use to you? That's owner talk—as if you were better than other people!" And Dr. Yeron said, "I will believe equality is for all when I see it written in the Constitution of Yeowe." For our Constitution, ratified by a world vote during the time I was at Hagayot, spoke of citizens only as men. That is finally what the demonstration became, a demand that the Constitution be amended to include women as citizens, provide for the secret ballot, and guarantee the right to free speech, freedom of the press and of assembly, and free education for all children.

I lay down on the train tracks along with seventy thousand women, that hot day. I sang with them. I heard what that sounds like, so many women singing together, what a big, deep sound it makes.

I had begun to speak in public again when we were gathering women for the great demonstration. It was a gift I had, and we made use of it. Sometimes gang boys or ignorant men would come to heckle and threaten me, shouting, "Bosswoman, Owner-woman, black cunt, go back where you came from!" Once when they were yelling that, go back, go back, I leaned into the microphone and said, "I can't go back. We used to sing a song on the plantation where I was a slave," and I sang it,

O, O, Ye-o-we,
Nobody never comes back.

The singing made them be still for a moment. They heard it, that awful grief, that yearning.

After the great demonstration the unrest never died down, but there were times that the energy flagged, the Movement didn't move, as Dr. Yeron said. During one of those times I went to her and proposed that we set up a printing house and publish books. This had been a dream of mine, growing from that day in Hagayot when Seugi had touched her words and wept.

"Talk goes by," I said, "and all the words and images in the net go by, and anybody can change them. But books are there. They last. They are the body of history, Mr. Yehedarhed says."

"Inspectors," said Dr. Yeron. "Until we get the free press amendment, the chiefs aren't going to let anybody print anything they didn't dictate themselves."

I did not want to give up the idea. I knew that in Yotebber Region we could not publish anything political, but I argued that we might print stories and poems by women of the region. Others thought it a waste of time. We discussed it back and forth for a long time. Mr. Yehedarhed came back from a trip to the Embassy, up north in the Old Capital. He listened to our discussions, but said nothing, which disappointed me. I had thought that he might support my project.

One day I was walking home from school to my apartment, which was in a big, old, noisy house not far from the levee. I liked the place because my windows opened into the branches of trees, and through the trees I saw the river, four miles wide here, easing along among sandbars and reedbeds and willow isles in the dry season, brimming up the levees in the wet season when the rainstorms scudded across it. That day as I came near the house, Mr. Yehedarhed appeared, with two sour-faced policewomen close behind him as usual. He greeted me and asked if we might talk. I was confused and did not know what to do but to invite him up to my room.

His guards waited in the lobby. I had just the one big room on the third floor. I sat on the bed and the Sub-Envoy sat in the chair. Owner went round and round his legs, saying roo? roo?

I had observed that the Sub-Envoy took pleasure in disappointing the expectations of the Chief and his cohorts, who were all for pomp and fleets of cars and elaborate badges and uniforms. He and his police-women went all over the city, all over Yotebber, in his government car or on foot. People liked him for it. They knew, as I knew now, that he had been assaulted and beaten and left for dead by a World Party gang his first day here, when he went out afoot alone. The city people liked his courage and the way he talked with everybody, anywhere. They had adopted him. We in the Liberation Movement thought of him as "our Envoy," but he was theirs, and the Chief's too. The Chief may have hated his popularity, but he profited from it.

"You want to start a publishing house," he said, stroking Owner, who fell over with his paws in the air.

"Dr. Yeron says there's no use until we get the Amendments."

"There's one press on Yeowe not directly controlled by the government," Mr. Yehedarhed said, stroking Owner's belly.

"Look out, he'll bite," I said. "Where is that?"

"At the University. I see," Mr. Yehedarhed said, looking at his thumb. I apologized. He asked me if I was certain that Owner was male. I said I had been told so, but never had thought to look. "My impression is that your Owner is a lady," Mr. Yehedarhed said, in such a way that I began to laugh helplessly.

He laughed along with me, sucked the blood off his thumb, and went on. "The University never amounted to much. It was a Corporation ploy—let the assets pretend they're going to college. During the last years of the War it was closed down. Since Liberation Day it's reopened and crawled along with no one taking much notice of it. The faculty are mostly old. They came back to it after the War. The National Government gives it a subsidy because it sounds well to have a University of Yeowe, but they don't pay it any attention, because it has no prestige. And because many of them are unenlightened men." He said this without scorn, descriptively. "It does have a printing house."

"I know," I said. I reached out for my old book and showed it to him.

He looked through it for a few minutes. His face was curiously tender as he did so. I could not help watching him. It was like watching a woman with a baby, a constant, changing play of attention and response.

"Full of propaganda and errors and hope," he said at last, and his voice too was tender. "Well, I think this could be improved upon. Don't you? All that's needed is an editor. And some authors."

"Inspectors," I warned, imitating Dr. Yeron.

"Academic freedom is an easy issue for the Ekumen to have some influence upon," he said, "because we invite people to attend the Ekumenical Schools on Hain and Ve. We certainly want to invite graduates of the University of Yeowe. But of course, if their education is severely defective because of the lack of books, of information . . ."

I said, "Mr. Yehedarhed, are you *supposed* to subvert government policies?" The question broke out of me unawares.

He did not laugh. He paused for quite a long time before he answered. "I don't know," he said. "So far the Ambassador has backed me. We may both get reprimanded. Or fired. What I'd like to do . . ." His strange eyes were right on me again. He looked down at the book he still held. "What I'd like is to become a Yeowan citizen," he said. "But my usefulness to Yeowe, and to the Liberation Movement, is my position with the Ekumen. So I'll go on using that, or misusing it, till they tell me to stop."

When he left I had to think about what he had asked me to do. That was to go to the University as a teacher of history, and once there to volunteer for the editorship of the press. That all seemed so preposterous, for a woman of my background and my little learning, that I thought I must be misunderstanding him. When he convinced me that I had understood him, I thought he must have very badly misunderstood who I was and what I was capable of. After we had talked about that for a little while, he left, evidently feeling that he was making me uncomfortable, and perhaps feeling uncomfortable himself, though in fact we laughed a good deal and I did not feel uncomfortable, only a little as if I were crazy.

I tried to think about what he had asked me to do, to step so far beyond myself. I found it difficult to think about. It was as if it hung over me, this huge choice I must make, this future I could not imagine. But what I thought about was him, Yehedarhed Havzhiva. I kept seeing him sitting there in my old chair, stooping down to stroke Owner. Sucking blood off his thumb. Laughing. Looking at me with his white-cornered eyes. I saw his red-brown face and red-brown hands, the color of pottery. His quiet voice was in my mind.

I picked up the kitten, half-grown now, and looked at its hinder end. There was no sign of any male parts. The little black silky body squirmed in my hands. I thought of him saying, "Your Owner is a lady," and I wanted to laugh again, and to cry. I stroked the kitten and set her down, and she sat sedately beside me, washing her shoulder. "Oh poor little lady," I said. I don't know who I meant. The kitten, or Lady Tazeu, or myself.

He had said to take my time thinking about his proposal, all the time I wanted. But I had not really thought about it at all when, the next day but one, there he was, on foot, waiting for me as I came out of the school. "Would you like to walk on the levee?" he said.

I looked around.

"There they are," he said, indicating his cold-eyed bodyguards. "Everywhere I am, they are, three to five meters away. Walking with me is dull, but safe. My virtue is guaranteed."

We walked down through the streets to the levee and up onto it in the long early evening light, warm and pink-gold, smelling of river and mud and reeds. The two women with guns walked along just about four meters behind us.

"If you do go to the University," he said after a long silence, "I'll be there constantly."

"I haven't yet—" I stammered.

"If you stay here, I'll be here constantly," he said. "That is, if it's all right with you."

I said nothing. He looked at me without turning his head. I said without intending to, "I like it that I can see where you're looking."

"I like it that I can't see where you're looking," he said, looking directly at me.

We walked on. A heron rose up out of a reed islet and its great wings beat over the water, away. We were walking south, downriver. All the western sky was full of light as the sun went down behind the city in smoke and haze.

"Rakam, I would like to know where you came from, what your life on Werel was," he said very softly.

I drew a long breath. "It's all gone," I said. "Past."

"We are our past. Though not only that. I want to know you. Forgive me. I want very much to know you."

After a while I said, "I want to tell you. But it's so bad. It's so ugly. Here, now, it's beautiful. I don't want to lose it."

"Whatever you tell me I will hold valuable," he said, in his quiet voice that went to my heart. So I told him what I could about Shomeke compound, and then hurried on through the rest of my story. Sometimes he asked a question. Mostly he listened. At some time in my telling he had taken my arm, I scarcely noticing at the time. When he let me go, thinking some movement I made meant I wanted to be released, I missed that light touch. His hand was cool. I could feel it on my forearm after it was gone.

"Mr. Yehedarhed," said a voice behind us: one of the bodyguards. The sun was down, the sky flushed with gold and red. "Better head back?"

"Yes," he said, "thanks." As we turned I took his arm. I felt him catch his breath.

I had not desired a man or a woman—this is the truth—since Shomeke. I had loved people, and I had touched them with love, but never with desire. My gate was locked.

Now it was open. Now I was so weak that at the touch of his hand I could scarcely walk on.

I said, "It's a good thing walking with you is so safe."

I hardly knew what I meant. I was thirty years old but I was like a young girl. I had never been that girl.

He said nothing. We walked along in silence between the river and the city in a glory of failing light.

"Will you come home with me, Rakam?" he said.

Now I said nothing.

"They don't come in with us," he said, very low, in my ear, so that I felt his breath.

"Don't make me laugh!" I said, and began crying. I wept all the way back along the levee. I sobbed and thought the sobs were ceasing and then sobbed again. I cried for all my sorrows, all my shames. I cried because they were with me now and always would be. I cried because the gate was open and I could go through at last, go into the country on the other side, but I was afraid to.

When we got into the car, up near my school, he took me in his arms and simply held me, silent. The two women in the front seat never looked round.

We went into his house, which I had seen once before, an old mansion of some owner of the Corporation days. He thanked the guards and shut the door. "Dinner," he said. "The cook's out. I meant to take you to a restaurant. I forgot." He led me to the kitchen, where we found cold rice and salad and wine. After we ate he looked at me across the kitchen table and looked down again. His hesitance made me hold still and say nothing. After a long time he said, "Oh, Rakam! will you let me make love to you?"

"I want to make love to you," I said. "I never did. I never made love to anyone."

He got up smiling and took my hand. We went upstairs together, passing what had been the entrance to the men's side of the house. "I live in the beza," he said, "in the harem. I live on the woman's side. I like the view."

We came to his room. There he stood still, looking at me, then looked away. I was so frightened, so bewildered, I thought I could not go to him or touch him. I made myself go to him. I raised my hand and touched his face, the scars by his eye and on his mouth, and put my arms around him. Then I could hold him to me, closer and closer.

Some time in that night as we lay drowsing entangled I said, "Did you sleep with Dr. Yeron?"

I felt Havzhiva laugh, a slow, soft laugh in his belly, which was against my belly. "No," he said. "No one on Yeowe but you. And you, no one on Yeowe but me. We were virgins, Yeowan virgins. . . . Rakam, *araha*. . . ." He rested his head in the hollow of my shoulder and said something else in a foreign language and fell asleep. He slept deeply, silently.

Later that year I came up north to the University, where I was taken on the faculty as a teacher of history. By their standards at that time, I was competent. I have worked there ever since, teaching and as editor of the press.

As he had said he would be, Havzhiva was there constantly, or almost.

The Amendments to the Constitution were voted, by secret ballot, mostly, in the Yeowan Year of Liberty 18. Of the events that led to this, and what has followed, you may read in the new three-volume *History of Yeowe* from the University Press. I have told the story I was asked to tell. I have closed it, as so many stories close, with a joining of two people. What is one man's and one woman's love and desire, against the history of two worlds, the great revolutions of our lifetimes, the hope, the unending cruelty of our species? A little thing. But a key is a little thing, next to the door it opens. If you lose the key, the door may never be unlocked. It is in our bodies that we lose or begin our freedom, in our bodies that we accept or end our slavery. So I wrote this book for my friend, with whom I have lived and will die free.

OLD MUSIC
AND THE
SLAVE WOMEN

THE CHIEF INTELLIGENCE OFFICER OF THE EKUMENICAL embassy to Werel, a man who on his home world had the name Sohikelwenyanmurkeres Esdan, and who in Voe Deo was known by a nickname, Esdardon Aya or Old Music, was bored. It had taken a civil war and three years to bore him, but he had got to the point where he referred to himself in ansible reports to the Stabiles on Hain as the embassy's chief stupidity officer.

He had been able, however, to retain a few clandestine links with friends in the Free City even after the Legitimate Government sealed the embassy, allowing no one and no information to enter or leave it. In the third summer of the war, he came to the Ambassador with a request. Cut off from reliable communication with the embassy, Liberation Command had asked him (how? asked the Ambassador; through one of the men who delivered groceries, he explained) if the embassy would let one or two of its people slip across the lines and talk with them, be seen with them, offer proof that despite propaganda and disinformation, and though the embassy was stuck in Jit City, its staff had not been co-opted into supporting the Legitimates, but remained neutral and ready to deal with rightful authority on either side.

"Jit City?" said the Ambassador. "Never mind. But how do you get there?"

"Always the problem with Utopia," Esdan said. "Well, I can pass with contact lenses, if nobody's looking closely. Crossing the Divide is the tricky bit."

Most of the great city was still physically there, the government buildings, factories and warehouses, the university, the tourist attractions: the Great Shrine of Tual, Theater Street, the Old Market with its interesting display rooms and lofty Hall of Auction, disused since the sale and rental of assets had been shifted to the electronic marketplace; the numberless streets, avenues, and boulevards, the dusty parks shaded by purple-flowered beya trees, the miles and miles of shops, sheds, mills, tracks, stations, apartment buildings, houses, compounds, the neighborhoods, the suburbs, the exurbs. Most of it still stood, most of its fifteen million people were still there, but its deep complexity was gone. Connections were broken. Interactions did not take place. A brain after a stroke.

The greatest break was a brutal one, an axe-blow right through the pons, a kilo-wide no-man's-land of blown-up buildings and blocked streets, wreckage and rubble. East of the Divide was Legitimate territory: downtown, government offices, embassies, banks, communications towers, the university, the great parks and wealthy neighborhoods, the roads out to the armory, barracks, airports, and spaceport. West of the Divide was Free City, Dustyville, Liberation territory: factories, union compounds, the rentspeople's quarters, the old gareot residential neighborhoods, endless miles of little streets petering out into the plains at last. Through both ran the great East–West highways, empty.

The Liberation people successfully smuggled him out of the embassy and almost across the Divide. He and they had had a lot of practice in the old days getting runaway assets out to Yeowe and freedom. He found it interesting to be the one smuggled instead of one of the smugglers, finding it far more frightening yet less stressful, since he was not responsible, the package not the postman. But somewhere in the connection there had been a bad link.

They made it on foot into the Divide and partway through it and stopped at a little derelict truck sitting on its wheel rims under a gutted apartment house. A driver sat at the wheel behind the cracked, crazed windshield, and grinned at him. His guide gestured him into the back. The truck took off like a hunting cat, following a crazy route, zigzagging through the ruins. They were nearly across the Divide, jolting across a rubbled stretch which might have been a street or a marketplace, when the truck veered, stopped, there were shouts, shots, the vanback was flung open and men plunged in at him. "Easy," he said, "go easy," for they were manhandling him, hauling him, twisting his arm behind his back. They yanked him out of the truck, pulled off his coat and slapped him down searching for weapons, frogmarched him to a car waiting beside the truck. He tried to see if his driver was dead but could not look around before they shoved him into the car.

It was an old government state-coach, dark red, wide and long, made for parades, for carrying great estate owners to the Council and ambassadors from the spaceport. Its main section could be curtained to separate men from women passengers, and the driver's compartment was sealed off so the passengers wouldn't be breathing in what a slave breathed out.

One of the men had kept his arm twisted up his back until he shoved him headfirst into the car, and all he thought as he found himself sitting between two men and facing three others and the car starting up was, "I'm getting too old for this."

He held still, letting his fear and pain subside, not ready yet to move even to rub his sharply hurting shoulder, not looking into faces nor too obviously at the streets. Two glances told him they were passing Rei Street, going east, out of the city. He realised then he had been hoping they were taking him back to the embassy. What a fool.

They had the streets to themselves, except for the startled gaze of people on foot as they flashed by. Now they were on a wide boulevard, going very fast, still going east. Although he was in a very bad situation, he still found it absolutely exhilarating just to be out of the embassy, out in the air, in the world, and moving, going fast.

Cautiously he raised his hand and massaged his shoulder. As cautiously, he glanced at the men beside him and facing him. All were dark-skinned, two blue-black. Two of the men facing him were young. Fresh, stolid faces. The third was a veot of the third rank, an oga. His face had the quiet inexpressiveness in which his caste was trained. Looking at him, Esdan caught his eye. Each looked away instantly.

Esdan liked veots. He saw them, soldiers as well as slaveholders, as part of the old Voe Deo, members of a doomed species. Businessmen and bureaucrats would survive and thrive in the Liberation and no doubt find soldiers to fight for them, but the military caste would not. Their code of loyalty, honor, and austerity was too like that of their slaves, with whom they shared the worship of Kamye, the Swordsman, the Bondsman. How long would that mysticism of suffering survive the Liberation? Veots were intransigent vestiges of an intolerable order. He trusted them, and had seldom been disappointed in his trust.

The oga was very black, very handsome, like Teyeo, a veot Esdan had particularly liked. He had left Werel long before the war, off to Terra and Hain with his wife, who would be a Mobile of the Ekumen one of these days. In a few centuries. Long after the war was over, long after Esdan was dead. Unless he chose to follow them, went back, went home.

Idle thoughts. During a revolution you don't choose. You're carried, a bubble in a cataract, a spark in a bonfire, an unarmed man in a car with seven armed men driving very fast down the broad, blank East Arterial Highway. . . . They were leaving the city. Heading for the East Provinces. The Legitimate Government of Voe Deo was now reduced to half the capital city and two provinces, in which seven out of eight people were what the eighth person, their owner, called assets.

The two men up in the front compartment were talking, though they couldn't be heard in the owner compartment. Now the bullet-headed man to Esdan's right asked a muttered question to the oga facing him, who nodded.

"Oga," Esdan said.

The veot's expressionless eyes met his.

"I need to piss."

The man said nothing and looked away. None of them said anything for a while. They were on a bad stretch of the highway, torn up by fighting during the first summer of the Uprising or merely not maintained since. The jolts and shocks were hard on Esdan's bladder.

"Let the fucking white-eyes piss himself," said one of the two young men facing him to the other, who smiled tightly.

Esdan considered possible replies, good-humored, joking, not offensive, not provocative, and kept his mouth shut. They only wanted an excuse, those two. He closed his eyes and tried to relax, to be aware of the pain in his shoulder, the pain in his bladder, merely aware.

The man to his left, whom he could not see clearly, spoke: "Driver. Pull off up there." He used a speakerphone. The driver nodded. The car slowed, pulled off the road, jolting horribly. They all got out of the car. Esdan saw that the man to his left was also a veot, of the second rank, a zadyo. One of the young men grabbed Esdan's arm as he got out, another shoved a gun against his liver. The others all stood on the dusty roadside and pissed variously on the dust, the gravel, the roots of a row of scruffy trees. Esdan managed to get his fly open but his legs were so cramped and shaky he could barely stand, and the young man with the gun had come around and now stood directly in front of him with the gun aimed at his penis. There was a knot of pain somewhere between his bladder and his cock. "Back up a little," he said with plaintive irritability. "I don't want to wet your shoes." The young man stepped forward instead, bringing his gun right against Esdan's groin.

The zadyo made a slight gesture. The young man backed off a step. Esdan shuddered and suddenly pissed out a fountain. He was pleased, even in the agony of relief, to see he'd driven the young man back two more steps.

"Looks almost human," the young man said.

Esdan tucked his brown alien cock away with discreet promptness and slapped his trousers shut. He was still wearing lenses that hid the whites of his eyes, and was dressed as a rentsman in loose, coarse clothes of dull yellow, the only dye color that had been permitted to urban slaves. The banner of the Liberation was that same dull yellow. The wrong color, here. The body inside the clothes was the wrong color too.

Having lived on Werel for thirty-three years, Esdan was used to being feared and hated, but he had never before been entirely at the mercy of those who feared and hated him. The aegis of the Ekumen had sheltered him. What a fool, to leave the embassy where at least he'd been harmless, and let himself be got hold of by these desperate defenders of a lost cause, who might do a good deal of harm not only to but with him. How much resistance, how much endurance, was he capable of? Fortunately they couldn't torture any information about Liberation plans from him, since he didn't know a damned thing about what his friends were doing. But still, what a fool.

Back in the car, sandwiched in the seat with nothing to see but the young men's scowls and the oga's watchful nonexpression, he shut his eyes again. The highway was smooth here. Rocked in speed and silence he slipped into a post-adrenaline doze.

When he came fully awake the sky was gold, two of the little moons glittering above a cloudless sunset. They were jolting along on a side road, a driveway that wound past fields, orchards, plantations of trees and building-cane, a huge field-worker compound, more fields, another compound. They stopped at a checkpoint guarded by a single armed man, were checked briefly and waved through. The road went through

an immense, open, rolling park. Its familiarity troubled him. Lacework
of trees against the sky, the swing of the road among groves and glades.
He knew the river was over that long hill.

"This is Yaramera," he said aloud.

None of the men spoke.

Years ago, decades ago, when he'd been on Werel only a year or so,
they'd invited a party from the embassy down to Yaramera, the greatest
estate in Voe Deo. The Jewel of the East. The model of efficient slavery.
Thousands of assets working the fields, mills, factories of the estate, living in enormous compounds, walled towns. Everything clean, orderly,
industrious, peaceful. And the house on the hill above the river, a palace, three hundred rooms, priceless furnishings, paintings, sculptures,
musical instruments—he remembered a private concert hall with walls
of gold-backed glass mosaic, a Tualite shrine-room that was one huge
flower carved of scented wood.

They were driving up to that house now. The car turned. He caught
only a glimpse, jagged black spars against the sky.

The two young men were allowed to handle him again, haul him out
of the car, twist his arm, push and shove him up the steps. Trying not
to resist, not to feel what they were doing to him, he kept looking about
him. The center and the south wing of the immense house were roofless,
ruinous. Through the black outline of a window shone the blank clear
yellow of the sky. Even here in the heartland of the Law, the slaves had
risen. Three years ago, now, in that first terrible summer when thousands of houses had burned, compounds, towns, cities. Four million
dead. He had not known the Uprising had reached even to Yaramera.
No news came up the river. What toll among the Jewel's slaves for that
night of burning? Had the owners been slaughtered, or had they survived to deal out punishment? No news came up the river.

All this went through his mind with unnatural rapidity and clarity
as they crowded him up the shallow steps towards the north wing of

the house, guarding him with drawn guns as if they thought a man of sixty-two with severe leg cramps from sitting motionless for hours was going to break and run for it, here, three hundred kilos inside their own territory. He thought fast and noticed everything.

This part of the house, joined to the central house by a long arcade, had not burned down. The walls still bore up the roof, but he saw as they came into the front hall that they were bare stone, their carved panelling burnt away. Dirty sheetflooring replaced parquet or covered painted tile. There was no furniture at all. In its ruin and dirt the high hall was beautiful, bare, full of clear evening light. Both veots had left his group and were reporting to some men in the doorway of what had been a reception room. He felt the veots as a safeguard and hoped they would come back, but they did not. One of the young men kept his arm twisted up his back. A heavy-set man came towards him, staring at him.

"You're the alien called Old Music?"

"I am Hainish, and use that name here."

"Mr. Old Music, you're to understand that by leaving your embassy in violation of the protection agreement between your Ambassador and the Government of Voe Deo, you've forfeited diplomatic immunity. You may be held in custody, interrogated, and duly punished for any infractions of civil law or crimes of collusion with insurgents and enemies of the State you're found to have committed."

"I understand that this is your statement of my position," Esdan said. "But you should know, sir, that the Ambassador and the Stabiles of the Ekumen of the Worlds consider me protected both by diplomatic immunity and the laws of the Ekumen."

No harm trying, but his wordy lies weren't listened to. Having recited his litany the man turned away, and the young men grabbed Esdan again. He was hustled through doorways and corridors that he was now in too much pain to see, down stone stairs, across a wide, cobbled courtyard, and into a room where with a final agonising jerk on his arm and his feet knocked from under him so that he fell sprawling, they slammed the door and left him belly-down on stone in darkness.

He dropped his forehead onto his arm and lay shivering, hearing his breath catch in a whimper again and again.

LATER ON HE REMEMBERED THAT NIGHT, AND OTHER THINGS from the next days and nights. He did not know, then or later, if he was tortured in order to break him down or was merely the handy object of aimless brutality and spite, a sort of plaything for the boys. There were kicks, beatings, a great deal of pain, but none of it was clear in his memory later except the crouchcage.

He had heard of such things, read about them. He had never seen one. He had never been inside a compound. Foreigners, visitors, were not taken into slave quarters on the estates of Voe Deo. They were served by house-slaves in the houses of the owners.

This was a small compound, not more than twenty huts on the women's side, three longhouses on the gateside. It had housed the staff of a couple of hundred slaves who looked after the house and the immense gardens of Yaramera. They would have been a privileged set compared to the fieldhands. But not exempt from punishment. The whipping post still stood near the high gate that sagged open in the high walls.

"There?" said Nemeo, the one who always twisted his arm, but the other one, Alatual, said, "No, come on, it's over here," and ran ahead, excited, to winch the crouchcage down from where it hung below the main sentry station, high up on the inside of the wall.

It was a tube of coarse, rusty steel mesh sealed at one end and closable at the other. It hung suspended by a single hook from a chain. Lying on the ground it looked like a trap for an animal, not a very big animal. The two young men stripped off his clothes and goaded him to crawl into it headfirst, using the fieldhandlers, electric prods to stir up lazy slaves, which they had been playing with the last couple of days.

They screamed with laughter, pushing him and jabbing the prods in his anus and scrotum. He writhed into the cage until he was crouching in it head-down, his arms and legs bent and jammed up into his body. They slammed the trap end shut, catching his naked foot between the wires and causing a pain that blinded him while they hoisted the cage back up. It swung about wildly and he clung to the wires with his cramped hands. When he opened his eyes he saw the ground swinging about seven or eight meters below him. After a while the lurching and circling stopped. He could not move his head at all. He could see what was below the crouchcage, and by straining his eyes round he could see most of the inside of the compound.

In the old days there had been people down there to see the moral spectacle, a slave in the crouchcage. There had been children to learn the lesson of what happens to a housemaid who shirked a job, a gardener who spoiled a cutting, a hand who talked back to a boss. Nobody was there now. The dusty ground was bare. The dried-up garden plots, the little graveyard at the far edge of the women's side, the ditch between the two sides, the pathways, a vague circle of greener grass right underneath him, all were deserted. His torturers stood around for a while laughing and talking, got bored, went off.

He tried to ease his position but could move only very slightly. Any motion made the cage rock and swing so that he grew sick and increasingly fearful of falling. He did not know how securely the cage was balanced on that single hook. His foot, caught in the cage-closure, hurt so sharply that he longed to faint, but though his head swam he kept conscious. He tried to breathe as he had learned how to breathe a long time ago on another world, quietly, easily. He could not do it here now in this world in this cage. His lungs were squeezed in his ribcage so that each breath was extremely difficult. He tried not to suffocate. He tried not to panic. He tried to be aware, only to be aware, but awareness was unendurable.

When the sun came around to that side of the compound and shone full on him, the dizziness turned to sickness. Sometimes then he fainted for a while.

There was night and cold and he tried to imagine water, but there was no water.

He thought later he had been in the crouchcage two days. He could remember the scraping of the wires on his sunburned naked flesh when they pulled him out, the shock of cold water played over him from a hose. He had been fully aware for a moment then, aware of himself, like a doll, lying small, limp, on dirt, while men above him talked and shouted about something. Then he must have been carried back to the cell or stable where he was kept, for there was dark and silence, but also he was still hanging in the crouchcage roasting in the icy fire of the sun, freezing in his burning body, fitted tighter and tighter into the exact mesh of the wires of pain.

At some point he was taken to a bed in a room with a window, but he was still in the crouchcage, swinging high above the dusty ground, the dusties' ground, the circle of green grass.

The zadyo and the heavy-set man were there, were not there. A bondswoman, whey-faced, crouching and trembling, hurt him trying to put salve on his burned arm and leg and back. She was there and not there. The sun shone in the window. He felt the wire snap down on his foot again, and again.

Darkness eased him. He slept most of the time. After a couple of days he could sit up and eat what the scared bondswoman brought him. His sunburn was healing and most of his aches and pains were milder. His foot was swollen hugely; bones were broken; that didn't matter till he had to get up. He dozed, drifted. When Rayaye walked into the room, he recognised him at once.

They had met several times, before the Uprising. Rayaye had been Minister of Foreign Affairs under President Oyo. What position he had now, in the Legitimate Government, Esdan did not know. Rayaye was short for a Werelian but broad and solid, with a blue-black polished-looking face and greying hair, a striking man, a politician.

"Minister Rayaye," Esdan said.

"Mr. Old Music. How kind of you to recall me! I'm sorry you've been unwell. I hope the people here are looking after you satisfactorily?"

"Thank you."

"When I heard you were unwell I inquired for a doctor, but there's no one here but a veterinarian. No staff at all. Not like the old days! What a change! I wish you'd seen Yaramera in its glory."

"I did." His voice was rather weak, but sounded quite natural. "Thirty-two or -three years ago. Lord and Lady Aneo entertained a party from our embassy."

"Really? Then you know what it was," said Rayaye, sitting down in the one chair, a fine old piece missing one arm. "Painful to see it like this, isn't it! The worst of the destruction was here in the house. The whole women's wing and the great rooms burned. But the gardens were spared, may the Lady be praised. Laid out by Meneya himself, you know, four hundred years ago. And the fields are still being worked. I'm told there are still nearly three thousand assets attached to the property. When the trouble's over, it'll be far easier to restore Yaramera than many of the great estates." He gazed out the window. "Beautiful, beautiful. The Aneos' housepeople were famous for their beauty, you know. And train-ing. It'll take a long time to build up to that kind of standard again."

"No doubt."

The Werelian looked at him with bland attentiveness. "I expect you're wondering why you're here."

"Not particularly," Esdan said pleasantly.

"Oh?"

"Since I left the embassy without permission, I suppose the Govern-ment wanted to keep an eye on me."

"Some of us were glad to hear you'd left the embassy. Shut up there—a waste of your talents."

"Oh, my talents," Esdan said with a deprecatory shrug, which hurt his shoulder. He would wince later. Just now he was enjoying himself. He liked fencing.

"You're a very talented man, Mr. Old Music. The wisest, canniest alien on Werel, Lord Mehao called you once. You've worked with us—and against us, yes—more effectively than any other offworlder. We understand one another. We can talk. It's my belief that you genuinely wish my people well, and that if I offered you a way of serving them—a hope of bringing this terrible conflict to an end—you'd take it."

"I would hope to be able to."

"Is it important to you that you be identified as a supporter of one side of the conflict, or would you prefer to remain neutral?"

"Any action can bring neutrality into question."

"To have been kidnapped from the embassy by the rebels is no evidence of your sympathy for them."

"It would seem not."

"Rather the opposite."

"It could be so perceived."

"It can be. If you like."

"My preferences are of no weight, Minister."

"They're of very great weight, Mr. Old Music. But here. You've been ill, I'm tiring you. We'll continue our conversation tomorrow, eh? If you like."

"Of course, Minister," Esdan said, with a politeness edging on submissiveness, a tone that he knew suited men like this one, more accustomed to the attention of slaves than the company of equals. Never having equated incivility with pride, Esdan, like most of his people, was disposed to be polite in any circumstance that allowed it, and disliked circumstances that did not. Mere hypocrisy did not trouble him. He was perfectly capable of it himself. If Rayaye's men had tortured him and Rayaye pretended ignorance of the fact, Esdan had nothing to gain by insisting on it.

He was glad, indeed, not to be obliged to talk about it, and hoped not to think about it. His body thought about it for him, remembered it precisely, in every joint and muscle, now. The rest of his thinking about it he would do as long as he lived. He had learned things he had not known. He had thought he understood what it was to be helpless. Now he knew he had not understood.

When the scared woman came in, he asked her to send for the veterinarian. "I need a cast on my foot," he said.

"He does mend the hands, the bondsfolk, master," the woman whispered, shrinking. The assets here spoke an archaic-sounding dialect that was sometimes hard to follow.

"Can he come into the house?"

She shook her head.

"Is there anybody here who can look after it?"

"I will ask, master," she whispered.

An old bondswoman came in that night. She had a wrinkled, seared, stern face, and none of the crouching manner of the other. When she first saw him she whispered, "Mighty Lord!" But she performed the reverence stiffly, and then examined his swollen foot, impersonal as any doctor. She said, "If you do let me bind that, master, it will heal."

"What's broken?"

"These toes. There. Maybe a little bone in here too. Lotsalot bones in feet."

"Please bind it for me."

She did so, firmly, binding cloths round and round until the wrapping was quite thick and kept his foot immobile at one angle. She said, "You do walk, then you use a stick, sir. You put down only that heel to the ground."

He asked her name.

"Gana," she said. Saying her name she shot a sharp glance right at him, full-face, a daring thing for a slave to do. She probably wanted to get a good look at his alien eyes, having found the rest of him, though a strange color, pretty commonplace, bones in the feet and all.

"Thank you, Gana. I'm grateful for your skill and kindness."

She bobbed, but did not reverence, and left the room. She herself walked lame, but upright. "All the grandmothers are rebels," somebody had told him long ago, before the Uprising.

THE NEXT DAY HE WAS ABLE TO GET UP AND HOBBLE TO THE broken-armed chair. He sat for a while looking out the window.

The room looked out from the second floor over the gardens of Yaramera, terraced slopes and flowerbeds, walks, lawns, and a series of ornamental lakes and pools that descended gradually to the river: a vast pattern of curves and planes, plants and paths, earth and still water, embraced by the broad living curve of the river. All the plots and walks and terraces formed a soft geometry centered very subtly on an enormous tree down at the riverside. It must have been a great tree when the garden was laid out four hundred years ago. It stood above and well back from the bank, but its branches reached far out over the water and a village could have been built in its shade. The grass of the terraces had dried to soft gold. The river and the lakes and pools were all the misty blue of the summer sky. The flowerbeds and shrubberies were untended, overgrown, but not yet gone wild. The gardens of Yaramera were utterly beautiful in their desolation. Desolate, forlorn, forsaken, all such romantic words befitted them, yet they were also rational and noble, full of peace. They had been built by the labor of slaves. Their dignity and peace were founded on cruelty, misery, pain. Esdan was Hainish, from a very old people, people who had built and destroyed Yaramera a thousand times. His mind contained the beauty and the terrible grief of the place, assured that the existence of one cannot justify the other, the destruction of one cannot destroy the other. He was aware of both, only aware.

And aware also, sitting in some comfort of body at last, that the lovely sorrowful terraces of Yaramera may contain within them the terraces of Darranda on Hain, roof below red roof, garden below green garden, dropping steep down to the shining harbor, the promenades and piers and sailboats. Out past the harbor the sea rises up, stands up as high as his house, as high as his eyes. Esi knows that books say the sea lies down. "The sea lies calm tonight," says the poem, but he knows better. The sea stands, a wall, the blue-grey wall at the end of the world. If you sail out on it it will seem flat, but if you see it truly it's as tall as the hills of Darranda, and if you sail truly on it you will sail through that wall to the other side, beyond the end of the world.

The sky is the roof that wall holds up. At night the stars shine through the glass air roof. You can sail to them, too, to the worlds beyond the world.

"Esi," somebody calls from indoors, and he turns away from the sea and the sky, leaves the balcony, goes in to meet the guests, or for his music lesson, or to have lunch with the family. He's a nice little boy, Esi: obedient, cheerful, not talkative but quite sociable, interested in people. With very good manners, of course; after all he's a Kelwen and the older generation wouldn't stand for anything less in a child of the family, but good manners come easy to him, perhaps because he's never seen any bad ones. Not a dreamy child. Alert, present, noticing. But thoughtful, and given to explaining things to himself, such as the wall of the sea and the roof of the air. Esi isn't as clear and close to Esdan as he used to be; he's a little boy a long time ago and very far away, left behind, left at home. Only rarely now does Esdan see through his eyes, or breathe the marvelous intricate smell of the house in Darranda—wood, the resinous oil used to polish the wood, sweetgrass matting, fresh flowers, kitchen herbs, the sea wind—or hear his mother's voice: "Esi? Come on in now, love. The cousins are here from Dorased!"

Esi runs in to meet the cousins, old Iliawad with crazy eyebrows and hair in his nostrils, who can do magic with bits of sticky tape, and Tuitui who's better at catch than Esi even though she's younger, while Esdan falls asleep in the broken chair by the window looking out on the terrible, beautiful gardens.

FURTHER CONVERSATIONS WITH RAYAYE WERE DEFERRED. THE zadyo came with his apologies. The Minister had been called back to speak with the President, would return within three or four days. Esdan realised he had heard a flyer take off early in the morning, not far away. It was a reprieve. He enjoyed fencing, but was still very tired, very shaken, and welcomed the rest. No one came into his room but the scared woman, Heo, and the zadyo who came once a day to ask if he had all he needed.

When he could he was permitted to leave his room, go outside if he wished. By using a stick and strapping his bound foot onto a stiff old sandal-sole Gana brought him, he could walk, and so get out into the gardens and sit in the sun, which was growing milder daily as the summer grew old. The two veots were his guards, or more exactly guardians. He saw the two young men who had tortured him; they kept at a distance, evidently under orders not to approach him. One of the veots was usually in view, but never crowded him.

He could not go far. Sometimes he felt like a bug on a beach. The part of the house that was still usable was huge, the gardens were vast, the people were very few. There were the six men who had brought him, and five or six more who had been here, commanded by the heavy-set man Tualenem. Of the original asset population of the house and estate there were ten or twelve, a tiny remnant of the house-staff of cooks, cooks' helpers, washwomen, chambermaids, ladies' maids, bodyservants,

shoe-polishers, window-cleaners, gardeners, path-rakers, waiters, foot-
men, errandboys, stablemen, drivers, usewomen and useboys who had
served the owners and their guests in the old days. These few were no
longer locked up at night in the old house-asset compound where the
crouchcage was, but slept in the courtyard warren of stables for horses
and people where he had been kept at first, or in the complex of rooms
around the kitchens. Most of these remaining few were women, two of
them young, and two or three old, frail-looking men.

He was cautious of speaking to any of them at first lest he get them
into trouble, but his captors ignored them except to give orders, evidently considering them trustworthy, with good reason. Troublemakers,
the assets who had broken out of the compounds, burned the great
house, killed the bosses and owners, were long gone: dead, escaped, or
re-enslaved with a cross branded deep on both cheeks. These were good
dusties. Very likely they had been loyal all along. Many bondspeople,
especially personal slaves, as terrified by the Uprising as their owners,
had tried to defend them or had fled with them. They were no more
traitors than were owners who had freed their assets and fought on the
Liberation side. As much, and no more.

Girls, young fieldhands, were brought in one at a time as use-women
for the men. Every day or two the two young men who had tortured
him drove a landcar off in the morning with a used girl and came back
with a new one.

Of the two younger house bondswomen, the one called Kamsa
always carried her little baby around with her, and the men ignored her.
The other, Heo, was the scared one who had waited on him. Tualenem
used her every night. The other men kept hands off.

When they or any of the bondspeople passed Esdan in the house
or outdoors they dropped their hands to their sides, chin to the chest,
looked down, and stood still: the formal reverence expected of personal
assets facing an owner.

"Good morning, Kamsa."

Her reply was the reverence.

It had been years now since he had been with the finished product of generations of slavery, the kind of slave described as "perfectly trained, obedient, selfless, loyal, the ideal personal asset," when they were put up for sale. Most of the assets he had known, his friends and colleagues, had been city rentspeople, hired out by their owners to companies and corporations to work in factories or shops or at skilled trades. He had also known a good many fieldhands. Fieldhands seldom had any contact with their owners; they worked under gareot bosses and their compounds were run by cutfrees, eunuch assets. The ones he knew had mostly been runaways protected by the Hame, the underground railroad, on their way to independence in Yeowe. None of them had been as utterly deprived of education, options, any imagination of freedom, as these bondspeople were. He had forgotten what a good dusty was like. He had forgotten the utter impenetrability of the person who has no private life, the intactness of the wholly vulnerable.

Kamsa's face was smooth, serene, and showed no feeling, though he heard her sometimes talking and singing very softly to her baby, a joyful, merry little noise. It drew him. He saw her one afternoon sitting at work on the coping of the great terrace, the baby in its sling on her back. He limped over and sat down nearby. He could not prevent her from setting her knife and board aside and standing head and hands and eyes down in reverence as he came near.

"Please sit down, please go on with your work," he said. She obeyed. "What's that you're cutting up?"

"Dueli, master," she whispered.

It was a vegetable he had often eaten and enjoyed. He watched her work. Each big, woody pod had to be split along a sealed seam, not an easy trick; it took a careful search for the opening-point and hard, repeated twists of the blade to open the pod. Then the fat edible seeds had to be removed one by one and scraped free of a stringy, clinging matrix.

"Does that part taste bad?" he asked.

"Yes, master."

It was a laborious process, requiring strength, skill, and patience. He was ashamed. "I never saw raw dueli before," he said.

"No, master."

"What a good baby," he said, a little at random. The tiny creature in its sling, its head lying on her shoulder, had opened large bluish-black eyes and was gazing vaguely at the world. He had never heard it cry. It seemed rather unearthly to him, but he had not had much to do with babies.

She smiled.

"A boy?"

"Yes, master."

He said, "Please, Kamsa, my name is Esdan. I'm not a master. I'm a prisoner. Your masters are my masters. Will you call me by my name?"

She did not answer.

"Our masters would disapprove."

She nodded. The Werelian nod was a tip back of the head, not a bob down. He was completely used to it after all these years. It was the way he nodded himself. He noticed himself noticing it now. His captivity, his treatment here, had displaced, disoriented him. These last few days he had thought more about Hain than he had for years, decades. He had been at home on Werel, and now was not. Inappropriate comparisons, irrelevant memories. Alienated.

"They put me in the cage," he said, speaking as low as she did and hesitating on the last word. He could not say the whole word, crouchcage.

Again the nod. This time, for the first time, she looked up at him, the flick of a glance. She said soundlessly, "I know," and went on with her work.

He found nothing more to say.

"I was a pup, then I did live there," she said, with a glance in the direction of the compound where the cage was. Her murmuring voice was profoundly controlled, as were all her gestures and movements. "Before that time the house burned. When the masters did live here. They did often hang up the cage. Once, a man for until he did die there. In that. I saw that."

Silence between them.

"We pups never did go under that. Never did run there."

"I saw the . . . the ground was different, underneath," Esdan said, speaking as softly and with a dry mouth, his breath coming short. "I saw, looking down. The grass. I thought maybe . . . where they . . ." His voice dried up entirely.

"One grandmother did take a stick, long, a cloth on the end of that, and wet it, and hold it up to him. The cutfrees did look away. But he did die. And rot some time."

"What had he done?"

"Enna," she said, the one-word denial he'd often heard assets use—I don't know, I didn't do it, I wasn't there, it's not my fault, who knows. . . .

He'd seen an owner's child who said "enna" be slapped, not for the cup she broke but for using a slave word.

"A useful lesson," he said. He knew she'd understand him. Underdogs know irony like they know air and water.

"They did put you in that, then I did fear," she said.

"The lesson was for me, not you, this time," he said.

She worked, carefully, ceaselessly. He watched her work. Her downcast face, clay-color with bluish shadows, was composed, peaceful. The baby was darker-skinned than she. She had not been bred to a bondsman, but used by an owner. They called rape "use." The baby's eyes closed slowly, translucent bluish lids like little shells. It was small and delicate, probably only a month or two old. Its head lay with infinite patience on her stooping shoulder.

No one else was out on the terraces. A slight wind stirred in the flow-ering trees behind them, streaked the distant river with silver.

"Your baby, Kamsa, you know, he will be free," Esdan said.

She looked up, not at him, but at the river and across it. She said, "Yes. He will be free." She went on working.

It heartened him, her saying that to him. It did him good to know she trusted him. He needed someone to trust him, for since the cage he could not trust himself. With Rayaye he was all right; he could still fence; that wasn't the trouble. It was when he was alone, thinking, sleep-ing. He was alone most of the time. Something in his mind, deep in him, was injured, broken, had not mended, could not be trusted to bear his weight.

He heard the flyer come down in the morning. That night Rayaye invited him down to dinner. Tualenem and the two veots ate with them and excused themselves, leaving him and Rayaye with a half-bottle of wine at the makeshift table set up in one of the least damaged down-stairs rooms. It had been a hunting-lodge or trophy-room, here in this wing of the house that had been the azade, the men's side, where no women would ever have come; female assets, servants and usewomen, did not count as women. The head of a huge packdog snarled above the mantel, its fur singed and dusty and its glass eyes gone dull. Crossbows had been mounted on the facing wall. Their pale shadows were clear on the dark wood. The electric chandelier flickered and dimmed. The generator was uncertain. One of the old bondsmen was always tinker-ing at it.

"Going off to his usewoman," Rayaye said, nodding towards the door Tualenem had just closed with assiduous wishes for the Minister to have a good night. "Fucking a white. Like fucking turds. Makes my skin crawl. Sticking his cock into a slave cunt. When the war's over there'll be no more of that kind of thing. Halfbreeds are the root of this revolu-tion. Keep the races separate. Keep the ruler blood clean. It's the only answer." He spoke as if expecting complete accord, but did not wait to receive any sign of it. He poured Esdan's glass full and went in his resonant politician's voice, kind host, lord of the manor, "Well, Mr. Old Music, I hope you've been having a pleasant stay at Yaramera, and that your health's improved."

A civil murmur.

"President Oyo was sorry to hear you'd been unwell and sends his wishes for your full recovery. He's glad to know you're safe from any further mistreatment by the insurgents. You can stay here in safety as long as you like. However, when the time is right, the President and his cabinet are looking forward to having you in Bellen."

Civil murmur.

Long habit prevented Esdan from asking questions that would reveal the extent of his ignorance. Rayaye like most politicians loved his own voice, and as he talked Esdan tried to piece together a rough sketch of the current situation. It appeared that the Legitimate Government had moved from the city to a town, Bellen, northeast of Yaramera, near the eastern coast. Some kind of command had been left in the city. Rayaye's references to it made Esdan wonder if the city was in fact semi-independent of the Oyo government, governed by a faction, perhaps a military faction.

When the Uprising began, Oyo had at once been given extraordinary powers; but the Legitimate Army of Voe Deo, after their stunning defeats in the west, had been restive under his command, wanting more autonomy in the field. The civilian government had demanded retaliation, attack, and victory. The army wanted to contain the insurrection. Rega-General Aydan had established the Divide in the city and tried to establish and hold a border between the new Free State and the Legitimate Provinces. Veots who had gone over to the Uprising with their asset troops had similarly urged a border truce to the Liberation Command. The army sought armistice, the warriors sought peace. But "So

long as there is one slave I am not free," cried Nekam-Anna, Leader of
the Free State, and President Oyo thundered, "The nation will not be
divided! We will defend legitimate property with the last drop of blood
in our veins!" The Rega-General had suddenly been replaced by a new
Commander-in-Chief. Very soon after that the embassy was sealed, its
access to information cut.

Esdan could only guess what had happened in the half year since.
Rayaye talked of "our victories in the south" as if the Legitimate Army
had been on the attack, pushing back into the Free State across the
Devan River, south of the city. If so, if they had regained territory, why
had the government pulled out of the city and dug in down at Bellen?
Rayaye's talk of victories might be translated to mean that the Army
of the Liberation had been trying to cross the river in the south and
the Legitimates had been successful in holding them off. If they were
willing to call that a victory, had they finally given up the dream of
reversing the revolution, retaking the whole country, and decided to
cut their losses?

"A divided nation is not an option," Rayaye said, squashing that hope.
"You understand that, I think."

Civil assent.

Rayaye poured out the last of the wine. "But peace is our goal. Our
very strong and urgent goal. Our unhappy country has suffered enough."

Definite assent.

"I know you to be a man of peace, Mr. Old Music. We know the Ekumen fosters harmony among and within its member states. Peace is what
we all desire with all our hearts."

Assent, plus faint indication of inquiry.

"As you know, the Government of Voe Deo has always had the power
to end the insurrection. The means to end it quickly and completely."

No response but alert attention.

"And I think you know that it is only our respect for the policies of the Ekumen, of which my nation is a member, that has prevented us from using that means."

Absolutely no response or acknowledgment.

"You do know that, Mr. Old Music."

"I assumed you had a natural wish to survive."

Rayaye shook his head as if bothered by an insect. "Since we joined the Ekumen—and long before we joined it, Mr. Old Music—we have loyally followed its policies and bowed to its theories. And so we lost Yeowe! And so we lost the West! Four million dead, Mr. Old Music. Four million in the first Uprising. Millions since. Millions. If we had contained it then, many, many fewer would have died. Assets as well as owners."

"Suicide," Esdan said in a soft mild voice, the way assets spoke.

"The pacifist sees all weapons as evil, disastrous, suicidal. For all the age-old wisdom of your people, Mr. Old Music, you have not the experiential perspective on matters of war we younger, cruder peoples are forced to have. Believe me, we are not suicidal. We want our people, our nation, to survive. We are determined that it shall. The bibo was fully tested, long before we joined the Ekumen. It is controllable, targetable, containable. It is an exact weapon, a precise tool of war. Rumor and fear have wildly exaggerated its capacities and nature. We know how to use it, how to limit its effects. Nothing but the response of the Stabiles through your Ambassador prevented us from selective deployment in the first summer of the insurrection."

"I had the impression the high command of the Army of Voe Deo was also opposed to deploying that weapon."

"Some generals were. Many veots are rigid in their thinking, as you know."

"That decision has been changed?"

"President Oyo has authorised deployment of the bibo against forces massing to invade this province from the west."

Such a cute word, bibo. Esdan closed his eyes for a moment.

"The destruction will be appalling," Rayaye said.

Assent.

"It is possible," Rayaye said, leaning forward, black eyes in black face, intense as a hunting cat, "that if the insurgents were warned, they might withdraw. Be willing to discuss terms. If they withdraw, we will not attack. If they will talk, we will talk. A holocaust can be prevented. They respect the Ekumen. They respect you personally, Mr. Old Music. They trust you. If you were to speak to them on the net, or if their leaders will agree to a meeting, they will listen to you, not as their enemy, their oppressor, but as the voice of a benevolent, peace-loving neutrality, the voice of wisdom, urging them to save themselves while there is yet time. This is the opportunity I offer you, and the Ekumen. To spare your friends among the rebels, to spare this world untold suffering. To open the way to lasting peace."

"I am not authorised to speak for the Ekumen. The Ambassador—"

"Will not. Cannot. Is not free to. You are. You are a free agent, Mr. Old Music. Your position on Werel is unique. Both sides respect you. Trust you. And your voice carries infinitely more weight among the whites than his. He came only a year before the insurrection. You are, I may say, one of us."

"I am not one of you. I neither own nor am owned. You must redefine yourselves to include me."

Rayaye, for a moment, had nothing to say. He was taken aback, and would be angry. Fool, Esdan said to himself, old fool, to take the moral high ground! But he did not know what ground to stand on.

It was true that his word would carry more weight than the Ambassador's. Nothing else Rayaye had said made sense. If President Oyo wanted the Ekumen's blessing on his use of this weapon and seriously thought Esdan would give it, why was he working through Rayaye, and keeping Esdan hidden at Yaramera? Was Rayaye working with Oyo, or was he working for a faction that favored using the bibo, while Oyo still refused?

Most likely the whole thing was a bluff. There was no weapon. Esdan's pleading was to lend credibility to it, while leaving Oyo out of the loop if the bluff failed.

The biobomb, the bibo, had been a curse on Voe Deo for decades, centuries. In panic fear of alien invasion after the Ekumen first contacted them almost four hundred years ago, the Werelians had put all their resources into developing space flight and weaponry. The scientists who invented this particular device repudiated it, informing their government that it could not be contained; it would destroy all human and animal life over an enormous area and cause profound and permanent genetic damage worldwide as it spread throughout the water and the atmosphere. The government never used the weapon but was never willing to destroy it, and its existence had kept Werel from membership in the Ekumen as long as the Embargo was in force. Voe Deo insisted it was their guarantee against extraterrestrial invasion and perhaps believed it would prevent revolution. Yet they had not used it when their slave-planet Yeowe rebelled. Then, after the Ekumen no longer observed the Embargo, they announced that they had destroyed the stockpiles. Werel joined the Ekumen. Voe Deo invited inspection of the weapon sites. The Ambassador politely declined, citing the Ekumenical policy of trust. Now the bibo existed again. In fact? In Rayaye's mind? Was he desperate? A hoax, an attempt to use the Ekumen to back a bogey threat to scare off an invasion: the likeliest scenario, yet it was not quite convincing.

"This war must end," Rayaye said.

"I agree."

"We will never surrender. You must understand that." Rayaye had dropped his blandishing, reasonable tone. "We will restore the holy order of the world," he said, and now he was fully credible. His eyes, the dark Werelian eyes that had no whites, were fathomless in the dim light. He drank down his wine. "You think we fight for our property. To keep what we own. But I tell you, we fight to defend our Lady. In that fight is no surrender. And no compromise."

"Your Lady is merciful."

"The Law is her mercy."

Esdan was silent.

"I must go again tomorrow to Bellen," Rayaye said after a while, resuming his masterful, easy tone. "Our plans for moving on the southern front must be fully coordinated. When I come back, I'll need to know if you will give us the help I've asked you for. Our response will depend largely on that. On your voice. It is known that you're here in the East Provinces—known to the insurgents, I mean, as well as our people—though your exact location is of course kept hidden for your own safety. It is known that you may be preparing a statement of a change in the Ekumen's attitude toward the conduct of the civil war. A change that could save millions of lives and bring a just peace to our land. I hope you'll employ your time here in doing so."

He is a factionalist, Esdan thought. He's not going to Bellen, or if he is, that's not where Oyo's government is. This is some scheme of his own. Crackbrained. It won't work. He doesn't have the bibo. But he has a gun. And he'll shoot me.

"Thank you for a pleasant dinner, Minister," he said.

Next morning he heard the flyer leave at dawn. He limped out into the morning sunshine after breakfast. One of his veot guards watched him from a window and then turned away. In a sheltered nook just under the balustrade of the south terrace, near a planting of great bushes with big, blowsy, sweet-smelling white flowers, he saw Kamsa with her baby and Heo. He made his way to them, dot-and-go-one. The distances at Yaramera, even inside the house, were daunting to a lamed man. When he finally got there he said, "I am lonely. May I sit with you?"

The women were afoot, of course, reverencing, though Kamsa's reverence had become pretty sketchy. He sat on a curved bench splotched all over with fallen flowers. They sat back down on the flagstone path with the baby. They had unwrapped the little body to the mild sunshine. It was a very thin baby, Esdan thought. The joints in the bluish-dark arms and legs were like the joints in flowerstems, translucent knobs. The baby was moving more than he had ever seen it move, stretching its arms and turning its head as if enjoying the feel of the air. The head was large for the neck, again like a flower, too large a flower on too thin a stalk. Kamsa dangled one of the real flowers over the baby. His dark eyes gazed up at it. His eyelids and eyebrows were exquisitely delicate. The sunlight shone through his fingers. He smiled. Esdan caught his breath. The baby's smile at the flower was the beauty of the flower, the beauty of the world.

"What is his name?"

"Rekam."

Grandson of Kamye. Kamye the Lord and slave, huntsman and husbandman, warrior and peacemaker.

"A beautiful name. How old is he?"

In the language they spoke that was, "How long has he lived?" Kamsa's answer was strange. "As long as his life," she said, or so he understood her whisper and her dialect. Maybe it was bad manners or bad luck to ask a child's age.

He sat back on the bench. "I feel very old," he said. "I haven't seen a baby for a hundred years."

Heo sat hunched over, her back to him; he felt that she wanted to cover her ears. She was terrified of him, the alien. Life had not left much to Heo but fear, he guessed. Was she twenty, twenty-five? She looked forty. Maybe she was seventeen. Usewomen, ill-used, aged fast. Kamsa he guessed to be not much over twenty. She was thin and plain, but there was bloom and juice in her as there was not in Heo.

"Master did have children?" Kamsa asked, lifting up her baby to her breast with a certain discreet pride, shyly flaunting.

"No."

"*A yera yera,*" she murmured, another slave word he had often heard in the urban compounds: O pity, pity.

"How you get to the center of things, Kamsa," he said. She glanced his way and smiled. Her teeth were bad but it was a good smile. He thought the baby was not sucking. It lay peacefully in the crook of her arm. Heo remained tense and jumped whenever he spoke, so he said no more. He looked away from them, past the bushes, out over the wonderful view that arranged itself, wherever you walked or sat, into a perfect balance: the levels of flagstone, of dun grass and blue water, the curves of the avenues, the masses and lines of shrubbery, the great old tree, the misty river and its green far bank. Presently the women began talking softly again. He did not listen to what they said. He was aware of their voices, aware of sunlight, aware of peace.

Old Gana came stumping across the upper terrace towards them, bobbed to him, said to Kamsa and Heo, "Choyo does want you. Leave me that baby." Kamsa set the baby down on the warm stone again. She and Heo sprang up and went off, thin, light women moving with easy haste. The old woman settled down piece by piece and with groans and grimaces onto the path beside Rekam. She immediately covered him up with a fold of his swaddling-cloth, frowning and muttering at the foolishness of his mother. Esdan watched her careful movements, her gentleness when she picked the child up, supporting that heavy head and tiny limbs, her tenderness cradling him, rocking her body to rock him.

She looked up at Esdan. She smiled, her face wrinkling up into a thousand wrinkles. "He is my great gift," she said.

He whispered, "Your grandson?"

The backward nod. She kept rocking gently. The baby's eyes were closed, his head lay softly on her thin, dry breast. "I think now he'll die not long now."

After a while Esdan said, "Die?"

The nod. She still smiled. Gently, gently rocking. "He is two years of age, master."

"I thought he was born this summer," Esdan said in a whisper.

The old woman said, "He did come to stay a little while with us."

"What is wrong?"

"The wasting."

Esdan had heard the term. He said, "Avo?" the name he knew for it, a systemic viral infection common among Werelian children, frequently epidemic in the asset compounds of the cities.

She nodded.

"But it's curable!"

The old woman said nothing.

Avo was completely curable. Where there were doctors. Where there was medicine. Avo was curable in the city not the country. In the great house not the asset quarters. In peacetime not in wartime. Fool!

Maybe she knew it was curable, maybe she did not, maybe she did not know what the word meant. She rocked the baby, crooning in a whisper, paying no attention to the fool. But she had heard him, and answered him at last, not looking at him, watching the baby's sleeping face.

"I was born owned," she said, "and my daughters. But he was not. He is the gift. To us. Nobody can own him. The gift of the Lord Kamye of himself. Who could keep that gift?"

Esdan bowed his head down.

He had said to the mother, "He will be free." And she had said, "Yes."

He said at last, "May I hold him?"

The grandmother stopped rocking and held still a while. "Yes," she said. She raised herself up and very carefully transferred the sleeping baby into Esdan's arms, onto his lap.

"You do hold my joy," she said.

The child weighed nothing—six or seven pounds. It was like holding a warm flower, a tiny animal, a bird. The swaddling-cloth trailed down across the stones. Gana gathered it up and laid it softly around the baby, hiding his face. Tense and nervous, jealous, full of pride, she knelt there. Before long she took the baby back against her heart. "There," she said, and her face softened into happiness.

That night Esdan sleeping in the room that looked out over the terraces of Yaramera dreamed that he had lost a little round, flat stone that he always carried with him in a pouch. The stone was from the pueblo. When he held it in his palm and warmed it, it was able to speak, to talk with him. But he had not talked with it for a long time. Now he realised he did not have it. He had lost it, left it somewhere. He thought it was in the basement of the embassy. He tried to get into the basement, but the door was locked, and he could not find the other door.

He woke. Early morning. No need to get up. He should think about what to do, what to say, when Rayaye came back. He could not. He thought about the dream, the stone that talked. He wished he had heard what it said. He thought about the pueblo. His father's brother's family had lived in Arkanan Pueblo in the Far South Highlands. In his boyhood, every year in the heart of the northern winter, Esi had flown down there for forty days of summer. With his parents at first, later on alone. His uncle and aunt had grown up in Darranda and were not pueblo people. Their children were. They had grown up in Arkanan and belonged to it entirely. The eldest, Suhan, fourteen years older than Esdan, had been born with irreparable brain and neural defects, and it was for his sake that his parents had settled in a pueblo. There was a place for him there. He became a herdsman. He went up on the mountains with the yama, animals the South Hainish had brought over from O a millennium or so ago. He looked after the animals. He came back to live in the pueblo only in winter. Esi saw him seldom, and was glad of it, finding Suhan a fearful figure—big, shambling, foul-smelling, with a loud braying voice, mouthing incomprehensible words. Esi could not understand why Suhan's parents and sisters loved him. He thought they pretended to. No one could love him.

To adolescent Esdan it was still a problem. His cousin Noy, Suhan's sister, who had become the Water Chief of Arkanan, told him it was not a problem but a mystery. "You see how Suhan is our guide?" she said. "Look at it. He led my parents here to live. So my sister and I were born here. So you come to stay with us here. So you've learned to live in the pueblo. You'll never be just a city man. Because Suhan guided you here. Guided us all. Into the mountains."

"He didn't really guide us," the fourteen-year-old argued.

"Yes, he did. We followed his weakness. His incompleteness. Failure's open. Look at water, Esi. It finds the weak places in the rock, the openings, the hollows, the absences. Following water we come where we belong." Then she had gone off to arbitrate a dispute over the usage-rights to an irrigation system outside town, for the east side of the mountains was very dry country, and the people of Arkanan were contentious, though hospitable, and the Water Chief stayed busy.

But Suhan's condition had been irreparable, his weakness inaccesible even to the wondrous medical skills of Hain. This baby was dying of a disease that could be cured by a mere series of injections. It was wrong to accept his illness, his death. It was wrong to let him be cheated out of his life by circumstance, bad luck, an unjust society, a fatalistic religion. A religion that fostered and encouraged the terrible passivity of the slaves, that told these women to do nothing, to let the child waste away and die.

He should interfere, he should do something, what could be done?

"How long has he lived?"

"As long as his life."

There was nothing they could do. Nowhere to go. No one to turn to. A cure for avo existed, in some places, for some children. Not in this place, not for this child. Neither anger nor hope served any purpose. Nor grief. It was not the time for grief yet. Rekam was here with them, and they would delight in him as long as he was here. As long as his life. *He is my great gift. You do hold my joy.*

This was a strange place to come to learn the quality of joy. Water is my guide, he thought. His hands still felt what it had been like to hold the child, the light weight, the brief warmth.

HE WAS OUT ON THE TERRACE LATE THE NEXT MORNING, WAIT-ing for Kamsa and the baby to come out as they usually did, but the older veot came instead. "Mr. Old Music, I must ask you to stay indoors for a time," he said.

"Zadyo, I'm not going to run away," Esdan said, sticking out his swathed lump of a foot.

"I'm sorry, sir."

He stumped crossly indoors after the veot and was locked into a downstairs room, a windowless storage space behind the kitchens. They had fixed it up with a cot, a table and chair, a pisspot, and a battery lamp for when the generator failed, as it did for a while most days. "Are you expecting an attack, then?" he said when he saw these preparations, but the veot replied only by locking the door. Esdan sat on the cot and meditated, as he had learned to do in Arkanan Pueblo. He cleared dis-tress and anger from his mind by going through the long repetitions: health and good work, courage, patience, peace, for himself, health and good work, courage, patience, peace for the zadyo . . . for Kamsa, for baby Rekam, for Rayaye, for Heo, for Tualenem, for the oga, for Nemeo who had put him in the crouchcage, for Alatual who had put him in the crouchcage, for Gana who had bound his foot and blessed him, for people he knew in the embassy, in the city, health and good work, cour-age, patience, peace. . . . That went well, but the meditation itself was a failure. He could not stop thinking. So he thought. He thought about what he could do. He found nothing. He was weak as water, helpless as the baby. He imagined himself speaking on the holonet with a script saying that the Ekumen reluctantly approved the limited use of biological weapons in order to end the civil war. He imagined himself on the holonet dropping the script and saying that the Ekumen would never approve the use of biological weapons for any reason. Both imaginings were fantasies. Rayaye's schemes were fantasies. Seeing that his hostage was useless Rayaye would have him shot. How long has he lived? As long as sixty-two years. A much fairer share of time than Rekam was getting. His mind went on past thinking.

The zadyo opened the door and told him he could come out.

"How close is the Liberation Army, zadyo?" he asked. He expected no answer. He went out onto the terrace. It was late afternoon. Kamsa was there, sitting with the baby at her breast. Her nipple was in his mouth but he was not sucking. She covered her breast. Her face as she did so looked sad for the first time.

"Is he asleep? May I hold him?" Esdan said, sitting by her.

She shifted the little bundle over to his lap. Her face was still troubled. Esdan thought the child's breathing was more difficult, harder work. But he was awake, and looked up into Esdan's face with his big eyes. Esdan made faces, sticking out his lips and blinking. He won a soft little smile.

"The hands say, that army do come," Kamsa said in her very soft voice.

"The Liberation?"

"Enna. Some army."

"From across the river?"

"I think."

"They're assets—freedmen. They're your own people. They won't hurt you." Maybe.

She was frightened. Her control was perfect, but she was frightened. She had seen the Uprising, here. And the reprisals.

"Hide out, if you can, if there's bombing or fighting," he said. "Underground. There must be hiding places here."

She thought and said, "Yes."

It was peaceful in the gardens of Yaramera. No sound but the wind rustling leaves and the faint buzz of the generator. Even the burned, jagged ruins of the house looked mellowed, ageless. The worst has happened, said the ruins. To them. Maybe not to Kamsa and Heo, Gana and Esdan. But there was no hint of violence in the summer air. The baby smiled its vague smile again, nestling in Esdan's arms. He thought of the stone he had lost in his dream.

He was locked into the windowless room for the night. He had no way to know what time it was when he was roused by noise, brought stark awake by a series of shots and explosions, gunfire or handbombs. There was silence, then a second series of bangs and cracks, fainter. Silence again, stretching on and on. Then he heard a flyer right over the house as if circling, sounds inside the house: a shout, running. He lighted the lamp, struggled into his trousers, hard to pull on over the swathed foot. When he heard the flyer coming back and an explosion, he leapt in panic for the door, knowing nothing but that he had to get out of this deathtrap room. He had always feared fire, dying in fire. The door was solid wood, solidly bolted into its solid frame. He had no hope at all of breaking it down and knew it even in his panic. He shouted once, "Let me out of here!" then got control of himself, returned to the cot, and after a minute sat down on the floor between the cot and the wall, as sheltered a place as the room afforded, trying to imagine what was going on. A Liberation raid and Rayaye's men shooting back, trying to bring the flyer down, was what he imagined.

Dead silence. It went on and on.

His lamp flickered.

He got up and stood at the door.

"Let me out!"

No sound.

A single shot. Voices again, running feet again, shouting, calling. After another long silence, distant voices, the sound of men coming down the corridor outside the room. A man said, "Keep them out there for now," a flat, harsh voice. He hesitated and nerved himself and shouted out, "I'm a prisoner! In here!"

A pause.

"Who's in there?"

It was no voice he had heard. He was good at voices, faces, names, intentions.

"Esdardon Aya of the embassy of the Ekumen."

"Mighty Lord!" the voice said.

"Get me out of here, will you?"

There was no reply, but the door was rattled vainly on its massive hinges, was thumped; more voices outside, more thumping and banging. "Axe," somebody said. "Find the key," somebody else said; they went off. Esdan waited. He fought down a repeated impulse to laugh, afraid of hysteria, but it was funny, stupidly funny, all the shouting through the door and seeking keys and axes, a farce in the middle of a battle. What battle?

He had had it backwards. Liberation men had entered the house and killed Rayaye's men, taking most of them by surprise. They had been waiting for Rayaye's flyer when it came. They must have had contacts among the fieldhands, informers, guides. Sealed in his room, he had heard only the noisy end of the business. When he was let out, they were dragging out the dead. He saw the horribly maimed body of one of the young men, Alatual or Nemeo, come apart as they dragged it, ropy blood and entrails stretching out along the floor, the legs left behind.

The man dragging the corpse was nonplussed and stood there holding the shoulders of the torso. "Well, shit," he said, and Esdan stood gasping, again trying not to laugh, not to vomit.

"Come on," said the men with him, and he came on.

Early morning light slanted through broken windows. Esdan kept looking around, seeing none of the house people. The men took him into the room with the packdog head over the mantel. Six or seven men were gathered around the table there. They wore no uniforms, though some had the yellow knot or ribbon of the Liberation on their cap or sleeve. They were ragged, tough, hard. Some were dark, some had beige or clayey or bluish skin, all of them looked edgy and dangerous. One of those with him, a thin, tall man, said in the harsh voice that had said "Mighty Lord" outside the door: "This is him."

"I'm Esdardon Aya, Old Music, of the embassy of the Ekumen," he said again, as easily as he could. "I was being held here. Thank you for liberating me."

Several of them stared at him the way people who had never seen an alien stared, taking in his red-brown skin and deep-set, white-cornered eyes and the subtler differences of skull structure and features. One or two stared more aggressively, as if to test his assertion, show they'd believe he was what he said he was when he proved it. A big, broad-shouldered man, white-skinned and with brownish hair, pure dusty, pure blood of the ancient conquered race, looked at Esdan a long time. "We came to do that," he said.

He spoke softly, the asset voice. It might take them a generation or more to learn to raise their voices, to speak free.

"How did you know I was here? The fieldnet?"

It was what they had called the clandestine system of information passed from voice to ear, field to compound to city and back again, long before there was a holonet. The Hame had used the fieldnet and it had been the chief instrument of the Uprising.

A short, dark man smiled and nodded slightly, then froze his nod as he saw that the others weren't giving out any information.

"You know who brought me here, then—Rayaye. I don't know who he was acting for. What I can tell you, I will." Relief had made him stupid, he was talking too much, playing hands-around-the-flowerbed while they played tough guy. "I have friends here," he went on in a more neutral voice, looking at each of their faces in turn, direct but civil. "Bondswomen, house people. I hope they're all right."

"Depends," said a grey-haired, slight man who looked very tired.

"A woman with a baby, Kamsa. An old woman, Gana."

A couple of them shook their heads to signify ignorance or indifference. Most made no response at all. He looked around at them again, repressing anger and irritation at this pomposity, this tight-lipped stuff.

"We need to know what you were doing here," the brown-haired man said.

"A Liberation Army contact in the city was taking me from the embassy to Liberation Command, about fifteen days ago. We were intercepted in the Divide by Rayaye's men. They brought me here. I spent some time in a crouchcage," Esdan said in the same neutral voice. "My foot was hurt and I can't walk much. I talked twice with Rayaye. Before I say anything else I think you can understand that I need to know who I'm talking to."

The tall thin man who had released him from the locked room went around the table and conferred briefly with the grey-haired man. The brown-haired one listened, consented. The tall thin one spoke to Esdan in his uncharacteristically harsh, flat voice: "We are a special mission of the Advance Army of the World Liberation. I am Marshal Metoy." The others all said their names. The big brown-haired man was General Banarkamye, the tired older man was General Tueyo. They said their rank with their name, but didn't use it addressing one another, nor did they call him Mister. Before Liberation, rentspeople had seldom used any titles to one another but those of parentage: father, sister, aunty. Titles were something that went in front of an owner's name: Lord, Master, Mister, Boss. Evidently the Liberation had decided to do without them. It pleased him to find an army that didn't click its heels and shout Sir! But he wasn't certain what army he'd found.

"They kept you in that room?" Metoy asked him. He was a strange man, a flat, cold voice, a pale, cold face, but he wasn't as jumpy as the others. He seemed sure of himself, used to being in charge.

"They locked me in there last night. As if they'd had some kind of warning of trouble coming. Usually I had a room upstairs."

"You may go there now," Metoy said. "Stay indoors."

"I will. Thank you again," he said to them all. "Please, when you have word of Kamsa and Gana—?" He did not wait to be snubbed, but turned and went out.

One of the younger men went with him. He had named himself Zadyo Tema. The Army of the Liberation was using the old veot ranks, then. There were veots among them, Esdan knew, but Tema was not one. He was light-skinned and had the city-dusty accent, soft, dry, clipped. Esdan did not try to talk to him. Tema was extremely nervous, spooked by the night's work of killing at close quarters or by something else; there was an almost constant tremor in his shoulders, arms, and hands, and his pale face was set in a painful scowl. He was not in a mood for chitchat with an elderly civilian alien prisoner.

In war everybody is a prisoner, the historian Henennemores had written.

Esdan had thanked his new captors for liberating him, but he knew where, at the moment, he stood. It was still Yaramera.

Yet there was some relief in seeing his room again, sitting down in the one-armed chair by the window to look out at the early sunlight, the long shadows of trees across the lawns and terraces.

None of the housepeople came out as usual to go about their work or take a break from it. Nobody came to his room. The morning wore on. He did what exercises of the tanhai he could do with his foot as it was. He sat aware, dozed off, woke up, tried to sit aware, sat restless, anxious, working over words: *A special mission of the Advance Army of World Liberation.*

The Legitimate Government called the enemy army "insurgent forces" or "rebel hordes" on the holonews. It had started out calling itself the Army of the Liberation, nothing about World Liberation; but he had been cut off from any coherent contact with the freedom fighters ever since the Uprising, and cut off from all information of any kind since the embassy was sealed—except for information from other worlds light years away, of course, there'd been no end of that, the ansible was full of it, but of what was going on two streets away, nothing, not a word. In the embassy he'd been ignorant, useless, helpless, passive. Exactly as he was here. Since the war began he'd been, as Henennemores had said, a prisoner. Along with everybody else on Werel. A prisoner in the cause of liberty.

He feared that he would come to accept his helplessness, that it would persuade his soul. He must remember what this war was about. But let the Liberation come soon, he thought, come set me free!

In the middle of the afternoon the young zadyo brought him a plate of cold food, obviously scraps and leftovers they'd found in the kitchens, and a bottle of beer. He ate and drank gratefully. But it was clear that they had not released the housepeople. Or had killed them. He would not let his mind stay on that.

After sunset the zadyo came back and brought him downstairs to the packdog room. The generator was off, of course; nothing had kept it going but old Saka's eternal tinkering. Men carried electric torches, and in the packdog room a couple of big oil lamps burned on the table, putting a romantic, golden light on the faces round it, throwing deep shadows behind them.

"Sit down," said the brown-haired general, Banarkamye—Read-bible, his name could be translated. "We have some questions to ask you."

Silent but civil assent.

They asked how he had got out of the embassy, who his contacts with the Liberation had been, where he had been going, why he had tried to go, what happened during the kidnapping, who had brought him here, what they had asked him, what they had wanted from him. Having decided during the afternoon that candor would serve him best, he answered all the questions directly and briefly until the last one.

"I personally am on your side of this war," he said, "but the Ekumen is necessarily neutral. Since at the moment I'm the only alien on Werel free to speak, whatever I say may be taken, or mistaken, as coming from the embassy and the Stabiles. That was my value to Rayaye. It may be my value to you. But it's a false value. I can't speak for the Ekumen. I have no authority."

"They wanted you to say the Ekumen supports the Jits," the tired man, Tueyo, said.

Esdan nodded.

"Did they talk about using any special tactics, weapons?" That was Banarkamye, grim, trying not to weight the question.

"I'd rather answer that question when I'm behind your lines, General, talking to people I know in Liberation Command."

"You're talking to the World Liberation Army Command. Refusal to answer can be taken as evidence of complicity with the enemy." That was Metoy, glib, hard, harsh-voiced.

"I know that, Marshal."

They exchanged a glance. Despite his open threat, Metoy was the one Esdan felt inclined to trust. He was solid. The others were nervy, unsteady. He was sure now that they were factionalists. How big their faction was, how much at odds with Liberation Command it was, he could learn only by what they might let slip.

"Listen, Mr. Old Music," Tueyo said. Old habits die hard. "We know you worked for the Hame. You helped send people to Yeowe. You backed us then." Esdan nodded. "You must back us now. We are speaking to you frankly. We have information that the Jits are planning a counter-attack. What that means, now, it means that they're going to use the bibo. It can't mean anything else. That can't happen. They can't be let to do that. They have to be stopped."

"You say the Ekumen is neutral," Banarkamye said. "That is a lie. A hundred years the Ekumen wouldn't let this world join them, because we had the bibo. Had it, didn't use it, just had it was enough. Now they say they're neutral. Now when it matters! Now when this world is part of them! They have got to act. To act against that weapon. They have got to stop the Jits from using it."

"If the Legitimates did have it, if they did plan to use it, and if I could get word to the Ekumen—what could they do?"

"You speak. You tell the Jit President: the Ekumen says stop there. The Ekumen will send ships, send troops. You back us! If you aren't with us, you are with them!"

"General, the nearest ship is light years away. The Legitimates know that."

"But you can call them, you have the transmitter."

"The ansible in the embassy?"

"The Jits have one of them too."

"The ansible in the foreign ministry was destroyed in the Uprising. In the first attack on the government buildings. They blew the whole block up."

"How do we know that?"

"Your own forces did it. General, do you think the Legitimates have an ansible link with the Ekumen that you don't have? They don't. They could have taken over the embassy and its ansible, but in so doing they'd have lost what credibility they have with the Ekumen. And what good would it have done them? The Ekumen has no troops to send," and he added, because he was suddenly not sure Banarkamye knew it, "as you know. If it did, it would take them years to get here. For that reason and many others, the Ekumen has no army and fights no wars."

He was deeply alarmed by their ignorance, their amateurishness, their fear. He kept alarm and impatience out of his voice, speaking quietly and looking at them unworriedly, as if expecting understanding and agreement. The mere appearance of such confidence sometimes fulfills itself. Unfortunately, from the looks of their faces, he was telling the two generals they'd been wrong and telling Metoy he'd been right. He was taking sides in a disagreement.

Banarkamye said, "Keep all that a while yet," and went back over the first interrogation, repeating questions, asking for more details, listening to them expressionlessly. Saving face. Showing he distrusted the hostage. He kept pressing for anything Rayaye had said concerning an invasion or a counterattack in the south. Esdan repeated several times that Rayaye had said President Oyo was expecting a Liberation invasion of this province, downriver from here. Each time he added, "I have no idea whether anything Rayaye told me was the truth." The fourth or fifth time round he said, "Excuse me, General. I must ask again for some word about the people here—"

"Did you know anybody at this place before you came here?" a younger man asked sharply.

"No. I'm asking about housepeople. They were kind to me. Kamsa's baby is sick, it needs care. I'd like to know they're being looked after."

The generals were conferring with each other, paying no attention to this diversion.

"Anybody stayed here, a place like this, after the Uprising, is a collaborator," said the zadyo, Tema.

"Where were they supposed to go?" Esdan asked, trying to keep his tone easy. "This isn't liberated country. The bosses still work these fields with slaves. They still use the crouchcage here." His voice shook a little on the last words, and he cursed himself for it.

Banarkamye and Tueyo were still conferring, ignoring his question. Metoy stood up and said, "Enough for tonight. Come with me."

Esdan limped after him across the hall, up the stairs. The young zadyo followed, hurrying, evidently sent by Banarkamye. No private conversations allowed. Metoy, however, stopped at the door of Esdan's room and said, looking down at him, "The housepeople will be looked after."

"Thank you," Esdan said with warmth. He added, "Gana was caring for this injury. I need to see her." If they wanted him alive and undamaged, no harm using his ailments as leverage. If they didn't, no use in anything much.

He slept little and badly. He had always thrived on information and action. It was exhausting to be kept both ignorant and helpless, crippled mentally and physically. And he was hungry.

Soon after sunrise he tried his door and found it locked. He knocked and shouted a while before anybody came, a young fellow looking scared, probably a sentry, and then Tema, sleepy and scowling, with the door key.

"I want to see Gana," Esdan said, fairly peremptory. "She looks after this," gesturing to his swaddled foot. Tema shut the door without saying anything. After an hour or so, the key rattled in the lock again and Gana came in. Metoy followed her. Tema followed him.

Gana stood in the reverence to Esdan. He came forward quickly and put his hands on her arms and laid his cheek against hers. "Lord Kamye be praised I see you well!" he said, words that had often been said to him by people like her. "Kamsa, the baby, how are they?"

She was scared, shaky, her hair unkempt, her eyelids red, but she recovered herself pretty well from his utterly unexpected brotherly greeting. "They are in the kitchen now, sir," she said. "The army men, they said that foot do pain you."

"That's what I said to them. Maybe you'd re-bandage it for me."

He sat down on the bed and she got to work unwrapping the cloths. "Are the other people all right? Heo? Choyo?"

She shook her head once.

"I'm sorry," he said. He could not ask her more.

She did not do as good a job bandaging his foot as before. She had little strength in her hands to pull the wrappings tight, and she hurried her work, unnerved by the strangers watching.

"I hope Choyo's back in the kitchen," he said, half to her half to them. "Somebody's got to do some cooking here."

"Yes, sir," she whispered.

Not sir, not master! he wanted to warn her, fearing for her. He looked up at Metoy, trying to judge his attitude, and could not.

Gana finished her job. Metoy sent her off with a word, and sent the zadyo after her. Gana went gladly, Tema resisted. "General Banarkamye—" he began. Metoy looked at him. The young man hesitated, scowled, obeyed.

"I will look after these people," Metoy said. "I always have. I was a compound boss." He gazed at Esdan with his cold black eyes. "I'm a cutfree. Not many like me left, these days."

Esdan said after a moment, "Thanks, Metoy. They need help. They don't understand."

Metoy nodded.

"I don't understand either," Esdan said. "Does the Liberation plan to invade? Or did Rayaye invent that as an excuse for talking about deploying the bibo? Does Oyo believe it? Do you believe it? Is the Liberation Army across the river there? Did you come from it? Who are you? I don't expect you to answer."

"I won't," the eunuch said.

If he was a double agent, Esdan thought after he left, he was working for Liberation Command. Or he hoped so. Metoy was a man he wanted on his side.

But I don't know what my side is, he thought, as he went back to his chair by the window. The Liberation, of course, yes, but what is the Liberation? Not an ideal, the freedom of the enslaved. Not now. Never again. Since the Uprising, the Liberation is an army, a political body, a great number of people and leaders and would-be leaders, ambitions and greed clogging hopes and strength, a clumsy amateur semi-government lurching from violence to compromise, ever more complicated, never again to know the beautiful simplicity of the ideal, the pure idea of liberty. And that's what I wanted, what I worked for, all these years. To muddle the nobly simple structure of the hierarchy of caste by infecting it with the idea of justice. And then to confuse the nobly simple structure of the ideal of human equality by trying to make it real. The monolithic lie frays out into a thousand incompatible truths, and that's what I wanted. But I am caught in the insanity, the stupidity, the meaningless brutality of the event.

They all want to use me, but I've outlived my usefulness, he thought; and the thought went through him like a shaft of clear light. He had kept thinking there was something he could do. There wasn't.

It was a kind of freedom.

No wonder he and Metoy had understood each other wordlessly and at once.

The zadyo Tema came to his door to conduct him downstairs. Back to the packdog room. All the leader-types were drawn to that room, its dour masculinity. Only five men were there this time, Metoy, the two generals, the two who used the rank of rega. Banarkamye dominated them all. He was through asking questions and was in the order-giving vein. "We leave here tomorrow," he said to Esdan. "You with us. We will have access to the Liberation holonet. You will speak for us. You will tell the Jit government that the Ekumen knows they are planning to deploy banned weapons and warns them that if they do, there will be instant and terrible retaliation."

Esdan was light-headed with hunger and sleeplessness. He stood still—he had not been invited to sit down—and looked down at the floor, his hands at his sides. He murmured barely audibly, "Yes, master."

Banarkamye's head snapped up, his eyes flashed. "What did you say?"

"Enna."

"Who do you think you are?"

"A prisoner of war."

"You can go."

Esdan left. Tema followed him but did not stop or direct him. He made his way straight to the kitchen, where he heard the rattle of pans, and said, "Choyo, please, give me something to eat!" The old man, cowed and shaky, mumbled and apologised and fretted, but produced some fruit and stale bread. Esdan sat at the worktable and devoured it. He offered some to Tema, who refused stiffly. Esdan ate it all. When he was done he limped on out through the kitchen exit-ways to a side door leading to the great terrace. He hoped to see Kamsa there, but none of the housepeople were out. He sat on a bench in the balustrade that looked down on the long reflecting pool. Tema stood nearby, on duty.

"You said the bondspeople on a place like this, if they didn't join the Uprising, were collaborators," Esdan said.

Tema was motionless, but listening.

"You don't think any of them might just not have understood what was going on? And still don't understand? This is a benighted place, zadyo. Hard to even imagine freedom, here."

The young man resisted answering for a while, but Esdan talked on, trying to make some contact with him, get through to him. Suddenly something he said popped the lid.

"Usewomen," Tema said. "Get fucked by blacks, every night. All they are, fucks. Jits' whores. Bearing their black brats, yesmaster yesmaster. You said it, they don't know what freedom is. Never will. Can't liberate anybody lets a black fuck 'em. They're foul. Dirty, can't get clean. They got black jizz through and through 'em. Jit-jizz!" He spat on the terrace and wiped his mouth.

Esdan sat still, looking down over the still water of the pool to the lower terraces, the big tree, the misty river, the far green shore. May he be well and work well, have patience, compassion, peace. What use was I, ever? All I did. It never was any use. Patience, compassion, peace. They are your own people. . . . He looked down at the thick blob of spittle on the yellow sandstone of the terrace. Fool, to leave his own people a lifetime behind him and come to meddle with another world. Fool, to think you could give anybody freedom. That was what death was for. To get us out of the crouchcage.

He got up and limped towards the house in silence. The young man followed him.

The lights came back on just as it was getting dark. They must have let old Saka go back to his tinkering. Preferring twilight, Esdan turned the room light off. He was lying on his bed when Kamsa knocked and came in, carrying a tray. "Kamsa!" he said, struggling up, and would have hugged her, but the tray prevented him. "Rekam is—?"

"With my mother," she murmured.

"He's all right?"

The backward nod. She set the tray down on the bed, as there was no table.

"You're all right? Be careful, Kamsa. I wish I—They're leaving tomorrow, they say. Stay out of their way if you can."

"I do. Do you be safe, sir," she said in her soft voice. He did not know if it was a question or a wish. He made a little rueful gesture, smiling. She turned to leave.

"Kamsa, is Heo—?"

"She was with that one. In his bed."

After a pause he said, "Is there anywhere you can hide out?" He was afraid that Banarkamye's men might execute these people when they left, as "collaborators" or to hide their own tracks.

"We got a hole to go to, like you said," she said.

"Good. Go there, if you can. Vanish! Stay out of sight."

She said, "I will hold fast, sir."

She was closing the door behind her when the sound of a flyer approaching buzzed the windows. They both stood still, she in the doorway, he near the window. Shouts downstairs, outside, men running. There was more than one flyer, approaching from the southeast. "Kill the lights!" somebody shouted. Men were running out to the flyers parked on the lawn and terrace. The window flared up with light, the air with a shattering explosion.

"Come with me," Kamsa said, and took his hand and pulled him after her, out the door, down the hall and through a service door he had never even seen. He hobbled with her as fast as he could down ladderlike stone stairs, through a back passage, out into the stable warren. They came outdoors just as a series of explosions rocked everything around them. They hurried across the courtyard through overwhelming noise and the leap of fire, Kamsa still pulling him along with complete sureness of where she was going, and ducked into one of the storerooms at the end of the stables. Gana was there and one of the old bondsmen, opening up a trap door in the floor. They went down, Kamsa with a leap, the others slow and awkward on the wooden ladder, Esdan most awkward, landing badly on his broken foot. The old man came last and pulled the trap shut over them. Gana had a battery lamp, but kept it on only briefly, showing a big, low, dirt-floored cellar, shelves, an archway to another room, a heap of wooden crates, five faces: the baby awake, gazing silent as ever from its sling on Gana's shoulder. Then darkness. And for some time silence.

They groped at the crates, set them down for seats at random in the darkness.

A new series of explosions, seeming far away, but the ground and the darkness shivered. They shivered in it. "O Kamye," one of them whispered.

Esdan sat on the shaky crate and let the jab and stab of pain in his foot sink into a burning throb.

Explosions: three, four.

Darkness was a substance, like thick water.

"Kamsa," he murmured.

She made some sound that located her near him.

"Thank you."

"You said hide, then we did talk of this place," she whispered.

The old man breathed wheezily and cleared his throat often. The baby's breathing was also audible, a small uneven sound, almost panting.

"Give me him." That was Gana. She must have transferred the baby to his mother.

Kamsa whispered, "Not now."

The old man spoke suddenly and loudly, startling them all: "No water in this!"

Kamsa shushed him and Gana hissed, "Don't shout, fool man!"

"Deaf," Kamsa murmured to Esdan, with a hint of laughter.

If they had no water, their hiding time was limited; the night, the next day; even that might be too long for a woman nursing a baby. Kamsa's mind was running on the same track as Esdan's. She said, "How do we know, should we come out?"

"Chance it, when we have to."

There was a long silence. It was hard to accept that one's eyes did not adjust to the darkness, that however long one waited one would see nothing. It was cave-cool. Esdan wished his shirt were warmer.

"You keep him warm," Gana said.

"I do," Kamsa murmured.

"Those men, they were bondsfolk?" That was Kamsa whispering to him. She was quite near him, to his left.

"Yes. Freed bondsfolk. From the north."

She said, "Lotsalot different men come here, since the old Owner did die. Army soldiers, some. But no bondsfolk before. They shot Heo. They shot Vey and old Seneo. He didn't die but he's shot."

"Somebody from the field compound must have led them, showed them where the guards were posted. But they couldn't tell the bondsfolk from the soldiers. Where were you when they came?"

"Sleeping, back of the kitchen. All us housefolk. Six. That man did stand there like a risen dead. He said, Lie down there! Don't stir a hair! So we did that. Heard them shooting and shouting all over the house. Oh, mighty Lord! I did fear! Then no more shooting, and that man did come back to us and hold his gun at us and take us out to the old house-compound. They did get that old gate shut on us. Like old days."

"For what did they do that if they are bondsfolk?" Gana's voice said from the darkness.

"Trying to get free," Esdan said dutifully.

"How free? Shooting and killing? Kill a girl in the bed?"

"They do all fight all the others, mama," Kamsa said.

"I thought all that was done, back three years," the old woman said. Her voice sounded strange. She was in tears. "I thought that was freedom then."

"They did kill the master in his bed!" the old man shouted out at the top of his voice, shrill, piercing. "What can come of that!"

There was a bit of a scuffle in the darkness. Gana was shaking the old fellow, hissing at him to shut up. He cried, "Let me go!" but quieted down, wheezing and muttering.

"Mighty Lord," Kamsa murmured, with that desperate laughter in her voice.

The crate was increasingly uncomfortable, and Esdan wanted to get his aching foot up or at least level. He lowered himself to the ground. It was cold, gritty, unpleasant to the hands. There was nothing to lean against. "If you made a light for a minute, Gana," he said, "we might find sacks, something to lie down on."

The world of the cellar flashed into being around them, amazing in its intricate precision. They found nothing to use but the loose board shelves. They set down several of these, making a kind of platform, and crept onto it as Gana switched them back into formless simple night. They were all cold. They huddled up against one another, side to side, back to back.

After a long time, an hour or more, in which the utter silence of the cellar was unbroken by any noise, Gana said in an impatient whisper, "Everybody up there did die, I think."

"That would simplify things for us," Esdan murmured.

"But we are the buried ones," said Kamsa.

Their voices roused the baby and he whimpered, the first complaint Esdan had ever heard him make. It was a tiny, weary grizzling or fretting, not a cry. It roughened his breathing and he gasped between his frettings. "Oh, baby, baby, hush now, hush," the mother murmured, and Esdan felt her rocking her body, cradling the baby close to keep him warm. She sang almost inaudibly, *"Suna meya, suna na . . . Sura rena, sura na . . ."* Monotonous, rhythmic, buzzy, purring, the sound made warmth, made comfort.

He must have dozed. He was lying curled up on the planks. He had no idea how long they had been in the cellar.

I have lived here forty years desiring freedom, his mind said to him. That desire brought me here. It will bring me out of here. I will hold fast.

He asked the others if they had heard anything since the bombing raid. They all whispered no.

He rubbed his head. "What do you think, Gana?" he said.

"I think the cold air does harm that baby," she said in almost her normal voice, which was always low.

"You do talk? What do you say?" the old man shouted. Kamsa, next to him, patted him and quieted him.

"I'll go look," Gana said.

"I'll go."

"You got one foot on you," the old woman said in a disgusted tone. She grunted and leaned hard on Esdan's shoulder as she stood up. "Now be still." She did not turn on the light, but felt her way over to the ladder and climbed it, with a little whuff of breath at each step up. She pushed, heaved at the trap door. An edge of light showed. They could dimly see the cellar and each other and the dark blob of Gana's head up in the light. She stood there a long time, then let the trap down. "Nobody," she whispered from the ladder. "No noise. Looks like first morning."

"Better wait," Esdan said.

She came back and lowered herself down among them again. After a time she said, "We go out, it's strangers in the house, some other army soldiers. Then where?"

"Can you get to the field compound?" Esdan suggested.

"It's a long road."

After a while he said, "Can't know what to do till we know who's up there. All right. But let me go out, Gana."

"For what?"

"Because I'll know who they are," he said, hoping he was right.

"And they too," Kamsa said, with that strange little edge of laughter. "No mistaking you, I guess."

"Right," he said. He struggled to his feet, found his way to the ladder, and climbed it laboriously. "I'm too old for this," he thought again. He pushed up the trap and looked out. He listened for a long time. At last he whispered to those below him in the dark, "I'll be back as soon as I can," and crawled out, scrambling awkwardly to his feet. He caught his breath: the air of the place was thick with burning. The light was strange, dim. He followed the wall till he could peer out of the store-room doorway.

What had been left of the old house was down like the rest of it, blown open, smouldering and masked in stinking smoke. Black embers and broken glass covered the cobbled yard. Nothing moved except the smoke. Yellow smoke, grey smoke. Above it all was the even, clear blue of dawn.

He went around onto the terrace, limping and stumbling, for his foot shot blinding pains up his leg. Coming to the balustrade he saw the blackened wrecks of the two flyers. Half the upper terrace was a raw crater. Below it the gardens of Yaramera stretched beautiful and serene as ever, level below level, to the old tree and the river. A man lay across the steps that went down to the lower terrace; he lay easily, restfully, his arms outflung. Nothing moved but the creeping smoke and the white-flowered bushes nodding in a breath of wind.

The sense of being watched from behind, from the blank windows of the fragments of the house that still stood, was intolerable. "Is anybody here?" Esdan suddenly called out.

Silence.

He shouted again, louder.

There was an answer, a distant call, from around in front of the house. He limped his way down onto the path, out in the open, not seeking to conceal himself; what was the use? Men came around from the front of the house, three men, then a fourth—a woman. They were assets, roughly clothed, fieldhands they must be, come down from their compound. "I'm with some of the housepeople," he said, stopping when they stopped, ten meters apart. "We hid out in a cellar. Is anybody else around?"

"Who are you?" one of them said, coming closer, peering, seeing the wrong color skin, the wrong kind of eyes.

"I'll tell you who I am. But is it safe for us to come out? There's old people, a baby. Are the soldiers gone?"

"They are dead," the woman said, a tall, pale-skinned, bony-faced woman.

"One we found hurt," said one of the men. "All the housepeople dead. Who did throw those bombs? What army?"

"I don't know what army," Esdan said. "Please, go tell my people they can come up. Back there, in the stables. Call out to them. Tell them who you are. I can't walk." The wrappings on his foot had worked loose, and the fractures had moved; the pain began to take away his breath. He sat down on the path, gasping. His head swam. The gardens of Yaramera grew very bright and very small and drew away and away from him, farther away than home.

He did not quite lose consciousness, but things were confused in his mind for a good while. There were a lot of people around, and they were outdoors, and everything stank of burnt meat, a smell that clung in the back of his mouth and made him retch. There was Kamsa, the tiny bluish shadowy sleeping face of the baby on her shoulder. There was Gana, saying to other people, "He did befriend us." A young man with big hands talked to him and did something to his foot, bound it up again, tighter, causing terrible pain and then the beginning of relief.

He was lying down on his back on grass. Beside him a man was lying down on his back on grass. It was Metoy, the eunuch. Metoy's scalp was bloody, the black hair burned short and brown. The dust-colored skin of his face was pale, bluish, like the baby's. He lay quietly, blinking sometimes.

The sun shone down. People were talking, a lot of people, somewhere nearby, but he and Metoy were lying on the grass and nobody bothered them.

"Were the flyers from Bellen, Metoy?" Esdan said.

"Came from the east." Metoy's harsh voice was weak and hoarse. "I guess they were." After a while he said, "They want to cross the river."

Esdan thought about this for a while. His mind still did not work well at all. "Who does?" he said finally.

"These people. The fieldhands. The assets of Yaramera. They want to go meet the Army."

"The Invasion?"

"The Liberation."

Esdan propped himself up on his elbows. Raising his head seemed to clear it, and he sat up. He looked over at Metoy. "Will they find them?" he asked.

"If the Lord so wills," said the eunuch.

Presently Metoy tried to prop himself up like Esdan, but failed. "I got blown up," he said, short of breath. "Something hit my head. I see two for one."

"Probably a concussion. Lie still. Stay awake. Were you with Banarkamye, or observing?"

"I'm in your line of work."

Esdan nodded, the backward nod.

"Factions will be the death of us," Metoy said faintly.

Kamsa came and squatted down beside Esdan. "They say we must go cross the river," she told him in her soft voice. "To where the people-army will keep us safe. I don't know."

"Nobody knows, Kamsa."

"I can't take Rekam cross a river," she whispered. Her face clenched up, her lips drawing back, her brows down. She wept, without tears and in silence. "The water is cold."

"They'll have boats, Kamsa. They'll look after you and Rekam. Don't worry. It'll be all right." He knew his words were meaningless.

"I can't go," she whispered.

"Stay here then," Metoy said.

"They said that other army will come here."

"It might. More likely ours will."

She looked at Metoy. "You are the cutfree," she said. "With those others." She looked back at Esdan. "Choyo got killed. All the kitchen is blown in pieces burning." She hid her face in her arms.

Esdan sat up and reached out to her, stroking her shoulder and arm.

He touched the baby's fragile head with its thin, dry hair.

Gana came and stood over them. "All the fieldhands are going cross the river," she said. "To be safe."

"You'll be safer here. Where there's food and shelter." Metoy spoke in short bursts, his eyes closed. "Than walking to meet an invasion."

"I can't take him, mama," Kamsa whispered. "He has got to be warm. I can't, I can't take him."

Gana stooped and looked into the baby's face, touching it very softly with one finger. Her wrinkled face closed like a fist. She straightened up, but not erect as she used to stand. She stood bowed. "All right," she said. "We'll stay."

She sat down on the grass beside Kamsa. People were on the move around them. The woman Esdan had seen on the terrace stopped by Gana and said, "Come on, grandmother. Time to go. The boats are ready waiting."

"Staying," Gana said.

"Why? Can't leave that old house you worked in?" the woman said, jeering, humoring. "It's all burned up, grandmother! Come on now. Bring that girl and her baby." She looked at Esdan and Metoy, a flick-glance. They were not her concern. "Come on," she repeated. "Get up now."

"Staying," Gana said.

"You crazy housefolk," the woman said, turned away, turned back, gave it up with a shrug, and went on.

A few others stopped, but none for more than a question, a moment. They streamed on down the terraces, the sunlit paths beside the quiet pools, down towards the boathouses beyond the great tree. After a while they were all gone.

The sun had grown hot. It must be near noon. Metoy was whiter than ever, but he sat up, saying he could see single, most of the time.

"We should get into the shade, Gana," Esdan said. "Metoy, can you get up?"

He staggered and shambled, but walked without help, and they got to the shade of a garden wall. Gana went off to look for water. Kamsa was carrying Rekam in her arms, close against her breast, sheltered from the sun. She had not spoken for a long time. When they had settled down she said, half questioning, looking around dully, "We are all alone here."

"There'll be others stayed. In the compounds," Metoy said. "They'll turn up."

Gana came back; she had no vessel to carry water in, but had soaked her scarf, and laid the cold wet cloth on Metoy's head. He shuddered. "You can walk better, then we can go to the house-compound, cutfree," she said. "Places we can live in, there."

"House-compound is where I grew up, grandmother," he said.

And presently, when he said he could walk, they made their halt and lame way down a road which Esdan vaguely remembered, the road to the crouchcage. It seemed a long road. They came to the high compound wall and the gate standing open.

Esdan turned to look back at the ruins of the great house for a moment. Gana stopped beside him.

"Rekam died," she said under her breath.

He caught his breath. "When?"

She shook her head. "I don't know. She wants to hold him. She's done with holding him, then she will let him go." She looked in the open gateway at the rows of huts and longhouses, the dried-up garden patches, the dusty ground. "Lotsalot little babies are in there," she said. "In that ground. Two of my own. Her sisters." She went in, following Kamsa. Esdan stood a while longer in the gateway, and then he went in to do what there was for him to do: dig a grave for the child, and wait with the others for the Liberation.

THE FINDER

I. In the Dark Time

THIS IS THE FIRST PAGE OF THE *BOOK OF THE DARK*, WRITTEN some six hundred years ago in Berila, on Enlad:

"After Elfarran and Morred perished and the Isle of Soléa sank beneath the sea, the Council of the Wise governed for the child Serriadh until he took the throne. His reign was bright but brief. The kings who followed him in Enlad were seven, and their realm increased in peace and wealth. Then the dragons came to raid among the western lands, and wizards went out in vain against them. King Akambar moved the court from Berila in Enlad to the City of Havnor, whence he sent out his fleet against invaders from the Kargad Lands and drove them back into the East. But still they sent raiding ships even as far as the Inmost Sea. Of the fourteen Kings of Havnor the last was Maharion, who made peace both with the dragons and the Kargs, but at great cost. And after the Ring of the Runes was broken, and Erreth-Akbe died with the great dragon, and Maharion the Brave was killed by treachery, it seemed that no good thing happened in the Archipelago.

"Many claimed Maharion's throne, but none could keep it, and the quarrels of the claimants divided all loyalties. No commonwealth was left and no justice, only the will of the wealthy. Men of noble houses, merchants, and pirates, any who could hire soldiers and wizards called himself a lord, claiming lands and cities as his property. The warlords made those they conquered slaves, and those they hired were in truth slaves, having only their masters to safeguard them from rival warlords seizing the lands, and sea-pirates raiding the ports, and bands and hordes of lawless, miserable men dispossessed of their living, driven by hunger to raid and rob."

The *Book of the Dark*, written late in the time it tells of, is a compilation of self-contradictory histories, partial biographies, and garbled legends. But it's the best of the records that survived the dark years. Wanting praise, not history, the warlords burnt the books in which the poor and powerless might learn what power is.

But when the lore-books of a wizard came into a warlord's hands he was likely to treat them with caution, locking them away to keep them harmless or giving them to a wizard in his hire to do with as he wished. In the margins of the spells and word lists and in the endpapers of these books of lore a wizard or his prentice might record a plague, a famine, a raid, a change of masters, along with the spells worked in such events and their success or unsuccess. Such random records reveal a clear moment here and there, though all between those moments is darkness. They are like glimpses of a lighted ship far out at sea, in darkness, in the rain.

And there are songs, old lays and ballads from small islands and from the quiet uplands of Havnor, that tell the story of those years.

Havnor Great Port is the city at the heart of the world, white-towered above its bay; on the tallest tower the sword of Erreth-Akbe catches the first and last of daylight. Through that city passes all the trade and commerce and learning and craft of Earthsea, a wealth not hoarded. There the King sits, having returned after the healing of the Ring, in sign of healing. And in that city, in these latter days, men and women of the islands speak with dragons, in sign of change.

But Havnor is also the Great Isle, a broad, rich land; and in the villages inland from the port, the farmlands of the slopes of Mount Onn, nothing ever changes much. There a song worth singing is likely to be sung again. There old men at the tavern talk of Morred as if they had known him when they too were young and heroes. There girls walking out to fetch the cows home tell stories of the women of the Hand, who are forgotten everywhere else in the world, even on Roke, but remembered among those silent, sunlit roads and fields and in the kitchens by the hearths where housewives work and talk.

In the time of the kings, mages gathered in the court of Enlad and later in the court of Havnor to counsel the king and take counsel together, using their arts to pursue goals they agreed were good. But in the dark years, wizards sold their skills to the highest bidder, pitting their powers one against the other in duels and combats of sorcery, careless of the evils they did, or worse than careless. Plagues and famines, the failure of springs of water, summers with no rain and years with no summer, the birth of sickly and monstrous young to sheep and cattle, the birth of sickly and monstrous children to the people of the isles—all these things were charged to the practices of wizards and witches, and all too often rightly so.

So it became dangerous to practice sorcery, except under the protection of a strong warlord; and even then, if a wizard met up with one whose powers were greater than his own, he might be destroyed. And if a wizard let down his guard among the common folk, they too might destroy him if they could, seeing him as the source of the worst evils they suffered, a malign being. In those years, in the minds of most people, all magic was black.

It was then that village sorcery, and above all women's witchery, came into the ill repute that has clung to it since. Witches paid dearly for practicing the arts they thought of as their own. The care of pregnant beasts and women, birthing, teaching the songs and rites, the fertility and order of field and garden, the building and care of the house and its furniture, the mining of ores and metals—these great things had always been in the charge of women. A rich lore of spells and charms to ensure the good outcome of such undertakings was shared among the witches. But when things went wrong at the birth, or in the field, that would be the witches' fault. And things went wrong more often than right, with the wizards warring, using poisons and curses recklessly to gain immediate advantage without thought for what followed after. They brought drought and storm, blights and fires and sicknesses across the land, and the village witch was punished for them. She didn't know why her charm of healing caused the wound to gangrene, why the child she brought into the world was imbecile, why her blessing seemed to burn the seed in the furrows and blight the apple on the tree. But for these ills, somebody had to be to blame: and the witch or sorcerer was there, right there in the village or the town, not off in the warlord's castle or fort, not protected by armed men and spells of defense. Sorcerers and witches were drowned in the poisoned wells, burned in the withered fields, buried alive to make the dead earth rich again.

So the practice of their lore and the teaching of it had become perilous. Those who undertook it were often those already outcast, crippled, deranged, without family, old—women and men who had little to lose. The wise man and wise woman, trusted and held in reverence, gave way to the stock figures of the shuffling, impotent village sorcerer with his trickeries, the hag-witch with her potions used in aid of lust, jealousy, and malice. And a child's gift for magic became a thing to dread and hide.

This is a tale of those times. Some of it is taken from the *Book of the Dark*, and some comes from Havnor, from the upland farms of Onn and the woodlands of Faliern. A story may be pieced together from such scraps and fragments, and though it will be an airy quilt, half made of hearsay and half of guesswork, yet it may be true enough. It's a tale of the Founding of Roke, and if the Masters of Roke say it didn't happen so, let them tell us how it happened otherwise. For a cloud hangs over the time when Roke first became the Isle of the Wise, and it may be that the wise men put it there.

II. Otter

There was an otter in our brook
That every mortal semblance took,
Could any spell of magic make,
And speak the tongues of man and drake.
So runs the water away, away,
So runs the water away.

OTTER WAS THE SON OF A BOATWRIGHT WHO WORKED IN THE shipyards of Havnor Great Port. His mother gave him his country name; she was a farm woman from Endlane village, around northwest of Mount Onn. She had come to the city seeking work, as many came. Decent folk in a decent trade in troubled times, the boatwright and his family were anxious not to come to notice lest they come to grief. And so, when it became clear that the boy had a gift of magery, his father tried to beat it out of him.

"You might as well beat a cloud for raining," said Otter's mother.

"Take care you don't beat evil into him," said his aunt.

"Take care he doesn't turn your belt on you with a spell!" said his uncle.

But the boy played no tricks against his father. He took his beatings in silence and learned to hide his gift.

It didn't seem to him to amount to much. It was such an easy matter to him to make a silvery light shine in a dark room, or find a lost pin by thinking about it, or true up a warped joint by running his hands over the wood and talking to it, that he couldn't see why they made a fuss over such things. But his father raged at him for his "shortcuts," even struck him once on the mouth when he was talking to the work, and insisted that he do his carpentry with tools, in silence.

His mother tried to explain. "It's as if you'd found some great jewel," she said, "and what's one of us to do with a diamond but hide it? Anybody rich enough to buy it from you is strong enough to kill you for it. Keep it hid. And keep away from great people and their crafty men!"

"Crafty men" is what they called wizards in those days.

One of the gifts of power is to know power. Wizard knows wizard, unless the concealment is very skillful. And the boy had no skills at all except in boat-building, of which he was a promising scholar by the age of twelve. About that time the midwife who had helped his mother at his birth came by and said to his parents, "Let Otter come to me in the evenings after work. He should learn the songs and be prepared for his naming day."

That was all right, for she had done the same for Otter's elder sister, and so his parents sent him to her in the evenings. But she taught Otter more than the song of the Creation. She knew his gift. She and some men and women like her, people of no fame and some of questionable reputation, had all in some degree that gift; and they shared, in secret, what lore and craft they had. "A gift untaught is a ship unguided," they said to Otter, and they taught him all they knew. It wasn't much, but there were some beginnings of the great arts in it; and though he felt uneasy at deceiving his parents, he couldn't resist this knowledge, and the kindness and praise of his poor teachers. "It will do you no harm if you never use it for harm," they told him, and that was easy for him to promise them.

At the stream Serrenen, where it runs within the north wall of the city, the midwife gave Otter his true name, by which he is remembered in islands far from Havnor.

Among these people was an old man whom they called, among themselves, the Changer. He showed Otter a few spells of illusion; and when the boy was fifteen or so, the old man took him out into the fields by Serrenen to show him the one spell of true change he knew. "First let's see you turn that bush into the seeming of a tree," he said, and promptly Otter did so. Illusion came so easy to the boy that the old man took alarm. Otter had to beg and wheedle him for any further teaching and finally to promise him, swearing on his own true and secret name, that if he learned the Changer's great spell he would never use it but to save a life, his own or another's.

Then the old man taught it to him. But it wasn't much use, Otter thought, since he had to hide it.

What he learned working with his father and uncle in the shipyard he could use, at least; and he was becoming a good craftsman, even his father would admit that.

Losen, a sea-pirate who called himself King of the Inmost Sea, was then the chief warlord in the city and all the east and south of Havnor. Exacting tribute from that rich domain, he spent it to increase his soldiery and the fleets he sent out to take slaves and plunder from other lands. As

Otter's uncle said, he kept the shipwrights busy. They were grateful to
have work in a time when men seeking work found only beggary, and rats
ran in the courts of Maharion. They did an honest job, Otter's father said,
and what the work was used for was none of their concern.

But the other learning he had been given had made Otter touchy in
these matters, delicate of conscience. The big galley they were building
now would be rowed to war by Losen's slaves and would bring back
slaves as cargo. It galled him to think of the good ship in that vicious
usage. "Why can't we build fishing boats, the way we used to?" he asked,
and his father said, "Because the fishermen can't pay us."

"Can't pay us as well as Losen does. But we could live," Otter argued.

"You think I can turn the King's order down? You want to see me sent
to row with the slaves in the galley we're building? Use your head, boy!"

So Otter worked along with them with a clear head and an angry
heart. They were in a trap. What's the use of a gift of power, he thought,
if not to get out of a trap?

His conscience as a craftsman would not let him fault the carpentry
of the ship in any way; but his conscience as a wizard told him he could
put a hex on her, a curse woven right into her beams and hull. Surely
that was using the secret art to a good end? For harm, yes, but only to
harm the harmful. He did not talk to his teachers about it. If he was
doing wrong, it was none of their fault and they would know nothing
about it. He thought about it for a long time, working out how to do it,
making the spell very carefully. It was the reversal of a finding charm: a
losing charm, he called it to himself. The ship would float, and handle
well, and steer, but she would never steer quite true.

It was the best he could do in protest against the misuse of good
work and a good ship. He was pleased with himself. When the ship
was launched (and all seemed well with her, for her fault would not
show up until she was out on the open sea) he could not keep from his
teachers what he had done, the little circle of old men and midwives,

the young hunchback who could speak with the dead, the blind girl who knew the names of things. He told them his trick, and the blind girl laughed, but the old people said, "Look out. Take care. Keep hidden."

In Losen's service was a man who called himself Hound, because, as he said, he had a nose for witchery. His employment was to sniff Losen's food and drink and garments and women, anything that might be used by enemy wizards against him; and also to inspect his warships. A ship is a fragile thing in a dangerous element, vulnerable to spells and hexes. As soon as Hound came aboard the new galley he scented something. "Well, well," he said, "who's this?" He walked to the helm and put his hand on it. "This is clever," he said. "But who is it? A newcomer, I think." He sniffed appreciatively. "Very clever," he said.

They came to the house in Boatwright Street after dark. They kicked the door in, and Hound, standing among the armed and armored men, said, "Him. Let the others be." And to Otter he said, "Don't move," in a low, amicable voice. He sensed great power in the young man, enough that he was a little afraid of him. But Otter's distress was too great and his training too slight for him to think of using magic to free himself or stop the men's brutality. He flung himself at them and fought them like an animal till they knocked him on the head. They broke Otter's father's jaw and beat his aunt and mother senseless to teach them not to bring up crafty men. Then they carried Otter away.

Not a door opened in the narrow street. Nobody looked out to see what the noise was. Not till long after the men were gone did some neighbors creep out to comfort Otter's people as best they could. "Oh, it's a curse, a curse, this wizardry!" they said.

† † †

HOUND TOLD HIS MASTER THAT THEY HAD THE HEXER IN A
safe place, and Losen said, "Who was he working for?"

"He worked in your shipyard, your highness." Losen liked to be
called by kingly titles.

"Who hired him to hex the ship, fool?"

"It seems it was his own idea, your majesty."

"Why? What was he going to get out of it?"

Hound shrugged. He didn't choose to tell Losen that people hated
him disinterestedly.

"He's crafty, you say. Can you use him?"

"I can try, your highness."

"Tame him or bury him," said Losen, and turned to more important
matters.

OTTER'S HUMBLE TEACHERS HAD TAUGHT HIM PRIDE. THEY
had trained into him a deep contempt for wizards who worked for such
men as Losen, letting fear or greed pervert magic to evil ends. Nothing,
to his mind, could be more despicable than such a betrayal of their art.
So it troubled him that he couldn't despise Hound.

He had been stowed in a storeroom of one of the old palaces that
Losen had appropriated. It had no window, its door was cross-grained
oak barred with iron, and spells had been laid on that door that would
have kept a far more experienced wizard captive. There were men of
great skill and power in Losen's pay.

Hound did not consider himself to be one of them. "All I have is a
nose," he said. He came daily to see that Otter was recovering from his
concussion and dislocated shoulder, and to talk with him. He was, as far
as Otter could see, well-meaning and honest. "If you won't work for us
they'll kill you," he said. "Losen can't have fellows like you on the loose.
You'd better hire on while he'll take you."

"I can't."

Otter stated it as an unfortunate fact, not as a moral assertion. Hound looked at him with appreciation. Living with the pirate king, he was sick of boasts and threats, of boasters and threateners.

"What are you strongest in?"

Otter was reluctant to answer. He had to like Hound, but didn't have to trust him. "Shape-changing," he mumbled at last.

"Shape-taking?"

"No. Just tricks. Turn a leaf to a gold piece. Seemingly."

In those days they had no fixed names for the various kinds and arts of magic, nor were the connections among those arts clear. There was—as the wise men of Roke would say later—no science in what they knew. But Hound knew pretty surely that his prisoner was concealing his talents.

"Can't change your own form, even seemingly?"

Otter shrugged.

It was hard for him to lie. He thought he was awkward at it because he had no practice. Hound knew better. He knew that magic itself resists untruth. Conjuring, sleight of hand, and false commerce with the dead are counterfeits of magic, glass to the diamond, brass to the gold. They are fraud, and lies flourish in that soil. But the art of magic, though it may be used for false ends, deals with what is real, and the words it works with are the true words. So true wizards find it hard to lie about their art. In their heart they know that their lie, spoken, may change the world.

Hound was sorry for him. "You know, if it was Gelluk questioning you, he'd have everything you know out of you just with a word or two, and your wits with it. I've seen what old Whiteface leaves behind when he asks questions. Listen, can you work with the wind at all?"

Otter hesitated and said, "Yes."

"D'you have a bag?"

Weatherworkers used to carry a leather sack in which they said they kept the winds, untying it to let a fair wind loose or to capture a contrary one. Maybe it was only for show, but every weatherworker had a bag, a great long sack or a little pouch.

"At home," Otter said. It wasn't a lie. He did have a pouch at home. He kept his fine-work tools and his bubble level in it. And he wasn't altogether lying about the wind. Several times he had managed to bring a bit of magewind into the sail of a boat, though he had no idea how to combat or control a storm, as a ship's weatherworker must do. But he thought he'd rather drown in a gale than be murdered in this hole.

"But you wouldn't be willing to use that skill in the King's service?"

"There is no king in Earthsea," the young man said, stern and righteous.

"In my master's service, then," Hound amended, patient.

"No," Otter said, and hesitated. He felt he owed this man an explanation. "See, it's not so much won't as can't. I thought of making plugs in the planking of that galley, near the keel—you know what I mean by plugs? They'd work out as the timbers work when she gets in a heavy sea." Hound nodded. "But I couldn't do it. I'm a shipbuilder. I can't build a ship to sink. With the men aboard her. My hands wouldn't do it. So I did what I could. I made her go her own way. Not his way."

Hound smiled. "They haven't undone what you did yet, either," he said. "Old Whiteface was crawling all over her yesterday, growling and muttering. Ordered the helm replaced." He meant Losen's chief mage, a pale man from the North named Gelluk, who was much feared in Havnor.

"That won't do it."

"Could you undo the spell you put on her?"

A flicker of complacency showed in Otter's tired, battered young face. "No," he said. "I don't think anybody can."

"Too bad. You might have used that to bargain with."

Otter said nothing.

"A nose, now, is a useful thing, a salable thing," Hound went on. "Not that I'm looking for competition. But a finder can always find work, as they say . . . You ever been in a mine?"

The guesswork of a wizard is close to knowledge, though he may not know what it is he knows. The first sign of Otter's gift, when he was two or three years old, was his ability to go straight to anything lost, a dropped nail, a mislaid tool, as soon as he understood the word for it. And as a boy one of his dearest pleasures had been to go alone out into the countryside and wander along the lanes or over the hills, feeling through the soles of his bare feet and throughout his body the veins of water underground, the lodes and knots of ore, the lay and interfolding of the kinds of rock and earth. It was as if he walked in a great building, seeing its passages and rooms, the descents to airy caverns, the glimmer of branched silver in the walls; and as he went on, it was as if his body became the body of earth, and he knew its arteries and organs and muscles as his own. This power had been a delight to him as a boy. He had never sought any use for it. It had been his secret.

He did not answer Hound's question.

"What's below us?" Hound pointed to the floor, paved with rough slate flags.

Otter was silent a while. Then he said in a low voice, "Clay, and gravel, and under that the rock that bears garnets. All under this part of the city is that rock. I don't know the names."

"You can learn 'em."

"I know how to build boats, how to sail boats."

"You'll do better away from the ships, all the fighting and raiding. The King's working the old mines at Samory, round the mountain. There you'd be out of his way. Work for him you must, if you want to stay alive. I'll see that you're sent there. If you'll go."

After a little silence Otter said, "Thanks." And he looked up at Hound, one brief, questioning, judging glance.

Hound had taken him, had stood and seen his people beaten sense-less, had not stopped the beating. Yet he spoke as a friend. Why? said Otter's look. Hound answered it.

"Crafty men need to stick together," he said. "Men who have no art at all, nothing but wealth—they pit us one against the other, for their gain not ours. We sell 'em our power. Why do we? If we went our own way together, we'd do better, maybe."

HOUND MEANT WELL IN SENDING THE YOUNG MAN TO SAMORY, but he did not understand the quality of Otter's will. Nor did Otter himself. He was too used to obeying others to see that in fact he had always followed his own bent, and too young to believe that anything he did could kill him.

He planned, as soon as they took him out of his cell, to use the old Changer's spell of self-transformation and so escape. Surely his life was in danger, and it would be all right to use the spell? Only he couldn't decide what to turn himself into—a bird, or a wisp of smoke, what would be safest? But while he was thinking about it, Losen's men, used to wizard's tricks, drugged his food and he ceased to think of anything at all. They dumped him into a mule-cart like a sack of oats. When he showed signs of reviving during the journey, one of them bashed him on the head, remarking that he wanted to make sure he got his rest.

When he came to himself, sick and weak from the poison and with an aching skull, he was in a room with brick walls and bricked-up win-dows. The door had no bars and no visible lock. But when he tried to get to his feet he felt bonds of sorcery holding his body and mind, resilient, clinging, tightening as he moved. He could stand, but could not take a step towards the door. He could not even reach his hand out. It was a horrible sensation, as if his muscles were not his own. He sat down again and tried to hold still. The spellbonds around his chest kept him from breathing deeply, and his mind felt stifled too, as if his thoughts were crowded into a space too small for them.

After a long time the door opened and several men came in. He could do nothing against them as they gagged him and bound his arms behind him. "Now you won't weave charms nor speak spells, young 'un," said a broad, strong man with a furrowed face, "but you can nod your head well enough, right? They sent you here as a dowser. If you're a good dowser you'll feed well and sleep easy. Cinnabar, that's what you're to nod for. The King's wizard says it's still here somewhere about these old mines. And he wants it. So it's best for us that we find it. Now I'll walk you out. It's like I'm the water finder and you're my wand, see? You lead on. And if you want to go this way or that way you dip your head, so. And when you know there's ore underfoot, you stamp on the place, so. Now that's the bargain, right? And if you play fair I will."

He waited for Otter to nod, but Otter stood motionless. "Sulk away," the man said. "If you don't like this work, there's always the roaster."

The man, whom the others called Licky, led him out into a hot, bright morning that dazzled his eyes. Leaving his cell he had felt the spellbonds loosen and fall away, but there were other spells woven about other buildings of the place, especially around a tall stone tower, filling the air with sticky lines of resistance and repulsion. If he tried to push forward into them his face and belly stung with jabs of agony, so that he looked at his body in horror for the wound; but there was no wound. Gagged and bound, without his voice and hands to work magic, he could do nothing against these spells. Licky had tied one end of a braided leather cord around his neck and held the other end, following him. He let Otter walk into a couple of the spells, and after that Otter avoided them. Where they were was plain enough: the dusty pathways bent to miss them.

Leashed like a dog, he walked along, sullen and shivering with sickness and rage. He stared around him, seeing the stone tower, stacks of wood by its wide doorway, rusty wheels and machines by a pit, great heaps of gravel and clay. Turning his sore head made him dizzy.

"If you're a dowser, better dowse," said Licky, coming up alongside him and looking sidelong into his face. "And if you're not, you'd better dowse all the same. That way you'll stay above ground longer."

A man came out of the stone tower. He passed them, walking hurriedly with a queer shambling gait, staring straight ahead. His chin shone and his chest was wet with spittle leaking from his lips.

"That's the roaster tower," said Licky. "Where they cook the cinnabar to get the metal from it. Roasters die in a year or two. Where to, dowser?"

After a bit Otter nodded left, away from the grey stone tower. They walked on towards a long, treeless valley, past grass-grown dumps and tailings.

"All under here's worked out long since," Licky said. And Otter had begun to be aware of the strange country under his feet: empty shafts and rooms of dark air in the dark earth, a vertical labyrinth, the deepest pits filled with unmoving water. "Never was much silver, and the watermetal's long gone. Listen, young 'un, do you even know what cinnabar is?"

Otter shook his head.

"I'll show you some. That's what Gelluk's after. The ore of watermetal. Watermetal eats all the other metals, even gold, see. So he calls it the King. If you find him his King, he'll treat you well. He's often here. Come on, I'll show you. Dog can't track till he's had the scent."

Licky took him down into the mines to show him the gangues, the kinds of earth the ore was likely to occur in. A few miners were working at the end of a long level.

Because they were smaller than men and could move more easily in narrow places, or because they were at home with the earth, or most likely because it was the custom, women had always worked the mines of Earthsea. These miners were free women, not slaves like the workers in the roaster tower. Gelluk had made him foreman over the miners, Licky said, but he did no work in the mine; the miners forbade it, earnestly believing it was the worst of bad luck for a man to pick up a shovel or shore a timber. "Suits me," Licky said.

A shock-haired, bright-eyed woman with a candle bound to her forehead set down her pick to show Otter a little cinnabar in a bucket, brownish red clots and crumbs. Shadows leapt across the earth face at which the miners worked. Old timbers creaked, dirt sifted down. Though the air ran cool through the darkness, the drifts and levels were so low and narrow the miners had to stoop and squeeze their way. In places the ceilings had collapsed. Ladders were shaky. The mine was a terrifying place; yet Otter felt a sense of shelter in it. He was half sorry to go back up into the burning day.

Licky did not take him into the roaster tower, but back to the barracks. From a locked room he brought out a small, soft, thick, leather bag that weighed heavy in his hands. He opened it to show Otter the little pool of dusty brilliance lying in it. When he closed the bag the metal moved in it, bulging, pressing, like an animal trying to get free.

"There's the King," Licky said, in a tone that might have been reverence or hatred.

Though not a sorcerer, Licky was a much more formidable man than Hound. Yet like Hound he was brutal not cruel. He demanded obedience, but nothing else. Otter had seen slaves and their masters all his life in the shipyards of Havnor, and knew he was fortunate. At least in daylight, when Licky was his master.

He could eat only in the cell, where they took his gag off. Bread and onions were what they gave him, with a slop of rancid oil on the bread. Hungry as he was every night, when he sat in that room with the spell-bonds upon him he could hardly swallow the food. It tasted of metal, of ash. The nights were long and terrible, for the spells pressed on him, weighed on him, waked him over and over terrified, gasping for breath,

and never able to think coherently. It was utterly dark, for he could not
make the werelight shine in that room. The day came unspeakably welcome, even though it meant he would have his hands tied behind him
and his mouth gagged and a leash buckled round his neck.

Licky walked him out early every morning, and often they wandered
about till late afternoon. Licky was silent and patient. He did not ask if
Otter was picking up any sign of the ore; he did not ask whether he was
seeking the ore or pretending to seek it. Otter himself could not have
answered the question. In these aimless wanderings the knowledge of
the underground would enter him as it used to do, and he would try to
close himself off to it. "I will not work in the service of evil!" he told
himself. Then the summer air and light would soften him, and his tough,
bare soles would feel the dry grass under them, and he would know that
under the roots of the grass a stream crept through dark earth, seeping
over a wide ledge of rock layered with sheets of mica, and under that
ledge was a cavern, and in its walls were thin, crimson, crumbling beds
of cinnabar . . . He made no sign. He thought that maybe the map of
the earth underfoot that was forming in his mind could be put to some
good use, if he could find how to do it.

But after ten days or so, Licky said, "Master Gelluk's coming here. If
there's no ore for him, he'll likely find another dowser."

Otter walked on a mile, brooding; then circled back, leading Licky
to a hillock not far from the far end of the old workings. There he nodded downward and stamped his foot.

Back in the cell room, when Licky had unleashed him and untied his
gag, he said, "There's some ore there. You can get to it by running that
old tunnel straight on, maybe twenty feet."

"A good bit of it?"

Otter shrugged.

"Just enough to keep going on, eh?"

Otter said nothing.

"Suits me," said Licky.

Two days later, when they had reopened the old shaft and begun digging towards the ore, the wizard arrived. Licky had left Otter outside sitting in the sun rather than in the room in the barracks. Otter was grateful to him. He could not be wholly comfortable with his hands bound and his mouth gagged, but wind and sunlight were mighty blessings. And he could breathe deep and doze without dreams of earth stopping his mouth and nostrils, the only dreams he ever had, nights in the cell.

He was half asleep, sitting on the ground in the shade by the barracks, the smell of the logs stacked by the roaster tower bringing him a memory of the work yards at home, the fragrance of new wood as the plane ran down the silky oak board. Some noise or movement roused him. He looked up and saw the wizard standing before him, looming above him.

Gelluk wore fantastic clothes, as many of his kind did in those days. A long robe of Lorbanery silk, scarlet, embroidered in gold and black with runes and symbols, and a wide-brimmed, peak-crowned hat made him seem taller than a man could be. Otter did not need to see his clothes to know him. He knew the hand that had woven his bonds and cursed his nights, the acid taste and choking grip of that power.

"I think I've found my little finder," said Gelluk. His voice was deep and soft, like the notes of a viol. "Sleeping in the sunshine, like one whose work has been well done. So you've sent them digging for the Red Mother, have you? Did you know the Red Mother before you came here? Are you a courtier of the King? Here, now, there's no need for ropes and knots." Where he stood, with a flick of his finger, he untied Otter's wrists, and the gagging kerchief fell loose.

"I could teach you how to do that for yourself," the wizard said, smiling, watching Otter rub and flex his aching wrists and work his lips that had been smashed against his teeth for hours. "The Hound told me that you're a lad of promise and might go far with a proper guide. If you'd like to visit the Court of the King, I can take you there. But maybe you don't know the King I'm talking of?"

Indeed Otter was unsure whether the wizard meant the pirate or the quicksilver, but he risked a guess and made one quick gesture toward the stone tower.

The wizard's eyes narrowed and his smile broadened.

"Do you know his name?"

"The watermetal," Otter said.

"So the vulgar call it, or quicksilver, or the water of weight. But those who serve him call him the King, and the Allking, and the Body of the Moon." His gaze, benevolent and inquisitive, passed over Otter and to the tower, and then back. His face was large and long, whiter than any face Otter had seen, with bluish eyes. Grey and black hairs curled here and there on his chin and cheeks. His calm, open smile showed small teeth, several of them missing. "Those who have learned to see truly can see him as he is, the lord of all substances. The root of power lies in him. Do you know what we call him in the secrecy of his palace?"

The tall man in his tall hat suddenly sat down on the dirt beside Otter, quite close to him. His breath smelled earthy. His light eyes gazed directly into Otter's eyes. "Would you like to know? You can know anything you like. I need have no secrets from you. Nor you from me," and he laughed, not threateningly, but with pleasure. He gazed at Otter again, his large, white face smooth and thoughtful. "Powers you have, yes, all kinds of little traits and tricks. A clever lad. But not too clever; that's good. Not too clever to learn, like some . . . I'll teach you, if you like. Do you like learning? Do you like knowledge? Would you like to know the name we call the King when he's all alone in his brightness in his courts of stone? His name is Turres. Do you know that name? It's a word in the language of the Allking. His own name in his own language. In our base tongue we would say Semen." He smiled again and patted Otter's hand. "For he is the seed and fructifier. The seed and source of might and right. You'll see. You'll see. Come along! Come along! Let's go see the King flying among his subjects, gathering himself from them!" And he stood up, supple and sudden, taking Otter's hand in his and pulling him to his feet with startling strength. He was laughing with excitement.

Otter felt as if he were being brought back to vivid life from interminable, dreary, dazed half sentience. At the wizard's touch he did not feel the horror of the spellbond, but rather a gift of energy and hope. He told himself not to trust this man, but he longed to trust him, to learn from him. Gelluk was powerful, masterful, strange, yet he had set him free. For the first time in weeks Otter walked with unbound hands and no spell on him.

"This way, this way," Gelluk murmured. "No harm will come to you." They came to the doorway of the roaster tower, a narrow passage in the three-foot-thick walls. He took Otter's arm, for the young man hesitated.

Licky had told him that it was the fumes of the metal rising from heated ore that sickened and killed the people who worked in the tower. Otter had never entered it nor seen Licky enter it. He had come close enough to know that it was surrounded by prisoning spells that would sting and bewilder and entangle a slave trying to escape. Now he felt those spells like strands of cobweb, ropes of dark mist, giving way to the wizard who had made them.

"Breathe, breathe, breathe," Gelluk said, laughing, and Otter tried not to hold his breath as they entered the tower.

The roasting pit took up the center of a huge domed chamber. Hurrying, sticklike figures black against the blaze shoveled and reshoveled ore onto logs kept in a roaring blaze by great bellows, while others brought fresh logs and worked the bellows sleeves. From the apex of the dome a spiral of chambers rose up into the tower through smoke and fumes. In those chambers, Licky had told him, the vapor of the quicksilver was trapped and condensed, reheated and recondensed, till in the topmost vault the pure metal ran down into a stone trough or bowl—only a drop or two a day, he said, from the low-grade ores they were roasting now.

"Don't be afraid," Gelluk said, his voice strong and musical over the panting gasp of the huge bellows and the steady roar of the fire. "Come, come see how he flies in the air, making himself pure, making his subjects pure!" He drew Otter to the edge of the roasting pit. His eyes shone in the flare and dazzle of the flames. "Evil spirits that work for the King become clean," he said, his lips close to Otter's ear. "As they slaver, the dross and stains flow out of them. Illness and impurities fester and run free from their sores. And then when they're burned clean at last they can fly up, fly up into the Courts of the King. Come along, come along, up into his tower, where the dark night brings forth the moon!"

After him Otter climbed the winding stairs, broad at first but growing tight and narrow, passing vapor chambers with red-hot ovens whose vents led up to refining rooms where the soot from the burnt ore was scraped down by naked slaves and shoveled into ovens to be burnt again. They came to the topmost room. Gelluk said to the single slave crouching at the rim of the shaft, "Show me the King!"

The slave, short and thin, hairless, with running sores on his hands and arms, uncapped a stone cup by the rim of the condensing shaft. Gelluk peered in, eager as a child. "So tiny," he murmured. "So young. The tiny Prince, the baby Lord, Lord Turres. Seed of the world! Soul-jewel!"

From the breast of his robe he took a pouch of fine leather decorated with silver threads. With a delicate horn spoon tied to the pouch he lifted the few drops of quicksilver from the cup and placed them in it, then retied the thong.

The slave stood by, motionless. All the people who worked in the heat and fumes of the roaster tower were naked or wore only breechclout and moccasins. Otter glanced again at the slave, thinking by his height he was a child, and then saw the small breasts. It was a woman. She was bald. Her joints were swollen knobs in her bone-thin limbs. She looked up once at Otter, moving her eyes only. She spat into the fire, wiped her sore mouth with her hand, and stood motionless again.

"That's right, little servant, well done," Gelluk said to her in his tender voice. "Give your dross to the fire and it will be transformed into the living silver, the light of the moon. Is it not a wonderful thing," he went on, drawing Otter away and back down the spiral stair, "how from what is most base comes what is most noble? That is a great principle of the art! From the vile Red Mother is born the Allking. From the spittle of a dying slave is made the silver Seed of Power."

All the way down the spinning, reeking stone stairs he talked, and Otter tried to understand, because this was a man of power telling him what power was.

But when they came out into the daylight again his head kept on spinning in the dark, and after a few steps he doubled over and vomited on the ground.

Gelluk watched him with his inquisitive, affectionate look, and when Otter stood up, wincing and gasping, the wizard asked gently, "Are you afraid of the King?"

Otter nodded.

"If you share his power he won't harm you. To fear a power, to fight a power, is very dangerous. To love power and to share it is the royal way. Look. Watch what I do." Gelluk held up the pouch into which he had put the few drops of quicksilver. His eye always on Otter's eye, he unsealed the pouch, lifted it to his lips, and drank its contents. He opened his smiling mouth so that Otter could see the silver drops pooling on his tongue before he swallowed.

"Now the King is in my body, the noble guest of my house. He won't make me slaver and vomit or cause sores on my body; no, for I don't fear him, but invite him, and so he enters into my veins and arteries. No harm comes to me. My blood runs silver. I see things unknown to other

men. I share the secrets of the King. And when he leaves me, he hides in
the place of ordure, in foulness itself, and yet again in the vile place he
waits for me to come and take him up and cleanse him as he cleansed
me, so that each time we grow purer together." The wizard took Otter's
arm and walked along with him. He said, smiling and confidential, "I
am one who shits moonlight. You will not know another such. And
more than that, more than that, the King enters into my seed. He is my
semen. I am Turres and he is me . . ."

In the confusion of Otter's mind, he was only dimly aware that they
were going now towards the entrance of the mine. They went underground. The passages of the mine were a dark maze like the wizard's
words. Otter stumbled on, trying to understand. He saw the slave in the
tower, the woman who had looked at him. He saw her eyes.

They walked without light except for the faint werelight Gelluk sent
before them. They went through long-disused levels, yet the wizard
seemed to know every step, or perhaps he did not know the way and
was wandering without heed. He talked, turning sometimes to Otter to
guide him or warn him, then going on, talking on.

They came to where the miners were extending the old tunnel. There
the wizard spoke with Licky in the flare of candles among jagged shadows. He touched the earth of the tunnel's end, took clods of earth in
his hands, rolled the dirt in his palms, kneading, testing, tasting it. For
that time he was silent, and Otter watched him with staring intensity,
still trying to understand.

Licky came back to the barracks with them. Gelluk bade Otter goodnight in his soft voice. Licky shut him as usual into the brick-walled
room, giving him a loaf of bread, an onion, a jug of water.

Otter crouched as always in the uneasy oppression of the spellbond.
He drank thirstily. The sharp earthy taste of the onion was good, and
he ate it all.

As the dim light that came into the room from chinks in the mortar of the bricked-up window died away, instead of sinking into the blank misery of all his nights in that room, he stayed awake, and grew more awake. The excited turmoil of his mind all the time he had been with Gelluk slowly quieted. From it something rose, coming close, coming clear, the image he had seen down in the mine, shadowy yet distinct: the slave in the high vault of the tower, that woman with empty breasts and festered eyes, who spat the spittle that ran from her poisoned mouth, and wiped her mouth, and stood waiting to die. She had looked at him.

He saw her now more clearly than he had seen her in the tower. He saw her more clearly than he had ever seen anyone. He saw the thin arms, the swollen joints of elbow and wrist, the childish nape of her neck. It was as if she was with him in the room. It was as if she was in him, as if she was him. She looked at him. He saw her look at him. He saw himself through her eyes.

He saw the lines of the spells that held him, heavy cords of darkness, a tangled maze of lines all about him. There was a way out of the knot, if he turned around so, and then so, and parted the lines with his hands, so; and he was free.

He could not see the woman any more. He was alone in the room, standing free.

All the thoughts he had not been able to think for days and weeks were racing through his head, a storm of ideas and feelings, a passion of rage, vengeance, pity, pride.

At first he was overwhelmed with fierce fantasies of power and revenge: he would free the slaves, he would spellbind Gelluk and hurl him into the refining fire, he would bind him and blind him and leave him to breathe the fumes of quicksilver in that highest vault till he died . . . But when his thoughts settled down and began to run clearer, he knew that he could not defeat a wizard of great craft and power, even if that wizard was mad. If he had any hope it was to play on his madness, and lead the wizard to defeat himself.

He pondered. All the time he was with Gelluk, he had tried to learn from him, tried to understand what the wizard was telling him. Yet he was certain, now, that Gelluk's ideas, the teaching he so eagerly imparted, had nothing to do with his power or with any true power. Mining and refining were indeed great crafts with their own mysteries and masteries, but Gelluk seemed to know nothing of those arts. His talk of the Allking and the Red Mother was mere words. And not the right words. But how did Otter know that?

In all his flood of talk the only word Gelluk had spoken in the Old Tongue, the language of which wizards' spells were made, was the word *turres*. He had said it meant semen. Otter's own gift of magery had recognised that meaning as the true one. Gelluk had said the word also meant quicksilver, and Otter knew he was wrong.

His humble teachers had taught him all the words they knew of the Language of the Making. Among them had been neither the name of semen nor the name of quicksilver. But his lips parted, his tongue moved. *"Ayezur,"* he said.

His voice was the voice of the slave in the stone tower. It was she who knew the true name of quicksilver and spoke it through him.

Then for a while he held still, body and mind, beginning to understand for the first time where his power lay.

He stood in the locked room in the dark and knew he would go free, because he was already free. A storm of praise ran through him.

After a while, deliberately, he re-entered the trap of spellbonds, went back to his old place, sat down on the pallet, and went on thinking. The prisoning spell was still there, yet it had no power over him now. He could walk into it and out of it as if it were mere lines painted on the floor. Gratitude for this freedom beat in him as steady as his heartbeat.

He thought what he must do, and how he must do it. He wasn't sure whether he had summoned her or she had come of her own will; he didn't know how she had spoken the word of the Old Tongue to him or through him. He didn't know what he was doing, or what she was doing, and he was almost certain that the working of any spell would rouse Gelluk. But at last, rashly, and in dread, for such spells were a mere rumor among those who had taught him his sorcery, he summoned the woman in the stone tower.

He brought her into his mind and saw her as he had seen her, there, in that room, and called out to her; and she came.

Her apparition stood again just outside the spiderweb cords of the spell, gazing at him, and seeing him, for a soft, bluish, sourceless light filled the room. Her sore, raw lips quivered but she did not speak.

He spoke, giving her his true name: "I am Medra."

"I am Anieb," she whispered.

"How can we get free?"

"His name."

"Even if I knew it . . . When I'm with him I can't speak."

"If I was with you, I could use it."

"I can't call you."

"But I can come," she said.

She looked round, and he looked up. Both knew that Gelluk had sensed something, had wakened. Otter felt the bonds close and tighten, and the old shadow fall.

"I will come, Medra," she said. She held out her thin hand in a fist, then opened it palm up as if offering him something. Then she was gone.

The light went with her. He was alone in the dark. The cold grip of the spells took him by the throat and choked him, bound his hands, pressed on his lungs. He crouched, gasping. He could not think; he could not remember. "Stay with me," he said, and did not know who he spoke to. He was frightened, and did not know what he was frightened of. The wizard, the power, the spell . . . It was all darkness. But in his body, not in his mind, burned a knowledge he could not name any more, a certainty that was like a tiny lamp held in his hands in a maze of caverns underground. He kept his eyes on that seed of light.

Weary, evil dreams of suffocation came to him, but took no hold on him. He breathed deep. He slept at last. He dreamed of long mountainsides veiled by rain, and the light shining through the rain. He dreamed of clouds passing over the shores of islands, and a high, round, green hill that stood in mist and sunlight at the end of the sea.

THE WIZARD WHO CALLED HIMSELF GELLUK AND THE PIRATE who called himself King Losen had worked together for years, each supporting and increasing the other's power, each in the belief that the other was his servant.

Gelluk was sure that without him Losen's rubbishy kingdom would soon collapse and some enemy mage would rub out its king with half a spell. But he let Losen act the master. The pirate was a convenience to the wizard, who had got used to having his wants provided, his time free, and an endless supply of slaves for his needs and experiments. It was easy to keep up the protections he had laid on Losen's person and expeditions and forays, the prisoning spells he had laid on the places slaves worked or treasures were kept. Making those spells had been a different matter, a long hard work. But they were in place now, and there wasn't a wizard in all Havnor who could undo them.

Gelluk had never met a man he feared. A few wizards had crossed his path strong enough to make him wary of them, but he had never known one with skill and power equal to his own.

Of late, entering always deeper into the mysteries of a certain lorebook brought back from the Isle of Way by one of Losen's raiders, Gelluk had become indifferent to most of the arts he had learned or had discovered for himself. The book convinced him that all of them were only shadows or hints of a greater mastery. As one true element controlled all substances, one true knowledge contained all others.

Approaching ever closer to that mastery, he understood that the crafts of wizards were as crude and false as Losen's title and rule. When he was one with the true element, he would be the one true king. Alone among men he would speak the words of making and unmaking. He would have dragons for his dogs.

In the young dowser he recognised a power, untaught and inept, which he could use. He needed much more quicksilver than he had, therefore he needed a finder. Finding was a base skill. Gelluk had never practiced it, but he could see that the young fellow had the gift. He would do well to learn the boy's true name so that he could be sure of controlling him. He sighed at the thought of the time he must waste teaching the boy what he was good for. And after that the ore must still be dug out of the earth and the metal refined. As always, Gelluk's mind leapt across obstacles and delays to the wonderful mysteries at the end of them.

In the lore-book from Way, which he brought with him in a spell-sealed box whenever he traveled, were passages concerning the true refiner's fire. Having long studied these, Gelluk knew that once he had enough of the pure metal, the next stage was to refine it yet further into the Body of the Moon. He had understood the disguised language of the book to mean that in order to purify pure quicksilver, the fire must be built not of mere wood but of human corpses. Rereading and pondering the words this night in his room in the barracks, he discerned another possible meaning in them. There was always another meaning in the words of this lore. Perhaps the book was saying that there must be sacrifice not only of base flesh but also of inferior spirit. The great fire in the tower should burn not dead bodies but living ones. Living and conscious. Purity from foulness: bliss from pain. It was all part of the great principle, perfectly clear once seen. He was sure he was right, had at last understood the technique. But he must not hurry, he must be patient, must make certain. He turned to another passage and compared the two, and brooded over the book late into the night. Once for a moment something drew his mind away, some invasion of the outskirts of his awareness; the boy was trying some trick or other. Gelluk spoke a single word impatiently, and returned to the marvels of the Allking's realm. He never noticed that his prisoner's dreams had escaped him.

Next day he had Licky send him the boy. He looked forward to seeing him, to being kind to him, teaching him, petting him a bit as he had done yesterday. He sat down with him in the sun. Gelluk was fond of children and animals. He liked all beautiful things. It was pleasant to have a young creature about. Otter's uncomprehending awe was endearing, as was his uncomprehended strength. Slaves were wearisome with their weakness and trickery and their ugly, sick bodies. Of course Otter was his slave, but the boy need not know it. They could be teacher and prentice. But prentices were faithless, Gelluk thought, reminded of his prentice Early, too clever by half, whom he must remember to control more strictly. Father and son, that's what he and Otter could be. He would have the boy call him Father. He recalled that he had intended to find out his true name. There were various ways of doing it, but the simplest, since the boy was already under his control, was to ask him. "What is your name?" he said, watching Otter intently.

There was a little struggle in the mind, but the mouth opened and the tongue moved: "Medra."

"Very good, very good, Medra," said the wizard. "You may call me Father."

"YOU MUST FIND THE RED MOTHER," HE SAID, THE DAY AFTER that. They were sitting side by side again outside the barracks. The autumn sun was warm. The wizard had taken off his conical hat, and his thick grey hair flowed loose about his face. "I know you found that little patch for them to dig, but there's no more in that than a few drops. It's scarcely worth burning for so little. If you are to help me, and if I am to teach you, you must try a little harder. I think you know how." He smiled at Otter. "Don't you?"

Otter nodded.

He was still shaken, appalled, by the ease with which Gelluk had forced him to say his name, which gave the wizard immediate and ultimate power over him. Now he had no hope of resisting Gelluk in any way. That night he had been in utter despair. But then Anieb had come into his mind: come of her own will, by her own means. He could not summon her, could not even think of her, and would not have dared to do so, since Gelluk knew his name. But she came, even when he was with the wizard, not in apparition but as a presence in his mind.

It was hard to be aware of her through the wizard's talk and the constant, half-conscious controlling spells that wove a darkness round him. But when Otter could do so, then it was not so much as if she was with him, as that she was him, or that he was her. He saw through her eyes. Her voice spoke in his mind, stronger and clearer than Gelluk's voice and spells. Through her eyes and mind he could see, and think. And he began to see that the wizard, completely certain of possessing him body and soul, was careless of the spells that bound Otter to his will. A bond is a connection. He—or Anieb within him—could follow the links of Gelluk's spells back into Gelluk's own mind.

Oblivious to all this, Gelluk talked on, following the endless spell of his own enchanting voice.

"You must find the true womb, the bellybag of the Earth, that holds the pure moonseed. Did you know that the Moon is the Earth's father? Yes, yes; and he lay with her, as is the father's right. He quickened her base clay with the true seed. But she will not give birth to the King. She is strong in her fear and wilful in her vileness. She holds him back and hides him deep, fearing to give birth to her master. That is why, to give him birth, she must be burned alive."

Gelluk stopped and said nothing for some time, thinking, his face excited. Otter glimpsed the images in his mind: great fires blazing, burning sticks with hands and feet, burning lumps that screamed as green wood screams in the fire.

"Yes," Gelluk said, his deep voice soft and dreamy, "she must be burned alive. And then, only then, he will spring forth, shining! Oh, it's time, and past time. We must deliver the King. We must find the great lode. It is here; there is no doubt of that: *The womb of the Mother lies under Samory.*"

Again he paused. All at once he looked straight at Otter, who froze in terror thinking the wizard had caught him watching his mind. Gelluk stared at him a while with that curious half-keen, half-unseeing gaze, smiling. "Little Medra!" he said, as if just discovering he was there. He patted Otter's shoulder. "I know you have the gift of finding what's hidden. Quite a great gift, were it suitably trained. Have no fear, my son. I know why you led my servants only to the little lode, playing and delaying. But now that I've come, you serve me, and have nothing to be afraid of. And there's no use trying to conceal anything from me, is there? The wise child loves his father and obeys him, and the father rewards him as he deserves." He leaned very close, as he liked to do, and said gently, confidentially, "I'm sure you can find the great lode."

"I know where it is," Anieb said.

Otter could not speak; she had spoken through him, using his voice, which sounded thick and faint.

Very few people ever spoke to Gelluk unless he compelled them to. The spells by which he silenced, weakened, and controlled all who approached him were so habitual to him that he gave them no thought. He was used to being listened to, not to listening. Serene in his strength and obsessed with his ideas, he had no thought beyond them. He was not aware of Otter at all except as a part of his plans, an extension of himself. "Yes, yes, you will," he said, and smiled again.

But Otter was intensely aware of Gelluk, both physically and as a presence of immense controlling power; and it seemed to him that Anieb's speaking had taken away that much of Gelluk's power over him, gaining him a place to stand, a foothold. Even with Gelluk so close to him, fearfully close, he managed to speak.

"I will take you there," he said, stiffly, laboriously.

Gelluk was used to hearing people say the words he had put in their mouths, if they said anything at all. These were words he wanted but had not expected to hear. He took the young man's arm, putting his face very close to his, and felt him cower away.

"How clever you are," he said. "Have you found better ore than that patch you found first? Worth the digging and the roasting?"

"It is the lode," the young man said.

The slow stiff words carried great weight.

"The great lode?" Gelluk looked straight at him, their faces not a hand's breadth apart. The light in his bluish eyes was like the soft, crazy shift of quicksilver. "The womb?"

"Only the Master can go there."

"What Master?"

"The Master of the House. The King."

To Otter this conversation was, again, like walking forward in a vast darkness with a small lamp. Anieb's understanding was that lamp. Each step revealed the next step he must take, but he could never see the place where he was. He did not know what was coming next, and did not understand what he saw. But he saw it, and went forward, word by word.

"How do you know of that House?"

"I saw it."

"Where? Near here?"

Otter nodded.

"Is it in the earth?"

Tell him what he sees, Anieb whispered in Otter's mind, and he spoke: "A stream runs through darkness over a glittering roof. Under the roof

is the House of the King. The roof stands high above the floor, on high
pillars. The floor is red. All the pillars are red. On them are shining
runes."

Gelluk caught his breath. Presently he said, very softly, "Can you
read the runes?"

"I cannot read them." Otter's voice was toneless. "I cannot go there.
No one can enter there in the body but only the King. Only he can read
what is written."

Gelluk's white face had gone whiter; his jaw trembled a little. He
stood up, suddenly, as he always did. "Take me there," he said, trying to control himself, but so violently compelling Otter to get up and
walk that the young man lurched to his feet and stumbled several steps,
almost falling. Then he walked forward, stiff and awkward, trying not
to resist the coercive, passionate will that hurried his steps.

Gelluk pressed close beside him, often taking his arm. "This way,"
he said several times. "Yes, yes! This is the way." Yet he was following
Otter. His touch and his spells pushed him, rushed him, but in the
direction Otter chose to go.

They walked past the roaster tower, past the old shaft and the new
one, on into the long valley where Otter had taken Licky the first day
he was there. It was late autumn now. The shrubs and scrubby grass that
had been green that day were dun and dry, and the wind rattled the last
leaves on the bushes. To their left a little stream ran low among willow
thickets. Mild sunlight and long shadows streaked the hillsides.

Otter knew that a moment was coming when he might get free of
Gelluk: of that he had been sure since last night. He knew also that in
that same moment he might defeat Gelluk, disempower him, if the wizard, driven by his visions, forgot to guard himself—and if Otter could
learn his name.

The wizard's spells still bound their minds together. Otter pressed
rashly forward into Gelluk's mind, seeking his true name. But he did not

know where to look or how to look. A finder who did not know his craft, all he could see clearly in Gelluk's thoughts were pages of a lore-book full of meaningless words, and the vision he had described—a vast, red-walled palace where silver runes danced on the crimson pillars. But Otter could not read the book or the runes. He had never learned to read.

All this time he and Gelluk were going on farther from the tower, away from Anieb, whose presence sometimes weakened and faded. Otter dared not try to summon her.

Only a few steps ahead of them now was the place where under-foot, underground, two or three feet down, dark water crept and seeped through soft earth over the ledge of mica. Under that opened the hollow cavern and the lode of cinnabar.

Gelluk was almost wholly absorbed in his own vision, but since Otter's mind and his were connected, he saw something of what Otter saw. He stopped, gripping Otter's arm. His hand shook with eagerness.

Otter pointed at the low slope that rose before them. "The King's House is there," he said. Gelluk's attention turned entirely away from him then, fixed on the hillside and the vision he saw within it. Then Otter could call to Anieb. At once she came into his mind and being, and was there with him.

Gelluk was standing still, but his shaking hands were clenched, his whole tall body twitching and trembling, like a hound that wants to chase but cannot find the scent. He was at a loss. There was the hillside with its grass and bushes in the last of the sunlight, but there was no entrance. Grass growing out of gravelly dirt; the seamless earth.

Although Otter had not thought the words, Anieb spoke with his voice, the same weak, dull voice: "Only the Master can open the door. Only the King has the key."

"The key," Gelluk said.

Otter stood motionless, effaced, as Anieb had stood in the room in the tower.

"The key," Gelluk repeated, urgent.

"The key is the King's name."

That was a leap in the darkness. Which of them had said it?

Gelluk stood tense and trembling, still at a loss. "Turres," he said, after a time, almost in a whisper.

The wind blew in the dry grass.

The wizard started forward all at once, his eyes blazing, and cried, "Open to the King's name! I am Tinaral!" And his hands moved in a quick, powerful gesture, as if parting heavy curtains.

The hillside in front of him trembled, writhed, and opened. A gash in it deepened, widened. Water sprang up out of it and ran across the wizard's feet.

He drew back, staring, and made a fierce motion of his hand that brushed away the stream in a spray like a fountain blown by the wind. The gash in the earth grew deeper, revealing the ledge of mica. With a sharp rending crack the glittering stone split apart. Under it was darkness.

The wizard stepped forward. "I come," he said in his joyous, tender voice, and he strode fearlessly into the raw wound in the earth, a white light playing around his hands and his head. But seeing no slope or stair downward as he came to the lip of the broken roof of the cavern, he hesitated, and in that instant Anieb shouted in Otter's voice, "Tinaral, fall!"

Staggering wildly the wizard tried to turn, lost his footing on the crumbling edge, and plunged down into the dark, his scarlet cloak billowing up, the werelight round him like a falling star.

"Close!" Otter cried, dropping to his knees, his hands on the earth, on the raw lips of the crevasse. "Close, Mother! Be healed, be whole!" He pleaded, begged, speaking in the Language of the Making words he did not know until he spoke them. "Mother, be whole!" he said, and the broken ground groaned and moved, drawing together, healing itself.

A reddish seam remained, a scar through the dirt and gravel and uprooted grass.

The wind rattled the dry leaves on the scrub-oak bushes. The sun was behind the hill, and clouds were coming over in a low, grey mass.

Otter crouched there at the foot of the hillslope, alone.

The clouds darkened. Rain passed through the little valley, falling on the dirt and the grass. Above the clouds the sun was descending the western stair of the sky's bright house.

Otter sat up at last. He was wet, cold, bewildered. Why was he here?

He had lost something and had to find it. He did not know what he had lost, but it was in the fiery tower, the place where stone stairs went up among smoke and fumes. He had to go there. He got to his feet and shuffled, lame and unsteady, back down the valley.

He had no thought of hiding or protecting himself. Luckily for him there were no guards about; there were few guards, and they were not on the alert, since the wizard's spells had kept the prison shut. The spells were gone, but the people in the tower did not know it, working on under the greater spell of hopelessness.

Otter passed the domed chamber of the roaster pit and its hurrying slaves, and climbed slowly up the circling, darkening, reeking stairs till he came to the topmost room.

She was there, the sick woman who could heal him, the poor woman who held the treasure, the stranger who was himself.

He stood silent in the doorway. She sat on the stone floor near the crucible, her thin body greyish and dark like the stones. Her chin and breasts were shiny with the spittle that ran from her mouth. He thought of the spring of water that had run from the broken earth.

"Medra," she said. Her sore mouth could not speak clearly. He knelt down and took her hands, looking into her face.

"Anieb," he whispered, "come with me."

"I want to go home," she said.

He helped her stand. He made no spell to protect or hide them. His strength had been used up. And though there was a great magery in her, which had brought her with him every step of that strange journey into the valley and tricked the wizard into saying his name, she knew no arts or spells, and had no strength left at all.

Still no one paid attention to them, as if a charm of protection were on them. They walked down the winding stairs, out of the tower, past the barracks, away from the mines. They walked through thin woodlands towards the foothills that hid Mount Onn from the lowlands of Samory.

ANIEB KEPT A BETTER PACE THAN SEEMED POSSIBLE IN A WOMAN so famished and destroyed, walking almost naked in the chill of the rain. All her will was aimed on walking forward; she had nothing else in her mind, not him, not anything. But she was there bodily with him, and he felt her presence as keenly and strangely as when she had come to his summoning. The rain ran down her naked head and body. He made her stop to put on his shirt. He was ashamed of it, for it was filthy, he having worn it all these weeks. She let him pull it over her head and then walked right on. She could not go quickly, but she went steadily, her eyes fixed on the faint cart track they followed, till the night came early under the rain clouds, and they could not see where to set their feet.

"Make the light," she said. Her voice was a whimper, plaintive. "Can't you make the light?"

"I don't know," he said, but he tried to bring the werelight round them, and after a while the ground glimmered faintly before their feet.

"We should find shelter and rest," he said.

"I can't stop," she said, and started to walk again.

"You can't walk all night."

"If I lie down I won't get up. I want to see the Mountain."

Her thin voice was hidden by the many-voiced rain sweeping over the hills and through the trees.

They went on through darkness, seeing only the track before them

in the dim silvery glow of werelight shot through by silver lines of rain.
When she stumbled he caught her arm. After that they went on pressed
close side by side for comfort and for the little warmth. They walked
slower, and yet slower, but they walked on. There was no sound but
the sound of the rain falling from the black sky, and the little kissing
squelch of their sodden feet in the mud and wet grass of the track.

"Look," she said, halting. "Medra, look."

He had been walking almost asleep. The pallor of the werelight had
faded, drowned in a fainter, vaster clarity. Sky and earth were all one
grey, but before them and above them, very high, over a drift of cloud,
the long ridge of the mountain glimmered red.

"There," Anieb said. She pointed at the mountain and smiled. She
looked at her companion, then slowly down at the ground. She sank
down kneeling. He knelt with her, tried to support her, but she slid
down in his arms. He tried to keep her head at least from the mud of
the track. Her limbs and face twitched, her teeth chattered. He held her
close against him, trying to warm her.

"The women," she whispered, "the hand. Ask them. In the village. I
did see the Mountain."

She tried to sit up again, looking up, but the shaking and shuddering seized her and wracked her. She began to gasp for breath. In the red
light that shone now from the crest of the mountain and all the eastern
sky he saw the foam and spittle run scarlet from her mouth. Sometimes
she clutched at him, but she did not speak again. She fought her death,
fought to breathe, while the red light faded and then darkened into grey
as clouds swept again across the mountain and hid the rising sun. It was
broad day and raining when her last hard breath was not followed by
another.

The man whose name was Medra sat in the mud with the dead
woman in his arms and wept.

A carter walking at his mule's head with a load of oakwood came upon them and took them both to Woodedge. He could not make the young man let go of the dead woman. Weak and shaky as he was, he would not set his burden down on the load, but clambered into the cart holding her, and held her all the miles to Woodedge. All he said was "She saved me," and the carter asked no questions.

"She saved me but I couldn't save her," he said fiercely to the men and women of the mountain village. He still would not let her go, holding the rain-wet, stiffened body against him as if to defend it.

Very slowly they made him understand that one of the women was Anieb's mother, and that he should give Anieb to her to hold. He did so at last, watching to see if she was gentle with his friend and would protect her. Then he followed another woman meekly enough. He put on dry clothing she gave him to put on, and ate a little food she gave him to eat, and lay down on the pallet she led him to, and sobbed in weariness, and slept.

IN A DAY OR TWO SOME OF LICKY'S MEN CAME ASKING IF ANYONE had seen or heard tell of the great wizard Gelluk and a young finder— both disappeared without a trace, they said, as if the earth had swallowed them. Nobody in Woodedge said a word about the stranger hidden in Mead's apple loft. They kept him safe. Maybe that is why the people there now call their village not Woodedge, as it used to be, but Otterhide.

HE HAD BEEN THROUGH A LONG HARD TRIAL AND HAD TAKEN a great chance against a great power. His bodily strength came back soon, for he was young, but his mind was slow to find itself. He had lost something, lost it forever, lost it as he found it.

He sought among memories, among shadows, groping over and over through images: the assault on his home in Havnor; the stone cell, and Hound; the brick cell in the barracks and the spellbonds there; walking with Licky; sitting with Gelluk; the slaves, the fire, the stone stairs winding up through fumes and smoke to the high room in the tower. He had to regain it all, to go through it all, searching. Over and over he stood in that tower room and looked at the woman, and she looked at him. Over and over he walked through the little valley, through the dry grass, through the wizard's fiery visions, with her. Over and over he saw the wizard fall, saw the earth close. He saw the red ridge of the mountain in the dawn. Anieb died while he held her, her ruined face against his arm. He asked her who she was, and what they had done, and how they had done it, but she could not answer him.

Her mother Ayo and her mother's sister Mead were wise women. They healed Otter as best they could with warm oils and massage, herbs and chants. They talked to him and listened when he talked. Neither of them had any doubt but that he was a man of great power. He denied this. "I could have done nothing without your daughter," he said.

"What did she do?" Ayo asked, softly.

He told her, as well as he could. "We were strangers. Yet she gave me her name," he said. "And I gave her mine." He spoke haltingly, with long pauses. "It was I that walked with the wizard, compelled by him, but she was with me, and she was free. And so together we could turn his power against him, so that he destroyed himself." He thought for a long time, and said, "She gave me her power."

"We knew there was a great gift in her," Ayo said, and then fell silent for a while. "We didn't know how to teach her. There are no teachers left on the mountain. King Losen's wizards destroyed the sorcerers and witches. There's no one to turn to."

"Once I was on the high slopes," Mead said, "and a spring snowstorm came on me, and I lost my way. She came there. She came to me, not in the body, and guided me to the track. She was only twelve then."

"She walked with the dead, sometimes," Ayo said very low. "In the forest, down towards Faliern. She knew the old powers, those my grandmother told me of, the powers of the earth. They were strong there, she said."

"But she was only a girl like the others, too," Mead said, and hid her face. "A good girl," she whispered.

After a while Ayo said, "She went down to Firn with some of the young folk. To buy fleece from the shepherds there. A year ago last spring. That wizard they spoke of came there, casting spells. Taking slaves."

Then they were all silent.

Ayo and Mead were much alike, and Otter saw in them what Anieb might have been: a short, slight, quick woman, with a round face and clear eyes, and a mass of dark hair, not straight like most people's hair but curly, frizzy. Many people in the west of Havnor had hair like that.

But Anieb had been bald, like all the slaves in the roaster tower.

Her use-name had been Flag, the blue iris of the springs. Her mother and aunt called her Flag when they spoke of her.

"Whatever I am, whatever I can do, it's not enough," he said.

"It's never enough," Mead said. "And what can anyone do alone?"

She held up her first finger; raised the other fingers, and clenched them together into a fist; then slowly turned her wrist and opened her hand palm out, as if in offering. He had seen Anieb make that gesture. It was not a spell, he thought, watching intently, but a sign. Ayo was watching him.

"It is a secret," she said.

"Can I know the secret?" he asked after a while.

"You already know it. You gave it to Flag. She gave it to you. Trust."

"Trust," the young man said. "Yes. But against—Against them?— Gelluk's gone. Maybe Losen will fall now. Will it make any difference? Will the slaves go free? Will beggars eat? Will justice be done? I think there's an evil in us, in humankind. Trust denies it. Leaps across it. Leaps the chasm. But it's there. And everything we do finally serves evil, because that's what we are. Greed and cruelty. I look at the world, at the forests and the mountain here, the sky, and it's all right, as it should be. But we aren't. People aren't. We're wrong. We do wrong. No animal does wrong. How could they? But we can, and we do. And we never stop."

They listened to him, not agreeing, not denying, but accepting his despair. His words went into their listening silence, and rested there for days, and came back to him changed.

"We can't do anything without each other," he said. "But it's the greedy ones, the cruel ones who hold together and strengthen each other. And those who won't join them stand each alone." The image of Anieb as he had first seen her, a dying woman standing alone in the tower room, was always with him. "Real power goes to waste. Every wizard uses his arts against the others, serving the men of greed. What good can any art be used that way? It's wasted. It goes wrong, or it's thrown away. Like slaves' lives. Nobody can be free alone. Not even a mage. All of them working their magic in prison cells, to gain nothing. There's no way to use power for good."

Ayo closed her hand and opened it palm up, a fleeting sketch of a gesture, of a sign.

A man came up the mountain to Woodedge, a charcoal burner from Firn. "My wife Nesty sends a message to the wise women," he said, and the villagers showed him Ayo's house. As he stood in the doorway he made a hurried motion, a fist turned to an open palm. "Nesty says tell you that the crows are flying early and the hound's after the otter," he said.

Otter, sitting by the fire shelling walnuts, held still. Mead thanked the messenger and brought him in for a cup of water and a handful of shelled nuts. She and Ayo chatted with him about his wife. When he had gone she turned to Otter.

"The Hound serves Losen," he said. "I'll go today."

Mead looked at her sister. "Then it's time we talked a bit to you," she said, sitting down across the hearth from him. Ayo stood by the table, silent. A good fire burned in the hearth. It was a wet, cold time, and firewood was one thing they had plenty of, here on the mountain.

"There's people all over these parts, and maybe beyond, who think, as you said, that nobody can be wise alone. So these people try to hold to each other. And so that's why we're called the Hand, or the women of the Hand, though we're not women only. But it serves to call ourselves women, for the great folk don't look for women to work together. Or to have thoughts about such things as rule or misrule. Or to have any powers."

"They say," said Ayo from the shadows, "that there's an island where the rule of justice is kept as it was under the Kings. Morred's Isle, they call it. But it's not Enlad of the Kings, nor Éa. It's south, not north of Havnor, they say. There they say the women of the Hand have kept the old arts. And they teach them, not keeping them secret each to himself, as the wizards do."

"Maybe with such teaching you could teach the wizards a lesson," Mead said.

"Maybe you can find that island," said Ayo.

Otter looked from one to the other. Clearly they had told him their own greatest secret and their hope.

"Morred's Isle," he said.

"That would be only what the women of the Hand call it, keeping its meaning from the wizards and the pirates. To them no doubt it would bear some other name."

"It would be a terrible long way," said Mead.

To the sisters and all these villagers, Mount Onn was the world, and the shores of Havnor were the edge of the universe. Beyond that was only rumor and dream.

"You'll come to the sea, going south, they say," said Ayo.

"He knows that, sister," Mead told her. "Didn't he tell us he was a ship carpenter? But it's a terrible long way down to the sea, surely. With this wizard on your scent, how are you to go there?"

"By the grace of water, that carries no scent," Otter said, standing up. A litter of walnut shells fell from his lap, and he took the hearth broom and swept them into the ashes. "I'd better go."

"There's bread," Ayo said, and Mead hurried to pack hard bread and hard cheese and walnuts into a pouch made of a sheep's stomach. They were very poor people. They gave him what they had. So Anieb had done.

"My mother was born in Endlane, round by Faliern Forest," Otter said. "Do you know that town? She's called Rose, Rowan's daughter."

"The carters go down to Endlane, summers."

"If somebody could talk to her people there, they'd get word to her. Her brother, Littleash, used to come to the city every year or two."

They nodded.

"If she knew I was alive," he said.

Anieb's mother nodded. "She'll hear it."

"Go on now," said Mead.

"Go with the water," said Ayo.

He embraced them, and they him, and he left the house.

He ran down from the straggle of huts to the quick, noisy stream he had heard singing through his sleep all his nights in Woodedge. He prayed to it. "Take me and save me," he asked it. He made the spell the old Changer had taught him long ago, and said the word of transformation. Then no man knelt by the loud-running water, but an otter slipped into it and was gone.

III. Tern

There was a wise man on our hill
Who found his way to work his will.
He changed his shape, he changed his name,

> *But ever the other will be the same.*
> *So runs the water away, away,*
> *So runs the water away.*

ONE WINTER AFTERNOON ON THE SHORE OF THE ONNEVA River where it fingers out into the north bight of the Great Bay of Havnor, a man stood up on the muddy sand: a man poorly dressed and poorly shod, a thin brown man with dark eyes and hair so fine and thick it shed the rain. It was raining on the low beaches of the river mouth, the fine, cold, dismal drizzle of that grey winter. His clothes were soaked. He hunched his shoulders, turned about, and set off towards a wisp of chimney smoke he saw far down the shore. Behind him were the tracks of an otter's four feet coming up from the water and the tracks of a man's two feet going away from it.

Where he went then, the songs don't tell. They say only that he wandered, "he wandered long from land to land." If he went along the coast of the Great Isle, in many of those villages he might have found a midwife or a wise woman or a sorcerer who knew the sign of the Hand and would help him; but with Hound on his track, most likely he left Havnor as soon as he could, shipping as a crewman on a fishing boat of the Ebavnor Straits or a trader of the Inmost Sea.

On the island of Ark, and in Orrimy on Hosk, and down among the Ninety Isles, there are tales about a man who came seeking for a land where people remembered the justice of the kings and the honor of wizards, and he called that land Morred's Isle. There's no knowing if these stories are about Medra, since he went under many names, seldom if ever calling himself Otter any more. Gelluk's fall had not brought Losen down. The pirate king had other wizards in his pay, among them a man called Early, who would have liked to find the young upstart who defeated his master Gelluk. And Early had a good chance of tracing him. Losen's power stretched all across Havnor and the north of the

Inmost Sea, growing with the years; and the Hound's nose was as keen as ever.

Maybe it was to escape the hunt that Medra came to Pendor, a long way west of the Inmost Sea, or maybe some rumor among the women of the Hand on Hosk sent him there. Pendor was a rich island, then, before the dragon Yevaud despoiled it. Wherever Medra had gone until then, he had found the lands like Havnor or worse, sunk in warfare, raids, and piracy, the fields full of weeds, the towns full of thieves. Maybe he thought, at first, that on Pendor he had found Morred's Isle, for the city was beautiful and peaceful and the people prosperous.

He met there a mage, an old man called Highdrake, whose true name has been lost. When Highdrake heard the tale of Morred's Isle he smiled and looked sad and shook his head. "Not here," he said. "Not this. The Lords of Pendor are good men. They remember the kings. They don't seek war or plunder. But they send their sons west dragon hunting. In sport. As if the dragons of the West Reach were ducks or geese for the killing! No good will come of that."

Highdrake took Medra as his student, gratefully. "I was taught my art by a mage who gave me freely all he knew, but I never found anybody to give that knowledge to, until you came," he told Medra. "The young men come to me and they say, 'What good is it? Can you find gold?' they say. 'Can you teach me how to make stones into diamonds? Can you give me a sword that will kill a dragon? What's the use of talking about the balance of things? There's no profit in it,' they say. No profit!" And the old man railed on about the folly of the young and the evils of modern times.

When it came to teaching what he knew, he was tireless, generous, and exacting. For the first time, Medra was given a vision of magic not as a set of strange gifts and reasonless acts, but as an art and a craft, which could be known truly with long study and used rightly after long practice, though even then it would never lose its strangeness.

Highdrake's mastery of spells and sorcery was not much greater than his pupil's, but he had clear in his mind the idea of something very much greater, the wholeness of knowledge. And that made him a mage.

Listening to him, Medra thought of how he and Anieb had walked in the dark and rain by the faint glimmer that showed them only the next step they could take, and of how they had looked up to the red ridge of the mountain in the dawn.

"Every spell depends on every other spell," said Highdrake. "Every motion of a single leaf moves every leaf of every tree on every isle of Earthsea! There is a pattern. That's what you must look for and look to. Nothing goes right but as part of the pattern. Only in it is freedom."

Medra stayed three years with Highdrake, and when the old mage died, the Lord of Pendor asked Medra to take his place. Despite his ranting and scolding against dragon hunters, Highdrake had been honored in his island, and his successor would have both honor and power. Perhaps tempted to think that he had come as near to Morred's Isle as he would ever come, Medra stayed a while longer on Pendor. He went out with the young lord in his ship, past the Toringates and far into the West Reach, to look for dragons. There was a great longing in his heart to see a dragon. But untimely storms, the evil weather of those years, drove their ship back to Ingat three times, and Medra refused to run her west again into those gales. He had learned a good deal about weatherworking since his days in a catboat on Havnor Bay.

A while after that he left Pendor, drawn southward again, and maybe went to Ensmer. In one guise or another he came at last to Geath in the Ninety Isles.

There they fished for whales, as they still do. That was a trade he wanted no part of. Their ships stank and their town stank. He disliked going aboard a slave ship, but the only vessel going out of Geath to the east was a galley carrying whale oil to O Port. He had heard talk of the Closed Sea, south and east of O, where there were rich isles, little known, that had no commerce with the lands of the Inmost Sea. What he sought might be there. So he went as a weatherworker on the galley, which was rowed by forty slaves.

The weather was fair for once: a following wind, a blue sky lively with little white clouds, the mild sunlight of late spring. They made good way from Geath. Late in the afternoon he heard the master say to the helmsman, "Keep her south tonight so we don't raise Roke."

He had not heard of that island, and asked, "What's there?"

"Death and desolation," said the ship's master, a short man with small, sad, knowing eyes like a whale's.

"War?"

"Years back. Plague, black sorcery. The waters all round it are cursed."

"Worms," said the helmsman, the master's brother. "Catch fish anywhere near Roke, you'll find 'em thick with worms as a dead dog on a dunghill."

"Do people still live there?" Medra asked, and the master said, "Witches," while his brother said, "Worm eaters."

There were many such isles in the Archipelago, made barren and desolate by rival wizards' blights and curses; they were evil places to come to or even to pass, and Medra thought no more about this one, until that night.

Sleeping out on deck with the starlight on his face, he had a simple, vivid dream: it was daylight, clouds racing across a bright sky, and across the sea he saw the sunlit curve of a high green hill. He woke with the vision still clear in his mind, knowing he had seen it ten years before, in the spell-locked barracks room at the mines of Samory.

He sat up. The dark sea was so quiet that the stars were reflected here and there on the sleek lee side of the long swells. Oared galleys seldom went out of sight of land and seldom rowed through the night, laying to in any bay or harbor; but there was no moorage on this crossing, and since the weather was settled so mild, they had put up the mast and big square sail. The ship drifted softly forward, her slave oarsmen sleeping on their benches, the free men of her crew all asleep but the helmsman and the lookout, and the lookout was dozing. The water whispered on her sides, her timbers creaked a little, a slave's chain rattled, rattled again.

"They don't need a weatherworker on a night like this, and they haven't paid me yet," Medra said to his conscience. He had waked from his dream with the name Roke in his mind. Why had he never heard of the isle or seen it on a chart? It might be accursed and deserted as they said, but wouldn't it be set down on the charts?

"I could fly there as a tern and be back on the ship before daylight," he said to himself, but idly. He was bound for O Port. Ruined lands were all too common. No need to fly to seek them. He made himself comfortable in his coil of cable and watched the stars. Looking west, he saw the four bright stars of the Forge, low over the sea. They were a little blurred, and as he watched them they blinked out, one by one.

The faintest little sighing tremor ran over the slow, smooth swells.

"Master," Medra said, afoot, "wake up."

"What now?"

"A witchwind coming. Following. Get the sail down."

No wind stirred. The air was soft, the big sail hung slack. Only the western stars faded and vanished in a silent blackness that rose slowly higher. The master looked at that. "Witchwind, you say?" he asked, reluctant.

Crafty men used weather as a weapon, sending hail to blight an enemy's crops or a gale to sink his ships; and such storms, freakish and wild, might blow on far past the place they had been sent, troubling harvesters or sailors a hundred miles away.

"Get the sail down," Medra said, peremptory. The master yawned and cursed and began to shout commands. The crewmen got up slowly and slowly began to take the awkward sail in, and the oarmaster, after asking several questions of the master and Medra, began to roar at the slaves and stride among them rousing them right and left with his knotted rope. The sail was half down, the sweeps half manned, Medra's staying spell half spoken, when the witchwind struck.

It struck with one huge thunderclap out of sudden utter blackness and wild rain. The ship pitched like a horse rearing and then rolled so hard and far that the mast broke loose from its footing, though the stays held. The sail struck the water, filled, and pulled the galley right over, the great sweeps sliding in their oarlocks, the chained slaves struggling and shouting on their benches, barrels of oil breaking loose and thundering over one another—pulled her over and held her over, the deck vertical to the sea, till a huge storm wave struck and swamped her and she sank. All the shouting and screaming of men's voices was suddenly silent. There was no noise but the roar of the rain on the sea, lessening as the freak wind passed on eastward. Through it one white seabird beat its wings up from the black water and flew, frail and desperate, to the north.

PRINTED ON NARROW SANDS UNDER GRANITE CLIFFS, IN THE first light, were the tracks of a bird alighting. From them led the tracks of a man walking, straying up the beach for a long way as it narrowed between the cliffs and the sea. Then the tracks ceased.

Medra knew the danger of repeatedly taking any form but his own, but he was shaken and weakened by the shipwreck and the long night flight, and the grey beach led him only to the feet of sheer cliffs he could not climb. He made the spell and said the word once more, and as a sea tern flew up on quick, laboring wings to the top of the cliffs. Then, possessed by flight, he flew on over a shadowy sunrise land. Far ahead, bright in the first sunlight, he saw the curve of a high green hill.

To it he flew, and on it landed, and as he touched the earth he was a man again.

He stood there for a while, bewildered. It seemed to him that it was not by his own act or decision that he had taken his own form, but that in touching this ground, this hill, he had become himself. A magic greater than his own prevailed here.

He looked about, curious and wary. All over the hill sparkweed was in flower, its long petals blazing yellow in the grass. Children on Havnor knew that flower. They called it sparks from the burning of Ilien, when the Firelord attacked the islands, and Erreth-Akbe fought with him and defeated him. Tales and songs of the heroes rose up in Medra's memory as he stood there: Erreth-Akbe and the heroes before him, the Eagle Queen, Heru, Akambar who drove the Kargs into the east, and Serriadh the peacemaker, and Elfarran of Soléa, and Morred, the White Enchanter, the beloved king. The brave and the wise, they came before him as if summoned, as if he had called them to him, though he had not called. He saw them. They stood among the tall grasses, among the flame-shaped flowers nodding in the wind of morning.

Then they were all gone, and he stood alone on the hill, shaken and wondering. "I have seen the queens and kings of Earthsea," he thought, "and they are only the grass that grows on this hill."

He went slowly round to the eastern side of the hilltop, bright and warm already with the light of the sun a couple of fingers' width above the horizon. Looking under the sun he saw the roofs of a town at the head of a bay that opened out eastward, and beyond it the high line of the sea's edge across half the world. Turning west he saw fields and pastures and roads. To the north were long green hills. In a fold of land southward a grove of tall trees drew his gaze and held it. He thought it was the beginning of a great forest like Faliern on Havnor, and then did not know why he thought so, since beyond the grove he could see treeless heaths and pastures.

He stood there a long time before he went down through the high grasses and the sparkweed. At the foot of the hill he came into a lane. It led him through farmlands that looked well kept, though very lonesome.

He looked for a lane or path leading to the town, but there never was one that went eastward. Not a soul was in the fields, some of which were newly ploughed. No dog barked as he went by. Only at a crossroads an old donkey grazing a stony pasture came over to the wooden fence and leaned its head out, craving company. Medra stopped to stroke the grey-brown, bony face. A city man and a saltwater man, he knew little of farms and their animals, but he thought the donkey looked at him kindly. "Where am I, donkey?" he said to it. "How do I get to the town I saw?"

The donkey leaned its head hard against his hand so that he would go on scratching the place just above its eyes and below its ears. When he did so, it flicked its long right ear. So when he parted from the donkey he took the right hand of the crossroad, though it looked as if it would lead back to the hill; and soon enough he came among houses, and then onto a street that brought him down at last into the town at the head of the bay.

It was as strangely quiet as the farmlands. Not a voice, not a face. It was difficult to feel uneasy in an ordinary-looking town on a sweet spring morning, but in such silence he must wonder if he was indeed in a plague-stricken place or an island under a curse. He went on. Between a house and an old plum tree was a wash line, the clothes pinned on it flapping in the sunny breeze. A cat came round the corner of a garden, no abandoned starveling but a white-pawed, well-whiskered, prosperous cat. And at last, coming down the steep little street, which here was cobbled, he heard voices.

He stopped to listen, and heard nothing.

He went on to the foot of the street. It opened into a small market square. People were gathered there, not many of them. They were not buying or selling. There were no booths or stalls set up. They were waiting for him.

Ever since he had walked on the green hill above the town and had seen the bright shadows in the grass, his heart had been easy. He was expectant, full of a sense of great strangeness, but not frightened. He stood still and looked at the people who came to meet him.

Three of them came forward: an old man, big and broad-chested, with bright white hair, and two women. Wizard knows wizard, and Medra knew they were women of power.

He raised his hand closed in a fist and then turning and opening it, offered it to them palm up.

"Ah," said one of the women, the taller of the two, and she laughed. But she did not answer the gesture.

"Tell us who you are," the white-haired man said, courteously enough, but without greeting or welcome. "Tell us how you came here."

"I was born in Havnor and trained as a shipwright and a sorcerer. I was on a ship bound from Geath to O Port. I was spared alone from drowning, last night, when a witchwind struck." He was silent then. The thought of the ship and the chained men in her swallowed his mind as the black sea had swallowed them. He gasped, as if coming up from drowning.

"How did you come here?"

"As . . . as a bird, a tern. Is this Roke Island?"

"You changed yourself?"

He nodded.

"Whom do you serve?" asked the shorter and younger of the women, speaking for the first time. She had a keen, hard face, with long black brows.

"I have no master."

"What was your errand in O Port?"

"In Havnor, years ago, I was in servitude. Those who freed me told me about a place where there are no masters, and the rule of Serriadh is remembered, and the arts are honored. I have been looking for that place, that island, seven years."

"Who told you about it?"

"Women of the Hand."

"Anyone can make a fist and show a palm," said the tall woman, pleasantly. "But not everyone can fly to Roke. Or swim, or sail, or come in any way at all. So we must ask what brought you here."

Medra did not answer at once. "Chance," he said at last, "favoring long desire. Not art. Not knowledge. I think I've come to the place I sought, but I don't know. I think you may be the people they told me of, but I don't know. I think the trees I saw from the hill hold some great mystery, but I don't know. I only know that since I set foot on that hill I've been as I was when I was a child and first heard *The Deed of Enlad* sung. I am lost among wonders."

The white-haired man looked at the two women. Other people had come forward, and there was some quiet talk among them.

"If you stayed here, what would you do?" the black-browed woman asked him.

"I can build boats, or mend them, and sail them. I can find, above and under ground. I can work weather, if you have any need of that. And I'll learn the art from any who will teach me."

"What do you want to learn?" asked the taller woman in her mild voice.

Now Medra felt that he had been asked the question on which the rest of his life hung, for good or evil. Again he stood silent a while. He started to speak, and didn't speak, and finally spoke. "I could not save one, not one, not the one who saved me," he said. "Nothing I know could have set her free. I know nothing. If you know how to be free, I beg you, teach me!"

"Free!" said the tall woman, and her voice cracked like a whip. Then she looked at her companions, and after a while she smiled a little. Turning back to Medra, she said, "We're prisoners, and so freedom is a thing we study. You came here through the walls of our prison.

Seeking freedom, you say. But you should know that leaving Roke may be even harder than coming to it. Prison within prison, and some of it we have built ourselves." She looked at the others. "What do you say?" she asked them.

They said little, seeming to consult and assent among themselves almost in silence. At last the shorter woman looked with her fierce eyes at Medra. "Stay if you will," she said.

"I will."

"What will you have us call you?"

"Tern," he said; and so he was called.

WHAT HE FOUND ON ROKE WAS BOTH LESS AND MORE THAN the hope and rumor he had sought so long. Roke Island was, they told him, the heart of Earthsea. The first land Segoy raised from the waters in the beginning of time was bright Éa of the northern sea, and the second was Roke. That green hill, Roke Knoll, was founded deeper than all the islands. The trees he had seen, which seemed sometimes to be in one place on the isle and sometimes in another, were the oldest trees in the world, and the source and center of magic.

"If the Grove were cut, all wizardry would fail. The roots of those trees are the roots of knowledge. The patterns the shadows of their leaves make in the sunlight write the words Segoy spoke in the Making."

So said Ember, his fierce, black-browed teacher.

All the teachers of the art magic on Roke were women. There were no men of power, few men at all, on the island.

Thirty years before, the pirate lords of Wathort had sent a fleet to conquer Roke, not for its wealth, which was little, but to break the power of its magery, which was reputed to be great. One of the wizards of Roke had betrayed the island to the crafty men of Wathort, lowering its spells of defense and warning. Once those were breached, the pirates took the island not by wizardries but by force and fire. Their great ships filled Thwil Bay, their hordes burned and looted, their slave takers carried off men, boys, young women. Little children and the old they slaughtered. They fired every house and field they came to. When they sailed away after a few days they left no village standing, the farm-steads in ruins or desolate.

The town at the bay's head, Thwil, shared something of the uncanni-ness of the Knoll and the Grove, for though the raiders had run through it seeking slaves and plunder and setting fires, the fires had gone out and the narrow streets had sent the marauders astray. Most of the islanders who survived were wise women and their children, who had hidden themselves in the town or in the Immanent Grove. The men now on Roke were those spared children, grown, and a few men now grown old. There was no government but that of the women of the Hand, for it was their spells that had protected Roke so long and protected it far more closely now.

They had little trust in men. A man had betrayed them. Men had attacked them. It was men's ambitions, they said, that had perverted all the arts to ends of gain. "We do not deal with their governments," said tall Veil in her mild voice.

And yet Ember said to Medra, "We were our own undoing."

Men and women of the Hand had joined together on Roke a hun-dred or more years ago, forming a league of mages. Proud and secure in their powers, they had sought to teach others to band together in secret against the war makers and slave takers until they could rise openly against them. Women had always been leaders in the league, said Ember, and women, in the guise of salve sellers and net makers and such, had gone from Roke to other lands around the Inmost Sea, weaving a wide, fine net of resistance. Even now there were strands and knots of that net left. Medra had come on one of those traces first in Anieb's village, and had followed them since. But they had not led him here. Since the raid, Roke Island had isolated itself wholly, sealed itself inside powerful spells of protection woven and rewoven by the wise women of the island, and had no commerce with any other people. "We can't save them," Ember said. "We couldn't save ourselves."

Veil, with her gentle voice and smile, was implacable. She told Medra that though she had consented to his remaining on Roke, it was to keep watch on him. "You broke through our defenses once," she said. "All that you say of yourself may be true, and may not. What can you tell me that would make me trust you?"

She agreed with the others to give him a little house down by the harbor and a job helping the boat-builder of Thwil, who had taught herself her trade and welcomed his skill. Veil put no difficulties in his path and always greeted him kindly. But she had said, "What can you tell me that would make me trust you?" and he had no answer for her.

Ember usually scowled when he greeted her. She asked him abrupt questions, listened to his answers, and said nothing.

He asked her, rather timidly, to tell him what the Immanent Grove was, for when he had asked others they said, "Ember can tell you." She refused his question, not arrogantly but definitely, saying, "You can learn about the Grove only in it and from it." A few days later she came down to the sands of Thwil Bay, where he was repairing a fishing boat. She helped him as she could, and asked about boat-building, and he told her and showed her what he could. It was a peaceful afternoon, but after it she went off in her abrupt way. He felt some awe of her; she was incalculable. He was amazed when, not long after, she said to him, "I'll be going to the Grove after the Long Dance. Come if you like."

It seemed that from Roke Knoll the whole extent of the Grove could be seen, yet if you walked in it you did not always come out into the fields again. You walked on under the trees. In the inner Grove they were all of one kind, which grew nowhere else, yet had no name in Hardic but "tree." In the Old Speech, Ember said, each of those trees had its own name. You walked on, and after a time you were walking

again among familiar trees, oak and beech and ash, chestnut and walnut and willow, green in spring and bare in winter; there were dark firs,
and cedar, and a tall evergreen Medra did not know, with soft reddish
bark and layered foliage. You walked on, and the way through the trees
was never twice the same. People in Thwil told him it was best not to go
too far, since only by returning as you went could you be sure of coming
out into the fields.

"How far does the forest go?" Medra asked, and Ember said, "As far
as the mind goes."

The leaves of the trees spoke, she said, and the shadows could be read.
"I am learning to read them," she said.

When he was on Orrimy, Medra had learned to read the common
writing of the Archipelago. Later, Highdrake of Pendor had taught him
some of the runes of power. That was known lore. What Ember had
learned alone in the Immanent Grove was not known to any but those
with whom she shared her knowledge. She lived all summer under the
eaves of the Grove, having no more than a box to keep the mice and
wood rats from her small store of food, a shelter of branches, and a cook
fire near a stream that came out of the woods to join the little river running down to the bay.

Medra camped nearby. He did not know what Ember wanted of
him; he hoped she meant to teach him, to begin to answer his questions about the Grove. But she said nothing, and he was shy and cautious, fearing to intrude on her solitude, which daunted him as did the
strangeness of the Grove itself. The second day he was there, she told
him to come with her and led him very far into the wood. They walked
for hours in silence. In the summer midday the woods were silent. No
bird sang. The leaves did not stir. The aisles of the trees were endlessly
different and all the same. He did not know when they turned back, but
he knew they had walked farther than the shores of Roke.

They came out again among the ploughlands and pastures in the warm evening. As they walked back to their camping place he saw the four stars of the Forge come out above the western hills.

Ember parted from him with only a "Good night."

The next day she said, "I'm going to sit under the trees." Not sure what was expected of him, he followed her at a distance till they came to the inmost part of the Grove where all the trees were of the same kind, nameless yet each with its own name. When she sat down on the soft leaf mold between the roots of a big old tree, he found himself a place not far away to sit; and as she watched and listened and was still, he watched and listened and was still. So they did for several days. Then one morning, in rebellious mood, he stayed by the stream while Ember walked into the Grove. She did not look back.

Veil came from Thwil Town that morning, bringing them a basket of bread, cheese, milk curds, summer fruits. "What have you learned?" she asked Medra in her cool, gentle way, and he answered, "That I'm a fool."

"Why so, Tern?"

"A fool could sit under the trees forever and grow no wiser."

The tall woman smiled a little. "My sister has never taught a man before," she said. She glanced at him, and gazed away, over the summery fields. "She's never looked at a man before," she said.

Medra stood silent. His face felt hot. He looked down. "I thought," he said, and stopped.

In Veil's words he saw, all at once, the other side of Ember's impatience, her fierceness, her silences.

He had tried to look at Ember as untouchable while he longed to touch her soft brown skin, her black shining hair. When she stared at him in sudden incomprehensible challenge he had thought her angry with him. He feared to insult, to offend her. What did she fear? His desire? Her own?—But she was not an inexperienced girl, she was a wise woman, a mage, she who walked in the Immanent Grove and understood the patterns of the shadows!

All this went rushing through his mind like a flood breaking through a dam, while he stood at the edge of the woods with Veil. "I thought mages kept themselves apart," he said at last. "Highdrake said that to make love is to unmake power."

"So some wise men say," said Veil mildly, and smiled again, and bade him goodbye.

He spent the whole afternoon in confusion, angry. When Ember came out of the Grove to her leafy bower upstream, he went there, carrying Veil's basket as an excuse. "May I talk to you?" he said.

She nodded shortly, frowning her black brows.

He said nothing. She squatted down to find out what was in the basket. "Peaches!" she said, and smiled.

"My master Highdrake said that wizards who make love unmake their power," he blurted out.

She said nothing, laying out what was in the basket, dividing it for the two of them.

"Do you think that's true?" he asked.

She shrugged. "No," she said.

He stood tongue-tied. After a while she looked up at him. "No," she said in a soft, quiet voice, "I don't think it's true. I think all the true powers, all the old powers, at root are one."

He still stood there, and she said, "Look at the peaches! They're all ripe. We'll have to eat them right away."

"If I told you my name," he said, "my true name—"

"I'd tell you mine," she said. "If that . . . if that's how we should begin."

They began, however, with the peaches.

They were both shy. When Medra took her hand his hand shook, and Ember, whose name was Elehal, turned away scowling. Then she touched his hand very lightly. When he stroked the sleek black flow of her hair she seemed only to endure his touch, and he stopped. When he tried to embrace her she was stiff, rejecting him. Then she turned and, fierce, hasty, awkward, seized him in her arms. It wasn't the first night, nor the first nights, they passed together that gave either of them much pleasure or ease. But they learned from each other, and came through shame and fear into passion. Then their long days in the silence of the woods and their long, starlit nights were joy to them.

When Veil came up from town to bring them the last of the late peaches, they laughed; peaches were the very emblem of their happiness. They tried to make her stay and eat supper with them, but she wouldn't. "Stay here while you can," she said.

The summer ended too soon that year. Rain came early; snow fell in autumn even as far south as Roke. Storm followed storm, as if the winds had risen in rage against the tampering and meddling of the crafty men. Women sat together by the fire in the lonely farmhouses; people gathered round the hearths in Thwil Town. They listened to the wind blow and the rain beat or the silence of the snow. Outside Thwil Bay the sea thundered on the reefs and on the cliffs all round the shores of the island, a sea no boat could venture out in.

What they had they shared. In that it was indeed Morred's Isle. Nobody on Roke starved or went unhoused, though nobody had much more than they needed. Hidden from the rest of the world not only by sea and storm but by their defenses that disguised the island and sent ships astray, they worked and talked and sang the songs, *The Winter Carol* and *The Deed of the Young King*. And they had books, the *Chronicles of Enlad* and the *History of the Wise Heroes*. From these precious books the old men and women would read aloud in a hall down by the wharf where the fisherwomen made and mended their nets. There was a hearth there, and they would light the fire. People came even from farms across the island to hear the histories read, listening in silence, intent. "Our souls are hungry," Ember said.

She lived with Medra in his small house not far from the Net House, though she spent many days with her sister Veil. Ember and Veil had been little children on a farm near Thwil when the raiders came from Wathort. Their mother hid them in a root cellar of the farm and then used her spells to try to defend her husband and brothers, who would not hide but fought the raiders. They were butchered with their cattle. The house and barns were burnt. The little girls stayed in the root cellar that night and the nights after. Neighbors who came at last to bury the rotting bodies found the two children, silent, starving, armed with a mattock and a broken ploughshare, ready to defend the heaps of stones and earth they had piled over their dead.

Medra knew only a hint of this story from Ember. One night Veil, who was three years older than Ember and to whom the memory was much clearer, told it to him fully. Ember sat with them, listening in silence.

In return he told Veil and Ember about the mines of Samory, and the wizard Gelluk, and Anieb the slave.

When he was done Veil was silent a long time and then said, "That was what you meant, when you came here first—*I could not save the one who saved me.*"

"And you asked me, *What can you tell me that could make me trust you?*"

"You have told me," Veil said.

Medra took her hand and put his forehead against it. Telling his story he had kept back tears. He could not do so now.

"She gave me freedom," he said. "And I still feel that all I do is done through her and for her. No, not for her. We can do nothing for the dead. But for . . ."

"For us," said Ember. "For us who live, in hiding, neither killed nor killing. The dead are dead. The great and mighty go their way unchecked. All the hope left in the world is in the people of no account."

"Must we hide forever?"

"Spoken like a man," said Veil with her gentle, wounded smile.

"Yes," said Ember. "We must hide, and forever if need be. Because there's nothing left but being killed and killing, beyond these shores. You say it, and I believe it."

"But you can't hide true power," Medra said. "Not for long. It dies in hiding, unshared."

"Magic won't die on Roke," said Veil. "*On Roke all spells are strong.* So said Ath himself. And you have walked under the trees . . . Our job must be to keep that strength. Hide it, yes. Hoard it, as a young dragon hoards up its fire. And share it. But only here. Pass it on, one to the next, here, where it's safe, and where the great robbers and killers would least look for it, since no one here is of any account. And one day the dragon will come into its strength. If it takes a thousand years . . ."

"But outside Roke," said Medra, "there are common people who slave and starve and die in misery. Must they do so for a thousand years with no hope?"

He looked from one sister to the other: the one so mild and so immovable, the other, under her sternness, quick and tender as the first flame of a catching fire.

"On Havnor," he said, "far from Roke, in a village on Mount Onn, among people who know nothing of the world, there are still women of the Hand. That net hasn't broken after so many years. How was it woven?"

"Craftily," said Ember.

"And cast wide!" He looked from one to the other again. "I wasn't well taught, in the City of Havnor," he said. "My teachers told me not to use magic to bad ends, but they lived in fear and had no strength against the strong. They gave me all they had to give, but it was little. It was by mere luck I didn't go wrong. And by Anieb's gift of strength to me. But for her I'd be Gelluk's servant now. Yet she herself was untaught, and so enslaved. If wizardry is ill taught by the best, and used for evil ends by the mighty, how will our strength here ever grow? What will the young dragon feed on?"

"This is the center," said Veil. "We must keep to the center. And wait."

"We must give what we have to give," said Medra. "If all but us are slaves, what's our freedom worth?"

"The true art prevails over the false. The pattern will hold," Ember said, frowning. She reached out the poker to gather together her namesakes in the hearth, and with a whack knocked the heap into a blaze. "That I know. But our lives are short, and the pattern's very long. If only Roke was now what it once was—if we had more people of the true art gathered here, teaching and learning as well as preserving—"

"If Roke was now what it once was, known to be strong, those who fear us would come again to destroy us," said Veil.

"The solution lies in secrecy," said Medra. "But so does the problem."

"Our problem is with men," Veil said, "if you'll forgive me, dear brother. Men are of more account to other men than women and children are. We might have fifty witches here and they'll pay little heed. But if they knew we had five men of power, they'd seek to destroy us again."

"So though there were men among us we were the *women* of the Hand," said Ember.

"You still are," Medra said. "Anieb was one of you. She and you and all of us live in the same prison."

"What can we do?" said Veil.

"Learn our strength!" said Medra.

"A school," Ember said. "Where the wise might come to learn from one another, to study the pattern . . . The Grove would shelter us."

"The lords of war despise scholars and schoolmasters," said Medra.

"I think they fear them too," said Veil.

So they talked, that long winter, and others talked with them. Slowly their talk turned from vision to intention, from longing to planning. Veil was always cautious, warning of dangers. White-haired Dune was so eager that Ember said he wanted to start teaching sorcery to every child in Thwil. Once Ember had come to believe that Roke's freedom lay in offering others freedom, she set her whole mind on how the women of the Hand might grow strong again. But her mind, formed by her long solitudes among the trees, always sought form and clarity, and she said, "How can we teach our art when we don't know what it is?"

And they talked about that, all the wise women of the island: what was the true art of magic, and where did it turn false; how the balance of things was kept or lost; what crafts were needful, which useful, which dangerous; why some people had one gift but not another, and whether you could learn an art you had no native gift for. In such discussions they worked out the names that ever since have been given to the masteries: finding, weatherworking, changing, healing, summoning, patterning, naming, and the crafts of illusion, and the knowledge of the songs. Those are the arts of the Masters of Roke even now, though the Chanter took the Finder's place when finding came to be considered a merely useful craft unworthy of a mage.

And it was in these discussions that the school on Roke began.

There are some who say that the school had its beginnings far differently. They say that Roke used to be ruled by a woman called the Dark Woman, who was in league with the Old Powers of the earth. They say she lived in a cave under Roke Knoll, never coming into the daylight, but weaving vast spells over land and sea that compelled men to her evil will, until the first Archmage came to Roke, unsealed and entered the cave, defeated the Dark Woman, and took her place.

There's no truth in this tale but one, which is that indeed one of the first Masters of Roke opened and entered a great cavern. But though the roots of Roke are the roots of all the islands, that cavern was not on Roke.

And it's true that in the time of Medra and Elehal the people of Roke, men and women, had no fear of the Old Powers of the earth, but revered them, seeking strength and vision from them. That changed with the years.

Spring came late again that year, cold and stormy. Medra set to boat-building. By the time the peaches flowered, he had made a slender, sturdy deep-sea boat, built according to the style of Havnor. He called her *Hopeful*. Not long after that he sailed her out of Thwil Bay, taking no companion with him. "Look for me at the end of summer," he said to Ember.

"I'll be in the Grove," she said. "And my heart with you, my dark otter, my white tern, my love, Medra."

"And mine with you, my ember of fire, my flowering tree, my love, Elehal."

ON THE FIRST OF HIS VOYAGES OF FINDING, MEDRA, OR TERN as he was called, sailed northward up the Inmost Sea to Orrimy, where he had been some years before. There were people of the Hand there whom he trusted. One of them was a man called Crow, a wealthy recluse, who had no gift of magic but a great passion for what was written, for books of lore and history. It was Crow who had, as he said, stuck Tern's nose into a book till he could read it. "Illiterate wizards are the curse of Earthsea!" he cried. "Ignorant power is a bane!" Crow was a strange man, wilful, arrogant, obstinate, and, in defense of his passion, brave. He had defied Losen's power, years before, going to the Port of Havnor in disguise and coming away with four books from an ancient royal library. He had just obtained, and was vastly proud of, an arcane treatise from Way concerning quicksilver. "Got that from under Losen's nose too," he said to Tern. "Come have a look at it! It belonged to a famous wizard."

"Tinaral," said Tern. "I knew him."

"Book's trash, is it?" said Crow, who was quick to pick up signals if they had to do with books.

"I don't know. I'm after bigger prey."

Crow cocked his head.

"The Book of Names."

"Lost with Ath when he went into the west," Crow said.

"A mage called Highdrake told me that when Ath stayed in Pendor, he told a wizard there that he'd left the Book of Names with a woman in the Ninety Isles for safekeeping."

"A woman! For safekeeping! In the Ninety Isles! Was he mad?"

Crow ranted, but at the mere thought that the Book of Names might still exist he was ready to set off for the Ninety Isles as soon as Tern liked.

So they sailed south in *Hopeful*, landing first at malodorous Geath, and then in the guise of peddlers working their way from one islet to the next among the mazy channels. Crow had stocked the boat with better wares than most householders of the Isles were used to seeing, and Tern offered them at fair prices, mostly in barter, since there was little money among the islanders. Their popularity ran ahead of them. It was known that they would trade for books, if the books were old and uncanny. But in the Isles all books were old and all uncanny, what there was of them.

Crow was delighted to get a water-stained bestiary from the time of Akambar in return for five silver buttons, a pearl-hilted knife, and a square of Lorbanery silk. He sat in *Hopeful* and crooned over the antique descriptions of harikki and otak and icebear. But Tern went ashore on every isle, showing his wares in the kitchens of the housewives and the sleepy taverns where the old men sat. Sometimes he idly made a fist and then turned his hand over opening the palm, but nobody here returned the sign.

"Books?" said a rush plaiter on North Sudidi. "Like that there?" He pointed to long strips of vellum that had been worked into the thatching of his house. "They good for something else?" Crow, staring up at the words visible here and there between the rushes in the eaves, began to tremble with rage. Tern hurried him back to the boat before he exploded.

"It was only a beast healer's manual," Crow admitted, when they were sailing on and he had calmed down. "'Spavined,' I saw, and something about ewes' udders. But the ignorance! the brute ignorance! To roof his house with it!"

"And it was useful knowledge," Tern said. "How can people be anything but ignorant when knowledge isn't saved, isn't taught? If books could be brought together in one place . . ."

"Like the Library of the Kings," said Crow, dreaming of lost glories.

"Or your library," said Tern, who had become a subtler man than he used to be.

"Fragments," Crow said, dismissing his life's work. "Remnants!"

"Beginnings," said Tern.

Crow only sighed.

"I think we might go south again," Tern said, steering for the open channel. "Towards Pody."

"You have a gift for the business," Crow said. "You know where to look. Went straight to that bestiary in the barn loft . . . But there's nothing much to look for here. Nothing of importance. Ath wouldn't have left the greatest of all the lore-books among boors who'd make thatch of it! Take us to Pody if you like. And then back to Orrimy. I've had about enough."

"And we're out of buttons," Tern said. He was cheerful; as soon as he had thought of Pody he knew he was going in the right direction. "Perhaps I can find some along the way," he said. "It's my gift, you know."

Neither of them had been on Pody. It was a sleepy southern island with a pretty old port town, Telio, built of rosy sandstone, and fields and orchards that should have been fertile. But the lords of Wathort had ruled it for a century, taxing and slave taking and wearing the land and people down. The sunny streets of Telio were sad and dirty. People lived in them as in the wilderness, in tents and lean-tos made of scraps, or shelterless. "Oh, this won't do," Crow said, disgusted, avoiding a pile of human excrement. "These creatures don't have books, Tern!"

"Wait, wait," his companion said. "Give me a day."

"It's dangerous," Crow said, "it's pointless," but he made no further objection. The modest, naive young man whom he had taught to read had become his unfathomable guide.

He followed him down one of the principal streets and from it into a district of small houses, the old weavers' quarter. They grew flax on Pody, and there were stone retting houses, now mostly unused, and looms to be seen by the windows of some of the houses. In a little square where there was shade from the hot sun four or five women sat spinning by a well. Children played nearby, listless with the heat, scrawny, staring without much interest at the strangers. Tern had walked there unhesitating, as if he knew where he was going. Now he stopped and greeted the women.

"Oh, pretty man," said one of them with a smile, "don't even show us what you have in your pack there, for I haven't a penny of copper or ivory, nor seen one for a month."

"You might have a bit of linen, though, mistress? woven, or thread? Linen of Pody is the best—so I've heard as far as Havnor. And I can tell the quality of what you're spinning. A beautiful thread it is." Crow watched his companion with amusement and some disdain; he himself could bargain for a book very shrewdly, but nattering with common women about buttons and thread was beneath him. "Let me just open this up," Tern was saying as he spread his pack out on the cobbles, and the women and the dirty, timid children drew closer to see the wonders he would show them. "Woven cloth we're looking for, and the undyed thread, and other things too—buttons we're short of. If you had any of horn or bone, maybe? I'd trade one of these little velvet caps here for three or four buttons. Or one of these rolls of ribbon; look at the color of it. Beautiful with your hair, mistress! Or paper, or books. Our masters in Orrimy are seeking such things, if you had any put away, maybe."

"Oh, you are a pretty man," said the woman who had spoken first, laughing, as he held the red ribbon up to her black braid. "And I wish I had something for you!"

"I won't be so bold as to ask for a kiss," said Medra, "but an open hand, maybe?"

He made the sign; she looked at him for a moment. "That's easy," she said softly, and made the sign in return, "but not always safe, among strangers."

He went on showing his wares and joking with the women and children. Nobody bought anything. They gazed at the trinkets as if they were treasures. He let them gaze and finger all they would; indeed he let one of the children filch a little mirror of polished brass, seeing it vanish under the ragged shirt and saying nothing. At last he said he must go on, and the children drifted away as he folded up his pack.

"I have a neighbor," said the black-braided woman, "who might have some paper, if you're after that."

"Written on?" said Crow, who had been sitting on the well coping, bored. "Marks on it?"

She looked him up and down. "Marks on it, sir," she said. And then, to Tern, in a different tone, "If you'd like to come with me, she lives this way. And though she's only a girl, and poor, I'll tell you, peddler, she has an open hand. Though perhaps not all of us do."

"Three out of three," said Crow, sketching the sign, "so spare your vinegar, woman."

"Oh, it's you who have it to spare, sir. We're poor folk here. And ignorant," she said, with a flash of her eyes, and led on.

She brought them to a house at the end of a lane. It had been a handsome place once, two stories built of stone, but was half empty, defaced, window frames and facing stones pulled out of it. They crossed a courtyard with a well in it. She knocked at a side door, and a girl opened it.

"Ach, it's a witch's den," Crow said, at the whiff of herbs and aromatic smoke, and he stepped back.

"Healers," their guide said. "Is she ill again, Dory?"

The girl nodded, looking at Tern, then at Crow. She was thirteen or fourteen, heavyset though thin, with a sullen, steady gaze.

"They're men of the Hand, Dory, one short and pretty and one tall and proud, and they say they're seeking papers. I know you had some once, though you may not now. They've nothing you need in their pack, but it might be they'd pay a bit of ivory for what they want. Is it so?" She turned her bright eyes on Tern, and he nodded.

"She's very sick, Rush," the girl said. She looked again at Tern. "You're not a healer?" It was an accusation.

"No."

"She is," said Rush. "Like her mother and her mother's mother. Let us in, Dory, or me at least, to speak to her." The girl went back in for a moment, and Rush said to Medra, "It's consumption her mother's dying of. No healer could cure her. But she could heal the scrofula, and touch for pain. A wonder she was, and Dory bade fair to follow her."

The girl motioned them to come in. Crow chose to wait outside. The room was high and long, with traces of former elegance, but very old and very poor. Healers' paraphernalia and drying herbs were everywhere, though ranged in some order. Near the fine stone fireplace, where a tiny wisp of sweet herbs burned, was a bedstead. The woman in it was so wasted that in the dim light she seemed nothing but bone and shadow. As Tern came close she tried to sit up and to speak. Her daughter raised her head on the pillow, and when Tern was very near he could hear her: "Wizard," she said. "Not by chance."

A woman of power, she knew what he was. Had she called him there?

"I'm a finder," he said. "And a seeker."

"Can you teach her?"

"I can take her to those who can."

"Do it."

"I will."

She laid her head back and closed her eyes.

Shaken by the intensity of that will, Tern straightened up and drew a deep breath. He looked round at the girl, Dory. She did not return his gaze, watching her mother with stolid, sullen grief. Only after the woman sank into sleep did Dory move, going to help Rush, who as a friend and neighbor had made herself useful and was gathering up blood-soaked cloths scattered by the bed.

"She bled again just now, and I couldn't stop it," Dory said. Tears ran out of her eyes and down her cheeks. Her face hardly changed.

"Oh child, oh lamb," said Rush, taking her into her embrace; but though she hugged Rush, Dory did not bend.

"She's going there, to the wall, and I can't go with her," she said. "She's going alone and I can't go with her—Can't you go there?" She broke away from Rush, looking again at Tern. "You can go there!"

"No," he said. "I don't know the way."

Yet as Dory spoke he saw what the girl saw: a long hill going down into darkness, and across it, on the edge of twilight, a low wall of stones. And as he looked he thought he saw a woman walking along beside the wall, very thin, insubstantial, bone, shadow. But she was not the dying woman in the bed. She was Anieb.

Then that was gone and he stood facing the witch-girl. Her look of accusation slowly changed. She put her face in her hands.

"We have to let them go," he said.

She said, "I know."

Rush glanced from one to the other with her keen, bright eyes. "Not only a handy man," she said, "but a crafty man. Well, you're not the first."

He looked his question.

"This is called Ath's House," she said.

"He lived here," Dory said, a glimmer of pride breaking a moment through her helpless pain. "The Mage Ath. Long ago. Before he went into the west. All my foremothers were wise women. He stayed here. With them."

"Give me a basin," Rush said. "I'll get water to soak these."

"I'll get the water," Tern said. He took the basin and went out to the courtyard, to the well. Just as before, Crow was sitting on the coping, bored and restless.

"Why are we wasting time here?" he demanded, as Tern let the bucket down into the well. "Are you fetching and carrying for witches now?"

"Yes," Tern said, "and I will till she dies. And then I'll take her daughter to Roke. And if you want to read the Book of Names, you can come with us."

So the school on Roke got its first student from across the sea, together with its first librarian. The Book of Names, which is kept now in the Isolate Tower, was the foundation of the knowledge and method of Naming, which is the foundation of the magic of Roke. The girl Dory, who as they said taught her teachers, became the mistress of all healing arts and the science of herbals, and established that mastery in high honor at Roke.

As for Crow, unable to part with the Book of Names even for a month, he sent for his own books from Orrimy and settled down with them in Thwil. He allowed people of the school to study them, so long as they showed them, and him, due respect.

So the pattern of the years was set for Tern. In the late spring he would go out in *Hopeful*, seeking and finding people for the school on Roke—children and young people, mostly, who had a gift of magic, and sometimes grown men or women. Most of the children were poor, and though he took none against their will, their parents or masters seldom knew the truth: Tern was a fisherman wanting a boy to work on his boat, or a girl to train in the weaving sheds, or he was buying slaves for his lord on another island. If they sent a child with him to give it

opportunity, or sold a child out of poverty to work for him, he paid
them in true ivory; if they sold a child to him as a slave, he paid them
in gold, and was gone by the next day, when the gold turned back into
cow dung.

He traveled far in the Archipelago, even out into the East Reach. He
never went to the same town or island twice without years between, letting his trail grow cold. Even so he began to be spoken of. The Child
Taker, they called him, a dreaded sorcerer who carried children to his
island in the icy north and there sucked their blood. In villages on Way
and Felkway they still tell children about the Child Taker, as an encouragement to distrust strangers.

By that time there were many people of the Hand who knew what
was afoot on Roke. Young people came there sent by them. Men and
women came to be taught and to teach. Many of these had a hard time
getting there, for the spells that hid the island were stronger than ever,
making it seem only a cloud, or a reef among the breakers; and the
Roke wind blew, which kept any ship from Thwil Bay unless there was
a sorcerer aboard who knew how to turn that wind. Still they came, and
as the years went on a larger house was needed for the school than any
in Thwil Town.

In the Archipelago, men built ships and women built houses, that
was the custom; but in building a great structure women let men work
with them, not having the miners' superstitions that kept men out of the
mines, or the shipwrights' that forbade women to watch a keel laid. So
both men and women of great power raised the Great House on Roke.
Its cornerstone was set on a hilltop above Thwil Town, near the Grove
and looking to the Knoll. Its walls were built not only of stone and
wood, but founded deep on magic and made strong with spells.

Standing on that hill, Medra had said, "There is a vein of water, just
under where I stand, that will not go dry." They dug down carefully
and came to the water; they let it leap up into the sunlight; and the first

part of the Great House they made was its inmost heart, the courtyard of the fountain.

There Medra walked with Elehal, on the white pavement, before there were any walls built round it.

She had planted a young rowan from the Grove beside the fountain. They came to be sure it was thriving. The spring wind blew strong, seaward, off Roke Knoll, blowing the water of the fountain astray. Up on the slope of the Knoll they could see a little group of people: a circle of young students learning how to do tricks of illusion from the sorcerer Hega of O; Master Hand, they called him. The sparkweed, past flowering, cast its ashes on the wind. There were streaks of grey in Ember's hair.

"Off you go, then," she said, "and leave us to settle this matter of the Rule." Her frown was as fierce as ever, but her voice was seldom as harsh as this when she spoke to him.

"I'll stay if you want, Elehal."

"I do want you to stay. But don't stay! You're a finder, you have to go find. It's only that agreeing on the Way—or the Rule, Waris wants us to call it—is twice the work of building the House. And causes ten times the quarrels. I wish I could get away from it! I wish I could just walk with you, like this . . . And I wish you wouldn't go north."

"Why do we quarrel?" he said rather despondently.

"Because there are more of us! Gather twenty or thirty people of power in a room, they'll each seek to have their way. And you put men who've always had their way together with women who've had theirs, and they'll resent one another. And then, too, there are some true and real divisions among us, Medra. They must be settled, and they can't be settled easily. Though a little goodwill would go a long way."

"Is it Waris?"

"Waris and several other men. And they *are* men, and they make that important beyond anything else. To them, the Old Powers are abominable. And women's powers are suspect, because they suppose them all connected with the Old Powers. As if those Powers were to be controlled or used by any mortal soul! But they put men where we put the world. And so they hold that a true wizard must be a man. And celibate."

"Ah, that," Medra said, rueful.

"That indeed. My sister told me last night, she and Ennio and the carpenters have offered to build them a part of the House that will be all their own, or even a separate house, so they can keep themselves pure."

"Pure?"

"It's not my word, it's Waris's. But they've refused. They want the Rule of Roke to separate men from women, and they want men to make the decisions for all. Now what compromise can we make with them? Why did they come here, if they won't work with us?"

"We should send away the men who won't."

"Away? In anger? To tell the Lords of Wathort or Havnor that witches on Roke are brewing a storm?"

"I forget—I always forget," he said, downcast again. "I forget the walls of the prison. I'm not such a fool when I'm outside them . . . When I'm here I can't believe it is a prison. But outside, without you, I remember . . . I don't want to go, but I have to go. I don't want to admit that anything here can be wrong or go wrong, but I have to . . . I'll go this time, and I will go north, Elehal. But when I come back I'll stay. What I need to find I'll find here. Haven't I found it already?"

"No," she said, "only me . . . But there's a great deal of seeking and finding to be done in the Grove. Enough to keep even you from being restless. Why north?"

"To reach out the Hand to Enlad and Éa. I've never gone there. We know nothing about their wizardries. *Enlad of the Kings, and bright Éa, eldest of isles!* Surely we'll find allies there."

"But Havnor lies between us," she said.

"I won't sail my boat across Havnor, dear love. I plan to go around it. By water." He could always make her laugh; he was the only one who could. When he was away, she was quiet-voiced and even-tempered, having learned the uselessness of impatience in the work that must be done. Sometimes she still scowled, sometimes she smiled, but she did not laugh. When she could, she went to the Grove alone, as she had always done. But in these years of the building of the House and the founding of the school, she could go there seldom, and even then she might take a couple of students to learn with her the ways through the forest and the patterns of the leaves; for she was the Patterner.

Tern left late that year on his journey. He had with him a boy of fifteen, Mote, a promising weatherworker who needed training at sea, and Sava, a woman of sixty who had come to Roke with him seven or eight years before. Sava had been one of the women of the Hand on the isle of Ark. Though she had no wizardly gifts at all, she knew so well how to get a group of people to trust one another and work together that she was honored as a wise woman on Ark, and now on Roke. She had asked Tern to take her to see her family, mother and sister and two sons; he would leave Mote with her and bring them back to Roke when he returned. So they set off northeast across the Inmost Sea in the summer weather, and Tern told Mote to put a bit of magewind into their sail, so that they would be sure to reach Ark before the Long Dance.

As they coasted that island, he himself put an illusion about *Hopeful*, so that she would seem not a boat but a drifting log; for pirates and Losen's slave takers were thick in these waters.

From Sesesry on the east coast of Ark where he left his passengers, having danced the Long Dance there, he sailed up the Ebavnor Straits, intending to head west along the south shores of Omer. He kept the illusion spell about his boat. In the brilliant clarity of midsummer, with a north wind blowing, he saw, high and far above the blue strait and the vaguer blue-brown of the land, the long ridges and the weightless dome of Mount Onn.

Look, Medra. Look!

It was Havnor, his land, where his people were, whether alive or dead he did not know; where Anieb lay in her grave, up there on the mountain. He had never been back, never come this close. It had been how long? Sixteen years, seventeen years. Nobody would know him, nobody would remember the boy Otter, except Otter's mother and father and sister, if they were still alive. And surely there were people of the Hand in the Great Port. Though he had not known of them as a boy, he should know them now.

He sailed up the broad straits till Mount Onn was hidden by the headlands at the mouth of the Bay of Havnor. He would not see it again unless he went through that narrow passage. Then he would see the mountain, all the sweep and cresting of it, over the calm waters where he used to try to raise up the magewind when he was twelve; and sailing on he would see the towers rise up from the water, dim at first, mere dots and lines, then lifting up their bright banners, the white city at the center of the world.

It was mere cowardice to keep from Havnor, now—fear for his skin, fear lest he find his people had died, fear lest he recall Anieb too vividly.

For there had been times when he felt that, as he had summoned her living, so dead she might summon him. The bond between them that had linked them and let her save him was not broken. Many times she had come into his dreams, standing silent as she stood when he first saw her in the reeking tower at Samory. And he had seen her, years ago, in the vision of the dying healer in Telio, in the twilight, beside the wall of stones.

He knew now, from Elehal and others on Roke, what that wall was. It lay between the living and the dead. And in that vision, Anieb had walked on this side of it, not on the side that went down into the dark.

Did he fear her, who had freed him?

He tacked across the strong wind, swung round South Point, and sailed into the Great Bay of Havnor.

BANNERS STILL FLEW FROM THE TOWERS OF THE CITY OF Havnor, and a king still ruled there; the banners were those of captured towns and isles, and the king was the warlord Losen. Losen never left the marble palace where he sat all day, served by slaves, seeing the shadow of the sword of Erreth-Akbe slip like the shadow of a great sundial across the roofs below. He gave orders, and the slaves said, "It is done, your majesty." He held audiences, and old men came and said, "We obey, your majesty." He summoned his wizards, and the mage Early came, bowing low. "Make me walk!" Losen shouted, beating his paralysed legs with his weak hands.

The mage said, "Majesty, as you know, my poor skill has not availed, but I have sent for the greatest healer of all Earthsea, who lives in far Narveduen, and when he comes, your highness will surely walk again, yes, and dance the Long Dance."

Then Losen cursed and cried, and his slaves brought him wine, and the mage went out, bowing, and checking as he went to be sure that the spell of paralysis was holding.

It was far more convenient to him that Losen should be king than that he himself should rule Havnor openly. Men of arms didn't trust men of craft and didn't like to serve them. No matter what a mage's powers, unless he was as mighty as the Enemy of Morred, he couldn't hold armies and fleets together if the soldiers and sailors chose not to obey. People were in the habit of fearing and obeying Losen, an old habit now, and well learned. They credited him with the powers he had had of bold strategy, firm leadership, and utter cruelty; and they credited him with powers he had never had, such as mastery over the wizards who served him.

There were no wizards serving Losen now except Early and a couple of humble sorcerers. Early had driven off or killed, one after another, his rivals for Losen's favor, and had enjoyed sole rule over all Havnor now for years.

When he was Gelluk's prentice and assistant, he had encouraged his master in the study of the lore of Way, finding himself free while Gelluk was off doting on his quicksilver. But Gelluk's abrupt fate had shaken him. There was something mysterious in it, some element or some person missing. Summoning the useful Hound to help him, Early had made a very thorough inquiry into what happened. Where Gelluk was, of course, was no mystery. Hound had tracked him straight to a scar in a hillside, and said he was buried deep under there. Early had no wish to exhume him. But the boy who had been with him, Hound could not track: could not say whether he was under that hill with Gelluk, or had got clean away. He had left no spell traces as the mage did, said Hound, and it had rained very hard all the night after, and when Hound thought he had found the boy's tracks, they were a woman's; and she was dead.

Early did not punish Hound for his failure, but he remembered it. He was not used to failures and did not like them. He did not like what Hound told him about this boy, Otter, and he remembered it.

The desire for power feeds off itself, growing as it devours. Early suffered from hunger. He starved. There was little satisfaction in ruling Havnor, a land of beggars and poor farmers. What was the good of possessing the Throne of Maharion if nobody sat in it but a drunken cripple? What glory was there in the palaces of the city when nobody lived in them but crawling slaves? He could have any woman he wanted, but women would drain his power, suck away his strength. He wanted no woman near him. He craved an enemy: an opponent worth destroying.

His spies had been coming to him for a year or more muttering about a secret insurgency all across his realm, rebellious groups of sorcerers

that called themselves the Hand. Eager to find his enemy, he had one
such group investigated. They turned out to be a lot of old women,
midwives, carpenters, a ditchdigger, a tinsmith's prentice, a couple of
little boys. Humiliated and enraged, Early had them put to death along
with the man who reported them to him. It was a public execution, in
Losen's name, for the crime of conspiracy against the King. There had
perhaps not been enough of that kind of intimidation lately. But it went
against his grain. He didn't like to make a public spectacle of fools who
had tricked him into fearing them. He would rather have dealt with
them in his own way, in his own time. To be nourishing, fear must
be immediate; he needed to see people afraid of him, hear their terror,
smell it, taste it. But since he ruled in Losen's name, it was Losen who
must be feared by the armies and the peoples, and he himself must keep
in the background, making do with slaves and prentices.

Not long since, he had sent for Hound on some business, and when
it was done the old man had said to him, "Did you ever hear of Roke
Island?"

"South and west of Kamery. The Lord of Wathort's owned it for forty
or fifty years."

Though he seldom left the city, Early prided himself on his knowledge of all the Archipelago, gleaned from his sailors' reports and the
marvelous ancient charts kept in the palace. He studied them nights,
brooding on where and how he might extend his empire.

Hound nodded, as if its location was all that had interested him in
Roke.

"Well?"

"One of the old women you had tortured before they burned the lot,
you know? Well, the fellow who did it told me. She talked about her son
on Roke. Calling out to him to come, you know. But like as if he had
the power to."

"Well?"

"Seemed odd. Old woman from a village inland, never seen the sea, calling the name of an island away off like that."

"The son was a fisherman who talked about his travels."

Early waved his hand. Hound sniffed, nodded, and left.

Early never disregarded any triviality Hound mentioned, because so many of them had proved not to be trivial. He disliked the old man for that, and because he was unshakable. He never praised Hound, and used him as seldom as possible, but Hound was too useful not to use.

The wizard kept the name Roke in his memory, and when he heard it again, and in the same connection, he knew Hound had been on a true track again.

Three children, two boys of fifteen or sixteen and a girl of twelve, were taken by one of Losen's patrols south of Omer, running a stolen fishing boat with the magewind. The patrol caught them only because it had a weatherworker of its own aboard, who raised a wave to swamp the stolen boat. Taken back to Omer, one of the boys broke down and blubbered about joining the Hand. Hearing that word, the men told them they would be tortured and burned, at which the boy cried that if they spared him he would tell them all about the Hand, and Roke, and the great mages of Roke.

"Bring them here," Early said to the messenger.

"The girl flew away, lord," the man said unwillingly.

"Flew away?"

"She took bird form. Osprey, they said. Didn't expect that from a girl so young. Gone before they knew it."

"Bring the boys, then," Early said with deadly patience.

They brought him one boy. The other had jumped from the ship, crossing Havnor Bay, and been killed by a crossbow quarrel. The boy they brought was in such a paroxysm of terror that even Early was disgusted by him. How could he frighten a creature already blind and beshatten with fear? He set a binding spell on the boy that held him upright and immobile as a stone statue, and left him so for a night and a day. Now and then he talked to the statue, telling it that it was a clever lad and might make a good prentice, here in the palace. Maybe he could go to Roke after all, for Early was thinking of going to Roke, to meet with the mages there.

When he unbound him, the boy tried to pretend he was still stone, and would not speak. Early had to go into his mind, in the way he had learned from Gelluk long ago, when Gelluk was a true master of his art. He found out what he could. Then the boy was no good for anything and had to be disposed of. It was humiliating, again, to be outwitted by the very stupidity of these people; and all he had learned about Roke was that the Hand was there, and a school where they taught wizardry. And he had learned a man's name.

The idea of a school for wizards made him laugh. A school for wild boars, he thought, a college for dragons! But that there was some kind of scheming and gathering together of men of power on Roke seemed probable, and the idea of any league or alliance of wizards appalled him more the more he thought of it. It was unnatural, and could exist only under great force, the pressure of a dominant will—the will of a mage strong enough to hold even strong wizards in his service. There was the enemy he wanted!

Hound was down at the door, they said. Early sent for him to come up. "Who's Tern?" he asked as soon as he saw the old man.

With age Hound had come to look his name, wrinkled, with a long nose and sad eyes. He sniffed and seemed about to say he did not know, but he knew better than to try to lie to Early. He sighed. "Otter," he said. "Him that killed old Whiteface."

"Where's he hiding?"

"Not hiding at all. Went about the city, talking to people. Went to see his mother in Endlane, round the mountain. He's there now."

"You should have told me at once," Early said.

"Didn't know you were after him. I've been after him a long time. He fooled me." Hound spoke without rancor.

"He tricked and killed a great mage, my master. He's dangerous. I want vengeance. Who did he talk to here? I want them. Then I'll see to him."

"Some old women down by the docks. An old sorcerer. His sister."

"Get them here. Take my men."

Hound sniffed, sighed, nodded.

There was not much to be got from the people his men brought to him. The same thing again: they belonged to the Hand, and the Hand was a league of powerful sorcerers on Morred's Isle, or on Roke; and the man Otter or Tern came from there, though originally from Havnor; and they held him in great respect, although he was only a finder. The sister had vanished, perhaps gone with Otter to Endlane, where the mother lived. Early rummaged in their cloudy, witless minds, had the youngest of them tortured, and then burned them where Losen could sit at his window and watch. The King needed some diversions.

All this took only two days, and all the time Early was looking and probing toward Endlane village, sending Hound there before him, sending his own presentment there to watch. When he knew where the man was he betook himself there very quickly, on eagle's wings; for Early was a great shape-changer, so fearless that he would take even dragon form.

He knew it was well to use caution with this man. Otter had defeated Tinaral, and there was this matter of Roke. There was some strength in him or with him. Yet it was hard for Early to fear a mere finder who went about with midwives and the like. He could not bring himself to sneak and skulk. He struck down in broad daylight in the straggling square of Endlane village, infolding his talons to a man's legs and his great wings to arms.

A child ran bawling to its mammy. No one else was about. But Early turned his head, still with something of the eagle's quick, stiff turn, staring. Wizard knows wizard, and he knew which house his prey was in. He walked to it and flung the door open.

A slight, brown man sitting at the table looked up at him.

Early raised his hand to lay the binding spell on him. His hand was stayed, held immobile half lifted at his side.

This was a contest, then, a foe worth fighting! Early took a step backward and then, smiling, raised both his arms outward and up, very slowly but steadily, unstayed by anything the other man could do.

The house vanished. No walls, no roof, nobody. Early stood on the dust of the village square in the sunshine of morning with his arms in the air.

It was only illusion, of course, but it checked him a moment in his spell, and then he had to undo the illusion, bringing back the door frame around him, the walls and roof beams, the gleam of light on crockery, the hearth stones, the table. But nobody sat at the table. His enemy was gone.

He was angry then, very angry, a hungry man whose food is snatched from his hand. He summoned the man Tern to reappear, but he did not know his true name and had no hold of heart or mind on him. The summons went unanswered.

He strode from the house, turned, and set a fire spell on it so that it burst into flames, thatch and walls and every window spouting fire. Women ran out of it screaming. They had been hiding no doubt in the back room; he paid them no attention. "Hound," he thought. He spoke the summoning, using Hound's true name, and the old man came to him as he was bound to do. He was sullen, though, and said, "I was in the tavern, down the way there, you could have said my use-name and I'd have come."

Early looked at him once. Hound's mouth snapped shut and stayed shut.

"Speak when I let you," the wizard said. "Where is the man?"

Hound nodded northeastwards.

"What's there?"

Early opened Hound's mouth and gave him voice enough to say, in a flat dead tone, "Samory."

"What form is he in?"

"Otter," said the flat voice.

Early laughed. "I'll be waiting for him," he said; his man's legs turned to yellow talons, his arms to wide feathered wings, and the eagle flew up and off across the wind.

Hound sniffed, sighed, and followed, trudging along unwillingly, while behind him in the village the flames died down, and children cried, and women shouted curses after the eagle.

THE DANGER IN TRYING TO DO GOOD IS THAT THE MIND COMES to confuse the intent of goodness with the act of doing things well.

That is not what the otter was thinking as it swam fast down the Yennava. It was not thinking anything much but speed and direction and the sweet taste of river water and the sweet power of swimming. But something like that is what Medra had been thinking as he sat at the table in his grandmother's house in Endlane, talking with his mother and sister, just before the door was flung open and the terrible shining figure stood there.

Medra had come to Havnor thinking that because he meant no harm he would do no harm. He had done irreparable harm. Men and women and children had died because he was there. They had died in torment, burned alive. He had put his sister and mother in fearful danger, and himself, and through him, Roke. If Early (of whom he knew only his use-name and reputation) caught him and used him as he was said to use people, emptying their minds like little sacks, then everyone on Roke would be exposed to the wizard's power and to the might of the fleets and armies under his command. Medra would have betrayed

Roke to Havnor, as the wizard they never named had betrayed it to Wathort. Maybe that man, too, had thought he could do no harm.

Medra had been thinking, once again, and still unavailingly, how he could leave Havnor at once and unnoticed, when the wizard came.

Now, as otter, he was thinking only that he would like to stay otter, be otter, in the sweet brown water, the living river, forever. There is no death for an otter, only life to the end. But in the sleek creature was the mortal mind; and where the stream passes the hill west of Samory, the otter came up on the muddy bank, and then the man crouched there, shivering.

Where to now? Why had he come here?

He had not thought. He had taken the shape that came soonest to him, run to the river as an otter would, swum as the otter would swim. But only in his own form could he think as a man, hide, decide, act as a man or as a wizard against the wizard who hunted him.

He knew he was no match for Early. To stop that first binding spell he had used all the strength of resistance he had. The illusion and the shape-change were all the tricks he had to play. If he faced the wizard again he would be destroyed. And Roke with him. Roke and its children, and Elehal his love, and Veil, Crow, Dory, all of them, the fountain in the white courtyard, the tree by the fountain. Only the Grove would stand. Only the green hill, silent, immovable. He heard Elehal say to him, *Havnor lies between us.* He heard her say, *All the true powers, all the old powers, at root are one.*

He looked up. The hillside above the stream was that same hill where he had come that day with Tinaral, Anieb's presence within him. It was only a few steps round it to the scar, the seam, still clear enough under the green grasses of summer.

"Mother," he said, on his knees there, "Mother, open to me."

He laid his hands on the seam of earth, but there was no power in them.

"Let me in, Mother," he whispered in the tongue that was as old as the hill. The ground shivered a little and opened.

He heard an eagle scream. He got to his feet. He leapt into the dark.

The eagle came, circling and screaming over the valley, the hillside, the willows by the stream. It circled, searching and searching, and flew back as it had come.

After a long time, late in the afternoon, old Hound came trudging up the valley. He stopped now and then and sniffed. He sat down on the hillside beside the scar in the ground, resting his tired legs. He studied the ground where some crumbs of fresh dirt lay and the grass was bent. He stroked the bent grass to straighten it. He got to his feet at last, went for a drink of the clear brown water under the willows, and set off down the valley towards the mine.

MEDRA WOKE IN PAIN, IN DARKNESS. FOR A LONG TIME THAT was all there was. The pain came and went, the darkness remained. Once it lightened a little into a twilight in which he could dimly see. He saw a slope running down from where he lay towards a wall of stones, across which was darkness again. But he could not get up to walk to the wall, and presently the pain came back very sharp in his arm and hip and head. Then the darkness came around him, and then nothing.

Thirst: and with it pain. Thirst, and the sound of water running.

He tried to remember how to make light. Anieb said to him, plaintively, "Can't you make the light?" But he could not. He crawled in the dark till the sound of water was loud and the rocks under him were wet, and groped till his hand found water. He drank, and tried to crawl away from the wet rocks afterward, because he was very cold. One arm hurt and had no strength in it. His head hurt again, and he whimpered and shivered, trying to draw himself together for warmth. There was no warmth and no light.

He was sitting a little way from where he lay, looking at himself,

although it was still utterly dark. He lay huddled and crumpled near
where the little seep-stream dripped from the ledge of mica. Not far
away lay another huddled heap, rotted red silk, long hair, bones. Beyond
it the cavern stretched away. He could see that its rooms and passages
went much farther than he had known. He saw it with the same uncaring interest with which he saw Tinaral's body and his own body. He
felt a mild regret. It was only fair that he should die here with the man
he had killed. It was right. Nothing was wrong. But something in him
ached, not the sharp body pain, a long ache, lifelong.

"Anieb," he said.

Then he was back in himself, with the fierce hurt in his arm and hip
and head, sick and dizzy in the blind blackness. When he moved, he
whimpered; but he sat up. I have to live, he thought. I have to remember
how to live. How to make light. I have to remember. I have to remember
the shadows of the leaves.

How far does the forest go?

As far as the mind goes.

He looked up into the darkness. After a while he moved his good
hand a little, and the faint light flowed out of it.

The roof of the cavern was far above him. The trickle of water dripping from the mica ledge glittered in short dashes in the werelight.

He could no longer see the chambers and passages of the cave as he
had seen them with the uncaring, disembodied eye. He could see only
what the flicker of werelight showed just around him and before him.
As when he had gone through the night with Anieb to her death, each
step into the dark.

He got to his knees, and thought then to whisper, "Thank you,
Mother." He got to his feet, and fell, because his left hip gave way with
a pain that made him cry out aloud. After a while he tried again, and
stood up. Then he started forward.

It took him a long time to cross the cavern. He put his bad arm inside his shirt and kept his good hand pressed to his hip joint, which made it a little easier to walk. The walls narrowed gradually to a passage. Here the roof was much lower, just above his head. Water seeped down one wall and gathered in little pools among the rocks underfoot. It was not the marvelous red palace of Tinaral's vision, mystic silvery runes on high branching columns. It was only the earth, only dirt, rock, water. The air was cool and still. Away from the dripping of the stream it was silent. Outside the gleam of werelight it was dark.

Medra bowed his head, standing there. "Anieb," he said, "can you come back this far? I don't know the way." He waited a while.

He saw darkness, heard silence. Slow and halting, he entered the passage.

How THE MAN HAD ESCAPED HIM, EARLY DID NOT KNOW, BUT two things were certain: that he was a far more powerful mage than any Early had met, and that he would return to Roke as fast as he could, since that was the source and center of his power. There was no use trying to get there before him; he had the lead. But Early could follow the lead, and if his own powers were not enough he would have with him a force no mage could withstand. Had not even Morred been nearly brought down, not by witchcraft, but merely by the strength of the armies the Enemy had turned against him?

"Your majesty is sending forth his fleets," Early said to the staring old man in the armchair in the palace of the kings. "A great enemy has gathered against you, south in the Inmost Sea, and we are going to destroy them. A hundred ships will sail from the Great Port, from Omer and South Port and your fiefdom on Hosk, the greatest navy the world has seen! I shall lead them. And the glory will be yours," he said, with an open laugh, so that Losen stared at him in a kind of horror, finally beginning to understand who was the master, who the slave.

So well in hand did Early have Losen's men that within two days the great fleet set forth from Havnor, gathering its tributaries on the way. Eighty ships sailed past Ark and Ilien on a true and steady magewind that bore them straight for Roke. Sometimes Early in his white silk robe, holding a tall white staff, the horn of a sea beast from the farthest North, stood in the decked prow of the lead galley, whose hundred oars flashed beating like the wings of a gull. Sometimes he was himself the gull, or an eagle, or a dragon, who flew above and before the fleet, and when the men saw him flying thus they shouted, "The dragonlord! the dragonlord!"

They came ashore in Ilien for water and food. Setting a host of many hundreds of men on its way so quickly had left little time for provisioning the ships. They overran the towns along the west shore of Ilien, taking what they wanted, and did the same on Vissti and Kamery, looting what they could and burning what they left. Then the great fleet turned west, heading for the one harbor of Roke Island, the Bay of Thwil. Early knew of the harbor from the maps in Havnor, and knew there was a high hill above it. As they came nearer, he took dragon form and soared up high above his ships, leading them, gazing into the west for the sight of that hill.

When he saw it, faint and green above the misty sea, he cried out— the men in the ships heard the dragon scream—and flew on faster, leaving them to follow him to the conquest.

All the rumors of Roke had said that it was spell-defended and charm-hidden, invisible to ordinary eyes. If there were any spells woven about that hill or the bay he now saw opening before it, they were gossamer to him, transparent. Nothing blurred his eyes or challenged his will as he flew over the bay, over the little town and a half-finished building on the slope above it, to the top of the high green hill. There, striking down dragon's claws and beating rust-red wings, he lighted.

He stood in his own form. He had not made the change himself. He stood alert, uncertain.

The wind blew, the long grass nodded in the wind. Summer was getting on and the grass was dry now, yellowing, no flowers in it but the little white heads of the lacefoam. A woman came walking up the hill towards him through the long grass. She followed no path, and walked easily, without haste.

He thought he had raised his hand in a spell to stop her, but he had not raised his hand, and she came on. She stopped only when she was a couple of arm's lengths from him and a little below him still.

"Tell me your name," she said, and he said, "Teriel."

"Why did you come here, Teriel?"

"To destroy you."

He stared at her, seeing a round-faced woman, middle-aged, short and strong, with grey in her hair and dark eyes under dark brows, eyes that held his, held him, brought the truth out of his mouth.

"Destroy us? Destroy this hill? The trees there?" She looked down to a grove of trees not far from the hill. "Maybe Segoy who made them could unmake them. Maybe the earth will destroy herself. Maybe she'll destroy herself through our hands, in the end. But not through yours. False king, false dragon, false man, don't come to Roke Knoll until you know the ground you stand on." She made one gesture of her hand, downward to the earth. Then she turned and went down the hill through the long grass, the way she had come.

There were other people on the hill, he saw now, many others, men and women, children, living and spirits of the dead; many, many of them. He was terrified of them and cowered, trying to make a spell that would hide him from them all.

But he made no spell. He had no magic left in him. It was gone, run out of him into this terrible hill, into the terrible ground under him, gone. He was no wizard, only a man like the others, powerless.

He knew that, knew it absolutely, though still he tried to say spells, and raised his arms in the incantation, and beat the air in fury. Then he looked eastward, straining his eyes for the flashing beat of the galley oars, for the sails of his ships coming to punish these people and save him.

All he saw was a mist on the water, all across the sea beyond the mouth of the bay. As he watched it thickened and darkened, creeping out over the slow waves.

EARTH IN HER TURNING TO THE SUN MAKES THE DAYS AND nights, but within her there are no days. Medra walked through the night. He was very lame, and could not always keep up the werelight. When it failed he had to stop and sit down and sleep. The sleep was never death, as he thought it was. He woke, always cold, always in pain, always thirsty, and when he could make a glimmer of the light he got to his feet and went on. He never saw Anieb but he knew she was there. He followed her. Sometimes there were great rooms. Sometimes there were pools of motionless water. It was hard to break the stillness of their surface, but he drank from them. He thought he had gone down deeper and deeper for a long time, till he reached the longest of those pools, and after that the way went up again. Sometimes now Anieb followed him. He could say her name, though she did not answer. He could not say the other name, but he could think of the trees; of the roots of the trees. This was the kingdom of the roots of the trees. How far does the forest go? As far as forests go. As long as the lives, as deep as the roots of the trees. As long as leaves cast shadows. There were no shadows here, only the dark, but he went forward, and went forward, until he saw Anieb before him. He saw the flash of her eyes, the cloud of her curling hair. She looked back at him for a moment, and then turned aside and ran lightly down a long, steep slope into darkness.

Where he stood it was not wholly dark. The air moved against his face. Far ahead, dim, small, there was a light that was not werelight. He went forward. He had been crawling for a long time now, dragging the right leg, which would not bear his weight. He went forward. He smelled the wind of evening and saw the sky of evening through the branches and leaves of trees. An arched oak root formed the mouth of the cave, no bigger than a man or a badger needed to crawl through. He crawled through. He lay there under the root of the tree, seeing the light fade and a star or two come out among the leaves.

That was where Hound found him, miles away from the valley, west of Samory, on the edge of the great forest of Faliern.

"Got you," the old man said, looking down at the muddy, lax body. He added, "Too late," regretfully. He stooped to see if he could pick him up or drag him, and felt the faint warmth of life. "You're tough," he said. "Here, wake up. Come on. Otter, wake up."

He recognised Hound, though he could not sit up and could barely speak. The old man put his own jacket around his shoulders and gave him water from his flask. Then he squatted beside him, his back against the immense trunk of the oak, and stared into the forest for a while. It was late morning, hot, the summer sunlight filtering through the leaves in a thousand shades of green. A squirrel scolded, far up in the oak, and a jay replied. Hound scratched his neck and sighed.

"The wizard's off on the wrong track, as usual," he said at last. "Said you'd gone to Roke Island and he'd catch you there. I said nothing."

He looked at the man he knew only as Otter.

"You went in there, that hole, with the old wizard, didn't you? Did you find him?"

Medra nodded.

"Hmn," Hound went, a short, grunting laugh. "You find what you look for, don't you? Like me." He saw that his companion was in distress, and said, "I'll get you out of here. Fetch a carter from the village down there, when I've got my breath. Listen. Don't fret. I haven't hunted you all these years to give you to Early. The way I gave you to Gelluk. I was sorry for that. I thought about it. What I said to you about men of a craft sticking together. And who we work for. Couldn't see that I had much choice about that. But having done you a disfavor, I thought if I came across you again I'd do you a favor, if I could. As one finder to the other, see?"

Otter's breath was coming hard. Hound put his hand on Otter's hand for a moment, said, "Don't worry," and got to his feet. "Rest easy," he said.

He found a carter who would carry them down to Endlane. Otter's mother and sister were living with cousins while they rebuilt their burned house as best they could. They welcomed him with disbelieving joy. Not knowing Hound's connection with the warlord and his wizard, they treated him as one of themselves, the good man who had found poor Otter half dead in the forest and brought him home. A wise man, said Otter's mother Rose, surely a wise man. Nothing was too good for such a man.

Otter was slow to recover, to heal. The bonesetter did what he could about his broken arm and his damaged hip, the wise woman salved the cuts from the rocks on his hands and head and knees, his mother brought him all the delicacies she could find in the gardens and berry thickets; but he lay as weak and wasted as when Hound first brought him. There was no heart in him, the wise woman of Endlane said. It was somewhere else, being eaten up with worry or fear or shame.

"So where is it?" Hound said.

Otter, after a long silence, said, "Roke Island."

"Where old Early went with the great fleet. I see. Friends there. Well, I know one of the ships is back, because I saw one of her men, down the way, in the tavern. I'll go ask about. Find out if they got to Roke and what happened there. What I can tell you is that it seems old Early is late coming home. Hmn, hmn," he went, pleased with his joke. "Late coming home," he repeated, and got up. He looked at Otter, who was not much to look at. "Rest easy," he said, and went off.

He was gone several days. When he returned, riding in a horse-drawn cart, he had such a look about him that Otter's sister hurried in to tell him, "Hound's won a battle or a fortune! He's riding behind a city horse, in a city cart, like a prince!"

Hound came in on her heels. "Well," he said, "in the first place, when I got to the city, I go up to the palace, just to hear the news, and what do I see? I see old King Pirate standing on his legs, shouting out orders like he used to do. Standing up! Hasn't stood for years. Shouting orders! And some of 'em did what he said, and some of 'em didn't. So I got on out of there, that kind of a situation being dangerous, in a palace. Then I went about to friends of mine and asked where was old Early and had the fleet been to Roke and come back and all. Early, they said, nobody knew about Early. Not a sign of him nor from him. Maybe I could find him, they said, joking me, hmn. They know I love him. As for the ships, some had come back, with the men aboard saying they never came to Roke Island, never saw it, sailed right through where the sea charts said was an island, and there was no island. Then there were some men from one of the great galleys. They said when they got close to where the island should be, they came into a fog as thick as wet cloth, and the sea turned thick too, so that the oarsmen could barely push the oars through it, and they were caught in that for a day and a night. When they got out, there wasn't another ship of all the fleet on the sea, and the slaves were near rebelling, so the master brought her home as quick as he could. Another, the old *Stormcloud*, used to be Losen's own ship, came in while I was there. I talked to some men off her. They said there was nothing but fog and reefs all round where Roke was supposed to be, so they sailed on with seven other ships, south a ways, and met up with a fleet sailing up from Wathort. Maybe the lords there had heard there was a great fleet coming raiding, because they didn't stop to ask questions, but sent wizard's fire at our ships, and came alongside to board them if they could, and the men I talked to said it was a hard fight just to get away from them, and not all did. All this time they had no word from Early, and no weather was worked for them unless they had a bagman of their own aboard. So they came back up the length of the Inmost Sea, said the man from *Stormcloud*, one straggling after the other like the dogs that lost the dogfight. Now, do you like the news I bring you?"

Otter had been struggling with tears; he hid his face. "Yes," he said, "thanks."

"Thought you might. As for King Losen," Hound said, "who knows." He sniffed and sighed. "If I was him I'd retire," he said. "I think I'll do that myself."

Otter had got control of his face and voice. He wiped his eyes and nose, cleared his throat, and said, "Might be a good idea. Come to Roke. Safer."

"Seems to be a hard place to find," Hound said.

"I can find it," said Otter.

IV. Medra

> There was an old man by our door
> Who opened it to rich or poor;
> Many came there both small and great,
> But few could pass through Medra's Gate.
>   So runs the water away, away,
>   So runs the water away.

HOUND STAYED IN ENDLANE. HE COULD MAKE A LIVING AS A finder there, and he liked the tavern, and Otter's mother's hospitality.

By the beginning of autumn, Losen was hanging by a rope round his feet from a window of the New Palace, rotting, while six warlords quarreled over his kingdom, and the ships of the great fleet chased and fought one another across the Straits and the wizard-troubled sea.

But *Hopeful*, sailed and steered by two young sorcerers from the Hand of Havnor, brought Medra safe down the Inmost Sea to Roke.

Ember was on the dock to meet him. Lame and very thin, he came to her and took her hands, but he could not lift his face to hers. He said, "I have too many deaths on my heart, Elehal."

"Come with me to the Grove," she said.

They went there together and stayed till the winter came. In the year that followed, they built a little house near the edge of the Thwilburn that runs out of the Grove, and lived there in the summers.

They worked and taught in the Great House. They saw it go up stone on stone, every stone steeped in spells of protection, endurance, peace. They saw the Rule of Roke established, though never so firmly as they might wish, and always against opposition; for mages came from other islands and rose up from among the students of the school, women and men of power, knowledge, and pride, sworn by the Rule to work together and for the good of all, but each seeing a different way to do it.

Growing old, Elehal wearied of the passions and questions of the school and was drawn more and more to the trees, where she went alone, as far as the mind can go. Medra walked there too, but not so far as she, for he was lame.

After she died, he lived a while alone in the small house near the Grove.

One day in autumn he came back to the school. He went in by the garden door, which gives on the path through the fields to Roke Knoll. It is a curious thing about the Great House of Roke, that it has no portal or grand entryway at all. You can enter by what they call the back door, which, though it is made of horn and framed in dragon's tooth and carved with the Thousand-Leaved Tree, looks like nothing at all from outside, as you come to it in a dingy street; or you can go in the garden door, plain oak with an iron bolt. But there is no front door.

He came through the halls and stone corridors to the inmost place, the marble-paved courtyard of the fountain, where the tree Elehal had planted now stood tall, its berries reddening.

Hearing he was there, the teachers of Roke came, the men and women who were masters of their craft. Medra had been the Master Finder, until he went to the Grove. A young woman now taught that art, as he had taught it to her.

"I've been thinking," he said. "There are eight of you. Nine's a better number. Count me as a master again, if you will."

"What will you do, Master Tern?" asked the Summoner, a grey-haired mage from Ilien.

"I'll keep the door," Medra said. "Being lame, I won't go far from it. Being old, I'll know what to say to those who come. Being a finder, I'll find out if they belong here."

"That would spare us much trouble and some danger," said the young Finder.

"How will you do it?" the Summoner asked.

"I'll ask them their name," Medra said. He smiled. "If they'll tell me, they can come in. And when they think they've learned everything, they can go out again. If they can tell me my name."

So it was. For the rest of his life, Medra kept the doors of the Great House on Roke. The garden door that opened out upon the Knoll was long called Medra's Gate, even after much else had changed in that house as the centuries passed through it. And still the ninth Master of Roke is the Doorkeeper.

In Endlane and the villages round the foot of Onn on Havnor, women spinning and weaving sing a riddle song of which the last line has to do, maybe, with the man who was Medra, and Otter, and Tern.

Three things were that will not be:
Soléa's bright isle above the wave,
A dragon swimming in the sea,
A seabird flying in the grave.

ON THE

HIGH MARSH

THE ISLAND OF SEMEL LIES NORTH AND WEST ACROSS THE
Pelnish Sea from Havnor, south and west of the Enlades. Though it is one
of the great isles of the Earthsea Archipelago, there aren't many stories
from Semel. Enlad has its glorious history, and Havnor its wealth, and
Pain its ill repute, but Semel has only cattle and sheep, forests and little
towns, and the great silent volcano called Andanden standing over all.

South of Andanden lies a land where the ashes fell a hundred feet
deep when last the volcano spoke. Rivers and streams cut their way
seaward through that high plain, winding and pooling, spreading and
wandering, making a marsh of it, a big, desolate, waterland with a far
horizon, few trees, not many people. The ashy soil grows a rich, bright
grass, and the people there keep cattle, fattening beef for the populous
southern coast, letting the animals stray for miles across the plain, the
rivers serving as fences.

As mountains will, Andanden makes the weather. It gathers clouds
around it. The summer is short, the winter long, out on the high marsh.

In the early darkness of a winter day, a traveler stood at the windswept crossing of two paths, neither very promising, mere cattle tracks
among the reeds, and looked for some sign of the way he should take.

As he came down the last slope of the mountain, he had seen houses here and there out in the marshlands, a village not far away. He had thought he was on the way to the village, but had taken a wrong turning somewhere. Tall reeds rose up close beside the paths, so that if a light shone anywhere he could not see it. Water chuckled softly somewhere near his feet. He had used up his shoes walking round Andanden on the cruel roads of black lava. The soles were worn right through, and his feet ached with the icy damp of the marsh paths.

It grew darker quickly. A haze was coming up from the south, blotting out the sky. Only above the huge, dim bulk of the mountain did stars burn clearly. Wind whistled in the reeds, soft, dismal.

The traveler stood at the crossway and whistled back at the reeds.

Something moved on one of the tracks, something big, dark, in the darkness.

"Are you there, my dear?" said the traveler. He spoke in the Old Speech, the Language of the Making. "Come along, then, Ulla," he said, and the heifer came a step or two towards him, towards her name, while he walked to meet her. He made out the big head more by touch than sight, stroking the silken dip between her eyes, scratching her forehead at the roots of the nubbin horns. "Beautiful, you are beautiful," he told her, breathing her grassy breath, leaning against her large warmth. "Will you lead me, dear Ulla? Will you lead me where I need to go?"

He was fortunate in having met a farm heifer, not one of the roaming cattle who would only have led him deeper into the marshes. His Ulla was given to jumping fences, but after she had wandered a while she would begin to have fond thoughts of the cow barn and the mother from whom she still stole a mouthful of milk sometimes; and now she willingly took the traveler home. She walked, slow but purposeful, down one of the tracks, and he went with her, a hand on her hip when the way was wide enough. When she waded a knee-deep stream, he held on to her tail. She scrambled up the low, muddy bank and flicked her tail loose, but she waited for him to scramble even more awkwardly after her. Then she plodded gently on. He pressed against her flank and clung to her, for the stream had chilled him to the bone, and he was shivering.

"Moo," said his guide, softly, and he saw the dim, small square of yellow light just a little to his left.

"Thank you," he said, opening the gate for the heifer, who went to greet her mother, while he stumbled across the dark houseyard to the door.

It would be Berry at the door, though why he knocked she didn't know. "Come in, you fool!" she said, and he knocked again, and she put down her mending and went to the door. "Can you be drunk already?" she said, and then saw him.

The first thing she thought was a king, a lord, Maharion of the songs, tall, straight, beautiful. The next thing she thought was a beggar, a lost man, in dirty clothes, hugging himself with shivering arms.

He said, "I lost my way. Have I come to the village?" His voice was hoarse and harsh, a beggar's voice, but not a beggar's accent.

"It's a half mile on," said Gift.

"Is there an inn?"

"Not till you'd come to Oraby, a ten-twelve miles on south." She considered only briefly. "If you need a room for the night, I have one. Or San might, if you're going to the village."

"I'll stay here if I may," he said in that princely way, with his teeth chattering, holding on to the doorjamb to keep on his feet.

"Take your shoes off," she said, "they're soaking. Come in then." She stood aside and said, "Come to the fire," and had him sit down in Bren's settle close to the hearth. "Stir the fire up a bit," she said. "Will you have a bit of soup? It's still hot."

"Thank you, mistress," he muttered, crouching at the fire. She brought him a bowl of broth. He drank from it eagerly yet warily, as if long unaccustomed to hot soup.

"You came over the mountain?"

He nodded.

"Whatever for?"

"To come here," he said. He was beginning to tremble less. His bare feet were a sad sight, bruised, swollen, sodden. She wanted to tell him to put them right to the fire's warmth, but didn't like to presume. Whatever he was, he wasn't a beggar by choice.

"Not many come here to the High Marsh," she said. "Peddlers and such. But not in winter."

He finished his soup, and she took the bowl. She sat down in her place, the stool by the oil lamp to the right of the hearth, and took up her mending. "Get warm through, and then I'll show you your bed," she said. "There's no fire in that room. Did you meet weather, up on the mountain? They say there's been snow."

"Some flurries," he said. She got a good look at him now in the light of lamp and fire. He was not a young man, thin, not as tall as she had thought. It was a fine face, but there was something wrong, something amiss. He looks ruined, she thought, a ruined man.

"Why would you come to the Marsh?" she asked. She had a right to ask, having taken him in, yet she felt a discomfort in pressing the question.

"I was told there's a murrain among the cattle here." Now that he wasn't all locked up with cold his voice was beautiful. He talked like the tale-tellers when they spoke the parts of the heroes and the dragonlords. Maybe he was a teller or a singer? But no; the murrain, he had said.

"There is."

"I may be able to help the beasts."

"You're a curer?"

He nodded.

"Then you'll be more than welcome. The plague is terrible among the cattle. And getting worse."

He said nothing. She could see the warmth coming into him, untying him.

"Put your feet up to the fire," she said abruptly. "I have some old shoes of my husband's." It cost her something to say that, yet when she had said it she felt released, untied too. What was she keeping Bren's shoes for, anyhow? They were too small for Berry and too big for her. She'd given away his clothes, but kept the shoes, she didn't know what for. For this fellow, it would seem. Things came round if you could wait for them, she thought. "I'll set 'em out for you," she said. "Yours are perished."

He glanced at her. His dark eyes were large, deep, opaque like a horse's eyes, unreadable.

"He's dead," she said, "two years. The marsh fever. You have to watch out for that, here. The water. I live with my brother. He's in the village, at the tavern. We keep a dairy. I make cheese. Our herd's been all right," and she made the sign to avert evil. "I keep 'em close in. Out on the ranges, the murrain's very bad. Maybe the cold weather'll put an end to it."

"More likely to kill the beasts that sicken with it," the man said. He sounded a bit sleepy.

"I'm called Gift," she said. "My brother's Berry."

"Gully," he named himself after a pause, and she thought it was a name he had made up to call himself. It did not fit him. Nothing about him fit together, made a whole. Yet she felt no distrust of him. She was easy with him. He meant no harm to her. She thought there was kindness in him, the way he spoke of the animals. He would have a way with them, she thought. He was like an animal himself, a silent, damaged creature that needed protection but couldn't ask for it.

"Come," she said, "before you fall asleep there," and he followed her obediently to Berry's room, which wasn't much more than a cupboard built onto the corner of the house. Her room was behind the chimney. Berry would come in, drunk, in a while, and she'd put down the pallet

in the chimney corner for him. Let the traveler have a good bed for a
night. Maybe he'd leave a copper or two with her when he went on.
There was a terrible shortage of coppers in her household these days.

He woke, as he always did, in his room in the Great
House. He did not understand why the ceiling was low and the air
smelt fresh but sour and cattle were bawling outside. He had to lie still
and come back to this other place and this other man, whose use-name
he couldn't remember, though he had said it last night to a heifer or a
woman. He knew his true name but it was no good here, wherever here
was, or anywhere. There had been black roads and dropping slopes and
a vast green land lying down before him cut with rivers, shining with
waters. A cold wind blowing. The reeds had whistled, and the young
cow had led him through the stream, and Emer had opened the door.
He had known her name as soon as he saw her. But he must use some
other name. He must not call her by her name. He must remember what
name he had told her to call him. He must not be Irioth, though he was
Irioth. Maybe in time he would be another man. No; that was wrong;
he must be this man. This man's legs ached and his feet hurt. But it was
a good bed, a feather bed, warm, and he need not get out of it yet. He
drowsed a while, drifting away from Irioth.

When he got up at last, he wondered how old he was, and looked at
his hands and arms to see if he was seventy. He still looked forty, though
he felt seventy and moved like it, wincing. He got his clothes on, foul as
they were from days and days of travel. There was a pair of shoes under
the chair, worn but good, strong shoes, and a pair of knit wool stockings
to go with them. He put the stockings on his battered feet and limped
into the kitchen. Emer stood at the big sink, straining something heavy
in a cloth.

"Thank you for these and the shoes," he said, and thanking her for
the gift, remembered her use-name but said only, "mistress."

"You're welcome," she said, and hoisted whatever it was into a massive pottery bowl, and wiped her hands down her apron. He knew nothing at all about women. He had not lived where women were since he was ten years old. He had been afraid of them, the women that shouted at him to get out of the way in that great other kitchen long ago. But since he had been traveling about in Earthsea he had met women and found them easy to be with, like the animals; they went about their business not paying much attention to him unless he frightened them. He tried not to do that. He had no wish or reason to frighten them. They were not men.

"Would you like some fresh curds? It makes a good breakfast." She was eyeing him, but not for long, and not meeting his eyes. Like an animal, like a cat, she was, sizing him up but not challenging. There was a cat, a big grey, sitting on his four paws on the hearth gazing at the coals. Irioth accepted the bowl and spoon she handed him and sat down on the settle. The cat jumped up beside him and purred.

"Look at that," said the woman. "He's not friendly with most folk."

"It's the curds."

"He knows a curer, maybe."

It was peaceful here with the woman and the cat. He had come to a good house.

"It's cold out," she said. "Ice on the trough this morning. Will you be going on, this day?"

There was a pause. He forgot that he had to answer in words. "I'd stay if I might," he said. "I'd stay here."

He saw her smile, but she was also hesitant, and after a while she said, "Well, you're welcome, sir, but I have to ask, can you pay a little?"

"Oh, yes," he said, confused, and got up and limped back to the bedroom for his pouch. He brought her a piece of money, a little Enladian crownpiece of gold.

"Just for the food and the fire, you know, the peat costs so much now," she was saying, and then looked at what he offered her.

"Oh, sir," she said, and he knew he had done wrong.

"There's nobody in the village could change that," she said. She looked up into his face for a moment. "The whole village together couldn't change that!" she said, and laughed. It was all right, then, though the word "change" rang and rang in his head.

"It hasn't been changed," he said, but he knew that was not what she meant. "I'm sorry," he said. "If I stayed a month, if I stayed the winter, would that use it up? I should have a place to stay, while I work with the beasts."

"Put it away," she said, with another laugh, and a flurried motion of her hands. "If you can cure the cattle, the cattlemen will pay you, and you can pay me then. Call that surety, if you like. But put it away, sir! It makes me dizzy to look at it.—Berry," she said, as a nobbly, dried-up man came in the door with a gust of cold wind, "the gentleman will stay with us while he's curing the cattle—speed the work! He's given us surety of payment. So you'll sleep in the chimney corner, and him in the room. This is my brother Berry, sir."

Berry ducked his head and muttered. His eyes were dull. It seemed to Irioth that the man had been poisoned. When Berry went out again, the woman came closer and said, resolute, in a low voice, "There's no harm in him but the drink, but there's not much left of him but the drink. It's eaten up most of his mind, and most of what we have. So, do you see, put up your money where he won't see it, if you don't mind, sir. He won't come looking for it. But if he saw it, he'd take it. He often doesn't know what he's doing, do you see."

"Yes," Irioth said. "I understand. You are a kind woman." She was talking about him, about his not knowing what he was doing. She was forgiving him. "A kind sister," he said. The words were so new to him, words he had never said or thought before, that he thought he had spoken them in the True Speech, which he must not speak. But she only shrugged, with a frowning smile.

"Times I could shake his fool head off," she said, and went back to her work.

He had not known how tired he was until he came to haven. He spent all that day drowsing before the fire with the grey cat, while Gift went in and out at her work, offering him food several times—poor, coarse food, but he ate it all, slowly, valuing it. Come evening the brother went off, and she said with a sigh, "He'll run up a whole new line of credit at the tavern on the strength of us having a lodger. Not that it's your fault."

"Oh, yes," Irioth said. "It was my fault." But she forgave; and the grey cat was pressed up against his thigh, dreaming. The cat's dreams came into his mind, in the low fields where he spoke with the animals, the dusky places. The cat leapt there, and then there was milk, and the deep soft thrilling. There was no fault, only the great innocence. No need for words. They would not find him here. He was not here to find. There was no need to speak any name. There was nobody but her, and the cat dreaming, and the fire flickering. He had come over the dead mountain on black roads, but here the streams ran slow among the pastures.

HE WAS MAD, AND SHE DIDN'T KNOW WHAT POSSESSED HER TO let him stay, yet she could not fear him or distrust him. What did it matter if he was mad? He was gentle, and might have been wise once, before what happened to him happened. And he wasn't so mad as all that. Mad in patches, mad at moments. Nothing in him was whole, not even his madness. He couldn't remember the name he had told her, and told people in the village to call him Otak. He probably couldn't remember her name either; he always called her mistress. But maybe that was his courtesy. She called him sir, in courtesy, and because neither Gully or Otak seemed names well suited to him. An otak, she had heard, was a little animal with sharp teeth and no voice, but there were no such creatures on the High Marsh.

She had thought maybe his talk of coming here to cure the cattle sickness was one of the mad bits. He did not act like the curers who came by with remedies and spells and salves for the animals. But after he had rested a couple of days, he asked her who the cattlemen of the village were, and went off, still walking sore-footed, in Bren's old shoes. It made her heart turn in her, seeing that.

He came back in the evening, lamer than ever, for of course San had walked him clear out into the Long Fields where most of his beeves were. Nobody had horses but Alder, and they were for his cowboys. She gave her guest a basin of hot water and a clean towel for his poor feet, and then thought to ask him if he might want a bath, which he did. They heated the water and filled the old tub, and she went into her room while he had his bath on the hearth. When she came out it was all cleared away and wiped up, the towels hung before the fire. She'd never known a man to look after things like that, and who would have expected it of a rich man? Wouldn't he have servants, where he came from? But he was no more trouble than the cat. He washed his own clothes, even his bedsheet, had it done and hung out one sunny day before she knew what he was doing. "You needn't do that, sir, I'll do your things with mine," she said.

"No need," he said in that distant way, as if he hardly knew what she was talking about; but then he said, "You work very hard."

"Who doesn't? I like the cheese making. There's an interest to it. And I'm strong. All I fear is getting old, when I can't lift the buckets and the molds." She showed him her round, muscular arm, making a fist and smiling. "Pretty good for fifty years old!" she said. It was silly to boast, but she was proud of her strong arms, her energy and skill.

"Speed the work," he said gravely.

He had a way with her cows that was wonderful. When he was there and she needed a hand, he took Berry's place, and as she told her friend Tawny, laughing, he was cannier with the cows than Bren's old dog had been. "He talks to 'em, and I'll swear they consider what he says. And that heifer follows him about like a puppy." Whatever he was doing out on the ranges with the beeves, the cattlemen were coming to think well of him. Of course they would grab at any promise of help. Half San's herd was dead. Alder would not say how many head he had lost. The bodies of cattle were everywhere. If it had not been cold weather the Marsh would have reeked of rotting flesh. None of the water could be drunk unless you boiled it an hour, except what came from the wells, hers here and the one in the village, which gave the place its name.

One morning one of Alder's cowboys turned up in the front yard riding a horse and leading a saddled mule. "Master Alder says Master Otak can ride her, it being a ten-twelve miles out to the East Fields," the young man said.

Her guest came out of the house. It was a bright, misty morning, the marshes hidden by gleaming vapors. Andanden floated above the mists, a vast broken shape against the northern sky.

The curer said nothing to the cowboy but went straight to the mule, or hinny, rather, being out of San's big jenny by Alder's white horse. She was a whitey roan, young, with a pretty face. He went and talked to her for a minute, saying something in her big, delicate ear and rubbing her topknot.

"He does that," the cowboy said to Gift. "Talks at 'em." He was amused, disdainful. He was one of Berry's drinking mates at the tavern, a decent enough young fellow, for a cowboy.

"Is he curing the cattle?" she asked.

"Well, he can't lift the murrain all at once. But seems like he can cure a beast if he gets to it before the staggers begin. And those not struck yet, he says he can keep it off 'em. So the master's sending him all about the range to do what can be done. It's too late for many."

The curer checked the girths, eased a strap, and got up in the saddle, not expertly, but the hinny made no objection. She turned her long,

creamy-white nose and beautiful eyes to look at her rider. He smiled.
Gift had never seen him smile.

"Shall we go?" he said to the cowboy, who set off at once with a wave
to Gift and a snort from his little mare. The curer followed. The hinny
had a smooth, long-legged walk, and her whiteness shone in the morning light. Gift thought it was like seeing a prince ride off, like something out of a tale, the mounted figures that walked through bright mist
across the vague dun of the winter fields, and faded into the light, and
were gone.

IT WAS HARD WORK OUT IN THE PASTURES. "WHO DOESN'T DO
hard work?" Emer had asked, showing her round, strong arms, her hard,
red hands. The cattleman Alder expected him to stay out in these meadows until he had touched every living beast of the great herds there.
Alder had sent two cowboys along. They made a camp of sorts, with
a groundcloth and a half tent. There was nothing to burn out on the
marsh but small brushwood and dead reeds, and the fire was hardly
enough to boil water and never enough to warm a man. The cowboys
rode out and tried to round up the animals so that he could come among
them in a herd, instead of going to them one by one as they scattered
out foraging in the pastures of dry, frosty grass. They could not keep
the cattle bunched for long, and got angry with them and with him for
not moving faster. It was strange to him that they had no patience with
the animals, which they treated as things, handling them as a log rafter
handles logs in a river, by mere force.

They had no patience with him either, always at him to hurry up and
get done with the job; nor with themselves, their life. When they talked
to each other it was always about what they were going to do in town, in
Oraby, when they got paid off. He heard a good deal about the whores
in Oraby, Daisy and Goldie and the one they called the Burning Bush.
He had to sit with the young men because they all needed what warmth

there was to be got from the fire, but they did not want him there and he did not want to be there with them. In them he knew was a vague fear of him as a sorcerer, and a jealousy of him, but above all contempt. He was old, other, not one of them. Fear and jealousy he knew and shrank from, and contempt he remembered. He was glad he was not one of them, that they did not want to talk to him. He was afraid of doing wrong to them.

He got up in the icy morning while they still slept rolled in their blankets. He knew where the cattle were nearby, and went to them. The sickness was very familiar to him now. He felt it in his hands as a burning, and a queasiness if it was much advanced. Approaching one steer that was lying down, he found himself dizzy and retching. He came no closer, but said words that might ease the dying, and went on.

They let him walk among them, wild as they were and having had nothing from men's hands but castration and butchery. He had a pleasure in their trust in him, a pride in it. He should not, but he did. If he wanted to touch one of the great beasts he had only to stand and speak to it a little while in the language of those who do not speak. "Ulla," he said, naming them. "Ellu. Ellua." They stood, big, indifferent; sometimes one looked at him for a long time. Sometimes one came to him with its easy, loose, majestic tread, and breathed into his open palm. All those that came to him he could cure. He laid his hands on them, on the stiff-haired, hot flanks and neck, and sent the healing into his hands with the words of power spoken over and over. After a while the beast would give a shake, or toss its head a bit, or step on. And he would drop his hands and stand there, drained and blank, for a while. Then there would be another one, big, curious, shyly bold, muddy-coated, with the sickness in it like a prickling, a tingling, a hotness in his hands, a dizziness. "Ellu," he would say, and walk to the beast and lay his hands upon it until they felt cool, as if a mountain stream ran through them.

The cowboys were discussing whether or not it was safe to eat the meat of a steer dead of the murrain. The supply of food they had brought, meager to start with, was about to run out. Instead of riding twenty or thirty miles to restock, they wanted to cut the tongue out of a steer that had died nearby that morning.

He had forced them to boil any water they used. Now he said, "If you eat that meat, in a year you'll begin to get dizzy. You'll end with the blind staggers and die as they do."

They cursed and sneered, but believed him. He had no idea if what he said was true. It had seemed true as he said it. Perhaps he wanted to spite them. Perhaps he wanted to get rid of them.

"Ride back," he said. "Leave me here. There's enough food for one man for three or four days more. The hinny will bring me back."

They needed no persuasion. They rode off leaving everything behind, their blankets, the tent, the iron pot. "How do we get all that back to the village?" he asked the hinny. She looked after the two ponies and said what hinnies say. "Aaawww!" she said. She would miss the ponies.

"We have to finish the work here," he told her, and she looked at him mildly. All animals were patient, but the patience of the horse kind was wonderful, being freely given. Dogs were loyal, but there was more of obedience in it. Dogs were hierarchs, dividing the world into lords and commoners. Horses were all lords. They agreed to collude. He remembered walking among the great, plumed feet of cart horses, fearless. The comfort of their breath on his head. A long time ago. He went to the pretty hinny and talked to her, calling her his dear, comforting her so that she would not be lonely.

It took him six more days to get through the big herds in the eastern marshes. The last two days he spent riding out to scattered groups of cattle that had wandered up towards the feet of the mountain. Many of them were not infected yet, and he could protect them. The hinny carried him bareback and made the going easy. But there was nothing left for him to eat. When he rode back to the village he was light-headed and weak-kneed. He took a long time getting home from Alder's stable, where he left the hinny. Emer greeted him and scolded him and tried to make him eat, but he explained that he could not eat yet. "As I stayed there in the sickness, in the sick fields, I felt sick. After a while I'll be able to eat again," he explained.

"You're crazy," she said, very angry. It was a sweet anger. Why could not more anger be sweet?

"At least have a bath!" she said.

He knew what he smelled like, and thanked her.

"What's Alder paying you for all this?" she demanded while the water was heating. She was still indignant, speaking more bluntly even than usual.

"I don't know," he said.

She stopped and stared at him.

"You didn't set a price?"

"Set a price?" he flashed out. Then he remembered who he was not, and spoke humbly. "No. I didn't."

"Of all the innocence," Gift said, hissing the word. "He'll skin you." She dumped a kettleful of steaming water into the bath. "He has ivory," she said. "Tell him ivory it has to be. Out there ten days starving in the cold to cure his beasts! San's got nothing but copper, but Alder can pay you in ivory. I'm sorry if I'm meddling in your business. Sir." She flung out the door with two buckets, going to the pump. She would not use the stream water for anything at all, these days. She was wise, and kind. Why had he lived so long among those who were not kind?

"We'll have to see," said Alder, the next day, "if my beasts are cured. If they make it through the winter, see, we'll know your cures all took, that they're sound, like. Not that I doubt it, but fair's fair, right? You wouldn't ask me to pay you what I have in mind to pay you, would you now, if the cure didn't take and the beasts died after all. Avert the chance! But I wouldn't ask you to wait all that time unpaid, neither. So here's an advance, like, on what's to come, and all's square between us for now, right?"

The coppers weren't decently in a bag, even. Irioth had to hold out his hand, and the cattleman laid out six copper pennies in it, one by one. "Now then! That's fair and square!" he said, expansive. "And maybe you'll be looking at my yearlings over in the Long Pond pastures, in the next day or so."

"No," Irioth said. "San's herd was going down fast when I left. I'm needed there."

"Oh, no, you're not, Master Otak. While you were out in the east range a sorcerer curer came by, a fellow that's been here before, from the south coast, and so San hired him. You work for me and you'll be paid well. Better than copper, maybe, if the beasts fare well!"

Irioth did not say yes, or no, or thanks, but went off unspeaking. The cattleman looked after him and spat. "Avert," he said.

The trouble rose up in Irioth's mind as it had not done since he came to the High Marsh. He struggled against it. A man of power had come to heal the cattle, another man of power. But a sorcerer, Alder had said. Not a wizard, not a mage. Only a curer, a cattle healer. I do not need to fear him. I do not need to fear his power. I do not need his power. I must see him, to be sure, to be certain. If he does what I do here there is no harm. We can work together. If I do what he does here. If he uses only sorcery and means no harm. As I do.

He walked down the straggling street of Purewells to San's house, which was about midway, opposite the tavern. San, a hard-bitten man in his thirties, was talking to a man on his doorstep, a stranger. When they saw Irioth they looked uneasy. San went into his house and the stranger followed.

Irioth came up onto the doorstep. He did not go in, but spoke in the open door. "Master San, it's about the cattle you have there between the rivers. I can go to them today." He did not know why he said this. It was not what he had meant to say.

"Ah," San said, coming to the door, and hemmed a bit. "No need, Master Otak. This here is Master Sunbright, come up to deal with the murrain. He's cured beasts for me before, the hoof rot and all. Being as how you have all one man can do with Alder's beeves, you see . . ."

The sorcerer came out from behind San. His name was Ayeth. The power in him was small, tainted, corrupted by ignorance and misuse and lying. But the jealousy in him was like a stinging fire. "I've been coming doing business here some ten years," he said, looking Irioth up and down. "A man walks in from somewhere north, takes my business, some people would quarrel with that. A quarrel of sorcerers is a bad thing. If you're a sorcerer, a man of power, that is. I am. As the good people here well know."

Irioth tried to say he did not want a quarrel. He tried to say that there was work for two. He tried to say he would not take the man's work from him. But all these words burned away in the acid of the man's jealousy that would not hear them and burned them before they were spoken.

Ayeth's stare grew more insolent as he watched Irioth stammer. He began to say something to San, but Irioth spoke.

"You have—" he said—"you have to go. Back." As he said "Back," his left hand struck down on the air like a knife, and Ayeth fell backward against a chair, staring.

He was only a little sorcerer, a cheating healer with a few sorry spells. Or so he seemed. What if he was cheating, hiding his power, a rival hiding his power? A jealous rival. He must be stopped, he must be bound, named, called. Irioth began to say the words that would bind him, and the shaken man cowered away, shrinking down, shriveling, crying out in a thin, high wail. It is wrong, wrong, I am doing the wrong, I am the ill, Irioth thought. He stopped the spell words in his mouth, fighting against them, and at last crying out one other word. Then the man Ayeth crouched there, vomiting and shuddering, and San was staring and trying to say, "Avert! Avert!" And no harm was done. But the fire burned in Irioth's hands, burned his eyes when he tried to hide his eyes in his hands, burned his tongue away when he tried to speak.

For a long time nobody would touch him. He had fallen down in a fit in San's doorway. He lay there now like a dead man. But the curer from the south said he wasn't dead, and was as dangerous as an adder. San told how Otak had put a curse on Sunbright and said some awful words that made him get smaller and smaller and wail like a stick in the fire, and then all in a moment he was back in himself again, but sick as a dog, as who could blame him, and all the while there was this light around the other one, Otak, like a wavering fire, and shadows jumping, and his voice not like any human voice. A terrible thing.

Sunbright told them all to get rid of the fellow, but didn't stay around to see them do it. He went back down the south road as soon as he'd gulped a pint of beer at the tavern, telling them there was no room for two sorcerers in one village and he'd be back, maybe, when that man, or whatever he was, had gone.

Nobody would touch him. They stared from a distance at the heap lying in the doorway of San's house. San's wife wept aloud up and down the street. "Bad cess! Bad cess!" she cried. "Oh, my babe will be born dead, I know it!"

Berry went and fetched his sister, after he had heard Sunbright's tale at the tavern, and San's version of it, and several other versions already current. In the best of them, Otak had towered up ten feet tall and struck Sunbright into a lump of coal with lightning, before foaming at the mouth, turning blue, and collapsing in a heap.

Gift hurried to the village. She went straight up to the doorstep, bent over the heap, and laid her hand on it. Everybody gasped and muttered,

"Avert! Avert!" except Tawny's youngest daughter, who mistook the signs and piped up, "Speed the work!"

The heap moved, and roused up slowly. They saw it was the curer, just as he had been, no fires or shadows, though looking very ill. "Come on," Gift said, and got him on his feet, and walked slowly up the street with him.

The villagers shook their heads. Gift was a brave woman, but there was such a thing as being too brave. Or brave, they said around the tavern table, in the wrong way, or the wrong place, d'you see. Nobody should ought to meddle with sorcery that ain't born to it. Nor with sorcerers. You forget that. They seem the same as other folk. But they ain't like other folk. Seems there's no harm in a curer. Heal the foot rot, clear a caked udder. That's all fine. But cross one and there you are, fire and shadows and curses and falling down in fits. Uncanny. Always was uncanny, that one. Where'd he come from, anyhow? Answer me that.

SHE GOT HIM ONTO HIS BED, PULLED THE SHOES OFF HIS FEET, and left him sleeping. Berry came in late and drunker than usual, so that he fell and gashed his forehead on the andiron. Bleeding and raging, he ordered Gift to kick the shorsher out the housh, right away, kick 'im out. Then he vomited into the ashes and fell asleep on the hearth. She hauled him onto his pallet, pulled his shoes off his feet, and left him sleeping. She went to look at the other one. He looked feverish, and she put her hand on his forehead. He opened his eyes, looking straight into hers without expression. "Emer," he said, and closed his eyes again.

She backed away from him, terrified.

In her bed, in the dark, she lay and thought: He knew the wizard who named me. Or I said my name. Maybe I said it out loud in my sleep. Or somebody told him. But nobody knows it. Nobody ever knew my

name but the wizard, and my mother. And they're dead, they're dead . . .
I said it in my sleep . . .

But she knew better.

SHE STOOD WITH THE LITTLE OIL LAMP IN HER HAND, AND THE
light of it shone red between her fingers and golden on her face. He said
her name. She gave him sleep.

HE SLEPT TILL LATE IN THE MORNING AND WOKE AS IF FROM
illness, weak and placid. She was unable to be afraid of him. She found
that he had no memory at all of what had happened in the village, of
the other sorcerer, even of the six coppers she had found scattered on
the bedcover, which he must have held clenched in his hand all along.

"No doubt that's what Alder gave you," she said. "The flint!"

"I said I'd see to his beasts at . . . at the pasture between the rivers,
was it?" he said, getting anxious, the hunted look coming back into him,
and he got up from the settle.

"Sit down," she said. He sat down, but he sat fretting.

"How can you cure when you're sick?" she said.

"How else?" he said.

But he quieted down again presently, stroking the grey cat.

Her brother came in. "Come on out," he said to her as soon as he saw
the curer dozing on the settle. She stepped outside with him.

"Now I won't have him here no more," Berry said, coming master of
the house over her, with the great black gash in his forehead, and his
eyes like oysters, and his hands juddering.

"Where'll you go?" she said.

"It's him has to go."

"It's my house. Bren's house. He stays. Go or stay, it's up to you."

"It's up to me too if he stays or goes, and he goes. You haven't got all
the sayso. All the people say he ought to go. He's not canny."

"Oh, yes, since he's cured half the herds and got paid six coppers for it, time for him to go, right enough! I'll have him here as long as I choose, and that's the end of it."

"They won't buy our milk and cheese," Berry whined.

"Who says that?"

"San's wife. All the women."

"Then I'll carry the cheeses to Oraby," she said, "and sell 'em there. In the name of honor, brother, go wash out that cut, and change your shirt. You stink of the pothouse." And she went back into the house. "Oh, dear," she said, and burst into tears.

"What's the matter, Emer?" said the curer, turning his thin face and strange eyes to her.

"Oh, it's no good, I know it's no good. Nothing's any good with a drunkard," she said. She wiped her eyes with her apron. "Was that what broke you," she said, "the drink?"

"No," he said, taking no offense, perhaps not understanding.

"Of course it wasn't. I beg your pardon," she said.

"Maybe he drinks to try to be another man," he said. "To alter, to change . . ."

"He drinks because he drinks," she said. "With some, that's all it is. I'll be in the dairy, now. I'll lock the house door. There's . . . there's been strangers about. You rest yourself. It's bitter out." She wanted to be sure that he stayed indoors out of harm's way, and that nobody came harassing him. Later on she would go into the village, have a word with some of the sensible people, and put a stop to this rubbishy talk, if she could.

When she did so, Alder's wife Tawny and several other people agreed with her that a squabble between sorcerers over work was nothing new and nothing to take on about. But San and his wife and the tavern crew wouldn't let it rest, it being the only thing of interest to talk about for the rest of the winter, except the cattle dying. "Besides," Tawny said, "my man's never averse to paying copper where he thought he might have to pay ivory."

"Are the cattle he touched keeping afoot, then?"

"So far as we can see, they are. And no new sickenings."

"He's a true sorcerer, Tawny," Gift said, very earnest. "I know it."

"That's the trouble, love," said Tawny. "And you know it! This is no place for a man like that. Whoever he is is none of our business, but why did he come here, is what you have to ask."

"To cure the beasts," Gift said.

Sᴜɴʙʀɪɢʜᴛ ʜᴀᴅ ɴᴏᴛ ʙᴇᴇɴ ɢᴏɴᴇ ᴛʜʀᴇᴇ ᴅᴀʏꜱ when a new stranger appeared in town: a man riding up the south road on a good horse and asking at the tavern for lodging. They sent him to San's house, but San's wife screeched when she heard there was a stranger at the door, crying that if San let another witch-man in the door her baby would be born dead twice over. Her screaming could be heard for several houses up and down the street, and a crowd, that is, ten or eleven people, gathered between San's house and the tavern.

"Well, that won't do," said the stranger pleasantly. "I can't be bringing on a birth untimely. Is there maybe a room above the tavern?"

"Send him on out to the dairy," said one of Alder's cowboys. "Gift's taking whatever comes." There was some sniggering and shushing.

"Back that way," said the taverner.

"Thanks," said the traveler, and led his horse along the way they pointed.

"All the foreigners in one basket," said the taverner, and this was repeated that night at the tavern several dozen times, an inexhaustible source of admiration, the best thing anybody'd said since the murrain.

Gɪꜰᴛ ᴡᴀꜱ ɪɴ ᴛʜᴇ ᴅᴀɪʀʏ, ʜᴀᴠɪɴɢ ꜰɪɴɪꜱʜᴇᴅ ᴛʜᴇ ᴇᴠᴇɴɪɴɢ ᴍɪʟᴋ-ing. She was straining the milk and setting out the pans. "Mistress," said a voice at the door, and she thought it was the curer and said, "Just a minute while I finish this," and then turning saw a stranger and nearly dropped the pan. "Oh, you startled me!" she said. "What can I do for you, then?"

"I'm looking for a bed for the night."

"No, I'm sorry, there's my lodger, and my brother, and me. Maybe San, in the village—"

"They sent me here. They said, 'All the foreigners in one basket.'" The stranger was in his thirties, with a blunt face and a pleasant look, dressed plain, though the cob that stood behind him was a good horse. "Put me up in the cow barn, mistress, it'll do fine. It's my horse needs a good bed; he's tired. I'll sleep in the barn and be off in the morning. Cows are a pleasure to sleep with on a cold night. I'll be glad to pay you, mistress, if two coppers would suit, and my name's Hawk."

"I'm Gift," she said, a bit flustered, but liking the fellow. "All right, then, Master Hawk. Put your horse up and see to him. There's the pump, there's plenty of hay. Come on in the house after. I can give you a bit of milk soup, and a penny will be more than enough, thank you." She didn't feel like calling him sir, as she always did the curer. This one had nothing of that lordly way about him. She hadn't seen a king when she first saw him, as with the other one.

When she finished in the dairy and went to the house, the new fellow, Hawk, was squatting on the hearth, skillfully making up the fire. The curer was in his room asleep. She looked in, and closed the door.

"He's not too well," she said, speaking low. "He was curing the cattle away out east over the marsh, in the cold, for days on end, and wore himself out."

As she went about her work in the kitchen, Hawk lent her a hand now and then in the most natural way, so that she began to wonder if men from foreign parts were all so much handier about the house than the men of the Marsh. He was easy to talk with, and she told him about the curer, since there was nothing much to say about herself.

"They'll use a sorcerer and then ill-mouth him for his usefulness," she said. "It's not just."

"But he scared 'em, somehow, did he?"

"I guess he did. Another curer came up this way, a fellow that's been by here before. Doesn't amount to much that I can see. He did no good to my cow with the caked bag, two years ago. And his balm's just pig fat, I'd swear. Well, so, he says to Otak, you're taking my business. And maybe Otak says the same back. And they lose their tempers, and they did some black spells, maybe. I guess Otak did. But he did no harm to the man at all, but fell down in a swoon himself. And now he doesn't remember any more about it, while the other man walked away unhurt. And they say every beast he touched is standing yet, and hale. Ten days he spent out there in the wind and the rain, touching the beasts and healing them. And you know what the cattleman gave him? Six pennies! Can you wonder he was a little rageous? But I don't say . . ." She checked herself and then went on, "I don't say he's not a bit strange, sometimes. The way witches and sorcerers are, I guess. Maybe they have to be, dealing with such powers and evils as they do. But he is a true man, and kind."

"Mistress," said Hawk, "may I tell you a story?"

"Oh, are you a teller? Oh, why didn't you say so to begin with! Is that what you are then? I wondered, it being winter and all, and you being on the roads. But with that horse, I thought you must be a merchant. Can you tell me a story? It would be the joy of my life, and the longer the better! But drink your soup first, and let me sit down to hear . . ."

"I'm not truly a teller, mistress," he said with his pleasant smile, "but I do have a story for you." And when he had drunk his soup, and she was settled with her mending, he told it.

"In the Inmost Sea, on the Isle of the Wise, on Roke Island, where all magery is taught, there are nine Masters," he began.

She closed her eyes in bliss and listened.

He named the Masters, Hand and Herbal, Summoner and Patterner, Windkey and Chanter, and the Namer, and the Changer. "The Changer's and the Summoner's are very perilous arts," he said. "Changing, or transformation, you maybe know of, mistress. Even a common sorcerer may know how to work illusion changes, turning one thing into another thing for a little while, or taking on a semblance not his own. Have you seen that?"

"Heard of it," she whispered.

"And sometimes witches and sorcerers will say that they've summoned the dead to speak through them. Maybe a child the parents are grieving for. In the witch's hut, in the darkness, they hear it cry, or laugh . . ."

She nodded.

"Those are spells of illusion only, of seeming. But there are true changes, and true summonings. And these may be true temptations to the wizard! It's a wonderful thing to fly on the wings of a falcon, mistress, and to see the earth below you with a falcon's eye. And summoning, which is naming truly, is a great power. To know the true name is to have power, as you know, mistress. And the summoner's art goes straight to that. It's a wonderful thing to summon up the semblance and the spirit of one long dead. To see the beauty of Elfarran in the orchards of Soléa, as Morred saw it when the world was young . . ."

His voice had become very soft, very dark.

"Well, to my story. Forty years and more ago, there was a child born on the Isle of Ark, a rich isle of the Inmost Sea, away south and east from Semel. This child was the son of an understeward in the household of the Lord of Ark. Not a poor man's son, but not a child of much account. And the parents died young. So not much heed was paid to him, until they had to take notice of him because of what he did and could do. He was an uncanny brat, as they say. He had powers. He could light a fire or douse it with a word. He could make pots and pans fly through the air. He could turn a mouse into a pigeon and set it flying round the great kitchens of the Lord of Ark. And if he was crossed, or frightened, then he did harm. He turned a kettle of boiling water over a cook who had mistreated him."

"Mercy," whispered Gift. She had not sewn a stitch since he began.

"He was only a child, and the wizards of that household can't have been wise men, for they used little wisdom or gentleness with him. Maybe they were afraid of him. They bound his hands and gagged his mouth to keep him from making spells. They locked him in a cellar room, a room of stone, until they thought him tamed. Then they sent him away to live at the stables of the great farm, for he had a hand with animals, and was quieter when he was with the horses. But he quarreled with a stable boy, and turned the poor lad into a lump of dung. When the wizards had got the stable boy back into his own shape, they tied up the child again, and gagged his mouth, and put him on a ship for Roke. They thought maybe the Masters there could tame him."

"Poor child," she murmured.

"Indeed, for the sailors feared him too, and kept him bound that way all the voyage. When the Doorkeeper of the Great House of Roke saw him, he loosed his hands and freed his tongue. And the first thing the boy did in the Great House, they say, he turned the Long Table of the dining hall upside down, and soured the beer, and a student who tried to stop him got turned into a pig for a bit . . . But the boy had met his match in the Masters.

"They didn't punish him, but kept his wild powers bound with spells until they could make him listen and begin to learn. It took them a long time. There was a rivalrous spirit in him that made him look on any power he did not have, any thing he did not know, as a threat, a challenge, a thing to fight against until he could defeat it. There are many boys like that. I was one. But I was lucky. I learned my lesson young.

"Well, this boy did learn at last to tame his anger and control his power. And a very great power it was. Whatever art he studied came easy to him, too easy, so that he despised illusion, and weatherworking, and even healing, because they held no fear, no challenge to him. He saw no virtue in himself for his mastery of them. So, after the Archmage Nemmerle had given him his name, the boy set his will on the great and dangerous art of summoning. And he studied with the Master of that art for a long time.

"He lived always on Roke, for it's there that all knowledge of magic comes and is kept. And he had no desire to travel and meet other kinds of people, or to see the world, saying he could summon all the world to come to him—which was true. Maybe that's where the danger of that art lies.

"Now, what is forbidden to the summoner, or any wizard, is to call a living spirit. We can call to them, yes. We can send to them a voice or a presentment, a seeming, of ourself. But we do not summon them, in spirit or in flesh, to come to us. Only the dead may we summon. Only the shadows. You can see why this must be. To summon a living man is to have entire power over him, body and mind. No one, no matter how strong or wise or great, can rightly own and use another.

"But the spirit of rivalry worked in the boy as he grew to be a man. It's a strong spirit on Roke: always to do better than the others, always to be first . . . The art becomes a contest, a game. The end becomes a means to an end less than itself . . . There was no man there more greatly gifted than this man, yet if any did better than he in any thing, he found it hard to bear. It frightened him, it galled him.

"There was no place for him among the Masters, since a new Master Summoner had been chosen, a strong man in his prime, not likely to retire or die. Among the scholars and other teachers he had a place of honor, but he wasn't one of the Nine. He'd been passed over. Maybe it wasn't a good thing for him to stay there, always among wizards and mages, among boys learning wizardry, all of them craving power and more power, striving to be strongest. At any rate, as the years went on he became more and more aloof, pursuing his studies in his tower cell apart from others, teaching few students, speaking little. The Summoner would send gifted students to him, but many of the boys there scarcely knew of him. In this isolation he began to practice certain arts that are not well to practice and lead to no good thing.

"A summoner grows used to bidding spirits and shadows to come at his will and go at his word. Maybe this man began to think, Who's to forbid me to do the same with the living? Why have I the power if I cannot use it? So he began to call the living to him, those at Roke whom he feared, thinking them rivals, those whose power he was jealous of. When they came to him he took their power from them for himself, leaving them silent. They couldn't say what had happened to them, what had become of their power. They didn't know.

"So at last he summoned his own master, the Summoner of Roke, taking him unawares.

"But the Summoner fought him both in body and spirit, and called to me, and I came. Together we fought against the will that would destroy us."

Night had come. Gift's lamp had flickered out. Only the red glow of the fire shone on Hawk's face. It was not the face she had thought it. It was worn, and hard, and scarred all down one side. The hawk's face, she thought. She held still, listening.

"This is not a teller's tale, mistress. This is not a story you will ever hear anyone else tell.

"I was new at the business of being Archmage then. And younger than the man we fought, and maybe not afraid enough of him. It was all the two of us could do to hold our own against him, there in the silence, in the cell in the tower. Nobody else knew what was going on. We fought. A long time we fought. And then it was over. He broke. Like a stick breaking. He was broken. But he fled away. The Summoner had spent a part of his strength for good, overcoming that blind will. And

I didn't have the strength in me to stop the man when he fled, nor the wits to send anyone after him. And not a shred of power left in me to follow him with. So he got away from Roke. Clean gone.

"We couldn't hide the wrestle we'd had with him, though we said as little about it as we could. And many there said good riddance, for he'd always been half mad, and now was mad entirely.

"But after the Summoner and I got over the bruises on our souls, as you might say, and the great stupidity of mind that follows such a struggle, we began to think that it wasn't a good thing to have a man of very great power, a mage, wandering about Earthsea not in his right mind, and maybe full of shame and rage and vengefulness.

"We could find no trace of him. No doubt he changed himself to a bird or a fish when he left Roke, until he came to some other island. And a wizard can hide himself from all finding spells. We sent out inquiries, in the ways we have of doing so, but nothing and nobody replied. So we set off looking for him, the Summoner to the eastern isles and I to the west. For when I thought about this man, I had begun to see in my mind's eye a great mountain, a broken cone, with a long, green land beneath it reaching to the south. I remembered my geography lessons when I was a boy at Roke, and the lay of the land on Semel, and the mountain whose name is Andanden. So I came to the High Marsh. I think I came the right way."

There was a silence. The fire whispered.

"Should I speak to him?" Gift asked in a steady voice.

"No need," said the man like a falcon. "I will." And he said, "Irioth."

She looked at the door of the bedroom. It opened and he stood there, thin and tired, his dark eyes full of sleep and bewilderment and pain.

"Ged," he said. He bowed his head. After a while he looked up and asked, "Will you take my name from me?"

"Why should I do that?"

"It means only hurt. Hate, pride, greed."

"I'll take those names from you, Irioth, but not your own."

"I didn't understand," Irioth said, "about the others. That they are other. We are all other. We must be. I was wrong."

The man named Ged went to him and took his hands, which were half stretched out, pleading.

"You went wrong. You've come back. But you're tired, Irioth, and the way's hard when you go alone. Come home with me."

Irioth's head drooped as if in utter weariness. All tension and passion had gone out of his body. But he looked up, not at Ged but at Gift, silent in the hearth corner.

"I have work here," he said.

Ged too looked at her.

"He does," she said. "He heals the cattle."

"They show me what I should do," Irioth said, "and who I am. They know my name. But they never say it."

After a while Ged gently drew the older man to him and held him in his arms. He said something quietly to him and let him go. Irioth drew a deep breath.

"I'm no good there, you see, Ged," he said. "I am, here. If they'll let me do the work." He looked again at Gift, and Ged did also. She looked at them both.

"What say you, Emer?" asked the one like a falcon.

"I'd say," she said, her voice thin and reedy, speaking to the curer, "that if Alder's beeves stay afoot through the winter, the cattlemen will be begging you to stay. Though they may not love you."

"Nobody loves a sorcerer," said the Archmage. "Well, Irioth! Did I come all this way for you in the dead of winter, and must go back alone?"

"Tell them—tell them I was wrong," Irioth said. "Tell them I did wrong. Tell Thorion—" He halted, confused.

"I'll tell him that the changes in a man's life may be beyond all the arts we know, and all our wisdom," said the Archmage. He looked at Emer again. "May he stay here, mistress? Is that your wish as well as his?"

"He's ten times the use and company to me my brother is," she said. "And a kind true man, as I told you. Sir."

"Very well, then. Irioth, my dear companion, teacher, rival, friend, farewell. Emer, brave woman, my honor and thanks to you. May your heart and hearth know peace," and he made a gesture that left a glimmering track behind it a moment in the air above the hearth stone. "Now I'm off to the cow barn," he said, and he was.

The door closed. It was silent except for the whisper of the fire.

"Come to the fire," she said. Irioth came and sat down on the settle.

"Was that the Archmage? Truly?"

He nodded.

"The Archmage of the world," she said. "In my cow barn. He should have my bed—"

"He won't," said Irioth.

She knew he was right.

"Your name is beautiful, Irioth," she said after a while. "I never knew my husband's true name. Nor he mine. I won't speak yours again. But I like to know it, since you know mine."

"Your name is beautiful, Emer," he said. "I will speak it when you tell me to."

DRAGONFLY

I. Iria

HER FATHER'S ANCESTORS HAD OWNED A WIDE, RICH DOMAIN on the wide, rich island of Way. Claiming no title or court privilege in the days of the kings, through all the dark years after Maharion fell they held their land and people with firm hands, putting their gains back into the land, upholding some sort of justice, and fighting off petty tyrants. As order and peace returned to the Archipelago under the sway of the wise men of Roke, for a while yet the family and their farms and villages prospered. That prosperity and the beauty of the meadows and upland pastures and oak-crowned hills made the domain a byword, so that people said "as fat as a cow of Iria," or "as lucky as an Irian." The masters and many tenants of the domain added its name to their own, calling themselves Irian. But though the farmers and shepherds went on from season to season and year to year and generation to generation as steady and regenerative as the oaks, the family that owned the land altered and declined with time and chance.

A quarrel between brothers over their inheritance divided them. One

heir mismanaged his estate through greed, the other through foolishness. One had a daughter who married a merchant and tried to run her
estate from the city, the other had a son whose sons quarreled again,
redividing the divided land. By the time the girl called Dragonfly was
born, the domain of Iria, though still one of the loveliest regions of hill
and field and meadow in all Earthsea, was a battleground of feuds and
litigations. Farmlands went to weeds, farmsteads went unroofed, milk-
ing sheds stood unused, and shepherds followed their flocks over the
mountain to better pastures. The old house that had been the center of
the domain was half in ruins on its hill among the oaks.

Its owner was one of four men who called themselves Master of Iria.
The other three called him Master of Old Iria. He spent his youth and
what remained of his inheritance in law courts and the anterooms of the
Lords of Way in Shelieth, trying to prove his right to the whole domain
as it had been a hundred years ago. He came back unsuccessful and
embittered and spent his age drinking the hard red wine from his last
vineyard and walking his boundaries with a troop of ill-treated, under-
fed dogs to keep interlopers off his land.

He had married while he was in Shelieth, a woman no one at Iria
knew anything about, for she came from some other island, it was said,
somewhere in the west; and she never came to Iria, for she died in child-
birth there in the city.

When he came home he had a three-year-old daughter with him. He
turned her over to the housekeeper and forgot about her. When he was
drunk sometimes he remembered her. If he could find her, he made her
stand by his chair or sit on his knees and listen to all the wrongs that
had been done to him and to the house of Iria. He cursed and cried and
drank and made her drink too, pledging to honor her inheritance and
be true to Iria. She swallowed the mouthful of wine, but she hated the
curses and pledges and tears, and the slobbered caresses that followed
them. She would escape, as soon as she could, if she could, and go down

to the dogs and horses and cattle. She swore to them that she would be loyal to her mother, whom nobody knew or honored or was true to, except herself.

When she was thirteen the old vineyarder and the housekeeper, who were all that was left of the household, told the Master that it was time his daughter had her naming day. They asked if they should send for the sorcerer over at Westpool, or would their own village witch do. The Master of Iria fell into a screaming rage. "A village witch? A hex-hag to give Irian's daughter her true name? Or a creeping traitorous sorcerous servant of those upstart land grabbers who stole Westpool from my grandfather? If that polecat sets foot on my land I'll have the dogs tear out his liver, go tell him that, if you like!" And so on. Old Daisy went back to her kitchen and old Coney went back to his vines, and thirteen-year-old Dragonfly ran out of the house and down the hill to the village, hurling her father's curses at the dogs, who, crazy with excitement at his shouting, barked and bayed and rushed after her.

"Get back, you black-hearted bitch!" she yelled. "Home, you crawling traitor!" And the dogs fell silent and went sidling back to the house with their tails down.

Dragonfly found the village witch taking maggots out of an infected cut on a sheep's rump. The witch's use-name was Rose, like a great many women of Way and other islands of the Hardic Archipelago. People who have a secret name that holds their power the way a diamond holds light may well like their public name to be ordinary, common, like other people's names.

Rose was muttering a rote spell, but it was her hands and her little short sharp knife that did most of the work. The ewe bore the digging knife patiently, her opaque, amber, slotted eyes gazing into silence; only she stamped her small left front foot now and then, and sighed.

Dragonfly peered close at Rose's work. Rose brought out a maggot, dropped it, spat on it, and probed again. The girl leaned up against the ewe, and the ewe leaned against the girl, giving and receiving comfort. Rose extracted, dropped, and spat on the last maggot, and said, "Just hand me that bucket now." She bathed the sore with salt water. The ewe sighed deeply and suddenly walked out of the yard, heading for home. She had had enough of medicine. "Bucky!" Rose shouted. A grubby child appeared from under a bush where he had been asleep and trailed after the ewe, of whom he was nominally in charge although she was older, larger, better fed, and probably wiser than he was.

"They said you should give me my name," said Dragonfly. "Father fell to raging. So that's that."

The witch said nothing. She knew the girl was right. Once the Master of Iria said he would or would not allow a thing, he never changed his mind, priding himself on his intransigence, since in his view only weak men said a thing and then unsaid it.

"Why can't I give myself my own true name?" Dragonfly asked, while Rose washed the knife and her hands in the salt water.

"Can't be done."

"Why not? Why does it have to be a witch or a sorcerer? What do you *do?*"

"Well," Rose said, and dumped out the salt water on the bare dirt of the small front yard of her house, which, like most witches' houses, stood somewhat apart from the village. "Well," she said, straightening up and looking about vaguely as if for an answer, or a ewe, or a towel. "You have to know something about the power, see," she said at last, and looked at Dragonfly with one eye. Her other eye looked a little off to the side. Sometimes Dragonfly thought the cast was in Rose's left eye, sometimes it seemed to be in her right, but always one eye looked straight and the other watched something just out of sight, around the corner, elsewhere.

"Which power?"

"The one," Rose said. As suddenly as the ewe had walked off, she went into her house. Dragonfly followed her, but only to the door. Nobody entered a witch's house uninvited.

"You said I had it," the girl said into the reeking gloom of the one-roomed hut.

"I said you have a strength in you, a great one," the witch said from the darkness. "And you know it too. What you are to do I don't know, nor do you. That's to find. But there's no such power as to name yourself."

"Why not? What's more yourself than your own true name?"

A long silence.

The witch emerged with a soapstone drop spindle and a ball of greasy wool. She sat down on the bench beside her door and set the spindle turning. She had spun a yard of grey-brown yarn before she answered.

"My name's myself. True. But what's a name, then? It's what another calls me. If there was no other, only me, what would I want a name for?"

"But," said Dragonfly and stopped, caught by the argument. After a while she said, "So a name has to be a gift?"

Rose nodded.

"Give me my name, Rose," the girl said.

"Your dad says not."

"I say to."

"He's the master here."

"He can keep me poor and stupid and worthless, but he can't keep me nameless!"

The witch sighed, like the ewe, uneasy and constrained.

"Tonight," Dragonfly said. "At our spring, under Iria Hill. What he doesn't know won't hurt him." Her voice was half coaxing, half savage.

"You ought to have your proper nameday, your feast and dancing, like any young 'un," the witch said. "It's at daybreak a name should be given. And then there ought to be music and feasting and all. A party. Not sneaking about at night and no one knowing . . ."

"I'll know. How do you know what name to say, Rose? Does the water tell you?"

The witch shook her iron-grey head once. "I can't tell you." Her "can't" did not mean "won't." Dragonfly waited. "It's the power, like I said. It comes just so." Rose stopped her spinning and looked up with one eye at a cloud in the west; the other looked a little northward of the sky. "You're there in the water, together, you and the child. You take away the child-name. People may go on using that name for a use-name, but it's not her name, nor ever was. So now she's not a child, and she has no name. So then you wait. In the water there. You open your mind up, like. Like opening the doors of a house to the wind. So it comes. Your tongue speaks it, the name. Your breath makes it. You give it to that child, the breath, the name. You can't think of it. You let it come to you. It must come through you and the water to her it belongs to. That's the power, the way it works. It's all like that. It's not a thing you do. You have to know how to let it do. That's all the mastery."

"Mages can do more than that," the girl said after a while.

"Nobody can do more than that," said Rose.

Dragonfly rolled her head round on her neck, stretching till the vertebrae cracked, restlessly stretching out her long arms and legs. "Will you?" she said.

After some time, Rose nodded once.

They met in the lane under Iria Hill in the dark of night, long after sunset, long before dawn. Rose made a dim glow of werelight so that they could find their way through the marshy ground around the spring without falling in a sinkhole among the reeds. In the cold darkness under a few stars and the black curve of the hill, they stripped and waded into the shallow water, their feet sinking deep in velvet mud. The witch touched the girl's hand, saying, "I take your name, child. You are no child. You have no name."

It was utterly still.

In a whisper the witch said, "Woman, be named. You are Irian."

For a moment longer they held still; then the night wind blew across their naked shoulders, and shivering, they waded out, dried themselves as well as they could, struggled barefoot and wretched through the sharp-edged reeds and tangling roots, and found their way back to the lane. And there Dragonfly spoke in a ragged, raging whisper: "How could you name me that!"

The witch said nothing.

"It isn't right. It isn't my true name! I thought my name would make me be me. But this makes it worse. You got it wrong. You're only a witch. You did it wrong. It's *his* name. He can have it. He's so proud of it, his stupid domain, his stupid grandfather. I don't want it. I won't have it. It isn't me. I still don't know who I am. I'm not Irian!" She fell silent abruptly, having spoken the name.

The witch still said nothing. They walked along in the darkness side by side. At last, in a placating, frightened voice, Rose said, "It came so . . ."

"If you ever tell it to anyone I'll kill you," Dragonfly said.

At that, the witch stopped walking. She hissed in her throat like a cat. "*Tell* anyone?"

Dragonfly stopped too. She said after a moment, "I'm sorry. But I feel like—I feel like you betrayed me."

"I spoke your true name. It's not what I thought it would be. And I don't feel easy about it. As if I'd left something unfinished. But it is your name. If it betrays you, then that's the truth of it." Rose hesitated and then spoke less angrily, more coldly: "If you want the power to betray me, Irian, I'll give you that. My name is Etaudis."

The wind had come up again. They were both shivering, their teeth chattering. They stood face to face in the black lane, hardly able to see where the other was. Dragonfly put out her groping hand and met the witch's hand. They put their arms round each other in a fierce, long embrace. Then they hurried on, the witch to her hut near the village, the heiress of Iria up the hill to her ruinous house, where all the dogs, who had let her go without much fuss, received her back with a clamor and racket of barking that woke everybody for a half mile round except the master, sodden drunk by his cold hearth.

II. Ivory

THE MASTER OF IRIA OF WESTPOOL, BIRCH, DIDN'T OWN THE old house, but he did own the central and richest lands of the old domain. His father, more interested in vines and orchards than in quarrels with his relatives, had left Birch a thriving property. Birch hired men to manage the farms and wineries and cooperage and cartage and all, while he enjoyed his wealth. He married the timid daughter of the younger brother of the Lord of Wayfirth, and took infinite pleasure in thinking that his daughters were of noble blood.

The fashion of the time among the nobility was to have a wizard in their service, a genuine wizard with a staff and a grey cloak, trained on the Isle of the Wise; and so the Master of Iria of Westpool got himself a wizard from Roke. He was surprised how easy it was to get one, if you paid the price.

The young man, called Ivory, did not actually have his staff and cloak yet; he explained that he was to be made wizard when he went back to Roke. The Masters had sent him out in the world to gain experience, for all the classes in the school cannot give a man the experience he needs to be a wizard. Birch looked a little dubious at this, and Ivory reassured him that his training on Roke had equipped him with every kind of magic that could be needed in Iria of Westpool on Way. To prove it, he made it seem that a herd of deer ran through the dining hall, followed by a flight of swans, who marvelously soared in through the south wall and out through the north wall; and lastly a fountain in a silver basin sprang up in the center of the table, and when the master and his family cautiously imitated their wizard and filled their cups from it and tasted it, it was a sweet golden wine. "Wine of the Andrades," said the young man with a modest, complacent smile. By then the wife and daughters were entirely won over. And Birch thought the young man was worth his fee, although his own silent preference was for the dry red Fanian of his own vineyards, which got you drunk if you drank enough, while this yellow stuff was just honeywater.

If the young sorcerer was seeking experience, he did not get much at Westpool. Whenever Birch had guests from Kembermouth or from neighboring domains, the herd of deer, the swans, and the fountain of golden wine made their appearance. He also worked up some very pretty fireworks for warm spring evenings. But if the managers of the orchards and vineyards came to the master to ask if his wizard might put a spell of increase on the pears this year or maybe charm the black rot off the Fanian vines on the south hill, Birch said, "A wizard of Roke doesn't lower himself to such stuff. Go tell the village sorcerer to earn his keep!" And when the youngest daughter came down with a wasting cough, Birch's wife dared not trouble the wise young man about it, but sent humbly to Rose of Old Iria, asking her to come in by the back door and maybe make a poultice or sing a chant to bring the girl back to health.

Ivory never noticed that the girl was ailing, nor the pear trees, nor the vines. He kept himself to himself, as a man of craft and learning should. He spent his days riding about the countryside on the pretty black mare that his employer had given him for his use when he made it clear that he had not come from Roke to trudge about on foot in the mud and dust of country byways.

On his rides he sometimes passed an old house on a hill among great oaks. Once he turned off the village lane up the hill, but a pack of scrawny, evil-mouthed dogs came pelting and bellowing down at him. The mare was afraid of dogs and liable to buck and bolt, so after that he kept his distance. But he had an eye for beauty, and liked to look at the old house dreaming away in the dappled light of the early summer afternoons.

He asked Birch about the place. "That's Iria," Birch said—"Old Iria, I mean to say. I own that house by rights. But after a century of feuds and fights over it, my granddad let the place go to settle the quarrel. Though the master there would still be quarreling with me if he didn't keep too drunk to talk. Haven't seen the old man for years. He had a daughter, I think."

"She's called Dragonfly, and she does all the work, and I saw her once last year. She's tall, and as beautiful as a flowering tree," said the youngest daughter, Rose, who was busy crowding a lifetime of keen observation into the fourteen years that were all she was going to have for it. She broke off, coughing. Her mother shot an anguished, yearning glance at the wizard. Surely he would hear that cough, this time? He smiled at young Rose, and the mother's heart lifted. Surely he wouldn't smile so if Rose's cough was anything serious?

"Nothing to do with us, that lot at the old place," Birch said, displeased. The tactful Ivory asked no more. But he wanted to see the girl as beautiful as a flowering tree. He rode past Old Iria regularly. He tried stopping in the village at the foot of the hill to ask questions, but there was nowhere to stop and nobody would answer questions. A walleyed witch took one look at him and scuttled into her hut. If he went up to the house he would have to face the pack of hellhounds and probably a drunk old man. But it was worth the chance, he thought; he was bored out of his wits with the dull life at Westpool, and was never slow to take a risk. He rode up the hill till the dogs were yelling around him in a frenzy snapping at the mare's legs. She plunged and lashed out her hoofs at them, and he kept her from bolting only by a staying spell and all the strength in his arms. The dogs were leaping and snapping at his own legs now, and he was about to let the mare have her head when somebody came among the dogs shouting curses and beating them back with a strap. When he got the lathered, gasping mare to stand still, he saw the girl as beautiful as a flowering tree. She was very tall, very sweaty, with big hands and feet and mouth and nose and eyes, and a head of wild dusty hair. She was yelling, "Down! Back to the house, you carrion, you vile sons of bitches!" to the whining, cowering dogs.

Ivory clapped his hand to his right leg. A dogs tooth had ripped his breeches at the calf, and a trickle of blood came through.

"Is she hurt?" the woman said. "Oh, the traitorous vermin!" She was stroking down the mare's right foreleg. Her hands came away covered with blood-streaked horse sweat. "There, there," she said. "The brave girl, the brave heart." The mare put her head down and shivered all over with relief. "What did you keep her standing there in the middle of the dogs for?" the woman demanded furiously. She was kneeling at the horse's leg, looking up at Ivory. He was looking down at her from horseback, yet he felt short; he felt small.

She did not wait for an answer. "I'll walk her up," she said, standing, and put out her hand for the reins. Ivory saw that he was supposed to dismount. He did so, asking, "Is it very bad?" and peering at the horse's leg, seeing only bright, bloody foam.

"Come on then, my love," the young woman said, not to him. The mare followed her trustfully. They set off up the rough path round the hillside to an old stone and brick stableyard, empty of horses, inhabited only by nesting swallows that swooped about over the roofs calling their quick gossip.

"Keep her quiet," said the young woman, and left him holding the mare's reins in this deserted place. She returned after some time lugging a heavy bucket, and set to sponging off the mare's leg. "Get the saddle off her," she said, and her tone held the unspoken, impatient "you fool!"

Ivory obeyed, half annoyed by this crude giantess and half intrigued. She did not put him in mind of a flowering tree at all, but she was in fact beautiful, in a large, fierce way. The mare submitted to her absolutely. When she said, "Move your foot!" the mare moved her foot. The woman wiped her down all over, put the saddle blanket back on her, and made sure she was standing in the sun. "She'll be all right," she said. "There's a gash, but if you'll wash it with warm salt water four or five times a day, it'll heal clean. I'm sorry." She said the last honestly, though grudgingly, as if she still wondered how he could have let his mare stand there to be assaulted, and she looked straight at him for the first time. Her eyes were clear orange-brown, like dark topaz or amber. They were strange eyes, right on a level with his own.

"I'm sorry too," he said, trying to speak carelessly, lightly.

"She's Irian of Westpool's mare. You're the wizard, then?"

He bowed. "Ivory, of Havnor Great Port, at your service. May I—"

She interrupted. "I thought you were from Roke."

"I am," he said, his composure regained.

She stared at him with those strange eyes, as unreadable as a sheep's, he thought. Then she burst out: "You lived there? You studied there? Do you know the Archmage?"

"Yes," he said with a smile. Then he winced and stooped to press his hand against his shin for a moment.

"Are you hurt too?"

"It's nothing," he said. In fact, rather to his annoyance, the cut had stopped bleeding.

The woman's gaze returned to his face.

"What is it—what is it like—on Roke?"

Ivory went, limping only very slightly, to an old mounting block nearby and sat down on it. He stretched his leg, nursing the torn place, and looked up at the woman. "It would take a long time to tell you what Roke is like," he said. "But it would be my pleasure."

† † †

"THE MAN'S A WIZARD, OR NEARLY," SAID ROSE THE WITCH, "A Roke wizard! You must not ask him questions!" She was more than scandalized, she was frightened.

"He doesn't mind," Dragonfly reassured her. "Only he hardly ever really answers."

"Of course not!"

"Why of course not?"

"Because he's a wizard! Because you're a woman, with no art, no knowledge, no learning!"

"You could have taught me! You never would!"

Rose dismissed all she had taught or could teach with a flick of the fingers.

"Well, so I have to learn from him," said Dragonfly.

"Wizards don't teach women. You're besotted."

"You and Broom trade spells."

"Broom's a village sorcerer. This man is a wise man. He learned the High Arts at the Great House on Roke!"

"He told me what it's like," Dragonfly said. "You walk up through the town, Thwil Town. There's a door opening on the street, but it's shut. It looks like an ordinary door."

The witch listened, unable to resist the lure of secrets revealed and the contagion of passionate desire.

"And a man comes when you knock, an ordinary looking man. And he gives you a test. You have to say a certain word, a password, before he'll let you in. If you don't know it, you can never go in. But if he lets you in, then from inside you see that the door is entirely different—it's made out of horn, with a tree carved on it, and the frame is made out of a tooth, one tooth of a dragon that lived long, long before Erreth-Akbe, before Morred, before there were people in Earthsea. There were only dragons, to begin with. They found the tooth on Mount Onn, in

Havnor, at the center of the world. And the leaves of the tree are carved so thin that the light shines through them, but the door's so strong that if the Doorkeeper shuts it no spell could ever open it. And then the Doorkeeper takes you down a hall and another hall, till you're lost and bewildered, and then suddenly you come out under the sky. In the Court of the Fountain, in the very deepest inside of the Great House. And that's where the Archmage would be, if he was there . . ."

"Go on," the witch murmured.

"That's all he really told me, yet," said Dragonfly, coming back to the mild, overcast spring day and the infinite familiarity of the village lane, Rose's front yard, her own seven milch ewes grazing on Iria Hill, the bronze crowns of the oaks. "He's very careful how he talks about the Masters."

Rose nodded.

"But he told me about some of the students."

"No harm in that, I suppose."

"I don't know," Dragonfly said. "To hear about the Great House is wonderful, but I thought the people there would be—I don't know. Of course they're mostly just boys when they go there. But I thought they'd be . . ." She gazed off at the sheep on the hill, her face troubled. "Some of them are really bad and stupid," she said in a low voice. "They get into the school because they're rich. And they study there just to get richer. Or to get power."

"Well, of course they do," said Rose, "that's what they're there for!"

"But power—like you told me about—that isn't the same as making people do what you want, or pay you—"

"Isn't it?"

"No!"

"If a word can heal, a word can wound," the witch said. "If a hand can kill, a hand can cure. It's a poor cart that goes only one direction."

"But on Roke, they learn to use power well, not for harm, not for gain."

"Everything's for gain some way, I'd say. People have to live. But what do I know? I make my living doing what I know how to do. But I don't meddle with the great arts, the perilous crafts, like summoning the dead," and Rose made the hand sign to avert the danger spoken of.

"Everything's perilous," Dragonfly said, gazing now through the sheep, the hill, the trees, into still depths, a colorless, vast emptiness like the clear sky before sunrise.

Rose watched her. She knew she did not know who Irian was or what she might be. A big, strong, awkward, ignorant, innocent, angry woman, yes. But ever since Irian was a child Rose had seen something more in her, something beyond what she was. And when Irian looked away from the world like that, she seemed to enter that place or time or being beyond herself, utterly beyond Rose's knowledge. Then Rose feared her, and feared for her.

"You take care," the witch said, grim. "Everything's perilous, right enough, and meddling with wizards most of all."

Through love, respect, and trust, Dragonfly would never disregard a warning from Rose; but she was unable to see Ivory as perilous. She didn't understand him, but the idea of fearing him, him personally, was not one she could keep in mind. She tried to be respectful, but it was impossible. She thought he was clever and quite handsome, but she didn't think much about him, except for what he could tell her. He knew what she wanted to know and little by little he told it to her, and then it was not really what she had wanted to know, but she wanted to know more. He was patient with her, and she was grateful to him for his patience, knowing he was much quicker than she. Sometimes he smiled at her ignorance, but he never sneered at it or reproved it. Like the witch, he liked to answer a question with a question; but the answers to Rose's questions were always something she'd always known, while the answers to his questions were things she had never imagined and found startling, unwelcome, even painful, altering her beliefs.

Day by day, as they talked in the old stableyard of Iria, where they had fallen into the habit of meeting, she asked him and he told her more, though reluctantly, always partially; he shielded his Masters, she thought, trying to defend the bright image of Roke, until one day he gave in to her insistence and spoke freely at last.

"There are good men there," he said. "Great and wise the Archmage certainly was. But he's gone. And the Masters . . . Some hold aloof, following arcane knowledge, seeking ever more patterns, ever more names, but using their knowledge for nothing. Others hide their ambition under the grey cloak of wisdom. Roke is no longer where power is in Earthsea. That's the Court in Havnor, now. Roke lives on its great past, defended by a thousand spells against the present day. And inside those spell-walls, what is there? Quarreling ambitions, fear of anything new, fear of young men who challenge the power of the old. And at the center, nothing. An empty courtyard. The Archmage will never return."

"How do you know?" she whispered.

He looked stern. "The dragon bore him away."

"You saw it? You saw that?" She clenched her hands, imagining that flight, not even hearing his reply.

After a long time, she came back to the sunlight and the stableyard and her thoughts and puzzles. "But even if he's gone," she said, "surely some of the Masters are truly wise?"

When he looked up and spoke it was with reluctance, with a hint of a melancholy smile. "All the mystery and wisdom of the Masters, when it's out in the daylight, doesn't amount to so much, you know. Tricks of the trade—wonderful illusions. But people don't want to know that. They want the illusions, the mysteries. Who can blame them? There's so little in life that's beautiful or worthy."

As if to illustrate what he was saying, he had picked up a bit of brick from the broken pavement, and tossed it up in the air, and as he spoke it fluttered about their heads on delicate blue wings, a butterfly. He put out his finger and the butterfly lighted on it. He shook his finger and the butterfly fell to the ground, a fragment of brick.

"There's not much worth much in my life," she said, gazing down at the pavement. "All I know how to do is run the farm, and try to stand up and speak truth. But if I thought it was all tricks and lies even on Roke, I'd hate those men for fooling me, fooling us all. It can't be lies. Not all of it. The Archmage did go into the labyrinth among the Hoary Men and come back with the Ring of Peace. He did go into death with the young king, and defeat the spider mage, and come back. We know that on the word of the King himself. Even here, the harpers came to sing that song, and a teller came to tell it."

Ivory nodded. "But the Archmage lost all his power in the land of death. Maybe all magery was weakened then."

"Rose's spells work as well as ever," she said stoutly.

Ivory smiled. He said nothing, but she saw how petty the doings of a village witch appeared to him, who had seen great deeds and powers. She sighed and spoke from her heart—"Oh, if only I wasn't a woman!"

He smiled again. "You're a beautiful woman," he said, but plainly, not in the flattering way he had used with her at first, before she showed him she hated it. "Why would you be a man?"

"So I could go to Roke! And see, and learn! Why, why is it only men can go there?"

"So it was ordained by the first Archmage, centuries ago," said Ivory. "But . . . I too have wondered."

"You have?"

"Often. Seeing only boys and men, day after day, in the Great House and all the precincts of the school. Knowing that the townswomen are spell-bound from so much as setting foot on the fields about Roke Knoll. Once in years, perhaps, some great lady is allowed to come briefly into the outer courts . . . Why is it so? Are all women incapable of under-standing? Or is it that the Masters fear them, fear to be corrupted—No, but fear that to admit women might change the rule they cling to—the purity of that rule—"

"Women can live chaste as well as men can," Dragonfly said bluntly. She knew she was blunt and coarse where he was delicate and subtle, but she did not know any other way to be.

"Of course," he said, his smile growing brilliant. "But witches aren't always chaste, are they? . . . Maybe that's what the Masters are afraid of. Maybe celibacy isn't as necessary as the Rule of Roke teaches. Maybe it's not a way of keeping the power pure, but of keeping the power to themselves. Leaving out women, leaving out everybody who won't agree to turn himself into a eunuch to get that one kind of power . . . Who knows? A she-mage! Now that would change everything, all the rules!"

She could see his mind dance ahead of hers, taking up and playing with ideas, transforming them as he had transformed brick into butterfly. She could not dance with him, she could not play with him, but she watched him in wonder.

"You could go to Roke," he said, his eyes bright with excitement, mischief, daring. Meeting her almost pleading, incredulous silence, he insisted—"You could. A woman you are, but there are ways to change your seeming. You have the heart, the courage, the will of a man. You could enter the Great House. I know it."

"And what would I do there?"

"What all the students do. Live alone in a stone cell and learn to be wise! It might not be what you dream it to be, but that, too, you'd learn."

"I couldn't. They'd know. I couldn't even get in. There's the Doorkeeper, you said. I don't know the word to say to him."

"The password, yes. But I can teach it to you."

"You can? Is it allowed?"

"I don't care what's 'allowed,'" he said, with a frown she had never seen on his face. "The Archmage himself said, *Rules are made to be broken.* Injustice makes the rules, and courage breaks them. I have the courage, if you do!"

She looked at him. She could not speak. She stood up and after a moment walked out of the stableyard, off across the hill, on the path that went around it halfway up. One of the dogs, her favorite, a big, ugly, heavy-headed hound, followed her. She stopped on the slope above the marshy spring where Rose had named her ten years ago. She stood there. The dog sat down beside her and looked up at her face. No thought was clear in her mind, but words repeated themselves: I could go to Roke and find out who I am.

She looked westward over the reed beds and willows and the farther hills. The whole western sky was empty, clear. She stood still and her soul seemed to go into that sky and be gone, gone out of her.

There was a little noise, the soft clip-clop of the black mare's hoofs, coming along the lane. Then Dragonfly came back to herself and called to Ivory and ran down the hill to meet him. "I will go," she said.

HE HAD NOT PLANNED OR INTENDED ANY SUCH ADVENTURE, but crazy as it was, it suited him better the more he thought about it. The prospect of spending the long grey winter at Westpool sank his spirits like a stone. There was nothing here for him except the girl Dragonfly, who had come to fill his thoughts. Her massive, innocent strength had defeated him absolutely so far, but he did what she pleased in order to have her do at last what he pleased, and the game, he thought, was worth playing. If she ran away with him, the game was as good as won. As for the joke of it, the notion of actually getting her into the school on Roke disguised as a man, there was little chance of pulling it off, but it pleased him as a gesture of disrespect to all the piety and pomposity of the Masters and their toadies. And if somehow it succeeded, if he could actually get a woman through that door, even for a moment, what a sweet revenge it would be!

Money was a problem. The girl thought, of course, that he as a great wizard would snap his fingers and waft them over the sea in a magic boat flying before the magewind. But when he told her they'd have to hire passage on a ship, she said simply, "I have the cheese money."

He treasured her rustic sayings of that kind. Sometimes she frightened him, and he resented it. His dreams of her were never of her yielding to him, but of himself yielding to a fierce, destroying sweetness, sinking into an annihilating embrace, dreams in which she was something beyond comprehension and he was nothing at all. He woke from those dreams shaken and shamed. In daylight, when he saw her big, dirty hands, when she talked like a yokel, a simpleton, he regained his superiority. He only wished there were someone to repeat her sayings to, one of his old friends in the Great Port who would find them amusing. "I have the cheese money," he repeated to himself, riding back to Westpool, and laughed. "I do indeed," he said aloud. The black mare flicked her ear.

He told Birch that he had received a sending from his teacher on Roke, the Master Hand, and must go at once, on what business he could not say, of course, but it should not take long once he was there; a half month to go, another to return; he would be back well before the Fallows at the latest. He must ask Master Birch to provide him an advance on his salary to pay for ship passage and lodging, since a wizard of Roke should not take advantage of people's willingness to give him whatever he needed, but pay his way like an ordinary man. As Birch agreed with this, he had to give Ivory a purse for his journey, the first real money he had had in his pocket for years: ten ivory counters carved with the Otter of Shelieth on one side and the Rune of Peace on the other in honor of King Lebannen. "Hello, little namesakes," he told them when he was alone with them. "You and the cheese money will get along nicely."

He told Dragonfly very little of his plans, largely because he made few, trusting to chance and his own wits, which seldom let him down if he was given a fair chance to use them. The girl asked almost no questions. "Will I go as a man all the way?" was one.

"Yes," he said, "but only disguised. I won't put a semblance spell on you till we're on Roke Island."

"I thought it would be a spell of change," she said.

"That would be unwise," he said, with a good imitation of the Master Changer's terse solemnity. "If need be, I'll do it, of course. But you'll find wizards very sparing of the great spells. For good reason."

"The Equilibrium," she said, accepting all he said in its simplest sense, as always.

"And perhaps because such arts have not the power they once had," he said. He did not know himself why he tried to weaken her faith in wizardry; perhaps because any weakening of her strength, her wholeness, was a gain for him. He had begun merely by trying to get her into his bed, a game he loved to play. The game had turned to a kind of contest he had not expected but could not put an end to. He was determined now not to win her, but to defeat her. He could not let her defeat him. He must prove to her and himself that his dreams were meaningless.

Quite early on, impatient with wooing her massive physical indifference, he had worked up a charm, a sorcerer's seduction spell of which he was contemptuous even as he made it, though he knew it was effective. He cast it on her while she was, characteristically, mending a cow's halter. The result had not been the melting eagerness it had produced in girls he had used it on in Havnor and Thwil. Dragonfly had gradually become silent and sullen. She ceased asking her endless questions about Roke and did not answer when he spoke. When he very tentatively approached her, taking her hand, she struck him away with a blow to the head that left him dizzy. He saw her stand up and stride out of the stableyard without a word, the ugly hound she favored trotting after her. The hound looked back at him with a grin.

She took the path to the old house. When his ears stopped ringing he stole after her, hoping the charm was working and that this was only her particularly uncouth way of leading him at last to her bed. Nearing the house, he heard crockery breaking. The father, the drunkard, came wobbling out looking scared and confused, followed by Dragonfly's loud, harsh voice—"Out of the house, you drunken, crawling traitor! You foul, shameless lecher!"

"She took my cup away," the Master of Iria said to the stranger, whining like a puppy, while his dogs yammered around him. "She broke it."

Ivory departed. He did not return for two days. On the third day he rode experimentally past Old Iria, and she came striding down to meet him. "I'm sorry, Ivory," she said, looking up at him with her smoky orange eyes. "I don't know what came over me the other day. I was angry. But not at you. I beg your pardon."

He forgave her gracefully. He did not try a love charm on her again.

Soon, he thought now, he would not need one. He would have real power over her. He had finally seen how to get it. She had given it into his hands. Her strength and her willpower were tremendous, but fortunately she was stupid, and he was not.

Birch was sending a carter down to Kembermouth with six barrels of ten-year-old Fanian ordered by the wine merchant there. He was glad to send his wizard along as bodyguard, for the wine was valuable, and though the young king was putting things to rights as fast as he could, there were still gangs of robbers on the roads. So Ivory left Westpool on the big wagon pulled by four big cart horses, jolting slowly along, his legs dangling. Down by Jackass Hill an uncouth figure rose up from the wayside and asked the carter for a lift. "I don't know you," the carter said, lifting his whip to warn the stranger off, but Ivory came round the wagon and said, "Let the lad ride, my good man. He'll do no harm while I'm with you."

"Keep an eye on him then, master," said the carter.

"I will," said Ivory, with a wink at Dragonfly. She, well disguised in dirt and a farmhand's old smock and leggings and a loathsome felt hat, did not wink back. She played her part even while they sat side by side dangling their legs over the tailgate, with six great halftuns of wine jolting between them and the drowsy carter, and the drowsy summer hills and fields slipping slowly, slowly past. Ivory tried to tease her, but she only shook her head. Maybe she was scared by this wild scheme, now she was embarked on it. There was no telling. She was solemnly, heavily silent. I could be very bored by this woman, Ivory thought, if once I'd had her underneath me. That thought stirred him almost unbearably, but when he looked back at her, his desire died away before her massive, actual presence.

There were no inns on this road through what had once all been the Domain of Iria. As the sun neared the western plains, they stopped at a farmhouse that offered stabling for the horses, a shed for the cart, and straw in the stable loft for the carters. The loft was dark and stuffy and the straw musty. Ivory felt no lust at all, though Dragonfly lay not three feet from him. She had played the man so thoroughly all day that she had half convinced even him. Maybe she'll fool the old men after all! he thought. He grinned at the thought, and slept.

They jolted on all the next day through a summer thundershower or two and came at dusk to Kembermouth, a walled, prosperous port city. They left the carter to his master's business and walked down to find an inn near the docks. Dragonfly looked about at the sights of the city in a silence that might have been awe or disapproval or mere stolidity. "This is a nice little town," Ivory said, "but the only city in the world is Havnor."

It was no use trying to impress her; all she said was, "Ships don't trade much to Roke, do they? Will it take a long time to find one to take us, do you think?"

"Not if I carry a staff," he said.

She stopped looking about and strode along in thought for a while.

She was beautiful in movement, bold and graceful, her head carried high.

"You mean they'll oblige a wizard? But you aren't a wizard."

"That's a formality. We senior sorcerers may carry a staff when we're on Roke's business. Which I am."

"Taking *me* there?"

"Bringing them a student—yes. A student of great gifts!"

She asked no more questions. She never argued; it was one of her virtues.

That night, over supper at the waterfront inn, she asked with unusual timidity in her voice, "Do I have great gifts?"

"In my judgment, you do," he said.

She pondered—conversation with her was often a slow business—and said, "Rose always said I had power, but she didn't know what kind. And I . . . I know I do, but I don't know what it is."

"You're going to Roke to find out," he said, raising his glass to her. After a moment she raised hers and smiled at him, a smile so tender and radiant that he said spontaneously, "And may what you find be all you seek!"

"If I do, it will be thanks to you," she said. In that moment he loved her for her true heart, and would have foresworn any thought of her but as his companion in a bold adventure, a gallant joke.

They had to share a room at the crowded inn with two other travelers, but Ivory's thoughts were perfectly chaste, though he laughed at himself a little for it.

Next morning he picked a sprig of an herb from the kitchen garden of the inn and spelled it into the semblance of a fine staff, copper-shod and his own height exactly. "What is the wood?" Dragonfly asked, fascinated, when she saw it, and when he answered with a laugh, "Rosemary," she laughed too.

They set off along the wharves, asking for a ship bound south that might take a wizard and his prentice to the Isle of the Wise, and soon enough they found a heavy trader bound for Wathort, whose master would carry the wizard for goodwill and the prentice for half price. Even half price was half the cheese money; but they would have the luxury of a cabin, for *Sea Otter* was a decked, two-masted ship.

As they were talking with her master a wagon drew up on the dock and began to unload six familiar halftun barrels. "That's ours," Ivory said, and the ship's master said, "Bound for Hort Town," and Dragonfly said softly, "From Iria."

She glanced back at the land then. It was the only time he ever saw her look back.

The ship's weatherworker came aboard just before they sailed, no Roke wizard but a weatherbeaten fellow in a worn sea cloak. Ivory flourished his staff a little in greeting him. The sorcerer looked him up and down and said, "One man works weather on this ship. If it's not me, I'm off."

"I'm a mere passenger, Master Bagman. I gladly leave the winds in your hands."

The sorcerer looked at Dragonfly, who stood straight as a tree and said nothing.

"Good," he said, and that was the last word he spoke to Ivory.

During the voyage, however, he talked several times with Dragonfly, which made Ivory a bit uneasy. Her ignorance and trustfulness could endanger her and therefore him. What did she and the bagman talk about? he asked, and she answered, "What is to become of us."

He stared.

"Of all of us. Of Way and Felkway, and Havnor, and Wathort, and Roke. All the people of the islands. He says that when King Lebannen was to be crowned, last autumn, he sent to Gont for the old Archmage to come crown him, and he wouldn't come. And there was no new Archmage. So the King put on his crown himself. And some say that's wrong, and he doesn't rightly hold the throne. But others say the King himself is the new Archmage. But he isn't a wizard, only a king. So others say the dark years will come again, when there was no rule of justice, and wizardry was used for evil ends."

After a pause Ivory said, "That old weatherworker says all this?"

"It's common talk, I think," said Dragonfly, with her grave simplicity.

The weatherworker knew his trade, at least. *Sea Otter* sped south; they met summer squalls and choppy seas, but never a storm or a troublesome wind. They put off and took on cargo at ports on the north shore of O, at Ilien, Leng, Kamery, and O Port, and then headed west to carry the passengers to Roke. And facing the west Ivory felt a little hollow at the pit of his stomach, for he knew all too well how Roke was guarded. He knew neither he nor the weatherworker could do anything at all to turn the Roke wind if it blew against them. And if it did, Dragonfly would ask why? why did it blow against them?

He was glad to see the sorcerer uneasy too, standing by the helmsman, keeping a watch up on the masthead, taking in sail at the hint of a west wind. But the wind held steady from the north. A thunder squall came pelting on that wind, and Ivory went down to the cabin, but Dragonfly stayed up on deck. She was afraid of the water, she had told him. She could not swim; she said, "Drowning must be a horrible thing—Not to breathe the air—" She had shuddered at the thought. It was the only fear she had ever shown of anything. But she disliked the low, cramped cabin, and had stayed on deck every day and slept there on the warm nights. Ivory had not tried to coax her into the cabin. He knew now that coaxing was no good. To have her he must master her; and that he would do, if only they could come to Roke.

He came up on deck again. It was clearing, and as the sun set, the clouds broke all across the west, showing a golden sky behind the high dark curve of a hill.

Ivory looked at that hill with a kind of longing hatred.

"That's Roke Knoll, lad," the weatherworker said to Dragonfly, who stood beside him at the rail. "We're coming into Thwil Bay now. Where there's no wind but the wind they want."

By the time they were well into the bay and had let down the anchor it was dark, and Ivory said to the ship's master, "I'll go ashore in the morning."

Down in their tiny cabin Dragonfly sat waiting for him, solemn as ever but her eyes blazing with excitement. "We'll go ashore in the morning," he repeated to her, and she nodded, acceptant.

She said, "Do I look all right?"

He sat down on his narrow bunk and looked at her sitting on her narrow bunk; they could not face each other directly, as there was no room for their knees. At O Port she had bought herself a decent shirt and breeches, at his suggestion, so as to look a more probable candidate for the school. Her face was windburnt and scrubbed clean. Her hair was braided and the braid clubbed, like Ivory's. She had got her hands clean too, and they lay flat on her thighs, long strong hands, like a man's.

"You don't look like a man," he said. Her face fell. "Not to me. You'll never look like a man to me. But don't worry. You will to them."

She nodded, with an anxious face.

"The first test is the great test, Dragonfly," he said. Every night as he lay alone in this cabin he had planned this conversation. "To enter the Great House. To go through that door."

"I've been thinking about it," she said, hurried and earnest. "Couldn't I just tell them who I am? With you there to vouch for me—to say even if I am a woman, I have some gift—and I'd promise to take the vow and make the spell of celibacy, and live apart if they wanted me to—"

He was shaking his head all through her speech. "No, no, no, no. Hopeless. Useless. Fatal!"

"Even if you—"

"Even if I argued for you. They won't listen. The Rule of Roke forbids women to be taught any high art, any word of the Language of the Making. It's always been so. They will not listen. So they must be shown! And we'll show them, you and I. We'll teach them. You must have courage, Dragonfly. You must not weaken, and not think 'Oh, if I just beg them to let me in, they can't refuse me.' They can, and will. And if you reveal yourself, they will punish you. And me." He put a ponderous emphasis on the last word, and inwardly murmured, "Avert."

She gazed at him from her unreadable eyes, and finally asked, "What must I do?"

"Do you trust me, Dragonfly?"

"Yes."

"Will you trust me entirely, wholly—knowing that the risk I take for you is greater even than your risk in this venture?"

"Yes."

"Then you must tell me the word you will speak to the Doorkeeper."

She stared. "But I thought you'd tell it to me—the password."

"The password he will ask you for is your true name."

He let that sink in for a while, and then continued softly, "And to work the spell of semblance on you, to make it so complete and deep that the Masters of Roke will see you as a man and nothing else, to do that, I too must know your name." He paused again. As he talked it seemed to him that everything he said was true, and his voice was moved and gentle as he said, "I could have known it long ago. But I chose not to use those arts. I wanted you to trust me enough to tell me your name yourself."

She was looking down at her hands, clasped now on her knees. In the faint reddish glow of the cabin lantern her lashes cast very delicate, long shadows on her cheeks. She looked up, straight at him. "My name is Irian," she said.

He smiled. She did not smile.

He said nothing. In fact he was at a loss. If he had known it would be this easy, he could have had her name and with it the power to make her do whatever he wanted, days ago, weeks ago, with a mere pretense at this crazy scheme—without giving up his salary and his precarious respectability, without this sea voyage, without having to go all the way to Roke for it! For he saw the whole plan now was folly. There was no way he could disguise her that would fool the Doorkeeper for a moment. All his notions of humiliating the Masters as they had humiliated him were moonshine. Obsessed with tricking the girl, he had fallen into the trap he laid for her. Bitterly he recognised that he was always believing his own lies, caught in nets he had elaborately woven. Having once made a fool of himself on Roke, he had come back to do it all over again. A great, desolate anger swelled up in him. There was no good, no good in anything.

"What's wrong?" she asked. The gentleness of her deep, husky voice unmanned him, and he hid his face in his hands, fighting against the shame of tears.

She put her hand on his knee. It was the first time she had ever touched him. He endured it, the warmth and weight of her touch that he had wasted so much time wanting.

He wanted to hurt her, to shock her out of her terrible, ignorant kindness, but what he said when he finally spoke was "I only wanted to make love to you."

"You did?"

"Did you think I was one of their eunuchs? That I'd castrate myself with spells so I could be holy? Why do you think I don't have a staff? Why do you think I'm not at the school? Did you believe everything I said?"

"Yes," she said. "I'm sorry." Her hand was still on his knee. She said, "We can make love if you want."

He sat up, sat still.

"What are you?" he said to her at last.

"I don't know. It's why I wanted to come to Roke. To find out."

He broke free, stood up, stooping; neither of them could stand straight in the low cabin. Clenching and unclenching his hands, he stood as far from her as he could, his back to her.

"You won't find out. It's all lies, shams. Old men playing games with words. I wouldn't play their games, so I left. Do you know what I did?" He turned, showing his teeth in a rictus of triumph. "I got a girl, a town girl, to come to my room. My cell. My little stone celibate cell. It had a window looking out on a back street. No spells—you can't make spells with all their magic going on. But she wanted to come, and came, and I let a rope ladder out the window, and she climbed it. And we were at it when the old men came in! I showed 'em! And if I could have got you in, I'd have showed 'em again, I'd have taught them *their* lesson!"

"Well, I'll try," she said.

He stared.

"Not for the same reasons as you," she said, "but I still want to. And we came all this way. And you know my name."

It was true. He knew her name: Irian. It was like a coal of fire, a burning ember in his mind. His thought could not hold it. His knowledge could not use it. His tongue could not say it.

She looked up at him, her sharp, strong face softened by the shadowy lantern light. "If it was only to make love you brought me here, Ivory," she said, "we can do that. If you still want to."

Wordless at first, he simply shook his head. After a while he was able to laugh. "I think we've gone on past . . . that possibility . . ."

She looked at him without regret, or reproach, or shame.

"Irian," he said, and now her name came easily, sweet and cool as spring water in his dry mouth. "Irian, here's what you must do to enter the Great House . . ."

III. Azver

HE LEFT HER AT THE CORNER OF THE STREET, A NARROW, DULL, somehow sly-looking street that slanted up between featureless walls to a wooden door in a higher wall. He had put his spell on her, and she looked like a man, though she did not feel like one. She and Ivory took each other in their arms, because after all they had been friends, companions, and he had done all this for her. "Courage!" he said, and let her go. She walked up the street and stood before the door. She looked back then, but he was gone.

She knocked.

After a while she heard the latch rattle. The door opened. A middle-aged man stood there. "What can I do for you?" he said. He did not smile, but his voice was pleasant.

"You can let me into the Great House, sir."

"Do you know the way in?" His almond-shaped eyes were attentive, yet seemed to look at her from miles or years away.

"This is the way in, sir."

"Do you know whose name you must tell me before I let you in?"

"My own, sir. It is Irian."

"Is it?" he said.

That gave her pause. She stood silent. "It's the name the witch Rose of my village on Way gave me, in the spring under Iria Hill," she said at last, standing up and speaking truth.

The Doorkeeper looked at her for what seemed a long time. "Then it is your name," he said. "But maybe not all your name. I think you have another."

"I don't know it, sir."

After another long time she said, "Maybe I can learn it here, sir."

The Doorkeeper bowed his head a little. A very faint smile made crescent curves in his cheeks. He stood aside. "Come in, daughter," he said.

She stepped across the threshold of the Great House.

Ivory's spell of semblance dropped away like a cobweb. She was and looked herself.

She followed the Doorkeeper down a stone passageway. Only at the end of it did she think to turn back to see the light shine through the thousand leaves of the tree carved in the high door in its bone-white frame.

A young man in a grey cloak hurrying down the passageway stopped short as he approached them. He stared at Irian; then with a brief nod he went on. She looked back at him. He was looking back at her.

A globe of misty, greenish fire drifted swiftly down the corridor at eye level, apparently pursuing the young man. The Doorkeeper waved his hand at it, and it avoided him. Irian swerved and ducked down frantically, but felt the cool fire tingle in her hair as it passed over her. The Doorkeeper glanced round, and now his smile was wider. Though he said nothing, she felt he was aware of her, concerned for her. She stood up and followed him.

He stopped before an oak door. Instead of knocking he sketched a little sign or rune on it with the top of his staff, a light staff of some greyish wood. The door opened as a resonant voice behind it said, "Come in!"

"Wait here a little, if you please, Irian," the Doorkeeper said, and went into the room, leaving the door wide open behind him. She could see bookshelves and books, a table piled with more books and ink pots and writings, two or three boys seated at the table, and the grey-haired, stocky man the Doorkeeper spoke to. She saw the man's face change, saw his eyes shift to her in a brief, startled gaze, saw him question the Doorkeeper, low-voiced, intense.

They both came to her. "The Master Changer of Roke: Irian of Way," said the Doorkeeper.

The Changer stared openly at her. He was not as tall as she was. He stared at the Doorkeeper, and then at her again.

"Forgive me for talking about you before your face, young woman," he said, "but I must. Master Doorkeeper, you know I'd never question your judgment, but the Rule is clear. I have to ask what moved you to break it and let her come in."

"She asked to," said the Doorkeeper.

"But—" The Changer paused.

"When did a woman last ask to enter the school?"

"They know the Rule doesn't allow them."

"Did you know that, Irian?" the Doorkeeper asked her, and she said, "Yes, sir."

"So what brought you here?" the Changer asked, stern, but not hiding his curiosity.

"Master Ivory said I could pass for a man. Though I thought I should say who I was. I will be as celibate as anyone, sir."

Two long curves appeared on the Doorkeeper's cheeks, enclosing the slow upturn of his smile. The Changer's face remained stern, but he blinked, and after a little thought said, "I'm sure—yes—It was definitely the better plan to be honest. What Master did you speak of?"

"Ivory," said the Doorkeeper. "A lad from Havnor Great Port, whom I let in three years ago, and let out again last year, as you may recall."

"Ivory! That fellow that studied with the Hand?—Is he here?" the Changer demanded of Irian, wrathily. She stood straight and said nothing.

"Not in the school," the Doorkeeper said, smiling.

"He fooled you, young woman. Made a fool of you by trying to make fools of us."

"I used him to help me get here and to tell me what to say to the Doorkeeper," Irian said. "I'm not here to fool anybody, but to learn what I need to know."

"I've often wondered why I let that boy in," said the Doorkeeper. "Now I begin to understand."

At that the Changer looked at him, and after pondering said soberly, "Doorkeeper, what have you in mind?"

"I think Irian of Way may have come to us seeking not only what she needs to know, but also what we need to know." The Doorkeeper's tone was equally sober, and his smile was gone. "I think this may be a matter for talk among the nine of us."

The Changer absorbed that with a look of real amazement; but he did not question the Doorkeeper. He said only, "But not among the students."

The Doorkeeper shook his head, agreeing.

"She can lodge in the town," the Changer said, with some relief.

"While we talk behind her back?"

"You won't bring her into the Council Room?" the Changer said in disbelief.

"The Archmage brought the boy Arren there."

"But—But Arren was King Lebannen—"

"And who is Irian?"

The Changer stood silent, and then he said quietly, with respect, "My friend, what is it you think to do, to learn? What is she, that you ask this for her?"

"Who are we," said the Doorkeeper, "that we refuse her without knowing what she is?"

"A WOMAN," SAID THE MASTER SUMMONER.

Irian had waited some hours in the Doorkeeper's chamber, a low, light, bare room with a window seat at a small-paned window looking out on the kitchen gardens of the Great House—handsome, well-kept gardens, long rows and beds of vegetables, greens, and herbs, with berry canes and fruit trees beyond. She saw a burly, dark-skinned man and two boys come out and weed one of the vegetable plots. It eased her mind to watch their careful work. She wished she could help them at it. The waiting and the strangeness were very difficult. Once the Doorkeeper came in, bringing her a mug of water and a plate with cold meat and bread and scallions, and she ate because he told her to eat, but chewing and swallowing were hard work. The gardeners went away and there was nothing to watch out the window but the cabbages growing and the sparrows hopping, and now and then a hawk far up in the sky, and the wind moving softly in the tops of tall trees, on beyond the gardens.

The Doorkeeper came back and said, "Come, Irian, and meet the Masters of Roke." Her heart began to go at a cart-horse gallop. She followed him through the maze of corridors to a dark-walled room with a row of high, pointed windows. A group of men stood there. Every one of them turned to look at her as she came into the room.

"Irian of Way, my lords," said the Doorkeeper. They were all silent. He motioned her to come farther into the room. "The Master Changer you have met," he said to her. He named all the others, but she could not take in their names and masteries, except that the Master Herbal was the one she had supposed to be a gardener, and the youngest of them, a tall man with a stern, beautiful face that seemed carved out of dark stone, was the Master Summoner. It was he who spoke when the Doorkeeper was done. "A woman," he said.

The Doorkeeper nodded once, mild as ever.

"This is what you brought the Nine together for? This and no more?"

"This and no more," said the Doorkeeper.

"Dragons have been seen flying above the Inmost Sea. Roke has no archmage, and the islands no true-crowned king. There is real work to do," the Summoner said, and his voice too was like stone, cold and heavy. "When will we do it?"

There was an uncomfortable silence, as the Doorkeeper did not speak. At last a slight, bright-eyed man who wore a red tunic under his grey wizard's cloak said, "Do you bring this woman into the House as a student, Master Doorkeeper?"

"If I did, it would be up to you all to approve or disapprove," said he.

"Do you?" asked the man in the red tunic, smiling a little.

"Master Hand," said the Doorkeeper, "she asked to enter as a student, and I saw no reason to deny her."

"Every reason," said the Summoner.

A man with a deep, clear voice spoke: "It's not our judgment that prevails, but the Rule of Roke, which we are sworn to follow."

"I doubt the Doorkeeper would defy it lightly," said one whom Irian had not noticed till he spoke, though he was a big man, white-haired, rawboned, and crag-faced. Unlike the others, he looked at her as he spoke. "I am Kurremkarmerruk," he said to her. "As the Master Namer here, I make free with names, my own included. Who named you, Irian?"

"The witch Rose of our village, lord," she answered, standing straight, though her voice came out high-pitched and rough.

"Is she misnamed?" the Doorkeeper asked the Namer.

Kurremkarmerruk shook his head. "No. But . . ."

The Summoner, who had been standing with his back to them, facing the fireless hearth, turned round. "The names witches give each other are not our concern here," he said. "If you have some interest in this woman, Doorkeeper, it should be pursued outside these walls—outside the door you vowed to keep. She has no place here nor ever will. She can bring only confusion, dissension, and further weakness among us. I will speak no longer and say nothing else in her presence. The only answer to conscious error is silence."

"Silence is not enough, my lord," said one who had not spoken before. To Irian's eyes he was very strange-looking, having pale reddish skin, long pale hair, and narrow eyes the color of ice. His speech was also strange, stiff and somehow deformed. "Silence is the answer to everything, and to nothing," he said.

The Summoner lifted his noble, dark face and looked across the room at the pale man, but did not speak. Without a word or gesture he turned away again and left the room. As he walked slowly past Irian, she shrank back from him. It was as if a grave had opened, a winter grave, cold, wet, dark. Her breath stuck in her throat. She gasped a little for air. When she recovered herself, she saw the Changer and the pale man both watching her intently.

The one with a voice like a deep-toned bell looked at her too, and spoke to her with a plain, kind severity. "As I see it, the man who brought you here meant to do harm, but you do not. Yet being here, Irian, you do us and yourself harm. Everything not in its own place does harm. A note sung, however well sung, wrecks the tune it isn't part of. Women teach women. Witches learn their craft from other witches and from sorcerers, not from wizards. What we teach here is in a language not for women's tongues. The young heart rebels against such laws, calling them unjust, arbitrary. But they are true laws, founded not on what we want, but on what is. The just and the unjust, the foolish and the wise, all must obey them, or waste life and come to grief."

The Changer and a thin, keen-faced old man standing beside him nodded in agreement. The Master Hand said, "Irian, I am sorry. Ivory was my pupil. If I taught him badly, I did worse in sending him away. I thought him insignificant, and so harmless. But he lied to you and beguiled you. You must not feel shame. The fault was his and mine."

"I am not ashamed," Irian said. She looked at them all. She felt that she should thank them for their courtesy but the words would not come. She nodded stiffly to them, turned round, and strode out of the room.

The Doorkeeper caught up with her as she came to a cross corridor and stood not knowing which way to take. "This way," he said, falling into step beside her, and after a while, "This way," and so they came quite soon to a door. It was not made of horn and ivory. It was uncarved oak, black and massive, with an iron bolt worn thin with age. "This is the garden door," the mage said, unbolting it. "Medra's Gate, they used to call it. I keep both doors." He opened it. The brightness of the day dazzled Irian's eyes. When she could see clearly she saw a path leading from the door through the gardens and the fields beyond them; on past the fields were the high trees, and the swell of Roke Knoll was off to the right. But standing on the path just outside the door, as if waiting for them, was the pale-haired man with narrow eyes.

"Patterner," said the Doorkeeper, not at all surprised.

"Where do you send this lady?" said the Patterner in his strange speech.

"Nowhere," said the Doorkeeper. "I let her out as I let her in, at her desire."

"Will you come with me?" the Patterner said to Irian.

She looked at him and at the Doorkeeper and said nothing.

"I don't live in this House. In any house," the Patterner said. "I live there. The Grove.—Ah," he said, turning suddenly. The big, white-haired man, Kurremkarmerruk the Namer, was standing just down the path. He had not been standing there until the other mage said "Ah." Irian stared from one to the other in blank bewilderment.

"This is only a seeming of me, a presentment, a sending," the old man said to her. "I don't live here either. Miles off." He gestured northward. "You might come there when you're done with the Patterner here. I'd like to learn more about your name." He nodded to the other two mages and was not there. A bumblebee buzzed heavily through the air where he had been.

Irian looked down at the ground. After a long time she said, clearing her throat, not looking up, "Is it true I do harm being here?"

"I don't know," said the Doorkeeper.

"In the Grove is no harm," said the Patterner. "Come on. There is an old house, a hut. Old, dirty. You don't care, eh? Stay a while. You can see." And he set off down the path between the parsley and the bush beans. She looked at the Doorkeeper; he smiled a little. She followed the pale-haired man.

They walked a half mile or so. The round-topped knoll rose up full in the western sun on their right. Behind them the school sprawled grey and many-roofed on its lower hill. The grove of trees towered before them now. She saw oak and willow, chestnut and ash, and tall evergreens. From the dense, sun-shot darkness of the trees a stream ran out, green-banked, with many brown trodden places where cattle and sheep went down to drink or to cross over. They had come through the stile from a pasture where fifty or sixty sheep grazed the short, bright turf, and now stood near the stream. "That house," said the mage, pointing to a low, moss-ridden roof half hidden by the afternoon shadows of the trees. "Stay tonight. You will?"

He asked her to stay, he did not tell her to. All she could do was nod.

"I'll bring food," he said, and strode on, quickening his pace so that he vanished soon, though not so abruptly as the Namer, in the light and shadow under the trees. Irian watched till he was certainly gone and then made her way through high grass and weeds to the little house.

It looked very old. It had been rebuilt and rebuilt again, but not for a long time. Nor had anyone lived in it for a long time, from the still, lonesome air of it. Yet it had a pleasant air, as if those who had slept there slept peacefully. As for decrepit walls, mice, dust, cobwebs, and scant furniture, all that was quite homelike to Irian. She found a bald broom and swept out the mouse droppings. She unrolled her blanket on the plank bed. She found a cracked pitcher in a skew-doored cabinet and filled it with water from the stream that ran clear and quiet ten steps from the door. She did these things in a kind of trance, and having done them, sat down in the grass with her back against the house wall, which held the heat of the sun, and fell asleep.

When she woke, the Master Patterner was sitting nearby, and a basket was on the grass between them.

"Hungry? Eat," he said.

"I'll eat later, sir. Thank you," said Irian.

"I am hungry now," said the mage. He took a hard-boiled egg from the basket, cracked, shelled, and ate it.

"They call this the Otter's House," he said. "Very old. As old as the Great House. Everything is old, here. We are old—the Masters."

"You're not very," Irian said. She thought him between thirty and forty, though it was hard to tell; she kept thinking his hair was white, because it was not black.

"But I came far. Miles can be years. I am Kargish, from Karego. You know?"

"The Hoary Men!" said Irian, staring openly at him. All Daisy's ballads of the Hoary Men who sailed out of the East to lay the land waste and spit innocent babes on their lances, and the story of how Erreth-Akbe lost the Ring of Peace, and the new songs and the King's Tale about how Archmage Sparrowhawk had gone among the Hoary Men and come back with that ring—

"Hoary?" said the Patterner.

"Frosty. White," she said, looking away, embarrassed.

"Ah." Presently he said, "The Master Summoner is not old." And she got a sidelong look from those narrow, ice-colored eyes.

She said nothing.

"I think you feared him."

She nodded.

When she said nothing, and some time had passed, he said, "In the shadow of these trees is no harm. Only truth."

"When he passed me," she said in a low voice, "I saw a grave."

"Ah," said the Patterner.

He had made a little heap of bits of eggshell on the ground by his knee. He arranged the white fragments into a curve, then closed it into a circle. "Yes," he said, studying his eggshells; then, scratching up the earth a bit, he neatly and delicately buried them. He dusted off his hands. Again his glance flicked to Irian and away.

"You have been a witch, Irian?"

"No."

"But you have some knowledge."

"No. I don't. Rose wouldn't teach me. She said she didn't dare. Because I had power but she didn't know what it was."

"Your Rose is a wise flower," said the mage, unsmiling.

"But I know I have something to do. Something to be. That's why I wanted to come here. To find out. On the Isle of the Wise."

She was getting used to his strange face now and was able to read it. She thought that he looked sad. His way of speaking was harsh, quick, dry, peaceable. "The men of the Isle are not always wise, eh?" he said. "Maybe the Doorkeeper." He looked at her now, not glancing but squarely, his eyes catching and holding hers. "But there. In the wood. Under the trees. There is the old wisdom. Never old. I can't teach you. I can take you into the Grove." After a minute he stood up. "Yes?"

"Yes," she said uncertainly.

"The house is all right?"

"Yes—"

"Tomorrow," he said, and strode off.

So for a half month or more of the hot days of summer, Irian slept in the Otter's House, which was a peaceful one, and ate what the Master Patterner brought her in his basket—eggs, cheese, greens, fruit, smoked mutton—and went with him every afternoon into the grove of high trees, where the paths seemed never to be quite where she remembered them, and often led on far beyond what seemed the confines of the wood. They walked there in silence, and spoke seldom when they rested. The mage was a quiet man. Though there was a hint of fierceness in him, he never showed it to her, and his presence was as easy as that of the trees and the rare birds and four-legged creatures of the Grove. As he had said, he did not try to teach her. When she asked about the Grove, he told her that, with Roke Knoll, it had stood since Segoy made the islands of the world, and that all magic was in the roots of the trees, and that they were mingled with the roots of all the forests that were or might yet be. "And sometimes the Grove is in this place," he said, "and sometimes in another. But it is always."

She had never seen where he lived. He slept wherever he chose to, she imagined, in these warm summer nights. She asked him where the food they ate came from. What the school did not supply for itself, he said, the farmers round about provided, considering themselves well recompensed by the protections the Masters set on their flocks and fields and orchards. That made sense to her. On Way, the phrase "a wizard without his porridge" meant something unprecedented, unheard-of. But she was no wizard, and so, wanting to earn her porridge, she did her best to repair the Otter's House, borrowing tools from a farmer and buying nails and plaster in Thwil Town, for she still had half the cheese money.

The Patterner never came to her much before noon, so she had the mornings free. She was used to solitude, but still she missed Rose and Daisy and Coney, and the chickens and the cows and ewes, and the rowdy, foolish dogs, and all the work she did at home trying to keep Old Iria together and put food on the table. So she worked away unhurriedly every morning till she saw the mage come out from the trees with his sunlight-colored hair shining in the sunlight.

Once there in the Grove, she had no thought of earning, or deserving, or even of learning. To be there was enough, was all.

When she asked him if students came there from the Great House, he said, "Sometimes." Another time he said, "My words are nothing. Hear the leaves." That was all he said that could be called teaching. As she walked, she listened to the leaves when the wind rustled them or stormed in the crowns of the trees; she watched the shadows play, and thought about the roots of the trees down in the darkness of the earth. She was utterly content to be there. Yet always, without discontent or ugency, she felt that she was waiting. And that silent expectancy was deepest and clearest when she came out of the shelter of the woods and saw the open sky.

Once, when they had gone a long way and the trees, dark evergreens she did not know, stood very high about them, she heard a call—a horn blowing, a cry?—remote, on the very edge of hearing. She stood still, listening towards the west. The mage walked on, turning only when he realised she had stopped.

"I heard—" she said, and could not say what she had heard.

He listened. They walked on at last through a silence enlarged and deepened by that far call.

She never went into the Grove without him, and it was many days before he left her alone within it. But one hot afternoon when they came to a glade among a stand of oaks, he said, "I will come back here, eh?" and walked off with his quick, silent step, lost almost at once in the dappled, shifting depths of the forest.

She had no wish to explore for herself. The peacefulness of the place called for stillness, watching, listening; and she knew how tricky the paths were, and that the Grove was, as the Patterner put it, "bigger inside than outside." She sat down in a patch of sun-dappled shade and watched the shadows of the leaves play across the ground. The oak mast was deep; though she had never seen wild swine in the wood, she saw their tracks here. For a moment she caught the scent of a fox. Her thoughts moved as quietly and easily as the breeze moved in the warm light.

Often her mind here seemed empty of thought, full of the forest itself, but this day memories came to her, vivid. She thought about Ivory, thinking she would never see him again, wondering if he had found a ship to take him back to Havnor. He had told her he'd never go back to Westpool; the only place for him was the Great Port, the King's City, and for all he cared the island of Way could sink in the sea as deep as Soléa. But she thought with love of the roads and fields of Way. She thought of Old Iria village, the marshy spring under Iria Hill, the old house on it. She thought about Daisy singing ballads in the kitchen, winter evenings, beating out the time with her wooden clogs; and old Coney in the vineyards with his razor-edge knife, showing her how to prune the vine "right down to the life in it;" and Rose, her Etaudis, whispering charms to ease the pain in a child's broken arm. I have known wise people, she thought. Her mind flinched away from remembering her father, but the motion of the leaves and shadows drew it on. She saw him drunk, shouting. She felt his prying, tremulous hands on her. She saw him weeping, sick, shamed; and grief rose up through her body and dissolved, like an ache that melts away in a long stretch of the arms. He was less to her than the mother she had not known.

She stretched, feeling the ease of her body in the warmth, and her mind drifted back to Ivory. She had had no one in her life to desire. When the young wizard first came riding by so slim and arrogant, she wished she could want him; but she didn't and couldn't, and so she had thought him spell-protected. Rose had explained to her how wizards' spells worked "so that it never enters your head nor theirs, see, because it would take from their power, they say." But Ivory, poor Ivory, had been all too unprotected. If anybody was under a spell of chastity it must have been herself, for charming and handsome as he was she had never been able to feel a thing for him but liking, and her only lust had been to learn what he could teach her.

She considered herself, sitting in the deep silence of the Grove. No bird sang; the breeze was down; the leaves hung still. Am I ensorcelled? Am I a sterile thing, not whole, not a woman? she asked herself, looking at her strong bare arms, the soft swell of her breasts in the shadow under the throat of her shirt.

She looked up and saw the Hoary Man come out of a dark aisle of great oaks and come towards her across the glade.

He stopped in front of her. She felt herself blush, her face and throat burning, dizzy, her ears ringing. She sought words, anything to say, to turn his attention away from her, and could find nothing at all. He sat down near her. She looked down, as if studying the skeleton of a last-year's leaf by her hand.

What do I want? she asked herself, and the answer came not in words but throughout her whole body and soul: the fire, a greater fire than that, the flight, the flight burning—

She came back into herself, into the still air under the trees. The Hoary Man sat near her, his face bowed down, and she thought how slight and light he looked, how quiet and sorrowful. There was nothing to fear. There was no harm.

He looked over at her.

"Irian," he said, "do you hear the leaves?"

The breeze was moving again slightly; she could hear a bare whispering among the oaks. "A little," she said.

"Do you hear the words?"

"No."

She asked nothing and he said no more. Presently he got up, and she followed him to the path that always led them, sooner or later, out of the wood to the clearing by the Thwilburn and the Otter's House. When they came there, it was late afternoon. He went down to the stream and knelt to drink from it where it left the wood, above all the crossings. She did the same. Then sitting in the cool, long grass of the bank, he began to speak.

"My people, the Kargs, they worship gods. Twin gods, brothers. And the king there is also a god. But before the gods and after, always, are the streams. Caves, stones, hills. Trees. The earth. The darkness of the earth."

"The Old Powers," Irian said.

He nodded. "There, women know the Old Powers. Here too, witches. And the knowledge is bad—eh?"

When he added that little questioning "eh?" or "neh?" to the end of what had seemed a statement it always took her by surprise. She said nothing.

"Dark is bad," said the Patterner. "Eh?"

Irian drew a deep breath and looked at him eye to eye as they sat there. *"Only in dark the light,"* she said.

"Ah," he said. He looked away so that she could not see his expression.

"I should go," she said. "I can walk in the Grove, but not live there. It isn't my—my place. And the Master Chanter said I did harm by being here."

"We all do harm by being," said the Patterner.

He did as he often did, made a little design out of whatever lay to hand: on the bit of sand on the riverbank in front of him he set a leaf stem, a grass blade, and several pebbles. He studied them and rearranged them. "Now I must speak of harm," he said.

After a long pause he went on. "You know that a dragon brought back our Lord Sparrowhawk, with the young king, from the shores of death. Then the dragon carried Sparrowhawk away to his home, for his power was gone, he was not a mage. So presently the Masters of Roke met to choose a new archmage, here, in the Grove, as always. But not as always.

"Before the dragon came, the Summoner too had returned from death, where he can go, where his art can take him. He had seen our lord and the young king there, in that country across the wall of stones. He said they would not come back. He said Lord Sparrowhawk had told him to come back to us, to life, to bear that word. So we grieved for our lord.

"But then came the dragon, Kalessin, bearing him living.

"The Summoner was among us when we stood on Roke Knoll and saw the Archmage kneel to King Lebannen. Then, as the dragon bore our friend away, the Summoner fell down.

"He lay as if dead, cold, his heart not beating, yet he breathed. The Herbal used all his art, but could not rouse him. 'He is dead,' he said. 'The breath will not leave him, but he is dead.' So we mourned him. Then, because there was dismay among us, and all my patterns spoke of change and danger, we met to choose a new warden of Roke, an archmage to guide us. And in our council we set the young king in the Summoner's place. To us it seemed right that he should sit among us. Only the Changer spoke against it at first, and then agreed.

"But we met, we sat, and we could not choose. We said this and said that, but no name was spoken. And then I . . ." He paused a while. "There came on me what my people call the *eduevanu*, the other breath. Words came to me and I spoke them. I said, *Hama Gondun!*—And Kurremkarmerruk told them this in Hardic: 'A woman on Gont.' But when I came back to my own wits, I could not tell them what that meant. And so we parted with no archmage chosen.

"The king left soon after, and the Master Windkey went with him. Before the king was to be crowned, they went to Gont and sought our lord Sparrowhawk, to find what that meant, 'a woman on Gont.' Eh? But they did not see him, only my countrywoman Tenar of the Ring. She said she was not the woman they sought. And they found no one, nothing. So Lebannen judged it to be a prophecy yet to be fulfilled. And in Havnor he set his crown on his own head.

"The Herbal, and I too, judged the Summoner dead. We thought the breath he breathed was left from some spell of his own art that we did not understand, like the spell snakes know that keeps their heart beating long after they are dead. Though it seemed terrible to bury a breathing body, yet he was cold, and his blood did not run, and no soul was in him. That was more terrible. So we made ready to bury him. And then, as he lay beside his grave, his eyes opened. He moved, and spoke. He said, 'I have summoned myself again into life, to do what must be done.'"

The Patterner's voice had grown rougher. He suddenly brushed the little design of pebbles apart with the palm of his hand.

"So when the Windkey returned from the king's crowning, we were nine again. But divided. For the Summoner said we must meet again and choose an archmage. The king had had no place among us, he said. And 'a woman on Gont,' whoever she may be, has no place among the men on Roke. Eh? The Windkey, the Chanter, the Changer, the Hand, say he is right. And as King Lebannen is a man returned from death, fulfilling that prophecy, they say so will the archmage be a man returned from death."

"But—" Irian said, and stopped.

After a while the Patterner said, "That art, summoning, you know, is terrible. It is always danger. Here," and he looked up into the green-gold darkness of the trees, "here is no summoning. No bringing back across the wall. No wall."

His face was a warrior's face, but when he looked into the trees it was softened, yearning.

"So," he said, "now he makes you his reason for our meeting. But I will not go to the Great House. I will not be summoned."

"He won't come here?"

"I think he will not walk in the Grove. Nor on Roke Knoll. On the Knoll, what is, is so."

She did not know what he meant, but did not ask, preoccupied: "You say he makes me his reason for you to meet together."

"Yes. To send away one woman, it takes nine mages." He very seldom smiled, and when he did it was quick and fierce. "We are to meet to uphold the Rule of Roke. And so to choose an archmage."

"If I went away—" She saw him shake his head. "I could go to the Namer—"

"You are safer here."

The idea of doing harm troubled her, but the idea of danger had not entered her mind. She found it inconceivable. "I'll be all right," she said. "So the Namer, and you—and the Doorkeeper?—"

"—do not wish Thorion to be archmage. Also the Master Herbal, though he digs and says little."

He saw Irian staring at him in amazement. "Thorion the Summoner speaks his true name," he said. "He died, eh?"

She knew that King Lebannen used his true name openly. He too had returned from death. Yet that the Summoner should do so continued to shock and disturb her as she thought about it.

"And the . . . the students?"

"Divided also."

She thought about the school, where she had been so briefly. From here, under the eaves of the Grove, she saw it as stone walls enclosing one kind of being and keeping out all others, like a pen, a cage. How could any of them keep their balance in a place like that?

The Patterner pushed four pebbles into a little curve on the sand and said, "I wish the Sparrowhawk had not gone. I wish I could read what the shadows write. But all I can hear the leaves say is Change, change . . . Everything will change but them." He looked up into the trees again with that yearning look. The sun was setting. He stood up, bade her goodnight gently, and walked away, entering under the trees.

She sat on a while by the Thwilburn. She was troubled by what he had told her and by her thoughts and feelings in the Grove, and troubled that any thought or feeling could have troubled her there. She went to the house, set out her supper of smoked meat and bread and summer lettuce, and ate it without tasting it. She roamed restlessly back down the stream bank to the water. It was very still and warm in the late dusk, only the largest stars burning through a milky overcast. She slipped off her sandals and put her feet in the water. It was cool, but veins of sun warmth ran through it. She slid out of her clothes, the man's breeches and shirt that were all she had, and slipped naked into the water, feeling the push and stir of the current all along her body. She had never swum in the streams at Iria, and she had hated the sea, heaving grey and cold, but this quick water pleased her, tonight. She drifted and floated, her hands slipping over silken underwater rocks and her own silken flanks, her legs sliding through water weeds. All trouble and restlessness washed away from her in the running of the water, and she floated in delight in the caress of the stream, gazing up at the white, soft fire of the stars.

A chill ran through her. The water ran cold. Gathering herself together, her limbs still soft and loose, she looked up and saw on the bank above her the black figure of a man.

She stood straight up, naked, in the water.

"Get away!" she shouted. "Get away, you traitor, you foul lecher, or I'll cut the liver out of you!" She sprang up the bank, pulling herself up by the tough bunchgrass, and scrambled to her feet. No one was there. She stood afire, shaking with rage. She leapt back down the bank, found her clothes, and pulled them on, still swearing aloud—"You coward wizard! You traitorous son of a bitch!"

"Irian?"

"He was here!" she cried. "That foul heart, that Thorion!" She strode to meet the Patterner as he came into the starlight by the house. "I was bathing in the stream, and he stood there watching me!"

"A sending—only a seeming of him. It could not hurt you, Irian."

"A sending with eyes, a seeming with seeing! May he be—" She stopped, at a loss suddenly for the word. She felt sick. She shuddered, and swallowed the cold spittle that welled in her mouth.

The Patterner came forward and took her hands in his. His hands were warm, and she felt so mortally cold that she came close up against him for the warmth of his body. They stood so for a while, her face turned from him but their hands joined and their bodies pressed close. At last she broke free, straightening herself, pushing back her lank wet hair. "Thank you," she said. "I was cold."

"I know."

"I'm never cold," she said. "It was him."

"I tell you, Irian, he cannot come here, he cannot harm you here."

"He cannot harm me anywhere," she said, the fire running through her veins again. "If he tries to, I'll destroy him."

"Ah," said the Patterner.

She looked at him in the starlight, and said, "Tell me your name—Not your true name—Only a name I can call you. When I think of you."

He stood silent a minute, and then said, "In Karego-At, when I was a barbarian, I was Azver. In Hardic, that is a banner of war."

"Azver," she said. "Thank you."

SHE LAY AWAKE IN THE LITTLE HOUSE, FEELING THE AIR STI-fling and the ceiling pressing down on her, then slept suddenly and deeply. She woke as suddenly when the east was just getting light. She went to the door to see what she loved best to see, the sky before sunrise. Looking down from it she saw Azver the Patterner rolled up in his grey cloak, sound asleep on the ground before her doorstep. She withdrew noiselessly into the house. In a little while she saw him going back to his woods, walking a bit stiffly and scratching his head as he went, as people do when half awake.

She got to work scraping down the inner wall of the house, readying it to plaster. Just as the first sunlight struck in the window, there was a knock at her open door. Outside was the man she had thought was a gardener, the Master Herbal, looking solid and stolid, like a brown ox, beside the gaunt, grim-faced old Namer.

She came to the door and muttered some kind of greeting. They daunted her, these Masters of Roke; and also their presence meant that the peaceful time was over, the days of walking in the silent summer forest with the Patterner. That had come to an end last night. She knew it, but she did not want to know it.

"The Patterner sent for us," said the Master Herbal. He looked uncomfortable. Noticing a clump of weeds under the window, he said, "That's velver. Somebody from Havnor planted it here. Didn't know there was any on the island." He examined it attentively, and put some seed pods into his pouch.

Irian was studying the Namer covertly but equally attentively, trying to see if she could tell if he was what he had called a sending or was there in flesh and blood. Nothing about him appeared insubstantial, but she thought he was not there, and when he stepped into the slanting sunlight and cast no shadow, she knew it.

"Is it a long way from where you live, sir?" she asked.

He nodded. "Left myself halfway," he said. He looked up; the Patterner was coming towards them, wide awake now.

He greeted them and asked, "The Doorkeeper will come?"

"Said he thought he'd better keep the doors," said the Herbal. He closed his many-pocketed pouch carefully and looked around at the others. "But I don't know if he can keep a lid on the ant hill."

"What's up?" said Kurremkarmerruk. "I've been reading about dragons. Not paying attention to ants. But all the boys I had studying at the Tower left."

"Summoned," said the Herbal, drily.

"So?" said the Namer, more drily.

"I can tell you only how it seems to me," the Herbal said, reluctant, uncomfortable.

"Do that," the old mage said.

The Herbal still hesitated. "This lady is not of our council," he said at last.

"She is of mine," said Azver.

"She came to this place at this time," the Namer said. "And to this place, at this time, no one comes by chance. All any of us knows is how it seems to us. There are names behind names, my Lord Healer."

The dark-eyed mage bowed his head at that, and said, "Very well," evidently with relief at accepting their judgment over his own. "Thorion has been much with the other Masters, and with the young men. Secret meetings, inner circles. Rumors, whispers. The younger students are frightened, and several have asked me or the Doorkeeper if they may go—leave Roke. And we'd let them go. But there's no ship in port, and none has come into Thwil Bay since the one that brought you, lady, and sailed again next day for Wathort. The Windkey keeps the Roke wind against all. If the king himself should come, he could not land on Roke."

"Until the wind changes, eh?" said the Patterner.

"Thorion says Lebannen is not truly king, since no archmage crowned him."

"Nonsense! Not history!" said the old Namer. "The first archmage came centuries after the last king. Roke ruled in the kings' stead."

"Ah," said the Patterner. "Hard for the housekeeper to give up the keys when the owner comes home. Eh?"

"The Ring of Peace is healed," said the Herbal, in his patient, troubled voice, "the prophecy is fulfilled, the son of Morred is crowned, and yet we have no peace. Where have we gone wrong? Why can we not find the balance?"

"What does Thorion intend?" asked the Namer.

"To bring Lebannen here," said the Herbal. "The young men talk of 'the true crown.' A second coronation, here. By the Archmage Thorion."

"Avert!" Irian blurted out, making the sign to prevent word from becoming deed. None of the men smiled, and the Herbal belatedly made the same gesture.

"How does he hold them all?" the Namer said. "Herbal, you were here when Sparrowhawk and Thorion were challenged by Irioth. His gift was as great as Thorion's, I think. He used it to use men, to control them wholly. Is that what Thorion does?"

"I don't know," the Herbal said. "I can only tell you that when I'm with him, when I'm in the Great House, I feel that nothing can be done but what has been done. That nothing will change. Nothing will grow. That no matter what cures I use, the sickness will end in death." He looked around at them all like a hurt ox. "And I think it is true. There is no way to regain the Equilibrium but by holding still. We have gone too far. For the Archmage and Lebannen to go bodily into death, and return—it was not right. They broke a law that must not be broken. It was to restore the law that Thorion returned."

"What, to send them back into death?" the Namer said, and the Patterner, "Who is to say what is the law?"

"There is a wall," the Herbal said.

"That wall is not as deep-rooted as my trees," said the Patterner.

"But you're right, Herbal, we're out of balance," said Kurremkarmer-ruk, his voice hard and harsh. "When and where did we begin to go too far? What have we forgotten, turned our back on, overlooked?"

Irian looked from one to the other.

"When the balance is wrong, holding still is not good. It must get more wrong," said the Patterner. "Until—" He made a quick gesture of reversal with his open hands, down going up and up down.

"What's more wrong than to summon oneself back from death?" said the Namer.

"Thorion was the best of us all—a brave heart, a noble mind." The Herbal spoke almost in anger. "Sparrowhawk loved him. So did we all."

"Conscience caught him," said the Namer. "Conscience told him he alone could set things right. To do it, he denied his death. So he denies life."

"And who shall stand against him?" said the Patterner. "I can only hide in my woods."

"And I in my tower," said the Namer. "And you, Herbal, and the Doorkeeper, are in the trap, in the Great House. The walls we built to keep all evil out. Or in, as the case may be."

"We are four against him," said the Patterner.

"They are five against us," said the Herbal.

"Has it come to this," the Namer said, "that we stand at the edge of the forest Segoy planted and talk of how to destroy one another?"

"Yes," said the Patterner. "What goes too long unchanged destroys itself. The forest is forever because it dies and dies and so lives. I will not let this dead hand touch me. Or touch the king who brought us hope. A promise was made, made through me. I spoke it—'A woman on Gont.' I will not see that word forgotten."

"Then should we go to Gont?" said the Herbal, caught in Azver's passion. "Sparrowhawk is there."

"Tenar of the Ring is there," said Azver.

"Maybe our hope is there," said the Namer.

They stood silent, uncertain, trying to cherish hope.

Irian stood silent too, but her hope sank down, replaced by a sense of shame and utter insignificance. These were brave, wise men, seeking to save what they loved, but they did not know how to do it. And she had no share in their wisdom, no part in their decisions. She drew away from them, and they did not notice. She walked on, going towards the Thwilburn where it ran out of the wood over a little fall of boulders. The water was bright in the morning sunlight and made a happy noise. She wanted to cry, but she had never been good at crying. She stood and watched the water, and her shame turned slowly into anger.

She came back towards the three men, and said, "Azver."

He turned to her, startled, and came forward a little.

"Why did you break your Rule for me? Was it fair to me, who can never be what you are?"

Azver frowned. "The Doorkeeper admitted you because you asked," he said. "I brought you to the Grove because the leaves of the trees spoke your name to me before you ever came here. *Irian*, they said, *Irian*. Why you came I don't know, but not by chance. The Summoner too knows that."

"Maybe I came to destroy him."

He looked at her and said nothing.

"Maybe I came to destroy Roke."

His pale eyes blazed then. "Try!"

A long shudder went through her as she stood facing him. She felt herself larger than he was, larger than she was, enormously larger. She could reach out one finger and destroy him. He stood there in his small, brave, brief humanity, his mortality, defenseless. She drew a long, long breath. She stepped back from him.

The sense of huge strength was draining out of her. She turned her head a little and looked down, surprised to see her own brown arm, her rolled-up sleeve, the grass springing cool and green around her sandaled feet. She looked back at the Patterner and he still seemed a fragile being. She pitied and honored him. She wanted to warn him of the peril he was in. But no words came to her at all. She turned round and went back to the stream bank by the little falls. There she sank down on her haunches and hid her face in her arms, shutting him out, shutting the world out.

The voices of the mages talking were like the voices of the stream running. The stream said its words and they said theirs, but none of them were the right words.

IV. Irian

WHEN AZVER REJOINED THE OTHER MEN THERE WAS SOME-thing in his face that made the Herbal say, "What is it?"

"I don't know," he answered. "Maybe we should not leave Roke."

"Probably we can't," said the Herbal. "If the Windkey locks the winds against us . . ."

"I'm going back to where I am," Kurremkarmerruk said abruptly. "I don't like leaving myself about like an old shoe. I'll be here with you this evening." And he was gone.

"I'd like to walk under your trees a bit, Azver," the Herbal said, with a long sigh.

"Go on, Deyala. I'll stay here." The Herbal went off. Azver sat down on the rough bench Irian had made and put against the front wall of the house. He looked upstream at her, crouching motionless on the bank. Sheep in the field between them and the Great House blatted softly. The morning sun was getting hot.

His father had named him Banner of War. He had come west, leaving all he knew behind him. He had learned his true name from the trees of the Immanent Grove, and become the Patterner of Roke. All this year the patterns of the shadows and the branches and the roots, all the silent language of his forest, had spoken of destruction, of transgression, of all things changed. Now it was upon them, he knew. It had come with her.

She was in his charge, in his care, he had known that when he saw her. Though she came to destroy Roke, as she had said, he must serve her. He did so willingly. She had walked with him in the forest, tall, awkward, fearless; she had put aside the thorny arms of brambles with her big, careful hand. Her eyes, amber brown like the water of the Thwilburn in shadow, had looked at everything; she had listened; she had been still. He wanted to protect her and knew he could not. He had given her a little warmth when she was cold. He had nothing else to give her. Where she must go she would go. She did not understand danger. She had no wisdom but her innocence, no armor but her anger. Who are you, Irian? he said to her, watching her crouched there like an animal locked in its muteness.

The Herbal came back from the woods and sat with him a while, not speaking. In the middle of the day he went back to the Great House, agreeing to return with the Doorkeeper in the morning. They would ask all the other Masters to meet with them in the Grove. "But *he* won't come," Deyala said, and Azver nodded.

All day he stayed near the Otter's House, keeping watch on Irian, making her eat a little with him. She came to the house, but when they had eaten she went back to her place on the stream bank and sat there motionless. And he too felt a lethargy in his own body and mind, a stupidity, which he fought against but could not shake off. He thought of the Summoner's eyes, and then it was he that felt cold, cold through, though he was sitting in the full heat of the summer's day. We are ruled by the dead, he thought. The thought would not leave him.

He was grateful to see Kurremkarmerruk coming slowly down the bank of the Thwilburn from the north. The old man waded through the stream barefoot, holding his shoes in one hand and his tall staff in the other, snarling when he missed his footing on the rocks. He sat down on the near bank to dry his feet and put his shoes back on. "When I go back to the Tower," he said, "I'll ride. Hire a carter, buy a mule. I'm old, Azver."

"Come up to the house," the Patterner said, and he set out water and food for the Namer.

"Where's the girl?"

"Asleep." Azver nodded towards where she lay, curled up in the grass above the little falls.

The heat of the day was beginning to lessen and the shadows of the Grove lay across the grass, though the Otter's House was still in sunlight. Kurremkarmerruk sat on the bench with his back against the house wall, and Azver on the doorstep.

"We've come to the end of it," the old man said out of silence.

Azver nodded, in silence.

"What brought you here, Azver?" the Namer asked. "I've often thought of asking you. A long, long way to come. And you have no wizards in the Kargish lands."

"No. But we have the things wizardry is made of. Water, stones, trees, words . . ."

"But not the words of the Making."

"No. Nor dragons."

"Never?"

"Only in old tales from the farthest east, from the desert of Hur-at-Hur. Before the gods were. Before men were. Before men were men, they were dragons."

"Now that is interesting," said the old scholar, sitting up straighter. "I told you I've been reading about dragons. You know these rumors of them flying over the Inmost Sea as far east as Gont. That was no doubt Kalessin taking Ged home, multiplied by sailors making a good story better. But a boy here swore to me that his whole village had seen dragons flying, this spring, west of Mount Onn. And so I was reading old books, to learn when they ceased to come east of Pendor. And in an old Pelnish scroll, I came on your story, or something like it. That men and dragons were all one kind, but they quarreled. Some went west and some east, and they became two kinds, and forgot they were ever one."

"We went farthest east," Azver said. "But do you know what the leader of an army is, in my tongue?"

"*Edran,*" said the Namer promptly, and laughed. "Drake. Dragon . . ."

After a while he said, "I could chase an etymology on the brink of doom . . . But I think, Azver, that that's where we are. We won't defeat him."

"He has the advantage," Azver said, very dry.

"He does. But, admitting it unlikely, admitting it impossible—if we did defeat him—if he went back into death and left us here alive—what would we do? What comes next?"

After a long time, Azver said, "I have no idea."

"Your leaves and shadows tell you nothing?"

"Change, change," said the Patterner. "Transformation."

He looked up suddenly. The sheep, who had been grouped near the stile, were scurrying off, and someone was coming along the path from the Great House.

"A group of young men," said the Herbal, breathless, as he came to them. "Thorion's army. Coming here. To take the girl. To send her away." He stood and drew breath. "The Doorkeeper was speaking with them when I left. I think—"

"Here he is," said Azver, and the Doorkeeper was there, his smooth, yellow-brown face tranquil as ever.

"I told them," he said, "that if they went out Medra's Gate this day, they'd never go back through it into a house they knew. Some of them were for turning back, then. But the Windkey and the Chanter urged them on. They'll be along soon."

They could hear men's voices in the fields east of the Grove.

Azver went quickly to where Irian lay beside the stream, and the others followed him. She roused up and got to her feet, looking dull and dazed. They were standing around her, a kind of guard, when the group of thirty or more men came past the little house and approached them. They were mostly older students; there were five or six wizard's staffs among the crowd, and the Master Windkey led them. His thin, keen old face looked strained and weary, but he greeted the four mages courteously by their titles.

They greeted him, and Azver took the word—"Come into the Grove, Master Windkey," he said, "and we will wait there for the others of the Nine."

"First we must settle the matter that divides us," said the Windkey.

"That is a stony matter," said the Namer.

"The woman with you defies the Rule of Roke," the Windkey said. "She must leave. A boat is waiting at the dock to take her, and the wind, I can tell you, will stand fair for Way."

"I have no doubt of that, my lord," said Azver, "but I doubt she will go."

"My Lord Patterner, will you defy our Rule and our community, that has been one so long, upholding order against the forces of ruin? Will it be you, of all men, who break the pattern?"

"It is not glass, to break," Azver said. "It is breath, it is fire."

It cost him a great effort to speak.

"It does not know death," he said, but he spoke in his own language, and they did not understand him. He drew closer to Irian. He felt the warmth of her body. She stood staring, in that animal silence, as if she did not understand any of them.

"Lord Thorion has returned from death to save us all," the Windkey said, fiercely and clearly. "He will be Archmage. Under his rule Roke will be as it was. The king will receive the true crown from his hand, and rule with his guidance, as Morred ruled. No witches will defile sacred ground. No dragons will threaten the Inmost Sea. There will be order, safety, and peace."

None of the four mages with Irian answered him. In the silence, the men with him murmured, and a voice among them said, "Let us have the witch."

"No," Azver said, but could say nothing else. He held his staff of willow, but it was only wood in his hand.

Of the four of them, only the Doorkeeper moved and spoke. He took a step forward, looking from one young man to the next and the next. He said, "You trusted me, giving me your names. Will you trust me now?"

"My lord," said one of them with a fine, dark face and a wizard's oaken staff, "we do trust you, and therefore ask you to let the witch go, and peace return."

Irian stepped forward before the Doorkeeper could answer.

"I am not a witch," she said. Her voice sounded high, metallic, after the men's deep voices. "I have no art. No knowledge. I came to learn."

"We do not teach women here," said the Windkey. "You know that."

"I know nothing," Irian said. She took another step forward, facing the mage directly. "Tell me who I am."

"Learn your place, woman," the mage said with cold passion.

"My place," she said, slowly, the words dragging—"my place is on the hill. Where things are what they are. Tell the dead man I will meet him there."

The Windkey stood silent. The group of men muttered, angry, and some of them moved forward. Azver came between her and them, her words releasing him from the paralysis of mind and body that had held him. "Tell Thorion we will meet him on Roke Knoll," he said. "When he comes, we will be there. Now come with me," he said to Irian.

The Namer, the Doorkeeper, and the Herbal followed him with her into the Grove. There was a path for them. But when some of the young men started after them, there was no path.

"Come back," the Windkey said to the young men.

They turned back, uncertain. The low sun was still bright on the fields and the roofs of the Great House, but inside the wood it was all shadows.

"Witchery," they said, "sacrilege, defilement."

"Best come away," said the Master Windkey, his face set and somber, his keen eyes troubled. He set off back to the school, and they straggled after him, arguing and debating in frustration and anger.

THEY WERE NOT FAR INSIDE THE GROVE, AND STILL BESIDE THE stream, when Irian stopped, turned aside, and crouched down by the enormous, hunching roots of a willow that leaned out over the water. The four mages stood on the path.

"She spoke with the other breath," Azver said.

The Namer nodded.

"So we must follow her?" the Herbal asked.

This time the Doorkeeper nodded. He smiled faintly and said, "So it would seem."

"Very well," said the Herbal, with his patient, troubled look; and he went aside a little, and knelt to look at some small plant or fungus on the forest floor.

Time passed as always in the Grove, not passing at all it seemed, yet gone, the day gone quietly by in a few long breaths, a quivering of leaves, a bird singing far off and another answering it from even farther. Irian stood up slowly. She did not speak, but looked down the path, and then walked down it. The four men followed her.

They came out into the calm, open evening air. The west still held some brightness as they crossed the Thwilburn and walked across the fields to Roke Knoll, which stood up before them in a high dark curve against the sky.

"They're coming," the Doorkeeper said. Men were coming through the gardens and up the path from the Great House, the five mages, many students. Leading them was Thorion the Summoner, tall in his grey cloak, carrying his tall staff of bone-white wood, about which a faint gleam of werelight hovered.

Where the two paths met and joined to wind up to the heights of the Knoll, Thorion stopped and stood waiting for them. Irian strode forward to face him.

"Irian of Way," the Summoner said in his deep, clear voice, "that there may be peace and order, and for the sake of the balance of all things, I bid you now leave this island. We cannot give you what you ask, and for that we ask your forgiveness. But if you seek to stay here you forfeit forgiveness, and must learn what follows on transgression."

She stood up, almost as tall as he, and as straight. She said nothing for a minute and then spoke out in a high, harsh voice. "Come up onto the hill, Thorion," she said.

She left him standing at the waymeet, on level ground, and walked up the hill path for a little way, a few strides. She turned and looked back down at him. "What keeps you from the hill?" she said.

The air was darkening around them. The west was only a dull red line, the eastern sky was shadowy above the sea.

The Summoner looked up at Irian. Slowly he raised his arms and the white staff in the invocation of a spell, speaking in the tongue that all the wizards and mages of Roke had learned, the language of their art, the Language of the Making: "Irian, by your name I summon you and bind you to obey me!"

She hesitated, seeming for a moment to yield, to come to him, and then cried out, "I am not only Irian!"

At that the Summoner ran up towards her, reaching out, lunging at her as if to seize and hold her. They were both on the hill now. She towered above him impossibly, fire breaking forth between them, a flare of red flame in the dusk air, a gleam of red-gold scales, of vast wings—then that was gone, and there was nothing there but the woman standing on the hill path and the tall man bowing down before her, bowing slowly down to earth, and lying on it.

Of them all it was the Herbal, the healer, who was the first to move. He went up the path and knelt down by Thorion. "My lord," he said, "my friend."

Under the huddle of the grey cloak his hands found only a huddle of clothes and dry bones and a broken staff.

"This is better, Thorion," he said, but he was weeping.

The old Namer came forward and said to the woman on the hill, "Who are you?"

"I do not know my other name," she said. She spoke as he had spoken, as she had spoken to the Summoner, in the Language of the Making, the tongue the dragons speak.

She turned away and began to walk on up the hill.

"Irian," said Azver the Patterner, "will you come back to us?"

She halted and let him come up to her. "I will, if you call me," she said.

She reached out and touched his hand. He drew his breath sharply.

"Where will you go?" he said.

"To those who will give me my name. In fire, not water. My people."

"In the west," he said.

She said, "Beyond the west."

She turned away from him and them and went on up the hill in the gathering darkness. As she went farther from them they saw her, all of them, the great gold-mailed flanks, the spiked, coiling tail, the talons, the breath that was bright fire. On the crest of the knoll she paused a while, her long head turning to look slowly round the Isle of Roke, gazing longest at the Grove, only a blur of darkness in darkness now. Then with a rattle like the shaking of sheets of brass the wide, vaned wings opened and the dragon sprang up into the air, circled Roke Knoll once, and flew.

A curl of fire, a wisp of smoke drifted down through the dark air.

Azver the Patterner stood with his left hand holding his right hand, which her touch had burnt. He looked down at the men, who stood silent at the foot of the hill, staring after the dragon. "Well, my friends," he said, "what now?"

Only the Doorkeeper answered. He said, "I think we should go to our house, and open its doors."

PARADISES
LOST

This shaking keeps me steady. I should know.
What falls away is always. And is near.
I wake to sleep, and take my waking slow.
I learn by going where I have to go.
Theodore Roethke, The Waking

The Dirtball

THE BLUE PARTS WERE LOTS OF WATER, LIKE THE HYDRO TANKS
only deeper, and the other-colored parts were dirt, like the earth gardens
only bigger. Sky was what she couldn't understand. Sky was another
ball that fit around the dirtball, Father said, but they couldn't show it in
the model globe, because you couldn't see it. It was transparent, like air.
It was air. But blue. A ball of air, and it looked blue from underneath,
and it was outside the dirtball. Air outside. That was really strange. Was
there air inside the dirtball? No, Father said, just earth. You lived on the
outside of the dirtball, like evamen doing eva, only you didn't have to
wear a suit. You could breathe the blue air, just like you were inside. In

nighttime you'd see black and stars, like if you were doing eva, Father said, but in daytime you'd see only blue. She asked why. Because the light was brighter than the stars, he said. Blue light? No; the star that made it was yellow, but there was so much air it looked blue. She gave up. It was all so hard and so long ago. And it didn't matter.

Of course they would "land" on some other dirtball, but that wasn't going to happen till she was very old, nearly dead, sixty-five years old. By then, if it mattered, she'd understand.

Privative Definition

ALIVE IN THE WORLD ARE HUMAN BEINGS, PLANTS, AND BACTERIA.
The bacteria live in and on the human beings and the plants and the soils and other things, and are alive but not visible. The activity even of great numbers of bacteria is not often visible, or appears to be simply a property of their host. Their life is on another order. Orders, as a rule, cannot perceive one another except with instruments which allow perception of a different scale. With such an instrument one gazes in wonder at the world revealed. But the instrument has not revealed one's larger-order world to that smaller-order world, which continues orderly, undisturbed and unaware, until the drop dries suddenly on the glass slide. Reciprocity is a rare thing.

The smaller-order world revealed here is an austere one. No amoeba oozing along, or graceful paisley-paramecium, or vacuum-cleaning rotifer; no creature larger than bacteria, juddering endlessly under the impacts of molecules.

And only certain bacteria. No molds, no wild yeasts. No virus (down another order). Nothing that causes disease in human beings or in plants. Nothing but the necessary bacteria, the house-cleaners, the digesters, the makers of dirt—clean dirt. There is no gangrene in the world, no blood poisoning. No colds in the head, no flu, no measles, no plague, no typhus or typhoid or tuberculosis or AIDS or dengue or cholera or yellow fever or Ebola or syphilis or poliomyelitis or leprosy or bilharzia or herpes, no chickenpox, no cold sores, no shingles. No Lyme disease. No ticks. No malaria. No mosquitoes. No fleas or flies, no roaches or spiders, no weevils or worms. Nothing in the world has more or less than two legs. Nothing has wings. Nothing sucks blood. Nothing hides in tiny crevices, waves tendrils, scuttles into shadows, lays eggs, washes its fur, clicks its mandibles, or turns around three times before it lies down with its nose on its tail. Nothing has a tail. Nothing in the world has tentacles or fins or paws or claws. Nothing in the world soars. Nothing swims. Nothing purrs, barks, growls, roars, chitters, trills, or cries repeatedly two notes, a descending fourth, for three months of the year. There are no months of the year. There is no moon. There is no year. There is no sun. Time is divided into lightcycles, darkcycles, and tendays. Every 365.25 cycles there is a celebration and a number called The Year is changed. This Year is 141. It says so on the schoolroom clock.

The Tiger

OF COURSE THERE ARE PICTURES OF MOONS AND SUNS AND animals, all labelled with names. In the Library on the bookscreens you can watch big things running on all fours over some kind of hairy carpet and the voices say, "horses in wyoming," or "llamas in peru." Some of the pictures are funny. Some of them you wish you could touch. Some are frightening. There's one with bright hair all gold and dark, with terrible clear eyes that stare at you without liking you, without knowing you at all. "Tiger in zoo," the voice says. Then children are playing with some little "kittens" that climb on them and the children giggle and the kittens are cute, like dolls or babies, until one of them

looks right at you and there are the same eyes, the round, clear eyes that
do not know your name.

"I am Hsing," Hsing said loudly to the kitten-picture on the book-
screen. The picture turned its head away, and Hsing burst into tears.

Teacher was there, full of comfort and queries. "I hate it, I hate it!"
the five-year-old wailed.

"It's only a movie. It can't hurt you. It isn't real," said the
twenty-five-year-old.

Only people are real. Only people are alive. Father's plants are alive,
he says so, but people are really alive. People know you. They know your
name. They like you. Or if they don't, like Alida's cousin's little boy
from School Four, you tell them who you are and then they know you.

"I'm Hsing."

"Shing," the little boy said, and she tried to teach him the difference between saying Hsing and saying Shing, but the difference didn't
matter unless you were talking Chinese, and it didn't matter anyway,
because they were going to play Follow-the-Leader with Rosie and Lena
and all the others. And Luis, of course.

If Nothing Is Very Different from You, What Is a Little Different from You Is Very Different from You

LUIS WAS VERY DIFFERENT FROM HSING. FOR ONE THING, SHE
had a vulva and he had a penis. As they were comparing the two one
day, Luis remarked that he liked the word vulva because it sounded
warm and soft and round. And vagina sounded rather grand. But "Penis,
peee-niss," he said mincingly, "pee-piss! It sounds like a little dinky pissy
sissy thing. It ought to have a better name." They made up names for
it. Bobwob, said Hsing. Gowbondo! said Luis. Bobwob when it was

lying down and Gowbondo when it stood up, they decided, aching with laughter. "Up, up, Gowbondo!" Luis cried, and it raised its head a little from his slender, silky thigh. "See, it knows its name! You call it." And she called it, and it answered, although Luis had to help it a little, and they laughed until not only Bobwob-Gowbondo but both of them were limp all over, rolling on the floor, there in Luis's room where they always went after school unless they went to Hsing's room.

Putting on Clothes

SHE LOOKED FORWARD TO IT FOREVER AND COULDN'T SLEEP AT all the night before, lying awake forever. But there was Father standing there suddenly, wearing his dress-up clothes, black long pants and his white silky kurta. "Wake up, sleepyhead, are you going to sleep through your Ceremony?" She leaped up from bed in terror, believing him, so that he said at once, seriously, "No, no, I was only joking. You have plenty of time. You don't have to get dressed, yet!" She saw the joke, but she was too bewildered and excited to laugh. "Help me comb my *hair!*" she wailed, tugging her comb into a knot in the thick black tangles. He knelt to help her.

By the time they got to the Temenos her excitement only made everything clearer than usual, bright, distinct. The huge room seemed even bigger than usual. Music was playing, cheery and dancy. Lots and lots of people were coming, naked children, each one with a parent in dress-up clothes, some of them with two parents, many with grand-parents, a few with a little naked brother or sister or a big brother or sister in dress-up clothes. Luis's father was there, but he was only wearing workshorts and an old singlet, and she was sorry for Luis. Her mother Jael came through the big crowd of people. Jael's son Joel came with her from Quad Four, and both of them were wearing really, really dress-up clothes. Jael's had red zigzags and sparkles painted on, and Joel's shirt was purple with a gold zipper. They hugged and kissed, and Jael gave Father a package and said "For later," and Hsing knew what was in it, but didn't say anything. Father was hiding his package in one hand behind his back and she knew what was in it too.

The music was turning into the song they had all been learning, all the seven-year-olds in all four schools in the whole world: "I'm growing up! I'm growing up!" The parents pushed the children forward or led the shy ones by the hand, whispering, "Sing! Sing!" And all the little naked children, singing, came together in the center of the high round room. "I'm growing up! What a happy happy day!" they sang, and the grown-ups began to sing with them, so it got huge and loud and deep and made tears start in her eyes. "What a happy happy day!"

An old teacher talked a little while, and then a young teacher with a beautiful high clear voice said, "Now everyone sit down," and everyone sat down on the deck. "I will read each child's name. When I read your name, stand up. Your parent and relations will stand up too, and then you can go to them, and look at your clothes. But don't put them on till everybody in the world has their new clothes! I'll say when. So! Are you ready? So! 5-Adano Sita! Stand up and be clothed!"

A little tiny girl jumped up in the circle of sitting children. She was red in the face and looked around in terror for her mother, who stood up laughing and waving a beautiful red shirt. Little Sita ran headlong for her, and everybody laughed and clapped. "5-Alzs-Matteu Frans! Stand up and be clothed!" And so it went, till the clear voice said, "5-Liu Hsing! Stand up and be clothed!" and she stood up, her eyes fixed on Father, who was easy to see because of Jael and Joel glittering beside him. She ran to him and took something silky, something wonderful, into her arms, and the people from Peony Compound and Lotus Compound clapped specially hard. She turned and stood pressed against Father's legs, watching.

"5-Nova Luis! Stand up and be clothed," but he was up and over with his father almost before the words were said, so that people laughed again, and hardly had time to clap. Hsing tried to catch Luis's eye but he wouldn't look. He watched the rest of the Ceremony seriously, so she did too.

"These are the fifty-four seven-year-old children of the Fifth Generation," the teacher said when no more children were left in the center of the circle. "Let us welcome them to all the joys and responsibilities of growing up," and everybody cheered and clapped while the naked children, hurrying and inept, struggling with unfamiliar holes, getting things upside down, fumbling with buttons, put on their new clothes, their first clothes, and stood up again, resplendent.

Then all the teachers and grown-ups started singing "What a happy happy day" again and there was a lot more hugging and kissing. Hsing got enough of that pretty soon, but she noticed that Luis really liked it, and hugged back hard when grown-ups he hardly knew hugged him.

Ed had given Luis black shorts and a blue silky shirt, in which he looked absolutely different and absolutely himself. Rosa had all white clothes because her mother was an angel. Father had given Hsing dark blue shorts and a white shirt, and Jael's package was light blue pants and a blue shirt with white stars on it, to wear tomorrow. The cloth of the shorts rubbed her thighs when she moved and the shirt felt soft, soft on her shoulders and belly. She danced with joy, and Father took her hands and danced gravely with her. "So, my grown-up daughter!" he said, and his smile crowned the day.

Luis Being Different

THE PENIS-VULVA DIFFERENCE WAS SUPERFICIAL. SHE HAD learned that word from Father not long ago, and found it useful. Luis wasn't different only from her or only because of that superficial difference. He was different from everybody. Nobody said "ought to" the way Luis did. He wanted the truth. Not to lie. He wanted honor. That was the word. That was the difference. He had more honor than the others. Honor is hard and clear and Luis was hard and clear. And at the same time and in exactly the same way he was tender, he was soft. He got asthma and couldn't breathe, he got big headaches that knocked him out for days, he was sick before exams and performances and ceremonies. He was like the knife that wounds, and like the wound. Everybody treated Luis with a difference, respectfully, liking him but not trying to get close to him. Only she knew that he was also the touch that heals the wound.

V

WHEN THEY WERE TEN AND FINALLY WERE ALLOWED TO ENTER what the teachers called Virtual Earth and the Chi-Ans called V-Dichew, Hsing was overwhelmed and disappointed. V-Dichew was exciting and tremendously complicated, yet thin. It was superficial. It was programs.

There were infinite things in it, but one stupid real thing, her old toothbrush, had more being in it than all the swarming rush of objects and sensations in City or Jungle or Countryside. In Countryside, she was always aware that although there was nothing overhead but the blue air, and she was walking along on grass-stuff that carpeted the uneven deck for impossible distances rising up into impossible shapes (*hills*), and that the noises in her ears were air moving fast (*wind*) and a kind of high yit-yit sound sometimes (*birds*), and that those things on all fours way off on the winds, no, on the hills, were animals (*cattle*), all the same, all the time, she knew she was sitting in a chair in School Two V-Lab with some junk attached to her body, and her body refused to be fooled, insisting that no matter how strange and amazing and educational and important and historical V-Dichew was, it was a fake. Dreams could also be convincing, beautiful, frightening, important. But she didn't want to live in dreams. She wanted to be awake in her body touching true cloth, true metal, true skin.

The Poet

WHEN SHE WAS FOURTEEN, HSING WROTE A POEM FOR AN ENG-lish assignment. She wrote it in both the languages she knew. In English it went:

In the Fifth Generation
My grandfather's grandfather walked under heaven.
That was another world.

When I am a grandmother, they say, I may walk under heaven
On another world.

But I am living my life now joyously in my world
Here in the middle of heaven.

She had been learning Chinese with her father since she was nine; they had read some of the classics together. He smiled when he read the Chinese poem, read the characters "under heaven"—"t'ien hsia." She saw his smile and it made her happy, proud of her erudition and enormously proud that Yao had recognised it, that they shared this almost secret, almost private understanding.

The teacher asked her to read her poem aloud in both languages at first-quarter Class Day for second-year high-schoolers. The next day the editor of *Q-4*, the most famous literary magazine in the world, called her up and asked if he could publish it. Her teacher had sent it to him. He wanted her to read it for the audio. "It needs your voice," he said. He was a big man with a beard, 4-Bass Abby, imperious and opinionated, a god. He was rude to everybody else but kind to her. When they made the recording and she fluffed it, he just said, "Back up and take it easy, poet," and she did.

Then it seemed for a while that everywhere she was she heard her own voice saying "When I am a grandmother, they say. . . ." on the speaker, and people she hardly knew at school said, "Hey I heard your poem, it was zazz." All the angels liked it specially and told her so.

She was going to be a poet, of course. She would be really great, like 2-Eli Ali. Only instead of little short weird obscure poems like Eli's, she would write a great narrative poem about—actually the problem was what should it be about. It could be a great historical epic about the Zero Generation. It would be called *Genesis*. For a week she was excited, thinking about it all the time. But to do it she'd really have to learn all the history that she was sort of gliding through in History, she'd have to read hundreds of books. And she'd have to really go into V-Dichew to feel what it had been like to live there. It would all take years before she could even start writing it.

Maybe she could write love poems. There were an awful lot of love poems in the World Lit anthology. She had a feeling that you didn't need to really be in love with a person to write a love poem. Maybe in fact if you were really seriously in love it would interfere with the poetry. A sort of yearning, undemanding adoration like she felt for Bass Abby, or for Rosa at school, maybe was a good place to start from. So she wrote quite a few love poems, but for one reason or another she was embarrassed about turning them in to her teacher, and only showed them to Luis. Luis had acted all along like he didn't think she was a poet. She had to show him.

"I like this one," he said. She peered to see which one.

What is the sadness in you
that I see only in your smile?
I wish I could hold your sadness
in my arms like a sleeping child.

She hadn't thought much of the poem, it was so short, but now it seemed better than she'd thought.

"It's about Yao, isn't it?" Luis said.

"About my *father*?" Hsing said, so shocked she felt her cheeks burning. "No! It's a *love* poem!"

"Well, who do you actually love a lot besides your father?" Luis asked in his horrible matter-of-fact way.

"A whole lot of people! And love is—There are different *kinds*—"

"Are there?" He glanced up at her. He pondered. "I didn't say it was a sex poem. I don't think it is a sex poem."

"Oh, you are so weird," Hsing said, abruptly and deftly snatching her writer back and closing the folder labelled *Original Poems by 5-Liu Hsing.* "What makes you think you know anything about poetry anyhow?"

"I know about as much about it as you do," said Luis with his pedantic fairness, "but I can't *do* it at all. You can. Sometimes."

"Nobody can write great poetry all the time!"

"Well,"—her heart always sank when he said "Well"—"maybe not literally all the time, but the good ones have an amazingly high average. Shakespeare, and Li Po, and Yeats, and 2-Eli—"

"What's the use trying to be like *them*?" she wailed.

"I didn't mean you had to be like them," he said after a slight pause and in a different tone. He had realised that he might have hurt her. That made him unhappy. When he was unhappy he became gentle. She knew exactly how he felt, and why, and what he'd do, and she also knew the fierce, regretful tenderness for him that swelled up inside her, a sore tenderness, like a bruise. She said, "Oh, I don't care about all that anyway. Words are too sloppy, I like math. Let's go meet Lena at the gym."

As they jogged through the corridors it occurred to her that in fact the poem he had liked wasn't about Rosa, as she had thought, or about her father, as he had thought, but was about him, Luis. But it was all stupid anyhow and didn't matter. So she wasn't Shakespeare. But she loved quadratic equations.

4-Liu Yao

HOW SHELTERED THEY WERE, HOW PROTECTED! SAFER THAN any guarded prince or pampered child of the rich had ever been; safer than any child had ever been on Earth.

No cold winds to shiver in or heavy heat to sweat in. No plagues or coughs or fevers or toothaches. No hunger. No wars. No weapons. No danger. No danger from anything in the world but the danger the world itself was in. But that was a constant, a condition of being, and therefore hard to think about, except sometimes in dream; the horrible images. The walls of the world deformed, bulging, shattering. The soundless explosion. A spray of bloody mist, a tiny smear of vapor in the starlight. They were all in danger all the time, surrounded by danger. That is the essence of safety, the heart of it: that the danger is outside.

They lived inside. Inside their world with its strong walls and strong laws, shaped and bulwarked to protect and surround them with strength. There they lived, and there was no threat unless they made it.

"People are a risky business," Liu Yao said, smiling. "Plants mostly don't go crazy."

Yao's profession was gardening. He worked in hydroponic engineering and maintenance and in plant-genetic quality and control. He was in the gardens every workday and many evenings. The 4-5-Liu homespace was full of pet plants—gourdvines in carboys of water, flowering shrubs in pots of dirt, epiphytes festooning the vents and light-fixtures. Many of them were experimentals, which usually died. Hsing believed that her father was sorry for these genetic errors, felt guilty about them, and brought them home to die in peace. Occasionally one of the experiments thrived under his patient attendance and went back to the plant labs in triumph, accompanied by Yao's faint, deprecating smile.

4-Liu Yao was a short, slender, handsome man with a shock of black hair early going grey. He did not have the bearing of a handsome man. He was reserved, courteous, but shy. A good listener but a rare and low-voiced talker, when he was with more than one or two people he was almost entirely silent. With his mother 3-Liu Meiling or his friend 4-Wang Yuen or his daughter Hsing he would converse contentedly, unassertively. His passions were contained, restrained, powerful: the Chinese classics, his plants, his daughter. He thought a good deal and felt a good deal. He was mostly content to follow his thoughts and feelings alone, in silence, like a man going downstream in a small boat on a great river, sometimes steering, more often drifting. Of boats and rivers, of cliffs and currents, Yao knew only images in pictures, words in poems. Sometimes he dreamed that he was in a boat on a river, but the dreams were vague. He knew dirt, though, knew it exactly, bodily. Dirt was what he worked in. And water and air he knew, the humble, transparent things, on whose clarity, invisibility, life depended, the miracles. A bubble of air and water floated in the dry black vacuum, reflecting starlight. He lived inside it.

3-Liu Meiling lived in the group of homespaces called Peony Compound, a corridor away from her son's homespace. She led an extremely active social life limited almost entirely to the Chinese-Ancestry population of Quadrant Two. Her profession was chemistry; she worked in the fabric labs; she had never liked the work. As soon as she decently could she went on halftime and then retired. Didn't like any work, she said. Liked to look after babies in the baby-garden, play games, gamble for flower-cookies, talk, laugh, gossip, find out what was happening next door. She took great pleasure in her son and granddaughter and ran in and out of their homespace constantly, bringing dumplings, rice cakes, gossip. "You should move to Peony!" she said frequently, but knew they wouldn't, because Yao was unsociable, and that was fine, except she did hope that Hsing would stay with her own people when she decided to have a baby, which she also said frequently. "Hsing's mother is a fine woman, I like Jael," she told her son, "but I never will understand why you couldn't have had a baby from one of the Wong girls and then her mama would be right here in Quadrant Two, that would have been so nice for all of us. But I know you have to do things your way. And I must say even if Hsing is only half Chinese Ancestry nobody would ever know it, and what a beauty she's getting to be, so I suppose you did know what you were doing, if anyone ever does when it comes to falling in love or having a child, which I doubt. It's basically luck, is all it is. Young 5-Li has an eye on her, did you notice yesterday? He's twenty-three, a good solid boy. Here she is now! Hsing! How beautiful your hair is when it's long! You should let it grow longer!" The kind, practical, undemanding babble of his mother's talk was another stream on which Yao floated vaguely, peacefully, until all at once, in one moment, it was cut short. Silence. A bubble had burst. A bubble in an artery of the brain, the doctors said. For a few hours 3-Liu Meiling gazed in mute bewilderment at something no one else could see, and then died. She was only seventy. All life is in danger, from without, from within. People are a risky business.

The Floating World

THE BRIEF FUNERAL WAS HELD IN PEONY COMPOUND; THEN the body of 3-Liu Meiling was taken by her son and granddaughter and the technician to the Life Center to be recycled, a chemical process of breakdown and re-use with which as a chemist she had been perfectly familiar. She would still be part of their world, not as a being but as an endless becoming. She would be part of the children Hsing would bear. They were all part of one another. All used and users, all eaters, all eaten.

Inside a bubble where there is so much air and no more, so much water and no more, so much food and no more, so much energy and no more—in an aquarium, perfectly self-contained in its tiny balancing act: one catfish, two sticklebacks, three water-weeds, plenty of algae, three snails, maybe four, but no dragonfly larvae—inside a bubble, the population must be strictly controlled.

When Meiling dies she is replaced. But she is no more than replaced. Everybody can have a child. Some can't or won't or don't have children and some children die young, and so most of those who want two children can have two children. Four thousand isn't a great number. It is a carefully maintained number. Four thousand isn't a great gene pool, but it is a carefully selected and managed one. The anthrogeneticists are just as watchful and dispassionate as Yao in the plant labs. But they do not experiment. Sometimes they can catch a fault at the source, but they have not the resources to meddle with twists and recombinations. All such massive, elaborate technologies, supported by the continuous exploitation of the resources of a planet, were left behind by the Zero Generation. The anthrogeneticists have good tools and know their job, and their job is maintenance. They maintain the quality, literally, of life.

Everyone who wants to can have a child. One child, two at most. A woman has her motherchild. A man has his fatherchild.

The arrangement is unfair to men, who have to persuade a woman to bear a child for them. The arrangement is unfair to women, who are expected to spend three-quarters of a year of their life bearing somebody else's child. To women who want a child and cannot conceive or whose sexual life is with other women, so that they have to persuade both a

man and a woman to get and give them a child, the arrangement is
doubly unfair. The arrangement is, in fact, unfair. Sexuality and justice
have little if anything in common. Love and friendship and conscience
and kindness and obstinacy find ways to make the unfair arrangement
work, though not without anxiety, not without anguish, and not always.

Marriage and linking are informal options, often chosen while the
children are young, for many women find it hard to part with a fatherchild, and a homespace for four is luxuriously spacious.

Many women do not want to bear or bring up a child at all, many
feel their fertility to be a privilege and obligation, and some pride themselves on it. Now and then there is a woman who boasts of the number
of her fatherchildren, as of a basketball score.

4-Steinfeld Jael bore Hsing; she's Hsing's mother, but Hsing isn't
her child. Hsing is 4-Liu Yao's child, his fatherdaughter. Jael's child is
Joel, her motherson, six years older than his halfsister Hsing, two years
younger than his halfbrother 4-Adami Seth.

Everybody has a homespace. A single is one and one half rooms; a
room is a space of 960 cubic feet. The commonest shape is 10' x 12' x 8',
but since the partitions are movable the proportions can be altered freely
within the limits of the structural space. A double, like the 4-5 Lius', is
usually arranged as two little sleepcells and a large sharespace: two priva-
cies and a commonality. When people link, and if they each have one or
two children, their homespace may get quite large. The 3-4-5-Steinman-
Adamis, Jael and Joel and 3-Adami Manhattan, to whom she has been
linked for years, and his fatherson Seth, have 3,840 cubic feet of homespace. They live in Quad Four, where a lot of Nor-Ans live, Northameri-
can and European Ancestry people. With her usual flair for the dramatic,
Jael has found an area in the outer arc where there's room for ten-foot
ceilings. "Like the sky!" she cries. She has painted the ceilings bright blue.
"Feel the difference?" she says. "The sense of liberation—of freedom?" In
fact, when she goes to stay with Jael on visits, Hsing finds the rooms

rather disagreeable; they seem deep and cold, with all that waste space overhead. But Jael fills them with her warmth, her golden, inexhaustible voice, her bright clothing, her abundance of being.

When Hsing began menstruating and learning how to use prevention and brooding about sex, both Jael and Meiling told her that having a baby is a piece of luck. They were very different women, but they used the same word. "The best luck," Meiling said. "So interesting! Nothing else uses *all* of you." And Jael talked about how your relation to the baby in your womb and the newborn baby nursing was part of sex, an extension and completion of it that you were really lucky to know. Hsing listened with the modest, cynical reserve of the virgin. She'd make up her own mind about all that when the time came.

Many Chi-Ans had, more or less silently, disapproved of Yao's asking a woman of another quadrant and a different ancestry to bear his child. Many people of Jael's ancestry had asked her if she wanted an exotic experience or what. The fact was Jael and Yao had fallen desperately in love. They were old enough to realise that love was all they had in common. Jael had asked Yao if she could have his child. Moved to the heart, he had agreed. Hsing was born of an undying passion. Whenever Yao came to bring Hsing for a visit, Jael flung her arms about him crying "Oh Yao, it's you!" with such utter, ravished joy and delight that only a man as thoroughly satisfied and self-satisfied as Adami Manhattan could have escaped agonies of jealousy. Manhattan was a huge, hairy man. Perhaps being fifteen years older, eight inches taller, and a great deal hairier than Yao helped him to be unjealous of him.

Grandparents provided another way to increase the size of a homespace. Sometimes relatives, halfsibs, their parents, their children grouped together in still larger spaces. Next down the corridor from the 4-5 Lius' was the 3-4-5-Wangs'—Lotus Compound—eleven contiguous homespaces, the partitions arranged so as to provide a central atrium, the scene of ceaseless noise and activity. Peony Compound, where Meiling had lived all her life, always had from eight to eighteen homespaces. None of the other ancestries lived in such large groupings.

In fact by the fifth generation many people had lost any sense of what ancestry was, found it irrelevant, and disapproved of people who based their identity or their community on it. In Council, disapproval was frequently expressed of Chinese-Ancestry clannishness, referred to by its critics as "Quad Two separatism" or more darkly as "racism," and by those who practiced it as "keeping to our ways." The Chi-Ans protested the new Schools Administration policy of shifting teachers around from quad to quad, so that children would be taught by people from other ancestries, other communities; but they were outvoted in Council.

The Bubble

DANGERS, RISKS. IN THE GLASS BUBBLE, THE FRAGILE WORLD, the danger of schism, of conspiracy, the danger of aberrant behavior, madness, the violence of madness. No decision of any consequence at all was to be made by a single person acting without counsel. Nobody ever, since the beginning, had been allowed alone at any of the systems controls. Always a backup, a watcher. Yet there had been incidents. None had yet wreaked permanent damage.

But what of the merely normal, usual behavior of human beings? What is aberrant? Who's sane?

Read the histories, say the teachers. History tells us who we are, how we have behaved, therefore how we will behave.

Does it? The history in the bookscreens, Earth History, that appalling record of injustice, cruelty, enslavement, hatred, murder—that record, justified and glorified by every government and institution, of waste and misuse of human life, animal life, plant life, the air, the water, the planet? If that is who we are, what hope for us? History must be what we have escaped from. It is what we were, not what we are. History is what we need never do again.

The foam of the salt ocean has tossed up a bubble. It floats free.

To learn who we are, look not at history but at the arts, the record of our best, our genius. The elderly, sorrowful, Dutch faces gaze out of the darkness of a lost century. The mother's beautiful grave head is bowed above the dead son who lies across her lap. The old mad king cries over his murdered daughter, "Never, never, never, never, never!" With infinite gentleness the Compassionate One murmurs, "It does not last, it cannot satisfy, it has no being." "Sleep, sleep," say the cradle songs, and "Set me free" cry the yearning slave-songs. The symphonies rise, a glory out of darkness. And the poets, the crazy poets cry out, "A terrible beauty is born." But they're all crazy. They're all old and mad. All their beauty is terrible. Don't read the poets. They don't last, they can't satisfy, they have no being. They wrote about another world, the dirt world. That too, too solid world which the Zeroes made naught of.

Ti Chiu, Dichew, the dirt-ball. Earth. The "garbage" world. The "trash" planet.

These words are archaic, history-words, attached only to history-images: receptacles were filled with "dirty" "garbage" that was poured into vehicles which carried it to "trash dumps" to "throw away." What does that mean? Where is "away"?

Roxana and Rosa

WHEN SHE WAS SIXTEEN HSING READ THE DIARIES OF 0-FAYEZ Roxana. That self-probing mind, forever questioning its own honesty, was attractive to the adolescent. Roxana was rather like Luis, Hsing thought, but a woman. Sometimes she needed to be with a woman's mind, not a man's, but Lena was obsessed with her basketball scores, and Rosa had gone totally angel, and Grandmother had died. Hsing read Roxana's Diaries.

She realised for the first time that the people of the Zero Generation, the worldmakers, had believed that they were imposing an immense sacrifice on their descendants. What the Zeroes gave up, what they lost in leaving Earth—Roxana always used the English word—was compensated to them by their mission, their hope, and (as Roxana was well aware) by the tremendous power they had wielded in creating the very fabric of life for thousands of people for generations to come. "We are the gods of *Discovery*," Roxana wrote. "May the true gods forgive us our arrogance!"

But when she speculated on the years to come, she did not write of her descendants as children of the gods, but as victims, seeing them with fear, guilt, and pity, helpless prisoners of their ancestor's will and desire. "How will *they* forgive us?" she mourned. "We who took the world from them before they were ever born—we who took the seas, the mountains, the meadowlands, the cities, the sunlight from them, all their birthright? We have left them trapped in a cage, a tin can, a specimen box, to live and die like laboratory rats and never see the moon, never run across a field, never know what freedom is!"

I don't know what cages or tin cans or specimen boxes are, Hsing thought with impatience, but whatever a laboratory rat is, I'm not. I've run across a v-field in Countryside. You don't need fields and hills and all that stuff to be free! Freedom's what your mind does, what your soul is. It has nothing to do with all that Dichew-stuff. Don't worry, Grandmother! she said to the long-dead writer. It all worked out just fine. You made a wonderful world. You were a very wise, kind god.

When Roxana got depressed about her poor deprived descendants she also tended to go on and on about Shindychew, which she called the destination planet or just the Destination. Sometimes it cheered her up to imagine what it might be like, but mostly she worried about it. Would it be habitable? Would there be life on it? What kind of life? What would "the settlers" find, how would they cope with what they found, would they send the information back to Earth? That was so important to her. It was funny, poor Roxana worrying about what kind of signals her great-great-great-grandchildren would send "back" in two hundred years to a place they'd never been! But the bizarre idea was a great consolation to her. It was her justification for what they had done. It was the reason. *Discovery* would build a vast and delicate rainbow bridge across Space, and across it the true gods would walk: information, knowledge. The rational gods. That was Roxana's recurring image, her solace.

Hsing found her god-imagery tiresome. People with a monotheist ancestry seemed unable to get over it. Roxana's lower-case metaphorical deities were preferable to the capitalised Gods and Fathers in History and Lit, but she had very little patience with any of them.

Getting the Message

DISAPPOINTED WITH ROXANA, HSING QUARRELED WITH HER friend.

"Rosie, I wish you'd talk about other stuff," she said.

"I just want to share my happiness with you," Rosa said in her Bliss voice, soft, mild, and as flexible as a steel mainbeam.

"We used to be happy together without dragging in Bliss."

Rosa looked at her with a general lovingness that insulted Hsing obscurely but very deeply. We were *friends*, Rosie! she wanted to cry.

"Why do you think we're here, Hsing?"

Mistrusting the question, she pondered a bit before she answered. "If you mean that literally, we're here because the Zero Generation arranged that we should be here. If you mean it in some abstract sense, then I reject the question as loaded. To ask 'why' assumes purpose, a final cause. Zero Generation had a purpose: to send a ship to another planet. We're carrying it out."

"But where are we going?" Rosa asked with the intense sweetness, the sweet intensity, that made Hsing feel tight, sour, and defensive.

"To the Destination. Shindychew. And you and I will be old grannies when we get there!"

"Why are we going there?"

"To get information and send it back," Hsing said, having no answer ready except Roxana's, and then hesitated. She realised that it was a fair question, and that she had never really asked or answered it. "And to live there," she said. "To find out—about the universe. We are a—we are a voyage. Of discovery. The voyage of the *Discovery*."

She discovered the meaning of the name of the world as she said it.

"To discover—?"

"Rosie, this leading-question bit belongs in babygarden. 'And what do we call *this* nice curly letter?' Come on. Talk to me, don't manipulate me!"

"Don't be afraid, angel," Rosa said, smiling at Hsing's anger. "Don't be afraid of joy."

"Don't call me angel. I liked you when you were just you, Rosa."

"I never had any idea who I was before I knew Bliss," Rosa said, no longer smiling, and with such simplicity that Hsing felt both awed and ashamed.

But when she left Rosa, she was bereft. She had lost her friend for years, her beloved for a while. They wouldn't link when they grew up, as she had dreamed. She was damned if she'd be an angel! But oh, Rosie, Rosie. She tried to write a poem. Only two lines came:

We will always meet and never meet again.
Our corridors lead us forever apart.

What Does Apart Mean in a Closed World?

IT WAS HSING'S FIRST REAL LOSS. GRANDMOTHER MEILING had been such a cheerful, kindly presence, her death had been so unexpected, so quietly abrupt, that Hsing had never been entirely aware that she was gone. It seemed as if she still lived down the corridor. To think of her was not to grieve, but to be comforted. But Rosa was lost.

Hsing brought all the vigor and passion of her youth to her first grief. She walked in shadow. Certain parts of her mind might have been darkened permanently. Her fierce resentment of the angels for taking Rosa from her led her to think that some of the older people of her ancestry were right: it was no use trying to understand other-ancestry people. They were different. They were best avoided. Keep to our own kind. Keep to the middle, keep to the way.

Even Yao, tired of fellow-workers in the plantlabs preaching Bliss, quoted Old Long-Ears—"They talk, they don't know. They know, they don't talk."

Fools

"SO YOU KNOW?" LUIS SAID, WHEN SHE REPEATED THE LINE TO him. "You Chi-Ans?"

"No. Nobody knows. I just don't like preaching!"

"Lots of people do, though," Luis said. "They like preaching and they like being preached to. All kinds of people."

Not us, she thought, but didn't say. After all, Luis wasn't Chinese Ancestry.

"Just because you have a flat face," he said, "you don't have to make a wall out of it."

"I don't have a flat face. That's racist."

"Yes you do. The Great Wall of China. Come on out, Hsing. It's me. Hybrid Luis."

"You aren't any more hybrid than I am."

"Much more."

"You don't think Jael is Chinese!" she jeered.

"No, she's pure Nor-An. But my birthmother's half Euro and half Indo and my father's one quarter each Southamerican and Afro and the other half Japanese, if I have it straight. Whatever it all means. What it means is I have no ancestry. Only ancestors. But you! You look like Yao and your grandmother, and you talk like them, and you learned Chinese from them, and you grew up here in the heart of an ancestry, and you're in process right now of doing the old Chi-An Exclusion Act. Your ancestry comes from the most racist people in history."

"Not so! The Japanese—the Euros—the Northamericans—"

They argued amicably for a while on sketchy data, and agreed that probably everybody on Dichew had been racist, as well as sexist, classist, and obsessed with money, that incomprehensible but omnipresent element of all the histories. They got sidetracked into economics, which they had been trying to understand in history class. They talked about money for a while, very stupidly.

If everybody has access to the same food, clothing, furniture, tools, education, information, work, and authority, and hoarding is useless because you can have for the asking, and gambling is an idle sport because there's nothing to lose, so that wealth and poverty have become mere metaphors—"rich in love," "poor in spirit"—how is one to understand the importance of money?

"Really they were awful fools," Hsing said, voicing the heresy all intelligent young people arrived at sooner or later.

"Then we are too," Luis said, maybe believing it, maybe not.

"Oh Luis," Hsing said with a long, deep sigh, looking up at the mural on the wall of the High School snackery, currently an abstract of soft curving pinks and golds, "I don't know what I'd do without you."

"Be an awful fool."

She nodded.

4-Nova Ed

LUIS WASN'T TURNING OUT THE WAY HIS FATHER INTENDED. They both knew it. 4-Nova Ed was a kind man whose existence was centered in his genitals. Stimulation and relief was the pressing issue, but procreation was important to him too. He had wanted a son to carry his name and his genes into the future. He was glad to help make a child for any woman who asked him to, and did so three times; but he had looked long and carefully for the right woman to bear his father-son. He studied every word of several compatibility charts and genetic mixmatches, though reading wasn't his favorite occupation; and when he finally decided he'd found the one, he made sure she was willing to control the gender. "A daughter would be fine if I had two, but if it's one it's a son, right?"

"A son you want, a son you get," said 4-Sandstrom Lakshmi, and bore him one. An active, athletic woman, she found the experience of pregnancy so uncomfortable and time-consuming that she never repeated it. "It was your big, brown, Goddam eyes, Ed," she said. "Never again. Here you are. He's all yours." Every now and then Lakshmi turned up at the 4-5 Nova homespace, always bringing a toy appropriate to Luis's age a year ago or five years from now. Usually she and Ed had what she called commemorative sex. After it she would say, "I wonder what the hell I thought I was doing. Never again! But I guess he's OK, isn't he?"

"The kid's OK!" his father said, heartily and without conviction. "Your brains, my plumbing."

She worked in Central Communications; Ed was a physical therapist, a good one, but as he said, his ideas were all in his hands. "It's why I'm such a good lover," he told his partners, and he was right. He was also a good parent for a baby. He knew how to hold the baby and handle him, and loved to do so. He lacked the fear of the infant, the squeamish dissociation which paralyses less manly men. The delicacy and vigor of the tiny body delighted him. He loved Luis as flesh of his flesh, wholeheartedly and happily, for the first couple of years, and less happily for the rest of his life. As the years went on the pure delight got covered over and buried under a lot of other stuff, a lot of hard feelings.

The child had a deep, silent will and temper. He would never give in and never take things easy. He had colic forever. Every tooth was a battle. He wheezed. He learned to talk before he could walk. By the time he was three he was saying things that left Ed staring. "Don't talk so Goddam fancy!" he told the child. He was disappointed in his son and ashamed of his disappointment. He had wanted a companion, a double, a kid to teach racquetball to. Ed had been Quad Two racquetball champion six years running.

Luis dutifully learned to play racquetball, never very well, and tried to teach his father a word game called Grammary, which drove Ed nuts. He did outstandingly well at school, and Ed tried to be proud of him. Instead of running around with the kidherd, Luis always brought a Chi-An kid over, a girl, Liu Hsing, and they shut the room door and played for hours, silently. Ed checked, of course. They weren't up to anything more than all herdkids got up to, but he was glad when they got to their Ceremony and started wearing clothes. In shorts and shirts they looked like little adults. In their nakedness they had been somehow slippery, elusive, mysterious.

As all the growing-up rules came into force, Luis obeyed them. He still preferred the girl Hsing over all the boys and they still saw each other all the time, but never alone together with the door shut. Which meant that when Ed was home he had to listen to them as they did their homework or talked. Talked, talked, shit, how they talked. Until the girl was twelve. Then her ancestry's rule was that she could only meet a boy in public places and with other people around. Ed found this an excellent idea. He hoped Luis would take up with other girls, maybe get into some boy activities. Luis and Hsing did go around with a group of the Quad Two teens. But the two of them always ended up somewhere, talking.

"When I was sixteen, I'd slept with three girls," Ed said. "And a couple of guys." It didn't come out the way he meant. He meant to confide in Luis, to encourage him, but it sounded like a boast or a reproach.

"I don't want to have sex yet," the boy said, sounding stuffy. Ed couldn't blame him.

"It's not really a big deal," Ed said.

"It is for you," Luis said. "So I guess it is for me."

"No, what I mean—" But Ed could not say what he meant. "It's not just fun," he said lamely.

A pause.

"Beats jerking off," Ed said.

Luis nodded, evidently in full agreement.

A pause.

"I just want to figure out how to, maybe, you know, how to find my own way, in all that," the boy said, not as fast with the words as usual.

"That's OK," the father said, and they parted with mutual relief. The boy might be slow, Ed thought, but at least he'd grown up in a home-space with plenty of healthy, open, happy sex as an example.

On Nature

IT WAS INTERESTING TO KNOW THAT ED HAD SLEPT WITH MEN; it must have been youthful experiment, for he'd never to Luis's knowledge brought a man home. But he brought women home. Probably every woman of his own generation, Luis thought, and now he was bringing home some of the older Fives. Luis knew the sound of his orgasms by heart—a harsh, increasing hah! hah! HAH!—and had heard every conceivable form of ecstatic female shriek, wail, howl, grunt, gasp, and bellow. The most notable bellower was 4-Yep Sosi, a physical therapist from Quad Three. She had been coming over every now and then ever since Luis could remember. She always brought star-cookies for Luis, even now. Sosi started out going aah, like a lot of them, but her aahs got louder and louder and more and more continuous, rising to a relentless, mindless ululation, so piercing that once Granny 2-Wong down the corridor thought it was an alarm siren and roused up everybody in the Wong compound. It didn't embarrass Ed at all. Nothing did. "It's perfectly natural," he said.

It was a favorite phrase of his. Anything to do with the body was "perfectly natural." Anything to do with the mind wasn't.

So, what was "nature"?

As far as Luis could think it through, and he thought about it a good deal his last year in high school, Ed was quite correct. In this world—on this ship, he corrected himself, for he was trying to train his mind in certain habits—on this ship, "nature" was the human body. And to some extent the plants, soils, and water in hydroponics; and the bacterial population. Those only to some extent, because they were so closely controlled by the techs, even more closely controlled than human bodies were.

"Nature," on the original planet, had meant what was not controlled by human beings. "Nature" was what was substantially previous to control, the raw material for control, or what had escaped from control. Thus the areas of Dichew where few people lived, quadrants that were undesirably dry or cold or steep, had been called "nature," "wilderness," or "nature preserves." In these areas lived the animals, which were also called "natural" or "wild." And all the "animal" functions of the human body were therefore "natural"—eating, drinking, pissing, shitting, sex, reflex, sleep, shouting, and going off like a siren when somebody licked your clitoris.

Control over these functions wasn't called unnatural, however, except possibly by Ed. It was called civilisation. Control started affecting the natural body as soon as it was born. And it really began to click in, Luis saw, at seven when you put on clothes and undertook to be a citizen instead of one of the kidherd, the wild bunch, the naked little savages.

Wonderful words!—wild—savage—civilisation—citizen—

No matter how you civilised it, the body remained somewhat wild, or savage, or natural. It had to keep up its animal functions, or die. It could never be fully tamed, fully controlled. Even plants, Luis learned from listening to Hsing's father, however manipulated to serve their symbiotic functions, were not totally predictable or obedient; and the bacteria populations came up constantly with "wild" breeds, possibly dangerous mutations. The only things that could be perfectly controlled were inanimate, the matter of the world, the elements and compounds, solid, liquid, or gas, and the artifacts made from them.

What about the controller, the civiliser itself, the mind? Was it civilised? Did it control itself?

There seemed to be no reason why it should not; yet its failures to do so constituted most of what was taught as History. But that was inevitable, Luis thought, because on Dichew "Nature" had been so huge and so strong. Nothing there was really, absolutely under control, except v-stuff.

Oddly enough he had learned that interesting fact from a virtual. He hacked his way through a tropical jungle buzzing with things that flew, bit, crawled, stung, snapped, and tormented the flesh, gasping for breath in a malodorous clinging heat that took his strength away, until he came to an open place where a horrible little group of humans deformed by disease, malnutrition, and self-mutilation rushed out of huts, screaming at the sight of him, and shot poisoned darts at him through blowguns. It was part of a lesson in Ethical Dilemmas, using the V-Dichew program Jungle. The words tropic, jungle, trees, insects, sting, huts, tattoos, darts had been in the Preliminary Vocabulary yesterday. But right now the Ethical Dilemma was pressing. Should he run away? try to parley? ask for mercy? shoot back? His v-persona carried a lethal weapon and wore a heavy garment, which might deflect the darts or might not.

It was an interesting lesson, and they had a good debate in class afterwards. But what stuck with Luis long after was the sheer, overwhelming enormity of that "jungle," that "wild nature" in which the savage human beings seemed so insignificant as to be accidental, and the civilised human being was completely foreign. He did not belong there. No sane person did. No wonder the subzero generations had had trouble maintaining civilisation and self-control, against odds like that.

A Controlled Experiment

ALTHOUGH HE FOUND THE ARGUMENTS OF THE ANGELS BOTH rather silly and rather disturbing, he thought that they might be right in one fundamental matter: that the destination of this ship was not as important as the voyage itself. Having read history, and experienced Jungle and Inner City, Luis wondered if part of the Zero Generation's intent might have been to give at least a few thousand people a place where they could escape such horrors. A place where human existence could be controlled, as in a laboratory experiment. A controlled experiment in control.

Or a controlled experiment in freedom?

That was the biggest word Luis knew.

He mentally perceived words as having various sizes, densities, depths; words were dark stars, some small and dull and solid, some immense, complex, subtle, with a powerful gravity-field that attracted infinite meanings to them. *Freedom* was the biggest of the dark stars.

For what it meant to him personally he had a clear, precise image. His asthma attacks were infrequent, but vivid to his mind; and once when he was thirteen, in gymnastics, he had been under Big Ling at the wrong moment and Big Ling had come down right on him. Being about twice Luis's weight, Ling had squashed the air entirely out of Luis's lungs. After an endless time of gasping for air, the first breath, raw, dragging, searingly painful: that was freedom. Breath. What you breathed.

Without it you suffocated, went dark, and died.

People who had to live on the animal level might have been able to move around a lot, but never had enough air for their minds to breathe; they had no freedom. That was clear to him in the history readings and the historical v-worlds. Inner City 2000 was so shocking because it wasn't "wild nature" that made the people there crazy, sick, dangerous, and incredibly ugly, but their own lack of control over their own supposedly civilised "nature."

Human nature. A strange combination of words.

Luis thought about the man in Quad Three, last year, who had attacked a woman sexually, beaten her unconscious, and then killed himself by drinking liquid oxygen. He had been a Five, and the event, disturbing to everyone in the world, was particularly horrible and haunting to the people of his generation. They asked themselves *could I have done that? could that happen to me?* None of them seemed to know the answer. That man, 5-Wolfson Ad, had lost control over his "animal" or "natural" needs and so had ended up without any freedom at all, not making choices, not able even to stay alive. Maybe some people couldn't handle freedom.

The angels never talked about freedom. Follow orders, attain Bliss.

What would the angels do in the Year 201?

That was an interesting question, actually. What would any of them do, what would happen to the controlled experiment, when the laboratory ship reached the Destination? Shindychew was a planet—another huge mass of wild stuff, uncontrollable "nature," where they wouldn't even know what the rules were. On Dichew, at least their ancestors had been familiar with "nature," knew how to use it, how to get around in it, which animals were dangerous or poisonous, how to grow the wild plants, and so on. On the New Earth they wouldn't know anything.

The books talked about that, a little, not much. After all there was still half a century to go before they got there. But it would be interesting to find out what they did know about Shindychew.

When he asked his history teacher, 3-Tranh Eti, she said that the education program would provide Generation Six with a whole lot of education about the Destination and living there. Generation Five people would mostly be so old when they got there that it wasn't really their problem, she said, though of course they would be allowed to "land" if they wished to. The program was designed to keep the "middle generations" ("That's us," the old woman said drily) content with their world. A practical approach, she said, and well meant, but perhaps it had encouraged the mentality that was now so very prevalent among the proponents of Bliss.

She spoke frankly to Luis, her best student, and he told her as frankly that whether he got there or not, no matter how old he'd be if he got there, he wanted to find out now where he was going. He understood why; he didn't need to understand how; but he did want to understand where.

Tranh Eti gave him some help in accessing information, but it turned out that the education program for Generation Six was not accessible at present. It was being reviewed by the Educational Committee.

His other teachers advised him to finish his studies in high school and college and worry about the Destination later. If at all.

He went to the Head Librarian, old 3-Tan, his friend Bingdi's grandfather.

"To speculate about our destination," Tan said, "is to increase anxiety, impatience, and erroneous expectations." He smiled slightly. He spoke slowly, with pauses between sentences. "Our job is to travel. A different job from arrival." After a pause he went on, "But a generation that knows only how to travel—can they teach a generation how to arrive?"

The Garan

LUIS CONTINUED TO PURSUE HIS INTEREST. HE WENT BACK, ON his own, to Jungle.

He had to follow the trail, of course. However through-composed a virtual-reality program was, you could do in it only what there was to do. It was like a dream, any dream, especially a nightmare: only certain choices are offered, if any.

There was the trail. You had to take the trail. The trail would lead to the ugly, degraded little savages, and they would scream and shoot poisoned darts, and then he would have to make one of the choices. Methodically, Luis made them, one after another.

Attempts to reason with the savages or run away from them ended quickly in blackout, which was, of course, v-death.

Once when they attacked him he fired the gun and killed one of the men. This was horrible beyond anything he had ever imagined and he escaped the program within moments of firing the weapon. That night he dreamed that he had a secret name that nobody knew, not even himself. A woman he had never seen before came to him and said, "Add your name to the wolf."

He went back into Jungle, though it was not easy. He found that if he showed no fear, threatened them with the gun if they attacked but did not fire it, the little men eventually, very suddenly, accepted his presence. After that another set of choice-forks opened out. He could keep his weapon in evidence and force the savages to lead him to the Lost City (which was supposed to be why you'd entered the jungle). He could make them obey him, but always he blacked out before he got far; the savages had murdered him. Or, if he behaved without fear, not threatening them and asking nothing of them, he could stay with them, living in a half-ruined hut. They accepted him as some kind of crazy man. The women gave him food and showed him how to do things, and he began to learn their language and customs. These were surprisingly intricate, formal, and fascinating. It was only v-learning; it only went so far, and seemed more than it was; when you came out you didn't come out with much. A program could hold only so much, even in implication. But what little he recalled of it had strangely enriched his thinking. He intended to go back some time, work his way to that final choice, and redo living with the savages.

But he had a different purpose, this time. This time when he entered Jungle, he moved as slowly as he could, and once he was well in he stopped and stood still on the path. He was no longer afraid of meeting the savages. Now that he knew them, had lived among them, it would have been sad to see them come at him, as they inevitably would, screaming and trying to kill him. He wanted not to meet them, this time. They were virtual human beings made by human beings. He had come to try to experience a place where nothing was human.

As he stood there, beginning to sweat at once, smelling the stinks, slapping at the creatures that buzzed and flickered around him and landed on his skin and bit, listening to the uncanny noises, he thought about Hsing. She would not admit VR as experience. She never went to V-Dichew unless it was required by a teacher. She never played v-games, wouldn't even try the really interesting one Luis and Bingdi had worked out using "Borges's Garden" as a matrix. "I don't want to be in another person's world, I want to be in mine," she said.

"You read novels," he said.

"Sure. But *I* do reading. The writer puts the story there, and I do it. I make it be. The v-programmer uses me to do *his* story. Nobody uses my body and my mind but me. OK?" She always got fierce.

She had a point; but what struck Luis, standing alert and tense on the narrow incredibly intricate jungle pathway like a corridor gone crazy, watching something full of legs crawl away into the sinister darkness under a huge thing that he decided was a tree, but a tree lying down instead of standing up—what struck him was not only the choking, senseless complexity of this place, its quality of chaos, even though it was only a re-creation, the program of a sensation-field—but also how hostile it was. Dangerous, frightening. Was he experiencing the programmer's hostility?

There were plenty of sadistic programs; some people got hooked on them. How could he tell whether "nature" was in fact so terrible?

Certainly there were VR programs in which Dichew appeared simpler, more comprehensible—Countryside or Walking to the Mountains. And watching films, where the only sensations you had to cope with were sight and hearing, you could see that even though it was chaotic, "nature" could be pretty. Some people got hooked on those films, too, and were always watching sea turtles swimming in the sea and sky birds flying in the sky. But looking was one thing and feeling was another, even if it was only virtual feeling.

How could anybody actually live their whole life in a place like Jungle? The discomfort of the sensation-field was constant, the heat, the creatures, the changes of temperature, the rough, gritty, filthy surfaces of things, the endless unevenness—every step you took you had to look to see what your foot was going to land on. He remembered the natives' disgusting food. They killed animals and ate pieces of animal. The women chewed the root of some kind of plant, spat the chewed mass into a dish, let it rot a while, and then everybody ate it. If these stinging and biting poisonous animals were real not virtual, you'd come out of Jungle full of toxins. Indeed, what finally happened to you in the choice-fork where you lived with the savages was that you put your hand on a vine and it was a poisonous animal with no legs. It bit your hand, and within a few minutes you felt terrible pain and nausea, and then blackout. They had to end the program one way or another, of course; it was ten cycles subjective, ten actual hours, the maximum permitted length of a v-program. He had been not only virtually dead, but actually extremely stiff, hungry, thirsty, exhausted, and distressed when he came out of it.

Was the program honest? Did people on Dichew actually live in such misery? Not for ten cycles/hours, but for a lifetime? In constant fear of dangerous animals, fear of enemy savages, fear of each other, in constant pain from the thorns on plants, bites and stings, muscle strains from carrying heavy loads, feet bruised by the terrible uneven surfaces, and enduring still greater horrors, starvation, diseases, broken or deformed limbs, blindness? Not one of the savages, not even the baby and its young mother, was sound and clean. Their lesions and sores and scabs and calluses, bleared eyes, twisted limbs, filthy feet, filthy hair had only become more painful to look at as he began to know them as people. He had kept wanting to help them.

As he stood now on the v-path there was a noise near him in the darkness of the trees and long stringy plants, epiphytes like Yao's, only huge and knotted. Something among all these weird crowded-together lives that made the jungle had made a noise. He stood stiller than ever, remembering the garan.

He had gone with the men of the savage tribe, understanding that they were doing "hunting." They had glimpsed a flash of spotted golden light. One of the men had whispered a word, *garan*, which he remembered when he came back. He looked for it but it was not in the dictionary.

Now it came out of the chaos-darkness, the garan. It walked across the pathway from left to right a few meters in front of him. It was long, low, golden with black spots. It walked with indescribable softness and skill on four round feet, the head low, followed by a long graceful extension of itself, a tail, the tip just twitching as it vanished into the darkness again in utter silence. It never glanced at Luis.

He stood transfixed. It's VR, it's a program, he said to himself. Every time I came into Jungle, if I stood here just so long, the garan would walk across the path. If I was ready for it, if I wanted to, I could shoot at it with my v-gun. If the program includes "hunting," I would kill it. If the program doesn't include "hunting," my gun wouldn't fire. I could not make anything happen. The garan would walk on and vanish in silence, the tip of its tail just twitching as it disappears. This is not the wilderness. This is not nature. This is supreme control.

He turned around and walked out of the program.

He met Bingdi on his way to the gym to run laps. "I want to develop a technology for VU," he said.

"Sure," Bingdi said, after a moment, and grinned. "Let's do it."

Where Are We Going?

PROGRAMS, PHOTOGRAPHS, DESCRIPTIONS—ALL REPRESENTATIONS of Dichew were suspect, since they were products of technology, of the human mind. They were interpretations. The planet of origin was inaccessible to direct understanding.

The planet of destination was less even than that. As he continued to explore the Library, Luis began to understand why the Zero Generation had been so eager for information about Shindychew. They had none.

The discovery of what they called a "Terran planet" within "accessible range" had set off the whole *Discovery* project. The sub-Zeroes had studied it as exhaustively as their instruments permitted. But neither spectrum analysis nor any form of direct observation of a small non-self-luminous body at that distance could tell them all they needed to know. Life had been established as a universal emergent within certain parameters, and all the parameters they were able to establish were highly favorable. All the same, as he read in an ancient article called "Where Are They Going?" it was possible that a very small difference from "Earth" could make "New Earth" utterly uninhabitable for humans. Chemical incompatibility of the life forms with human chemistry, making everything there poisonous. A slightly different balance of the gases of the atmosphere, so that people could not breathe the air.

Air is freedom, Luis thought.

The Librarian was reading at a table nearby. Luis went over and sat down by him. He showed old Tan the article. "It says it's possible that we won't be able to breathe there."

The Librarian glanced over the article. "I certainly won't be able to," he observed. After the usual pause between sentences, he explained. "I'll be dead." He smiled a benign, semi-circular smile.

"What I'm trying to find," Luis said, "is something about what they expected us to do when we got there. Are there instructions somewhere—for the various possibilities—?"

"At present," the old man said, "if there are such instructions, they are sealed."

Luis started to speak, then stopped, waiting for Tan's pause to end.

"Information has always been controlled."

"By whom?"

"Primarily, by the decisions of the Zero Generation. Secondarily, by the decisions of the Educational Council."

"Why would the Zeroes hide information about our destination? Is it that bad?"

"Perhaps they thought, since so little was known, the middle generations needn't worry about it. And the Sixth Generation would find out. And send them the information. This is a voyage of scientific discovery." He looked up at Luis, his face impassive. "If the air is not breathable, or there are other problems, people can go out in suits. Evamen. Live inside, study outside. Observe. Send information to the *Discovery* in orbit. And thence back to Ti Chiu." He pronounced the Chinese word in Chinese. "There are Unreplaceable Supplies for twelve generations, not six. In case we could not stay there. Or chose not to. Chose to go back to Ti Chiu."

It took Tan quite a while to say all this. Luis's mind filled the pauses with imaginings, as if he were illustrating a text: the vast trajectory slowing, slowing towards a certain star; the little shipworld hovering above the surface of the immense planetworld; tiny figures in evasuits swarming out into Jungle. . . . Vivid, improbable. Virtual Unreality.

"'Back,'" he said. "What's 'back'? None of us came from Dichew. Back or forward, what's the difference?"

"'How much difference between yes and no? What difference between good and bad?'" the old man said, looking at him approvingly, yet with that expression in his eyes that Luis could not interpret. Was it sorrow?

He knew the quotation. Hsing and her father Yao had both studied with 3-Tan, who as well as being the Librarian was a scholar of the Chinese classics, and all three were fans of Old Long-Ears. Growing up in Quad Two, Luis had heard the book quoted till he read a translation of it in self-defense. Recently he had re-read it, trying to figure out how much of it made sense to him. Liu Yao had copied the whole thing out in the ancient Chinese characters. It had taken over a year. "Just practicing calligraphy," he said. Watching the complex, mysterious figures flow from Yao's brush, Luis had been moved more strongly than he ever had been moved by the seemingly comprehensible translated words. As if not to understand was to understand.

Circulation

PAPER, MADE FROM RICE STRAW, WAS RARE STUFF. LITTLE WRIT-
ing was done by hand. Yao had got permission to use several meters of
paper for his copying, but he could not keep it out of circulation for long.
He gave pieces of the scroll to Chi-An friends. They would put them
up on the wall for a while, then recycle them. No inessential artifact
could survive more than a few years. Clothes, artworks, paper copies of
texts, toys, all were given back to the cycle, sometimes with a ceremony
of grief. A funeral for the beloved doll. The portrait of Grandfather
might be copied into the electronic memory bank when the original was
recycled. Arts were practical or ephemeral or immaterial—a wedding
shirt, bodypaint, a song, a story in an all-net magazine. The cycle was
inexorable. The people of *Discovery* were their own raw material. They
had everything they needed, they had nothing they could keep. The
only poverty such a world could suffer would follow from the loss or
waste of energy/matter tied up in useless objects or ejected into space.

Or, in the very long run, from entropy.

Once upon a time a dermatologist doing eva to repair a slight
encounter-graze on the underhull had tossed his alloy gun to his companion a few meters away, who missed the catch. The film-story of the
Lost Gun was a dramatic moment in second-grade Ecology. Oh! the
children cried in horror as the tool, gently revolving, drifted among the
stars, farther and farther away. There—look—it's going to away! It's
going to away forever!

The light of the stars moved the world. Hydrogen acceptors fed the
tiny fusion reactors that powered the electrical and mechanical systems
and the Fresno accelerators that sped *Discovery* on its way. The little
world was affected from outside only by dust and photons. It accepted
nothing from outside but atoms of hydrogen.

Within itself it was entirely self-sustaining, self-renewing. Every cell shed by human skin, every speck of dust worn from a fabric or a bearing, every molecule of vapor from leaf or lung, was drawn into the filters and the reconverters, saved, recombined, re-used, reconfigured, reborn. The system was in equilibrium. There were reserves for emergencies, never yet called upon, and the store of Unreplaceable Supplies Tan had mentioned, some of them raw materials, others hi-tech items which the ship lacked the means to duplicate: a surprisingly small amount, stored in two cargobays. The effect of the second law of thermodynamics operating in this almost-closed system had been reduced to almost-nil.

Everything had been thought about, seen to, provided for. All the necessities of life. *Why am I here? Why am I?* A purpose for living: a reason. That, too, the Zeroes had tried to provide.

For all the middle generations of the two-century voyage, their reason for being was to be alive and well, to keep the ship in good running order, and to furnish it with another generation, so that it could accomplish its mission, their mission, the purpose to which they were all essential. A purpose which had meant so much to the Zeroes, the earthborn. Discovery. Exploration of the universe. Scientific information. Knowledge.

An irrelevant knowledge, useless, meaningless to people living and dying in the closed, complete world of the ship.

What did they need to know that they didn't know?

They knew that life was inside: light, warmth, breath, companionship. They knew that outside was nothing. The void. Death. Death silent, immediate, absolute.

Syndromes

"INFECTIOUS DISEASES" WERE SOMETHING YOU READ ABOUT OR saw hideous pictures of in history films. In every generation there were a few cancers, a few systemic disorders; kids broke their arms, athletes overdid it; hearts and other organs went wrong or wore out; cells followed their programs, aged, died; people aged, died. A major responsibility of doctors was seeing that death did not come too hard.

The angels spared them even that responsibility, being strong on "positive dying," which made of death a devout communal exercise, leading the dying person into trance induced by hypnosis, chanting, music, and other techniques; the death itself was greeted by ecstatic rejoicing.

Many doctors dealt almost entirely with gestation, birth, and death: "easy out, easy in." Diseases were words in textbooks.

But there were syndromes.

In the First and Second Generations many men in their thirties and forties had suffered rashes, lethargy, joint pains, nausea, weakness, inability to concentrate. The syndrome was tagged SD, somatic depression. The doctors judged it to be psychogenic.

It was in response to the SD syndrome that certain areas of professional work had been gender-restricted. A measure was put up for discussion and vote: men were to do all structural maintenance and dermatology. The last—repair and upkeep of the skin of the world where it interfaced with space—was the only job that required doing eva: going outside the world.

There were loud protests. The "division of labor," perhaps the oldest and deepest-founded of all the institutions of power-imbalance—was that irrational, fanciful set of prescriptions and proscriptions to be reinstituted here, where sanity and balance must, at the cost of life itself, be preserved?

Discussions in Council and quad meetings went on for a long time. The argument for gender-restriction was that men, unable to bear and nourish children, needed a compensatory responsibility to valorise their greater muscular strength as well as their hormone-related aggressivity and need for display.

A great many men and women found this argument insupportable in every sense of the word. A slightly larger number found it convincing. The citizens voted to restrict all evas to men.

After a generation had passed, the arrangement was seldom questioned. Its popular justification was that since men were biologically more expendable than women they should do the dangerous work. In fact no one had ever been killed doing eva, or even taken a dangerous dose of radiation; but the sense of danger glamorised the rule. Active, athletic boys volunteered for dermatology in numbers far larger than were needed, and so served on a reserve rota with regular training evas. Evamen had a distinctive way of dressing: brown canvas shorts, a carefully embroidered sleeve-patch of stars on black.

The outbreak of SD had leveled off eventually to a low endemic level, a drop that some said was connected to the eva restrictions and some said was not.

The Thirds had dealt with a high incidence of spontaneous abortions and stillbirths, never explained, and fortunately lasting only a few years. The episode had caused an increase in late pregnancies and two-child families until the optimum replacement ratio was recovered.

In the Fourth and Fifth generations a perhaps related, even more debilitating set of symptoms appeared, diagnosed but as yet unexplained, tagged TSS, tactile sensitivity syndrome. The symptoms were random pains and extreme neural sensitivity. TSS sufferers avoided crowds, could not eat in the refectories, complained that everything they touched hurt; they used dark glasses and earplugs and covered their hands and feet with things called sox. As no explanation or cure had been found, myths of prevention sprang up and folk remedies flourished. Quad Two had a low incidence of TSS, and so the Chi-An food style—rice, soy, ginger, garlic—was imitated. A reclusive life seemed to ease the symptoms, so some people with TSS tried to keep their children out of kidherd and school. But here the law intervened. No

parental decision was permitted to impair the welfare of the child and of
the community as determined by the Constitution and the judgment of
the Council on Education. The children went to school and suffered no
visible ill effects. Dark glasses, earplugs, and sox were a brief fad among
high-schoolers, but the disorder affected few people under twenty. The
angels asserted that no practitoner of Bliss suffered from TSS, and that
to escape it, all you had to do was learn to rejoice.

Ancestors of the Angels

o-Kim Jan had been the youngest of the Zeroes, ten days
old at Embarkation.

o-Kim Jan was a power in the Council for many years. Her genius
was for organisation, order, a firm, impartial administration. The Chi-
Ans called her Lady Confucius.

She had a late-born son, 1-Kim Terry. Her son led an obscure life,
interrupted by bouts of somatic depression, as a programmer for the
primary schools innet, until o-Kim died in the year 79. She was the last
of the Zeroes, the earthborn. Her death was felt as momentous.

Her funeral was attended by a very great crowd, far too many even
for the Temenos to hold. The ceremony was broadcast on the allnet.
Almost every person in the world watched it and so saw the inception
of a new religion.

Church and State

The Constitution was explicit in decreeing the abso-
lute separation of creed from polity. Article 4 specifically named the
monotheisms that figured so large in history, including the religion that

had controlled the dominant governments at the time the voyage of *Discovery* was planned. Any attempt "to influence an election or the deliberation of a legislative body by overt or covert invocation of the principles or tenets of Judaism, Christianity, Islam, Mormonism, or any other religious creed or institution," if confirmed by an ad hoc committee on Religious Manipulation, could be punished by public reprimand, loss of office, or permanent disqualification from any position of responsibility.

In the early decades there had been many challenges to Article 4. Though the planners had consciously tried to select *Discovery's* crew for what they saw as scientific impartiality of mind, the monotheist tendency to limit understanding to a single mode was already deeply embedded in much of their science. They had expected that in a deliberately, widely heterogeneous population the practice of tolerance would be not so much a virtue as a necessity. Still, in the Zero Generation, after several years of space travel people who had never given religion much thought, or who had thought of it as inimical, often took to identifying themselves as Mormon, Muslim, Christian, Jew, Buddhist, Hindu. They had found that religious affiliations and practices gave them needed support and comfort in their sudden, utter, irrevocable exile from everyone on Earth and from the Earth itself.

Faithful atheists were incensed by this outbreak of piety. Actual memories of the horrors of the Fundamentalist Purification and historical evidence of endless genocides in the name of God cast their shadows across the mildest forms of public worship. Eclecticism waved its ineffectual hands. Accusations were hurled, challenges made. Ad hoc Committees on Religious Manipulation were convened and reconvened.

But the generations after the Zeroes had no experience of exile; they lived where they were born, where their parents had been born. And miscegenation made ancestral pieties irrelevant. It was difficult for a Jewish Presbyterian Parsee to choose which of his Puritanisms to obey.

It was not difficult to forgo the incompatible righteousnesses of a Sunni-Mormon-Brahmin inheritance.

When o-Kim died, Article 4 had not been invoked for years. There were religious practices, but no religious institutions. Practice was private or familial. People sat vipassana or zazen, prayed for guidance or in praise. A family celebrated the birth of Jesus or the kindness of Ganesh or the memory of the Passover on more or less appropriate days of the monthless year. Of all ceremonies, funerals, which were always public, were the most likely to bring the trappings as well as the essentials of religion into play. Beautiful old words in beautiful old languages were spoken, and rites of mourning and consolation were observed.

The Funeral and the Birth of Bliss

o-Kim had been a militant atheist. She had said, "People need God the way a three-year-old needs a chainsaw." Her funeral was scrupulously free of references to the supernatural or quotations from holy books. People spoke briefly—some not briefly enough—about her effect on their life and everyone's life, about her charisma, her incorruptibility, her powerful, parental, practical care for the future generations. And they spoke with emotion of this death of the "Last of the Earthborn." Children of children watching this ceremony, they said, would be alive when the Mission that the Founders sent forth came at last to its fulfilment—when the Destination was reached. Kim Jan's spirit would be with them then.

Finally, as was customary, the child of the deceased rose to say the last words.

1-Kim Terry came up on the podium in front of the people and the innet camcorders beside the bier where his mother's body lay draped in white. There was great intensity and purposefulness in his movements. To people who knew him, he looked changed—assured, calm. He was not tearful or shaky-voiced. He looked out over the crowd that filled the whole floor of the Temenos. "He shone," several people said later.

"The last of those whose body was born of Earth is gone," he said in a clear, strong voice, which reminded many of his mother, a fine speaker in Council. "She has gone to the glory of which her body was the bright shadow. We here, now, travel away from the body into the realm of the soul. We are free. We are utterly free of darkness, of sin, of Earth. Through the corridors of the future I bring the message to you. I am the messenger, the angel. And you, you are angels. You are the chosen. God has called you, called you by name. You are the blessed. You are divine beings, sacred souls, who have been called to live in bliss. All that remains to us to do is to know who we are, that we are the inhabitants of heaven. That we are the blessed, the heavenborn, chosen for the eternal voyage. That we are, each one of us, sacred, born to live in bliss and die to greater bliss." He raised his arms in a great, dignified gesture of blessing over the startled, silent multitude.

He spoke on for another twenty minutes.

"Unhinged with grief," some people said as they left the Temenos or turned off the set; cynics responded, "Maybe with relief?" But many people discussed the ideas and images Kim Terry had put into their minds, feeling that he had given them something they had craved without knowing it, or felt without being able to say it.

Becoming Angels

THE FUNERAL HAD BEEN EPOCHAL. NOW THAT NO LIVING PERSON in the world remembered the planet of origin, was there any reason to think anyone there remembered them? Of course they sent out radio messages concerning the progress of the *Discovery* regularly, as specified in the Constitution, but was anybody listening?

"Orphans of the Void," a mawkish song with a good tune, sung by the Fourth Quad group Nubetels, became a rage overnight. And people talked about 1-Kim Terry's speech.

They went by his homespace to talk to him, some concerned, some curious. They were received by a couple named 2-Patel Jimmy and 2-Lung Yuko, his next-door neighbors. Terry is resting, they said, but he'll talk this evening. Did you feel the wonderful feelings while he was speaking in the Temenos? they asked. Did you see how different, how changed he is? We've watched him change, they said, watched him become wise, radiant, eloquent. Come hear him. He'll speak this evening.

For a while it was a kind of fad to go hear Terry speak about Bliss. There were jokes about it. Atheists railed about cult hysteria and hypocritical egotrippers. Then some people forgot about it, and others kept going to the Kim homespace cycle after cycle, year after year, for the evening meetings with Terry, Jimmy, and Yuko. People held meetings in their own homespaces, with little feasts, songs, meditations, devotions. They called these meetings angelic rejoicings, and called themselves friends in bliss, or angels.

When these followers of Kim Terry began to preface their kin-name with Angel as a kind of title, there was a good deal of disapproval and discussion in the councils. The angels agreed that such group identification was potentially divisive. Terry himself told his followers not to go against the will of the majority: "For, whether or not we know it, are we not all angels?"

Yuko, Jimmy, and Jimmy's little son Inbliss lived with Terry in the homespace he had shared with his mother. They led the nightly meetings. Kim Terry himself become increasingly reclusive. In the early years he now and then spoke to meetings held in the Quad One Circus or the Temenos, but as the years went by he appeared less and less often in public, speaking to his followers only over the innet. To those who

went to the meetings at his homespace he might appear briefly, blessing and encouraging them; but his followers believed that his bodily
presence was unimportant compared to his angelic presence, which was
continual. Bodily matters darkened bliss, obscuring the soul's needs.
"The corridors I walk are not these corridors," Terry said.

His death in the year 123 brought on a deep hysteria of mourning
combined with festivity, for his followers, embracing his doctrine of
Actuality as explained by his energetic interpreter, 3-Patel Inbliss, celebrated his apparent death as a rebirth into the Real World, to which the
shipworld was merely the means of access, the "vehicle of bliss."

Patel Inbliss lived on alone in the Kim homespace after Terry's and
his parents' death, holding meetings there, speaking at home Rejoicings, talking on the innet, working on and circulating the collection of
sayings and meditations called *The Angel to the Angels*. Patel Inbliss was
a man of great intelligence, ambition, and devotion, with a genius for
organisation. Under his guidance the Rejoicings had become less dis-
orderly and ecstatic, indeed were now quite sedate. He discouraged the
wearing of special clothing—undyed shorts and kurtas for men, white
clothing and headscarves for women—which many angels had adopted.
To dress differently was divisive, he said. Are we not all angels?

Under his leadership, indeed, more and more people declared themselves to be angels. The number of conversions in the first decades of the
second century brought on a call for an Article 4 hearing on Religious
Manipulation by a group who claimed that Patel Inbliss had formed
and promulgated a religious cult which worshipped Terry as a god, thus
threatening secular authority. The Central Council never actually called
a committee to investigate the charge. The angels asserted that, though
they venerated Kim Terry as a guide and teacher, they held him to be
no more divine than the least of them. Are we not all angels? And Patel
Inbliss argued cogently that the practice of Bliss in no way conflicted
with polity and governance, but on the contrary supported it in every

particular: for the laws and ways of the world were the laws and ways of Bliss. The Constitution of *Discovery* was holy writ. The life of the ship was bliss itself—the joyful mortal imitation of immortal reality. "Why would the followers of perfect law disobey it?" he asked. "Why would those who enjoy the angelic order seek disorder? Why would the inhabitants of heaven seek any other place or way to live?"

Angels were, in fact, extremely good citizens, active and cooperative in all civic duties, ready to fulfil communal obligations, diligent committee and Council members. In fact, more than half the Central Council at the time were angels. Not seraphim or archangels, as the very devout and those close to Patel Inbliss were nicknamed, but just everyday angels, enjoying the serenity and good fellowship of the Rejoicings, which were by now a familiar, accepted element of life for many people. The idea that the beliefs and practices of Bliss could in any way run counter to morality, that to be an angel was to be a rebel, was clearly ridiculous.

Patel Inbliss, now in his seventies, indomitably active, still occupied the Kim homespace.

Inside, Outside

"Could it be that there are two kinds of people . . ." Luis said to Hsing. Then he paused for so long that she replied crisply, "Yes. Possibly even three. Daring thinkers have postulated as many as five."

"No. Only two. People who can roll their tongue sideways into a tube and people who can't."

She stuck out her tongue at him. They had known since they were six that he could make his tongue into a tube and whistle through it, that she couldn't, and that it was genetically determined.

"One kind," he said, "has a need, a lack, they have to have a certain vitamin. The other kind doesn't."

"Well?"

"Vitamin Belief."

She considered.

"Not genetic," he said. "Cultural. Metaorganic. But as individually real and definite as a metabolic deficiency. People either need to believe or they don't."

She still pondered.

"The ones that do don't believe that the others don't. They don't believe that there are people who don't believe."

"Hope?" she offered, tentative.

"Hope isn't belief. Hope's contingent upon reality, even when it's not very realistic. Belief dismisses reality."

"'The name you can say isn't the right name,'" said Hsing.

"The corridor you can walk in isn't the right corridor," said Luis.

"What's the harm in believing?"

"It's dangerous to confuse reality with unreality," he said promptly. "To confuse desire with power, ego with cosmos. Extremely dangerous."

"Oooh." She made a face at his pomposity. After a while she said, "Is that what Terry's mother meant—'People need God like a three-year-old needs a chensa.' What was a chensa, I wonder?"

"A weapon, maybe."

"I used to go to Rejoicings sometimes with Rosa before she went seraph. I liked a lot of it, actually. The songs. And when they praise things, you know, just ordinary things, and say how everything you do is sacred. I don't know, I liked it," she said, a little defensive. He nodded. "But then they'd get into reading all the weird stuff out of the book, about what the 'voyage' really is, and what 'discovery' actually means, and I'd get claustro. Basically they were saying that there is nothing at all outside. The whole universe is inside. It was weird."

"They're right."

"Oh?"

"For us—they're right. There is nothing at all outside. Vacuum. Dust."

"The stars—the galaxies!"

"Light-specks on a screen. We can't reach them, we can't get to them. Not us. Not in our lifetime. Our universe is this ship."

It was an idea so familiar as to be banal and so strange it unnerved her. She pondered.

"And life here is perfect," Luis said.

"It is?"

"Peace and plenty. Light and warmth. Safety and freedom."

Well, of course, Hsing thought, and her face showed it.

Luis pressed on—"You did History. All that suffering. Did anybody in the subzero generations ever live as well as we live? Half as well? Most of them were afraid all the time. In pain. They were ignorant. They fought each other over money and religions. They died from diseases and wars and food shortage. It was all like Inner City 2000 or Jungle. It was hell. And this is heaven. Angel Terry was right."

She was puzzled by his intensity. "So?"

"So did our ancestors arrange to send us from one hell to another hell, by way of heaven? Do you see potential danger in that arrangement?"

"Well," Hsing said. She considered his metaphor. "Well, for the Sixes, maybe it'll seem kind of unfair. It's not going to make much difference to us. We'll be too doddering to go eva at all, I suppose. Although I'd like to dodder out and see what it looks like. Even if it is hell."

"That's why you're not an angel. You accept the fact that our life, our voyage, has a purpose outside itself. That we have a destination."

"Do I? I don't think so. I just sort of hope we do. It would be interesting to be somewhere else."

"But the angels believe there is nowhere else."

"Then they're in for a surprise when we reach Shindychew," Hsing said. "But then, I expect we all are. . . . Listen, I have to do that chart for Canaval. I'll see you in class."

They were second-year college students, nineteen years old, when they had this conversation. They did not know that sophomores had always discussed belief and unbelief and the purpose of existence.

Words from Earth

MESSAGES HAD FOLLOWED, OR PRECEDED, THEM, OF COURSE, ever since *Discovery* left the planet Dichew, Earth. During the First Generation many personal messages were received. *Descendants of Ross Betti: Everybody in Badgerwood is rooting for you!* Such transmissions had become rarer as the years went on, and finally vanished. Occasionally there had been major interruptions in reception, once lasting for nearly a year; and as the distance grew, and for some reason particularly during the last five years, distortions and delays and partial losses were the norm. Still, *Discovery* had not been forgotten. Words came. Images arrived. Somebody, or some program, on the Planet of Origin kept sending out a steady trickle of news, information, updates on technology, a poem or a fiction, occasionally whole periodicals or volumes of political commentary, literature, philosophy, criticism, art, documentaries; only all the definitions had changed and you couldn't be sure whether what you were watching or reading was invented or actual, because how could you possibly tell Earth reality from Earth fiction, and the science was just as bad, because they took discoveries for granted and forgot to define the terms they were using. Generations One and Two had spent a lot of time and passion and intelligence analysing and interpreting receptions from Dichew. There had been whole schools of opinion in Quads One and Four about the reports concerning apparent conflict between what were apparently philosophical-religious schools of thought, or possibly national or ethnic divisions, called (in Arabic) The True Followers and The Authentic Followers. Thousands or millions—the transmissions

spoke of billions but this was certainly a distortion or error—at any rate
a great number of people on Dichew had killed one another, had been
killed, because of this conflict of ideas or beliefs. On *Discovery*, there were
violent arguments about what the ideas, the beliefs, the conflicts were.
The arguments went on for decades, but nobody died because of them.

By the Third and Fourth Generations the general content of Earth
transmissions had become so arcane that only devotees followed them
closely; most people paid no attention to them at all. If something
important had happened on Dichew somebody or other would notice,
and in any case whatever was received went into the Archives. Or was
supposed to be going into the Archives.

4-Canaval

WHEN SHE CAME TO COLLEGE CENTER TO ENROLL FOR HER
first-year courses, Hsing found that the professor of Navigation,
4-Canaval Hiroshi, had requested that she be skipped over the first year
of his course and put into the second. "What if I wasn't intending to
take Nav at all?" she demanded of the registrar, indignant at this high-
handed order. But she was flattered; clearly Canaval had been watching
the High School math and astro classes, and had his eye on her. She
signed up for Nav 2.

Navigation was an honored profession but not a glamorous one, not
like being an evaman or an innet entertainer. To many people the idea
of navigation was a little threatening. They explained it by saying that
in most jobs you could make a mistake and of course it would cause
trouble (any event in a glass bowl is likely to affect everything in the
glass bowl), but in jobs like atmosphere control and navigation, a mistake could hurt or even kill people—hurt or kill *everybody*.

All the systems were full of failsafes and backups and redundancies, but there was, notoriously, no way to failsafe navigation. The computers, of course, were infallible, but they had to be operated by humans; the course had to be continually adjusted; all the navigators could do was check and re-check their calculations and the computers' calculations and operations, check and re-check input and feedback, check and correct for error, and keep on doing it, over and over and over. If the calculations and operations all agreed with each other, if it all checked out, then nothing happened. You just did it all over again forever.

Navigation was about as thrilling as running the bacteria counts, also an unpopular job. And the mathematical talent and training required to do it was formidable. Not many students took Nav for more than the required first year, and very few went on to specialise in it. 4-Canaval was looking for candidates, or victims, as some of his students said.

If the unpopularity of the subject rose from some deeper discomfort, some dread of what it dealt with—the voyage through space, the very movement of the shipworld, its course, its goal—nobody talked about it. But Hsing thought about it sometimes.

Canaval Hiroshi was in his forties, a short, straight-backed man with coarse, bushy black hair and a blunt face, like the pictures of Zen Masters, Hsing thought. He was related to Luis; they were half-cousins; at moments Hsing saw a resemblance. In class he was brusque, impatient, intolerant of error. Students complained: one insignificant mistake in a computer simulation and he tossed the whole thing out, hours of work—"worthless." He was certainly both arrogant and obsessive, but Hsing defended him against charges of megalomania. "It's not his ego," she said. "I don't think he has an ego. All he has is his work. And it does have to be right. Without error. I mean, if we get too close to a gravity sink, does it matter whether it's by a parsec or by a kilometer?"

"All right, but a millimeter isn't going to do any harm," said Aki, who had just had a beautiful charting deleted as "worthless."

"A millimeter now, a parsec in ten years," Hsing said priggishly. She saw Aki roll his eyes. She didn't care. Nobody else seemed to understand the excitement of doing what Canaval did, the thrill of getting it right—not nearly right, but *exactly* right. Perfection. It was beautiful, the work. It was abstract, yet human, even humble, because what you wanted didn't matter. And you couldn't rush it; you had to get all the small things right, take care of all the details, in order to get to the great thing. There was a way to follow. It took constant, ceaseless, alert attention to that way to stay on it. It was not a matter of following your wish or your will, but of following what was. Being aware, all the time, being centered. Celestial Navigation: heaven-sailing. Out there was infinity. Through it there was one way.

And if knowing this went to your head, you always got reminded, immediately and inarguably, that you were completely dependent on the computers.

In third-year Nav, Canaval always gave a problem: *The computers are down for five seconds. Using the coordinates and settings given, plot course for the next five seconds without using the computers.*—Students either gave it up within hours, or worked days at it and then gave it up as a waste of time. Hsing did not hand the problem back in. At the end of term, Canaval asked her for it. "I thought I'd play around with it in vacation," she said.

"Why?"

"I like the computations. And I want to know how long it'll take me."

"How long so far?"

"Forty-four hours."

He nodded so slightly that perhaps he didn't nod, and turned away. He was incapable of showing approval.

He did, however, have a capacity for pleasure, and laughed when he found things funny, usually quite simple things, silly mistakes, foolish mishaps. His laughter was a loud, childish ha! ha! ha! After he laughed he always said, smiling broadly, "Stupid! Stupid!"

"He really is a Zen Master," she told Luis in the snackery. "I mean really. He sits zazen. He gets up at four to sit. Three hours. I wish I could do that. But I'd have to go to bed at twenty, I'd never get any studying done." Observing a lack of response in Luis, she said, "And how is your v-corpse?"

"Reduced to a virtual skeleton," Luis said, still looking a bit absent.

College students chose a professional course in third year. Hsing was in Nav, Luis in Med. They no longer had any classes together, but they met daily in the snackery, the gyms, or the library. They no longer visited each other's room.

Sex in the Glass Bowl

LOVERS DO NOT RUN AWAY (WHERE IS AWAY?). LOVERS' MEET-ings are public matters. Your procreative capacity is a matter of intense and immediate social interest and concern. Contraception is guaranteed by an injection every twenty-five days, for girls from the onset of menstruation, for boys at a time determined by medical staff. Failure to come to the Clinic for your conshot at the due date and hour is followed by immediate public inquiry: Clinic staff people come to your class, your gym, your section, corridor, homespace, announcing your name and your delinquency loud and clear.

People are permitted to go without conshots on the following conditions or undertakings: sterilization, or completion of menopause; a pledge either of chastity or of strict homosexuality; or an intention to conceive, formally declared by both the man and the woman. A woman who violates her undertaking to be chaste or conceives a child with anyone but the declared partner can get a morning-after shot, but both she and her sexual partner must then go back to conshots for two years. Unauthorised conceptions are aborted. The inexorable social and

genetic reasons for all this are made clear during your education. But all
the reasons in the world wouldn't work if you could keep your sexual
life private. You can't.

Your corridor knows, your family knows, your section, your ancestry,
your whole quadrant knows who you are and where you are and what you
do and who you do it with, and they all talk. Shame and honor are powerful social engines. If enforced by total publicity and attached to rational
need, rather than to hierarchic fantasies and the will to dominate, shame
and honor can keep a society running steadily for a long time.

A teenager may move out of the parent's homespace and find a single
on another corridor, in another section, even change quadrants; but
everybody in that new corridor, section, quad will know who goes in
and out your door. They will be observant, and interested, and vigilant,
and curious, and mostly well-disposed, and always hoping for a scandal, and they will talk.

The Warn, or Warren, was the first place many young people moved
to when they left parentspace. It was a set of corridors in Quad Four,
close to the College; all the spaces were singles; due to the shape of
the housing of the main accelerator, walls in the Warn weren't all at
right angles, and some of the spaces were substandard size. The students
moved partitions around and created a maze of cubicles and sharespaces.
The Warn was noisy and disorganised and smelled of dirty clothes.
Sleep there was occasional, sex was casual. But everybody turned up on
time at Clinic for their conshot.

Luis lived near the Warn in a triple with two other medical students,
Tan Bingdi and Ortiz Einstein. Hsing was still in the Quad Two homespace with Yao. She had a twenty-minute walk to and from college daily.

After the usual adolescent period of experimenting around, when
she entered college Hsing had pledged chastity. She said she didn't want
conshots controlling her body's cycles, and didn't want emotion controlling her mind; not till she was through college.

Luis continued to get his conshot every twenty-five days, did not pledge, but did not go to bed with any of his friends. He never had. His only sexual experiences had been the general promiscuities of teenparties.

They knew all this about each other because it was public knowledge. When they were together they didn't talk about these matters. Their silences were as deeply and comfortably mutual as their conversations.

Their friendship was of course equally public. Their friends speculated freely about why Hsing and Luis didn't have sex and whether and when they'd get around to it.

Beneath their friendship was something that was not public, and was not friendship: a pledge made without words, but with the body; a non-action with profound results. They were each other's privacy. They had found where away was. The key to it was silence.

Hsing broke the pledge, broke the silence.

"Reduced to a virtual skeleton," Luis said absently, evidently thinking of something other than the v-cadaver which had been teaching him Anatomy. The cadaver had been programmed by its ghoulish author to guide and chastise the apprentice dissector. "The medulla, idiot!" it would whisper cavernously from moveless lips and lungless rib-cavity, or "Surely you don't take *that* for the caecum?" Hsing liked to hear what the cadaver had been saying. If you made no mistakes it occasionally rewarded you with bursts of poetry. "Soul clap hands and sing, and louder sing!" it had cried, even as Luis removed the larynx. But he had no cadaver-tales for her today, and went on sitting at the snackery table, brooding.

She said, "Luis, Lena—"

Luis held up his hand so quickly, so silently, that she fell silent, having said nothing but the name.

"No," he said.

There was a very long pause.

"Listen. Luis. You're free."

His hand was up again, warding off speech, defending silence.

She insisted: "I want you to know that you are—"

"You can't free me," he said. His voice was deepened by anger or some other emotion. "Yes. I'm free. We both are."

"I only—"

"Don't, Hsing! Don't!" He looked straight into her eyes for an instant. He stood up. "Let it be," he said. "I have to go." He strode off among the tables. People said "Hi, Luis" and he did not answer. People saw a quarrel. Hsing and Luis had a fight in the snackery today. Hey, what's up with Hsing and Luis?

Yin Yang

A YOUNG WOMAN MAY FIND IT DIFFICULT TO WITHSTAND THE urgent sexual advances of an older man in a position of power or authority. Her resistance is further compromised if she finds him attractive. She is likely to deny both the difficulty and the attraction, wishing to maintain her freedom of choice and that of other women. If her desire for independence is strong and clear, she will resist the pressure of his desire, she will resist her own longing to match the strength of her yielding to the strength of his aggression, to take him into herself while crying "Take me!"

Or she may come to see her freedom precisely in that yielding. Yin is her principle, after all. Yin is called the negative principle, but it is Yin that says "Yes."

They met again in the snackery a while after commencement. Both were in intense training in their chosen specialties, Luis interning at the Central Hospital, Hsing as an apprentice in the Bridge Crew. Their work consumed them. They had not seen each other alone for two or three tendays.

She said, "Luis, I'm living with Canaval."

"Somebody said you were." He still spoke with that vagueness, absentness, a kind of soft cover over something hard and set.

"I just decided to last week. I wanted to tell you."

"If it's a good thing for you . . ."

"Yes. It is. He wants us to marry."

"That's good."

"Hiroshi is—he's like the fusion core. It's exciting to be with him." She spoke earnestly, trying to explain, wanting him to understand. It was important that he understand. He looked up suddenly, smiling. Her face turned dusky red. "Intellectually, emotionally," she said.

"Hey, flatface, if it's good it's good," he said. He leaned over and lightly kissed her nose.

"You and Lena—" she said, eager.

He smiled a different smile and replied quietly, mildly, absolutely, "No."

Integrity

It wasn't that there were pieces missing from Hiroshi. He was complete. He was all one piece. Maybe that's what was missing— bits of the other Hiroshis who might have read novels, or played solitaire, or stayed in bed late mornings, or done anything but what he did, been anyone other than what he was.

Hiroshi did what he did and doing it was what he was.

Hsing had thought, as a young woman might think, that her being in his life would enlarge it, change it. She understood very soon after she came to live with him that the arrangement had changed her life greatly and his not at all. She had become part of what Hiroshi did. An essential part, certainly: because he did only what was essential. Only she had never truly understood what he did.

That understanding made a greater change in her thinking and her

life's course than having sex and living with him did. Not that the pleasures, tensions, and discoveries of sex didn't engage and delight and
often surprise her; but she found sex, like eating, a splendid physical
satisfaction which did not take up a great deal of her mind or even her
emotions. Those were occupied by her work.

And the discovery, the revelation Hiroshi brought her, had nothing
to do, or seemed to have nothing to do, with their partnership. It concerned the work he did, they did. Their whole life. The life of everybody
in the worldship.

"You got me to live with you so you could co-opt me," she said to him,
half a year or so later.

He replied with his usual honesty—for though everything he did
served to conceal and perpetuate a deception, he made scrupulous
efforts never to lie to a friend—"No, no. I trusted you. But it simplified
everything. Doesn't it?"

She laughed. "For you. Not for me! For me everything used to be
simple. Now everything's double . . ."

He looked at her without speaking for a while; then he took her hand
and gently put his lips against her palm. He was a formally courteous
sexual partner, whose ultimate surrender to passion always moved her to
tenderness, so that their lovemaking was a reliable and sometimes amazing joy. All the same she knew that to him she was ultimately only fuel
to the fusion core—an element in his overriding, single purpose. She
told herself that she did not feel used, or tricked, because she knew now
that everything was fuel to Hiroshi, including himself.

Errors

THEY HAD BEEN MARRIED FOR THREE DAYS WHEN HE TOLD HER
what the purpose of his work was—what he did.

"You asked me a year ago about discrepancies in the acceleration records," he said. They were eating alone together in their homespace. Honeymooning, it was called, a word that didn't have many reverberations in this world without honey or bees to make it, without months or a moon to make them. But a nice custom.

She nodded. "You showed me I'd left out some factor. I don't remember what it was."

"Falsehood," he said.

"No, that isn't what you said. The constant of—"

He interrupted her. "What I said was a falsehood," he said. "A deliberate deception. To lead you astray. Make you think you'd made an error. Your computations were perfectly correct, you omitted nothing. There are discrepancies. Much greater discrepancies than the one you found."

"In the acceleration records?" she said stupidly.

Hiroshi nodded once. He had stopped eating. She knew that when he spoke so quietly he was very tense.

She was hungry, and pushed in one good supply of noodles before she put her chopsticks down and said, through noodles, "All right, what are you telling me?"

His face was strained. His eyes lifted to hers for a moment with an expression of desperation? pleading?—so uncharacteristic that it shocked her, moved her as his vulnerability in lovemaking did. "What's wrong, Hiroshi?" she whispered.

"The ship has been decelerating for over four years," he said.

Her mind moved with terrific rapidity, running through implications, explanations, scenarios.

"What went wrong?" she asked at last, quite steadily.

"Nothing. The deceleration is controlled. Deliberate."

He was looking down at his bowl. When he glanced up at her and at once looked down again, she realised that he feared her judgment. That he feared her. Though, she thought, his fear would not influence his actions or his words to her.

"Deliberate?"

"A decision made four years ago," he said.

"By?"

"Four people on the Bridge. Later, two in Administration. Four people in Engineering and Maintenance also know about it now."

"Why?"

The question seemed to relieve him, perhaps because it was asked quietly, without protest or challenge. He answered in a tone more like his usual one, even with a touch of the lecturer's assurance and acerbity. "You asked what's wrong. Nothing is. Nothing went wrong. We have always been on course, with almost no deviance. But an error did occur. An extraordinary, massive error. Which allowed us to take advantage of it. Error is opportunity. Chierek and I spotted it. A fundamental, ongoing error in the trajectory approximations, dating from our passage through the CG440 sink, five years ago, in Year 154. What happened during that passage?"

"We lost speed," she answered automatically.

"We gained it," he said. He glanced up to meet her incredulity. "Our acceleration increase was so great and so abrupt that the computers assumed a factor-ten error and compensated for it." He paused to make sure that she was following him.

"Factor *ten*?"

"By the time Chierek came to me with the figures and I realised that it could only be explained as a computer compensation error, we'd accelerated to .82 and were forty years ahead of schedule."

She was indignant at his joking, trying to fool her, saying these enormities. "Point eight two is not possible," she said, cold, dismissive.

"Oh yes," Hiroshi said with a grin that was equally cold, "it's possible. It's actual. We did it. We traveled at .82 for ninety-one days.

Everything you know about acceleration, Gegaard's calculations, the massgain limit—it was all wrong. That's where the errors were! In the basic assumptions! Error is opportunity. It's all clear enough, once you have the records and can do the computations. We can tell the physicists back on Dichew all about it when we get to Shindychew. Tell them where they went wrong. Tell them how to use a sink to whiplash an object up to eight tenths lightspeed. This is the voyage of the *Discovery*, all right. We could have made it in eighty years." His face was hard with triumph, the conqueror's face. "We're going to arrive at the target system five years from now," he said. "In the first half of Year 164."

She felt nothing but anger.

"If this is true," she said at last, slowly and without expression, "why are you telling me now? Why are you telling me at all? You've kept this from everybody else. Why?"

It was not only the enormous shock of what he was telling her, it was his victorious look, his triumphant tone, that brought up the surge of rage in her—the opposition he had feared at the beginning, the question *How dare you?* But her anger now didn't affect him; he was unshaken, borne up by his conviction of rightness.

"It's the only power we have," he said.

"'We?' Who?"

"We who aren't angels."

To Count the Number of Angels

WHEN LUIS WAS TOLD THAT THE EDUCATIONAL AGENDA FOR the Sixth Generation was not accessible because it was being revised, he said, "But that's what I was told when I asked to see it eight years ago."

The woman on the Education Center info screen, a motherly sort, shook her head sympathetically. "Oh, it's always under revision or under consideration, angel," she said. "They have to keep updating it."

"I see," said Luis, "thank you," and switched out.

Old Tan had died two years ago, but his grandson was a promising replacement. "Listen, Bingdi," Luis said across their sharespace, "does the bodycount register angels?"

"How should I know?"

"Librarians are the masters of useful trivia."

"You mean, are angels listed as such? No. Why would they be? The old religious affiliations weren't ever listed. Listing would be divisive." Bingdi did not speak quite as slowly as his grandfather, but in a similar rhythm, each sentence followed by a small, thoughtful silence, a quarter-note rest. "I suppose Bliss is a religious affiliation. I don't know how else it could be defined. Though I'm not sure how religion is defined."

"So there's no way to know accurately how many angels there are. Or put it another way: There's no way to know who is an angel and who isn't."

"You could ask."

"Certainly. I will."

"You'll go from corridor to corridor throughout the world," Bingdi said, "inquiring of each person you pass, Are you an angel?"

"'Are we not all angels?'" said Luis.

"Sometimes it seems that way."

"It does indeed."

"What are you getting at?"

"It's what I can't get at that worries me. The education program for the Sixes, for instance."

Bingdi looked mildly startled. "Are you planning on procreating a baby Six?"

"No. I want to find out something about Shindychew. The Sixes are going to land on Shindychew. It seems reasonable to assume they'll be educated to do so. Informed of what to expect. How to cope with living outside. Trained in doing long-term eva on a planet surface. That's going to be their job, after all. The Zeroes must have included information on it in the education program. Your grandfather said they did. Where is it? And who is going to train them?"

"Well, there aren't any Sixes even wearing clothes yet," Bingdi said. "A bit soon to terrify the poor little noodles with tales of an unknown world, isn't it?"

"Better too soon than never," said Luis. "Destination Date is forty-four years from now. *We* might want to go do eva on Shindychew. Dodder forth, as Hsing put it."

"May I think about it after a couple of decades?" Bingdi said. "Just now I need to finish this bit of useful trivia."

He turned to his screen, but in a minute he looked round again at Luis. "What's the connection of that with the number of angels?" he said, in the voice of one who glimpses the answer as he asks the question.

Enemies of Bliss

SHE DID NOT KNOW 5-CHIN RAMON WELL, THOUGH HE WAS one of Hiroshi's circle. He had been on the Managerial Counsel for a couple of years now. She had not voted for him. He identified as Chinese Ancestry and lived in Pine Mountain Compound, which was mostly Chins and Lees. A lot of the Chins had become angels early on. Ramon had risen, as they said, high in Bliss. He seemed a colorless, conventional man; like many male angels he treated women in a defensive, distancing, facetious manner Hsing found despicable. She had been displeased as well as very surprised to find he was one of the ten—now eleven—people who knew that the ship was decelerating towards an early arrival at the Destination.

"So you made this tape without telling the people you were taping

them?" she asked him, not trying to keep contempt and distrust out of
her voice.

"Yes," Ramon said, without expression.

Ramon had had a crisis of conscience: so Hiroshi said. 5-Chatterji
Uma explained it to Hsing. Hsing liked and admired Uma, a bright,
elegant little woman, elected to chair the Managerial Counsel four
years running; she had to listen to her. Ramon, Uma explained, had
been admitted to Patel Inbliss's inner circle, the archangels; and what
he heard and learned there had so disturbed him that he had broken his
vow of secrecy, made notes of things said among the archangels, and
given them to Uma. She had taken his report to Canaval and the others.
They had requested Ramon to prove his allegations. So he had surrepti-
tiously taped a session of the archangels.

"How can you trust a person who would do such a thing?" Hsing had
demanded.

"It was the only way he could provide us evidence." Uma had looked
with sympathy at Hsing. "Paranoid suspicions—rumors of plots to take
over navigation, tamper with our genes, put untested drugs in the water
supply—how many have we all heard! This was the only way Ramon
could convince us that he wasn't paranoid, or simply malicious."

"Tapes are easy to fake."

"Fakes are easy to spot," said 4-Garcia Teo with a smile; he was a big,
craggy, kindly engineer whom Hsing could not help trusting, hard as
she was working to distrust everybody in this room. "It's real."

"Listen to it, Hsing," Canaval said, and she nodded, though with
a sullen heart. She hated it, this secrecy, lying, hiding, plotting. She
did not want to be part of it, did not want to be with these people, to
be one of them, to share the power they had seized—seized because
they had to, they kept saying; but nobody had to lie. Nobody had the
right to do what they were doing, to control everybody's life without
telling them.

The voices on the tape meant nothing to her. Men's voices, talking about some business she did not understand, none of her business in any case. Let the angels have their secrets, let Canaval and Uma have theirs, just leave me out of it, she thought.

But she was caught by the sound of Patel Inbliss's voice, a soft, old voice, iron-soft, familiar to her all her life. Through her resistance, her disgust at being forced to eavesdrop, her incredulity, she heard that voice say, "Canaval must be discredited before we can count on the Bridge. And Chatterji."

"And Tranh," said another voice, at which 5-Tranh Golo, also a member of the Counsel, nodded his head in a wry pantomime of thanks-very-much.

"What strategy have you formed?"

"Chatterji is easy," said the other, deeper voice, "she's indiscreet and arrogant. Whispers will cripple her influence. With Canaval it is going to have to be a matter of his health."

Hsing felt a curious chill. She glanced at Hiroshi. He sat as impassive as if in his morning meditation.

"Canaval is an enemy of bliss," said the old voice, Patel's.

"In a position of unique authority," said one of the others, to which the deep voice replied, "He must be replaced. On the Bridge, and in the College. We must have a good man in both those positions." The tone of the deep voice was mild, full of reasoned certainty.

The discussion went on; much of it was incomprehensible to Hsing, but she listened intently now, trying to understand. All at once the tape ended midword.

She started, looked around at the others: Uma, Teo, Golo, and Ramdas, whom she thought of as friends; Chin Ramon and two women, an engineer and a Counsel member, whom she knew as members of the secret circle but did not think of as friends. And Hiroshi, still sitting zazen. They were in Uma's homespace, furnished "nomad style," a recent fad, no biltins, only carpeting and pillows in bright paisleys.

"What was that about your health?" Hsing demanded. "And then they were talking about something about heart valves?"

"I have a congenital heart deformity," he said. "It's on my H-folder."

Everyone had an H-folder: genetic map, health record, school records, work history. You held the code on it; nobody could see your H-folder without your permission, until you died and the file went from Records to Archives. A considerable mystique of privacy surrounded these personal files. No one but a coparent or a doctor would ever ask to see your H-folder. That anyone could break or steal the code and look at it without your permission was unthinkable. Hsing had not seen Hiroshi's H-folder and had never asked to, since they weren't planning on a child. She did not understand why he had mentioned it.

"Records staff is about ninety percent angels," Ramon said, seeing her blank expression.

She resented his pushing her, forcing her to realise what Hiroshi had meant. She resented Ramon altogether, his too-soft voice, his tight, hard face. Whenever Ramon was around, Hiroshi got tense, too, tight-mouthed, obsessed with all this stuff about the angels taking over. Now Ramon had got control over her too, forcing her to collude, to listen to the tape he'd made betraying people who trusted him.

To her dismay she found that she felt like crying. She had not cried for years. What was there to cry about?

Chatterji Uma's sympathetic gaze was on her. "Hsing," she said quietly, as the others began talking, "when Ramon showed me his notes, I told him to get out. Then I threw up all night."

"But," Hsing said. "But. But *why* would they *do* all this?" Her voice came out unmodulated, loud. The others turned.

Both Ramon and Hiroshi answered: "Power," one said, the other said, "Control."

She did not look at either of them. She looked at the Counselwoman, the woman, for an answer that made sense.

"Because—if I understand it—" Uma said, "Patel Inbliss has taught the angels that our destination is not a stopping place—not a place at all."

Hsing stared. "You mean they think Shindychew doesn't exist?"

"Nothing exists outside the ship. Nothing exists but the Voyage."

Soul, Say What Death Is

"Rejoice in the voyage of life, from life, to life,
Life everlasting, bliss everlasting.
We are flying, O my angels, we will fly!"

ALL THE CELEBRANTS SANG OUT THE LAST LINE, SWEET AND exultant, and Rosa turned to smile at Luis. They sat in a row, Luis, Rosa with her baby Jellika, her husband Ruiz Jen holding his two-year-old Joy on his lap. Angels were strong on what they called "whole families" and "true brotherhood," couples who had and brought up both their children together. *Mother sweet to cherish, Father strong to guide, little boy, little girl, growing side by side.* Luis's head was full of tags and rhymes and sayings. He had read almost nothing but angelic literature for the last four tendays. He had read *The Angel to the Angels* through twice, and Patel Inbliss's *New Commentaries* three times, and many other texts; he had talked to angel friends and acquaintances, and listened much more than he talked. He had asked Rosa if he could come to Rejoicings with her, and she had of course told him happily that nothing could make her happier.

"I'm not going to become an angel, Rosie," he said, "that's not why I want to come," but she laughed and took his hands—"Oh, you already are an angel, Luis. Don't worry about that. I would just love to bring you into bliss!"

After the singing there was the Session in Peace, during which the celebrants sat in silence until one of them was moved to speak. Luis had come to look forward to these sessions. What was said was usually quite brief—a joy shared, or a fear or sorrow, in trustful expectation of sympathy. The first time he had come with Rosa, she stood up to say, "I am so glad because my dear friend Luis is here!" and people had turned and smiled at her and him. There were cut-and-dried speeches about thankfulness and remembering to be joyful, but often people spoke from the heart. Last meeting, an old man whose wife had died said, "I know Ada is flying in bliss, but I am lonely walking in the corridors without her. If you know how, please help me learn not to grieve her joy."

Today people were shy of talking and said only conventional things, probably because an archangel was present. Archangels visited home or sectional Rejoicings to give brief talks or teachings. Some of them were singers who performed the songs called "devotionals," to which the celebrants listened rapt. Luis had found these songs musically and intellectually rich and complex, and readied himself to listen with interest when the singer, 5-Van Wing, was introduced.

"I will sing a new song," Wing said with angelic simplicity, paused, and began. His unaccompanied voice was a strong, sure tenor. He sang a devotional of a kind Luis had not heard before. The tune was a free, ecstatic outpouring, evidently largely ex tempore, built on a few linked patterns, but the words were at odds with the music; they were allusive, brief, obscure.

> *Eye, what do you see?*
> *Blackness, the void.*
> *Ear, what do you hear?*
> *Silence, no voice.*
> *Soul, say what death is?*

Silent, black, outside.
Let life be purified!
Fly ever to rejoice,
O vehicle of bliss!

The last three lines rose in conventionally joyous cadences, but the song had lingered darkly on the words before them, repeating them many times, the singer imbuing them with a tremor of horror which Luis felt as strongly as the others.

It was a remarkable performance, and Van Wing was a real artist, he thought.

He recognised as he did so that he was defending himself against the song, trying to trivialise the effect those lines had had on him.

Soul, say what death is?
Silent, black, outside.

As he went back through the crowded corridors to his homespace in Four, the words kept singing their dark song in his head. When he woke next morning, he understood what they meant to him.

Sitting on his bed he began to write in a blank book Hsing had made for him as a birthday present when they were sixteen. Though he had always used it sparingly, over the years most of the pages had been covered top to bottom and edge to edge with his small clear handwriting. Only a few were left. The flyleaf was inscribed: "A Box to Hold Luis's Mind. Made with Love by Hsing," her name not in letters but in the ancient ideogram: 星. He read the inscription whenever he opened the book.

He wrote: "Life/ship/vehicle/passage: mortal means to immortality (true bliss). Destination metaphorical—for Destination read Destiny. All meaning is inside. Nothing is outside. Outside is nothing. Negation,

nil, void: Death. Life is inside. To go outside is denial, is blasphemy."
He stared at the last word a while, then leaned over and brought up the
OED on his innetscreen. He studied the definition and derivation of
"blasphemy" for some time. He then looked up "heresy, heretic, heretical,"
and then "orthodoxy," which he quit abruptly to begin writing again in
the blank book: "Hu. sp. highly ADAPTABLE! Bliss a psych./meta-
organic adaptation to existence in transit—near-perfect homeostasis.
Follow rules, live inside, live forever. Maladaptation to *arrival*. Arrival
equated with phys./spir. DEATH." He paused again, then wrote, "How
to counteract, causing least possible argument, factionalism, distress?"

He stopped writing and sat for a long time thinking, brooding. The
soft, steady, unvarying flow of air at 22° C from the atmosphere-intake
of his sleepspace stirred the thin leaves of the book and laid them gently
down to the right, revealing the flyleaf again. "A Box to Hold Luis's
Mind." The word love. The ideogram that meant Hsing, that meant
star. There really was nobody else to talk to.

She did not answer his first message, and when he got through to her
she was busy, sorry, things are so busy just now, I just can't get away from
work. . . . She could not possibly have become self-important. Canaval was
self-important, not without justification. But Hsing pompous, Hsing eva-
sive? No. Busy. Why so busy? What kind of work kept one from answering a friend? Probably she was still afraid of him. That grieved him, but it
was not a new grief. And since it was herself she feared, not him, it really
was her problem, not his. So he insisted. He refused to be put off. "I will
come tomorrow at ten," and at ten he was at the door of her homespace.
She was there; Canaval was not. She was brusque, awkward. They sat
down facing each other on the biltin couch. "Is something wrong, Luis?"

"I need to tell you what I've learned about the angels."

It was a strange thing to say after half a year of silence between
them, he knew that; still, he found her response even stranger. She
looked amazed, dismayed. She covered her shock, began to speak,

stopped, and finally, with what seemed suspicion, said, "Why me?"

"Who else?"

"What do you think I have to do with anything to do with them?"

Circuitous! Luis thought. He said only, "Nothing. And that's getting to be rare. This is important, and I need to talk it over with you. I want to know what you think about it. Your judgment. I've always thought best when I talked with you."

She did not loosen up at all. Tense, wary, she nodded grudgingly. She said, "Do you want tea?"

"No, thank you. I'll talk as fast as I can. Please interrupt if I'm not clear. Tell me if what I say is credible."

"I don't find much incredible lately," she said, dry, not looking at him. "Go ahead, then. I do have to be on the Bridge at ten-forty. I'm sorry."

"Half an hour will do."

In half that time he told her what he had to tell. He began with his realisation that the education committees and councils had been controlled for at least twenty years by a large, steady majority of angels. It was now impossible to find what curriculum the Zero Generation had originally planned for the Sixth. Those plans had evidently been deleted—possibly even from the Archives.

Every time he considered that possibility it still shocked Luis, and he did not try to minimise his concern. Hsing continued to conceal any reaction she felt. He began to wonder if she already knew everything he was telling her. If so, she wasn't admitting that either. He went on.

The elementary and high school curriculum had been scarcely altered since Hsing's and Luis's schooldays. The most striking change was a decrease in information and discussion concerning both Dichew and Shindychew. Children now in school spent very little time learning about the planets of origin and destination. Language concerning them was vague, with a curiously remote tone. In two recent texts Luis had found the phrase, "the planetary hypothesis."

"But in 43.5 years we will arrive at one of these hypotheses," Luis said. "What are we going to make of it?"

Hsing looked stricken again—frightened. He didn't know what to make of that, either. He went on.

"I've been trying to understand the elements in angelic theory or belief that lead them to deny the importance—the fact—of our origin on one planet and our destination on another. Bliss is a coherent system of thought that makes almost perfect sense in itself and as a belief-system for people living as we live. In fact, that's the problem. Bliss is a self-contained proposition, a closed system. It is a psychic adaptation to our life—ship life—an adaptation to a self-contained system, an unvarying artificial environment providing all necessities at all times. We of the middle generations have no goal except to stay alive and keep the ship running and on course, and to achieve it all we have to do is follow the rules—the Constitution. The Zeroes saw that as an important duty, a high obligation, because they saw it as an element of the whole voyage—the means glorified by the end. But for those who won't see the end, there's not much glory being the means. Self-preservation seems self-centered. The system's not only closed, but stifling. That was Kim Terry's vision—how to glorify the means, the voyage—how to make following the rules an end in itself. As he saw it, our true journey is not only to a material world outside in space, but also to a spiritual world of bliss—which we will attain, by living rightly *here*."

Hsing nodded.

"Over the last decades Patel Inbliss has gradually changed the emphasis of this vision. *Here* is all. There's nothing outside the ship—literally nothing, spiritually nothing. Origin and destination are now metaphors. They have no reality. Journey is the sole reality. The voyage is its own end."

She was still impassive, as if he was telling her nothing she didn't know; but she was alert.

"Patel isn't a theorist. He's an activist. Acting on his vision through his archangels and their disciples. I believe that in the last ten or fifteen years, angels have been making many of the decisions in Council, and most of the decisions about education."

Again she nodded, but warily.

"The schools teach almost nothing about the original purpose of the interstellar voyage—to study and perhaps settle a planet. The texts and programs still have information about the cosmos—star-charts, stellar types, planet formation, all that stuff we had in Tenth—but I've been talking to teachers and they tell me they skip most of it. The children 'aren't interested,' they 'find these old material-science theories confusing.' You realise that almost all school administrators and about 65 percent of the teachers—90 percent in Quad One—are members of Bliss?"

"So many?"

"At least that many. My impression is that some angels conceal their beliefs, deliberately, to keep their dominance from becoming too plain."

Hsing looked uneasy, disgusted, but said nothing.

"Meanwhile in the archangelic teachings, 'outside' is equated with danger, physical and spiritual—sin, evil—and with death. Nothing else. There is nothing good outside the ship. Inside is positive, outside negative. Pure dualism.—Not many young angels are going into dermatology these days, but there are some older ones who do eva. As soon as they're through the airlocks, they undergo a ritual of purification. Did you know that?"

"No," she said.

"It's called decontamination. An old material-science-theory word with a new meaning. The soul is contaminated by the silent black outside. . . . Well, that aside. Angels are eager to follow the rules, because our life lived well leads us directly to eternal happiness. They are eager for us all to follow the rules. We live in the Vehicle of Bliss. We can't miss bliss. Unless we break the one new rule. The big one: The ship can't stop."

He stopped. Hsing looked angry, as she always did when she was worried, troubled, or scared.

His gradual discovery of the change in the angelic teachings and the extent of angelic control over various councils had alarmed but not frightened him. He had seen it as a problem, a serious problem, that must be addressed. The way to solve it was to bring it out into the open, forcing the angels to explain their policies and making the non-angels aware that Patel Inbliss was trying to change the rules, and exerting clandestine power to do so. When they saw that, they'd react against it. There need be no crisis.

"We've got 43.5 years," he said. "Plenty of time to talk it over. It's a matter of getting things back in proportion. The more radical angels will have to agree that we *do* have a destination, that people *are* going to do eva there, and that they'll need to be trained to do eva, not to look on it as a sin."

"It's worse than that," Hsing said. The tight, stricken look had come over her again. She jumped up and walked across the room—a neat, severe room, not like the messy nest she used to live in—and stood with her back to him.

"Well, yes," Luis said, unsure what she meant, but encouraged at her saying anything at all. "We all need training. We'll be in our sixties at Arrival. If the planet's habitable, we've got to get used to the idea of at least some of us living there—staying there. While maybe some of us turn around and head back to Dichew. . . . The angels never mention that, by the way. Inbliss seems to think only in a straight line extending to infinity. The flaw in his reasoning is that he assumes a material vehicle is capable of an eternal journey. Entropy does not seem to be part of Bliss."

"Yes," Hsing said.

"That's all," he said after a minute. He was puzzled and worried by her non-response. He waited a little and said, "I think this must be talked about. So I came to you. To talk about it. And you might want to talk about it to non-angelic people in Management and on the Bridge. They need to be concerned about this revision of our mission." He paused. "Maybe they already are."

"Yes," she said again. She had not turned around.

Luis had very little anger in his temperament and was not given to fits of pique, but he felt let down flat. As he looked at Hsing's back, her pink cheongsam, her short-legs-no-butt (so she had described her Chi-An figure), her black hair falling bright and straight and cut off sharp at the shoulder, he also felt pain. A hard, deep, sore pain at the heart.

"There was a flaw in my reasoning too," he said. He stood up.

She turned around. She still looked worried beyond anything he had expected. It had taken him a long time to realise how powerful angelic thinking had become, and he had dumped all his discoveries on her at once—yet none of it had seemed to surprise her. So why this reaction? And why wouldn't she talk about it?

"What flaw?" she asked, but still distrustful, holding back.

"Nothing. I miss talking with you."

"I know. The work in Nav, it seems like it never lets up."

She was looking at him but not looking at him. He couldn't stand it.

"So. That's it. Just sharing my worries, as we say in Peace Session. Thanks for the time."

He was in the doorway when she said, "Luis."

He stopped, but didn't turn.

"I want to talk more about all this maybe with you later."

"Sure. Don't let it worry you."

"I have to talk to Hiroshi about it."

"Sure," he said again, and went out into the corridor.

He wanted to go somewhere else, not corridor 4-4, not any corridor, not any room, not any place he knew. But there was no place he didn't know. No place in the world.

"I want to go out," he said to himself. "Outside."

Silent, black, outside.

On the Bridge

"Tell your friend not to panic," Hiroshi said. "The angels aren't in control. Not as long as we are."

He turned back to his work.

"Hiroshi."

He did not answer.

She stood a while near his seat at the navigators' station. Her gaze was on *Discovery*'s one "window": a meter-square screen on which data from the epidermal sensors was represented in visible light. Blackness. Bright dots, dim dots, haze: the local starfield and, in the left lower corner, a bit of the remote central galactic disk.

Children in the third year of school are brought to see the "window."

Or they used to be.

"Is that actually what's ahead of us?" she had asked Teo not long ago, and he had said, smiling, "No. Some of it's behind us. It's a movie I made. It's where we'd be if we were on schedule. In case somebody noticed."

She stared at it now and remembered Luis's phrase, VU. Virtual Unreality.

Without looking at Hiroshi she began to speak.

"Luis thinks the angels are taking control. You think you're in control. I think the angels are controlling you. You don't dare tell people that we're decades ahead of schedule, because you think that if the arch-angels knew, they'd take over and change course so as to miss the planet. But if you go on hiding the truth, you're guaranteeing that they'll take over when we reach the planet. What are you planning to say? *Here we are! Surprise!* All the angels will have to say is, *These people are crazy, they made a navigation error and then tried to cover it up. We aren't at Shindychew—it's forty years too soon—this is some other solar system.* So they take over the Bridge and we go on. And on. To nowhere."

A long time passed, so that she thought he had not listened, had not heard her at all.

"Patel's people are extremely numerous," he said. His voice was low. "As your friend has been discovering. . . . It was not an easy decision, Hsing. We have no strength except in the accomplished fact. Actuality against wishful thinking. We arrive, we come into orbit, and we can say: *There's the planet. It's real. Our job is to land people on it.* But if we tell people now . . . four years or forty, it doesn't matter. Patel's people will discredit us, replace us, change course, and . . . as you say. . . go on to nowhere. To 'bliss.'"

"How can you expect anybody to believe you, to support you, if you've lied to them right up to the last moment? Ordinary people. Not angels. What justifies you in not telling them the truth?"

He shook his head. "You underestimate Patel," he said. "We cannot throw away our one advantage."

"I think you underestimate the people who would support you. Underestimate them to the point of contempt."

"We must keep personalities out of this matter," he said with sudden harshness.

She stared at him. "Personalities?"

The Plenary Council

"THANK YOU, CHAIRWOMAN. MY NAME IS NOVA LUIS. I REQUEST the Council discuss formation of an ad hoc Committee on Religious Manipulation, to investigate the educational curriculum, the contents and availability of certain materials in the Records and Archives, and the composition of the fourteen committees and deliberative bodies listed on the screen."

4-Ferris Kim was on his feet at once: "A Committee on Religious Manipulation can be convened, according to the Constitution, only to investigate 'an election or the deliberation of a legislative body.' School curriculum, the materials kept in Records and Archives, and the committees and councils listed cannot be defined as legislative bodies and thus are exempt from examination."

"The Constitutional Committee will decide that point," said Uma, chairing the meeting. Ferris sat down looking satisfied.

Luis stood up again. "Since the religion in question is the creed of Bliss, may I suggest that the Chair consider the Constitutional Committee as possibly biased, since five of the six members profess the creed of Bliss."

Ferris was up again: "Creed? Religion? What kind of misunderstanding is this? There are no creeds or cults in our world. Such words merely echo ancient history, divisive errors which we have long since left behind on our way." His deep voice grew mellow, gentle. "Do you call the air a 'creed,' Doctor, because you breathe it? Do you call life a 'religion,' because you live it? Bliss is the ground and goal of our existence. Some of us rejoice in that knowledge; for others that joy lies in the future. But there are no religions here, no warring creeds. We are all united in the fellowship of *Discovery*."

"And the goal appointed in our Constitution for *Discovery* and those who travel in it is to travel through a portion of space to a certain planet, to study that planet, to colonise it if possible, and to send or bring back information about it to our world of origin, Dichew, Earth. We are all united in the resolve to accomplish that goal. Do you agree, Councillor Ferris?"

"Surely the Plenary Council is not the place to quibble over linguistic and intellectual theories?" Ferris said with mild deprecation, turning to the Chair.

"An allegation of religious manipulation is more than a quibble, Councillor," Uma said. "I will discuss this matter with my advisory council. It will be on the agenda of the next meeting."

The Soup Thickens

"WELL," BINGDI SAID, "WE HAVE CERTAINLY PUT THE TURD IN the soup-bowl."

They were running the track. Bingdi had done twenty laps. Luis had done five. He was slowing down and breathing hard. "Soup of bliss," he panted.

Bingdi slowed down. Luis gasped and stopped. He stood awhile and wheezed. "Damn," he said.

They walked to the bench for their towels.

"What did Hsing say when you talked to her?"

"Nothing."

After a while Bingdi said, "You know, that bunch on the Bridge and Uma's advisory council, they're as tight as the archangels. They talk to each other and nobody else. They're a faction, as much as the archangels."

Luis nodded. "Well, so, we're the third faction," he said. "The turd faction. The soup thickens. Ancient history repeats itself."

The Great Rejoicing of Year 164, Day 88

TWO DAYS AFTER THE PLENARY COUNCIL ANNOUNCED THE formation of a Committee on Religious Manipulation to investigate ideological bias in educational curricula and the suppression and destruction of information in the Records and Archives, Patel Inbliss called for a Great Rejoicing.

The Temenos was packed. Everybody said, "It must have been like this when o-Kim died."

The old man stood up at the lectern. His face, dark, unwrinkled, the bones showing through the fragile skin, loomed on every screen in every homespace. He raised his arms in blessing.

The great crowd sighed, a sound like wind in a forest, but they did not know that; they had never heard the sound of wind in a forest; they had never heard any sigh, any voice but their own and the voices of machines.

He talked for nearly an hour. At first he spoke of the importance of learning and following the laws of life laid down in the Constitution and taught in the schools. He asserted with passion that only scrupulous observance of these rules could assure justice, peace, and happiness to all. He talked about cleanliness, about recycling, about parenthood, about athletics, about teachers and teaching, about specialized studies, about the importance of unglamorous professions such as labwork, soil-work, infant care. Speaking of the happiness to be found in what he called "the modest life," he looked younger; his dark eyes shone. "Bliss is to be found everywhere," he said.

That became his theme: the ship called "discovery," the ship of life, that travels across the void of death: the vehicle of bliss.

Within the ship, rules and laws and ways are provided by which each mortal being may, by learning to live in mortal harmony and happiness, learn also the way to the True Destination.

"There is no death," the old man said, and again that sigh ran through the forest of lives crowded in the round hall. "Death is nothing. Death is null, death is void. Life is all. Mortal life voyages onward, ever onward, straight and true on its course to everlasting life, and light, and joy. Our origin was in darkness, in pain, in suffering. On that black ground of evil, in that terrible place, our ancestors in their wisdom saw where true life, true freedom was. And they sent us, their children, forth, free of darkness, earth, gravity, negativity, to travel forever into the light."

He blessed them again, and some thought his sermon was done, but as if given new energy by his words he was speaking on: "Do not mistake the goal of our discovery, the purpose of our lives! Do not mistake symbol and metaphor for reality! Our ancestors did not send us on this great voyage only to return to where it began. They did not free us from gravity only to sink again into gravity. They did not free us from Earth to doom us to another earth! That is literalism—scientific fundamentalism—a dreadful mental myopia. Our origin was on a planet, in darkness and misery, yes, but that is not our destination! How could it be?

"Our ancestors spoke of the Destination as a world, because they knew nothing else. They had lived only in darkness, in filth, in fear, dragged down by gravity. When they tried to imagine bliss, they could only imagine a better, brighter world, and so they called it a 'new earth.' But we can see the meaning of that obscure symbol, and translate it into truth: not a planet, a world, a place of darkness, fear, pain, and death— but the bright journey of mortal life into endless life, the unceasing, everlasting pilgrimage into unceasing, everlasting bliss. O my fellow angels! our voyage is sacred, and it is eternal!"

"Ahh," sighed the forest leaves.

"Ah!" said Luis, watching and listening in his homespace with Bingdi and several friends, known among themselves as the Turd Group.

"Hah!" said Hiroshi, watching and listening in his homespace with Hsing.

On the Bridge, Year 164, Day 104

"DIAMANT ASKED ME YESTERDAY ABOUT AN ANOMALY HE noticed in the acceleration figures. He's been following up on it for a couple of tendays."

"Lead him astray," Hiroshi said, comparing two sets of figures.

"I will not."

After some minutes he said, "What will you do?"

"Nothing."

His hands were flickering over the workboard. "Leaving it to me."

"If you choose."

"I have no choice."

He worked on. Hsing worked on.

She stopped working and said, "When I was about ten I had a terrible dream. I dreamed I was in one of the cargo bays, wandering around, and I realised that there was a little hole in the wall, in the skin of the ship. A hole in the world. It was very small. Nothing was happening, but I knew what had to happen was that all the air would rush out the hole, because outside was vacuum. The nothing outside the ship. So I put my hand over the hole. My hand covered it. But if I took my hand away, I knew the air would begin to rush out. I called and called, but nobody was near. Nobody heard. And finally I thought I had to go get help, and tried to take my hand off the hole, but I couldn't. It was held there. By the nothing outside."

"A terrible dream," Hiroshi said. As she spoke he had turned from the workboard and sat facing her with his hands on his knees, straight-backed, expressionless. "Do you recall it because you feel yourself in a similar position now?"

"No. I see you in that position."

He considered this awhile. "And do you see a way out of that position?"

"Shout for help."

He shook his head very slightly.

"Hiroshi, one or another of the students or the engineers is going to find out what you've been doing and talk about it before you can mislead, or co-opt, or silence them. In fact, I think it's already happening. Diamant's been going after this as if he's trying to prove something.

He's very bright and extremely anti-authoritarian—I was in classes with him. He will not be easy to mislead or co-opt."

He made no reply.

"As I was," she added, dryly but without rancor.

"What do you mean by 'shout for help'?"

"Tell him the truth."

"Only him?"

She shook her head. She said in a low voice, "Tell the truth."

"Hsing," he said, "I know you think our tactics are mistaken. I'm grateful to you for bringing up your disagreement so seldom, and only with me. I wish we could agree on what is right. But I cannot put the power to change our course into the hands of the cultists until it is literally too late for them to do so."

"It's not your decision to make."

"Will you take it out of my hands?"

"Someone will. And when they do, it will appear that you've been lying for years, you and your friends, in order to have sole power. How else can they see it? You will be dishonored." Her voice still sounded low and rough. After a moment, biting her lip, she added, "Your question to me just now was dishonorable."

"It was rhetorical," he said.

There was another long silence.

He said, "It was dishonorable. I beg your pardon, Hsing."

She nodded. She sat looking down at her hands.

"What action do you recommend?" he asked.

"Talk to Tan Bingdi, Nova Luis, Gupta Lena—the group that's behind the ad hoc committee. They're working to expose Patel's power-tactics. Tell them whatever you like about how it happened, but tell them that we're going to be at the Destination in three years—unless Patel prevents it."

"Or Diamant," he said.

She winced. She spoke more cautiously, more patiently: "The danger isn't people like Diamant, Hiroshi. It's a fanatic gaining access to the Bridge for two minutes to damage, disable the course-computers—that's always been a possibility, but now there's a *reason* for somebody to do it. Now they *want* us never to arrive. At least that's out in the open, since Patel's speech. So now the fact that we *are* arriving has to come out in the open, because we need all the support we can get to make it happen. We must have support. You can't go on alone with your hand over the hole in the world!"

She had felt him withdraw when she said the name Nova Luis. She grew more urgent and eloquent as she spoke, losing ground; she ended up pleading. She waited and he made no response. Her arguments and urgency ebbed away slowly into a dry flatness of nonfeeling.

At last she said, drily and flatly, "Or perhaps you can. But I can't go on lying to colleagues and friends. I won't give you away, but I won't collude any more. I will say nothing at all to anyone."

"Not a very practical plan," he said, looking up at her with a stiff smile. "Be patient, Hsing. That's all I ask."

She stood up. "The evil of this is that we don't trust each other."

"I trust you."

"You don't. Me, or my silence, or my friends. The lie sucks trust out. Into nothing."

Again he did not speak; and presently she turned and left the Bridge. After she had walked a while she realised that she was at Quad Two, at Turning 2-3, heading for her old homespace, where her father lived alone. She wanted to see Yao, but felt it would be somehow disloyal to Hiroshi to go see him now. She turned around and started back to the Canaval-Liu homespace in Quad Four. The corridors seemed tight and narrow, crowded. She spoke to people who spoke to her. She remembered a part of her old nightmare dream that she had not thought to tell Hiroshi. The hole in the wall of the world had not been made by something from outside, a bit of dust or rock; when she saw it she knew, as one knows in a dream, that it had been there ever since the ship was made.

An Announcement of Extraordinary Importance, Year 161, Day 202

THE CHAIR OF THE PLENARY COUNCIL PUT A NOTICE ON THE innet of an "announcement of extraordinary importance" to be made at twenty hours. The last such announcement had been made over fifteen years ago to explain the necessity of an alteration in profession quotas.

People gathered in the homespace or compound or meetingspace or workplace to hear. The Plenary Council held session.

Chatterji Uma came on the screen precisely at twenty and said, "Dear fellow passengers of the ship *Discovery*, we must prepare ourselves for a great change. From this night forward, our lives will be different—will be transformed." She smiled; her smile was charming. "Do not be apprehensive. This is a matter for rejoicing. The great goal of our voyage, the destination for which this ship and its crew were intended from the very beginning of our voyage, is closer than we dreamed. Not our children, but we ourselves, may be the ones to set foot upon a new world. Now Canaval Hiroshi, our Chief Navigator, will tell you the great discovery he and others on the Bridge have made, and what it means, and what we may expect."

Hiroshi replaced Uma on the screens. The thickness and blackness of his eyebrows gave him a sometimes threatening, sometimes questioning look. His voice however was reassuring, quiet, positive, and rather pedantic. He began by telling them what had happened five years ago as the ship passed through a gravity sink near a very large area of cosmic dust.

Hsing, watching him alone in their livingspace, could tell when he began to lie, not only because she knew the actual figures and dates but because when he began lying he became both more authoritative and more persuasive. The lies concerned the rates of acceleration and deceleration, the time of the discovery of the computer error, and the navigators' response.

Without being specific about dates, Hiroshi implied that the first suspicions of anomalies in the ship's rate of acceleration had arisen less than a year ago. The magnitude of the computer error and its implications had been only gradually revealed. He sketched a scenario of incredulous but intrepid humans wresting their secrets from computers whose programming forced them to resist any override of their response to the original misreading, of navigators forced to try to outwit their instruments, trick them into re-compensating for their immense overcompensation, slowing the ship down from the incredible speed it had achieved.

Until this moment, he said, that struggle had been so chancy, they had been so unsure of what had happened and was happening, that they had felt it unwise to make any announcement. "To avoid causing panic by a premature or incorrect disclosure was our chief concern. We know now that there is no cause for alarm. None. Our operations were entirely successful. Just as the acceleration exceeded all speculative limits, we have been able to decelerate very much more quickly than had been thought possible. We are on course and in control. The only change is that we are well ahead of schedule."

He looked up, as if looking out of the screen, his black eyes unreadable. He was speaking slowly, carefully, a little monotonously, letting each sentence stand by itself. "We are continuing to decelerate, and will do so for the next 3.2 years.

"Late in the year 164, we will enter orbit around the planet of destination, Hsin Ti Chiu or New Earth.

"That event, as we all know, was scheduled to occur in the year 201. Our voyage of discovery has been shortened by nearly forty years.

"Ours is a fortunate generation. We will see the end of our long voyage. We will reach its goal.

"We have much work to do in these two years. We must prepare our minds and bodies to leave our little world and walk upon a wide new earth. We must prepare our eyes and souls for the light of a new sun."

The True Way

"It doesn't make sense, Luis," Rosa said. "It doesn't mean anything. The Zeroes just didn't understand. How could they? They thought we were too sinful to be able to live in heaven forever. They were earthen, they couldn't help it, so they thought we'd have to be earthen too. But we aren't—how could we be, born here, on the way? Why would we want to live any life other than this one? They made it perfect. They sent us to heaven. They made the world for us so we could learn the way to everlasting life in bliss by living in mortal bliss. How could we learn it on some kind of earthen black world? Outside, unprotected, unguided? How can we keep going on the True Way if we *leave* the True Way? How can we reach heaven by stopping on an earth?"

"Well, maybe we can't, but we do have a job to do," Luis said. "They sent us to learn about that earth. And to tell them what we learn. Learning was important to them. Discovery. They named our ship *Discovery.*"

"Exactly! The discovery of bliss! Learning the True Way! The archangels are sending back what we've learned all the time, you know, Luis. We're teaching them the way—just as they hoped we would. The goal is a spiritual goal. Don't you see, we've *attained* the Destination? Why do we have to stop our beautiful voyage at some evil, terrible, earthen place and do eva?"

An Election, Year 162, Day 112

5-Nova Luis was elected Chair of the Plenary Council. The general trust he had earned as a conciliator, negotiator, and peacemaker during the troubles of the past half-year made his election inevitable, and popular even among the angels. His year in office was indeed one of reconciliation and healing.

A Death, Year 162, Day 205

AT THE AGE OF EIGHTY-SEVEN, 4-PATEL INBLISS SUFFERED A
massive stroke and began to die, amid a continuous frenzy of tearful
prayer, song, and rejoicing. For thirteen days the celebrants occupied
all the corridors surrounding the Kim homespace in Quadrant One,
where Inbliss was born and had lived all his life. As his dying went
on and on, weariness and tension grew among the mourner-rejoicers.
People feared an outbreak of hysteria and violence like that which
had followed the announcement of Arrival. Many non-angel occupants of the quadrant went to stay with friends or relatives in other
quads.

When at last an archangel announced that the Father had passed
to Eternal Bliss, there was much weeping in the corridors, but no
violence, except for a man in Quad Four named 5-Garr Joyful who
beat his wife and her daughter to death "so that they could enter
Eternal Bliss with the Father," he said; he omitted, however, to kill
himself.

The Temenos was filled solid for the funeral of Patel Inbliss. There
were many speeches, but their tone was subdued. He had no child
to deliver the final speech. The archangel Van Wing sang the dark
devotional, "Eye, what do you see?" to end the ceremony. The crowd
dispersed in the silence of exhaustion. The corridors that night were
empty.

A Birth, Year 162, Day 223

5-CANAVAL HIROSHI'S CHILD WAS BORN TO HIS WIFE 5-LIU
Hsing, and was given the name 6-Canaval Alejo by his father.

Though Nova Luis was not practicing medicine during his term as council chair, Hsing had asked him to attend the birth, and he did so. It was an entirely uneventful delivery.

When he came the next day to see his patients, he sat for a while with them. Hiroshi was on the Bridge. Hsing's milk had not come in yet, but the baby was rooting diligently at her breast or anything else that offered itself. "What did you want me for?" Luis said. "You obviously know how to have a baby a lot better than I do."

"I guess I found out," she said. "*Learn by doing!*—remember Teacher Mimi in third grade?" She was sitting up in bed, still looking tired, triumphant, flushed, and soft. She looked down at the small head covered with very fine black hair. "It's so tiny, I can't believe it's the same species," she said. "What do you call this stuff I'm leaking?"

"Colostrum. It's the only thing his species eats."

"Amazing," she said, very softly touching the black fuzz with the back of a finger.

"Amazing," Luis agreed soberly.

"Oh Luis, it was so—To have you here. I did need you."

"It was my pleasure," he said, still soberly.

The baby went through some spasms, and was discovered to have had a miniature bowel movement. "Well done, well done. He'll be a member of the Turd Group yet," Luis said. "Give him here, I'll clean him up. Well, will you look at that? A bobwob! A veritable bobwob! A fine specimen, too."

"It's a gowbondo," Hsing whispered. He looked up at her and saw she was in tears.

He laid the baby, swallowed up by its clean diaper, in her arms; she went on crying. "I'm sorry," she said.

"New mothers cry, flatface."

She wept very bitterly for a moment, gasping, then got control.

"Luis, what is—have you noticed anything about Hiroshi—"

"As a doctor?"

"Yes."

"Yes."

"What's wrong with him?"

He said nothing for a while, then, "He won't go to a physician, so you're asking me for a spot diagnosis—is that it?"

"I guess so. I'm sorry."

"It's all right. Has he been particularly tired?"

She nodded. "He fainted twice last week," she said in a whisper.

"Well, my guess would be congestive heart failure. I know a good deal about it because as an asthmatic I'm liable to it myself, though I haven't managed to achieve it yet. You can live with it for a long time. There are medicines he can take, various treatments and regimes. Send him to Regis Chandra at the Hospital."

"I'll try," she whispered.

"Do it." Luis spoke sternly. "Tell him that he owes his son a father."

He stood up to leave. Hsing said, "Luis—"

"Take it easy, don't worry. It'll be all right. This fellow will see to it." He touched the baby's ear.

"Luis, when we land, will you go outside?"

"Of course I will, if we can. What do you think I'm insisting on all this education and training for? To watch a bunch of evajocks running around in space suits on a vidscreen?"

"It seems like so many people want to stay here."

"Well, we'll find out when we get there. It's going to be interesting. It already is interesting. We found out what a whole section in Storage D is. We thought it was very heavy protective clothing, but the pieces were too large. It's temporary livingspaces. You prop them up somehow and live inside them. And there are inflatable toruses which Bose thinks are meant to float on water. *Ships.* Imagine enough water to float a ship on! No. I wouldn't miss it for the world. . . . I'll look in tomorrow."

The Registry of Intent Upon Arrival

IN THE FIRST QUARTER OF YEAR 163, ALL PEOPLE OVER SIXTEEN were required to declare Intent Upon Arrival in an open registry on the innet. They could change their declaration any time, and it would not be binding upon them until a moment of ultimate decision, to be announced after investigations of the habitability of the planet were complete and had been fully tested.

> They were asked:
> *If the planet proved habitable, would you be willing to be*
> *   part of a team visiting the surface to gather information?*
> *Would you be willing to live on the planet while the ship*
> *   remained in orbit?*
> *If the ship left, would you be willing to stay on the planet*
> *   as colonists?*
>
> They were asked to state their opinion:
> *How long should the ship stay in orbit as a support to the*
> *   people on the planet?*
> *And finally, if the planet was not accessible or not*
> *   habitable, or if you chose to stay on the ship and not*
> *   visit or colonise the planet:*
> *If and when the ship left, should it return to the planet of*
> *   origin, or continue on into space?*

A return journey to Earth, according to Canaval and others, might take as little as seventy-five years if the whiplash effect of the gravity sink could be repeated. Some engineers were skeptical, but the navigators were confident that *Discovery* could return to Earth within a lifetime or two. This assertion met with little enthusiasm except among the navigators.

The open registry of Intent Upon Arrival, accessible on the innet at all times, went through interesting fluctuations. At first the number of people willing to visit the planet or live on it while the ship stayed in orbit—Visitors, they were dubbed—was pretty large. Very few, however, said they would be willing to stay there when the ship left. These die-hards got tagged Outsiders, and accepted the name.

The largest figure by far was those who wished not to land on the planet at all, and to continue the voyage out as soon as possible. Over two thousand people registered immediately as Voyagers.

This angelic vote was so strong that there was no real question of what the final decision would be. *Discovery* would not stay in orbit around its Destination, would not turn back to its Origin, but would go on to Eternity.

Urgent arguments about exhaustibility of supplies, about wear and tear, about accident and entropy, swayed some Voyagers; but the major-ity continued steadfast in their intention to live in bliss and die to Bliss.

As this became clear, the number of people who registered as willing to stay permanently on the planet began to grow, and kept growing. It was clear that the angelic majority, eager to continue its sacred journey, could not be kept tethered to the planet for very long. Few of the angels opted even to make an exploratory visit to the planet's surface. Many, following the teachings of the archangels, tried to persuade their friends that leav-ing the ship was unthinkably dangerous—not a bodily risk, but a sin, a temptation to seek unneeded knowledge at the cost of the immortal soul.

Gradually the choices narrowed, became absolute. Go out into the dark and be left there, or continue on the bright and endless voyage. The unknown, or the known. Risk, or safety. Exile, or home.

Throughout the year, the number of those who shifted their registry from Visitor to Outsider grew to over a thousand.

In the latter half of Year 163, the yellow star that was the primary of Shindychew's system appeared to the eye at magnitude -2. School-children were taken onto the Bridge to see it in the "window."

The education curriculum had been radically revised. Though teachers who were angels were unenthusiastic or hostile to the new material, they were required to allow "lay teachers" to present information about what the Destination might be like. The VRs of Old Earth—Jungle, Inner City, and so on—had allegedly deteriorated, and had been destroyed; but many educational films were salvaged, and others were found in Storage awaiting use by potential settlers.

Those who registered as Visitors or Outsiders formed learning groups, in which they studied and discussed these films and instructional books. Dictionaries were much called upon to settle misunderstandings and arguments over terms, though sometimes the arguments went on and on. Was a *ravine* a need for food, or a place where the floor went down into a hole? The dictionary offered gorge, gully, gulch, canyon, chasm, rift, abyss . . . . A low place in the floor, then. When you need food badly, that's *ravenous*. But why would you need food badly?

A Pragmatist

"No. I don't intend to leave the ship."

Luis stared at the Registry, where he had just discovered Tan Bingdi's name on the list of Voyagers. He looked around at his friend, and at the screen again.

"You don't?"

"I never did. Why?"

"You aren't an angel," Luis said at last, stupidly.

"Of course not. I'm a pragmatist."

"But you've worked so hard to keep the . . . the way out open . . ."

"Of course." After a minute he explained: "I don't like quarrels, divisions, enforced choices. They spoil the quality of life."

"You aren't curious?"

"No. If I want to know what living on a planet surface is like, I can watch the training videos and holos. And read all the books in the Library about Old Earth. But why do I want to know what living on a planet is like? I live here. And I like it. I like what I know and I know what I like."

Luis continued to look appalled.

"You have a sense of duty," Bingdi told him affectionately. "Ancestral duty—go find a new world . . . Scientific duty—go find new knowledge. . . . If a door opens, you feel it's your duty to go through it. If a door opens, I unquestioningly close it. If life is good, I don't seek to change it. Life is good, Luis." He spoke, as always, with little rests between the sentences. "I will miss you and a lot of other people. I'll get bored with the angels. You won't be bored, down on that dirtball. But I have no sense of duty and I rather enjoy being bored. I want to live my life in peace, doing no harm and receiving no harm. And, judging by the films and books, I think this may be the best place, in all the universe, to live such a life."

"It's a matter of control, finally, isn't it," Luis said.

Bingdi nodded. "We need to be in control. The angels and I. You don't."

"We aren't in control. None of us. Ever."

"I know. But we've got a good imitation of it, here. VR's enough for me."

A Death, Year 163, Day 202

AFTER RECURRENT EPISODES OF ILLNESS, NAVIGATOR CANAVAL Hiroshi died of heart failure. His wife Liu Hsing with their infant son, and many friends, all the staff of Navigation, and most of the Plenary Council, attended the funeral service. His colleague 4-Patel Ramdas spoke of his brilliance in his profession, and wept as he finished speaking. 5-Chatterji Uma spoke of how he laughed at silly jokes, and told one he had laughed at; she said how happy he had been to have a son, though he had known him so briefly. One of his students spoke last, in the place of the child, calling him a hard master but a great man. Hsing then went with the technicians, accompanying his body to the Life Center for recycling. She had not spoken at the service. The technicians left her alone for a moment, and she laid her hand very gently on Hiroshi's cheek, feeling the death-cold. She whispered only, "Goodbye."

Destination

IN THE YEAR 164, DAY 82, *DISCOVERY* ENTERED ORBIT AROUND the planet Shindychew, Hsin Ti Chiu, or New Earth.

As the ship made its first forty orbits, probes sent down to the surface of the planet provided vast amounts of information, much of which was unintelligible or barely intelligible to those receiving it on the ship.

They were soon able to state with certainty, however, that people would be able to do eva on the surface without respirators or suits. There was a growing body of evidence that the planet might be accessible to long-range inhabitation. That people could live there.

In the year 164, Day 93, the first ship-to-ground vehicle made a successful landing in the area designated Subquadrant Eight of the planetary surface.

After This There Are No More Headings, for the World Is Changed, Names Change, Time Is Not Measured as It Was, and the Wind Blows Everything Away.

TO LEAVE THE SHIP: TO GO THROUGH THE AIRLOCK INTO THE lander, that was a comprehensible thing—terrifying, fiercely exciting, absolute, an act of transgression, of defiance, of affirmation. The last act.

To leave the lander: to go down those five steps onto the surface of the planet, that was to leave comprehension behind, to lose understanding: to go mad. To be translated into a language where no word—ground, air—transgress, affirm—act, do—made sense. A world without words. Without meaning. A universe undefined.

Immediately perceiving the wall, the blessed needed only wall, the side of the lander, she backed up against it and at once turned to hide her face against it so that she could see it, the wall, curving metal, firm, limiting, see it and not see the other, the no walls, the vast.

She held her baby close against her, his face to her breast.

People were there with her, beside her, clinging to the wall, but she was only vaguely aware of them, even though they were all huddled close together they all seemed apart and distant. She heard people gasping, vomiting. She was dizzy and sick. She could not breathe. The ventilation was failing, the fans were far too strong. Turn down the fans! A spotlight shone down on her, she could feel the heat of it on her head and neck, see the glare of it in the skin of the wall when she opened her eyes.

The skin of the wall, the ship's epidermis. She was doing eva. That was all. She always wanted to be an evaman when she was little. She was doing eva. When it was done she could go back into the world. She tried to hold on to the skin of the world but it was smooth ceramic and would not let her hold it. Cold mother, hard mother, dead mother.

She opened her eyes again and looked down past Alejo's silky black head at her feet and saw her feet standing in dirt. She moved, then, to get out of the dirt, because you shouldn't walk in dirt. Father had told her when she was very young, no, it's not good to walk in the dirt gardens, the plants need all the room, and your feet might hurt the little plants. So she moved away from the wall to move out of the dirt garden. But there was only dirt garden, dirt, plants, everywhere, wherever she put her feet. Her feet hurt the plants and the dirt hurt the soles of her feet. She looked despairingly for a walkway, a corridor, a ceiling, walls, looked away from the wall and saw a great whirl of green and blue spin round a center of intolerable light. Blinded and unbalanced she fell to her knees and hid her face beside the baby's face. She wept in shame.

Wind, air moving fast, hard, endlessly blowing, making you cold, so you shivered, shuddered, like having a fever, the wind stopping and starting, restless, stupid, unpredictable, unreasonable, maddening, hateful, a torment. Turn it off, make it stop!

Wind, air moving softly, moving slender grasses in waves over the hills, carrying odors from a long way off, so you lifted your head and sniffed, breathed it in, the strange, sweet, bitter smell of the world.

The sound of wind in a forest.

Wind that moved colors in the air.

People who had never been of much account became prominent, respected, constantly in demand. 4-Nova Ed was good with the tenses. He was the first to figure out how to deploy them properly. Miraculously the shambles of plasticloth and cords rose and became walls, walls to shut out the wind—became rooms, rooms to enclose you in the marvelous familiarity of surfaces close by, a ceiling close overhead, a floor smooth underfoot, quiet air, an even, unblinding light. It made all the difference, it made life livable, to have a tense, to have a homespace, to know you could go in, be in, be inside.

"It's 'tent,'" Ed said, but people had heard the more familiar word and went on calling them tense, tenses.

A fifteen-year-old girl, Lee Meili, remembered from an ancient movie what foot coverings were called. People had tried syndrome-sox, those that had them, but they were thin and wore out at once. She hunted through the Stockpile, the immense and growing labyrinth of stores that the landers kept bringing down from the ship, till she found crates labelled SHOES. The shoes hurt the delicate-skinned feet of people who had gone barefoot on carpet all their lives, but they hurt less than the floor here did. The *ground*. The *stones*. The *rocks*.

But 4-Patel Ramdas, whose skills had put *Discovery* into orbit and guided the first lander from ship to surface, stood with a reading lamp in one hand, its cord and plug in the other, staring at the dark wrinkled wall-like surface of a huge plant, the *tree* under which he had set up his tense. He was looking for an electrical outlet. His gaze was vague and sad. Presently he straightened up; his expression became scornful. He walked back to the Stockpile with the lamp.

5-Lung Tirza's three-month-old baby lay in the starlight while Tirza worked on construction. When she came to feed him she shrieked, "He's blind!" The pupils of his eyes were tiny dots. He was red with fever. His face and scalp blistered. He had convulsions, went into coma. He died that night. They had to recycle him in the dirt. Tirza lay on the place in the dirt where the baby was lying inside it, underneath her. She moaned with her mouth against the dirt. Moaning aloud, she raised her face with brown wet dirt all over it, a terrible face made of dirt.

NOT STAR: SUN. STARLIGHT WE KNOW: SAFE, KIND, DIS- tant. Sun is a star too close. This one.

My name is Star, Hsing said in her mind. Star, not Sun.

She made herself look out of her tense in darkcycle to see the safe, kind, distant stars who had given her her name. Shining stars, bing hsing. Tiny bright dots. Many, many, many. Not one. But each . . . Her thoughts would not hold. She was so tired. The immensity of the sky, the uncountability of the stars. She crawled back into inside. Inside the tense, inside the bagbed beside Luis. He lay in the moveless sleep of exhaustion. She listened automatically to his breathing for a moment; soft, unlabored. She drew Alejo into her arms, against her breasts. She thought of Tirza's baby inside the dirt. Inside the dirtball.

She thought of Alejo running across the grass the way he had today, running in the sunlight, shouting for the joy of running. She had hurried to call him back into the shade. But he loved the warmth of sunlight.

LUIS HAD LEFT HIS ASTHMA ON THE SHIP, HE SAID, BUT HIS migraines were bad sometimes. Many people had headaches, sinus pain. Possibly it was caused by particles in the air, particles of dirt, plants' pollens, substances and secretions of the planet, its outbreath. He lay in his tense in the long heat of the day, in the long ebb of the pain, thinking about the secrets of the planet, imagining the planet breathing out and himself breathing in that outbreath, like a lover, like breathing in Hsing's breath. Taking it in, drinking it in. Becoming it.

UP HERE ON THE HILLSIDE, LOOKING DOWN ON THE *RIVER* BUT not close to it, had seemed a good place for the *settlement*, a safe distance, so that children would not be falling into the huge, fiercely rushing, deep mass of water. Ramdas measured the distance and said it was 1.7 kilos. People who carried water discovered a different definition of distance: 1.7 kilos was a long distance to carry water. Water had to be carried. There were no pipes in the ground, no faucets in the rocks. And when there were no pipes and faucets you discovered that water was necessary, constantly, imperatively necessary. Was wonderful, worshipful, a blessing, a bliss the angels had never dreamed of. You discovered thirst. To drink when you were thirsty! And to wash—to be clean! To be as you'd always been, not grainy-skinned and gritty and sticky with smears of dirt, but clean!

Hsing walked back from the fields with her father. Yao walked a little stooped. His hands were blackened, cracked, ingrained with dirt. She remembered how when he worked in the dirt gardens of the ship that fine soft dirt had clung to his fingers, lined his knuckles and fingernails, just while he was working; then he washed his hands and they were clean.

To be able to wash when you were dirty, to have enough to drink all the time, what a wonderful thing. At Meeting they voted to move the tenses closer to the river, farther from the Stockpile. Water was more important than things. The children must learn to be careful.

Everybody must learn to be careful, everywhere, all the time.

Strain the water, boil the water. What a bother. But the doctors with their cultures were unyielding. Some of the native bacteria flourished in media made with human secretions. Infection was possible.

Dig latrines, dig cesspools, what hard work, what a bother. But the doctors with their manuals were unyielding. The manual on cesspools and septic tanks (printed in English in New Delhi two centuries ago) was hard to understand, full of words that had to be figured out by context: drainage, gravel, bedrock, seep.

A bother, being careful, taking care, taking trouble, following the rules. Never! Always! Remember! Don't! Don't forget! Or else!

Or else what?

You died anyway. This world hated you. It hated foreign bodies.

Three babies now, an adolescent, two adults. All under the dirt in that place, close to the little first death, Tirza's baby, their guide to the underground. To the inside.

THERE WAS PLENTY TO EAT. WHEN YOU LOOKED AT THE FOOD section of the Stockpile, the huge walls and corridors of crates, it seemed it must be all the food a thousand people could eat forever, and the angels' generosity in letting them have it all seemed overwhelming. Then you saw the way the land went on and on, past the Stockpile, past the new sheds, and the sky went on and on over them; and when you looked back the pile of crates looked very small.

You listened to Liu Yao saying in Meeting, "We must continue to test the native plants for edibility," and Chowdry Arvind saying, "We should be making gardens now, while the time of the revolu—of the year is the most advantageous time—the *growing season*."

You came to see that there was not plenty to eat. That there might not ever be plenty to eat. That (the beans did not flower, the rice did not come up out of the dirt, the genetic experiment did not succeed) there might not be enough to eat. In time. Time was not the same here.

Here, to every thing there was a season.

5-NOVA LUIS, A DOCTOR, SAT BESIDE THE BODY OF 5-CHANG Berto, a soil technician, who had died of blood poisoning from a blister on his heel. The doctor suddenly shouted at Berto's tense-mates, "He neglected it! You neglected him! You could see that it was infected! How could you let this happen? Do you think we're in a sterile environment? Don't you listen? Can't you understand that the dirt here is *dangerous*. Do you think I can work miracles?" Then he began to cry, and Berto's tense-mates all stood there with their dead companion and the weeping doctor, dumb with fear and shame and sorrow.

CREATURES. THERE WERE CREATURES EVERYWHERE. THIS world was made of creatures. The only things not alive were the rocks. Everything else was alive with creatures.

Plants covered the dirt, filled the waters, endless variety and number of plants (4-Liu Yao working in the makeshift plant test lab felt sometimes through the mist of exhaustion an incredulous delight, a sense of endless wealth, a desire to shout aloud—*Look! Look at this! How extraordinary!*)—and of animals, endless variety and number of animals (4-Steinman Jael, one of the first to sign up as an Outsider, had to go back permanently to the ship, driven into fits of shuddering and screaming by the continual sight and touch of the innumerable tiny crawling and flying creatures on the ground and in the air, and her uncontrollable fear of seeing them and being touched by them).

People were inclined at first to call the creatures cows, dogs, lions, remembering words from Earth books and holos. Those who read the manuals insisted that all the Shindychew creatures were much smaller than cows, dogs, lions, and were far more like what they called insects, arachnids, and worms on Dichew. "Nobody here has invented the backbone," said young Garcia Anita, who was fascinated by the creatures, and studied the Earth Biology archives whenever her work as an electrical engineer left her time to do so. "At least nobody in this part of the world. But they certainly have invented wonderful shells."

The creatures about a millimeter long with green wings that followed people about persistently and liked to walk on your skin, tickling slightly, got called dogs. They acted friendly, and dogs were supposed to be man's best friend. Anita said they liked the salt in human sweat, and weren't intelligent enough to be friendly, but people went on calling them dogs. Ach! what's that on my neck? Oh, it's just a dog.

THE PLANET REVOLVED AROUND THE STAR.

But at evening, the sun set. The same thing, but a different matter. With it as it set the sun took colors, colors of clouds moved through air by wind.

At daybreak the sun rose, bringing with it all the mutable, fierce, subtle colors of the world, restored, brought back to life, reborn.

Continuity here did not depend on human beings. Though they might depend on it. It was a different matter.

THE SHIP HAD GONE ON. IT WAS GONE.

Outsiders who had changed their minds about living outside had mostly gone back up in the first few tendays. When the Plenary Council, now chaired by the Archangel 5-Ross Minh, announced that *Discovery* would leave orbit on Day 256, Year 164, a number of people in the Settlement asked to be taken back to the ship, unable to endure the finality of permanent exile, or the painful realities of life outside. About as many shipsiders asked to join the Settlement, unable to accept the futility of an endless pilgrimage, or the government of the archangels.

When the ship left, the nine hundred and four people on the planet had chosen to be there. To die there. Some of them had already died there.

They talked about it very little. There wasn't a lot to say, and when you were tired all the time all you wanted was to eat and get into your bedbag and sleep. It had seemed like a big event, the ship going on, but it wasn't. They couldn't see it from the ground anyway. For days and days before the leaving date the radios and the hooknet carried a lot of talk about the journey into bliss, and exhortations telling the people on the ground that they were still all angels and were welcome back to joy. Then there was a flurry of personal messages, pleadings, blessings, goodbyes, and then the ship was gone.

For a long time *Discovery* kept sending news and messages to the Settlement, births, deaths, sermons, prayers, and reports of the unanimous joyfulness of the voyage. Personal messages went back to the ship from the Settlement, along with the same informational and scientific reports that were sent to Earth. Attempts at dialogue, at response, rarely successful, were mostly abandoned after a few years.

Obeying the mandates of the Constitution, the Settlers collected and organised the information they gathered concerning Shindychew and sent it to the planet of origin as often as the work of survival allowed them time to do so. A committee worked on keeping and transmitting methodical annals of the Settlement. People also sent observations and thoughts, images, poems.

You couldn't help wondering if anyone would listen to them. But that was nothing new.

Transmissions intended for the ship continued to come in to the receivers in the Settlement, since the people on Dichew wouldn't hear about the early arrival for years to come, and then their response would take years to arrive. The transmissions continued to be as confusing as ever, almost entirely irrelevant, and increasingly difficult to understand, due to changes in thought and vocabulary. What was a withheld E.O. and why had there been riots about it in Milak? What was faring technology? Why were they saying that it was essential to know about the 4:10 ratio in pankogenes?

The vocabulary problem was nothing new, either. All your life inside the ship you had known words that had no meaning at all. Words that signified nothing in the world. Words such as *cloud, wind, rain, weather.* Poets' words, explained in notes at the foot of the page, or that found a brief visual equivalent in films, sometimes a brief sensory equivalent in VRs. Words whose reality was imaginary, or virtual.

But here, the word that had no meaning, the concept without content, was the word virtual. Here nothing was virtual.

Clouds came over from the west. West, another reality: direction: a crucially important reality in a world you could get lost in.

Rain fell out of a certain kind of cloud, and the rain wet you, you were wet, the wind blew and you were cold, and it went on and didn't stop because it wasn't a program, it was the weather. It went on being. But you didn't, unless you acquired the sense to come in out of the rain.

Probably people on Earth already knew that.

The big, thick, tall plants, the trees, consisted largely of the very rare and precious substance wood, the material of certain instruments and ornaments ontheship. (One word: ontheship.) Wood objects had seldom been recycled, because they were irreplaceable; plastic copies were quite different in quality. Here plastic was rare and precious, but wood stood around all over the *hills* and *valleys*. With peculiar, ancient tools provided in the Landing Stock, fallen trees could be cut into pieces. (The meaning of the word *chensa*, spelled *chainsaw* in the manuals, was rediscovered.) All the pieces of tree were solid wood: an excellent material for building with, which could also be shaped into all kinds of useful devices. And wood could be set fire to, to create warmth.

This discovery of enormous importance, would it be news on Earth?

Fire. The stuff at the end of a welding torch. The active point in a bunsenburner.

Most people had never seen a fire burning. They gathered to it. Don't touch! But the air was cold now, full of cloud and wind, full of weather. Fire-warmth felt good. Lung Jo, who had set up the Settlement's first generator, gathered bits of tree and piled them inside his tense and set fire to them and invited his buddies to come get warm. Presently everybody poured out of the tense coughing and choking, which was fortunate, because the fire liked the tense as well as it liked the wood, and ate with its red and yellow tongues till nothing was left but a black stinking mess in the rain. A disaster. (Another disaster.) All the same, it was funny when they all rushed out weeping and coughing in a cloud of smoke.

Cloud. Smoke. Words full, crammed, jammed with meaning, with meanings. Life-and-death meanings, signifying life, signifying death. The poets had not been talking virtually, after all.

I wandered lonely as a cloud . . .

What is the weather in a beard?
It's windy there and rather weird . . .

THE 0-2 STRAIN OF OATS CAME UP OUT OF THE DIRT, SPRANG UP (*spring*), shot up, put out leaves and beautiful hanging grain-heads, was green, was yellow, was harvested. The seeds flowed between your fingers like polished beads, fell (*fall*) back into the heap of precious food.

ABRUPTLY, THE MATERIAL RECEIVED FROM THE SHIP CEASED to contain any personal messages or information, consisting of rebroadcasts of the three recorded talks given by Kim Terry, talks by Patel Inbliss, sermons by various archangels, and a recording of a male choir chanting, played over and over.

"WHY AM I SIX LO MEILING?"

When the child understood her mother's explanation, she said, "But that was ontheship. We live here. Aren't we all Zeroes?"

5-Lo Ana told this story in Meeting, and it went through the whole community causing pleasure, like the flight of one of the creatures with fluttering transparent wings edged with threads of gold, at which everybody looked up and stopped work and said, "Look!" Mariposas, somebody called them, and the pretty name stuck.

There had been a good deal of talk, during the cold weather when work wasn't so continuous, about the names of things. About naming things. Such as the dogs. People agreed that naming should be done seriously. But it was no good looking in the records and finding that on Dichew there had been creatures that looked something like this brown creature here so we'll call it *beetle*. It wasn't beetle. It ought to have its own name. Treecrawler, clickclicker, leaf-chewer. And what about us? Ana's kid is right, you know? 4's, 5's, 6's—what's that got to do with us now, here? The angels can go on to 100. . . . Lucky if they get to 10. . . . What about Zerin's baby? She isn't 6-Lahiri Padma. She's 1-Shindychew-Lahiri-Padma. . . . Maybe she's just Lahiri Padma. Why do we need to count the steps? We aren't going anywhere. She's here. She lives here. This is Padma's world.

SHE FOUND LUIS IN THE PATTY-GARDENS BEHIND THE WEST compound. It was his day off from the hospital. A beautiful day of early summer. His hair shone in the sunlight. She located him by that silver nimbus.

He was sitting on the ground, on the dirt. On his day off he did a shift at the irrigation system of little ditches, dikes, and watergates, which required constant but unlaborious supervision and maintenance. Patty grew well only when watered but not overwatered. The tubers, baked whole or milled, had become a staple since Liu Yao's success at breeding the edible strain. People who had trouble digesting native seeds and cereals thrived on patty.

Children of ten or eleven, old people, damaged people, mostly did irrigation shifts; it took no strength, just patience. Luis sat near the watergate that diverted the flow from West Creek into one or the other of the main channel systems. His legs, thin and brown, were stretched out and his crutch lay beside them. He leaned back on his arms, hands flat on the black dirt, face turned to the sun, eyes shut. He wore shorts and a loose, ragged shirt. He was both old and damaged.

Hsing came up beside him and said his name. He grunted but did not move or open his eyes. She squatted down by him. After a while his mouth looked so beautiful to her that she leaned over and kissed it.

He opened his eyes.

"You were asleep."

"I was praying."

"Praying!"

"Worshipping?"

"Worshipping what?"

"The sun?" he said, tentative.

"Don't ask me!"

He looked at her, exactly the Luis look, tenderly inquisitive, noncommittal, unreserved; ever since they were five years old he had been looking at her that way. Looking into her.

"Who else would I ask?" he asked her.

"If it's about praying and worshipping, not me."

She made herself more comfortable, settling her rump on the berm of an irrigation channel, facing Luis. The sun was warm on her shoulders. She wore a hat Luisita had inexpertly woven of grain-straw.

"A tainted vocabulary," he said.

"A suspect ideology," she said.

And the words suddenly gave her pleasure, the big words—
vocabulary! ideology!—Talk was all short, small, heavy words: food,
roof, tool, get, make, save, live. The big words they never used any
more, the long, airy words carried her mind up for a moment like a
mariposa, fluttering aloft on the wind.

"Well," he said, "I don't know." He pondered. She watched him ponder. "When I smashed my knee, and had to lie around," he said, "I
decided there was no use living without delight."

After a silence she said, in a dry tone, "Bliss?"

"No. Bliss is a form of VU. No, I mean delight. I never knew it on the
ship. Only here. Now and then. Moments of unconditional existence.
Delight."

Hsing sighed.

"Hard earned," she said.

"Oh yes."

They sat in silence for some time. The south wind gusted, ceased,
blew softly again. It smelled of wet earth and bean-flowers.

Luis said:

> *"When I am a grandmother, they say, I may walk under*
>   *heaven,*
>   *On another world."*

"Oh," Hsing said.

Her breath caught in another, deeper sigh, a sob. Luis put his hand
over hers.

"Alejo went fishing with the children, upstream," she said.

He nodded.

"I worry so much," she said. "I worry the delight away."

He nodded again. Presently he said, "But I was thinking . . . when I was worshipping, or whatever, what I was thinking, was about the dirt." He picked up a palmful of the crumbly, dark flood-plain soil, and let it fall from his hand, watching it fall. "I was thinking that if I could, I'd get up and dance on it. . . . Dance for me," he said, "will you, Hsing?"

She sat a moment, then stood up—it was a hard push up off the low berm, her own knees were not so good these days—and stood still.

"I feel stupid," she said.

She raised her arms up and outward, like wings, and looked down at her feet on the dirt. She pushed off her sandals, pushed them aside, and was barefoot. She stepped to the left, to the right, forward, back. She danced up to him holding her hands forward, palms down. He took them, and she pulled him up. He laughed; she did not quite smile. Swaying, she lifted her bare feet from the dirt and set them down again while he stood still, holding her hands. They danced together that way.

ABOUT THE AUTHOR

URSULA KROEBER LE GUIN was born in 1929 in Berkeley, and currently lives in Portland, Oregon. As of 2017 she will have published twenty-three novels, twelve collections of stories, five books of essays, thirteen books for children, nine volumes of poetry and four of translation. Among her numerous honors and awards are the Hugo Award, Nebula Award, PEN-Malamud Award, National Book Award, and Library of Congress Living Legends, and National Book Foundation Medal.

Her recent publications include *Steering the Craft* and *Late in the Day*, as well as the forthcoming title *Words Are My Matter*.